THE DAGGER OF ADENDIGAETH

The Dagger of Adendigaeth A Pattern of Shadow & Light Book 2 All Rights Reserved.

Copyright © 2012 Melissa McPhail v1.0

Copyright © 2014 Melissa McPhail v2.0

Map art by Ramah Palmer and Brandon Lidgard

Paperback ISBN: 978-1-4327-9824-6

Hardback ISBN: 978-1-4787-2013-3

THE DAGGER OF ADENDIGAETH

A PATTERN OF SHADOW AND LIGHT

— BOOK 2 —

ALL THINGS ARE FORMED OF PATTERNS...

MELISSA McPHAIL

BOOKS BY
MELISSA McPHAIL

Cephrael's Hand

The Dagger of Adendigaeth

Paths of Alir

ACKNOWLEDGEMENTS

TO MY INCREDIBLY loyal and supportive friends and family—for your patience and unconditional love despite my becoming a missing person so often during the writing of this novel; for the endless discussions and conjecturing that so often spurred new threads of storyline, for your amazing feedback, for tea and quiet moments of inspiration, for your constant, unwavering support. And to Sarah, Juliet and Shon, for loving me in spite of my many hours spent creating with the characters in this tale instead of with you. Thank you—a hundred times, thank you.

CONTENTS

Books by Melissa McPhail. v

Acknowledgements vii

Map of Alorin xiii

Author's Note xvii

Prologue 1

One. .13

Two. .21

Three .37

Four 44

Five. .48

Six 64

Seven. .76

Eight .95

Nine 113

Ten. 118

Eleven 131

Twelve 143

Thirteen 157

Fourteen 160

Fifteen 166

Sixteen 177

Seventeen 185

Eighteen 197

Nineteen 209

Twenty 225

Twenty-One 231

Twenty-Two 237

Twenty-Three 251

Twenty-Four 259

Twenty-Five 273

Twenty-Six 293

Twenty-Seven 301

Twenty-Eight 311

Twenty-Nine 326

Thirty 338

Thirty-One 342

Thirty-Two 354

Thirty-Three 369

Thirty-Four 388

Thirty-Five 398

Thirty-Six 422

Thirty-Seven 435

Thirty-Eight 447

Thirty-Nine 459

Forty 472

Forty-One 496

Forty-Two 508

Forty-Three 520

Forty-Four 528

Forty-Five 542

Forty-Six 549

Forty-Seven 564

Forty-Eight 586

Forty-Nine 599

Fifty 615

Fifty-One 621

Fifty-Two 632

Fifty-Three 643

Fifty-Four 652

Fifty-Five 674

Fifty-Six 693

Epilogue 718

Keep in Touch 729

Glossary of Terms 731

Dramatis Personae 737

On the kingdoms of Myacene, Avatar and Vest and travel between the Middle Kingdoms and the East: The waters of the Fire Sea are navigable along the coastline of the Middle Kingdoms paying regular heed to wind and weather. Storm surges are likely during the deep winter months along the north Saldarian coast and all of Dannym and Myacene.

MAP OF ALORIN

sulfuric geysers and vortices are often reported along with other volcanic disturbances along this unstable coast. Myacene is particularly dangerous at the 45th parallel, where electrical storms powered by the consistently active volcano of Mt. Veul have been known to generate cyclone several miles wide.

Myacene

Fire Sea

Eastwatch

Wynne

ndo

Tambarré

Saldaria

M'Nador

Avatar

Tal'Shira

Nahavand   Taj al'Jahanna

Sand Sea

Raku

Abu'Dhan   Kai'alil

Sakkalaah

Qar'imali

Akkad
Emirates

Duan'Bai

Vest

At the time of this charting, the Slave Trade is active between Avatar, Vest and the Forsaken Lands. Ships suspected of piracy and kidnapping are known to ply the southern waters of the Fire Sea. Captains are warned to run armed and must be ready to fend off attack at all hours of the watch.

The Middle Kingdoms
of Alorin

Charted on behalf of the Empress by the Imperial Cartographer on
this date of 517aV to reflect the missing island of Cair Tiern aval,
which vanished from the Bay of Jewels circa 497aV.

Additional maps can be found online at MelissaMcPhail.com

disturbances along this unstable coast. *Mnacene is*
45th parallel, where electrical storms spawned by t
of Mt. Veul have been known to generate cyclones

M'NADOR &
SURROUNDING
KINGDOMS

Fire S

Saldaria

Dhakarr Range

M'Nador

Wynne

Tambarré

ness Range

Tal'Shira

Nahavand

• Taj al'Jahanna

Sand Sea

Raku

Kulzaret'Mor

Abu'Dhan

Haden Gorge

Kai'alil

Qar'imali

Sakkalaah

Cry R.

Akkad
Emirates

Duan'Bai

At the time of this charting, th
Avatar, Vest and the Forsaken
kidnapping are known to ply the
Captains are warned to run an
attack at all hours of the wate

Lands

AUTHOR'S NOTE

WHEN DEALING WITH an epic fantasy spanning multiple books—especially when said books are published over a period of years—some authors choose to include within the story of each subsequent book a sort of refresher on what happened in the book just before it, finding a way (they hope) to seamlessly integrate the back-story of say, Book One, into the forward story of Book Two.

But the tale encompassed by a Pattern of Shadow & Light does not stop, rewind and auto-generate a summary every hundred-thousand words. Therefore, you won't find any cagey attempt on my part to bring you up to speed on what you may or may not remember. Yet I realize it may have been some years since you visited the realm of Alorin. So if you desire a quick refresher, I've provided that information here, within this Author's Note.

For those of you who are well versed in the story of *Cephrael's Hand*, by all means, skip this orientation and continue on to *The Dagger of Adendigaeth*.

At the end of *Cephrael's Hand*, Prince Ean had recovered from his near-death episode with the Malorin'athgul, Rinokh, only to face him again at the Temple of the Vestals in Rethynnea. Teaming up with his blood-brother Creighton (now a Shade), and the Espial Franco Rohre, Ean defeated Rinokh by holding onto his pattern while Creighton pulled him, unprotected, through an open node. This exposed the Malorin'athgul to the raw power of the pattern of the world, which unmade the form he'd been using in Alorin, but not before Rinokh cast his dark power, *deyjiin*, into the temple to destroy it. Aided by Franco, Ean and Creighton then used the same node to escape the crumbling temple as well as the pursuing forces of the Vestal Raine D'Lacourte.

Raine was fighting in the fray when Rinokh revealed himself. In facing the Malorin'athgul, the Vestal was finally forced to admit that the creatures *do* exist. With the assistance of the pirate Nodefinder Carian vran Lea, and accompanied by the avieth Gwynnleth, Raine pursued Ean and Franco Rohre across the node. However, he and the others did not end up in the same location as Ean and Franco. They found themselves instead in the desolate landscape of T'khendar.

When we left the Adept Healer Alyneri d'Giverny, she'd been taken hostage by men sworn to the Duke of Morwyk, aided by the wielder Sandrine du Préc. That same night, their fleeing coach was caught in a landslide, and Alyneri fell off a cliff and into a river raging in flood.

Meanwhile, our young truthreader, Tanis, was waiting for his lady in a café when he noticed a fiery-eyed man, whose gruesome thoughts accosted Tanis's sensitive mind during a chance meeting of gazes. Compelled by a sudden inexplicable sense of duty, Tanis followed the man from the tavern, departing without a word of explanation for the Lord Captain Rhys val Kincaide or Alyneri.

Finally, when we left the soldier Trell, he had just pulled a nameless girl from a flooded river and was bringing her back to the old desert woman, Yara, for help.

"Knowledge is the dagger of Adendigaeth.
Forgiveness is the balm."

– The Fifth Vestal Björn van Gelderan

PROLOGUE

THREE MOONS AGO IN ALORIN...

T HE HERMIT CLOSED his eyes against the blinding afternoon
sun and shifted his position on the rocky cliff. He'd been sitting
there for hours, his way of relaxing, of meditating...of atoning. His
deeply tanned skin testified to this habit. While his iron-grey hair and the
lines at his brown eyes proclaimed a man who'd seen a half-century of life,
the sinewy muscles beneath his linen tunic and wide-legged pants seemed
to belong to a much younger man—indeed, much, *much* younger than
his actual age, though he had long ago forgotten how many centuries that
numbered.

Far below his seaside cliff, surrounded by olive orchards and pastures
and farmland, the Agasi village of Talieri appeared as a dusting of tiny red-
roofed houses cramped up against the sparkling inland sea. Toy fishing boats
puttered through glassy waters, leaving wakes twenty times their length,
while larger craft hoisted breezy sails to head south toward the violet-hazed
mountains on the far horizon.

The hermit's home comprised a landscape of chalk cliffs, green hills,
and depthless blue sea-lakes that beckoned to fishermen and barefoot boys
with equal appeal. Further north, in the foothills of the high mountains of
Tirycth Mir, lay the Solvayre, a region of lush pastures and vineyards where
grapes were grown and pressed and fermented into Agasan's famous wines.

Even on cold days, like this one, the hermit liked to come down to the bluffs where the easterly wind always blew, where the only sound was the call of the birds circling midway between cliff and sea. Peace dwelled in the wide-open spaces of the world, where freedom seemed a birthright to man and eagles alike. Only there, naked beneath the vast expanse of mountain and sky, did the hermit's overactive mind find rest.

For he was a man possessed.

Possessed by demons of his own devising—as is so often true—tormented by the chains of obligation that weighed heavily upon his conscientious soul. *We are the sculptors of our destiny*, his mentor had often told him, *as much as the victims of it.*

His mentor had taught him this truth, unpalatable as it might be, so many ages ago. The hermit smiled at the thought of his mentor, his confidant…his friend, who was renowned as Alorin's enemy yet remained its only hope of salvation. Could one man be so many things?

Yes, he thought, *if his name is Björn van Gelderan.*

And where are you now, my old friend? What role have you assigned yourself during these darkest of days?

The hermit knew Björn had returned to Alorin, though he'd found only the briefest trace of him on the currents—Björn's card of calling to those who watched and waited for his coming. The Fifth Vestal had mastered the art of hiding his presence on the tides of *elae*—the most difficult of any undertaking with the lifeforce. Even Raine D'Lacourte would not find him on the currents unless Björn himself allowed it.

The hermit closed his eyes and exhaled a sigh echoic of the ages he'd witnessed. Björn van Gelderan had forever changed the course of his life, and the hermit was bound to him now, for good or for ill.

And you are Markal Morrelaine, he reminded himself, *not some witless recluse gone mad in his old age. You have work to do.*

He did, though he dreaded it—especially of late. The things he'd been seeing on the currents were shocking enough to bring an agonizing sense of fear into his daily work. He should have felt a measure of vindication—were not their earliest suspicions now justified?—but his heart knew only a dire sense of unease and a nagging guilt that had been tormenting him for ages like an indigestible, poisonous root. That everything was proceeding according to plan offered no solace; after all, Alorin's Fifth Vestal had devised it.

Our plan.

Markal too well remembered the days of its making; long days and even longer nights secluded in Björn's tower with the few they could trust while the other Vestals played at being important. Björn's zanthyr had both stood guard for their gathering and run Björn's bidding, returning with meals, ancient texts, weldmaps…or Sundragons.

This memory brought a smile to Markal's face, crinkling the deep lines at his eyes.

They had been so shocked—he and Malachai and the others—when the illustrious Ramuhárihkamáth walked into the room on the heels of the First Lord's zanthyr—for no feat was so monumental that Phaedor would not accomplish it if such was Björn's will—and even more astonished when Ramu bent his knee to Björn and swore his oath in front of them all. So many centuries ago now, yet the memory still tasted of the excitement and promise they'd all felt in those days.

The memory brought sadness, also. Of those original nine, who remained? Malachai was vanquished, his madness a terrible sacrifice. As far as Markal knew, Cristien and Anglar fell with Arion at the Citadel, and Dunglei and Parcifal before them at Gimlalai. Their smiles, their sarcastic wit, their brilliant minds—all lost, casualties of the larger war.

The best and the brightest of Alorin's wielders had died defending the realm against the threat Malachai became. Would that any of them might've foreseen this most tragic consequence.

Of the other survivors now sworn to their cause, Dagmar was in T'khendar, reportedly held prisoner by Björn—though Markal knew that was fantasy. The First Lord's zanthyr no doubt was off pursuing his own motives, as ever he did when not doing his master's bidding. Of the rest, he knew nothing; he only suspected that, like him, they were waiting to be summoned. To be *Called.*

And you're still stalling, he told himself while gazing off across the sparkling blue sea-lake toward the hazy mountains beyond. The Geborahs, they called them, named for the formless power that roamed the treacherous passes of Mount Ijssmarmöen. Far beyond, across the city-states of Navárre, nestled against the lush Caladrian Coast, lay the sacred city of Faroqhar, the Seat of the Empress Valentina van Gelderan, Björn's great, great, many-times-great grand-niece.

Markal had hidden from the Empress as much as any other. He'd known she would seek him ruthlessly for questioning once the war ended. Isolation and anonymity had been his foremost priorities, so he'd chosen Talieri to house his retreat from the world, in no small part because of the disinclination of anyone from the Imperial Court to travel there. While heavy traffic clogged the sea-lakes along their southern coasts, only fishermen and traders found their way to the sparsely populated northern shores.

The Empress left the region alone due to its proximity to the highly-prized wineries of Solvayre, whose owning families wielded great political power and were touchy about over-governance. That meant few, if any, visits from the Imperial Guard to Talieri, and no visits from Agasan's ruling class, who were far too important to pay a stop to an isolated fishing village with nothing to boast but an old hermit living atop their highest hill.

A foghorn sounded from afar, stirring Markal back to the present. The horn meant that Talieri was calling its fishermen home. The sea-lakes of Ijssmar became dangerous with the fall of night, and a ship caught on the lakes after sundown might never make it back to harbor. But the horn held a different meaning for Markal. Had he really been sitting there for so long, accomplishing nothing? Was he so afraid of what the currents would show him?

Afraid? No. Regretful perhaps, wary of the coming days, weary from his centuries of waiting for a time he now dreaded had arrived. Night would soon fall, and he could no longer count on the morning's arrival; in such troubled times, tomorrow belonged to no man.

Thus setting himself to task, Markal formed in his mind the pattern that would reveal the currents to him. Unlike Adepts, who might train themselves to see the currents even as a swimmer trained his lungs to hold breath, Markal had no Adept gift. But few could match his skill at Patterning.

Releasing the pattern to compel its *intent* into *becoming*, the currents opened to his sight. He no longer focused on the high mountains across the sea; instead, he studied the swirling eddies that swept along in great rosy funnels from the sky, like cyclones stained a pastel pink. The Life currents of the first strand. These pale whirlwinds brought to him the stories of countless lives jumbled together in a vortex of confused moments, disjointed vignettes he would have to piece together to discern the whole.

From the second strand, which he identified as a burnished copper sheen upon the land, Markal pieced together the travels of Nodefinders in whose activities he took an interest. One caught his eye: the Espial Franco Rohre. From Franco's frequent travels, and from the other life pattern accompanying Franco's upon the tides of the second strand, Markal inferred that Franco acted in the service of Raine D'Lacourte, taking the Vestal on a confusingly disjointed tour of the realm. Markal might've liked to delve deeper into their activities, for he felt it prudent to keep an eye on Raine D'Lacourte, but this was not his task for that day.

Releasing a new pattern, the merest whisper of intent, Markal's sight changed to view the fourth strand, the one comprising the patterns of thought. On these tides he learned of recent workings of *elae*, of twisted truth-patterns from the Prophet's temple in Tambarré...of magical battles in the Kutsamak and the balance of power in M'Nador's violent war.

All these varied strands of the lifeforce he studied and pondered, traced and deciphered. Night fell and the moon rose, but still he sat on the edge of his mountain. The night's cold could not touch him. Even the rain, had it come, would have splashed well above his head, beading as if on glass to run in rivulets to the ground in a circle at least two paces from his crossed legs.

These small comforts he allowed himself, trifling patterns of little regard; they did nothing to ease his cramping muscles, dull the ache behind his eyes, or allay the gnawing emptiness in his stomach. To study the currents in the detail to which he was accustomed required rigor and determination. Days sometimes passed before Markal had learned all he must know.

For some, such study was a pleasurable task. In their time together, Markal had known Björn to spend a week or more sitting on his tower roof studying the currents. He would come back inside lean and hardened from his fast, his brilliant blue eyes even more dazzling than usual. For Björn, this undertaking provided a means of edification; for Markal, it felt more like torture. This was but one fundamental difference between them. Björn reveled in the laborious study of Patterning, while Markal endured it through iron-willed self-discipline and a passion for order and method. This variance evidenced the innate difference between an Adept, like Björn, and a wielder, like Markal. For Björn, the touch of *elae* came as life itself; for Markal, it was always a battle of will, a mental marathon.

Order and method. This was his mantra.

He studied through the night, sitting without moving while the moon set and the stars fled the coming dawn. Soon the paling in the east became a glow, then a fire that burned in an orange-gold sky, flaming rose-hued clouds above a silver sea. And still he studied.

The townspeople called him *va dänstaty*, which meant 'the statue man' in the Talieri dialect. They'd called him other things, too, over the centuries: *warlock, sorcerer, necromancer.* They didn't know the difference between such words, or that in all his days, he would never have deigned even to acknowledge a necromancer's dark delving. They knew only that he'd once orchestrated magical workings there upon his mountain, that he'd caused the earth itself to rise up into his current home, and that through all the generations, he never aged beyond his seeming fifty years.

At the end of the Adept Wars, in the early days of his retreat from the world, the township had been frightened of him, worried that his immortality came from the vampiric demons of myth. Children had thrown rocks at him, and the village people shut their doors whenever he came to town. Those children had long since grown and lived and died, telling their stories to grandchildren and great-grandchildren, and he'd become a living legend.

Once they'd feared him; now they tolerated him—still a mystery, but no longer a threat.

He found none of this surprising. What did surprise him was how long he'd remained a subject of gossip and speculation. Had he made his home in the east, where few living wielders remained and magic was synonymous with myth, the people would long ago have forgotten him. Here, in an empire where the workings of *elae* were prevalent, even commonplace, where wielders walked the Imperial Court of the Sacred City with the status of nobility...here, people remembered his *one* long-ago working and feared it.

Perhaps a people who know magic know also to respect it, he often reasoned.

Perhaps. Or perhaps he merely gave the people of this remote village something to talk about. He didn't begrudge them their intrigues; if nothing else, they ensured his solitude.

Solitude indeed, Markal mused. There was nothing like studying events elsewhere in the realm to reinforce one's own sense of isolation.

He sighed and shifted his position. An annoying pebble had worked its way beneath his thigh, and he brushed it away before settling back to task. He'd learned all that he could from the first four strands. Time now to embark upon his most dreaded duty: the study of the fifth strand, the most ancient of elemental magics.

The fifth's golden flows had begun to carry upon them a taint heretofore unknown to *elae's* currents. Even when Malachai's Shades had hunted Alorin with genocidal blood on their blades, the fifth strand had not carried such a stain upon its tides.

This evil was not unexpected—indeed, he'd been watching signs of it fomenting for the last three-hundred years. Yet his lack of surprise did nothing to quell his instinctual flinch each time he found evidence of it— evidence of *their* presence.

Markal's heart broke to think of the terrible ramifications of Malorin'athgul in Alorin. He wanted more than anything to track them down, to stop them with any means available, even should it mean his life. But the First Lord had given him a different role to play, one just as important, or so Björn assured him. Yet this role his conscience—his heart—would never have chosen.

Order and method.

These cornerstones kept him aligned with a vital purpose, long disguised within a web of apparent treachery. They kept him primed through all the centuries for his most crucial of tasks. Thus he studied the fifth strand, observing its golden flows with a heavy heart and a troubled soul.

By midday, Markal had seen all he came to see. But as he began the weary process of focusing back on his surroundings, his *elae*-heightened senses perceived the near presence of another.

Impossible! Here?

The shocking discovery nearly shattered his rapport with *elae*, but he was Markal Morrelaine, a man who counted an unshakable composure as one of his most famous attributes.

Markal released *elae* and turned to look behind him just as the man rounded a rise, climbing the narrow bluff with the ease Markal remembered of him. The man saw Markal looking and waved.

Dagmar Ranneskjöld.

Markal sat rooted to the earth, his pulse quickening. The Second Vestal looked exactly as Markal remembered, and yet…more than he remembered. Dagmar also seemed to possess a certain weariness of spirit, one that Markal too often saw revealed in his own reflection. Strange to observe it now in a man he remembered as having an inexhaustible eagerness for confrontation.

All these thoughts passed in a single moment, the space of an indrawn breath, and then Markal was on his feet and waving in return. He bent to retrieve his polished rowan staff and walked with long strides to greet Alorin's Second Vestal.

They met near the edge of the high bluff, two tall silhouettes against the azure sky. Dagmar flashed his famous smile and opened his arms. "Markal, it has been a long time."

Markal grabbed the Second Vestal in a rough embrace. *Incredible* to find Dagmar here, in Alorin. "What of Raine?" He pulled back to take Dagmar's shoulders with both hands. "He will see you on the currents."

"Raine is otherwise engaged." Dagmar winked one pale-green eye. "Besides, have a little faith, my old friend. Might not the First Lord have taught me some *few* things in our long years together?"

Markal noted the dry humor in his tone, but his attention shifted more to the Vestal's oathring as it caught the sunlight, the jewel sparkling with blue fire. There was something ominous about seeing the ring and knowing what it meant that Dagmar wore it still, even as Björn no doubt did. Moreover, that the stone's color remained as true as the day of its forging.

He suddenly felt again the urgency they'd all shared during those last days of the Adept Wars. The frustration, the ineptitude, the guilt—the emotions welled up to claim him in one fierce moment, unprepared as he was for their return. He relived them now, prompted by the mere sight of a square blue stone set in a heavy silver band worn upon a man's middle finger.

Perceptive to Markal's state of mind, Dagmar placed a hand on his shoulder and captured his gaze with his own. "What is it? What burdens you?"

Markal shook his head. "Seeing your ring, remembering the time before, I wonder…" He gave Dagmar a troubled look. "I wonder if I am the man I once was. If I am still the right man for the task assigned me. It's been decades since I commanded the lifeforce beyond a whisper."

Dagmar laughed. "What's this? The great Markal Morrelaine doubting his ability? By Cephrael's Great Book, I never thought I'd see the day!"

Markal frowned at him.

Dagmar chuckled, wrapped an arm around his shoulders, and said with a twinkle in his eye, "Come now, don't begrudge my moment of gloating. Surely you remember how insufferable you were."

Markal grunted. "Humility has a way of creeping in unannounced."

They started off together, walking the stony path toward Markal's villa.

"It's amazing to be back in Alorin," Dagmar confessed after a moment. "Björn said it would be marvelous, that I would want to hold *elae* until I couldn't breathe, until I exhausted myself trying to contain it…until it consumed me." He glanced Markal's way, catching his gaze. "The lifeforce flows in T'khendar, but it never feels the same. To be so long away from Alorin…" His cheery smile faded. "It was difficult."

They strolled away from the cliffs, trading the open vista of blue waters and sky for Markal's orchard of olive and pear trees, the latter bare save for a few brown remnants, fodder for the east wind. Once they passed beyond the bluff, the wind died to a gentle breeze, as it always did, and other sounds returned: the distant bleating of sheep and goats, the myriad chirping of birds, a quiet rustling of tiny animals in the underbrush. Dagmar grew quiet, as if relishing the harmony of nature.

Markal, however, was brimming with questions. Yet as they headed down a stony path bordered with long, silver-green grass, only one question mattered. "How long do we have?"

A gusting breeze sent a cascade of golden-brown leaves sweeping across their path, and Dagmar caught a leaf as it fluttered down. He gazed at it pinned against his palm. "Events progress quickly." He glanced Markal's way as he closed the leaf in his fist. "We are pebbles of warning, you and I, announcing the avalanche that follows."

"And Björn…?" He let the thought trail off, not really wanting to voice such questions.

"You wonder if time has changed him?" Dagmar filled in the rest anyway, arching a flaxen brow. "Changed him, perhaps, as it changed Malachai?"

Markal looked away, shamed by his own doubts.

"Fret thee not." Dagmar's tone could not have been more confident, nor his gaze more genuine. "Björn solved the mystery of *deyjiin*. It can be worked safely now by a select few, when due precaution is taken. And my oath-brother, your mentor...he is as immutable as the fifth itself. But come, there is so much to tell you. Much has changed in T'khendar since Malachai's day, and many we thought lost were spared in the end. So let us enjoy what time is given us here. At dawn we must depart, for Björn needs you."

Markal spun him a concerned look. "So soon?"

With sober acceptance in his green eyes, Dagmar nodded. Then he flashed that famous smile and grabbed Markal around the shoulders again. "But that's tomorrow, eh? For tonight, let's you and I make a cavernous dent in your wine cellar!"

Markal could only smile and nod acquiescence, for in his heart, he had accepted the truth, and it was precisely as he'd feared.

Tomorrow was no longer his own.

PART ONE

ONE

"Nobility is birthed not of blood but of the heart."

– Gydryn val Lorian, King of Dannym

THE TEMPLE OF the Prophet Bethamin in Tambarré was built upon the ruins of a much older structure, one that first belonged to the ancient, and ultimately corrupt, Quorum of the Sixth Truth. For two long millennia, the massive complex stood crumbling atop its lonely mountain, a stark reminder of the Adept race's darkest days. During all the intervening years, none had seen fit to approach it, much less build something new from its ashes.

But time thins the cloth of memory. As the ages pass, its rich colors fade. Strong wool is beaten by the elements until the pattern of its lesson disintegrates, leaving holes in the truths it was meant to carry on. Even the stains of blood blend and bleed, leaving but faded blotches without meaning, mere shadows of lessons that came before, their warnings lost within the obscure impression that remains.

As the strong Saldarian sun dove westward, the Agasi truthreader Kjieran van Stone stood upon the newly rebuilt walls of the Prophet's temple, staring north. The wind blew his shoulder-length black hair into his eyes, so he held up a hand to hold it back, that it might not distract him from the view. In the distance, the upper crescent of the Dhahari mountain range merged with the Iverness range of southeastern Dannym to form jutting, snowcapped peaks as impassable as they were forbidding. Only the

Pass of Dharoym permitted travel between Dannym and Saldaria, and it was guarded day and night by hardened men sworn to the Duke of Morwyk.

Kjieran missed Dannym. He missed its green hills and misty grey mornings, its forbidding forests and charcoal seas. He missed the heavy snows of winter, and the north wind that scoured the land; and he missed the people—especially his king. In his years of service to Gydryn val Lorian, the monarch had become like a father to him, and his sons like the brothers Kjieran never had. In many ways, he missed Dannym more than his homeland of Agasan.

Though to be fair, he would've just as willingly served ten years before the mast on an Avataren slaver than spend even one more night in Tambarré.

At the behest of his king and the Fourth Vestal Raine D'Lacourte, Kjieran had been truth-bound to secrecy and sent to serve the Prophet as a spy for the north. He was afraid to do it—he'd nearly wept the night Raine truth-bound him—but they had no one better suited to go in his stead, and their need was dire.

The Fourth Vestal believed—they all believed—that the plot to end the val Lorian reign encompassed more than a single throne, and had not the king and queen already sacrificed enough with the loss of two of their sons? Kjieran could hardly refuse them, though he suspected that Tambarré would be his doom.

Little did he realize then that there were so many shades of grey within the spectrum of imminent death…that when a man might pluck any variety of poisoned fruit from the Tree of Dying and suffer the ending through myriad torments—drawing it out for months, even years—that death itself might become a mercy.

But he understood that much better now.

Kjieran had served the Prophet for six moons, and every day of it had been a waking horror. Every day he reminded himself of his vital purpose, of their desperate need—not just Dannym's, but all of Alorin. For without this hope to ground him, to shore up his fortitude and replenish his courage, he knew he would long ago have fled. Instead, each night he warded his dreams before laying down his head, loath to close his eyes for fear of the visions that lurked beyond his sight. But despite his best efforts, when dawn broke each morning, he still woke with a stifled scream.

They all did, the occupants of Tambarré—that is, those who slept at all.

At the sound of a voice raised in anger, Kjieran turned from his wistful study of the mountains. The conversation floated to him on the stagnant air that came seeping out of the temple hall, where large copper braziers glowed day and night. The Ascendants burned incense on those coals, and the oily smoke stained the walls and filled the air with a foul, fetid haze. When he heard the Prophet's voice, however, Kjieran hurried inside, for Bethamin misliked when his acolytes were not hovering close.

"Those patterns are bound with the fifth strand," the Prophet was saying in a tone of cold censure as Kjieran crept soundlessly through the vestry. "My hold upon a Marquiin should've been impossible to break—unless you've been misleading me, Dore."

"My lord, I wouldn't dream of misleading you," came the sycophantic voice of Dore Madden, an Adept wielder and advisor to the Prophet. Kjieran stifled a shudder as he drew up just short of the temple nave. Dore Madden made his skin crawl, and he would rather the man didn't know he was there.

He inched his head around the archway to see Dore and the Prophet standing about ten paces away. Dore Madden's cadaverous frame stood in profile to Kjieran, facing the Prophet as he continued, "The fifth strand acts as the sand in concrete, my lord. Any time one layers patterns of differing strands, they must be bound with the fifth if they are to endure. And like sand into the concrete mix, once bound, they cannot be separated."

"Then you tell me how it was done!" the Prophet hissed. Kjieran had never seen him so infuriated. Usually Bethamin was all cold dispassion no matter the horrific deeds happening in his name…or in his midst. Bethamin turned away from Dore and stood with hands clasped behind his back, his stance conveying his ultimate displeasure.

The Prophet was tall and broad of shoulder. He wore his long black hair in hundreds of braids, each strand bound four times with tiny gold bands, the mass contained by more elaborate braids encircling the whole. He went bare-chested to better display his immaculate form, only wearing white desert pants—or a shendyt for ceremonies—but the wide gold torc around his neck always shone brightly against his caramel skin. He was imposing. He was coldly arrogant. And he was terrifying.

"My lord, there is no way for me to know how it was done without inspecting the Marquiin who died or interrogating the perpetrator," Dore said in a soothingly obsequious tone. He smoothed his white hair back from his wide forehead and licked his lips, which he had a habit of doing. Kjieran thought the man just one generation removed from the foulest of desert lizards. "You heard the testimony of your Ascendant as well as I, my lord," Dore continued. "He saw this northern prince sully your Marquiin right before his own eyes, resulting in the untimely death of one of your most loyal servants. 'Tis surely the divine grace that is upon you, my lord, that your Ascendant found his way back to us with the terrible news. We must send someone in search of this treacherous wielder who thinks himself above you and seeks to undo your great work. Such a man could cause all manner of mischief while sullying the purity of your name, my lord."

The Prophet turned Dore a piercing look over his shoulder.

"But more importantly," Dore continued, leaning towards the Prophet with a wild look in his reptilian gaze and dropping his voice, "this happenstance surely proves the validity of my concerns, my lord. We need stronger stock to carry your sigil."

This issue was a bone of contention between Dore and the Prophet— Kjieran had overheard the argument many times. The Prophet turned away again, but Dore continued, his voice rising in pitch, "Wielders and men of the fifth are better suited to your Fire than these feeble fourth-stranders, my lord. Your power is too strong for them, as they're inborn of frail innocence. Only those born of the fifth might withstand the Fire's brilliance. They would become beacons for its radiance, my lord! A far more fitting receptacle than a truthreader's fragile shell."

"This is not the first time you've expressed this sentiment, Dore Madden," the Prophet observed uninterestedly. "The problem is the resources available."

"Yes, but I may have solved that problem, my lord."

Kjieran could tell from the dreadful eagerness in Dore's tone that the man had been waiting for just the right moment to reveal this new information. Kjieran loathed Dore Madden. Dore was the one who'd taught the Prophet what patterns could be twisted and snarled, perverted or adapted to host the power of his Fire. Every day the wielder brought Bethamin new patterns to try, having first tested them on the dungeons of doomed souls he kept as experimental rats scattered about Saldaria, many of them inexorably bound to him with the fifth.

Much to Kjieran's chagrin, the Prophet took Dore's bait. "Indeed? How?"

"There is a man—my most prized student—whom I've been working on for some years now. With the right compulsion patterns, I have succeeded in waking him to the currents of *elae*."

"*Elae*," the Prophet hissed. "An abomination."

"Indeed, indeed," Dore clucked, "but one must do things in their proper order, my lord. First my protégé had to learn to sense *elae* in its natural channels. Then he could be taught to work its patterns and *then*, my lord," and here he leveled his snake-eyed gaze at the Prophet's back, "then he could be taught to work *your* power."

The Prophet turned to him. "A common man?"

"Yes, my lord." Dore's eyes were alight with fervor. "But we're yet in the early stages of this sequence. Still, I have succeeded in my use of compulsion. I have made a common man into a wielder."

"A fine accomplishment," the Prophet noted. "I do not see how he could be brought to work my Fire. A man is but a man."

"Yes, my lord, but there *is* a way."

Dore had the Prophet's full attention now. "Tell me how."

Dore's black eyes veritably glowed with malice. He licked his lips. "Long have we dreamed of a force of wielders, an army worthy of carrying your sigil, an army to spearhead our vital quest to rid this world of the offensive abomination that is *elae* and all of its accursed offspring."

"Indeed," remarked the Prophet in annoyance. "Do not sermonize to me on my own cause, Dore Madden."

"My lord," Dore continued unctuously, "such a force exists already, though they are small and of no use to us. Yet they work a similar power to your own—*deyjiin* it is called."

The Prophet's expression darkened. "What army is this?"

"The Shades, my lord," Dore whispered with dutiful awe. He licked his lips again. "Long have Shades dwelled in the anathematized realm of T'khendar, bound to the Fifth Vestal, Björn van Gelderan. We cannot use them for our purposes, no, but we can learn from the Fifth Vestal's skill—indeed, indeed," he rubbed his hands together and gazed up at the Prophet with wild-eyed glee, "for three centuries I have been working to discover the patterns the Fifth Vestal used to bind the Shades to him—for make no mistake, my lord. They are not merely under compulsion, as your Marquiin, with only a small tendril of power available to do your great work. No, the Shades are bound to Björn van Gelderan *body and soul.* Through him, they are able to wield his dark power in all its fullness."

"*Deyjiin*," murmured the Prophet. Kjieran shivered from the ominous interest in his eyes. Abruptly Bethamin focused his gaze upon Dore. "You've found these patterns?"

"Not entirely." A momentary frown flickered across Dore's cadaverous features. "But my work progresses at great speed." He licked his lips again. "It won't be long now, my lord."

The Prophet regarded him intently. "And the man who vilified my Marquiin?"

"*Yes*," Dore said, drawing the word into a hiss. "This Ean val Lorian— he must be brought to face your justice, my lord. The job of retrieving him will be a most fitting quest for my star pupil—a *most* fitting quest—and a proving ground for his newfound skills. You will see, my lord." Dore licked his lips and rubbed his hands with savage delight. "You will see then how our plans may finally be accomplished!"

Kjieran inwardly swore. The news was both baffling and grave. A host of factions already sought Ean's death. Now to have Dore Madden after him as well? *And how in Tiern'aval did Ean unbind a Marquiin?* From what Kjieran knew of the young prince, he had no Adept talent.

I must get word to the Fourth Vestal at once.

Bethamin meanwhile was considering Dore with his darkly piercing eyes. At last, and much to Kjieran's mounting horror, he said, "Let it be done."

Dore's expression came as close to ecstasy as a cadaver could manage, as though death had claimed him in the last moments of coitus, just as release shuddered through him. "Thank you, my lord." Dore bowed eagerly and headed off.

The Prophet turned to look directly at Kjieran then. The truthreader had no doubt that the man had known he was there all the while. "Come, Kjieran," he commanded.

Kjieran exited the vestry into the nave where the Prophet stood wreathed in haze. He seemed an unearthly creature with his braids like serpents and his bare chest as muscled as the finest marble statue, with his dark eyes and exotic features. The Prophet was terrible and bewitching and darkly compelling, and Kjieran had never been so afraid of any living man.

What disturbed him the most was that though he knew Bethamin to be wholly without compassion and intent upon the destruction of their world—Kjieran saw the corruptive influence of his Fire and the horrific anguish it caused—yet still he was drawn to the man in spite of these!

Yea, what terrified Kjieran van Stone the most about the Prophet Bethamin was the sure knowledge that he was no more immune to the Prophet's seductive power than anyone else.

Kjieran knelt before the Prophet, head bowed. "My lord," he whispered.

"Kjieran, you told me you were trained in Patterning," said the Prophet.

Kjieran kept his eyes on the floor. The Prophet misliked the colorless eyes of a truthreader, yet he kept a few unsullied ones around to advise him, as if knowing that his Marquiin, once touched by his own fell power, were tainted and thereby useless for discerning the truth. The hypocrisy sickened Kjieran. "Yes, my lord. I trained in Agasan's Sormitáge."

"Dore would have me believe there is such a pattern as he describes. Is it so?"

"If there is, I do not know it."

"And these Shades of which he spoke? They exist?"

"I have never seen one, my lord, but they were a terrifying force during the Adept Wars. Dore would know them better than I, my lord. He survived the fall of the Citadel and is one of the Fifty Companions."

The tragedy of this anguished Kjieran no end. That Dore Madden had survived while so many good men fell—it was a bitter irony how the treacherous walked unharmed while thousands of innocents went to their deaths.

The Prophet reached down and took Kjieran by the chin, guiding him to rise. His touch felt as deeply cold as a river stone long caressed by the glacial melt; achingly cold, like flesh held too long to the snow. Kjieran kept his eyes downcast while the Prophet considered him, only praying that whatever Bethamin found in his countenance would satisfy him enough to let him be on his way again.

In the privacy of his chambers, the Prophet liked to experiment with the darkest of workings—bindings and compulsions and corrupted first-strand patterns that tormented rather than healed—and he maintained the utmost reserve throughout the process, no matter how insanely a man or woman screamed. Kjieran saw no rhyme or reason to who was chosen for these intervals, nor even any way to predict who would survive them. He merely prayed that Fate would close its eye to him while his heart beat frantically and he sipped his breath in tiny measures.

The Prophet at last released Kjieran's chin. "Thank you, Kjieran. That will be all."

"Your will be done, my lord." Kjieran barely managed to mumble the words for the ache in his jaw. He retreated to the vestry as quickly as he dared and then raced down the hall and into a prayer alcove, snatching its curtain roughly into place. He collapsed against the wall then, shaking uncontrollably, and fighting back the tension and fear that clenched his chest in a death-like vise. Sinking down to the floor, Kjieran hugged his knees to his chest and wept in silence. He wept in relief and he wept in despair.

For in that moment when the Prophet held him fast, an overpowering yearning to please his lord had possessed him. It felt wholly wrong—he *knew* this—a compulsion laid upon him so expertly that he couldn't tell anything was being worked at all. Yet he had been unable to resist it—to resist *him*. Kjieran knew that had the Prophet asked him in that moment to do anything—*anything*—he would have done it willingly. So Kjieran wept in gratitude that Fate's hand had passed him by, and he wept with the terrible understanding that the next time Fate's eye fell upon him, he might not be so graced.

TWO

"Seek not to know where the path may lead,

only to keep your feet upon it."

— Isabel van Gelderan, Epiphany's Prophet

SEVERAL DAYS AGO...

AS TANIS WALKED along Faring East following the man with the fiery eyes, the lad wondered if he was perhaps in a trance, if the dark-haired man in the amber cloak had somehow enchanted him, and now he was spellcast to follow him without any determinism whatsoever, like those tales of Fhorg blood magic where people are possessed by demons under the command of the Fhorgs' Red Priests.

Certainly it made no sense to be leaving his Lady Alyneri, still in the apothecary next door, without even a message to say where he was going, and he knew the Lord Captain Rhys would be furious. Yet these thoughts were but crumbs left behind on the café table where Tanis had been sitting, for the lad now knew only a driving sense of duty.

Whether or not it was fell magic that had propelled Tanis after the imposing stranger from the café, the lad did have enough sense to understand that following this man was dangerous. So he trailed a good half-block behind him, keeping him in sight through the crowd, but only just. Luckily the man was easy to spot, with his striking black hair and elegant amber cloak, not to mention the way the crowd inexplicably parted before him as the seas give way to the prow of a ship.

Tanis was keeping well back of him when four men emerged from a store and fell into step just behind the stranger, forming a phalanx. Their cloaks obscured the quivers on their backs, but Tanis saw their outline clear enough, likewise the blue tattoos that adorned their bald heads. The hair rose on the back of Tanis's neck, and gooseflesh sprouted down his arms like an evil rash, for he saw no mystery as to *their* origins.

Fhorgs.

Tanis thought it an uncomfortable coincidence that he had just been thinking of Fhorgs and now here appeared four of them. The Wildling race was well known for exploring occult arts; pieced with the visions Tanis had plucked from the stranger's mind, it seemed they were all involved in evil work. Suddenly frightened anew, Tanis knew there could be no wisdom to this decision, yet he couldn't bring himself to turn back.

A moment later, all of them were gone.

Tanis's heart nearly stopped. He sprinted through the crowd, pushing past commoner and noble alike, coming to a skidding halt as he passed a narrow alley that appeared as a mere crevice between the buildings. He thought he saw movement in the dimness beyond, so he slipped in to follow.

The confined space smelled dank and foul. Tanis swallowed his unease at the nearness of the slimy walls, which ended high above in only the barest strip of sky. He walked carefully on the muddied earth and cringed as his boots squished with every step—sure they would hear him following. Though it felt like an eternity, he soon saw the walls opening ahead, where the two adjacent buildings angled away from one another. He slowed just in time, for near voices floated back to him.

Tanis inched his head around the corner until he saw the five men standing ten paces away. The stranger held up one hand, Tanis saw a flash of silver slice down through the air, and then they all stepped forward, seemingly into the wall.

Tanis rushed after them, but he found only empty brick covered with yellow-green ooze. He pushed one hand against the slimy rock, but the wall was impenetrable. He spun around in frustration looking for any other way in and spotted an opportunity further down: a basement window low to the ground, its glass long shattered.

The opening was boarded over from within, but a stout kick proved the wood rotten. A few well-placed thrusts then with his boot gained him entry, and moments later he was pushing through the opening, which was just large enough to accommodate his slender frame.

He fell five paces and landed in an ungraceful heap upon the earthen floor, covered in cobwebs. Coughing, Tanis got to his feet and pulled the sticky cobwebs from his face. He wondered if he'd gone completely insane. Never mind that he didn't know if he was even in the same building as the stranger and his men, but what did he think he would do when and if he found them? The trancelike state—or whatever it had been—had fully worn off now, and any novelty of a grand adventure had evaporated beneath the gritty reality of the moment.

Yet that feeling of duty remained.

Berating himself for his obscenely foolish choices, Tanis glowered around in the dimness wondering what to do next. His Lady would've told him to turn around and leave. Rhys would say he never should've left the café to begin with. Prince Ean would probably ask why he felt compelled to follow the man, and the zanthyr…

What *would* the zanthyr tell him?

The truth was, the zanthyr probably wouldn't say a word, expecting Tanis to work it out on his own.

You'll never accomplish anything one way or the other if you just keep standing here, he told himself. Then he realized there was someone else who might advise him, and the idea cheered him. If Fynnlar had been there, he would no doubt have said, *'Well, Tanis lad, you've already come this far. Might as well keep going and dig your grave deep enough to keep the damned coyotes away.'*

Heartened then that at least one of his companions would be on his side, and despite his many misgivings, Tanis mustered his courage and surveyed the dim room, eventually spotting a rickety-looking staircase. It seemed so decrepit and fragile…hardly able to support a mouse. He gazed fretfully at it, debating whether to risk it, but it appeared to be the only way out. To his relief, the steps held his weight, and he made it to the floor above.

No sooner had he gained the dark hallway than he heard voices from down the nearly pitch-black passage. Feeling along the wall, he followed the sounds until he grew close enough to realize that what he'd thought was mumbling was actually men speaking a different language. Eventually he saw flickering torchlight reflected on the passage walls ahead. Tanis instinctively held his breath as he edged his eyes around the corner of the doorway through which the torchlight spilled. Thus he made no sound when he saw the shocking scene.

He faced a cavernous warehouse, empty of all storage save a few crates upended and used just then as chairs by a couple of the Fhorgs, who sat with their backs to him. The other two stood near the stranger, who held a torch low to the earth, the three of them peering down at the floor as if trying to read some inscription there. But the sight beyond them made Tanis's flesh crawl.

She hung from chains attached to the high ceiling, her body swinging slightly. She was clothed only in her own blood and the deep gouges of their foul craft—long gashes across her arms and thighs…and other places, crueler places that Tanis's eyes shied away from. Blood matted her long brown hair and stained her pale flesh. But when he saw her twitching and realized she was still alive…that's when he knew the intimacy of real fear.

Tanis saw what had been done, though his innocent mind rebelled against the knowledge. They'd bled her carefully, strategically, and now they studied the pools with discerning gazes, her blood lit by the stranger's torch held low. Tanis felt sick, both of stomach and of heart. Who was the poor woman that had endured such torment? And why had they put her to it?

The terrors he'd seen in the stranger's eyes flashed back to mind. Now Tanis understood them better.

Suddenly the stranger stiffened. He spun in a swirl of his cloak, and his hand flashed outward, fingers splayed.

Tanis abruptly sank to his knees in the earthen floor—*in* the floor!

Letting out a little shriek, the lad pulled frantically at his knees, but the unyielding earth had closed around his legs. Clawing at his thighs, his heart pounding, Tanis felt a chill descend like the bitter wind that precedes winter's first storm, and when he looked up, the stranger was standing over him.

"So…" He stared down at Tanis with those fiery eyes pinning him as surely as the earth around his legs.

The others came to see what their master had caught, and in the torchlight, Tanis saw their faces more clearly. Tattoos covered them; blue inscriptions in long lines of daemonic symbols reaching from forehead to chin and beyond.

Tanis shuddered.

"Aw, 'tis nawt bu'a laddie," one of them noted in the Common Tongue, though so heavily accented that Tanis could barely make out what he'd said.

The stranger leveled Tanis a narrow look. "No…" he determined, "it's the boy from the café." He also had a strange accent that Tanis couldn't place. "You followed me? Why?"

Tanis knew he couldn't have answered even if he'd thought of something to say.

The stranger grabbed his arm and pulled sharply. Tanis yowled, expecting his legs to be torn from his knees, but the man must've reversed his working in the same moment, for the lad found himself standing—if weakly—on the floor again. He craned his neck to look up at him, for he was really quite tall.

The stranger leaned to ask quietly in his ear, "What are you doing here, boy?" His breath was ice, his hand was a vice around his arm, and the terrible intimacy of his whisper made Tanis shudder again. "Answer me truthfully, or you may yet see the same fate as the Healer we've just bled." He tightened his grip painfully and shook Tanis, demanding again, "Tell me! Why have you followed me? *Who* sent you?"

Tanis tried to work some moisture into his mouth, but still he barely croaked out the words, "N-no one, milord. I just…I was just…" *Gods and devils*—what *was* he doing? "I just…just follow people…sometimes."

"This is no idle game!" the stranger hissed, emphasizing his point with yet a third squeeze of Tanis's arm. That time his nails drew blood. Tanis felt the heat of their punctures, but it seemed a welcome contrast to the awful cold of the man's touch.

"Pelas, 'e's just some urchin off the street," one of the Fhorgs said, amazingly in Tanis's defense.

The man named Pelas looked Tanis up and down fiercely, assessing him. The lad felt the power in his gaze, and not merely because of the threat he exuded. Rather, Tanis got the strange sensation that the man was much larger even than his tall frame, as if his body was merely the face of something massive and deadly that hunched in the darkness behind him. "This is no gamin," Pelas disagreed, "not dressed like this." Abruptly he shoved Tanis into the arms of the nearest Fhorg. "Bind him. We'll see if he remembers how to tell the truth with some carnal encouragement."

They all headed into the warehouse with Tanis being prodded between two Fhorgs. "Wha' about 'er?" asked one of the others, indicating the woman.

"The blood is cold," Pelas returned in annoyance. "We'll need a fresh extraction."

The Fhorg holding Tanis put a hand on his shoulder and forced him to his knees. Another grabbed his hands and began binding them behind his back. The gouges on his arm where Pelas's nails had cut him stung, but this pain was nothing compared to what the woman must be enduring.

Tanis felt her blood soaking through his britches as he knelt on the sodden floor, and he braved another look up at her. She'd been beautiful, once. Now she seemed a macabre sculpture, a sort of dark offering. It was vicious and terrible what they'd done to her.

"Not that," Pelas said to the Fhorg binding Tanis's hands. "Use the *goracrosta*."

"On '*im*?" The Fhorg's voice rose in protest. "But 'e's just a wee sprite!"

Pelas walked over to a table of knives. "We don't know *what* he is," he said while looking over his daggers, "or who he's working for."

Someone unwrapped the rough rope in several quick turns and rewound Tanis's hands with a silken cord instead. At first the *goracrosta* felt cool around his wrists, but soon it began to sting. Tanis sucked in his breath and clenched his teeth.

"Tis a waste of magic rope on a lit'l thing as 'im," the same Fhorg complained. "Just kill him and be done with it, Pelas. Darshan said—"

Pelas was growing irritated. It was clear from the tone of his voice as he shot back, "*Look* at his eyes and tell me he's just a boy from the street!"

A gruesome face appeared in front of Tanis then, close enough that he could have read the dark language tattooed upon it had he known its alphabet. He noted with grim fascination that even the Fhorg's eyelids held the blue inscriptions, thus creating an unbroken verse from hairline to chin. The eyes that gazed into his were as blue as the woad that stained the Fhorg's skin, and for a moment, Tanis saw the face beneath the tattoo, a rather unremarkable face that wore an expression of irritation. Straightening out of view again, the Fhorg told Pelas, "Yer right. A 'reader, this'un. But 'e cannae lie t'ye, Pelas."

Pelas selected a dagger from his collection and began eyeing down the blade. "Lying and telling the truth are not mutually exclusive. The absence of one does not ensure the presence of the other."

Tanis had to admit that was true—indeed, who knew it better than a truthreader? There were a dozen ways to avoid telling the whole truth without inserting a lie into the equation. That's why a truthreader learned to make his questions so exact. Ask a question the right way, and there could be no ambiguity to the answer.

"Who sent you, lad?" Pelas asked again without lifting his gaze from inspecting his blade.

The *goracrosta* around Tanis's wrist was growing colder, but with Pelas's question, pain flared up his arms and even beyond, stealing his breath. "No one!" Tanis gasped as tears sprang unbidden to his eyes.

"Suit yourself." Pelas murmured. He replaced the blade in its place and resumed his search for the perfect instrument.

"It's true!" Tanis wailed. The cord was so cold it burned, and painful pin-like stabs flared into his chest, like the *goracrosta* was somehow attacking his heart, making every breath painful to manage.

"Maybe, maybe not," Pelas muttered as he plucked another dagger from his table and turned towards him.

If ever Tanis needed courage, it was then. He tried scolding himself to be brave, but that just made him feel more desperate. He tried reminding himself that he'd chosen this path, but that just made him want to cry. *If only Phaedor was here,* the boy thought with a tremulous inhale, blinking back tears of pain, *he would know what to do!*

While one part of him tried not to think about the zanthyr for fear of imagining the tirade he'd endure over his incalculable stupidity, another part wondered: what *would* the zanthyr tell him if he were there? Tanis could almost hear Phaedor's resonant voice answering his need.

'This is a thing of magic they bind you with,' he would say. *'Its pain is mental, not physical. It attacks your mind, for this—not steel, not magic, not flesh—is your greatest weapon. Push the pain aside and focus instead on finding out what you can about this man, so that when you escape—'*

Escape? It seemed ridiculous to think escape was possible, but dying while strung up like a slaughtered steer seemed even more incredible—too incredible for so young a boy with such innocent views of the world.

Pelas approached, holding his weapon of choice. It was a black-bladed Merdanti dagger, a type Tanis knew well, for he had a similar blade strapped beneath the sleeve of his tunic—for all the good it was doing him! Yet Phaedor's imagined words had given him hope. He thought perhaps the pain *was* diminishing just a bit. That, or the terrible chill Pelas emitted was numbing all feeling.

Tanis drew in a shuddering breath and encouraged his lungs to expand against the pain that clenched his chest. "That's an interesting dagger you hold," the lad braved as boldly as he dared. "What careless zanthyr trusted you with his life?"

"Know you a zanthyr's blade, boy?" Pelas observed, turning the dagger from side to side as he regarded Tanis with brows lifted. "You're not entirely the innocent you would have us believe. Who sent you to spy on me?"

Despite it being cold enough now to see his breath on the air, an unexpected resurgence of determination fueled Tanis's defiance. "You're a w-wielder," he challenged through chattering teeth, "can you not f-find out yourself?"

Pelas pinned him with a predatory stare and shook his head to the negative. "Guess again."

The name came to him then without understanding, without knowing whence it had come or how he'd learned it, perhaps a word remembered from a whispered conversation, or plucked from the thoughts of one companion whose fears spoke too loudly. "My m-mistake," Tanis stammered. "Malorin'athgul, I mean."

Pelas's fiery eyes widened, and Tanis knew he'd guessed rightly. The man gave him an acknowledging nod...and a look of approval. But there was nothing safe about his admiration; rather it seemed the hungry sort of look a wolf gave its intended prey.

Tanis felt his insides tremble. *What in Tiern'aval is a Malorin'athgul?*

Abruptly Pelas grabbed Tanis by the hair and pressed his dagger to the lad's neck. The blade felt cool, the smooth stone impossibly sharp, and yet this was something familiar to him. Tanis didn't fear the blade, though he feared the man who wielded it.

"Pelas, the 'ealer cannae last much longer," one of the Fhorgs remarked from across the way. He had a hand to her wrist, and he dropped her arm as he looked to his master.

"*Duikhan nas*, Pelas," the blue-eyed Fhorg protested, thus far the only one of them to come to Tanis's defense. "The li'l truthreader is fresh, the witch ain't, and Darshan said—"

Pelas hissed something in a fiery tongue and spun away from Tanis, only to snare the outspoken Fhorg into the deadly circle of his arm instead. He jammed the dagger precariously beneath the Wildling's jawbone, drawing blood. "I am *tired* of hearing what my brother says," he murmured with venom aplenty. "Darshan is not my keeper, no matter what he may think. You'll do what *I* say and be grateful for the chance to serve."

"I serve Darshan," the Fhorg snarled, but his blue eyes kept darting towards Pelas's dagger.

"My brother will find little value in a tongueless spy, I assure you."

The Fhorg glared, a last act of defiance, but it was clear who would win this fight. "To die is to serve thee best, my master," he intoned in flat hatred.

Pelas shoved him forcefully away. The Fhorg barely caught himself before he pitched chest-first onto the bloody floor.

"You might try at least sounding sincere, Riod," Pelas remarked as he walked over to the captive Healer. "Darshan has such enduring admiration for courage in the face of one's enemies, does he not?"

Even Tanis could hear the sarcasm dripping from his tone.

"Rouse her," Pelas ordered the other Fhorg.

He jerked her head up by the hair and slapped her face hard. She gasped, and her eyes flew open.

"Now then." Pelas fixed her with an assessing look. "Where can I find the pattern, Camilla?"

The Healer named Camilla closed her eyes, but there was no denying the horror that stared at her. "...For the...thousandth...time," she whispered, the words finding their excruciating way across a threshold all but blockaded by pain, "...there is...no such pattern. These creatures are...lying to yo—"

The Fhorg closest to her punched her in the mouth, and she cried out even as her head snapped sideways.

"We've been over this, Camilla." Pelas frowned at her. He paced with hands behind his back. "These Fhorgs have no reason to lie to me, while you have every reason to do so."

Weeping now, the Healer named Camilla looked at Pelas and begged, "…ask…the boy."

"The boy?" Pelas looked at her strangely. "Why would I care for the opinion of a spy?"

Tanis watched in horror as Camilla's eyes rolled back in her head.

"Rouse her," Pelas said irritably.

One of the Fhorgs pitched a bucket of water in her face, and she jerked awake with a start, only to hang her head again. "*Please…*" she wept, a barely audible plea. "*Please…*I don't know…*ask* him."

Pelas looked at Tanis again. He seemed genuinely puzzled. "Did you come here to save her?"

"I…don't even know her," Tanis gasped, for he was enduring his own sort of torment from the rope binding his wrists.

Pelas turned to Riod. "What does she mean, 'ask the boy'?"

"Like I said, Pelas, 'e's a truthreader. He cannae lie t'ye and 'e knows when yer telling the truth."

Pelas fixed Tanis with an unsettling look. "I've heard that, of course," he mused, "but none of the Prophet's Marquiin have ever known what *I* was thinking. I doubt very much their veracity." He considered Tanis for a moment, and the boy tried not to cringe beneath his inspection. It was nearly too much to bear, holding his gaze, knowing the vicious beast that lurked behind it. "Still…it *would* be a useful skill if it exists. Very well. Let's give it a try. Ask me something, little spy."

Tanis scrambled to form a coherent thought. "Are you…are you going to let her go if she tells you what you want to know?" he sent a desperate glance towards Camilla, but her head was lolling.

"I hadn't really thought about it," Pelas said. The he decided, "Probably not. But that was too easy. Ask again."

Tanis sucked in his breath. "How many people have you murdered?"

"I've lost count, and this is becoming tedious. Prove your value to me or she dies as painful a death as my entertainment dictates."

In desperation, Tanis racked his brain for a real question, and when he posed it, he put all of the force of his truthreader's fourth-strand compulsion behind it. "What do you intend to do when you find the pattern you're looking for?"

Pelas's eyebrows rose. "Now that *is* interesting," he murmured, and

Tanis knew he'd felt the compulsion. "When I find the pattern," Pelas replied slowly then, "my brothers and I shall use it to unmake the world."

Even as he gazed in horror at the man, Tanis knew he'd spoken the truth.

"How very interesting..." Pelas eyed Tanis with new appreciation. Abruptly he spun back to the Healer. "Where can I find the pattern, Camilla?"

Head bowed, she whispered, "I...don't...know."

Pelas looked to Tanis. "So *truthreader*, is she telling the truth? Does she know this pattern for which I search?"

Tanis had never been more horrified than in hearing himself answer, "She knows the pattern you're looking for, but she doesn't know how to show it to you, and...and she wouldn't show it to you, even if she knew how." He dropped his gaze miserably then, hating himself in every way in that moment, but most of all, hating his inability to lie to this treacherous man.

Pelas's eyes lit with his smile. "Interesting." He lifted the knife to caress Camilla's cheek. "Let's see if we can help you change your mind, shall we?" Then he drove the blade into the flesh of her shoulder.

Her head flew up and she screamed, even as Tanis yelled, "*Stop!*" He'd never felt such desperation and horror combined into one overwhelming urge.

Pelas drew the blade down through the meat of Camilla's shoulder. She screamed and screamed. Blood poured from her arm across Pelas's hand, steaming where it touched his flesh.

Tanis screamed repeatedly as well, but Pelas never so much as spared a glance in his direction, so intent was he upon his craft.

Over the next half-hour, Tanis screamed until his throat was shredded and raw, until he cried himself into gasping hiccups. He pleaded and protested and shouted anything he could think of to distract the man, but Pelas could not be bothered once set upon his work.

Finally, when the Healer's upper arm was in shreds, Pelas set down his dagger. "Rouse her." He took up his torch and began studying the blood on the floor. One Fhorg set to waking Camilla while the others joined Pelas in peering at the pool.

Tanis was sitting on his heels crying when a jumble of images accosted his mind. He'd been doing his best to protect himself from the twisted thoughts that Pelas constantly spouted, and at first he cringed away from this new assault. But as he saw the pictures better, he realized these new images didn't belong to Pelas.

Tanis lifted his head and found the Healer staring at him.

The moment their eyes met, he understood.

Help me! Please!

Camilla was shouting her thoughts so loudly that Tanis worried Pelas would somehow hear her. Suddenly a torrent of images came to him, visions of Camilla as a girl, studying to be a Healer, kissing a dark-haired boy with a wide smile, giving birth—

Tears brimmed in the boy's eyes and fell down his cheeks. He dropped his head and squeezed his eyes shut, but the images didn't fade. Camilla was giving him her last confession, recalling all of the memories of her life as though to make him the receptacle for all that she was, placing her life's knowledge within his memory to carry forward, willing him to end her pain.

Tanis couldn't take any more—he couldn't bear to harbor her suffering, knowing the loving life she'd led, knowing of the children and husband who would mourn her.

DO something, Tanis!

Tanis knew he had to try.

Somewhere in the last hour, Tanis's arms had gone so numb he could barely move them. He suspected the silken cord with the vicious bite would not easily yield to the steel of men, but he had a different sort of weapon beneath his sleeve. *Merdanti.*

If he could get to the dagger.

In his favor was the preoccupation of his captors with studying the bloody floor. The difficulty came in removing the dagger from its casing through the thick wool of his tunic with fingers that had lost circulation. So he spent precious moments flexing his fingers working some blood back into them. Of course, with the return of feeling came the return of the pain, but Tanis clenched his teeth and endured it. Once he managed to push his sleeve out of the way, his fingers found the dagger and slowly—so slowly that he agonized over every passing moment—maneuvered the dagger into his hand.

Tanis kept his eyes pinned on the others as he positioned the blade to saw through the rope. For a harrowing second he nearly dropped the weapon—the smooth stone slipped through his numb fingers, only to be desperately caught and held tightly while his heart raced—but at last, he got the blade around into position again. To his immense relief, the moment Phaedor's dagger touched the *goracrosta*, it sliced through it like parting cream.

Just like that, Tanis was free.

He fixed his gaze on Camilla and kept his hands hidden behind him as he moved slowly to his feet. Then, knowing he couldn't think about it or he'd never be able to do it, Tanis ran to her. His legs were stiff under him, and he slipped as he sprinted across the slippery floor. In the end, he slammed into Camilla, who couldn't help but scream as he clung to her damaged body and brought the dagger down deep into her heart.

In the next instant, strong hands ripped him off the girl and cast him flying through the air. He crashed against a table and toppled backwards over it, landing hard on his belly on the floor. Before he even found his breath, someone snatched him up by his hair. Tanis made a choked shriek and grabbed onto the hand that was hauling him to his feet.

The lad brought up his head to see blue eyes staring at him, and then a fist hit his face and his head snapped back. Stars flared, and pain blackened the edges of his sight, making him feel instantly sick.

"Again," Pelas said.

Another fist took him in the mouth, bringing a fiery spill of blood.

"Again."

His abdomen became a pit of agony.

After the fifth time, Tanis blacked out.

When he regained consciousness, the first thing Tanis saw was Camilla's dead, staring eyes, for her body lay in a pool of blood, nearly nose to nose with his own. Even hurting as he was, even waking to such macabre conditions, Tanis didn't regret his decision to help her. He hadn't been able to save the boy Piper back in Acacia from Bethamin's corruptive touch, but he had been able to help Camilla find peace. He wasn't sure why he thought of the doomed young truthreader in that moment. Somehow the two experiences just seemed related.

As awareness returned to him, Tanis heard Pelas talking to one of the Fhorgs and was just grateful to no longer be the subject of the man's grim attentions. The position he was in didn't do much to alleviate the pain that throbbed through his body, but he dreaded doing anything to remind Pelas he was alive.

Lying still then, Tanis took stock of his situation: his hands were bound again, although this time they'd used regular rope. His right eye was swollen shut, and his bottom lip had swelled to the size of a slug. His belly felt like someone had cut half of it out and left the other to sicken, and his entire right side was a dull throbbing ache.

Not bad for a day's work, Tanis. Now what are you going to do?

For the life of him he couldn't imagine what had driven him to follow this corrupted, vicious man. Yet, no sooner did the lad wonder about it than that same sense of duty flared, a beacon he could neither ignore nor deny. It called to him, and Tanis was compelled to follow.

Not that the sensation offered any moral support; nor did it provide a sense of conviction which he might've fallen back on when courage ran low. Instead, it was just relentlessly there, as merciless in its insistence as Pelas was in his malevolent ministrations.

"Get him up." Pelas sounded dangerously vexed.

Tanis braced himself as they hauled him to his feet, but still a whimper escaped his clenched teeth. He half expected the man to put him into the chains that Camilla's body had just vacated, and was only hoping that somehow the zanthyr might still find him in time, but Pelas didn't seem of a mind to torture him—at least not right then.

He came up to Tanis and gazed down upon him with detached dispassion. "If you knew my nature, you knew what would befall you if you crossed me, yet you knowingly damaged my property." Pelas eyed him curiously. "Have you no fear of death, boy?"

Tanis spoke as carefully as he could to keep from tearing open the wounds in his lip where his teeth had speared through. "I never…thought much about it."

Pelas leaned close to peer at him, and Tanis noted—now that he was so close to the man—that his eyes were the color of molten copper. With his face just inches from Tanis's, Pelas inquired, "Do you accept that death is your ultimate destination?"

Tanis thought it a really strange question. "Everybody d-dies eventually," he said by way of agreement, though his swollen lips caused him to stumble a bit over the words. Too, he couldn't seem to stop shaking, and this was also affecting his speech.

Pelas straightened. "Interesting." He peered down at him again like a vulture assessing a bit of carrion, perhaps deciding whether or not it was worth the effort to gain it. "I think when I have completed my mission with the Healers I shall investigate the truthreaders." He looked to the Fhorg beside him to note, "My brother Darshan has no monopoly upon them, after all, despite his making a religion out of torturing them. There are still plenty to go around."

Tanis felt dismayed by this news.

"Well then." Pelas looked back to him. "I suppose it's time to say our good-byes, young spy. I would've liked to know for whom you were spying, but I have more pressing business."

"Like slaughtering Healers," Tanis offered bitterly.

"Exactly that," he agreed. Settling copper eyes quietly on Tanis then, Pelas licked his thumb and pressed it to the lad's forehead.

Tanis screwed up his eyes to watch the man's thumb, wondering what this was all about. It seemed a crazy means of farewell.

"What'd ye do wrong?" one of the Fhorgs asked after a moment of silence, wherein they'd all just stood there staring at him.

"Nothing!" Pelas sounded amazed. He grabbed Tanis by the neck, shoved his palm to the lad's head and growled something in a foreign tongue. Tanis had never imagined he could get any colder, but when his teeth started chattering loud enough to echo in the empty room, and his head starting hurting *really* badly—like after the time he'd been swept off a rock into Mieryn Bay in the dead of winter and took far too long to swim back to shore—he realized how far he'd been from knowing what it really felt like to be cold.

"It's nae working," the Fhorg Riod eventually pointed out. "Is yer power deserting ye, Pelas?"

Pelas turned Riod a piercing look. Then he tore away from Tanis and slammed his palm into Riod's chest. The Fhorg flew ten paces through the air and landed roughly on his back, already convulsing. His head bashed repeatedly into the blood-soaked earth while a guttural moan escaped in ghastly cadence.

Pelas eyed him quietly. "It would seem my power is not the issue. Regretfully, my brother will have to send a new spy." He looked back to Tanis then, and his gaze reflected both fury and intense curiosity. "You are an anomaly." He pushed a finger under Tanis's fragile chin while he looked him over. "I do believe you should not exist."

Tanis thought Pelas meant to say more, but something distracted him. He seemed to lose focus and for a long time looked for all the world to have completely vacated his body. Finally he blinked and released Tanis's chin.

"Well…it seems my investigation of you will have to wait. Watch him." He turned in a swirl of his cloak and vanished into the deep darkness beyond their circle of torchlight.

The three remaining Fhorgs found seats on several upended crates and settled in to wait. After a while, Tanis tried asking a few questions of them, but when none of them answered, he gave up and sat down on the ground next to Camilla, feeling heartsick and tormented and altogether rotten.

Yet in the back of his mind something connected. The Marquiin's power hadn't worked on him. Pelas's power hadn't worked on him. Therefore, it could be the same power.

But what power was it?

THREE

"Nothing of this world could be worthy of trust."
— The Prophet Bethamin

KJIERAN VAN STONE locked the door of his room and then leaned against it cautiously, listening for footsteps, for motion, for anyone who might be interested in his activities. While Bethamin saw fit to keep some unsullied truthreaders around, those who'd been spared his Fire—like Kjieran—were considered in the lowest regard and were always looked upon with suspicion by the Prophet's Ascendants. The Ascendants acted both as administrators and as the priests proselytizing Bethamin's faith, but since they were not themselves Adepts, they were quick to distrust all who were. Many times, Kjieran had endured several hours of interrogation just because he'd looked an Ascendant in the eye, and their probing was never pleasant, even when the Marquiin weren't involved.

So Kjieran was exceptionally careful when he prepared his reports to the Fourth Vestal. He did not like to envision what would happen to him if a Marquiin or one of the Ascendants discovered him spying, but he did know that under such a circumstance, death would be a mercy most certainly denied him.

There were many patterns that enabled communication across distances if one had the right medium, but any working of *elae* within the temple would bring the Prophet's Marquiin swarming down on Kjieran. Having anticipated such a problem, the Fourth Vestal had set up an elaborate network of contacts to forward Kjieran's communications out of the temple. They were all of them spies in the Brotherhood of the Seven Stones, professionals ready to die for their cause. Kjieran never came into contact with any of them, so he couldn't be questioned about their identities, nor they about his. He could only trust that his reports were being found and forwarded on, that the information he was risking his life to smuggle out of the temple was reaching those who needed it.

Sitting down at his desk, Kjieran wrote everything he'd overheard that morning in a complicated double-strand helix code the Vestal had made him learn before leaving Dannym. Then he rolled the letter tightly and placed it inside the hollowed-out center of a pillar candle—one of the thousands in use around the temple. Kjieran spent his free evenings digging out the candles' centers for this use, so he always had one ready. With the report safely coiled inside, Kjieran settled the bottom plug of wax back inside the candle and then warmed the wax all the way around the circular base, covering any evidence of his tampering. Then he dropped the candle to dent the bottom edge.

Now it would have to be replaced, for the Prophet unfailingly remarked upon the least imperfection in his temple.

Kjieran took his candle and some other items he'd brought from the vestry to be swapped, cleaned or repaired and made his way out of his dormitory.

Epiphany's grace had landed him the position of acolyte. He'd come in fully prepared—inasmuch as anyone could be prepared—to face Bethamin's Fire. Raine had even crafted a talisman to aid him in overcoming the deleterious effects of the Fire—provided he survived the working to begin with—but Kjieran hadn't needed to use it. The talisman remained sheltered in the false bottom of his trunk, protected by trace seals too minute to be noticed on the currents.

Kjieran believed it was divine intervention alone that had spared him the Prophet's 'purifying' fire, but he also knew—as did anyone who'd survived more than a week in Bethamin's temple—that no one was wholly safe from it. Kjieran had watched the Prophet enough to know that he was erratic in choosing his Marquiin. There were whispers, of course—from the other acolytes and the less discerning brothers—who believed that the Marquiin were chosen only after they'd displeased the Prophet during one of his midnight dalliances. Those 'chosen few' who were invited to the Prophet's bedchambers in the dead of night were just as likely to be mortals as Adepts, however, so Kjieran suspected there was slightly more to the decision of who was 'elevated' to the rank of Marquiin.

He only prayed it would never be him.

This fear more than anything kept him awake at night and invaded his thoughts during every moment of his day. So Kjieran kept his nose to his duties and his eyes on his toes, and he never gave anyone a reason to doubt the veracity of his belief or his devotion to the Prophet—least of all the man himself.

Shuddering as he recalled the icy touch of the Prophet's hand holding his chin, Kjieran turned a corner and came face to face with Dore Madden. He drew up short with a muttered apology and waited for the man to motion him on, but Dore merely stared at Kjieran with his two dark eyes like bright coals burning in an emaciated skull.

"Advisor Madden," Kjieran finally greeted once it became clear that the man wasn't willing to step aside and let Kjieran move on. He shifted his assortment of items in his arms and asked, "Was there something you needed?"

"You overheard my conversation with the Prophet this morning, did you not, acolyte?"

"I was there to attend the Prophet at his behest, Advisor," Kjieran replied, appreciating Dore's accusatory tone about as much as he liked the rest of the cadaverous man.

Dore licked his lips—thin, spindly lips spider-webbed with lines. "I asked about you." His gaze flicked over Kjieran aggressively. "You hailed from Dannym."

"I am Agasi, Advisor," Kjieran corrected, "but I was assigned to the King's court in Dannym for many years."

"Gydryn val Lorian is a known heretic who defames the Prophet's name and seeks to deny his people the benefit of our true faith. How then did you come to escape the kingdom?"

Kjieran gave him the line he'd practiced so many times with Raine that the half-truths had become as truth to him. He dropped his eyes in shame and confessed, "His majesty was…disappointed in my failure to identify the factions behind the deaths of his sons. I left his service in disgrace."

"And how did you find your way to the Light of Bethamin?"

"An Ascendant found me in Tregarion where I was awaiting passage to Agasan. His words, his passion…enlightened me." That much was true—Kjieran had only needed to wait a fortnight in Tregarion before he crossed paths with the Ascendant, who'd been eager to claim him in Bethamin's name.

Dore eyed him surreptitiously. "I am told you are a devoted servant."

"I am most honored to be in the Prophet's service as acolyte." Kjieran wished the man would be about whatever business he had and be done with him. It was one thing to dissemble before the Prophet, who made it impossible not to cower at his feet, and another thing altogether to stand two paces from Dore Madden and hide the utter revulsion that throbbed in every fiber of his being.

"No doubt you look forward to being elevated to the rank of Marquiin one day."

"As much as you must surely desire it, Advisor," Kjieran returned.

Dore licked his lips. "Alas, I am no truthreader to gain such an exalted position."

And aren't you endlessly thankful for it! "What did you need, Advisor?" Kjieran said, anxiously hurrying the man along. "I am about the Prophet's business and should not delay."

Dore gave him a look of indignant annoyance. "You heard, no doubt, that the prince whose family you once served has done the unthinkable."

"I know little of what transpired, Advisor."

"I'll tell you what *transpired*," Dore said vehemently. "Ean val Lorian broke the bond between the Prophet and one of his Marquiin—a profanation of both our doomed brother and our exalted Prophet!"

"It is unbelievable," Kjieran said, meaning it. He didn't believe a word of Dore's account. Kjieran hadn't seen Ean since he was a boy of thirteen, but if he'd had any Adept talent, it would've presented by then.

"I would know anything *you* might tell me of the prince." Dore finally got to the point. His eyes bored into Kjieran, and he licked his lips again. "You knew him as a child. You knew his family. Where would he go?"

Kjieran loathed giving Dore any information about the young prince, but he knew he would have to come up with something. "He is not in Calgaryn then?" he asked, stalling for time.

"After his treacherous misdeed, the heretic fled the kingdom. He was seen in Chalons-en-Les Trois but vanished before the hand of the Prophet's justice could apprehend him."

Kjieran frowned at the man. What to tell him when any information was likely too much?

"You seem reticent to speak, acolyte. Have you some misplaced loyalty to this heathen recusant?"

"You mistake my silence, Advisor." It took an immense force of will to keep his expression neutral. "I am merely considering what information might be most helpful." *That I might better keep it from you.*

"Has he any contacts outside of the kingdom?"

"His uncle Prince Ryan is Dannym's ambassador to Agasan," Kjieran supplied, confident this known fact would be of little value. "His cousin Fynnlar val Lorian is a known renegade who deals with pirates. Last I knew Fynnlar had been apprehended by the Empress's Imperial Navy and was being held for questioning."

Dore looked less than pleased. "What else? Surely you know more than this!"

Kjieran affected a thoughtful expression. "There is an heiress to whom the prince is betrothed. He may have gone to her estates."

Dore latched onto this avidly. "Where?"

"I was told she has holdings in M'Nador, Advisor. I do not know what part."

Dore's expression fell again. He frowned thunderously at Kjieran. "What about the man himself. How might I recognize him?"

Kjieran had no way of double-talking his way out of that question. "The young prince is handsome," he reluctantly admitted. "He would stand out in a crowd. He travels always with his blood-brother, Creighton Khelspath, son of Kristophe Khelspath of Agasan." Kjieran shifted his bundles again and shot Dore an agonized look. "Please, Advisor, I really must continue on my duties."

"Fine, fine." Dore stepped aside to give Kjieran leave. "But I may have more questions for you later."

"Anything I can do to be of service to the Prophet," Kjieran replied as he headed quickly down the hall, not looking back.

As soon as he was around the next corner he shuddered involuntarily. As much as the Prophet terrified him, Dore Madden disgusted him. The

man was like a fetid boil, oozing a malignant taint that infected everything
it touched. He delighted in working in the most profligate and repulsive
patterns imaginable. Kjieran suspected that Dore was responsible for more
evil works than just providing the Prophet with an ever-growing repertoire
of compulsion patterns, but he was certain of one thing: Dore Madden was
the only one in Tambarré that slept soundly.

Regaining his composure before someone saw him in such a state
of anxiety and remarked upon it, Kjieran continued on his way to the
temple repertory. Two scribes were just departing as he neared the massive
storeroom, which was a repository for supplies and materials vast and varied.
Entering, he saw two Lesser Brothers talking further down an adjoining
aisle.

Kjieran made his way first to the shelves where candles were stored
and switched out his damaged one for a pristine candle more befitting the
Prophet's temple. The former could still be used in the fellowship halls or
the scriptorium, where the Prophet rarely ventured, so it was not unusual to
leave a broken candle for others to use. Only Kjieran knew his candle would
somehow find its way outside the temple. For the briefest of moments as
he set it upon the lowest shelf in a particular spot behind the others, he
desperately envied the candle its escape.

He never knew who was retrieving his candles, but by the time he'd
finished his other errands, he passed by the shelf and saw the candle had
been taken. It gave him hope, however small, to see it gone.

It was too easy to lose sight of the world beyond Tambarré, too easy
to fall prey to the Prophet's seductive workings and lose oneself in the
hypnotically repetitious pattern of temple life. Too easy to overlook the evil
taking place all around one.

Kjieran had seen it happen often with Adepts and *na'turna* alike. The
simpler a man, in fact, the faster his mind was subverted. Too soon the
man would be incorporated into the massive cogwheel and gears that was
Tambarré, just one more mindless spoke turning on the Prophet's axis,
bound as much by his own failure to maintain vigilance upon his thoughts
as by Bethamin's spells of compulsion. Such a man walked freely among the
shadowed corridors of Tambarré, but he was no less a slave.

As Kjieran walked back to his room that day, he prayed for Ean, that
Epiphany would keep him safe; he prayed for his king and queen, that they

might find happiness together again; and he prayed that Raine was receiving his reports and putting together the pieces of this vast and complicated plot. But most of all he prayed that his sacrifice would result in a future for the realm, one without the Prophet Bethamin.

This he prayed for most fervently of all.

FOUR

"If a secret is to keep, let none know of its possession."

– Aristotle of Cyrene, cir. 101aF

THE MAN DRESSED in black sat in the chair of his small room staring at his hands. He had nice hands. His fingers were long and straight—good for picking up tiny things—and his nails had a pleasing shape, even after enduring so much for so long.

His hands were the only part of himself he still recognized.

Too many years in the salt mines of N'ghorra had left him twisted and bent. His left leg had been broken once when scaffolding had collapsed upon him, and it hadn't healed correctly. There were no Healers in N'ghorra. No whores either, unless you considered the *bacchasi,* but he preferred his hand over young boys when such urges came to him in the night.

His face, once handsome, had become the canvas for a long scar ranging from jaw to cheekbone. It flamed when the weather turned hot. The man who'd given him that scar lost an eye in the exchange, so the man in black considered he'd won that fight. He had other scars, too, related to other conflicts, but the scars that ran the deepest were the ones that couldn't be seen.

Scars of treachery. Scars of betrayal. Scars of abandonment and rejection from those who neither loved nor cared any longer. These were the scars that rooted the deepest, cleaving muscle and bone, twisting his memories into abominable, unbearable things.

He hadn't always been full of regret. He remembered being different once. He'd still had a name then—before bondage and the salt mines had taken it from him. He remembered standing for something, believing in something so strongly that it drove him to survive one of the most hellish places in the living realm.

That was before Dore Madden found him. Now he couldn't remember those convictions that had once given him strength.

Now the salt mines of N'ghorra were his fondest memories.

Dore Madden.

The name was a curse to him, but a curse that bound him more securely than the chains of N'ghorra ever had. Dore had found him and bound him with the fifth before they'd even left the mines—'ensuring his cooperation' the man liked to claim. That working still haunted his dreams, a nightmare from which he found no escape. No compulsive binding was ever gentle, but to be bound to a lunatic like Dore Madden meant feeling the touch of his mind intimately, and this...*this* was a torment the man in black would not wish upon his gravest enemy.

He'd come to accept his fate the way one accepts any torture over time, eventually becoming inured to the crawling sense in his skull, to the man's howling insanity, to his perverted desires and compulsions laid so deep as to scald his very bones.

He liked to think that if Dore had found him before N'ghorra, his pride would've led him to take his own life before serving such depravity. But the salt mines changed a man, stripped him of everything, even his will to live. When there was no hope in life, there was no reason to care what you did on your way towards death.

It had been a very, very long time since the man in black remembered what hope felt like.

So he sat in his chair, bound beneath patterns of compulsion like heavy webs smothering body and soul, and he gazed at his hands and tried not to think about the constant feeling of worms crawling inside his skull or the twisted acts Dore might require of him next.

Sometimes he would sit for days on end waiting on the wielder's pleasure. Dore had ordered him to stay in his chair, and no matter how intensely he concentrated, no matter how desperately he tried, he could not move from the chair until the wielder gave him leave.

Beneath his hands on the table lay a length of string tied into elaborate knots. When Dore allowed it, and even sometimes when he didn't, the man in black would lose himself in their construction. He could sit for hours in utter silence while his deft fingers wove those knots. It had always been a habit of his, for as long as he could remember.

He'd lost track of how many hours he'd been sitting there when Dore finally entered looking uncharacteristically gleeful, which never boded well for anyone.

"It is done," the wielder announced as he walked into the room. "The Prophet has agreed to send you in search of the prince."

"Good," said the man in black. It wouldn't do to let Dore know how desperately he wanted this, how he would agree to most anything if it meant escaping Dore's constant oversight. People were *things* to Dore Madden. Possessions. He was tired of being a lunatic's favorite toy.

Dore looked him over with a violent light burning out of the holes in his head that passed for eyes. "We'll leave soon for Bemoth. Niko van Amstel has called all of the Fifty Companions to his estate—those of us left alive, that is." The violent light abruptly turned wild, frantic. It was a look that came into Dore's eyes at the merest mention Björn van Gelderan. Dore Madden feared no one as much as he feared him—*this*, the man in black knew as intimately as he knew Dore's own mind. The Prophet Bethamin, in all of his malfeasance, engendered but a pale shadow of discomfort next to Dore's deep-rooted terror of the Fifth Vestal.

"Niko has contacts throughout the realm," Dore continued, unaware that the man in black saw the shadows of his deepest secrets, the horrors that writhed within his own soul each night. "He will help us to discover the whereabouts of this northern prince."

"Good," was all the man in black said. With Dore Madden, the less said the better.

In the silence that followed, the man in black could feel Dore's hot gaze scouring him; he could feel the wielder testing the strength of the patterns binding him to his will. It made his skin crawl, even after so long, but he didn't let it show. It was never prudent to let Dore Madden know anything about you—not if it could be helped. "You're ready for this?" Dore asked after a moment. "No hesitation?"

The man in black lifted his eyes to Dore. "Why should I hesitate? You have instructed me well enough."

Dore smiled. He always looked hideous when he smiled. "Ah, my star pupil." He came and took the man's face in his hands. Bony white fingers smoothed back his black hair and caressed the scar that he hated so. "You will show them what brilliant work I have done. It is the dawn of a new era, and you will be the one to usher in the light. That's why I have decided to name you *Işak'getirmek*, Light-bringer."

The man in black closed his eyes as the worms of Dore's binding writhed eternally in his skull. At least now he had a name.

FIVE

"Be wary the treasure you pluck is not attached
to the toe of a dragon."

– An old Kandori saying

TRELL FROWNED AT the river. His storm-grey eyes were both slightly accusing and deeply searching, as if expecting the murky waters to hold explanation if not remorse. Gendaia was still lame, and Trell inexplicably blamed the river—or more specifically, the River Goddess Naiadithine.

Though he had no proof of her complicity in his horse's condition, instinct told him there was more to this confluence of events than mere chance. That Gendaia went lame during a shallow river fording—while neither impossible nor unheard of—was yet suspicious beyond measure where he and the River Goddess were both involved. What chance then that Gendaia's injury had prevented him from leaving only days before a mysterious girl rode the river's swollen waves to be deposited at his feet?

Okay, not exactly deposited. He'd put himself in harm's way to save her life, but that only strengthened his feeling of providence surrounding the matter.

Not that he didn't owe Naiadithine a great deal—more than he could ever repay even if it meant the offering of his life, for the goddess had saved him several times over, and Gendaia too. So he knew he owed her his trust—providing she did have a hand in laming Gendaia, for which there was no proof but Trell's instinct—but he still couldn't bring himself to forgive her.

Take from me what you will, my goddess, he thought, leveling a heated look at the chill waters, *but leave my horse out of it.*

Trell pushed fingers through his unruly black hair and then shoved hands into pockets as he turned to wander upriver. The dervish of his thoughts whirled endlessly, each leaf upon the twisting wind representative of a different mystery. Naiadithine's latest intervention in his life was just one among several strange events.

First, what to make of Yara's response?

As Trell had staggered into the farmhouse on that morning several days ago, drenched and muddied and with the cold weight of the unconscious lass in his arms, the old woman had turned from the fire, rocked back on her heels and remarked in astonishment, "It's *her!*"

Trell had been too preoccupied to register this pronouncement at the time—being so focused on getting the girl inside—and in the rush that followed there'd been little opportunity for questions. But since then he'd had plenty of time to consider it.

Stranger still, Yara had refused to let him help get the lass cleaned up, though it was quite a chore for the old woman to manage on her own. She'd mumbled some absurdity about it not being proper for Trell to see the girl disrobed. Trell refilled the tub twice before Yara deemed the lass clean enough for mending and allowed him to help her.

He remembered that moment with vivid clarity.

Walking into the bedroom to see the girl lying upon his bed with her long flaxen hair spread damply across the pillow...Yara was tending her broken arm as he came around to look down upon her face. Even maimed and bruised and with one eye swollen shut, even with that great ugly gash in her head, there was something...familiar about her.

It struck a memory.

The flash of an image—a young girl stood upon the seashore bundled in a violet cloak as much as silence, the wind whipping her flaxen hair as Trell watched from the stern of a skiff rowing laboriously out to sea... There were others on the shore, many others, but Trell only saw the girl's face, round-eyed and full of sorrow.

That briefest snatch of memory, yet he felt tied to her still, the nameless girl on a wintry beach. It was a tenuous link forged by a rope so frayed it was by miracle alone that it still held true. Nor could he say why he felt tied to her, only that he did.

Looking down upon the girl in his bed, Trell thought this could be the same girl who had watched him forlornly across windswept tides, for beneath the bruises he saw a similar likeness. But it was too much to hope for, so he let the idea fade.

"You going to keep standing there gaping like a brainless carp," Yara had grumbled, "or did you have a mind to help me save her life?"

Trell had jumped to help then, and together they'd reset her broken bone, splinted the arm and bandaged her wounds. Only once did the girl resurface, and then it was just to offer a brief glimpse of lovely amber eyes—albeit bloodshot and unfocused. The lass had retreated to unconsciousness the moment Yara set needle to the gash in her temple, which Trell supposed was just as well.

When all was said and done, Trell and Yara had returned to the kitchen where Yara prepared *czai* tea for them. As they sat together at the scrubbed wooden table, Trell had time to consider the moment of his arrival and had asked, "Do you know this girl, Yara?"

"*Pshaw.*" She dismissed his question as utter folly in that way women have of indicating with a simple wordless utterance how perfectly foolish men are in general.

But Trell was not to be put off so easily. "Why did you say, 'It's her' when I walked in?"

"What?" She settled him a doleful eye. "I never said such a thing."

He arched a dubious brow. "You certainly did."

"Certain are you of quite a few things you ought not to be, Ama-Kai'alil," she returned. She'd taken to calling him Man of the Tides since they spoke almost exclusively in the desert tongue, and in that language, the moniker was easier than using his name.

With the image of the young girl on the beach still vivid in his mind, Trell captured Yara's dark-eyed gaze and pressed, "*Do* you know this girl, Yara?"

Returning his stare, she lifted her chin and ascertained, "I have never laid eyes on her before."

It wasn't the answer he'd hoped for, but Trell admitted it was all he was likely to get. The wily old woman only ever explained what it suited her for a man to know, and that wasn't a great deal—as the episode with Carian vran Lea had proven.

But her affected indignation was hardly reassuring, and the memory was but one of the leaves circling his mind.

Trell scratched at his dark beard, which was growing unkempt and itchy and probably needed shaving off. A wind off the river teased Trell's hair into his eyes and the next curious leaf swept before his mind's eye…another day, another mystery…

It was a day or so after her rescue, and the girl lay in a fevered sleep. She had not resurfaced since that initial foray into consciousness, so they remained in mystery about who she was and whence she'd come—save, lately, the river—or at least Trell had no idea. Yara merely said she didn't, which Trell believed less and less as time progressed.

But on that day, Trell had just arrived in the nearby town of L'Aubernay to gather supplies for Yara's journey to Tregarion and beyond. As he was securing the wagon, his attention caught on a stranger who was conversing with the local tavern-keeper Jean-Claude, a big barrel-chested man Trell had come to know moderately well since his arrival at Yara's. Trell was close enough to hear their discussion, especially since the stranger was speaking abominable Veneisean with a heavy northern accent and was attempting to compensate for his ineptitude by shouting.

"…expected days ago but there's been no sign of her coach," the man was all but yelling. He was expensively attired, though his longish moustache and pointed chin-beard made him look somewhat akin to a goat and decidedly untrustworthy. Trell suspected he wouldn't have much luck getting answers from the townspeople of L'Aubernay, who misliked Northmen in general and especially the ones who couldn't be bothered to learn their language. "My lord will pay well for any news of her," the man meanwhile offered. "She is of importance to him personally."

"*Oui*," muttered Jean-Claude. He shoved hands into his considerable pockets. "And you'd be?"

The man puffed up with his own importance. "I am Lord Brantley."

Jean-Claude frowned. "Never heard of you."

"The Earl of Pent," Lord Brantley clarified.

"Never heard of Pent neither. Is it near L'Aubernay?"

Lord Brantley looked affronted. "Assuredly not."

"Tregarion then?"

"No, it's—"

"Chalons-en-Les Trois?"

"*No*, it—"

Jean-Claude scratched his head. "Jeune?"

"In the Maker's name, man, it's in Dannym!"

"Dannym." Jean-Claude repeated the name as if the kingdom was a distant land and not Veneisea's closest neighbor.

"*I* am from Dannym," the earl reasoned, "the woman I seek is from Dannym, and my lord hails from Dannym. We're all from Dannym."

"Pent is near Calgaryn then?" Jean-Claude asked, still pondering the mystery of Lord Brantley's origins.

"No—"

"Acacia?"

"Never mind where Pent is! I'm looking for a woman—blonde, brown eyes, about yea tall," and he motioned with his hand. "She was expected through here several nights ago."

Trell stiffened at the description, for the man had just described the girl lying unconscious in his bed.

"Hmm…" Jean-Claude meanwhile screwed up his face in thought. "*Ah oui*, had a storm three nights back. Road's washed out few miles to the south. Was the mademoiselle coming from the south?"

"Possibly." Lord Brantley turned suddenly close-mouthed, as if wary of saying too much about her origins.

"They'd be up from Rethynnea then." Jean-Claude nodded sagaciously.

Lord Brantley gave him an aggravated look. "I'm not certain of their exact point of departure."

"Oh. Xerses, you think?"

"I just said, I don't—"

"Thessalonia? Cause that would bring them in by the east road, not the south road. Did the mademoiselle come from the south, do you know?"

Lord Brantley looked nearly apoplectic. "Is there any other tavern in town?" he asked in desperation.

"Just the one. Did you need a room?"

The earl sort of stared at him. When he realized the question was actually genuine, he answered defeatedly, "No. I'm looking for a woman—blonde, about yea tall—"

"What'd you say her name was?"

"Her name isn't important! What's important for *you* to remember is that my lord will pay handsomely for news of her—any news at all."

"Who'd be your lord then? The Earl of Pent?"

"No, you dimwitted fop! *I am*—oh, never mind!" He spun on his heel and stalked across the square.

Jean-Claude watched the earl stomp away. Then he noticed Trell and grinned at him by way of greeting before heading back inside his tavern. Trell nodded politely in return, but his attention remained fixed on the Earl of Pent.

Should he tell him of the girl?

Yara had been suspiciously adamant that they should say nothing of her until she woke and could speak for herself. Trell wasn't sure why Yara felt so inclined, but he trusted the old woman's instincts far more than he trusted Lord Brantley.

As he continued about his business that day—or rather, Yara's business—Trell caught sight of Lord Brantley several times, but he didn't cross paths with him again until they bumped into each other accidentally as the earl was exiting the cobbler's shop.

"You there!" He waved a dictatorial hand for Trell to approach him. "I've seen you about town today, haven't I, fellow?"

Trell found something in the earl's manner to be decidedly insulting, as if the man thought himself considerably higher in both station and quality of character than anyone he was likely to meet in L'Aubernay.

"I'm looking for a woman. She might've passed through here a few nights ago. Someone might've seen her. *You* might've seen her?"

Trell hugged his sack of milled amaranth to his chest and considered Lord Brantley. He didn't like what he'd seen of the man thus far—the earl wore arrogance as a pale substitute for the livery of the mysterious lord he served—but Trell knew that a servant did not always accurately represent his lord. He was cautious not to judge in haste and deny the girl better help than he and Yara might provide. To buy himself more time to consider, he asked, "What did she look like, your mademoiselle?"

The earl was apparently too preoccupied with his own avarice to notice

Trell's cultured, elegant Veneisean, such a contrast to the earl's own speech—and indeed, everyone else in L'Aubernay. "Long blonde hair, skin the color of caramel. She stands no taller than your shoulder. Some might consider her lovely in a...a strange sort of way."

"I think I'd remember such a woman."

"Oh, she's memorable." The earl's tone held considerable heat, and Trell guessed there was a story there. "My lord is desperate to find her. Her coach never arrived at its intended rendezvous, so my men and I are backtracking."

"She could've passed right through L'Aubernay," Trell pointed out. "If she stayed in town, Jean-Claude the tavern-keeper would know."

"That man wouldn't know his own dog if bit him on his arse," the earl grumbled.

At this remark, Trell determined he was not fond of Lord Brantley.

"She's young and fair," the earl went on, heedless of Trell's low impression of him, "unworldly. She'd be lost here in this foreign land, not speaking the language as you and I."

Trell regarded him steadily. "She's kin to your lord?"

"No, a...a friend of the family."

"He must be benevolent indeed to send his men so far in search of a family friend."

"Lord Stefan val Tryst is a great man, a powerful man," the earl boasted, but Trell thought there was more air than substance to his praise. "He's next in line for the Eagle Throne and will soon be upon it."

Trell arched brows at this, startled by both the seditious pronouncement and the earl's lack of prudence in declaring it. "It was my understanding the Eagle Throne already has a king upon it."

"That's open to interpretation." Lord Brantley might've donned a mask of hatred, so changed did his countenance become at this reference.

Or rather, perhaps, the mask has finally come off and the true face surfaces?

Trell decided he'd seen enough of Lord Brantley. "I must be on my way. Good day to you, monsieur."

But the earl was not to be put off so quickly. Perhaps Trell had not hidden the truth from his gaze well enough, or perhaps the man was just that tenacious, but he grabbed Trell's arm and demanded hotly, "Might you have seen her then?" The voracious look in his gaze gave Trell the certainty he'd theretofore been lacking.

He cast an unfriendly eye upon the earl's hand on his arm, and the man released his hold. Trell slowly repeated then, "Have I seen a blonde woman standing about as tall as my shoulder?"

Lord Brantley nodded, his gaze full of predatory anticipation.

"No," Trell said, and it was true—the girl had never stood up at all.

He could tell from the earl's expression that he didn't entirely believe him—that, or he wasn't willing to give up the one thread of hope he'd latched onto.

"You seem an educated sort," Lord Brantley said with an undercurrent of urgency now fueling his speech, "and you seem to know these people, this area. I can pay you well to help me, and this woman…well, she's the type…" He leaned in and added in a low voice, "Between you and me, there might be more in it for you should you be the one to find her. My lord doesn't care if she's returned to him in *exactly* the same condition, if you catch my drift."

Trell gazed at him coldly. All he could think of was that while he'd imagined he'd been saving the girl from a raging river, in fact he'd been saving her from the despicable Lord Brantley.

"Good day, monsieur." Trell blatantly did not wish him luck as they parted. In fact, as he was walking away, Trell asked Thalma, the Goddess of Luck, to turn her eye far afield of the Earl of Pent.

Lord Brantley called after him in a decidedly menacing tone, "That's quite the sword you've got there. It speaks rather loudly, to those who know its like."

Trell felt a jolt at these words, but he didn't stop walking, and he didn't turn around.

That had been yesterday, and all of today he'd been wrestling with Lord Brantley's comment and the mystery of the sleeping girl. Now he walked the river's edge with trepidation, and his grey eyes saw only trouble as he gazed into the greenish waters.

Why must serving you be so difficult, my goddess?

Fhionna's voice seemed to answer, a bit of wisdom conferred a lifetime ago. *Naiadithine's ways are as twisted as a river's path, but her heart is as true to her chosen ones as the river is to its course. If you walk in Naiadithine's eye, you must trust that the river is taking you where you need to go. Even if all else seems false, you must trust the river, Trell of the Tides.*

Trell turned from his thoughts at the sound of pounding feet just moments before a boy came sprinting out of the forest. It was Deon, the youngest son of Yara's closest neighbor, who often came by to help around the farmstead.

"Trell!" His brown eyes were bright and his cheeks flushed from his sprint. "She's awake!"

Alyneri dreamed of dark water. She floated upon a starless sea whose massive waves carried her, cradled her, swept her onward through the night. In her dream, the darkness was complete, yet she felt no fear of it, only a lingering regret now mostly dissolved. Her heart felt at peace for the first time since her early childhood, before the politics of kings had shattered it.

For a long time, she knew the loss of self was imminent, that the moment would come when she would cease to exist, and she welcomed such release. This life had been a winding stream of painful experiences, too painful for a sensitive young soul. She had dared to love and was mercilessly punished for it. Obeyed her king, and was exploited as due reward. Everyone she loved had been taken from her. In the numb of unconsciousness, the final sacrifice of her life seemed the logical denouement.

The first time Alyneri realized she was still alive came as a shock. Out of the peaceful ebb of her life, lightning struck the dark water. Blinding light flared, the starless sea webbed with crackling heat, and pain bolted her back to consciousness.

She saw a hand and arm moving in front of her, blurry and crimson tinged. Voices spoke in hushed tones, one male, one female. Her head felt like a cauldron burning in the furnace of its forging. One arm was a lesser fire, and the rest of her body was cold and terrifyingly unresponsive, a doll body encased in ice.

Someone moaned, and she was horrified to realize it had been her.

"Be still child," she heard a woman say. Then to another, "Hold her now while I stitch the wound."

Warm hands pressed against her, and she felt the heat melting through her icy flesh. Then a needle speared her temple, a blinding sheet of lightning flared across her vision, and everything went black.

The second time Alyneri found consciousness was much like the first. Only this time, as pain and ice and fire drew her from numb sleep, she couldn't open her eyes at all. The voices were far off and strange, and her body was too heavy to move. In time, she heard someone approaching and felt a cool hand touch her cheek.

"The fever is still upon her," the same woman said, her voice pitched in such a way as to indicate she was speaking to someone in another room. Alyneri caught something else odd in her voice, but she couldn't pin thought to what it was. As the woman left her side, she tried to move her upper body. Pain like lightning flared, and down she tumbled once more into the midnight water.

On her third resurfacing, Alyneri awoke in darkness. Her body felt comfortably cool. Remembering the last time she'd tried to move her head, she decided to start this time with a more benign appendage. She wiggled her toes and was happy to find no pain in the doing. Legs and fingers followed, to equally safe result. Finally, after lying still for several long breaths trying to work up the courage, she braved moving her head ever-so-slightly from side to side and was rewarded with only a dull ache. Relief flooded her.

Moving other parts, she recognized that one arm was strapped to her chest, and she lifted a hand to feel the splint that held it safe. Then she gingerly explored the bandage wrapped around her head and across her eyes.

What happened to me?

The last thing she remembered with any clarity was going into the apothecary. She followed herself in memory as she walked through the store and found—

The image of Sandrine brought a sudden nauseous chagrin, and other memories followed in a flood: the drugged tea, the strange man in the coach—kidnapping her in the name of the Duke of Morwyk, though the details remained fuzzy—and then the violent storm. She felt again that dizzying moment when the coach had lurched and pitched her into the storm. After that, she remembered only brief glimpses of waking.

So who had saved her?

She was debating whether she might try to sit up when a door opened and a woman came inside singing a tune Alyneri immediately recognized.

Come rain, come rain,
Come wash my hands of these dusty years.
My love has gone, my life is long,

Come wash away these burning tears
My love has gone, but I live on.

Come rain, come rain.
Come christen me for I am bare
A life anew is one denied
She lives and dies while I have cried
My love is gone, but I live on.
Come rain, come rain.

"My father used to sing that song to me," Alyneri said when the woman paused at the end of the verse. Her own voice sounded so weak and hoarse it seemed barely a whisper, but the woman moved straight to her side.

"Ah *soraya*, you're awake at last." The voice, throaty and deep, reminded Alyneri with a pang of loss of Farshideh. The woman took Alyneri's free hand. Hers was a rough and calloused hand, and Alyneri could tell that it was also an old hand, one that had perhaps seen many babes born and lost.

"I love that song." Alyneri felt so oddly blind to the world due to her bandage, but she envisioned the kindly face of the woman at her side. "*Naeb's Lament*, isn't it?"

"It is an old Kandori song," the woman replied. Alyneri heard surprise as well as pleasure in her tone. "You were brought up well if your father sang it to you."

"I fell asleep to the sound of his voice singing every night," Alyneri recalled wistfully, wishing as ever that her father, Prince Jair, was still alive. That her charming, beautiful father had been stolen from her while she was still so young was one of the cruelest hands Fate had ever dealt her.

The woman patted her hand. "How do you feel, *soraya*?"

"Strange," she answered honestly. "Better than before. Thank you for helping me."

"All praise is due to Ama-Kai'alil. He's the one who dragged you from the river."

Alyneri drew in a long breath and exhaled slowly, settling herself to receive the news of her condition. "I don't remember the river. Am…am I—"

"No lasting harm, I think," the old woman assured her. "A broken rib, a fractured arm which we reset well for you. You took a bad hit to your head. As Azerjaiman blows west, that one worried us, but I see you've kept your wits about you. Daughters of the sand are strong."

Alyneri realized she'd been holding her breath and let it out in relief. "Thank you. I am…" she grunted and caught her lower lip between her teeth. "Well, I'm alive. That's a start, isn't it?"

"A good start, to be sure."

"But where am I?"

"Safe, child. In my home. I am Yara."

"You're Kandori," Alyneri said with a smile—not a difficult assertion considering they were speaking the desert tongue. She was surprised though that the speaking of it brought her such joy.

"As are you, it would seem," and Alyneri could hear the smile in Yara's voice. "The gods work in mysterious ways."

"But we're not in Kandori—we couldn't be?"

"Nay, child, a good deal west. Near the border of Veneisea and the town of L'Aubernay. Two days north of the Free City of Rethynnea."

So close…

Alyneri bit her lip again. So close to Ean still. It was such a relief. She reached her free hand to touch the bandages across her eyes. "Can these come off?"

"A while yet." Yara tapped her hand gently to leave the bandage alone. "I stitched the one wound, but your eye was in a bad way. There is bruising and swelling yet. It's been but days since you came to us. A few more for the healing, I would think."

Alyneri nodded her understanding, though her helplessness rankled. The one pattern a Healer couldn't see was her own. It was akin to not seeing the forest for the trees—how could one see the pattern of the entire forest when standing deep within it?

"A moment, *soraya*." Yara released her hand, and Alyneri heard her cross the room and then the sounds of a far door opening and closing. A moment later, the door sounded again and the woman returned. "There." She retook her chair at Alyneri's bedside. "I've called for Ama-Kai'alil. He'll be here soon to see you—been quite concerned, we have. I feared Inithiya would come for you when your fever ran so high, but She moved on. Angharad looked favorably upon you, child."

At least this once, Alyneri thought with a heavy heart. "Is Ama-Kai'alil your husband, Yara?"

"Lands, no!" Yara laughed an old woman's cackle. "Handsome and whip-smart to boot, he has even an old woman like me thinking things I haven't dreamed of in decades. If only I had a few less years on these old bones…"

Alyneri smiled. "You make him sound very nice."

Yara laughed at herself and added with pat of Alyneri's hand, "He's the son I might've had if Jai'Gar had seen fit to give me sons instead of daughters."

Alyneri smiled too, imagining what Yara's ideal man would look like. She envisioned someone like her father—tall and raven-haired, with almond skin and deep, dark eyes. "It's a strange naming though."

"That it is," Yara agreed. "There's a story there, to be sure. He'll tell you if you ask him right." She paused for a moment and then added quietly, "I imagine you both have some stories to share."

"*Yara?*"

Alyneri heard the man's call just before she heard the outer door close, and her breath caught in her throat. She'd recognized something in his voice, and yet…

"Ama-Kai'alil, friend of my heart, come and meet our charge."

She heard footsteps, and then, in the Common Tongue, he said, "Well…I guess I should say welcome back."

"Thank you." Alyneri managed a meek smile. It was disconcerting being blind to the world, trusting only lesser-used perceptions to provide the images her eyes were denied. "And thank you for saving me. Yara told me you risked your life."

He grunted derisively but with humor. "It was the least I could do."

Yara stood and walked across the room and announced in the desert tongue, "I'm off to see to dinner. Soraya, you make him stay here now and tell you his tale."

"Wait, you—" he said, surprised, "you speak the desert tongue?"

"My father was Kandori." Alyneri tried to put a face to his voice, which resonated with her in a way that struck her deeply, but oddly no face would form. "I hope—I mean…that doesn't bother you, does it?"

"Far from it." She could hear in fact how this pleased him. "You speak the Kandori tongue well," he said, coming closer. "Which language do you prefer?"

"I…I am pleased to use the language of my father…if it pleases you," she added, feeling herself blushing for no identifiable reason. She heard him sit down beside her then, and his presence made her feel strangely…safe. "Yara said there was a story to your name?"

"Yes, she likes to imagine greater things of me than I ever have hope of realizing."

"Greatness is as greatness does, Ama-Kai'alil," Yara admonished from the other room.

He chuckled. "But I would know of *you, azizam,* and then I must share some news—though I hope…well, we'll cross that bridge soon enough."

Alyneri felt at once thrilled and anxious by his attentions—*azizam* meant 'darling one.' "All right," she said after a moment. She caught her lip between her teeth and wished she had a clue what she looked like to him—then decided it was best that she didn't know. "What would you learn of me?"

"What if we started with your name?"

His tone was so kind, he put her at ease at once. "I am Alyneri. Alyneri d'Giverny."

She sensed a tension filling the silence that followed and became immediately dismayed. "Is…is something wrong?"

"I'm sorry," he sounded almost breathless. "Sometimes—it's only that certain words bring on memories…"

Alyneri waited, unsure how to proceed.

"Your name," he said after a moment. "I know it somehow. I don't know how I know it."

"I'm a Healer," she offered. "I'm not famous, but I served my king, as my mother and grandmother did before me. I have traveled some, and the Giverny name is known. I'm…well, I'm a duchess."

"I see," he replied, and then he added to himself, "that would explain some things."

"What kind of things?"

"We'll get to that," he said gently. "Can you tell me what happened to you? How you came to need rescuing by a ne'er-do-well like me?"

At which Yara snorted loudly from the other room.

"I was…" but she wasn't sure how much she should say—or how much she really even understood of what had happened. "There was a storm…and a mudslide. Our coach was caught. I don't remember it clearly." *Laudanum has that effect on a mind.*

"The road washed out about six miles south of L'Aubernay," he advised as she was mentally cringing from memories of Sandrine and the drugged tea. "Could be your coach was caught then."

"That sounds plausible."

"Were you traveling with others? Is there anyone we can notify? Surely a duchess has a retinue?"

"I…" but as much as she wanted to tell him of Ean and the others, as much as she wanted to trust this man with the golden voice, she dared not. "No." She turned her head away, though her eyes were already hidden from him. "There is no one," and the equal truth of this stung bitterly.

He took her hand with unexpected compassion. His was warm, calloused like a soldier's, strong. "Alyneri d'Giverny…" he her name as if testing it on his tongue, perhaps trying to remember where he'd tasted of it before. "It's a lovely name."

"Ama-Kai'alil," she said, turning to face him again, though the bandages quite prevented their eyes from meeting. "It's a…really strange name," and they both laughed at the truth of this.

He told her then of being lost at sea and washing up on the shore of Kai'alil, how they'd taken him to Duan'Bai and called him Man of the Tides.

"And upon waking in Duan'Bai? You remembered nothing?"

"Only my given name," he confessed, "but Yara likes calling me Ama-Kai'alil. She says it reminds her of home, and I don't mind, either way."

"Then I shall call you that as well. It has a certain cadence, I suppose." Her hand felt warm in his, and she hoped he wouldn't let go too quickly. "So…Duan Bai. How long ago was that?"

"Five years," and she heard the hollow ache in this confession.

"How did you come to Veneisea then?" she asked gently, not wanting to pry into the tender places of his soul any more than she'd want him poking at hers. "Did you cross the Assifiyahs with Yara?"

"No," and she heard his smile again.

"I suspect there's another story there."

"Indeed there is, *soraya*," Yara said, re-entering the room.

"Ah…" Alyneri sighed with delight as the heady fragrance of stew wafted to her senses. "That smells heavenly!"

Yara shooed Ama-Kai'alil from her side and sat in his place. Sad as she was to lose the touch of his hand, Alyneri found that she was quite famished.

"Some stew now," Yara admonished, "and then back to sleep with you."

"*Balé*, Yara," Alyneri dutifully submitted, though she wanted nothing more than to spend all night talking with Ama-Kai'alil.

"*Salam aleikom*, Alyneri d'Giverny," he said. *Peace be with you.* "*Shab be kheyr.*"

"Good night to you also, Ama-Kai'alil," she returned, missing his touch already.

SIX

*"The realm offers no mysteries greater than the soul. The
richest adventure lies in discovering ourselves."*

– D'Nofrio of Rogue, Sormitáge Scholar, circa 341aV

CARIAN VRAN LEA draped his arms around bent knees and
squinted into the distance. He could just make out the wavering
form of the Vestal Raine D'Lacourte making his way back up the
long sand dune, his image distorted by the morning's heat. Balls of Belloth
but that truthreader was obstinate. Carian had told him there was nothing
around for miles, but *no*, he had to go see for himself—and take all damned
night doing it.

"Who's the one that's been here before?" Carian demanded indignantly
of Gwynnleth's unconscious form, which was lying in the sand beside him.
"Yeah, that's what *I* said."

To be fair, Raine had also once been to T'khendar, but that had been
three hundred years ago, so Carian didn't think it counted.

He glanced over at Gwynnleth again. She didn't look so good. He'd
kept an eye on her all the while the Vestal was gone—that is, in between
his tirades of alternately cursing Raine and Franco Rohre—so he knew she
lived, but he felt unnerved sitting next to her for so long without her saying
a bloody word. The avieth always had something to say to a man—most of
it uncomplimentary, but that just made her more interesting.

Carian still didn't know what he thought about being in T'khendar.
True, it had been his plan to go there soon enough—had he not been

drawn into service by Raine D'Lacourte, he'd have left the moment he got the weldmap from that wily old Kandori woman. But being *tricked* into traveling to T'khendar...well, that just rankled. Never mind that he could blame their situation entirely on Raine—as he'd said many times, if the Vestal had let him *travel* the node to find out where it went, he'd probably have realized how dangerous it was. Then again, he might not have. It had been *exquisitely* done.

A doubleback, by Belloth's black balls!

Carian fancied himself one of the best Nodefinders in the thousand realms, yet he doubted he could've managed such a complicated and difficult working. The skill needed to pin two nodes to the same nodepoint...you might as well try to move two rivers and make them converge at the same mouth. It was practically Nodefinder mythology to speak of it at all. What's more, this doubleback ran between Alorin and T'khendar, two *entirely separate realms!* If Franco Rohre had truly created it, as Carian suspected he had, then the Espial deserved his most profound respect.

Still, Carian had imagined a more triumphant return to T'khendar, one where they didn't end up in the middle of the bloody Wyndlass Desert.

Raine was near enough now that Carian could see the sand on his britches and the chagrined look on his face. The pirate leaned back on his elbows and extended long legs in the sand, crossing his boots at the ankle. "Well?" he inquired cheerily.

"You were right." Raine trudged up the last ten feet of the dune looking exhausted.

Carian gave him a hard look. "You didn't walk all bloody night, did you?"

Raine threw himself down in the sand beside the pirate and draped arms over knees, hanging his head. "What in Tiern'aval do we do now?"

Carian had prepared a number of pithy remarks for use upon Raine's return, but seeing the Vestal so morose took all the fun out of gloating. "Like I said last night. We walk—*that* way," and he pointed west.

"But the mountains—" Raine made to protest again.

"Look, poppet, I know you think you know *all* about T'khendar—'*ooh, I was here during the Adept Wars,*'" he mimicked in a high-pitched voice, waving his hands in the air, "but I've been here *recently*, savvy? I actually *know* where I'm going."

Raine turned him a flat look. Then he turned and looked behind them at the empty air where the node had been. Then he looked at Gwynnleth's unconscious form. Then he looked back to Carian. "All right," he said, sounding defeated. "We'll do it your way."

"Might've reached that conclusion last night, you know," Carian complained as he got to his feet. It really was bloody hot. He wasn't looking forward to carrying the damned avieth either, but Raine sure didn't look like he was worth much that morning.

Hitching up his britches, Carian dropped to his knees in the sand, grabbed Gwynnleth's arm and shouldered her up, then exhaled an oath as he straightened again. She weighed a good deal more than he thought any self-respecting female should.

He blew the hair out of his eyes—hers, not his; his was tied in a knot behind his head—and looked to Raine. "Ready?"

"Lead on, Captain," Raine murmured, his eyes hard.

Carian turned them west and headed off. With every step he sank up to his ankles in the sand. To pass the time, he started a stream of invective that only got more creative as the sun got higher.

It was a long morning.

Round about midday, they found a copse of withered looking date palms and stopped to rest in the meager shade they provided. They'd been taking turns carrying the avieth, but Carian's back and shoulders were still aching. He was really starting to despise her.

He took a swig from his flagon and handed it to Raine. It wasn't smart to drink rum in the middle of the desert, but it sure as silver was smarter than drinking nothing at all.

Raine accepted the flagon and took a sip, somewhat gasping as the rum flamed his throat, "How many days did you say to cross this desert?"

"A fortnight on foot."

Raine looked around at the barren landscape and held his tongue. "Tell me about the node," he said as he handed Carian's flagon back.

Carian laid his head in the small bit of shade and stretched out on his back. "Best I can tell, it was a doubleback."

They'd done little talking about the node before Raine set off into the night to prove himself wrong. Mostly shouting, actually. Besides which,

Carian hadn't known how Franco had done it at first, but in the intervening hours, he'd figured it out. He'd had all night to think about it, hadn't he?

"What's a doubleback?"

"Well, to describe it in layman's terms, you take two nodes and you pin them to the same nodepoint. Since a nodepoint can only ever open into one node at a time, there's a switch that occurs as soon as one is traveled."

Raine considered this. "So the minute Franco took Ean across the one node…"

"Righto, my handsome. As soon as he stepped off the node, the first one switched off and the second one switched on. Then, once we traveled the second node, it switched back to the first, which is why we're trapped in this wretched hole of Belloth's burning arse."

Raine looked frustrated. "Then where did Franco take Ean?"

"Dunno, but they're here somewhere." *Probably enjoying a good meal and a smoke in Björn's bloody palace.*

"How do you know they're here? In T'khendar?"

Carian closed his eyes and tried to imagine himself swimming in the sea caves of Jamaii with a dozen naked maidens waiting on the shore to attend to his pleasure. "The nodes have to be close together to start with," he murmured. "At least in the same realm."

"That's some comfort," Raine remarked. He wiped his brow with his forearm and looked up at the sky. Then he frowned. "When did it turn blue?"

"Ages ago," the pirate muttered.

"Come to think of it," Raine looked around, really frowning now, "how is it we're still on our feet at all?"

"You're quick, aren't you?" Carian remarked with eyes still closed. "All night and you just figured out things are a bit different since you visited last?"

"Carian, your manner becomes tiresome."

"Sarcasm is just one of my diverse talents," the pirate returned unrepentantly. The man had made him wait all night in the damned sand. He could bloody well listen to him complaining about it for at least a commensurate amount of time.

Raine leveled him a long, steady stare.

Carian could feel his eyes like a hot lamp. "Oh, all *right*." He sat up to give the Vestal an annoyed scowl. "Like I tried telling you last night: there's *elae* here now. Go ahead, truthread me or something." Then he grimaced. Who'd have thought he'd ever offer to endure such torture?

But Raine clearly didn't want to test his theory. "Gwynnleth—"

"Yeah, there's got to be some other explanation for what happened to her," Carian muttered with an absent wave of his hand, "because I'm telling you, there's *elae* all over the place. Not that it'll help us much right now, unless you can work the fifth and call the wind to carry us out of here."

Raine still looked unconvinced.

Carian shrugged. "Suit yourself. Believe me, don't believe me. I don't give a rat's arse. But you're going to have to face it sometime, you know."

Raine gave him a strange look. "Face what?"

"The truth." Carian climbed to his feet and grabbed the avieth's arms again, hauling her up onto his shoulders. "Fortune prick me," he hissed as he shifted her dead weight across his back, "I vow she's gained ten pounds just lying there." He pushed his face close to where hers dangled below his shoulder and told her, "You're going to owe me big time when this is over, birdie." Then he smoothed a tangled strand of auburn hair away from her cheek and turned to Raine. "Ready?"

"As ever," remarked the Vestal, sounding anything but.

Perhaps an hour of walking later, something caught Carian's eye. He paused, hitched the avieth higher on his shoulders, and squinted towards the horizon. He could just make out a dark spec moving across the sky. It would have to be as big as a galleon ship for him to be able to see it from that distance. As the spec gradually grew in substance and shape, Carian arched brows. "Is that what I think it is?"

Following Carian's gaze, Raine sighed resignedly. "Very likely."

"Winds blow me proper," the pirate muttered.

"The *drachwyr* have always served my oath-brother," Raine noted unhappily. "He'll know we're here now."

Carian grinned sardonically. "Poppet, I hate to break this to you, but I'm sure he's known from the beginning. We came through *his* trap, remember?"

Raine looked wearily to him and then back to the *drachwyr* soaring in the far distance. He sighed. "No doubt he'll have us walk all the way to Niyadbakir just to make his point."

"And what point would that be?"

"Whatever his point is in bringing us here," Raine grumbled. Then he leveled Carian a heated look. "Rest you assured, Carian vran Lea, there's a reason we're here."

"Yep," the pirate agreed. "It's because you refused to let me travel the goddamned node." He hitched Gwynnleth up on his shoulders, hitched his britches up over his butt, and started off in the direction of the flying dragon. "At least we've got a heading now."

Wearing a black scowl, Raine followed.

They made steady but slow progress through the deep sand, seeing nothing and no one until the sun fell low in the western sky and Carian vowed he would go no farther. The wind had picked up as the sun fell, and now a steady furnace breeze accosted them. They'd trudged to the top of a dune to get a feel for the lay of things, and Carian decided that was as good a place as any to stop for the night. He slung the avieth off his shoulders somewhat ungently, trusting the soft sand to be more of a friend to her than it had been to his aching legs and ankles, and threw himself down beside her.

"Shade and bloody darkness, but do you owe me big-time, birdie." He rolled in exhaustion onto his back and flung his arms to either side.

Raine stood at the edge of the dune gazing at the line of mountains on the horizon. They didn't seem even one inch closer.

"I've been giving some thought to what you've told me, Carian," Raine observed while the wind tossed his brown hair into his eyes.

Carian noted that the Vestal had been quiet for most of the afternoon and seemed to have regained his composure. Perhaps realizing he wasn't about to keel over and die had something to do with it. Carian could see how facing imminent death by *elae*-denial could impact a man's disposition— especially a man like Raine.

"Mmm-hmm?" Carian murmured.

"If you were truthful in telling me how many people are living here…"

Carian felt the tiniest touch of Raine's power in his head and smiled. "There are five cities the size of Rethynnea," he returned with eyes still closed, "and Niyadbakir is easily as large as the Sacred City of Faroqhar."

Raine eyed him cynically. "Why weren't you forthcoming with this knowledge before, Carian? A man like you…I would've thought at least the guild would know about it."

Carian grimaced, said a few silent curses and returned peevishly, "It's because of that damned zanthyr."

"Ah…" Raine seemed to need little else by way of explanation.

"We had a bit of a misunderstanding the last time I was here." Carian felt like the truth was being scraped out of his pride with a dull-edged spoon. "He—well…he was in a position to demand a certain measure of discretion that I wouldn't usually agree to."

"I see."

"Yeah."

"Considering the number of people living here now," Raine observed then, blessedly not pushing Carian for more details about his prior interaction with Phaedor, "it would only follow that there would be *elae*. I decided to trust you and looked, and the currents have formed a natural pattern, though it is quite different from Alorin's…which I suppose is to be expected."

Wearing a thoughtful frown, the Vestal sat down and draped elbows over knees. "There is much I do not understand about all of this."

"It's all seems pretty obvious to me."

Raine gave him a heated look. "Indeed, Carian vran Lea? Tell me then: why did Malachai beseech the Council of Realms for their help in bringing life to T'khendar if merely populating the place would've accomplished the deed?" He exhaled heavily and shook his head. "No…my oath-brother still has much to explain."

Carian left that one alone. He knew his boundaries, and Raine knew he had *elae* back now. You didn't taunt a cornered skunk unless you wanted to walk around reeking skunk odor for a week and with your eyes and throat half-burned out.

"Carian…" When the pirate didn't respond, Raine said again, more insistently, "*Carian*," and knocked him on the leg—hard. "What is that?"

Carian opened one eye to look. Then he bolted upright. "I'll be scuppered and sunk if that ain't—" He jumped to his feet.

A vessel was approaching in the distance. At first, all Carian could see of it was the long tail of sand rising in its wake, but as it neared, he recognized it as a sailcraft. He whooped a shout and clapped Raine on the shoulder. "We're saved, poppet! I won't have to eat you after all."

"I'm so relieved," the Vestal remarked bleakly.

Soon the craft had sailed close enough to make out the details of its construction. Its hull was slightly curved across the beam, and more so along the keel, though the bottom lay flat and smooth to allow for quick slippage across the sand. The gaff-rigged mainsail looked massive by comparison to the craft. But it was the man standing at the helm that had Carian grinning from ear to ear.

The captain turned his sailcraft into the wind and eased off the sails, and the vessel slowed before them.

Instantly Carian grabbed Gwynnleth up into his arms and went skipping and sliding down the dune. The captain slung himself out of the boat and landed in the deep sand just as Carian reached him. The pirate shoved the avieth into the other man's large arms, let out a whooping holler and grabbed the both of them into a bear hug.

"Balearic de Parma! What in Tiern'aval are *you* doing in T'khendar?" Carian drew back and grabbed Balearic by the shoulders. "Last I heard, half the imperial armada was in pursuit of the *Black Gryphon*! I thought I'd surely seen the last of you!"

Balearic was such a beast of a man—broad-chested and thick armed—that the long-limbed avieth seemed frail in his grasp. He boasted wild black hair as long as Carian's and more earrings than flesh in his ears. "We'll get to that later," he answered with a grin that jingled the charms braided into his beard. He arched an unruly black eyebrow and hefted Gwynnleth in his arms. "Who's this then?"

"That's Gwynnleth." Carian gave her a sooty look. "She's a pain in the arse, apparently in any state of consciousness."

"And your friend?" Balearic lifted kohl-lined blue eyes to Raine, who was finally descending the dune.

"Oh. That's Raine D'Lacourte."

Balearic really arched brows at that. "Ah so..." He eyed Raine speculatively.

"You gonna invite us on board, Balearic, or did you just stop to gloat like the gypsy you are?"

"To be sure, to be sure." Balearic nodded towards the ship. "Climb aboard, and I'll hand your lass up to ye. What did ye do to her anyway?"

Carian clambered into the sailcraft and then reached down to take Gwynnleth from the captain. "I think she's allergic to your lovely realm.

Soon as we got here, she started screaming." Carian exhaled a grunt of protest as he hefted the avieth up and laid her carefully down again on a bench to one side of the helm. "I thought *that* was annoying," he said as he straightened and brushed hands against his britches, "but I'd willingly trade a ranting and screaming Gwynnleth for this one. At least the other version could walk."

Raine reached the bottom of the dune and approached Balearic. "Thank you for stopping for us, Captain," he said solemnly, extending his hand. "I am Raine D'Lacourte."

"Balearic de Parma, Your Excellency." The gypsy clasped wrists with the Vestal. "Welcome aboard," and he motioned Raine towards his ship.

Raine jumped up, grabbed the railing and easily swung his legs up and over the side to land gracefully on the deck.

"Who knew you were so spry?" Carian gave him a black look. "*You* should've been carrying her all this time!"

Balearic climbed back aboard and took the helm. "Carian, you want to grab that sheet?" He indicated the line that controlled the mainsail.

Carian jumped to, and shortly he'd maneuvered the sail back to catch the wind. The craft lurched into motion, and then the ship was spinning around and beating west, with a spray of sand rising in a tempest behind them.

Carian happily sank down onto a bench built into the side of the sailcraft and took off his boots. "What are you doing out here, Balearic?" he asked as he emptied a small mountain of sand onto the deck. "Don't tell me it was Fortune's eye alone guided you to us."

Balearic nodded knowingly towards dark spec, which was just then flying low along the horizon.

Carian followed his gaze and noted the Sundragon with a frown. "Oh. I suppose I should've guessed."

"The *drachwyr* sent you to retrieve us?" Raine stood in the stern leaning against the railing and holding onto one of the lines for support.

"Oh, no." Balearic shot him a look over his shoulder. "He told us you two were out here, and when I heard my old friend Carian vran Lea had finally made it to T'khendar, well…I came as soon as the wind picked up."

"Told you I was popular," Carian quipped with a toothy grin. He leaned back and clasped hands behind his head.

"What do you do in this desert?" Raine inquired of the captain. "If you don't mind my asking?"

"Our troupe is Iluminari, Your Excellency. With the solstice celebration of Adendigaeth beginning soon, we're preparing the fire candles. The Wyndlass is the only place in T'khendar for certain of the composites we need."

"Retired from the account, eh?" Carian gave Balearic a consoling look. "That have something to do with the imperial navy?"

"Aye, I have abandoned the sweet life," Balearic admitted, shooting Carian a broad grin, "but it's good here, too."

"I bet you find the part where half of the Empress's fleet isn't after you especially appealing, eh?"

"I admit that is a dominant factor." Balearic grinned at him. "Fortune must've had her eye on you though, lad," he noted then, "for tomorrow we return to the cities. One day later tripping through that node, and you'd have been at the mercy of the First Lord's *drachwyr*."

"One place I vow never to be! I suppose you have room for us to tag along with the troupe?"

"Oh, aye." Balearic looked him up and down with his bright blue eyes. "Always have room for working hands. It's six days to Renato, and about the same from there to Niyadbakir. You really found your way to the far edge of the realm."

"You can blame Franco Rohre for that," Carian grumbled. He was going to have words with that man if they ever met. Right after he kissed the hallowed ground he walked on.

"If I may ask, Captain," Raine said then, "how long have you been in T'khendar?"

"Nine years, Your Excellency."

"And how did you come to be here at all?" When Balearic didn't immediately reply, Raine added, "I assure you, Captain, my interest is purely scholarly. I won't be tracking anyone down in the name of justice."

A frown narrowed Balearic's gaze as he guided the ship. "There's those that will bring you here any time—for a price, my lord."

"How?"

"On the nodes, of course," Carian supplied. "I *told* you—"

"I know, I know," Raine held up a hand to quiet the pirate. "You traveled to T'khendar and lived to speak of it—only you *didn't* speak of it, Carian, or I might've asked many more questions when my need to understand wasn't nearly as dire."

Balearic gave the Vestal a considering glance. "From what I understand, Your Excellency, there's times of the year when the nodes can be traveled safely. Then again, I don't know as the First Lord doesn't just decide to untwist them twice a year and let it be known thusly. There's lots goes on here in T'khendar that you learn to take with a grain of salt."

"And when attempting to understand my oath-brother's activities," Raine muttered, "it must be taken by the handful."

The sun was hanging low on the horizon when they reached the Iluminari camp. Ten colorful wagons formed a circle around a large stone well, and campfires were already going when Balearic eased off the wind and drifted in. A host of sailcraft were anchored off to the south of the campsite, and Balearic guided their own craft smoothly into place beside the outermost of these.

"Come," he said to his guests, "join our camp. Eat and be welcome."

Raine and Carian disembarked—for all his complaining, the pirate collected the avieth the moment the craft was moored, even though Raine seemed of a mind to do so as well—and followed Balearic into the camp.

The Iluminari made them welcome, showering them with hot food and water and strong drink and finding beds for them in their wagons. As the stars came out to embellish the heavens, the gypsy camp broke into spirited celebration, with much singing and dancing within the circle of campfires.

Though always polite, Raine remained quiet throughout the evening. Carian kept his eye on the man as much as he did on the avieth. Though he'd never have admitted it to anyone—least of all to Raine—he was concerned about the Vestal. Carian had swallowed more than a few harsh realities in his time, but he knew these same truths would be even harder for Raine to digest.

So after scraping his plate clean and draining Balearic's bottle of rum, the pirate made his way to where Raine sat on the steps of a wagon. "You know," Carian said as he settled down on the step beside Raine, "that Rohre character did say that the Fifth Vestal would tell you everything."

"I recall the moment, Carian."

"I only *mean*," the pirate replied, giving him an aggravated look—*you try to be nice to people!* "I only mean that he's likely still willing to 'tell you his mind' as Rohre put it. Don't you think?"

"I have long stopped trying to predict what Björn will do, Carian," Raine replied resignedly. "Good night to you." He stood and went inside the wagon.

Staring after him, Carian decided that was the last time he would ever feel sorry for the damned Vestal, even though he knew it probably wasn't.

And over the course of the following weeks as they traveled with the Iluminari, he proved himself entirely right.

SEVEN

"A man is best judged by the reputation of his enemies."
— The Adept wielder Viernan hal'Jaitar

THE ESPIAL FRANCO Rohre stood staring at the doorknocker on a pair of black lacquered doors, trying to make up his mind to use it. Cast of rubbed iron in the shape of a roaring lion, the device was nearly as big as his head. Of course, it quite had to be if anyone was to notice it at all upon the massive doors leading into Niko van Amstel's Bemothi estate.

Niko...

It had been three centuries since Franco laid eyes on the Nodefinder Niko van Amstel, though their names were often spoken of in the same circles. But most of the Fifty Companions went out of their way to avoid one another and shared little conviviality, for at the basis of their acquaintanceship lay the knowledge that each knew the other's most wretched secret. It was ever more comfortable to associate with strangers than to see one's own conscience mirrored in another's haunted gaze.

But it wasn't seeing Niko again that troubled Franco so much as the reason for his visit. Only that morning—yet an entire world away—the Second Vestal had called Franco to chambers...

"Franco, welcome!" Dagmar had risen from his chair to greet Franco as a chrome-faced Shade was escorting him into Björn van Gelderan's library in T'khendar.

Franco had barely recovered his strength from his ordeal in Rethynnea's

Temple of the Vestals, where he and Ean val Lorian had helped unravel the physical form of the Malorin'athgul named Rinokh. Yet he might've been on his deathbed for all that his condition mattered—when the Great Master summoned, you went.

The tall stacks of Björn's three-story library dwarfed Franco as he strode across Akkadian carpets to clasp wrists with his mentor. "Great Master." Franco felt wary and exhausted and not a little awed to be standing in the personal library of Björn van Gelderan in the presence of the greatest Nodefinder who'd ever lived.

"Come, sit—drink," said Dagmar with an amiable smile, bright beneath his pale green eyes.

Franco was still trying to get used to the idea of conversing with the Great Master in person—three hundred years of knowing him only in his dreams made their more recent, fleshly meetings seem perpetually surreal. Dagmar poured a goblet of wine for him and indicated an armchair across the table for Franco to take a seat. Maps that looked old enough to have been penned on the day of the Genesis littered the polished tabletop between them.

"You called for me, my lord?" Franco inquired as he accepted the wine and sat.

Dagmar retook his chair as well. "Indeed. To congratulate you on a job well done."

Franco didn't consider the job exactly *well* done. He'd barely survived the encounter with the Malorin'athgul. Holding open a node while a volatile creature capable of unmaking the realm was dragged across the aether between worlds and partly unmade wasn't an experience he'd wish upon his worst enemy. That their plan had been successful only somewhat lessened his latent sense of horror over it.

"Um…thank you, milord."

"And you've recovered fully I hear?"

"So they tell me." Franco had taken more than a few blows during the battle in the temple against Raine's forces, but someone had healed his injuries while he slept.

Too bad they couldn't heal the lunatic in your head, yea?

Shut up.

"The First Lord is pleased with your work thus far."

In other words, you're still in his debt, the mad voice in his head goaded.

"What does the Vestal need from me?"

Would that he needed nothing!

For the millionth time, Franco wished that he might've shoved a dagger into Niko van Amstel's twisted heart rather than follow him to the eventual doom of owing an eternal debt to Björn van Gelderan.

The quirk of a smile hinted on Dagmar's lips, perhaps in perceiving Franco's less than enthusiastic inquiry of service. "It's Niko van Amstel."

Franco's eyes flew to Dagmar's. It was as if the Vestal had plucked Niko's name from his very consciousness.

"So you remember him," the Great Master observed sardonically.

Franco's wine tasted suddenly sour. He set the goblet back on the table. He didn't feel the need to comment on his memories.

"I called you here today, Franco, because I need you to find out what Niko is involved in." Dagmar pushed a map idly aside and drummed the fingers of one hand on the table. "I have my suspicions, and lately I've sought his dreams, but the man eludes me."

Franco gaped at him. "He wards his dreams from *you*? Doesn't that shout his crimes just as effectively as announcing them in person?"

Dagmar swirled the wine in his goblet and considered the liquid with a frown of pale brows. "To be certain; yet announcing them would at least be a confession. Now I must seek him out to discover his actions for myself."

"Buying time," Franco said suddenly, realizing Niko's likely tactic. "He's betting it will take you longer to discover what he's about than it will take him to go about it."

Dagmar looked up under his brows. "That's my fear. The man has ever been as crafty as he is morally indiscriminate."

The reference caught Franco off guard, for few knew this truth about Niko. Franco had to keep reminding himself that Dagmar knew the truth of what had happened three centuries ago on Tiern'aval. He knew the crime that had led Franco and the other Fifty Companions to flee to the catacombs during the Battle of the Citadel; events which had resulted in their binding and loathsome oath of fealty to Björn van Gelderan.

The Fifth Vestal had—for reasons unknown—truthbound them all as well, preventing them from ever revealing their mutual crime; thus they'd lived on as heroes—survivors of a great battle—when all any of them truly deserved was a coward's execution.

For centuries, Franco had been desperate to tell Raine and Alshiba the truth. Now Dagmar knew it, but Franco found it no easier to look him in the eye. He swallowed and dropped his gaze. "What would you have me do, my lord?"

The Second Vestal picked up a black envelope sealed with gold wax and handed it over. "You've received a summons to Niko's estate in Bemoth."

Franco looked the envelope over, not bothering to wonder how a letter addressed to his home in the Agasi province of Ma'hrkit had found its way to T'khendar. Björn had spies and allies everywhere.

"There's a pattern upon the seal," Dagmar advised as Franco was studying the signet pressed into the wax. "If anyone other than you opens the message, the letter will turn to ash and the sender will be alerted."

Franco looked back to him. "Then how do you know what it says?"

Dagmar gave him a quirk of a grin. "Is there any pattern the First Lord cannot unwork and refashion better than its original, Franco?"

Franco grimaced at this obvious truth. He broke the seal and unfolded the four corners of the envelope to reveal the invitation within. As Franco read the particulars, the Great Master advised, "Others have received such missives—voting Guild members, and many of your compatriots who once called themselves the Fifty Companions."

"That sounds ominous." Franco knew too well Niko's conniving temperament. He was only amazed it had taken the man this long to fashion another plan to doom them all.

"Attend him," Dagmar said. "Gain his confidence in whatever way you must. Find out what he's plotting and who conspires with him."

Now Franco stood upon Niko's doorstep feeling entirely too sober for the coming confrontation. But he dared not drown his wits in wine, no matter the screaming lunatic in his head. His wits were the only protection he had.

Franco lifted the lion knocker's iron tongue and banged three times. A moment later the doors opened to reveal a solemn-faced woman of indeterminate age. Arching an imperious eyebrow as her only greeting, she stepped aside to permit him to enter a cavernous hall tiled from floor to ceiling in rose-hued marble. The room might've been transported from a sultan's palace for the sheer amount of gilt covering every imaginable surface. Raine's truth, but Niko wore ostentation as a cloak.

The dour woman led him at a stately pace across the entry hall and into a suite of connected rooms. "You may wait here," she droned in a heavy Bemothi accent.

Franco headed through into a long gallery overlooking the jungle canopy. Further along the way, a man and a woman stood before the tall windows, observing the mountain view. A squall was shedding rain in the distance, striating the sky in great charcoal strokes, while the long rays of the setting sun enflamed the closer clouds.

"Majestic," Franco said.

The others turned.

He knew them both—of course, for all of them had been forced to work the same pattern while kneeling wretchedly at the feet of the Fifth Vestal. The petite Healer Mian Gartelt wore a gown in Queen Indora's colors, while the jet-haired Nodefinder Devangshu Vita stood as regal as ever, scowling down his aristocratic nose with typical disdain. Franco had never been friends with the man, but neither had they been enemies. Mian was another story.

"Franco Rohre." Devangshu's pale brown eyes looked him over as Franco came to stand of a height with the tall Bemothi. "I see the years since the war have treated you with tolerable grace."

The war. *The* war. The only war that mattered to them.

Franco smiled crookedly. "I hide my imperfections well."

Devangshu snorted.

"Did you just arrive, Franco?" Mian asked. She had the cherubic manner of a kindly farmer's wife, with plump rosy cheeks and a tiny button nose, but Franco knew she was as devious as they came and was willing to bet Niko had already taken her into his confidence.

"Yes, Mian. You're looking well."

"I serve Queen Indora of Veneisea now," she expressed proudly.

"A fulfilling position for you, no doubt." Franco was all too familiar with the rampant backstabbing and vindictiveness of Indora's court.

"Yes, quite," she agreed cheerfully, missing completely the subtle subtext of his comment. "And you? Whose service are you in?"

No one that I dare tell you about, my dear. "I am currently between contracts."

"That's good for you, then, right?" She gave him a chipper little smile, but upon noting Devangshu's stare, she added, "I only meant to say that I understand how you Nodefinders might loathe the restrictions of Espial patrons and their whims. Is it not so?"

"Most of the time." Franco gave her his most charming smile. In his many years masquerading as a minstrel, he'd become quite skilled at dissembling for the benefit of a lady's favor. More importantly, these people would be expecting a certain pattern of profligate behavior from him. Meeting their expectations would provide his best disguise.

"Mian, you were saying something about Laira di Giancora?" Devangshu remarked.

"Oh, yes, I was—"

"Laira di Giancora?" asked Franco.

"Yes, she's here," Mian informed him. "Quite a few of us have come already. You'll see them all no doubt at dinner—*oh!*" she pressed a hand to her cheek. "I was meant to help with the seating arrangements. Do excuse me."

When Mian had vanished out of hearing, Devangshu grumbled, "*Finally.* That woman is naught but a receptacle for the trashiest sort of gossip, which she spouts in an unbearably endless fount." He walked to a long sideboard where the wine service had been set. "Have a drink, Franco? I make no promises for the quality of Niko's wine."

Franco nodded, and Devangshu returned with two goblets, handing one to him. "So…Niko roped you into coming here as well, I see."

"How could I resist when he's re-routed a leis to his door just to celebrate the occasion?" Franco returned with some asperity.

"Haughty bastard," Devangshu grumbled. "That's the sort of thing I'd expect from Markal Morrelaine, but Niko has only ever aspired to the notable role of Markal's lesser second, a bastardized copy matching the original neither in skill nor arrogance."

"We share at least in our disdain for our host," Franco murmured. "Speaking of, do you know what this 'important briefing' is about? Have you met with him?"

Devangshu snorted dubiously. "He's been locked away with Dore since I arrived, no doubt plotting some nefarious scheme to damn us all yet again."

"Dore Madden is *here?*" Franco couldn't have been more dismayed to receive this news. If Niko van Amstel was a tornado, Dore Madden was the hurricane that had spawned him. "...I thought Dore was pretending to be Björn van Gelderan," Franco recovered his composure with difficulty, "waging his own private little war in Avatar, safe across the Fire Sea."

Devangshu grunted. "If what Niko says about Björn is true, nowhere is safe for any of us."

"Niko has been known to exaggerate."

They alluded, of course, to the most pressing concern on any Companion's mind—that of being *Called.* The task Björn assigned each of them individually on that ill-fated night was a secret never to be shared. None of them knew who among the others—if any—had done as Björn bade them. Yet they all knew that Björn had returned to Alorin to call in their debts, and his price for disobedience was the life he'd spared so long ago.

Franco had accepted his Calling. He'd resigned himself to the understanding that his treason might never be repaid, nor the First Lord's mercy in sparing his life that night at on Tiern'aval. He'd crossed paths in recent weeks with a few other Companions who were also upon the First Lord's business, but otherwise, he had no way of knowing who had been Called, save the ones who turned up slashed to a pulp.

"Well...Dore's back from Avatar, and we're none the better for it," Devangshu meanwhile muttered. It seemed even talk of Dore Madden was easier to stomach than contemplations of Björn van Gelderan and his Calling—which was only fitting, in Franco's estimation.

Devangshu turned to gaze back out at the distant storm. The clouds were broadening and had embraced most of the horizon, now a dark sheet sporadically backlit with lightning flares. "Dore Madden," he repeated disdainfully, shaking his head. "Would that in three centuries someone had acquired the fortitude to end the man's life and spare us all his odious scheming. But no one does." He turned Franco a heated look, his brown eyes sharp with criticism. "No one does—and do you know why? For fear that he might still claim their souls from the afterlife." He gestured with his wine as he added, "It's certain that if there was a way to accomplish so despicable a deed, Dore Madden would be the one to discover it."

"An astute observation," Franco replied soberly, wishing it was only jest and not completely true.

Franco felt that Niko carried much of the blame—he'd been the one that pushed them to hide in the catacombs, where Björn had eventually found them, rather than turning themselves in and begging for mercy—but that was only after Dore's even more lunatic plan to assault the Hundred Mages had failed miserably.

Franco wondered how much he could trust Devangshu. It would be helpful to have an ally. "Devangshu…" he began, but whatever else he might've said was preempted just then by the arrival of their host.

"Ah, the inimitable Franco Rohre, minstrel and bard, Nodefinder extraordinaire!"

Swallowing a grimace, Franco turned to acknowledge his host. He gave him a wan smile and a nod of greeting. "Niko."

Clearly Niko had been vigilant at working the Pattern of Life, which all of them had been forced to work the first time while kneeling at Björn's feet. Blonde and blue-eyed, square-jawed and broad-shouldered, Niko was the consummate embodiment of nobility in form and the vilest low-city scoundrel in deed.

They'd been good friends once, back when they were still in university together at Agasan's famous Sormitáge. Franco had even looked up to Niko—who'd always boasted enormous popularity, despite his lesser talent—but that was before Franco learned that the handsome façade concealed such an unscrupulous core.

"How pleased I am to find you've accepted my invitation for the weekend, Franco," Niko said. His blue-eyed gaze shifted to the other Nodefinder then. "And Devangshu Vita. Your venerated presence doubly honors my halls."

"Of course it does." Devangshu stared at him balefully and drank his wine.

Niko smiled that cultured, humorless smile that was so polite and yet so insulting at the same time. "Do make yourself at home, Vita. I won't be but a moment with Rohre here, and then it is my hope we may all share a bountiful meal and become happily reacquainted. Come, Franco?"

Franco cast an inquiring look at Devangshu, but the latter only nodded a farewell and turned his back on their host.

Franco fell into step with Niko as they walked through the wide halls of his mansion. "You seem to have done well for yourself." Franco's gaze took in the vaulted hallways decorated with myriad statues, tapestries and works of art.

"I've become a collector of sorts," Niko returned amiably. "Nothing so notable as the Sormitáge's *Primär Insamling* or Veneisea's *Musée d'art historitée*, yet my humble collection has garnered the notice of many like-minded souls. My home has become a melting pot where artists and their philanthropic patrons can meet. Most recently I entertained the Empress of Agasan's cousin and his retinue."

Franco understood this rhetoric as Niko's way of insinuating that he'd become powerful and politically well-connected—or at least he wanted Franco to believe he was, which at the moment was the more salient point.

"And what of your craft?" Franco inquired. "Traveled anywhere notable lately?'

Nowhere as notable as you, sneered the mad voice of his conscience.

Niko's eyes veritably glowed. "Oh, I've done my share of exploring, weld-hopping and such—haven't we all? No doubt we could both exchange stories of the distant realms now within our reach." He took Franco by the shoulder as he joked, "I'll bet we could reconstruct half a weldmap just between the two of us! And of course, I've assisted the Alorin Seat on numerous occasions when she's had need of a Nodefinder." Niko was so absorbed with boasting that he missed completely Franco's revulsion at his touch, despite it flowing off him in waves. "I've made a number of visits to Illume Belliel on the Alorin Seat's behalf."

Franco found this news less than heartening. Niko gaining the acquaintanceship of Alshiba Torinin meant he'd set his sights on bigger games than the politics of kings. Franco managed to maneuver out of Niko's reach and kept his expression benign. "It is indeed an honor to be granted access to the cityworld."

Niko did not hide his disappointment well. "Oh…you've been there also?"

Franco knew he had to flatter the man, though it galled him to play to that particular vice. He gave a self-deprecating smile. "On rare occasion."

"Then you also have made the fair acquaintance of the Alorin Seat?"

Franco felt himself far too closely acquainted with every Vestal, but he merely replied with a modest smile, "Only through association with others."

They continued small talk while they walked, with Franco balancing on the precarious line of appealing to Niko's vanity without divulging anything about his own activities and contacts.

When they reached a long gallery overlooking a line of forbidding mountains, two men were awaiting them. Franco took one look at Dore Madden and realized that he regretting making Dore's acquaintance even more than he regretted Björn van Gelderan's.

Dore had never been a hale figure, but the years since the wars had hollowed the man until he looked positively corpselike. His deep-set eyes seemed even more shadowed than before, and were now little more than dark pools beneath black brows, giving his countenance a certain ferocity. His skin had grown tan during his years in Avatar, with deep, hard lines etched around his eyes and thin, spiteful ones spider-webbing his mouth. Rail-thin and with hair as white as the desert sand, he looked nearly his considerable age, though he held his shoulders incongruously straight.

"Ah, Franco Rohre." Dore took note of him with too much satisfaction for Franco's comfort—the man taking note of him at all was disturbing enough. "We gain the attention of a big fish in the little pond that is our modest guild."

"Dore," Franco said by way of greeting. His gaze strayed to the man standing beside Dore, a black-clad, cold-eyed stranger with a notable scar across his cheek. Scar or not, he might've still been handsome had he not radiated such ill-humor.

Niko placed a hand on Franco's shoulder, drawing his attention. "Come, sit and have wine with us while we talk, Franco."

Franco had to physically restrain himself from grabbing Niko's hand off his shoulder and twisting it in a maneuver that would've had the man on the floor in seconds. Instead, he forced a shallow smile and replied, "Certainly, Niko, wine would be welcome."

The four of them moved towards a grouping of armchairs overlooking a balcony and the encroaching storm. It was there, as Niko was handing him a goblet of wine, that Franco noticed the scent of magic in the room.

It isn't that *elae* can actually be smelled; rather, the awareness of the lifeforce is its own perception—no different from taste or touch—that must be honed like any other sense. Franco's recent travels with the Fourth Vestal had brought him repeatedly into contact with the fourth strand of *elae*, and he knew it unmistakably now. Someone in that room was wielding the fourth.

A quick glance around as the others were taking their seats confirmed that the man in black was working the fourth strand. The fact that no one had introduced the man reinforced this conclusion. A quick leap landed Franco on the motive of this gathering then.

The working of fourth-strand patterns to discover the truth of a man's words came naturally to a truthreader, but as was the case for most patterns intrinsic to the various strands, these same patterns were unwieldy and difficult to master by one not born of that strand. The complexity of wielding fourth-strand truth patterns by someone other than a truthreader made the patterns untrustworthy. Only the basest sort of individual hired a wielder to pattern the fourth instead of hiring a truthreader for the same purpose.

But Franco understood immediately why a truthreader would be unwelcome in this gathering: a truthreader in the room meant *everyone's* thoughts were potentially open to display, while a wielder might settle his truth pattern on but one individual. It went without saying that Niko and Dore had agendas they didn't wish known even to each other, much less to an Adept truthreader. To this end, having a wielder there to work the fourth made perfect sense, loathsome though it might be.

"Franco, Franco," Dore sat with his spindly fingers clasping the arms of his chair like lion claws gripping the balls of a claw-foot tub, "we hear great things about you."

Franco shifted his gaze to the man somewhat unwillingly. "That seems unlikely."

"No, indeed," Dore insisted. "It has come to our attention that you were recently in the employ of the Fourth Vestal—an honor, no doubt, for one such as yourself."

Franco knew what Dore insinuated, a reminder that his noble family line had fallen from grace. It might've rankled once, but Franco had long progressed past such vanities. He was far more concerned about the man in black's cold-eyed gaze upon him, which he could feel as surely as the flow of the fourth.

But Franco had been skilled in compartmenting his thoughts many years before he came into close association with Raine D'Lacourte, and his months with the Vestal had honed this skill to a razor point.

Franco naturally detested any wielder who would work fourth-strand truth patterns—knowing their inherent fallibility—and it both infuriated and disgusted him that this stranger would wield such patterns upon him. He was loath to allow the man to garner even the least impression of his true thoughts, but he knew to affect this end he would have to drive the man forcefully and quickly from the room.

So Franco, being only recently recovered from a near-fatal use of his own talent and thereby lacking a certain measure of decorum, conceived of decidedly vile imagery matching, he felt, his level of disgust towards the nameless—if vaguely familiar-looking—wielder.

While still holding Dore's gaze, Franco filled his head with lustful thoughts of Niko. The idea was so abhorrent to him that he felt certain he could easily transfer this intensity of feeling to the wielder who sought to know his mind. Knowing, too, just how 'loudly' he needed to think of these images in order to broadcast them to the wielder through the fourth-strand patterns he was working, Franco cast the images his way and was rewarded by sight of the man stiffening in his chair.

"Yes," Franco answered Dore while suppressing a potent grin that nearly made up for the disgust he felt himself. "I was asked to serve the Vestal in a matter of some importance."

"Might you tell us of this?" Niko inquired.

Franco turned to Niko and affected a regretful expression as he confessed, "If only I could." Let them decide what to make of that.

From Niko's understanding look, the man had interpreted Franco's reply as he'd intended. "I see, of course. It is only natural that Raine D'Lacourte would truth-bind you. Is there *anything* you can tell us?"

Franco set down his wine untouched. "Why are you so interested in the Fourth Vestal's activities, Niko?"

"We heard he was in search of Björn van Gelderan," Dore answered. As Franco turned him an unreadable look, Dore added, "Surely you are as eager as we are to know Björn's whereabouts."

"From what I hear, it's not Björn coming after all of us to call in his debt," Franco snapped, his composure momentarily lost at facing this man after so long and so much. Dore alone among the Companions had not fled to the catacombs. They'd all been sure he'd perished at the Citadel, yet somehow he'd escaped both the battle and Björn's justice. A galling irony.

"Be that as it may," Niko said evenly, "the more information we have, the better prepared we shall be."

Franco didn't think there would be much Niko could do to prepare for a Shade appearing at his bedside, but he said only, "We didn't find him, so there's not much I can offer." He felt the strength of the fourth-strand patterns leveled upon him intensifying, which only made him angry, so he fought back with images of Niko performing fellatio upon the man in black. This brought a grunt of disgust from the wielder, which in turn drew Dore's eye to the man with obvious annoyance.

"A few more questions, if you might indulge us, Franco," Niko proposed, ignorant of the depraved visions Franco was presenting on his behalf.

"Certainly, Niko," Franco said as unctuously as he could manage while upping the intensity of Niko's imagined pleasure at his work upon the stranger in black. The wielder squirmed in his chair.

Irritated ostensibly at the wielder writhing beside him like a man with imminent diarrhea, Dore said brusquely, "We hear that lately you've made the intimate acquaintance of the Fire Princess Ysolde Remalkhen."

Franco couldn't help but be impressed by the extent of their information. *Niko has spies deep in Calgaryn to know that—or Dore does.* The latter thought chilled him. "Just so," Franco admitted, for there was no point in denying it—and it certainly helped uphold the libertine image he was trying to present of himself.

"Did you then also encounter the crown prince upon his recent return?" *And what interest could you possibly have in Ean val Lorian, Dore?*

Franco did not like this unexpected turn of questioning, which brought him too close for comfort to his own recent activities on the First Lord's behalf.

It took incredible force of will, but he did what he must. He forced himself to imagine the most despicable visions of Niko he could stomach.

It took more fortitude than he imagined to refrain from shuddering as he mentally shouted the scene.

The wielder shuddered on his behalf, drawing a hostile glare from Dore.

Franco deemed the wielder too distracted now to be of much use to Dore, so he answered with careful duality, "I did cross paths with the young prince."

Dore brightened—that is, if the malicious intensity boiling within his gaze could be considered bright. "What do you know of him? This Prince Ean?"

"Very little," Franco lied. He eyed the wielder surreptitiously to be certain he noted nothing untoward in the comment. "Only that the prince seemed aggrieved by his mother's attempted assassination on the afternoon of his return." He added as an afterthought—to help perpetuate the lie, "And there seemed to be some trouble with an heiress? I really can't recall."

Dore's manic expression fell into obvious frustration. "Did the Fire Princess mention nothing of the prince to you? She did not share in his plans perhaps?"

"Conversation was not the focus of our evenings, Dore," Franco replied, while at the same time imagining the man in black kneeling now before Niko's bare form—

The wielder stifled a groan and launched abruptly out of his chair. He sped from the room looking unwell.

Franco felt immensely gratified.

While Dore stared after the man in bewilderment, Franco asked, "Why the interest in the prince, Niko?"

Niko waved a hand absently. "It's Dore who garners some fascination with the boy." He added brusquely, "*Dore?*"

The man tore his gaze from the retreating wielder and fastened it instead on Franco. He stared at him blankly for a moment, during which time Franco honestly wondered if the man had mentally vacated to another realm, and at last remarked, "The Prophet has his eye on the val Lorian prince."

Franco stilled. "The Prophet?" He schooled his voice to indifference, but inside he was screaming. "The Prophet is...a patron of yours, Dore?"

"I have long been Advisor to the Prophet Bethamin, even before he moved his temple from Myacene to Tambarré."

Franco went cold. *By Cephrael's Great Book, that would mean decades!* It was horrific news.

Dore said grimly, "The Prophet is most displeased that a certain prince has been lately killing his Marquiin."

It took a moment for Franco to understand his intimation. "You mean...you speak of Prince Ean?"

"The Prophet has reason to suspect him, yes. *Good* reason." He turned his gaze to the black-robed wielder, who stood outside on the balcony in the rain, and frowned again.

This was disheartening information to say the least. After everything Ean had already been through... Franco decided he'd best steer the conversation away from the prince before his true thoughts betrayed him— with or without the nameless wielder there to work the fourth. "What work do you do for Bethamin, Dore?" He let his tone betray his unease. "Is that what this meeting is about?"

"Dore's work is his own, Franco." Niko sensed his agitation but mistook the reason for it. "But you needn't worry. The Prophet is our ally."

"Oh indeed," Franco returned flatly. It was time to move this meeting along while the contents of his stomach remained within it. Franco looked to his host. "I tire of this questioning, Niko. Why have you invited me here? What's this about?"

Niko gave him a gratuitous smile saturated with insincerity. "We are but old friends getting reacquainted, Franco!" He opened palms in a beseeching gesture. "Surely you're not offended by our interest?"

'Gain his confidence in whatever way you must...'

Dagmar's command weighed heavily upon Franco's already overtaxed conscience. *Appearances, appearances!*

Franco reined in his anger and apprehension and dampened it beneath a shield of sour protest. "No...of course not, Niko."

Niko settled him a pleased smile. "To the point then, as you have so graciously requested." He crossed ankle over knee and clasped hands in his lap, a studied gesture intended to disarm the conversation. "Franco," he began then as his pale gold eyebrows furrowed with disingenuous concern, "you must know that the realm is out of Balance."

Franco nodded for him to continue.

"We believe," and he indicated Dore as part of the *we*, "that to rectify and restore Balance to the realm, we must have a full complement representing us in Illume Belliel. This is imperative, Franco." He leaned in to add with a conspiratorial frown, "I must tell you, we are not the only ones who trust to this solution."

Franco watched Niko's face for any hint of his deceitful nature, but the man was impressively vacant. "Let me see if I understand," he replied, taking a measured breath. "You believe the realm is out of Balance because all five Vestals aren't sitting in some chairs in Illume Belliel?"

"It is the only explanation that fits," Niko assured him. "Think about it: the timing of the war, the circumstances surrounding the Second Vestal's disappearance and the Fifth's betrayal…all of these events exactly correlate to the moment the Adept race began dying." He opened palms to the ceiling as if his logic was incontrovertible. "There really can be no other reason for it."

Franco sat dumbfounded. He was, in fact, so thoroughly flabbergasted that the moment left him entirely without response. It was so beyond the limits of reason! "I must…think on this," he said ineptly.

"Yes, it is astonishing, is it not?"

"Quite," Franco heartily agreed.

"We must know where you stand, Rohre," Dore demanded then, suddenly paying attention to the conversation again. "Are you with us?"

Franco was so unbalanced that it took him precious moments to derive what Dore was asking. The shock when he did realize it nearly thrust him from his chair. "You're…" he fought to control his fury, to suppress the urge to draw his blade and violently eviscerate them. "You're planning to *depose* the Second and Fifth Vestals?"

"That is a harsh word," Niko protested in an injured tone, "and not fair to our intentions. No, not fair at all."

"The Second Vestal could be dead for all we know," Dore pointed out curtly, "and the Fifth is disavowed. The Alorin Seat should have confronted the matter centuries ago. If she'd had the courage then to do what was needed, our race would not now be dying."

"It must be done." Niko clasped hands in his lap resolutely, as if he was well and truly regretful about their intended coup. "For the good of the realm, of course."

Franco fervently wanted a drink, but he'd be damned if he'd imbibe anything given him by Niko van Amstel.

'Gain his confidence in whatever way you must...'

Damn Dagmar for leveling such an order! *Damn Niko for his accursed plotting!* But above all, Franco knew he was truly damned because he hadn't had the courage three centuries ago when all might've gone quite differently. Now it was long too late.

"I confess..." Franco managed, knowing he had to say something, "I am most...concerned by this course of action. What if it fails?"

"We have powerful allies," Dore assured him with a wicked smile.

Franco cringed inside. "What allies?"

"They prefer to remain anonymous," Niko said, "but I assure you they are most capable of following through at their end of things."

"And..." *By Cephrael's Great Book!* Franco felt dry-throated with panic and fury both. "And what does this plan involve?"

Niko gave him a reassuring smile. "Right now, nothing is needed from you save knowing that you stand with us. When the time comes, of course..." and his smile broadened, "well...then you need only vote as your conscience dictates, yes?"

'Others have received such invitations—voting Guild members...' Dagmar's words took on a deeper and far more ominous meaning.

"Who?" Franco managed. "Who will replace the Great Master?"

Niko cast him a knowing look of abashed acceptance.

Franco very nearly lost his composure entirely. "You," he croaked.

Niko nodded in false modesty. "We searched for others—even your name was upon the list of candidates—but in the last, this burden was thrust upon me. Dore and the others eventually convinced me—over great protest, I must say, for surely others are equally worthy—that it is my duty to accept the role, for the good of the realm."

Franco couldn't help himself asking, "And the Alorin Seat? She also trusts to this solution?" He remembered Alshiba's calm determination at Mark Lavin's abandoned manor and her resolute unwillingness to believe ill of the Fifth Vestal.

"Alshiba and I have an understanding," Niko replied with a smile that was too smug for Franco's ease. "As I said, we've spent *much* time together."

Franco wanted to strangle him. *So it's not enough to propose unseating the Second and Fifth Vestals, but let's slander the First while you're at it by insinuating shared intimacy with the likes of you?* Niko's audacity defied comprehension.

"And what of Björn?" Franco kept his emotions in close check. "Who will replace him?"

"We have several wielders in mind. As you know, it will take a guild vote to elect the candidates for the Second Vestal, but the Alorin Seat alone may propose the Fifth. Even then, the appointment must go to the Council of Realms and can only be ratified by the Speaker."

"And you intend to influence that decision? You think you *can?*"

"We are certain of the matter," Dore intoned in a voice like gravel.

Franco was ready to impale him with the closest sharp object at hand. He knew he had to get out of there before he lost control and killed the both of them—or at least himself in trying. "Well…" he called up a smile as sincere as Niko's own, "when the time comes, Niko, you have my word that I will vote as my conscience dictates."

Niko opened arms. "That is all we can ask of any of our guild brothers, is it not, Dore?"

Dore grunted disagreeably, no doubt disgruntled by the fact that his wielder wasn't there to disprove Franco's fealty. The cadaverous wielder shoved out of his chair and stalked out onto the balcony, where the storm was now raging. Franco noticed that the rain formed a sheet around Dore. The faintest tingling reached his awareness as well, one he'd come to know of late—through recent association with Björn van Gelderan—as wielding of the fifth strand of *elae.*

If Franco's instincts had been dismayed before, now they were veritably howling.

A man was mistaken who thought that wielders weren't able to learn fifth strand patterns. Some of the simpler patterns, such as those that shift the density of the air, were easily mastered by a studied wielder. Rather, the problem with wielding the fifth—as any *sane* man knew—is that every endeavor involving fifth-strand patterns requires an enormous understanding of Balance and its play on the realm. Few wielders had ever mastered the fifth *and* achieved the necessary understanding of Balance, though many had tried and died in the attempt. Every wielder knows that to dabble in the fifth is courting disaster. Yet here was Dore using the fifth to keep his boots dry. Franco gazed at him in horror.

"I know it can be a lot to take in, my old friend." Niko once more misinterpreted Franco's silence. He placed a hand on Franco's arm again. "I look forward to putting these dark times behind us, to a day when we might renew the friendship we once shared."

Franco looked to him. *One day I will do it*, he promised himself as his eyes met Niko's. *One day I will make you regret all of the lives you've so callously ruined in pursuit of your own vanity.* "I look forward to that day," Franco replied, thinking of an entirely different scene than the one Niko proposed.

Niko smiled and squeezed his shoulder. "Good." He dropped his arm and turned to frown at Dore. "It's a relief to me that you're with us, Franco. With the dark times ahead—surely to mirror on some level those that lie behind—we must separate our friends from our enemies, the craven from the courageous; we must surround ourselves with those who would place the realm's survival above their own."

Franco thought that demarcation had long ago been made by the Fifth Vestal, who was far more qualified to sort through such allegiances. "I must go, Niko."

Niko turned in surprise. "You will not stay for dinner? For the festivities? At week's end I am throwing a grand fête—many of our old acquaintances will be attending, as well as some illustrious personages you would do well to meet, Franco."

"I fear I cannot stay. I have an…engagement," and he managed his best wanton grin.

Niko's gaze turned knowing. "In all these years…you haven't changed."

Franco clapped a hand on his shoulder and replied with daggers in mind, "Neither have you." Then he turned his back on the man and left as quickly as he dared.

EIGHT

"Let not the eyes deceive the mind; the heart is a truer guide."
— Jayachándranáptra, Rival of the Sun

TANIS DREAMED OF his mother.

In his dream, he was naught but a babe wrapped in blankets against the brisk sea air. His mother was holding him in her arms, and he could smell the ocean and feel the breeze on his face...

"Now, Tanis love," his mother murmured lovingly as she held him close and rocked gently back and forth, "never be afraid. Fear is the mask of capricious apparitions meaning only to deceive. It haunts and teases and torments, but its threats are empty. If you follow fear, if you let its whispers turn you from your path, fear will lead you to your doom. There's nothing in this world that can hurt you unless you first decide that it can. Even death is only another beginning. What then is there to fear?"

"Wise words from the wisest woman alive, Tanis lad," came the solemn voice of his father. Tanis couldn't only see the underside of his beard. He watched his father press a kiss into his mother's hair. "What has Tanis to fear in life with you for his mother?"

To which his mother replied, "We all must walk our paths..."

When Tanis woke, he was in a strange room.

He vaguely recalled the Fhorgs hauling him off in the middle of the night, but these memories were hazy and difficult to reach, blurred as they were by pain.

Pain.

Tanis sat straight up on the narrow bed, suddenly alert.

Why didn't he feel any pain?

He wasn't sure how long he'd slept—it could've been a day or longer—but he still ought to be experiencing *some* pain. He pushed at his eye and lip, which should've been swollen or at least bruised, and then yanked up his tunic to assess his ribs and belly. He found no bruises. No swelling, no tenderness. Nothing to show he'd been beaten.

The realization came as a shock. Had someone healed him? Surely no other explanation made sense, yet it seemed impossible that Pelas would've allowed it.

Then who?

And what would the others do when they found out?

Tanis didn't have long to wait for this answer, because it was just a moment later that one of the Fhorgs barged into his small room. The Wildling took one look at him and his face went wooden. He spun on his heel and stormed out, slamming and locking the door behind him.

Three minutes later, two of them showed up. The newest Fhorg grabbed Tanis's chin and looked him over with his woad-stained face. He snatched up the lad's clothing even as Tanis had done himself and eyeballed his bare belly. Then he stepped back looking suspicious.

"How did you do it?" the Fhorg demanded.

Tanis shrugged helplessly.

The Fhorg slapped him. "How did you do it?" he shouted.

"I don't know!"

The man's second cuff knocked Tanis sideways on the bed, and he tasted blood. Tanis glared up at him. "The truth doesn't change just because you hit me!"

"You'd be surprised," remarked the Fhorg coldly. "We'll see what Pelas says about this."

They stalked out.

Alone on the bed in a strange room, Tanis promised himself he wouldn't cry, but he felt shaken and frightened and altogether miserable. He was so angry at himself! Why had he followed Pelas? *Why?* He'd known the horrible, malicious things the man was involved in before he'd even left the café—he'd *known* the man was terribly dangerous. Why then? It made no sense whatsoever!

Yet every time Tanis thought back to that moment, the same sense of duty resurfaced. It was as palpable a feeling as hunger or heartbreak, and it called to him purposefully, though it made no impression on the fear quickening his heart.

Tanis didn't understand what it meant that he kept feeling as if he had a duty to carry out in regards to Pelas, but he imagined it must mean something—that much he knew from his training with Master o'Reith.

"We're all capable of knowing much more about the world and each other than we allow ourselves, Tanis youth," his master had often lectured. *"The Fifth Law of Patterning states that a wielder is limited by what he can envision. Likewise, the First Truth is based on the principle that a man may know what he envisions himself capable of knowing."*

Tanis only ever understood about ten percent of anything Master o'Reith talked about.

"Instinct comes from many sources, Tanis youth: conscience, long-buried truths often denied, and even earlier memories from our past Returnings resurfacing to influence our decisions for good or ill." The old man had been giving this lecture while cleaning his spectacles with a corner of his robe and thus squinting across the table at Tanis. *"Most people inherently ignore instinct, but that doesn't change instinct's inherent truth. Often instinct is all that stands between a man choosing a ship destined to falter in the storm and one that will safely reach port."*

Tanis had summated this lengthy lecture to mean that when instinct guided you, you'd be smart to do what it said. But that didn't make it easy, and instinct certainly didn't keep his stomach from growling.

Feeing terribly forlorn and even more hungry, Tanis laid down on the bed again and curled into a ball, still fighting off tears. His hand slipped up underneath his pillow, and—

Tanis bolted upright and shoved the pillow aside.

His dagger glinted dully atop the mattress.

Tanis stared at the weapon while his mind tried to make sense of what he saw. Of course, there was *no way* that Pelas would've returned his dagger. Which left only one explanation.

Phaedor must've enchanted the blade.

Suddenly choked with gratitude, Tanis inhaled a shuddering breath and clutched Phaedor's dagger close to his chest. That he carried with him something of the zanthyr, something Pelas couldn't take away from him—at least not for long—it was so incredibly important and special to him. *Thank you, my lord!* He cast the desperate thought, his heartfelt appreciation, towards the zanthyr, wherever he was.

Tanis could easily see Phaedor placing some kind of working upon the blade before giving it to him. *Imagine*—a boomerang dagger that always came back to where it had started.

What really twisted his mind into knots, however, was wondering *why* Phaedor had put the spell on the dagger. Had he known, even then, what Tanis would face? He wouldn't put it past the zanthyr to know such things. Phaedor stood leagues above others in most every imaginable way.

After hugging the dagger for longer than he would've been comfortable admitting, Tanis slipped it into his boot. Then he got up from the bed and walked to the room's only window. A rough shove pushed it open. Cold air flooded in, thick with brine and laden with the sound of the crashing sea. Charcoal waves thundered at the base of a cliff a hundred paces beneath his high room, and nothing but rugged, rocky coastline extended for miles.

Tanis sank to his knees and rested arms on the windowsill. Well, they weren't in the Cairs anymore.

Resting his chin on his hands, he watched the waves crashing below. He felt as if he'd been split in half: one side of him wanted to do one thing, while the other knew it had to do just the opposite. This duality manifested in several ways. For instance, part of him really wanted to be afraid, but another part knew he couldn't afford to be—the part that remembered his dream and his mother's important words.

Part of him wanted to mourn the loss of his friends and the safety that came in their company, while another knew his friends would get along fine without him and there was something he was meant to do meanwhile.

Part of him felt guilty and morose and worried what his lady must be thinking, how afraid for him she must be and how all of his companions must feel he'd betrayed them by sneaking off, but the practical part insisted that the others would understand.

That's good, because I certainly don't.

Mostly Tanis felt uncertain and sad and really regretted his decision while at the same time knowing he would make the same decision again if it presented itself.

These were complicated and inexplicable feelings, much too complex for an innocent boy of fourteen to make sense of right away.

As it turned out, he had all day to think on them.

He'd been back and forth from the window a dozen times when the sun finally slunk to hover between the overcast and the darkening sea. He was kneeling glumly at the window again, timing the growling of his stomach against the crash of the waves at high tide, when the door to his room banged open. Tanis let out a startled yelp and spun to find a Fhorg standing in the portal.

"Pelas wants ye, lad."

Feeling suddenly apprehensive, Tanis got to his feet and shut the window. Then he followed the Fhorg from the room. Three flights down a grand, curving staircase landed them in long hallway. As Tanis passed an open door, he glimpsed a circle of red candles burning around two Fhorgs, who sat cross-legged with their backs against each other and their palms bleeding onto the floor. Tanis caught whispers of their thoughts and shuddered.

Tanis's Fhorg guide escorted him through a large hall and out onto a stone patio that bordered the edge of the cliff. Pelas stood at the far end of the patio, facing the sea with his hands clasped behind his back. He wore a jacquard burgundy coat with belled sleeves, and his long hair blew wildly on the wind of a rising storm. He looked altogether unearthly and frightening, a creature of lightning and thunder.

Terribly nervous now but trying not to be, Tanis watched the Fhorg heading back inside and sort of stood there uncertainly, wondering what to do.

Eventually Pelas turned and pinned his coppery eyes on the boy. "Come here, little spy."

Tanis swallowed. He came to an uneasy halt at his side.

"Who sent you to spy on me? Tell me all, this time. I mislike lies of omission, truthreader, and believe me," he added, suddenly pinning Tanis with an intense coppery-eyed gaze, "I'll know when you're holding back."

Tanis swallowed as he looked up at him. The man seemed less menacing than he had the day before, and his thoughts were calmer. Tanis could barely hear them.

"The truth is…" He had no idea how to put into words the incomprehensible sense of duty that had compelled him to follow Pelas. "The truth is I don't *know* why I followed you, sir. I mean—" Suddenly it all came tumbling out. "I saw your thoughts back in the café, and then I—I just had this feeling—I can't explain it—and…and I *had* to follow you. I don't know why. I really wish I hadn't!" he added pitifully.

Pelas turned him a shadowy smile. "I'm sure that you do." He looked back to the rising storm just as lightning flared, splitting down through the sky between clouds and sea. The wind blew his long hair into crazy, twisting designs. Gazing at him, Tanis wondered if he might be not of their world at all.

"Do you like storms, little spy?" Pelas asked as thunder sounded, a vast gong of the heavens.

Tanis turned back to the choppy sea and hugged his arms to his chest. Between the wind and the chill Pelas emitted, he was getting really cold. "Where I live, we don't have many storms like this, not with lightning and thunder. The winds though…they can be terrifying fierce."

"I like the storms here," Pelas mused. "Aspects of them remind me of home."

"Where is that, sir?" Tanis asked through chattering teeth.

Pelas pinned him with one coppery eye. "Far from here." Then he frowned at the boy. "Are you cold, little spy?"

Tanis nodded. In fact, he was shivering.

Pelas spun on his heel and walked for the door. When Tanis didn't immediately follow, he called without turning, "Coming?"

Tanis ran to catch up.

Pelas breezed inside the hall and led away down a corridor, and Tanis followed, feeling confused. Where was the Pelas who'd viciously tormented the Healer Camilla just the night before? The Pelas whose thoughts were so twisted and dark, who'd tried to kill him with his power?

This couldn't be the same man.

Pelas led him to a circular room overlooking the sea. The waves crashed against the chalky cliffs below them, such that they seemed to be breaking against the foundations of the manor itself. A table abutting the windows had been set with a meal. Pelas took a chair there and motioned to Tanis to join him. "The Fhorgs never eat, you know," he said as they sat, then added as an afterthought, "in any event, not with me."

Tanis slowly sank down onto the other chair. He kept waiting for the man to strike him for no reason, for his thoughts to suddenly turn volatile, for something unexpected to happen. This anticipation made him jumpy and upset his stomach. It did not, however, prevent him from eating when Pelas offered to share his meal.

They sat in the dark together, eating in silence. It wasn't until Pelas had finished and pushed his plate away that he sat back in his chair and regarded Tanis significantly. "So, little spy." He called Tanis's gaze to his. "How is it you are quite healed since our altercation of last eve?"

Here it comes, Tanis thought. "I don't know, sir," he said with a wince, anticipating a blow.

But Pelas merely frowned at him. "Have you been this way all your life?"

Tanis opened one eye to peer cautiously at him. Then, seeing Pelas's mild expression, he relaxed and opened both eyes. He was relieved that Pelas hadn't hit him but more baffled than ever. "Um…I think I must've been, sir." Tanis had been putting quite a bit of thought to the idea all afternoon. "I mean…I've never really been hurt badly before, so I can't say for certain—not like…"

"Like yesterday," Pelas supplied quietly.

"Yes, sir." Tanis had never thought much on the subject before—he'd never had a reason to—but he'd realized during the afternoon that he couldn't remember ever really even being sick. Maybe he'd had a cold once…

"It would seem you are as confused as I am about yourself," Pelas remarked, noting the boy's perplexed frown.

Tanis looked to him uncertainly. "I guess so."

Abruptly Pelas grabbed his wrist in a tight hold. He pinned his eyes upon the boy, and Tanis felt that cold chill descend upon him again. He immediately started shivering. "W-what is sup-posed to h-happen?" he managed through chattering teeth, feeling unsettled and intensely discomfited by this mercurial man.

You ought to be happy he's not a raving lunatic tonight, Tanis! But instead, he wondered if maybe that's exactly what Pelas was.

Pelas released him and barked a laugh as he sat back in his chair again. "It's incredible! I wonder if Darshan has ever seen such a thing?"

Tanis eyed him fretfully.

Pelas noted his frightened look. "I find you uniquely interesting, little spy," he confessed by way of reassuring Tanis that he wasn't going to kill him right away. "But you must let me touch you like that from time to time, for I find it such an impossibility that I have to remind myself that you do in fact exist."

Thunder sounded outside, closer than before. Tanis looked out and saw a shock of lightning seem to strike the sea. Another rumble soon followed. He hugged his arms to his chest. "Why don't the Fhorgs eat with you, sir?"

Pelas grunted. "They are all my brother's spies, though only one was bold enough to claim it, and you saw how he fared. The others are more prudent."

It was such a strange concept that Tanis couldn't help but ask, "Why does your brother spy on you?"

"Clearly he doesn't trust me. Why else?"

"Trust you with what?"

Pelas shrugged. "Darshan fashions himself our leader, and being that he is older than I, he concludes this makes him twice my superior." Pelas eyed him narrowly. "My brother is a consummate prick. Pray *you* never cross paths with him. He has a particular fascination with truthreaders."

Tanis swallowed, for he heard more than Pelas had probably intended in his words. "You mean…" he braved in a small voice, "you mean the way *you're* attracted to Healers?"

Pelas settled him a telling look. "In a very deadly way, yes."

"But *why?*" The words came out in a plea. Tanis remembered all too clearly the man Pelas had been the night before, and here he sat with him at a table in the dark—it was like a nightmare story! His heart beat an unhealthy patter, and panic simmered at the fringes of his thoughts.

"We are what we are," Pelas mused. He waved a hand in annoyance and remarked, "Darshan has expansive theories and dwells upon our nature incessantly. Purpose! Purpose! *Pshaw!* Purpose *is.* It doesn't change, and it isn't imperiled simply because I choose to amuse myself with other diversions." Pelas rested a hand on the table and idly traced an impression in the wood with a furrow between his brows. "There are things to be observed about this world before we destroy it. Darshan doesn't understand the value of that, but observation...experience in new and varied ways...these things do have value. I have tried to make him understand this."

Tanis sort of stared at him feeling more than a little sick. "How can you say that," he asked meekly, trying not to cry, "and then just...just *slaughter* innocent people?"

Pelas looked at him strangely. "You are all dead already, little spy. You just don't know it."

"We're not dead!"

"But of course you are." Pelas placed his icy hand on Tanis's and leaned towards him, but there was only instruction in his tone as he explained, "All your lives are aimed in but one direction: death. Everything that comes between is simply delaying the inevitable. All your talk of feelings—your 'honor this' and 'love that'—naught but illusions, little spy. Your greatest impulse is to die, and you hurtle yourselves towards it relentlessly."

This viewpoint was so antipathetic to everything Tanis had ever believed that he just gaped at the man.

Pelas leaned back and released his hand. "I thought you understood," he said, looking puzzled. "Last night...*you* killed her. Not I."

"Because you were torturing her!" Tanis wailed. He glared hurtfully at Pelas while trying to rub some feeling back into his hand.

"Pain is but one expression of the inevitable end. It needn't be abhorrent. It can even be a release for some."

"It wasn't a release for Camilla!" Tanis blurted, nearly in tears.

Pelas frowned at him. "I can see that her fate truly disturbs you. I do not understand this reaction, but I admit it intrigues me." He drew in his breath and let it out slowly. "A Healer's blood speaks to me," he said after a moment, referencing Tanis's earlier question. "Even without the work I do for my brother in search of this pattern, their blood would call me inexorably forth. And when I find such women..." he paused, frowned. Tanis felt a terrible darkness filling the silence of Pelas's thoughts. The enormity of it made him shudder. Suddenly Pelas gave him a tragic smile, and the darkness dissipated as he confessed, "I cannot help this nature any more than you can change being a truthreader."

"You still have a choice," Tanis pointed out timidly. He felt overwhelmed by the horrific truths becoming clear to him.

"Choice is but an illusion." There was a certain remorselessness in Pelas's tone that was dreadful to experience. "One of many such illusions. You will see this too, eventually." Then his expression lightened, became even… amiable. "But off with you now. Back to your room for tonight. Tomorrow we will see about something else to wear. I can't take you anywhere all covered in…Camilla," and he waved nebulously at Tanis's blood-drenched clothes.

Tanis cringed at these callous words, but he did as Pelas bade him. As Tanis was walking away, however, he heard Pelas observe thoughtfully, "I've never had my own truthreader before."

The man's parting comment gave him such a chill that he was long beneath his covers before it finally left him.

A storm was raging when Tanis woke. The rain was falling in great sheets and making rivulets down his window pane. His room was very cold, so Tanis wrapped himself in the blanket from his cot and walked to the window to look out at the storm.

Beneath the cliff-side mansion, waves battered charcoal rocks, churning foam, and the wind, lacking any decent target upon the barren land, whipped and tore at the water. The storm's violent nature reminded him of Pelas.

Tanis thought he might be starting to understand his captor better, though the understanding brought no comfort. Something in Pelas's nature compelled him to seek out Healers and destroy them, but the man was also searching for a pattern that would help him and his brothers unmake their world.

The very idea made Tanis sick with fear. He only hoped no such pattern truly existed. From everything Master o'Reith had taught him, it didn't seem possible that such a pattern could be found, even if it did exist, for it would be too vast to be held within the ken of a single man—or even a few men. This seemed elementary to Tanis…but then, why did Pelas think there was such a pattern, and why would he think it could be found in the blood of Healers?

As thunder reverberated overhead, rattling the windowpanes, Tanis reflected on his grim thoughts. He had unexpectedly involved himself in a conflict that was far above his understanding. He thought of Prince Ean and the terrible guilt His Highness harbored over his own path. His prince, too, had been caught in a battle between forces greater than him, and he'd nearly died as a result.

Tanis felt a lump forming in his throat with these memories, so he decided not to think about Prince Ean just then. He didn't know if his prince lived, and he didn't think he could bear any more fear on top of what he was already shouldering.

Still, thoughts of Ean reminded Tanis of the terrible man who'd come to their camp that night, a man who might've signaled the end of them all if not for the zanthyr's quick protection.

And that's when it occurred to him that the dark-eyed stranger must also have been Malorin'athgul. The man had something of the look of Pelas, now that Tanis thought about it. Which brought another terrible question to mind.

Just how many brothers did Pelas have?

Abruptly the door of his room banged open, and a Fhorg stood in the doorway. "Let's go, spy."

Lest he rouse the Wildling's ire, Tanis quickly grabbed his boots and followed the Fhorg from the room. "I'm not a spy, you know," he grumbled under his breath as he followed down the passage. His

The Fhorg cast him a dubious eye. "What mission are ye upon then, if not spy'n?"

Tanis was about to answer 'none,' but he surprisingly couldn't make the word cross his tongue. To cover his dismay, he answered, "I serve a prince."

"Oh aye? Which one?"

"The Prince of Dannym."

The Fhorg shot him a wry look. "Serving him well, are ye?"

Tanis dropped his head. "No," he admitted. "I...snuck away to follow Pelas. I wasn't thinking."

"Oh aye," the Fhorg agreed with a grin, "clearly ye weren't. Lucky ye are t'was Lord Pelas ye chose to follow 'stead of his brother Darshan."

"Yes," Tanis muttered, "so he told me."

The Fhorg led him to the second floor of the sprawling manor and down a hallway where the rooms were larger and more elegantly appointed. He paused before an open doorway. "In there y'go. Yer new room. Off w'ye now."

Tanis entered a sitting room with a small balcony that fronted the sea and the storm. A serving woman was just coming out of the bed chamber as Tanis reached the door, and she pointed inside and nodded, saying something in a language that sounded, to Tanis's uneducated ear, like some dialect of Agasi. He walked in the direction she'd indicated and found a hot bath drawn and a fire burning in the hearth.

I suppose a nice bedroom is the reward for becoming Pelas's new truthreader, the lad thought with a fearful shudder.

The idea really made him cold inside.

Tanis quickly discarded his blanket and climbed into the tub. He didn't even mind that the water was scalding enough to turn his skin pink. He was still soaking when the maidservant returned carrying a linen-wrapped bundle. Leaving him to his bath, she went about her business in an orderly fashion, unwrapping each of the items and hanging the clothes they contained in the armoire. She laid out an outfit upon the bed, draped a robe over a chair for him, and gave him a naughty wink as she left.

He blushed a little in spite of himself.

When his skin was as shriveled as a prune's and he'd scrubbed away all the detritus from his first hellish confrontation with Pelas, Tanis climbed out of the tub and reflected that it *was* nice to feel clean. His lady was always going on about bathing, but Tanis had never truly appreciated the benefits of hot water until he'd had to scrub off three-day-old blood.

He shuddered at his own grim thoughts.

The maidservant had chosen a silk shirt and soft wool britches for him, but it was the jacket that really caught his attention. It was as fine as the beautiful coat Prince Ean had given him, though very different in style. The navy damask silk was woven in a recurring *fleur de lis* pattern, and the sleeves were belled like Pelas's own coat. The bottom hem flared slightly, and when Tanis put it on, it fit him almost too well. This was definitely not a coat for everyday use, which only made the boy more uneasy in wondering what Pelas had in store for him that day.

Tanis had just managed to get a comb through his hair, which he admitted was getting a bit shaggy, when Pelas came in. He wore his long locks pulled back into a plaited club and looked incredibly sophisticated and refined.

"Ah, good," he said, remarking upon Tanis's improved condition. "Is the coat to your liking?"

Tanis dropped his eyes to his hands. "It is very fine, sir. Thank you."

"Of course, it is your due. You cannot be seen with me dressed in bloodied rags. What will people think?"

Tanis couldn't tell if Pelas was teasing him or not, but he sensed a dry humor in the man's tone.

"Are you ready, little spy?"

Tanis bent and put on his boots, taking care with the one that still concealed his dagger. "Ready for what, sir?"

"For the day ahead."

"I don't know," Tanis answered uneasily. "That depends."

Pelas gave him a curious half smile. "On what?"

Tanis straightened and regarded him fretfully. "On whether or not you're planning to torture and kill anyone today."

Pelas considered him with his coppery eyes. "You really are an interesting little bird, aren't you? I would love to know what Darshan would think of you, save that it would be entirely too dangerous for you to meet him."

Tanis caught something of his thoughts in this statement and braved the question, "For me, sir, or for you?"

Pelas gave him a wondering look. "For both of us, I believe. You really can read my mind," he added appreciatively then. "How interesting that none of the Marquiin have ever managed it."

"Their talent has been corrupted by Bethamin's Fire," Tanis said without thinking, only remembering his foray into Piper's thoughts and what he'd perceived from the Marquiin who'd died in his arms back in Acacia.

"What do *you* know of Marquiin?" Pelas hissed.

The sudden fire in his gaze made Tanis take a reflexive step backwards. He felt trapped beneath his inspection and hurried to explain, "It's not what you're thinking, sir." He knew that Pelas loathed his brother Darshan's intervention in his activities and suspected everyone of being Darshan's spy. "When our company was traveling through Acacia on our way to the Cairs, my lady and I were taken hostage and handed over to an Ascendant. I was supposed to be tested, only..."

"Only it didn't work?" Pelas's manner thankfully softened.

"Yes, sir. The Ascendant was furious and he and the Marquiin started fighting."

Looking fascinated now, Pelas threw himself down into a near armchair and extended long legs before him. "Tell me, how did you escape them?"

"Prince—" Tanis caught himself and cursed his loose tongue, but it was out there now. Wincing, he finished, "Prince Ean showed up and rescued us."

"Prince Ean..." Pelas mused, "and which one would he be? There are so many princes in this realm."

"He's the Crown Prince of Dannym." Tanis feared that Pelas would attach some significance to Ean's name, but he seemed entirely unimpressed by it.

"But this does not explain how you know what my brother does to create the Marquiin, young spy."

"I'll tell you what I know sir, of course I will, but...it's just..."

Pelas gave him a tolerant look. "But?"

"Well, I *do* have a name," he grumbled.

Pelas grinned at him. "Do you?"

"Yes. It's Tanis."

"But I rather like the epithet I gave you. It seems entirely too fitting to discard it for something so trite as a name anyone might know."

Tanis sighed. "Yes, sir."

"Come then." Pelas launched himself out of the chair and headed off. "You can tell me of your deep knowledge of the Marquiin over breakfast."

Tanis caught up with him in the hall. Pelas was tall and long-legged, and he was as difficult to keep up with as Rhys or the zanthyr. As Tanis hurried along beside him, he noted that Pelas wore an aubergine coat of the same cut and cloth as Tanis's own. Clearly they were both heading somewhere important that day.

"I tire of the storm," Pelas remarked as they descended the manor's grand staircase. "Let us break our fast somewhere that has recently seen the sun."

With that, he took Tanis's upper arm and tugged him to a stop. Tanis watched him concentrate upon a distant point in the room, and then he saw a silver line spear down through the air. The line broadened to reveal a glossy blackness. Tanis didn't have time to formulate a fearful thought before they were into it and the darkness enveloped him completely. If not for Pelas's firm hold upon his arm, Tanis would've thought himself lost out of time.

A heartbeat later, another line split down out of the nothingness, and Pelas ushered him out into an alley. A slim band of blue sky showed overhead.

Pelas guided him between tall buildings and out onto a wide cobblestone street. It was still early morning wherever they were. Merchants were just setting up their carts or opening stores. All around him, Tanis heard a language being spoken that sounded somewhat like Agasi.

Pelas drew in a deep breath and sighed happily. "Much better. Come, little spy, I know a place that makes excellent meat pies, and their wine is unmatched."

"Where are we, sir?" Tanis asked as he walked at Pelas's side down the increasingly busy street.

Pelas turned him a smile, and Tanis realized that he was actually nice-looking—handsome even, in a darkly exotic way. His copper eyes could seem quite mysterious and intriguing when they weren't harboring maniacal intentions.

"The Solvayre," Pelas told him. "You've heard of the region, no doubt?"

"Yes, but…" he frowned, confused. "You didn't travel upon a node just then."

Pelas arched a sly brow. "Do I seem a Nodefinder to you?"

"No," Tanis muttered. It was not a heartening thought to know Malorin'athgul could skip around the realm at will. How were they traveling if not on the nodes? What was that black place? "If not the nodes, sir, then how?"

"Now, now, little spy." Pelas shot him a grin. "You have only just gained my good graces. That is far too soon to be prying into such important secrets."

Well, it had been worth a try.

They broke their fast at a winery's café. The patio overlooked a vineyard, which spread in tailored rows across the near rolling hills. "Sir," Tanis said when they were done with their meal and enjoying the vineyard's rich wine beneath a strong early-winter sun, "if you can travel anywhere without the nodes, why not just bring us right to this café?"

Pelas was sitting with his long legs extended to the side of their table, looking out towards the hills and a long line of cypress trees. Tanis was terribly confused by his manner, which was so...*likeable* now, so incongruous with the man he'd first met.

"Perhaps I appreciate the walk." Pelas cast him a sidelong glance. "Did you never think of that?"

"No," Tanis grumbled. "It seemed too benign."

Pelas chucked. "There are things to be observed in this world, little spy. I told you that. I'm in no hurry to destroy it."

"You seemed awfully hurried the other night," Tanis pointed out, feeling unexpectedly resentful of Pelas's callous and disconnected view.

Pelas turned to look straight at him, and something shifted in his gaze. It was like a lamp suddenly coming to light—or, rather, being instantly extinguished, replaced by a crushing darkness. The feeling of menace that overcame Pelas's thoughts made the hairs rise on Tanis's arms, and the boy suddenly felt pinned to his chair, just like at the café in Rethynnea.

"That is my work," Pelas murmured. The man Tanis had just been speaking with seemed far away now, replaced by an alarming personage that shouted his crimes with images of blood. "Sometimes..." Pelas whispered, scaring Tanis with his change of manner, "most times...it overtakes me." Then the moment was past, the beast retreating to its dark lair, and Pelas turned to gaze idly across the hills as if nothing had happened.

Tanis sucked in his breath in a little shuddering gasp. That Pelas could so readily become that *other*...

"So..." Pelas eyed Tanis inquisitively. "What do you know of the Marquiin?"

Tanis was still trembling a little, but he could tell the beast had been caged again and the likable man returned. "The Marquiin who tried to test me died in my arms."

Tanis would've rather not remembered those moments, for the man had been releasing all of the torment of several years into his expiring thoughts. Yet...something in the way Pelas had asked the question made Tanis feel like he had to answer it. It felt similar to a truthreader's compulsion, though more potent, a sort of quiet threat—yet a very clear, very real threat, like a stiletto pressed to your temple. This intimation of threat came from the lucid Pelas, the one who was otherwise amiable and even kind in his way, which only made the threat all the more potent.

The boy realized what he was sensing was the talent of a skilled interrogator. Pelas's power, whatever it was, did not merely compel Tanis to answer, it made him *want* to tell him all.

Helpless to resist, Tanis remembered that night, though it pained him greatly to dwell on those moments. "It's just…perceptions, really," he said then, glancing up to find Pelas regarding him intently.

"I'm interested in your perceptions."

Tanis wet his lips. "Very well. I…I'm not sure, but I think that the Prophet's power corrupts a truthreader's mind, and it only follows that this would inhibit his ability to wield *elae*. The Marquiin…" Tanis paused and rubbed uneasily at one eye. "Well… Prince Ean restored him in the end, and I saw some of his thoughts as he died. I didn't wholly understand them, but it seemed like he'd been under some sort of fourth-strand compulsion. I don't think he could actually work *elae's* fourth strand any more at all, even though it should've been within his nature as an Adept." Tanis looked up at Pelas, feeling heartbroken all over again. "Once Bethamin's Fire took him, he lost all contact with *elae*."

"So *that's* how he's doing it," Pelas murmured, eyes alight. "Oh, Darshan…" Abruptly he focused on Tanis again. "This Prince Ean, the prince you served, he's a wielder?"

Tanis shrugged. "I don't really know what he is. I think he's still trying to figure that out himself."

"Fascinating." Pelas shook his head wondrously. "Who knew when you appeared out of nowhere that you would prove such an intriguing diversion!"

Tanis frowned at him. "I'm honored to provide your entertainment, sir."

Pelas leveled him a quiet look. "Better this kind than the other."

At which point Tanis paled considerably.

Pelas drank more of his wine and eyed Tanis over the rim. "And what of your parentage, young spy? Perhaps that will tell us something of your nature and why you are immune both to my power and…Bethamin's Fire."

Tanis had been certain Pelas meant to say something else in his moment of hesitation, but he kept close hold on the thought, whatever it had been. The lad shook his head. "I'm sorry, sir. I know nothing of my parents."

"Nothing?" Pelas leaned towards him. "I sense more than nothing in your thoughts."

Tanis caught his lip between his teeth and gave him a tense look. Whatever power Pelas wielded over him was agonizingly effective; yet the man was requiring such private thoughts…every secret felt a bitter sacrifice.

"You're correct, sir." Tanis dropped his eyes to the goblet of wine sitting on the table before him. "I do know a…little more." He fought the urge to speak with every fiber of his being, but Pelas's power drew it out of him nonetheless. "I know that my mother and father lived by the sea. I know she was a truthreader, and I know that my father called her Renaii."

Pelas sat silent for a long time, considering him, while Tanis suffered a sick feeling in his stomach…consequence of giving in to whatever fell power Pelas had been working upon him. He imagined this was the way one might feel after taking an opiate and succumbing to pleasures debased and reviled. His self-respect lay crumpled in a sullied heap, stained with fluids better left unidentified. He hated the man in that moment for ripping the truth out of him so heartlessly.

Yet how does this differ from a truthreader's working? In truth, there was probably little difference save that a truthreader had kings and queens justifying his actions when he tore the truth forcefully out of a man.

"Renaii…" Pelas pressed a long finger to his lips. "I know that word. Do you?"

Tanis shook his head.

"It means 'light of my soul' in Old Alæic, the first language of this world, that of the zanthyrs and the *drachwyr*…among others."

Tanis frowned. "I was told it was an Agasi name."

"I suppose it is—but more like a term of endearment, like 'darling' or 'my love' yet revealing of deeper affection and regard." He glanced to the sky and the sun at its zenith. "But see here; it will be nearing sunset where we're heading. The party will be starting soon." Pelas stood and looked down at him in a way that seemed almost friendly. "What do you say, little spy? Shall we be fashionably late?"

Right then, Tanis loathed himself for following Pelas anywhere, but he went with him nonetheless.

NINE

"A brave man is one who recognizes Death waiting
upon the path and walks with him anyway."
— The Second Vestal Dagmar Ranneskjöld

KJIERAN VAN STONE woke to a pounding on his door. He stumbled out of bed and threw the bolt to find an Ascendant waiting on the other side. A pageboy behind him held a torch, his eyes downcast.

"Yes, Ascendant?"

"The Prophet calls for you, acolyte."

Kjieran's heart immediately leapt into a panic. "I should...I should dress."

"No, come as you are. Dare not keep the Prophet waiting."

Kjieran wore naught but thin linen breeks, but he followed all the same. One simply did not question Bethamin's Ascendants, and especially not within the confines of the temple.

To Kjieran's rising horror, the Ascendant led him towards the Prophet's private chambers. A multitude of fears bombarded him upon this realization, and he followed with effort, just concentrating on placing one foot before the other. It wouldn't do to stumble and give the Ascendant reason to question his faith.

You're still thinking you might come out of there intact.

Hope grew in scarce commodity in the Tempe of Tambarré, but he could do no less than cling to its fragile stalk. He held the last bastion between Bethamin and the world, and duty bound him to this task, even if it meant his death. This, he had long accepted. He just hoped it would *be* death and not one of the many other torments the Prophet meted as due reward to the faithful.

The towering doors that marked the Prophet's chambers stood open, but the Ascendant stopped without. "Go now, acolyte," he ordered stiffly. "The Prophet awaits."

Kjieran kept his gaze on his feet and headed into the Prophet's private dwelling, cringing as he heard the doors closing behind him. He pushed a hand to smooth back his shoulder-length black hair and braved a look around.

The hall was large, with a wall of arches open to the breeze, while a vast room spread away to the left, its tall ceilings supported by rounded columns inscribed with strange writing that Kjieran thought might be the language of Myacene, from whence the Prophet hailed. Through this chamber he made his way, seeing no one until he reached the end and an octagonal rotunda of arched windows beneath a frescoed dome. It was there that the Prophet sat, bare-chested, with one arm thrown over the back of a canvas chair and his long legs splayed before him.

"Come, Kjieran."

Kjieran tried to hide his rising unease. He kept his eyes on his feet, yet still he felt the Prophet's gaze upon filing across him like the razor edge of an icy knife. In each moment that Kjieran endured Bethamin's inspection, he could feel the knife caressing his skin, as if to determine which places were most likely to yield to gentle pressure and which would require a concentrated assault.

With downcast eyes, Kjieran saw the Prophet rise from his chair. A heartbeat later he felt the man's icy hands on his bare shoulders. The Prophet turned him to face away. Then his cold hands slipped around onto his chest in a sort of embrace. Kjieran gasped in a shuddering breath.

"Look there, Kjieran." The Prophet's deep voice, coming so close in his ear, cast a thrumming jolt through Kjieran, while the man's breath felt a chill breeze on his neck.

Trembling, Kjieran lifted his eyes to look where the Prophet had indicated. He saw a naked man lying face-down on the marble floor. It was hard to know how death had claimed the man, for no blood marred his white skin. Kjieran had cleaned up after many encounters that had not resolved so neatly—but never in his skivvies, and never in the middle of the night.

"I am most interested in this thing you call desire," the Prophet observed into his ear. "I've been studying it lately." He grasped his own elbows around Kjieran's bare chest and pulled his body close against his own. The touch of Bethamin's flesh was like the bitter north wind's kiss. Kjieran held himself taut, that the Prophet might not notice him shaking.

"This desire...it seems a wasted use of one's energies, yet your kind appear to thrive on it."

"Yes, my lord," Kjieran whispered.

"How does one create desire, Kjieran? What is it?"

Kjieran knew better than to give the Prophet some answer he just imagined the man would want to hear. There was no predicting his mind. And Bethamin had an uncanny ability to tell when a man was lying to him. "Desire is a quest, my lord."

"A quest for what?" The Prophet sounded earnestly intrigued.

Kjieran worked hard to keep his teeth from chattering. "For...for pleasure," he offered in a bare whisper, so afraid that at any moment the man would desire something more of him.

"What is pleasure then? Is seems to me this nebulous idea takes many forms, and all of them equally useless when death is the only end."

"Perhaps..." Kjieran tried to draw in a breath, but he was shaking so dreadfully, that all he managed was a gasp. "P-perhaps it is just a way of p-passing the hours until death."

"My doctrine," the Prophet stated, clearly displeased with this answer. He drew away from Kjieran. "I mislike platitudes drawn from my own teachings."

Kjieran swayed in place. He stared hard at his toes. "I beg your pardon, my lord."

The Prophet took hold of Kjieran's jaw and lifted his head to look upon his face. Kjieran closed his eyes and prayed like he'd never prayed in his life. "I have seen your faces when desire is upon them," the Prophet observed as he studied Kjieran's countenance with his darkly scalding eyes. "But I have not been able to engender it myself. Some emotions are so simple— fear, anger, desperation...these you seem to find easily. But desire...that the emotion eludes my understanding makes it intriguing. I would know it better, Kjieran."

"Yes, my lord," Kjieran whispered.

The Prophet ran his thumb across Kjieran's lips, the soft kiss of ice. "What do you desire, Kjieran?"

The compulsion to answer was so complete that only Raine's earlier binding saved him from telling everything. "To please you, my lord," he heard himself reply in a desperate gasp. Did he really mean to say it, or had Bethamin dragged it out of him? He honestly didn't know.

The Prophet released him. "You see? It is empty when I require it, but I know there is desire in you."

Kjieran dropped his head and stared hard at his feet, fervently wishing he might be anywhere else.

The Prophet returned to his chair radiating restlessness and malcontent. He settled his chin on his fist and watched Kjieran quietly. "If I don't require it of you, Kjieran, what answer will I get from you? The same?"

"Do you…wish me to desire you, my lord?" Kjieran braved.

The Prophet was silent for a long time, considering this question. "An intriguing concept. Am I something to be desired?"

Trapped in this, Kjieran answered, "Desire takes many forms, my lord."

"Ah, a safe response. You hide from me. Why?"

Kjieran nearly cried for wanting to answer him *because you rape our minds and destroy everything that we are!* But he answered truthfully, "Because I fear you, my lord."

"Yes, fear," the Prophet grumbled. "That one is easily managed. Here then, we return to my first question. What is it you truly desire, Kjieran? What drives that fire within you which I have so often seen in other men's eyes? How do I waken it in you?"

The Prophet laid no compulsion upon him that time, and Kjieran knew this was a gift from him, the gift of his trust. He also knew that should he disappoint the man with his answer, it might be the last thing he ever did.

So he drew in a tremulous breath and answered honestly, feeling stripped and naked in the telling, "Freedom, my lord."

"Freedom." The Prophet deep voice resonated in the chamber, which stood empty save for themselves and the dead man on the floor. Bethamin rose again from his chair, and once more Kjieran felt him approach. He stood helpless before him, merely his pawn to be used or discarded.

Bethamin stopped behind Kjieran and turned his body to face him again. He placed one icy hand on Kjieran's shoulder while another held his bare hip firmly. It was an intimate stance.

"Freedom," the Prophet murmured again, clearly considering the concept while his eyes assessed Kjieran's face. Kjieran could not see his expression, but he felt the man's thoughts. For once they were not riotous, but this didn't mean they were pleasant.

The Prophet cupped Kjieran's face with one hand again and ran his thumb across his lips. "This discussion has been fascinating," he said after a moment. "We must do it again."

"Yes, my lord," Kjieran whispered, feeling the Prophet's thumb binding his lips even as his nets of compulsion hovered hungrily above Kjieran's consciousness, just waiting to be cast.

The Prophet released him then, and Kjieran fled.

TEN

"How deep does the alabaster go?"

– A popular saying in T'khendar

EAN WOKE TO sunlight streaming through mullioned windows. As he lay in a four-poster bed large enough to comfortably accommodate five, he reviewed what he remembered: too well he recalled the battle at the Temple of the Vestals in Rethynnea…of holding desperately onto the tiniest thread of Rinokh's pattern as Creighton's Shade pulled the volatile man across a node…of the entire temple structure disintegrating around them.

It was everything else that was fuzzy.

He had a vague memory of crossing the node with Franco, both of them near collapse, and being greeted by a host of obsidian-eyed Shades who amazingly were trying to help them. He recalled being led down an endless hallway that seemed an acute form of torture in itself. He remembered a steaming bathtub, a plate of food he could barely find the energy to touch, and after that…nothing.

Feeling much restored that morning, however, Ean sat up and looked around. The room was palatial. A soaring ceiling displayed colorful frescoes above walls paneled in blue silk. His feet sank into soft Akkadian carpets as he rose from the bed. He walked to an armoire the size of a small house and opened one of its five doors to find more clothing than any one man should possess. He found his sword hanging inside the second door he opened. He stood for a moment marveling at the assortment of clothing in fine silks, velvets and wools—all, he suspected, tailored specifically for him.

Ean selected a soft blue-grey tunic whose cuffs were worked with silver thread and a pair of black pants that fit him like a glove. Three pairs of boots waited his pleasure, but he chose the ones that clearly were his own. Once he'd belted on his sword, he felt…

He wasn't sure how he felt.

Hale. Restored, certainly. Confused beyond belief. Relieved. Tormented by guilt. Apprehensive. Fearful for those he'd left behind.

It was hard to imagine one soul could feel so myriad and varied emotions at once.

He wandered the room, seeing the remains of a meal left upon the table, food he didn't remember eating. He saw a chair still bearing the impression of the man who'd sat within it, and an empty goblet on a marble-topped table.

He walked out onto his balcony, and the sight stole his breath.

From the varied tales circulating about T'khendar—perpetuated by those who'd never been there—Ean had expected to see a black basalt castle lording over a red desert that stretched for miles. Instead, he found an alabaster city of surpassing beauty, surrounded by lush green mountains.

Niyadbakir.

The name floated to him from the recesses of memory—whether recent or distant, he couldn't say.

The city crowned the entire mountainside—domes and spires lifting to spear the clear sky, gardens everywhere in between, and bridges arching from building to building, tower to elegant tower.

Leaning across his balcony railing to peer around a cupola, he saw a distant waterfall cascading down into mist, its length crossed by three grey-white stone bridges. Far below him at the palace's base, a vast garden drank in the morning sunlight, its fountains glittering.

And east of the white city, farmland stretched for miles—huge blocks of green and gold patchworking the eastern horizon—while jagged mountains rose from a forested base to form the valley's southern border.

The city bustled beneath him, and Ean watched from on high as men and women—who seemed but tiny, industrious ants—went about their business.

T'khendar.

Incredible to realize this view, this scene of productivity and…normalcy, was in T'khendar—that *he* was in T'khendar!

Ean's stomach growled voraciously, reminding him that he couldn't remember the last time he'd actually eaten a meal. Heading back inside then, he found his way through his apartments, and after choosing several wrong doors, finally found one that led into a hallway. Though nothing looked familiar, he went left, following the music of a tiered fountain chiming in a central atrium.

As he walked, more images returned to him.

He remembered Franco hugging him farewell, Creighton's Shade helping him into bed, a man's face—Björn's?—staring closely at his. A hand reaching to cover his eyes…

With the vision of Björn came a sudden acute anxiety. Apprehension and uncertainty flooded him, and he unconsciously slowed his pace.

It was so much to take in.

Before the battle in the temple, Creighton had told Ean more than he could easily assimilate in one month of conversation, much less a single hour.

Between Creighton's rushed explanation—which had resulted in Ean's sudden defection from Raine and his companions—and the present moment, Ean had betrayed his friends, abandoned his cousin in a petrified state, and openly defied the Fourth Vestal. He'd been blasted, threatened with annihilation, and nearly killed just holding onto Rinokh's pattern.

Reckless and brash?

Absolutely. He'd proven Morin d'Hain right time and time again, and it rankled that the man's assessment had been so inescapably accurate.

Ean stood still in the hallway considering all that had come before. Despite the thick, clinging cobwebs of guilt, he…well, while he felt regretful, he thought he'd made the right choice that night with Creighton—Raine's truth, he *hoped* he had anyway, for he'd certainly alienated himself from all who loved him in the doing. The feeling came with no reassurance, only a hollow sense of solitude.

'Players make their moves at will,' the zanthyr's words, ever wise, ever true. *'…reassured only by their own resolve…protected by no one, and shielded by nothing but the force of their conviction.'*

As he started off again, Ean wondered resentfully if Phaedor was ever wrong about anything. These spiraling thoughts absorbed his attention as he reached the atrium and—

Came face to face with a Shade.

The prince drew back with a startled intake of breath. He instantly recognized the Shade who'd taken him hostage. The shock of that remembered moment compelled Ean to draw his blade and smite the man, and he had to consciously restrain himself from reaching for his weapon.

How many months had he dreamed of confronting this creature face to face? How many nights envisioning the moment and what he would do, what he would say? All of it wasted, in vain…the ignorant dream of a naïve boy. Every conception he'd had of the Shade had been completely *wrong!*

"Be welcome, Ean," the Shade finally said, trying to ease the awkward tension that bound them in that indefinite moment while the winds of Ean's emotion blasted and buffeted them. The Shade placed palms together, pressed fingertips to his lips and bowed.

Ean called his composure to heel, feeling awkward and embarrassed. "Reyd…wasn't it?" he managed.

"That's correct." The Shade regarded him solemnly. "Do you feel rested? Recovered?"

"Yes." Ean had to remind himself in every moment that this man was not his enemy. "Very much so."

"That is excellent news. The First Lord will be pleased to know it. If it would not be too unpleasant for you to walk with me, I will escort you to him now."

"No, definitely not." Then he grimaced. "I mean, it's certainly not unpleasant for me. It's just that when I saw you…" Suddenly tongue-tied, he tried to find the words.

"It is only reasonable for you to wish me ill," Reyd observed gravely.

"Oh, for Epiphany's sake!" Ean pushed a hand through his hair and gave the Shade an imploring look. "You saved my blood-brother from the permanence of death. I should feel naught but…gratitude."

"I also assaulted you, took you hostage, threatened you and punched you in the face."

Ean cracked a smile. "I supposed I deserved it—at least that last part."

They stood staring at one another for a moment more, and then

Ean motioned them onward, mostly because he couldn't stand feeling so awkward and unbalanced.

The Shade acquiesced with a nod.

As they walked in silence, Ean's tension ebbed. Somehow, in that brief moment of reconciliation—even as clumsy as it had been—some part of him had yet been…righted.

In recent weeks, he'd started feeling like every piece in the game of Kings that was his life had been upended and cast haphazardly across the board. Now, one piece had been placed back in position, rightness restored to that small degree. Things were becoming—

Oddly, it seemed that things were becoming…as they should be.

It was the strangest experience.

"How long have I been asleep?" Ean had the sense that he'd lost a day or two since staggering across the node arm in arm with Franco.

"Six days," Reyd answered.

"*Six* days?"

"The First Lord felt you needed the rest and commanded you into the dreamless sleep of healing. You rose only to eat and drink twice a day but never woke."

"*Six days*," Ean said again, both startled and amazed. "I don't remember anything."

"No, you wouldn't. Such is the nature of the healing sleep."

"Are the others here? Creighton? Franco Rohre?"

"The Nodefinder left some days ago on an errand for the Second Vestal, and your blood-brother is on assignment. Ironic, because he spent every night at your bedside in case you woke early, and now upon the day he has been set to task, you rouse."

They passed through a vast atrium brightened by a glass-domed ceiling. "He is glad you are awake now, however," Reyd added, glancing Ean's way. The prince must've looked confused, for the Shade clarified, "All Shades are connected via the shared mind. Was this not explained to you?"

"I suppose Creighton said something about it," Ean muttered, "but I barely understood half of what he told me. Everything happened so quickly…" Ean shook his head. He had so many holes in his understanding.

"It's well that you've come here then," Reyd said, glancing at him. "The First Lord will make many things clearer."

Ean thought of how long he'd been desperate for answers and how most everyone who'd advised him only seemed to provide the information that most suited their own agendas. Would he even be able to accept *real* answers if Björn offered them?

Just then they reached a pair of immense doors. Seeing them, Ean forgot everything else.

Exquisitely carved with scenes of the Genesis, all manner of creatures and men seemed to explode out of them. Ean stopped short in their shadow, captured not merely by their beauty and expert craftsmanship. No, he was startled because—

"I've seen these doors before." He extended a hand tentatively towards them, yet oddly wary that if he touched them they would vanish like the dream they seemed.

"They are the Extian Doors."

Ean turned to him. "I don't mean I've seen something like this." He stared hard at the creature. "I mean I've seen *these exact* doors—I'm sure of it—but..." He looked back to them and pushed a hand through his hair, grabbing cinnamon waves into his fist as he gazed with wonder. "But that's not possible, is it?"

Reyd waved to the doors and they opened, swinging inward with stately silence. He walked through and then looked back to the prince. "Come, Ean val Lorian. The First Lord would greet you in the Hall of Games."

Ean followed, but he suddenly felt his entire Kings board wavering under him again, and him a single tiny knight fighting to stay upright.

Björn van Gelderan.

Ean remembered how the zanthyr had spoken of him so long ago. How he'd so quickly roused to anger when Ean, in all innocence, had spoken ill of the man. He remembered the way Raine D'Lacourte's diamondine gaze had filled with frustration at the mere mention of Björn, the way his manner had shifted from calm determination to anger and dismay, how he'd radiated his inability to outthink the Fifth Vestal as much as his guilt and resentment over it.

He remembered all of the stories he'd ever heard about the man—not a one depicted him as anything but a heinous traitor. And he recalled Raine's account of the sacrifice of the Citadel's Hundred Mages...

What in Tiern'aval were you thinking, *coming here?*

He'd betrayed everyone to join Björn. And why? For Creighton? Because through Björn's intervention, both of their lives had been spared? Because the Fifth Vestal could teach him to use his talent?

Because Björn is fighting the same people I'm fighting.

But Ean knew the intensity of feeling that drew him to Björn van Gelderan ran far deeper even than these reasons.

This is what you wanted all along—to seek him out, to confront him.

In the beginning, Ean had blamed Björn for Creighton's death. Now he knew that to be a terrible misconception. Now he knew that Björn had been helping him all along.

And yet…a glimmer of truth still demanded acknowledgment: he *had* wanted to seek out Björn. He'd felt the need pushing at him since the very first moment the Vestal's name was restored to his consciousness as a living man instead of a myth.

Well, now it's done…you've gone to him.

But as he pushed on, following the Shade, Ean faced so many unknowns that everything inside him was trembling.

The Hall of Games spread expansively, its black and white marble floor playing counterpoint to soaring ceilings and gigantic alabaster columns. The far wall of arched windows overlooked a garden patio, and beyond it spread the whole of Niyadbakir. Between the windows and Ean, groupings of chairs and tables offered players a space to congregate and partake in any manner of games.

At that time of the morning, only a few of the tables were occupied. Ean looked around as he followed Reyd, taking in the scene with wonder riding the tide of his apprehension until—

He saw *her.*

She stood near the balcony doors talking to two men. A black blindfold concealed her eyes and bound her long chestnut hair, and she held a raven-black staff taller than she was. Her simple, yet elegant, dress gleamed with hues of the deepest, richest wine.

Ean stood transfixed.

He didn't even realize he'd stopped walking, for the sight of her so riveted him. At the same time, he felt a painful compulsion to go immediately to her side. Most of all, he felt an overwhelming jealously towards the other men standing with her, simply because they had her attention. These emotions were incredibly strong, inexplicable, and disconcerting.

Reyd prodded Ean's elbow with a gentle touch, and the prince, still somewhat mesmerized, starting walking again.

While Ean watched, a black-haired man whose back was to him kissed the woman on both cheeks and said something quietly to her. She smiled tenderly at him and cupped his cheek in her palm. Then she placed her left hand upon the arm of a robust man with silver-grey hair cut just above his shoulders, and he led her away.

Then the dark-haired man was turning, and Ean stood face to face with Björn van Gelderan.

A memory came unbidden...

Ean looked up at the stranger, and taking a deep breath, he stepped upon the bridge. "Can we...walk together?" he asked the blue-eyed man.

"If you would have me at your side..."

There was no denying it...this man had drawn him back from the steppes of death, where even the zanthyr had not ventured.

Ean couldn't bring himself to take a single step more. He stood paralyzed—by apprehension, by doubt, by gratitude and regret and strange feelings of lingering resentment that seemingly had no place.

Björn crossed the distance between them in five long strides and grabbed Ean into a strong embrace. "Ean, at last!" He hugged him tightly. Pulling back, he took the prince by both shoulders. "Be welcome!"

As Ean gazed at the Vestal, a flurry of emotions choked him. He inexplicably felt another knight right itself upon his game board. He didn't know why or how, but he knew this was not a meeting.

It was a reunion.

Björn seemed to perceive Ean's delicate mental state, or perhaps he was used to people standing in speechless awe of him; he held Ean's gaze with infinite compassion. One hand squeezed the prince's shoulder. "Come. Will you break your fast with me?"

When Ean didn't object—verily, he couldn't find words of any sort—Björn nodded to Reyd, who left them, and then the Vestal led Ean out onto a sundrenched patio.

Ean had never witnessed such an impressive display of creation. The alabaster city, the deep lush valley, the jagged emerald mountains all around. It seemed like…paradise.

Björn led Ean towards a marble table that had been set with a meal, and Ean slowly sank into a chair, feeling dazed.

Could he really just eat? Just like that? He had so many questions, but they all seemed to demand justification in the answering, and Ean couldn't bring himself to demand such from this man—not now that he'd met him in the flesh.

Standing face to face with Björn had instantly recalled powerful emotions that seemingly had no source—feelings of profound loyalty and friendship, and of the immense weight of duty.

Everything seemed so disjointed, his mind was spinning… spinning…

"Have a drink, Ean." Björn was watching him in a quietly intense way that was very much like the zanthyr's in manner.

Ean shifted his gaze to meet the Vestal's. His eyes were quite impossibly blue. It was the first thing Ean had noticed about him, even before he noticed how striking he looked, even before the force of Björn's presence jarred him to the bone.

"Ean?"

Ean realized the man was trying to hand him a goblet of something, so he took it, and he drank all of it, noting after the fact that the wine had been strong. It warmed his stomach and brought some color back to his face, but it couldn't quiet the storm of his thoughts.

The Vestal put a plate of fruit in front of him. It looked just like ordinary Alorin fruit, not something born of an heretical realm of darkness and shadows governed by a traitorous villain. Ean felt the fool just sitting there, but he couldn't bring himself to eat. He had so many questions that he couldn't conceive of where to begin.

And then there was that feeling of reunion. Ean couldn't even think about that.

He wondered suddenly what the zanthyr would say if he saw him sitting there so frozen by his own insecurities. But thoughts of the zanthyr gave him a way to open the conversation at least.

"Is Phaedor…" Ean heard his own voice as if it were far away, drowned by waves of anticipation crashing on the treacherous rocks of curiosity. "Is he sworn into your service?"

Björn was slicing a pear. "Yes."

Ean drew in a slow breath and let it out again. The confirmation strangely pained him. "Wholly?"

Björn glanced his way. The intensity of his gaze was unsettling. "Phaedor is my most trusted companion."

Ean forced a swallow. *So Raine had the right of it. That much of what he said was true.*

"Thus did the zanthyr aid you at my behest," Björn added quietly. "I hope you were benefited by his service."

"I was—am," Ean corrected, feeling bruised and bare beneath the Vestal's acute inspection. He looked down at his lap. "Very much so."

"To carry the oath of a zanthyr is the gravest of responsibilities," Björn said by way of acknowledgement. He set down his knife, folded hands in his lap, and regarded Ean seriously. "Knowing an eternal creature is yours to command, that even while doing your bidding they're depending on you to care for their eternity and all this implies—that they must live forever with the choices they make on your orders—this knowledge drives me in my purpose every day." He exhaled a thoughtful breath and shifted his gaze out over the valley. "It is intolerable to imagine disappointing him."

"I know what you mean," Ean muttered, feeling as though he'd done little else. He considered Björn's words as he stared at his plate. Ean could hardly imagine the zanthyr swearing into the service of anyone, much less a traitor to his own race. There had to be much more to the story than he knew—than *anyone* knew. Björn's side.

He thought of others who served the First Lord: Franco, Creighton… Dagmar.

Ean drew in a deep breath and asked, "Do all who serve you do so willingly?"

Still regarding him with hands in his lap, calm and relaxed and yet exuding a confidence unlike anyone Ean had ever known, Björn replied simply but with conviction, "I would have no man's oath otherwise."

The intensity of his attention was unmatched. It was like sitting next to the sun. Ean pushed a hand through his hair and looked off over the city towards the mountains.

"Have something to eat, Ean."

Out of respect, Ean made an attempt at the plate before him, but the food tasted empty, his mind too preoccupied.

Björn watched him quietly and refilled Ean's goblet for him. "Everything you're feeling, Ean, is likely in some way justified." The prince gave him a tormented look, whereupon the Vestal continued, "Often in the past few months the truth was denied you, while in other circumstances you were intentionally misled. Balance is a dangerous game."

"Forgive me," Ean countered, feeling frustration welling at the familiar comment, "but it seems terribly convenient, this excuse of Balance."

Björn broke into a rueful smile. "No doubt it does. In truth it is highly vexing." He captured Ean's gaze with a compelling look. "How simple it would've been to approach you, explain the situation, tell you how much danger you're in and from whom and why, tell you how we intend to help you Awaken your talent, get your agreement and be done with it."

The cavalier nature of this comment twisted Ean's emotions into sudden turmoil. He knew the Vestal wasn't making light of his ordeal, but he couldn't keep from challenging tightly, "And why couldn't you?"

"In point of fact, that's exactly what we did—the first time."

Ean sort of stared at him. It seemed suddenly difficult to take a breath. "The…first time?"

Björn confirmed this with a nod.

Ean shoved a hand through his hair and stared at the Vestal. "And… what happened?"

"You died."

"I see." The prince reached urgently for his goblet. He gulped down the wine, wishing it was a stronger stuff. "I see…" he murmured again.

All those dreams…memories of dying.

How glib he'd been in his belief. For most people of Dannym, the Returning offered hope when loved ones were lost, an opportunity to know them again in another life. Yet even after realizing that he'd Awakened—even after Dagmar had explained that his pattern indicated his own wrongful death—Ean had never connected all the pieces.

He certainly hadn't imagined that he might've already once played a role in the Fifth Vestal's game!

Björn went back to his meal. "Now the second time—"

"The *second* time?" Ean protested weakly.

"—we were much more careful of not upsetting the Balance." He glanced up at Ean under his brows. "We approached you via intermediaries. We helped you come to your own conclusions. You had already Awakened and were eager to use your talents in aid of the realm. You sought us out."

"But it didn't matter," Ean said. It was easier if he didn't think of this conversation as truly being about him—*in some other life!*

"No," Björn answered gravely. "We had still interfered too greatly. We'd overstepped the Balance again."

"What makes it different this time?" It wasn't a heartening idea to ponder, that his death might already be foreordained by the ultimate checks and balances system of the universe.

"Many things," Björn assured him.

"I'd like to believe you." Ean felt like a harp strung too tightly, needing only the slightest sharp pluck to snap. "It's…a lot to take in."

"In time, more will become clear." Björn observed the prince's morose expression and reached to lay a hand on his arm. "You have a choice, Ean. Even now, on the brink of a critical juncture in the game…should you choose to walk away, none of us will stop you."

He didn't have to say that others might—the Duke of Morwyk, *Malorin'athgul*—that *Balance* might. Ean knew these truths already.

He lifted his gaze to meet the Vestal's. He thought about the Extian Doors and the certainty that he'd seen them before. He thought about his sense of reunion when Björn had embraced him. He thought of the intensity of his determination to seek Björn out in the early days of his vengeance, even knowing how absurd the idea had been.

"No," he whispered, turning away to hide the grief that suddenly choked him. He swallowed against a painful constriction in his throat. "I think I made that choice a long time ago."

Björn was watching him quietly, chin in hand. "So it would seem."

Ean clenched his jaw and cast burning eyes out across the vista again. For some reason, he really wished the zanthyr could've been there—if only to ridicule and chastise him. It was easier to face Phaedor's reproach than the depth of Björn van Gelderan's understanding.

"But ah…look," said the Vestal brightly. "What timing you possess, Julian."

Ean composed himself with effort and turned to find a youth close to his own age approaching. He wore a silver circlet around his longish blonde hair, and he boasted the early growth of a beard slightly darker in hue.

"Ean, may I present Julian D'Artenis of Jeune."

Julian pressed palms together, fingertips to lips, and bowed. "Be welcome, Ean." He smiled as he straightened. "I'm so pleased to meet you." His words betrayed the slightest hint of a Veneisean accent.

"Julian is also a fifth-strand Adept," Björn said. "He's come to T'khendar to train in his craft, but today he is simply a guide."

"Your guide," Julian clarified brightly.

Ean gave Julian a smile that he didn't feel in the least. "Well met, Julian. I fear I shan't be the best of company today."

"Not to worry. I was you once." Then he flashed a grin. "Well...sort of."

Ean looked back to his plate as if to give his food a regretful farewell, but he blinked when he found the plate empty. Only then did he realize that he'd eaten it all. His eyes darted to Björn, whose reply was a knowing half-smile beneath a quietly sparkling gaze.

Ean stood and looked down at the Vestal. "Thank you, for...everything." He didn't know all the things he was thanking Björn for, and part of him still resisted thanking him at all—that deluded part still prey to falsehoods and tales—but he felt that a show of gratitude was the least he could do.

Björn nodded graciously. "Enjoy your tour."

Julian clapped him on the shoulder. "Come, Ean. There's so much to see."

ELEVEN

"A rose without thorns is too like a shallow heart. One
cannot find love without pricking a few fingers."
– Errodan val Lorian, Queen of Dannym and the Shoring Isles

ALYNERI WOKE TO the smell of *czai*. Because the blindfold still obscured her sight, she imagined morning light filling the little bedroom and tried to envision the farmstead where Yara made her home. She could hear chickens and goats making friendly in the yard outside. The braying of a mule occasionally disturbed the ordered cacophony. The outside door opened and closed a few times while she lay quietly, and voices floated to her from the other room.

"…concerned for her," Ama-Kai'alil was saying as he and Yara came inside together. "It's been too long. I checked on her earlier and her condition still hasn't improved."

Alyneri's breath caught in her throat. *But I feel so much better!*

"No better, but no worse," Yara pointed out.

"Still, she should've healed by now. I fear for her. If things don't change soon…"

Alyneri went cold. *Am I dying?* Had they just been humoring her the other night?

She couldn't stand the idea of being fooled about her condition, and a sudden determination drove her from the bed. It was something of a challenge, sitting up with her injured head and her left arm strapped across her chest, but with persistence she made it upright. As the dizziness faded, she inched her way to standing. Her feet and legs felt stiff yet wobbly at the same time, and she noticed the twinges of bruises as muscles tensed to support her.

Had she not been so driven to understand the ongoing conversation in the other room, she would've been quite happy to lie back down and call it a day. Instead, she shuffled towards the voices, right hand extended blindly before her, feeling for the doorway. She made it to the door before they noticed her, whereupon a commotion ensued.

"Stones for breakfast! What are you doing up, child?" Yara exclaimed in the desert tongue.

Then, suddenly, *he* was at her side with his arm around her shoulder, supporting her. He smelled like the early morning—dew and fresh strewn hay—and a little like cinnamon, but that might've just been the *czai* tea.

"You shouldn't be out of bed, *soraya*." Yara chided her as Ama-Kai'alil was helping her into a chair. It felt good to sit down, but it also felt good to be moving around.

"I heard voices," she said as a feeble explanation for disobeying Yara's strict orders. "And I smelled *czai*."

"We could've brought it to you." Yara still sounded disgruntled by her appearance.

"And I..." Alyneri caught her lower lip between her teeth and then braved, "I heard you talking."

A confused silence met this. Then Ama-Kai'alil said, as understanding dawned, "You thought we were talking about you."

Alyneri sagged with relief. "You—you weren't?"

"*Pshaw!*" Yara grumbled. "Don't be ridiculous."

"But then..."

"It's my horse," Ama-Kai'alil explained. "She fell lame more than a fortnight ago and doesn't seem to be getting better. I..." He hesitated. "Well, suffice it to say I couldn't bear to lose her."

Alyneri straightened in her chair. "You must take me to see her."

"It's kind of you to want to see her," he answered, sounding puzzled, "but we've done all we can."

"*You* have perhaps." A surge of energy fueled into her at this newfound purpose. "But I am an Adept Healer. Please...let me see her."

"But *soraya*," Yara protested, "you're so weak yourself."

"I will be careful," Alyneri promised.

A moment of silence followed, and she imagined they were exchanging meaningful looks. "Well…" Ama-Kai'alil said finally, "if you think you could help…"

She could feel hope radiating off of him. "Will you guide me, Ama-Kai'alil?" She made to stand up again.

"Just a minute there," Yara pressed her shoulder back against the chair. "You'll not be going anywhere until you've put some food into that little body—you're like to float away on the slightest breeze as it is."

Alyneri admitted this was likely a fair assertion. Her body went from slim to emaciated with naught but five pounds lost from her frame, and Ean's condition had stolen her appetite long before her own accident.

Ean. Oh, Ean…

Thoughts of the prince necessarily brought thoughts of Tanis and the zanthyr, too, the three of them inextricably connected now in memory for reasons she didn't fully comprehend. Her throat constricted, and a tightness came to her chest. Her dear friends…they must be so worried!

"Alyneri?" Ama-Kai'alil's voice was close, full of concern. Images of the warm light of a Gandrel summer pierced through her grim thoughts. "Are you all right?"

"Oh, I'm fine," she whispered. "I'm sorry. It's just that I was reminded suddenly of friends who are dear to me."

He placed a hand upon hers. "Is there someone we should help you contact?"

The same question as before, but she shook her head. "There is no way to reach them." She felt suddenly the grave weight of all that had come to pass. "For now…no."

"As you will."

"Food then!" Yara placed a bowl in front of Alyneri and made to shoo Ama-Kai'alil away from her side.

"No, I'll do it," he said so gently that Alyneri's heart fluttered. Being next to him wakened marvelous feelings. Her breath always came a little faster when he was near.

Alyneri felt a unique and thrilling energy as he fed her with slow care, one hand holding hers, the other doling out Alyneri-size bites of Yara's hearty porridge. She tasted cinnamon and clove, apple, plum and fig, all of it drenched with honey and churned butter, but none as sweet as the feel of his hand on hers.

How strange to be so appended to a man she barely knew…yet something in his voice spoke to her with the warmth of a childhood memory.

The morning's conversation concerned preparations for Yara's impending trip, and not long after Yara began discussing the packing, Alyneri asked, "Where are you going, Yara?"

"To visit my grand-children in Agasan."

"Rimaldi and then the Solvayre," Ama-Kai'alil added with a smile in his voice.

"How wonderful!" Alyneri aimed a smile in her direction. "I have always wanted to see Agasan, especially the Rimaldi Coast. Will you be sad to leave Veneisea? It's a beautiful kingdom, from what I saw of it."

"*Pshaw*," grunted the old woman. "There are plenty of lovely places in the world, and I've had enough of Veneisean 'virtue' to last me twelve lifetimes. Do you know where the word *virtue* comes from?"

Alyneri opened her mouth to accept another bite of porridge—half listening to the old woman and half reflecting on how mortified she would've been if it had been Ean feeding her instead of Ama-Kai'alil, and how strange to find herself comparing them at all. "No, Yara," Alyneri managed through her mouthful.

Ama-Kai'alil supplied in a sardonic tone, "*Virtue* from the Veneisean root *vertu* from Old Cyrenaic, *vir*, meaning man."

"Man!" Yara grumbled. "Who generally exemplifies no virtues and countless vices. I guarantee you, a *man* devised the Veneisean Virtues and required *wo*man to follow them or be labeled a whore and a tramp."

"When I am king of Veneisea," Ama-Kai'alil teased, "I will recommend that men follow the Virtues as well as women."

Yara paused in her shuffling, and Alyneri got the sense she had pinned him with a wily eye. "When you are king, Ama-Kai'alil, you will do much greater things than that."

"I was only making a jest, Yara." Alyneri could tell the old woman's praise had embarrassed him.

"Yes, but there is something about you, Ama-Kai'alil," Yara insisted. "You are a man above men—a *leader* of men—not merely in deed and stature but in ideals…born to stand above others that they might aspire to better themselves merely by walking in your shadow."

He sat quietly beside Alyneri after this startling pronouncement. She wondered what he was thinking and wished for the tenth time that morning alone that she could've looked upon him. After a moment, he remarked softly, "A selfless deed doesn't make me royalty, Yara," and he sounded both uncomfortable and tormented.

"Perhaps not," she conceded, "but it does make you noble in the most meaningful sense."

Who is *he?* Alyneri wondered, herself caught now in the mystery of his heritage. She believed Yara's assessment of him. Even when speaking gently, he communicated with an air of competence and a calm certainty that compelled compliance. Knowing that he spoke more languages than she did only heightened her admiration. She quite believed she would do anything he asked of her, and she barely knew him.

When Alyneri had eaten all she could, he helped her from the table and back to her room, where Yara took over to help her dress. "This is one of my daughter Habivi's old dresses," she advised as she did up the buttons on the frock. "A bit loose through the hips, but it'll do."

"Do you think we can remove the bandage over my eyes?"

Yara checked with a peek beneath the bandages. "Not yet, *soraya*. There is still some swelling." At Alyneri's crestfallen sigh, Yara offered, "But we might do a little with your hair."

Thus did Alyneri emerge from the bedroom with a new dress, her hair braided, and feeling much restored, even if mainly in dignity.

He walked her out to the barn with one arm around her waist, keeping her close against him for support, her free hand in his. Being close to him served to bring a heady sense to the day.

Inside the barn, they stopped in front of a stall where a horse was already attentive to his arrival. "Alyneri," he said, "this is Gendaia."

"Oh, what a lovely name!" Alyneri extended her hand tentatively towards the horse.

"It means daybreak in Old Alæic."

"You speak the Old Tongue as well?"

"No, but those who named her do."

Gendaia placed her nose into Alyneri's outstretched palm. "Have you owned her long?"

"A Hallovian is owned by no man," he corrected with that particular golden tone in his voice that Alyneri had come to love, "but she's been my companion for several moons now."

"A Hallovian." She thought at once of Caldar's noble form.

He chuckled. "You've known one yourself, I take it."

"They're incredible animals. Can you let me inside with her?"

"Of course." He opened the stall and guided Alyneri within.

She reached out, and he guided her hand to the horse's withers. Then he stood close to her holding one hand protectively against the small of her back—the quiet assurance of his near presence—and his other hand across Gendaia's muzzle. Thus connected within this tactile circle, Alyneri sank into rapport.

The sudden light of *elae* dazzled her. She'd never before realized how much light *elae* encompassed—she'd never endured multiple days without sight—but it both astonished and rejuvenated her. Within Gendaia's energy, she gained a clear sense of her surroundings and of the three of them connected in their circle of touch.

All things are formed of patterns. Alyneri needed only to gain Gendaia's pattern to heal her. Except...the horse's pattern hid from her—perhaps some aspect of her Hallovian nature caused this. Alyneri went deeper into *elae,* deeper into the horse's own lifeforce, and found something truly astonishing.

Within the rushing, rosy stream of animal life, she saw a faint and distant pattern—a *human* pattern—and beyond it, the shadow of another. She spent a moment trying to understand these visions, but once she did...

It can't be possible!

He must've sensed her sudden astonishment and misinterpreted it, for she felt Ama-Kai'alil stiffen beside her. As if with concern, he pressed his hand tighter against her back.

Suddenly the most distant pattern flared.

"Ama-Kai'alil," she managed, breathless and barely keeping herself in rapport for the force of her sudden excitement, "please place your left hand upon mine."

He did so, and his pattern came into clear focus.

So, too, did the one beyond it.

Her own.

Alyneri remained immobile, unable at first even to process the enormity of her discovery. Finally, she gathered her wits and returned to the task at hand. A brief foray into uninspected corners of Gendaia's lifeforce resulted in the animal's pattern at last surfacing. Alyneri saw at once where Gendaia's pattern had been frayed, an injury so minimal that it took just the slightest gift of her own energy to mend it.

Gendaia nickered softly, and Alyneri smiled, unknowingly reassuring the man beside her, who had grown quite tense in the intervening minutes.

But she didn't release *elae*. Two tasks she had yet to do, so long as her energy held up. First to study his pattern, then to memorize her own.

His pattern she saw easily, for she had direct contact with him and could've looked upon it even without Gendaia's presence, but she dared not change anything about their configuration. Thus, Ama-Kai'alil's pattern remained distant but still within view. Its integrity shone uncompromised, though it had clearly been mended not too long ago. Whoever had Healed him had not simply rewoven the frayed strands; he or she had shored up Ama-Kai'alil's entire life pattern. Beside her stood a man whose entire constitution had been *improved*—made stronger, sturdier, more completely whole than nature had managed.

Alyneri didn't know how it had been done—how it *could* have been done.

Feeling her own energy draining, she pushed on, now turning her attention to herself. It was both exhilarating and terrifying to look upon her own pattern, to see its weaknesses and frayed strands, to see it—even so distantly—as its vitality ebbed even from her use of her own energy in viewing it.

She felt faintness coming on and knew she had to hurry. Using the last of her strength, she committed the pattern to memory.

She withdrew from rapport just as her legs buckled.

He caught her around the waist with a muttered oath and lowered her gently to the straw. "I'm—it's fine," she managed barely a whisper.

"I shouldn't have let you do this." He tone resonated fury, though his voice remained calm. "You shouldn't have risked your health this way—"

She pushed a hand feebly towards his lips to silence him. "It's done.

Gendaia is healed. It's only that I…discovered something, and I had to stay longer in rapport to study it."

"Then…" hope and amazement warred for purchase in his tone. "Gendaia is well? Truly?"

"Truly." Alyneri smiled. "See for yourself." When he hesitated to release her, she laughed. "Go on, then. I'm certainly not going anywhere."

Reluctantly he moved to the horse. After a moment, he said, "You're right. The swelling is already abating."

"By tomorrow I should be surprised if she is not ready to run again and quite fighting you to do so."

"Alyneri…" She felt him kneel once more at her side, and her heart took a little leap. He drew her hand into his own. "Alyneri, how can I ever thank you?"

"Thank me?" she laughed. "Did you not save my own life, Ama-Kai'alil? I fear I am still very much in your debt."

"No." His tone was quite serious and sincere. "There is no gift you might've given greater than this."

She smiled softly. She wished she could look upon him, this man who made her feel at once safe and cherished and whose presence filled her with such excitement. She realized with not a little apprehension that she might just be falling in love with a man she'd never laid eyes upon.

But why am I surprised? I'm doomed to love men who can never love me in return.

"We should get you back to bed." And before she had time to formulate a protest—not that she'd intended to—he'd scooped her up into his arms and was carrying her from the barn.

She rested her head against his strong shoulder. "Ama-Kai'alil, once I've rested and eaten, might you sit with me again? I have a favor to ask of you."

"Anything, Alyneri."

She caught her lip between her teeth and smiled.

Later that afternoon he came to her bedside. After food and rest, she felt restored and eager to tell him her plan. As he sank down onto the mattress at her side, she reached for his hand, and he twined her fingers within his own. She waited until the thrill of his touch abated to a manageable simmer and asked then, "Do you know much about the Healer's art?"

"I've a cursory understanding—that you find a man's pattern and repair it, and in doing so, repair his body."

"That is a fair representation. One of the harshest realities of being a Healer is the knowledge that you can't heal yourself."

"I've heard that, but I don't really understand why."

"It's the inability to see your own pattern. It's part of you, you see. Like standing within a forest, you're never able to be exterior enough to yourself to see the entire framework."

"Ah."

"And yet…" She caught her bottom lip between her teeth. The knowledge and her excitement over it were fairly bursting out of her. "And yet, this morning when you and Gendaia and I were linked, I saw Gendaia's pattern, your pattern…and my own."

"But how can that be?"

She'd been thinking hard about how to explain it to him. "Imagine looking into a mirror. You'd see only yourself and what's behind you, right?"

"Yes."

"Now imagine looking through a window at a mirror on a distant wall. You'd see not only yourself, but also the outside of the wall that supported the window, and maybe even a reflection from the window itself."

He understood immediately. "Gendaia was reflecting your own pattern back to you?"

"I think it was something like that. I don't fully understand it. I've been linked in rapport with other Healers and never experienced that mirroring effect. I suspect it has something to do with her animal nature—her pattern being different enough from a human pattern that she isn't merely a mirror but a window to a mirror. I definitely looked through her lifeforce to see your pattern and then my own."

"Is that what you were looking at when you almost fell?"

She nodded.

He relaxed his tense grip on her hand. "I thought you were over-taxing yourself. I was worried."

"No. I was just so surprised, I nearly lost my composure. Sloppy of me. My mother would've given me a hard ear's lashing."

"Where is your mother now?"

"She died when I was thirteen."

"Oh…I'm sorry."

"It's all right. I miss her terribly, but the ache of her loss isn't as it once was."

He squeezed her hand to convey his condolence. After a moment of silence, he admitted, "I know so little about you."

She laughed. "I am as forthcoming about my past as you are, I fear."

"Yes…we must change that." Something in the way he said this made her heart beat faster in her chest.

He told her then how the Emir had taken him in and treated him as an adopted son. How he'd come to wage war against the Nadoriin and their allies, and how he'd become a leader of the Converted.

When his tale ended, Alyneri sat in stunned silence. His story was both adventuresome and heartbreaking—to have lived for so many years alone in a strange land, knowing nothing of his past… She couldn't imagine how hard that would've been. And here she'd imagined him looking like her father— almond-skinned and dark-eyed—when in fact he could be as like any man she met on the streets of Calgaryn.

"You're shocked." He sounded uncertain, dismayed.

She shook her head. "I'm startled…staggered by your courage. All that Yara says about you is true."

She felt his lips press a kiss against the back of her hand. "Thank you for that," came his soft reply.

She braved a smile and let out her breath. "I…suppose it's my turn now."

"Only if you desire—"

"I do. I want to tell you." So she told him of the past five years of her own life. How her mother had died when her ship was lost at sea, how the boy she'd been betrothed to had died upon the same ship, while the boy she'd loved had been spirited away for his safety, and how she'd lived an orphan among the peerage in Calgaryn, never accepted, only tolerated for her talent and for the grace of her king.

He gave a slow exhale. "It seems we've both been alone."

"It becomes a part of you, I think," she observed, "that sense of isolation."

"Yes, it does." In the silence that followed, she felt the warmth of his gaze. She smiled and blushed beneath her bandage, thinking herself ridiculous to feel so attracted to this man, who by some definition might still be called a stranger.

"But you said you'd a favor to ask of me," he finally said, rescuing her from thoughts that were rapidly spiraling away.

"Yes, I…I need your help—and your trust."

"You have it."

"What I mean is…I'm going to do something I've never attempted before, and it might be a little dangerous, but I don't think too dangerous."

"You're going to try to heal yourself."

His quick deduction amazed her. "Yes."

"If I agree to help, will you promise to do nothing that risks yourself in the process?"

"Yes. I promise."

"Very well." He squeezed her hand. "What should I do?"

"Sit with me. Stay with me."

He did, and she began, not realizing until much later that in the process she was healing more than just her body.

Now that Alyneri knew what to look for, she found her own pattern quickly, and with Ama-Kai'alil at her side for support, she began smoothing her own pattern's frayed edges.

It required minimal skill but was incredibly taxing. As she used her energy to repair herself, she depleted her own reserves, so the process in the beginning was slow. Yet once she'd repaired a strand of her own pattern, she was that much closer to being fully healed—and that much stronger. Thus she made steady progress.

In between sessions, as she was resting but before sleep claimed her, they would talk. Sometimes they spoke about little things, like how much he loved thunderstorms, or how she thought goats looked a little like dragons, which really made him laugh for reasons he wouldn't explain. But sometimes they spoke of deeper things and fragile moments held closer to their hearts.

One time as she was drifting into sleep, he asked her, almost too softly for her to hear—as if both desirous and fretful of her answer, "Alyneri, what of the boy you said you loved?"

"Mmm…?"

"What happened with him?"

She roused herself somewhat and then settled back into her pillow. "Oh…I thought I loved him."

"Did he love you back?"

She considered the question from the fringes of sleep. "He humored me, I think."

"That seems cruel."

"No, he's not unkind," she said, lulled by her exhaustion into admitting things she might not otherwise have had the courage to confess. "He's compassionate when he wants to be, and generous…and quite unexpectedly brave. I think he just never understood how much I cared for him, else he might have realized that it was worse what he did—sort of pretending to adore me. When I turned thirteen, I was betrothed to his brother—however unwillingly at first…and I tried to forget loving him. Only that didn't work out…neither of them did, actually." Rousing to sudden awareness, she admitted with an embarrassed laugh, "I don't know why I'm telling you all this. I never speak my mind so openly."

He chuckled and replied in the Common Tongue, "I find that hard to believe, Your Grace."

She felt an odd and inexplicable thrill at hearing him call her by her title. "Well," she remitted, blushing profusely, "…at least not about a thing so close to my heart."

After a minute of quiet where Alyneri heard nothing but the rapid thrumming of her pulse, he caressed her hand with a brush of his lips and murmured, "Women…endure, don't they?"

"What do you mean?"

"I knew a woman—a most amazing woman—who harbored great sadness in her soul. She said that men came into her life and left again, but she endured. I knew another woman, a slip of a girl, who braved her father's considerable wrath and exile for love." He pressed his lips to her hand again, letting their closeness linger so she felt the warmth of his breath upon her skin. "You're miraculous creatures. The strength you possess…it's a tensile, pliant strength, like the pine saplings that bend to the capricious north wind but never break…"

But Alyneri missed the end of this thought, for she'd slipped away into sleep.

TWELVE

"The lion and the lamb may lie down together,
but the lamb won't get much sleep."

— An old desert proverb

TANIS WALKED WITH Pelas down from the Solvayre hills and through a quaint provincial town that boasted a different winery's café on every corner. He had to admit that it *was* a lovely walk.

Tanis just didn't understand the enigma that was Pelas.

Worse, he didn't understand his own response to the man. In some ways, the latter troubled him more than the former. He'd seen Pelas do terrible things. He knew he was intent on destroying their world—albeit perhaps not immediately—yet Tanis...*liked* him.

When he wasn't consumed by the darker side of his nature, Pelas resonated amiability. He laughed easily and often, and he gave money and compliments with equal generosity. Several times that day alone, Tanis had looked at him and wondered how he could've ever been afraid of such a genteel man. It really frightened him that he could become so quickly appended to someone who had just days ago tried to kill him.

This dual aspect of Pelas's nature had Tanis terribly confused.

Pelas spoke of new experiences like Tanis spoke of adventure, yet he claimed any emotion he felt as a result—even obvious joy—was only an illusion. Tanis thought that the pursuit of happiness was in itself a purpose for life—it certainly seemed enough of a purpose for a lot of people—but

Pelas only saw any urge to gain happiness as an expression of fear of death, an attempt to delay the inevitable.

He liked to converse on the matter though, and Tanis held out hope that one day he might find something smart enough to say to change his mind. He still had no idea why that sense of duty never left him, only driving him to stay close to Pelas, but Tanis thought getting the man to see anything true about their world would certainly be a worthwhile endeavor.

Pelas was giving a dissertation on how all men secretly craved death as they walked the back streets of town in search of an isolated place where he could call his doorway, and Tanis was absorbed in trying to find a way to counter his argument; so neither of them noticed a group of men coming out of a tavern. The men noticed them, however, if told from the way their eyes lit up. Eying Pelas and Tanis hungrily, the men split up and moved to follow.

Pelas had just turned down an alley that looked promising when Tanis saw the thieves. He spun a look over his shoulder and found more men coming up from behind. They all carried sharp blades and looked none too respectable, and they were coming fast.

"Sir?" Tanis said urgently.

His wary tone alerted Pelas. At once he swept the lad between himself and the wall and turned to receive the first man, just as the latter raised his sword. Pelas caught the blade with his bare hand and ripped it from the other's grasp. He flipped the weapon in the air, caught the hilt, and drove it deep into his assailant's chest.

Another man launched at him, and Pelas once again ripped his sword from his attacker's startled grasp. Pelas flipped the weapon and caught the hilt. Now he had two blades.

Minutes later, five men lay dead or dying—in either condition, they were no longer a threat. Pelas tossed their weapons into the dirt and brushed his hands together. His copper eyes mercilessly scanned the defeated. "I think this proves my point on men craving death, don't you?"

Tanis admitted it certainly seemed true in this case.

"Come, little spy." Pelas found an abandoned corner in which to call his doorway, and moments later they were emerging from darkness onto a jungle track. What sky could be seen between breaks in the high green canopy was flamed a brilliant orange-red, but among the trees, night had already fallen.

"Where are we, sir?" Tanis misliked the myriad foreign and frightening sounds accosting them from the jungle's depths.

"Bemoth." Pelas looked around wearing a smile. "Is this not a fantastic jungle, little spy? Can you hear all of the animals making their twilight calls? It is a most impressive display of life."

Tanis found this remark utterly baffling. "But I thought you said everyone only headed towards death."

"Oh indeed, indeed," he agreed, "yet there is something fascinating to me about forests and jungles, the way their creatures carry out their doomed lives entrenched upon a pattern too broad for them to comprehend, always flying towards the light but never reaching their freedom before the ice can claim them."

Tanis felt that sometimes Pelas's philosophies were as indecipherable as Master o'Reith's.

Pelas placed an icy hand on the lad's shoulder. "Come, we're just in time to make a grand entrance."

Tanis asked as they walked along the trail, "Sir, why didn't you just use your power to kill those men?"

Pelas cast him a discerning look. "I cannot use my power indiscriminately. My brothers and I are all agreed upon this point. If I destroyed those men with my power, others would find their bodies. Soon come the Empress's Red Guard to investigate, and the next thing we know, all of Agasan is looking for us. That's why we had to leave Rethynnea so quickly."

Tanis arched brows in surprise. "What do you mean? Why?"

Pelas's gaze darkened. "My brother Rinokh…" He shook his head. "He was fine so long as he played his games in the deserts of Avatar, but to bring him in among the cities…Shail should have known better than to involve him—except, now I *wonder*…" but he didn't finish this thought, only pressed a finger to his lips and frowned heavily instead. Tanis could tell the wheels of his intelligent mind were spinning, for he caught flashes of forceful thoughts full of fire and fury. But the images made no sense to him.

"What did he do?" Tanis prodded after a moment's pause. The unsettling jungle noises seemed to increase in inverse proportion to the volume of their own conversation. "Your brother Rinokh, I mean."

Pelas cast him a look. "Worked our power—and destroyed most of the Temple of the Vestals in Rethynnea in the process."

Tanis's heart fluttered at this news. The pirate Carian vran Lea had been investigating a node in the Temple of the Vestals, and Raine D'Lacourte had been preparing a small army for some kind of confrontation. The lad couldn't help wondering: if Rinokh was the one who'd nearly killed Prince Ean at their villa, what had happened at the temple to make him work his power again?

"I don't know how they stopped it," Pelas went on, heedless of Tanis's spiraling thoughts. "I can't imagine Rinokh used any kind of control in releasing his working to begin with, which means there is someone else in this world who can manage our power." He turned Tanis a dark eye. "My brother Shail is looking into that mystery."

Tanis gulped a swallow. He was almost certain that whatever had happened at the Temple of the Vestals, the zanthyr and Raine had been involved, and possibly the pirate and Prince Ean also. Tanis so wished he could have any news of his friends. Once again came that crushing sense of guilt for abandoning them.

Followed by the sense of duty, which provided shallow comfort.

They emerged from the jungle and gained a stone-paved path that meandered through a large garden, splitting and rejoining to form some sort of pattern too vast to be observed while walking upon it. The flames of the sky were dying into the dense, dark blue of early evening, and the night was balmy. After they headed up a flight of wide stone stairs marking the end of the lawn, Tanis turned to look behind him and saw the pattern of the path in its fullness. He didn't recognize it, but it looked pretty.

Turning back, he faced a massive mansion, reached by way of four sets of long stairs. Tanis wondered why Pelas couldn't have found somewhere closer to land them and decided he must've wanted the walk again.

He just couldn't understand the man.

When they finally reached a long patio that ran along one side of the manse, a crowd of well-dressed people was just beginning to filter outside to enjoy the night air. Surpassing them all in splendor, Pelas approached as if he'd just been out for a walk and headed on inside.

"Quickly now, little spy," he whispered in Tanis's ear as they were joining the party-goers, "give me a name—any name but your own."

"Tad," Tanis said, thinking immediately of his friend, which only then made him wonder how Tad was faring and what was happening back in Dannym. It seemed like they'd been gone so long.

"Ah, Signore di Nostri!" A diminutive woman who was just then approaching addressed Pelas with a smile. "We are so fortunate that you grace us with your presence tonight. Did you just arrive?"

"Lady Gartelt." Pelas took her hand and kissed it with a slight bow. "We were just enjoying the gardens. May I present my associate, Tad. A truthreader I am sponsoring."

"You are always so benevolent." She barely spared a glance for Tanis but gave Pelas a generously appreciative look.

"Your words, as ever, fill my heart with gladness, Mian. And how fares your Queen?"

"Troubled, my lord. I'm sure you know of the many Healers who have gone missing. Her Majesty counts nine vanished in recent moons. The queen has closed the holy city of Jeune to all but those upon Crown business."

"Dreadful," Pelas clucked.

Tanis's astonishment at the man's duplicity was surpassed only by his admiration for the perfection of its delivery.

"And where is our host this evening, lovely Mian?"

"Oh..." Mian looked off with a frown. "Niko is somewhere about. Shall I find him for you?"

"No, no—trouble yourself not. We're happy wanderers this evening."

"Well," she looked him up and down rather unsubtly, "if you think of any way I can help..."

"Of course, you will be the first one I call."

Mian smiled, curtsied, and departed without another glance at Tanis.

For once, Tanis appreciated Master o'Reith's making him memorize long lists of tedious names. "Sir," Tanis murmured as Mian was departing, "was that really Mian Gartelt of the Fifty Companions?"

Pelas frowned after the Healer. "Yes."

"But...?" He didn't understand why nothing had happened to Pelas, why his thoughts remained quiet. "But isn't she a Healer?"

Still gazing after Mian, Pelas arched a solitary ebon brow. "Indeed."

"Then...?"

He turned Tanis an unreadable look, just a slight tightening around his eyes to indicate his distaste. "She has Dore Madden's taint upon her," and he moved off again into the crowd.

Tanis walked attentively at Pelas's side as the man idled among the partygoers. He knew many people, most of whom addressed him as Signore di Nostri. To others, Pelas introduced himself as Immanuel di Nostri. But whether they were old acquaintances or new ones, Pelas always greeted them graciously.

Everyone who met Pelas immediately took to him. Tanis stood with his mouth half agape at the intimate and privileged things people randomly shared with Pelas—even people he'd only just met—and the lad noticed men and women both crossing the room just to say hello. Tanis grew ever more wary of him.

Pelas had power. It was subtle, hidden, but terribly potent. People uniformly were attracted to him, and something in his presence drew forth their deepest confessions. Tanis saw this part of him as a harmonic of his darker nature, and he understood how these traits were two sides of the same coin.

It frightened him to wonder if Pelas had worked some power upon him in the café that fateful afternoon...if indeed that's why Tanis had been compelled to follow him. What if it wasn't duty that drove him at all, but merely a subtle form of compulsion?

But it couldn't be, for Pelas would've expected me to follow him if he'd worked compulsion upon me—and why would he do that?

Yet the idea had lodged spiny tendrils into Tanis's head, and he couldn't entirely weed it out.

They'd finally made their way across the largest of the rooms when Tanis heard strains of music and laughter. Pelas heard it too, and he gave Tanis a bright smile, whispered, "Dancers!" with a wink and pulled Tanis eagerly towards the music.

They exited into a stone-paved court to the rhythmic beating of tambourines and the jingle of bells, to the plucking of sitars and the plaintive melody of reed pipes. And to a contingent of veiled dancers spinning and undulating upon a circular dais.

Tanis gaped at the women, who seemed practically naked to the northern boy, what with their cropped, bejeweled vests and low-slung skirts hung with tassels and fringe, navels sporting jewels or pierced with silver chains. And the way they moved… Tanis's eyes were very wide.

Pelas cast him an amused look. "I imagine you don't see many dancers like this in Dannym."

"No sir," Tanis whispered without removing his eyes from one girl wearing sheer red silk and whose belly was undulating like a snake.

They watched the dancers until two men flipped onto the dais and began a complicated saber dance. Tanis appreciated their skill, but he didn't find them nearly as interesting as the women. Pelas laughed at his disappointed look and motioned them on with a frosty but consoling pat on the lad's shoulder.

They followed along a patio lined with tall statues, each pair demarking a staircase leading down to the gardens. Pelas admired the sculptures as they passed, his gaze rapt, a slight smile curving the corners of his mouth.

"Sir," Tanis remarked as Pelas was inspecting a statue of a maiden being seduced by a fawn, "it looks like you're kind of enjoying yourself."

Pelas cast him an amused eye. "Does it?" He ran his fingers lightly across the woman's marble leg. "I suppose it could be said that I enjoy the experiences of this place. Darshan says joy is an illusion, but I'm willing to be deceived by beauty."

Tanis gave him a curious look. "Is that not a choice, sir?"

Pelas turned to him, looking surprised. "I'm…not sure. It is certainly an interesting idea." He was about to say more when his eyes narrowed and he hissed an expletive.

He grabbed Tanis close into the loop of one arm and swept his other hand through the air. Tanis watched the world subtly darken, even as a chilling veil descended. The lad knew this sensation; the last time he'd felt it, he'd been in the zanthyr's protection.

They remained perfectly still and watched three men emerge from the mansion to halt just feet from where he and Pelas were concealed. The first man boasted a tall frame and was blonde and handsome. The man beside him stood taller and broader still. Silk cording bound his long ebony hair, and he wore three red-gold bangles in each ear. The third was white-haired and looked emaciated, and his thoughts were riotous.

"I must be certain of success before I will act," said the man with the long black hair. His voice was close enough to Pelas's in timbre and inflection that Tanis could only assume he was one of Pelas's brothers.

"To be sure," the white-haired man agreed. He licked his lips and looked furtively around. Then he murmured, "The Prophet is fully in support of our plan."

"Be that as it may, *I* must be assured of it."

"We understand your requirements, Lord Abanachtran," the blonde man said. "We will keep you apprised of our progress."

"And what of the other matter?" demanded the white-haired man. A sort of gruesome excitement glinted from the dark pools that were his eyes.

The Lord Abanachtran looked him over critically. "It suits our purposes to aid you in apprehending this Ean val Lorian. Send your emissary to the Karakurt in Rethynnea. I believe your man will find her at his *complete* disposal." With that, he cast the both of them a piercing eye and departed. The two remaining men exchanged a look and then separated as if reluctant to be seen with one another.

Only when they were well away did Pelas release his spell.

Tanis rubbed his arms ardently and relaxed his clenched teeth while Pelas stared after his them with his eyes narrowed. "My younger brother, Shail," he muttered. "He has his sticky fingers in far too many pies. Come, my little spy." He touched Tanis gently upon the shoulder. "I mislike the taste of the air now."

Tanis could sense his tension. He wished he better understood what had just happened and why Shail made Pelas so uneasy. Not that the Lord Abanachtran didn't strike an imposing figure, and certainly he wore menace like a cloak.

"I think it is time we took our leave," Pelas remarked as they headed back into the crowded hall. "Stay close to me, lad."

Tanis had no intention of doing anything else, not with *another* Malorin'athgul wandering around, and then there was that other man...the cadaverous one with the storm of malevolent thoughts. Tanis could tell he was treacherous just from encountering the space of his mind.

They were making their way across the hall, weaving amongst the elegant crowd, when Pelas slowed his pace and then abruptly stiffened. His eyes latched onto a woman who was walking with a man towards the patio that Tanis and Pelas had just left. Pelas turned abruptly and followed her like a snared fish.

Tanis watched the darkness descending upon him with growing trepidation, yet he suspected that to disturb Pelas now might mean the end of both of them—especially with the Lord Abanachtran so close. He fretted over what to do and prayed as he followed Pelas that Epiphany might grant a moment's inspiration.

Just as they emerged back out onto the patio, the Lord Abanachtran appeared. Tanis could feel the man's malice preceding him in waves. The darkness meanwhile had wholly consumed Pelas—his thoughts had descended to that cold, merciless place that Tanis knew too well—and his eyes remained pinned upon the Healer and her escort, who were now heading down into the gardens.

Seeing Shail approaching, Tanis dropped his eyes and stared hard at his boots, desperately wishing he might become invisible again.

The man who called himself Lord Abanachtran stopped beside his brother. "Pelas," he greeted darkly.

"Shail," Pelas replied without turning his piercing gaze from the departing Healer.

"I see your bloodlust still consumes you, clouding your judgment as ever it has."

"As does your quest for dominion, brother," Pelas replied with cold disinterest. Perhaps it was an unexpected boon that Pelas was in the darkness, for he seemed ever as frightening as Shail. "I didn't expect to see you here," Pelas remarked.

"You should have. My field, after all, is intelligence."

"Sedition seems more apt."

Shail's lips spread in a feral smile. "Are they not one and the same?"

"I suppose we each pursue our purpose in unique ways." The condescension was heavy in Pelas's tone. He had not once bothered to look at his brother. Even Tanis felt himself excluded from rarified air. "So it's the Lord Abanachtran now, is it? That's bold, using your true name. Think you'll succeed in your little rebellion?"

Shail stiffened, and Tanis caught the tumble of his thoughts—a flash of confusion and the slightest startle of fear glimpsed amid boiling anger.

Pelas smiled, cool beneath the fire of his brother's furious gaze. "Ah, but you didn't think I knew so much of your affairs, did you? Yet I am not without my own spies."

Though he was clearly outraged, Shail reeled in his anger behind a contemptuous gaze. "And who's this?" He shifted the force of his attention onto Tanis, who in turn stared harder at his boots. "Your protégé?"

"The son of one of my subjects," Pelas replied with such perfect derision that even Tanis would have believed him. "He serves me now."

"A fitting duty in exchange for the service you bestowed on his mother."

Ignoring the sneer in this remark, Pelas returned, "I noted your experiment with Rinokh did not fare so well."

"Did it not?" Tanis felt Shail's chilling smile like slime creeping down the back of his neck. He suppressed a shudder. "Good to see you, brother," Shail murmured. Then he left.

Pelas struck off after the Healer.

Tanis fretted the entire time he followed Pelas through the garden, all the while imagining terrible consequences. They came upon the Healer abruptly in a rose court. She sat upon the edge of a fountain, laughing with her escort. Pelas approached the Healer and dropped to one knee.

"Pardon my intrusion," he murmured with his head bowed, "my deepest apologies, but I have followed you here." Looking up at the woman, who wore an expression of surprised interest, he continued, "When I saw you inside, I was taken aback. I felt certain that some part of me recognized you. Is it...could it be possible...do you recall if perhaps you might have healed me once?"

Tanis watched this courtship in terror, for the darkness had firm hold of Pelas, yet he remained immensely compelling...perhaps even slightly dangerous, but in a way that drew curiosity as a needle draws blood. This was the Pelas that Tanis had first glimpsed back in the café in Rethynnea, and with a gulp, the boy realized what must've drawn the darkness upon Pelas that day—or rather *who*—for he and Her Grace had walked by only moments before Tanis took up a chair near the man. Had Pelas been responding to the Lady Alyneri in the same way he now responded to this poor woman?

Tanis shuddered to think so. The idea of Pelas's darker nature having even glanced upon his lady filled Tanis with a sense of dread so complete that his stomach turned sickly over it.

The Healer had a round face that was not unkind. Her hair was dark, and she seemed in the fullness of her years. "I'm not sure, my lord," she replied. She exchange a glance with her companion. "Let me look upon you."

The smile Pelas gave her in reply broke Tanis's heart. Their conversation continued, with Pelas gaining her name and what city she hailed from, but the boy hardly heard it, for the sound of his soul crying out in protest was too loud in his ears.

Fate had worked a cruel twist indeed to force a man who was capable of engendering such admiration to subvert his talent to the detriment of all. Tanis wanted Pelas to be *good*, but he patently wasn't.

The Healer and her escort laughed at something Pelas said, drawing Tanis back into their conversation. Pelas gave her a charming smile, kissed her hand, and stood. "It was most wonderful to meet you, Merida," he said, proclaiming her doom as he bowed in farewell. Then he turned and left them.

Tanis followed, feeling agonized. Would that he had some magical potion that would cure Pelas of his dark desires! It was so hard to be with him, knowing what he intended, yet Tanis *wanted* to be with him. In their short time together, Tanis had come to know this man, and though they considered each other equally delusional, Tanis genuinely liked Pelas.

Why—oh why—in Epiphany's name did you follow him, you stupid boy?

Pelas did not head back to the mansion but led them deeper into the moonlit gardens. When they were far out of earshot and Pelas had surfaced from the darkness, Tanis braved timidly, "You're going to go after her aren't you, sir?"

Pelas glanced at him, but his gaze remained distant. "Very likely."

"But sir," Tanis protested desperately, "you could still choose not to do so."

"Such a choice is quite impossible, little spy."

"*No.* It's not—you simply decide that you won't do it!"

Pelas gave him a soft look, and Tanis felt real tenderness in it. "I could decide, as you say," he admitted, clearly giving due thought to the idea, "but in the end, it would make no difference. I would still find myself there someday, hungering, waiting to claim her." He shook his head and sighed resignedly. "I cannot change my nature. The end is inevitable."

"What if you could?" Tanis asked, stubbornly clinging to hope.

Pelas arched a curious brow. "What do you mean?"

"What if you *could* change your nature. *Would* you?"

"The question holds no merit. It is hypothetical."

"What if it wasn't?" Tanis persisted. Then he added suddenly, "There is much in our world that you haven't yet experienced."

Pelas frowned.

Tanis could tell his question had finally impinged, and he asked again, using all of his truthreader's power, "What would you choose if the choice was given to you, sir?"

Pelas turned him a swift look, for he'd felt the compulsion in it. "I..." his gaze became puzzled, intense. "I don't...know." Abruptly his expression softened. There was even a little admiration in it. "I will think upon it, little spy."

"Do that," Tanis grumbled. Then, as they started walking again, he asked, "Do we head—" but the words never made it off his tongue, for that's when things went from miserable to disastrous.

They had just emerged from a path leading between high boxwoods onto an open lawn, where seven armed men were fanning out to block their path.

Pelas slowed. Tanis felt his thoughts go still.

"Sir?" Tanis whispered. When Pelas didn't answer, the lad asked uncertainly, "Can you fight them the same as you did the thieves in the Solvayre?"

"These men carry Merdanti weapons," Pelas murmured ominously. "If I tried that trick again, I'd lose my hand."

Tanis stared fretfully at him. "Can't you use your power?"

"He knows I won't." Pelas kept a steely gaze fastened on the approaching men. "I can't afford to reveal myself here any more than Shail can."

Tanis felt the flutters of ill apprehension. *Seven* men carrying Merdanti blades, when even *one* could mean Pelas's death. He had no choice. He hurriedly drew his dagger from inside his boot and pushed it into Pelas's hand.

"What...?" Pelas's eyes went wide. "Where did you get this?"

"It's my own blade, sir."

"I can see it's the same blade—" But he pursed his lips and shook his head, knowing now was not the time to question the mystery. He turned and focused a calculating gaze upon the men then. "You may have just saved our lives, little spy." He shrugged out of his coat and handed it to Tanis, explaining, "It is always preferable to fight unencumbered; likewise to imagine each of your opponents is your most hated nemesis." His gaze narrowed dangerously. "I shall be envisioning both of my brothers. Run now into the thicket, little spy, and do not emerge until I call for you."

"Be careful, sir."

Pelas gave him a wondrous look. "Go!"

Tanis fled back along the boxwood path and forced his way through the hedge. The branches scratched deeply into his flesh, drawing blood. Concealed on the other side of the thicket then, Tanis hurried to find a vantage where he might peer back through.

He saw the men drawing near, saw Pelas go tense as a panther about to pounce, and then—

Pelas closed with the nearest man and blocked his advance with Phaedor's dagger. They struggled, and Pelas kicked him off.

Two more came at him. Pelas caught the upraised arm of the first man and twisted into his guard while slamming his dagger unerringly into the second man's heart. He grabbed the second mercenary's sword as the man collapsed, and he swung it up through the arm of the first man, which he still held trapped high. The now one-armed mercenary fell back with a scream.

Pelas relieved the severed arm of its sword and turned to met the next two men. He took them both together and beat them into a retreat using powerful, rapid strokes. One faltered and met his end with his throat and chest torn asunder. The second darted in as Pelas was turning and may have marked him in the motion, but Pelas finished his turn and severed his head.

Pelas must've sensed an attacker rushing up behind him then, for he dropped to one knee and parried the man's downward rushing blade with his two swords crossed over his head. Then he spun on his knees and swung both of his swords around with such power that he cut the man's body in half.

The armless man had found his feet and was staggering away. Pelas threw one of his swords and took him through the back. He slammed forcefully forward into the grass. The seventh man tried to flee, but Pelas caught him with his second blade thrown so powerfully that the man flew through the air and slammed into a tree, where he remained, staked gruesomely to the bark.

The night grew still. Pelas got to his feet and began collecting up the Merdanti weapons. He pitched them onto a cloak belonging to one of the fallen, hoisted the make-shift bag up over one shoulder and looked unerringly to where Tanis watched.

"Come little spy. We must away."

His voice remained tense, taught with senses on full alert, so the lad hastily pushed his way back through the boxwood, hissing a curse at the spiteful hedge, which grabbed hold of his boot in the end and nearly tripped him. He stumbled up to Pelas, looking frazzled.

Pelas looked over his scratched and disheveled appearance with laughter in his eyes. "I do believe you fared worse than me." He called his doorway, drew Tanis close within the circle of his arm, and spun them through.

They stood alone in the endless darkness, where the only sounds were the pounding of their hearts and the rush of their breath.

"Where do we go?" Tanis whispered.

"Not home. Not right away. The location of my home should be a secret, but I cannot trust that it hasn't been compromised."

"Where then?"

Pelas pulled him closer within the circle of his arm, reassuringly close, though his embrace was perilously cold. "I have an idea." His doorway appeared, slicing down through the lightless dark, and then they stepped out into a shipyard.

Tanis blinked in the bright sunlight, though the day's warmth was a welcome relief. Pelas looked quickly around, assured himself they were alone, and then turned the boy a smile. "Ready?" Without waiting for an answer, he led away.

THIRTEEN

"The hottest fire forges the sharpest steel."

– The Second Vestal Dagmar Ranneskjöld

I ŞAK GETIRMEK STOOD upon the balcony of Niko van Amstel's Bemothi manor gazing into the mist. The morning was tepid and damp, the air heavy from a late-night shower, and the mist rising out of the jungle enveloped the world in haze. Işak awaited Dore's permission to leave with an eager anticipation that he smothered beneath feelings of guilt—for he dared not let the man know his true thoughts.

The binding Dore had placed upon him so many years ago bound Işak to Dore and made his mind vulnerable to the wielder's inspection. That this working did not bind Dore to Işak in return was perhaps the only grace allowed him. To endure a mutual bond with Dore Madden would surely have driven him mad.

Işak felt cold. *So* cold. Cold enough that his fingers and lips were tinged blue, despite the balmy jungle climate; too cold to work the knots of his string as he whiled away the torturous hours. Standing in the rain through the night had leached all the warmth from his blood, but he welcomed the numbing chill, for it soothed the ever-constant, ever-painful fire that was Dore's bond.

He'd been waiting for more than a day on Niko's private balcony for his master to release him, but Dore was still vexed over the episode with Franco Rohre, days earlier. Işak had tried explaining why the Espial had so revolted him, but there was no explaining things to Dore—even had he been telling Dore the truth, which he patently had not.

Dore had punished Işak for his disobedience, punished him with blood and with pain laid in through the pattern of binding until Işak had wept—until he'd crawled, stripped and bleeding, to weep at Dore's feet, begging him for mercy. Dore had finally relented, but it was long after he'd made Işak beg him to punish him more; long after he'd sworn to his master that he deserved whatever Dore meted out.

Ironic. Had Franco chosen any other revolting pastime to focus upon, Işak could've easily ignored it, for he'd been privy to the worst sort of filth in N'ghorra and had become inured to all manner of depravities. Ill-chance alone led Franco Rohre to pick sodomy to accost Işak with—oh, clearly the man had recognized Işak's fourth-strand patterns and retaliated. Işak almost respected the Espial for that, but Franco's visions had been...

Işak closed his eyes.

Such vivid images were agonizing reminders of the shadows lurking in Işak's own past, memories long hidden from Dore, lest he exploit them ruthlessly. So he'd fled the room—even knowing his sure punishment—rather than risk Dore discovering such memories and subsequently using them to destroy the last vestiges of his humanity.

A wind blew, raising gooseflesh on Işak's already frigid skin. He shuddered as the wind raked across him. But it wasn't the air that chilled him now.

Memories drew forth that clenching fear that accompanied the rending of hope...memories of an adolescent who'd lost his innocence in the salt mines of N'ghorra at the hands of a cruel man who saw beauty and wished to destroy it, who thought nobility an outrage and honor an affront.

Many years later, Dore had repeatedly raped Işak's mind like the prisoner had raped his body, and now he couldn't decide which man he loathed more.

It was mid-morning before Dore appeared, but Işak hadn't moved—how could he, when Dore had forbidden it?

"Işak, come," Dore commanded, and Işak pulled himself away from the railing with effort. His muscles cramped sharply after so many stationary hours, but his face revealed none of this pain; nor did his thoughts betray the depths of his hatred for his master.

"Niko will take you to the Cairs today," Dore told him. "We have reason to believe the prince is there. You'll have the help of powerful allies loyal to Niko, loyal to me," and this last he stressed with a jolt upon the bond, a not-so-subtle warning that while Işak might soon be on his own in the world, he would still be watched. "You will have the Karakurt's network at your disposal and a company of Saldarians to aid in your task."

"Mercenaries," Işak growled.

"Skilled agents sworn to our cause," Dore corrected with a scowl and a lick of his spider-thin lips. "Radov has used the services of their leader many times. Now he loans them for our use."

"How magnanimous of him," Işak muttered ungraciously. The last thing he wanted was a host of spies watching his every move. "They are under my command?"

"I've said as much." Dore fixed Işak with a piercing look. "You will find the prince, and you will bring him back to Tambarré for questioning. You will do everything in your power to apprehend Ean val Lorian."

"I doubt he will come willingly, or easily."

"Bind him to you from the outset." Dore licked his lips with a flicker of a pale tongue. "It is the most effective way."

Işak also knew bindings were difficult to manage in the thick of battle. "And what if there is no way to gain him except through death? What then would you have me do?"

Dore scowled ferociously. Clearly he did not want to admit the possibility of failure, but Işak knew the man was no fool—never mind that he was entirely insane. "If there is no other way," Dore said finally, leveling his reptilian gaze upon Işak, "if he cannot be bound to your will and defies all attempts to apprehend him, then and only then, shall you slay him. If your only choice is mortal, you will stand over this upstart prince until his body is as cold as a camp-whore's tit."

Işak felt the stroke of compulsion laying itself upon him, new thorns of iron twining within the pattern of binding, spearing his already bleeding soul. Thus was Işak set to Dore's will like a clock wound each night, with no choice but to count the endless hours until time had all bled out and naught but emptiness remained.

"Go now," Dore murmured, eyeing him iniquitously. "Glory awaits."

FOURTEEN

KJIERAN WALKED THE long hall of his dormitory wrapped in a linen robe and with his body damp from the baths. Though he'd soaked for the better part of an hour, he still felt unclean. Earlier that day, he'd been called upon to attend three candidates while they were being tested for Bethamin's Fire. None had survived the testing.

Each time Kjieran watched another truthreader succumb to the Prophet's corruptive power, he saw the end of their race approaching. Easily as many truthreaders died as lived to become Marquiin—perhaps more. Kjieran feared that at this rate, Bethamin would destroy the entire strand of Adepts singlehandedly.

Yet even as he watched such men writhe and scream upon the Prophet's marble floor, he couldn't help but feel a measure of envy. They were the lucky ones.

It was Kjieran's job to dispose of such men, who were deemed unclean as a result of their failure to endure the Prophet's malignant attack upon their consciousness. Kjieran always handled his brothers of the fourth with the deepest sympathy and regard, whispering the Rite for the Departed over their bodies as he carted them to the crematorium. And while he knew he'd done as much as he could to guide them to the Returning, he still felt guilt. Guilt because he couldn't save them from being chosen, because he regularly stood by while the Prophet continued his wholesale slaughter of Kjieran's race—of his own Adept strand.

Guilt because he was so desperately relieved that *he* hadn't been tested that day.

With such memories so fresh in his mind, Kjieran thought the worst when he saw the Ascendant standing outside the open door of his bed chamber. Had they found him out? Was he being taken for questioning? He did a quick mental survey of items in his room, wondering if anything could incriminate him—yet he was always so careful! He slowed his approach, wondering if it was too late to turn around. But of course it was. The man had no doubt noticed him long since.

"How many I help you, Ascendant?" Kjieran asked with downcast eyes.

"It is well that you have bathed, acolyte." The Ascendant scoured him with a pale-eyed gaze. "The Prophet calls you to his chambers."

Remembering the last time he'd been called to attend the Prophet, Kjieran hesitated to ask, "May I dress, Ascendant?"

"I should hope so." The man looked Kjieran over like some kind of heathen.

Kjieran hurried to don his acolyte's robes and then followed the Ascendant to the Prophet's chambers. Once again the man stopped just before the towering doors, leaving Kjieran to find his own way.

This time the Prophet awaited him at a stone table set with a meal. Kjieran knelt at the Prophet's feet and bowed his head. "My lord," he murmured with his colorless eyes fixed on the marble tiles.

"Kjieran," replied the Prophet by way of welcome. "Take that seat there. You shall dine at my table tonight."

Kjieran received this news with a sinking feeling of dread, but he obediently stood and took his seat as instructed, keeping his eyes downcast. The plate before him held a varied display of Saldarian dishes, the aromas rich and heady after so long eating the diet of beans and bread they served at the acolytes' tables.

"You may eat, Kjieran."

He did so in silence, all too aware that the Prophet was studying him the entire time. Kjieran felt like a wild animal coaxed from safety with the promise of food so that the hunter might observe it more intimately. The idea made him shudder, and the food became suddenly unpalatable, but he didn't dare stop until the Prophet required it or until his plate was empty.

"I would know more about you, Kjieran," the Prophet said after a long time of just watching him.

Kjieran settled his hands in his lap, eyes downcast, but deep within he trembled. He bit the inside of his lip to keep himself focused, to keep above the raw desperation, for he'd realized while he was eating—the special attention, the late night rendezvous, this meal...

The Prophet was courting him.

"Tell me your story," Bethamin commanded with only the slightest hint of compulsion to sweeten the order. Even that feather-light touch made Kjieran almost heady with the need to tell his lord everything. Raine's protection allowed Kjieran to sense the Prophet's compulsion. Though he couldn't resist it, at least he wasn't tormented with guilt—as so many others were—over why he loved a man that was so dreadful in every way.

Somehow finding the courage to speak, Kjieran told his lord of growing up in Agasan, of training at the Sormitáge, and of his assignment to the Court of Dannym. He did not embellish, but neither did he make the story too thin, for he sensed that the Prophet was searching for deeper things. Bethamin asked questions of him that were tender and painful. He wanted Kjieran's most intimate thoughts and dug them out forcefully like deep-rooted tubers, leaving him feeling scraped and gaping in the retelling.

Finally the Prophet asked, "Do you resent this king for releasing you from his service?"

"How could I, my lord," Kjieran replied quietly, "when his expulsion brought me to you?"

"Of course," replied the Prophet dismissively, "but do you desire his death as retribution for how he wronged you?"

Kjieran thought fast to form a reply. He knew how easily one might avoid an answer without seeming to do so, how a skilled conversationalist could speak one thing and mean something else entirely and still have the statement resonate as truth. He chose his words carefully. "I desire that he should receive his due for the many crimes enacted during his reign, my lord."

The Prophet considered his answer. Then he stood and approached Kjieran, giving him ample time to appreciate the perfection of his form. He stopped, and Kjieran slipped from his chair onto his knees before the man, knowing this was expected.

He did not, however, expect the Prophet to sink his hands into his hair like a lover and pull him back to his feet. Bethamin placed his chilling hands on Kjieran's shoulders. His thumbs caressed the pulse points where Kjieran's blood throbbed in time with his racing heart. Kjieran's thoughts ran riotous with fear, and he struggled to overcome them.

"Why do you tremble beneath my touch?"

Kjieran braved haltingly, "Because…because your flesh is cold, my lord."

"And if it were not?" The Prophet's hands became warm upon his flesh. One hand moved around his throat while his other thumb found Kjieran's lips. "Then would you desire me?"

Kjieran felt no compulsion. The Prophet expected the truth from him, live or die by it. He sucked in a shuddering breath. "I do not think so, my lord."

Amazingly, the Prophet released him. Kjieran sagged in relief, yet fighting desperately to stifle his terror and grief.

"Look at me, Kjieran. Meet my gaze."

Kjieran lifted his eyes. The Prophet's gaze in return was fixed piercingly upon him. He took Kjieran's face in his hands and ran his thumbs over Kjieran's cheeks, over his lips. His darkly seductive gaze assessed Kjieran like a sculptor examining his work, searching for flaws. "I do not usually care for a truthreader's colorless eyes," the Prophet remarked. His voice had taken on the breathless, husky timbre of lust. "But there is something unique about you. I don't understand why I'm drawn to seek you out."

Kjieran held the man's gaze, too terrified to look away, though he felt scalded and sick with despair.

The Prophet stroked his lips with one thumb and then separated them. The same thumb parted Kjieran's teeth and hovered in the space between. "I have played games of desire with many men and women," he said as he ran his thumb slowly along the edge of Kjieran's teeth. "I can make my body respond to my will, make my phallus erect to give others the pleasure they claim they desire, but I do not know if these things are true, and I have never felt desire myself."

Kjieran's entire body was taut and quivering, and his breath came in ragged gasps.

"Yet I think I begin to feel desire for you." The Prophet hooked his thumb inside Kjieran's teeth and gently tugged his mouth apart, that his thumb might find Kjieran's tongue instead. He wet it with Kjieran's saliva and rubbed it across his lower lip, and the truthreader thought he might truly be sick. "Tell me, Kjieran…" Bethamin leaned to brush his nose along Kjieran's and whispered, "How can that be?"

"My…my lord?" Kjieran murmured wretchedly.

The Prophet straightened and ran his hand slowly through Kjieran's hair. Kjieran couldn't tell if the man enjoyed this or was merely exploring his body to satisfy some personal interest, for he was so deliberate in his motion.

"This concept fascinates me," the Prophet said as his hands continued their sensitive inspection of him. "If I desire you, what exactly do I desire? I do not desire your immediate death, for that would leave me without your company, and I find your company intriguing. I don't desire your obedience, for I have that already. I cannot compel you to desire me without knowing the falsehood of your kisses. What then am I desiring?" The Prophet eyed him circumspectly with his dark and potent gaze, clearly expecting a response.

Kjieran tried to gather his wits about him, but it was so hard hanging onto the fringes of his sanity while all manner of fearful visions assaulted him. "Perhaps… perhaps my lord wishes that I would also desire you?" he whispered.

"Yes, I believe that goes without saying. But is that all of it? Or is there something else?"

Suddenly the Prophet grabbed Kjieran's head and fastened his mouth upon his. The kiss thrilled electrifyingly through Kjieran, while Bethamin's tongue probed deeply. Just the slightest whisper of the Prophet's chill power bled through the seal of their lips, but even that gossamer wisp seared Kjieran. The Prophet's strong arms bound him, the entire encounter not one of pleasure but of tasting, testing… He embraced a feral creature who was deliberating on how well Kjieran would sate his hunger.

When the Prophet released him, Kjieran sucked in his breath with a gasp and fell to his knees. He dropped his head and stared hard at the floor, willing himself not to cry.

"How very interesting." The Prophet considered him during the silence that followed. "I wonder…desire is not effectively compelled, but can it be stoked, persuaded…enticed?"

Kjieran held his breath and prayed that the Prophet did not mean to explore these things tonight.

At last Bethamin said, "I must think further upon it." He stroked Kjieran's hair once more. "You may go, Kjieran."

"Your will be done, my lord," Kjieran all but wept, and as soon as he was beyond the doors of the Prophet's chambers, he ran.

FIFTEEN

"Come and kiss me here in plenty. Love's a stuff will not endure."
– The Immortal Bard Drake di Matteo

EAN MET JULIAN for breakfast. On the previous day, the ebullient youth had shown the prince around Björn's palace, which Julian and his fellows affectionately called the White Forest for the sheer number of turrets, cupolas and spires that graced its towers. Today he and Ean would be venturing into the city.

Niyadbakir.

Julian wanted Ean to know all of the 'best leisure places,' though Ean doubted he'd be seeing much leisure in any place once Björn deemed him ready to…what? Ean still didn't know what the man had in mind for him. It didn't weigh lightly on his conscience to face a future so wholly unknown.

Ean was still in awe, still confused, still slightly mistrustful and apprehensive of what each new day would bring—for certainly the other shoe had to drop any minute. Julian, on the other hand, seemed to take everything at face value. He'd been in T'khendar almost the entire time Ean had been dodging assassins. He eagerly answered any question Ean could dream up and always saw the brighter side of any conflict Ean shared with him. The prince wondered how long such a pure soul could stave off the cynicism that accumulates as innocent minds become corroded by the tarnish of hard experience. He felt he'd long passed that point himself.

Thoughts of innocence, however, necessarily reminded him of Tanis…

of Alyneri, and of the many others who no doubt felt he'd betrayed them. It didn't make for a pleasant contemplation to start his morning.

As they were readying to head off, Ean grabbed his sword and was belting it on when Julian said, "You won't need that, you know."

Ean looked at him uncomprehendingly.

"Your sword," he pointed to it with a smile. "No one wears weapons in Niyadbakir."

Pausing with his leather belt half threaded, Ean arched a brow. "I find that hard to believe."

"No, it's true. I mean, wear it if you like, but you'll be the only one doing so."

"Is that because of the First Lord," Ean asked skeptically, "or his Shades?"

Julian held his gaze quietly. "It's because of Isabel."

"Who's Isabel?"

Julian shook his head and flashed a grin. "You'll find out soon enough. Come."

Somewhat reluctantly, Ean left his sword hanging in the armoire.

To start their tour, Julian led Ean onto the ramparts of the Court Wall, one of several connecting walls that surrounded the palace and overlooked its many courts and gardens. The sun shone brilliantly in the sky, but the morning air felt cooler than it had the day before.

"What season is it here?" Ean asked as they were passing above a rose garden nearing the end of its bloom.

"Oh, it's winter," Julian said, "but the winters here are mild. This is about as cold as it gets, or so they tell me. It's almost Adendigaeth. You know—the Solstice Festival? It begins with the First Lord's Masquerade Ball." He turned Ean an excited smile. "I've been hearing about nothing else since I arrived—Adendigaeth is the biggest celebration of the year."

"Why not the harvest celebration?"

"Because Adendigaeth signifies rebirth and the Returning." When Ean just looked puzzled, Julian explained, "In ancient texts, Adendigaeth is a magical time. The *Sobra'Iternin* says this is the time when the *angiel* Cephrael and Epiphany return to Annwn, the Otherworld, where all life was formed and where the Maker resides. At the gates of Annwn stand the real Extian Doors. A crystalline as diamonds and standing a hundred paces high, they're actually formed of all the strands of *elae* woven together. Mortal eyes cannot look upon them, for their brilliance reflects the Maker's own essence. On the Longest Night, the *angiel* open the Extian Doors to allow all the waiting souls to journey through Annwn, that they may learn the secrets of death and Return."

Julian motioned them along the wall as he added, "We celebrated the Solstice in Jeune, where I'm from, and the Cairs celebrate it with Carnivále, but I don't think many people really pay attention to what they're celebrating. Here, Adendigaeth is sacred."

"Calgaryn celebrates the Longest Night with parties that last until dawn," Ean noted, "but I remember learning that the tradition grew out of a hallowed vigil."

"Exactly."

The more Ean heard, the stranger it all became. He shook his head. "This place is nothing like I'd imagined."

"I know!" Julian laughed. "You were expecting red skies and scorched earth and all, right?"

Ean gave him an intense look. "I suppose so."

Julian shrugged. "They say the city *was* basalt when Malachai raised it from the bedrock of the realm, but the First Lord changed it to alabaster a long time ago."

Not even bothering with the wonder inherent in that statement, Ean asked, "Why?" It seemed like such an enormous task to serve no purpose at all.

"Dunno." Julian shrugged. "I guess he thought it was prettier this way." When Ean gave him a dubious look, Julian laughed. "Master Morrelaine likes to say the First Lord did it to provide a lesson."

"Who is Master Morrelaine?"

"Markal Morrelaine?" Julian arched brows at him. "One of the most famous wielder's of the age before the Adept Wars? *He's* our instructor."

Ean sort of stared at him. *Markal Morrelaine.* How many more surprises were in store this day? Already he'd learned the Extian Doors—the ones he was sure he'd seen before—were the doors to the Otherworld where the dead souls went for rebirth. Now he'd learned that the most famous wielder in history—Björn and Malachai notwithstanding—was an instructor in T'khendar.

"So, Markal Morrelaine…" Ean tried to get a grip on his incredulity. "What about this lesson?"

"Well he has a saying: How deep does the alabaster go?"

Ean glanced at him curiously. "And the answer?"

Julian flashed a grin. "All the way to the other side. It's Master Morrelaine's way of telling us not to trust merely to surface phenomena but to look beneath the effect to view the cause—to find its source."

"Its pattern," Ean supplied.

"Just so." Julian looked pleased at his level of understanding. "It also means for us to look for deeper meanings in everything—not merely to trust that what we see is the truth. It means for us to evaluate what we're observing by comparing our observations against what we already know. And it means that no matter how complex things appear, there is a simple truth that once found will dissolve the complexity."

"He sure crammed a lot of meanings into one saying."

Julian gave a rueful sigh. "Master Morrelaine is fond of weighty proverbs." Then he brightened. "But oh—you'll be able to see him. This way!" He set off in a trot along the crenellated Court Wall, which wound like a massive snake embracing the multiple cloisters, yards and gardens that flanked the lower levels of the palace. Eventually he stopped at one of the crenels and rested elbows on the merlon, which was wide enough to accommodate both of them shoulder to shoulder and another besides.

As Ean joined Julian in gazing into the yard about thirty paces below, he saw a score of men and a few women—many of them seeming close to his own age—engaged in some form of physical training. They moved slowly through a sequence of exact poses, hands extended and knees bent, positions changing with each maneuver. It reminded Ean of the Dance of Swords his own swordmaster had taught him, only more complex.

"What are they chanting?" Ean asked, having noticed that the low murmur was actually words spoken in a different language.

"The Laws of Patterning," Julian supplied with a grimace. "Master Morrelaine feels we should know them verbatim—in Old Alæic." Suddenly he pointed. "That's him, there."

The silver-haired man Ean had seen the day before was just then emerging from beneath the sheltering roof of an adjacent loggia. But Ean hardly noticed him, for once again, *she* walked with him.

Just seeing her, Ean's heart bolted into a frantic race, for her presence captured him wholly.

That day she wore a flaxen dress with belled sleeves. As before, the black silk blindfold bound her hair, and she carried the same shadow-dark staff. Ean watched as she and Markal stopped in front of the group.

She tapped her staff lightly upon the stones, yet the result was a resounding clap that echoed in the court and brought the entire class to a standstill. They straightened and gave her their attention.

"Again, but like this," she said in a crystalline voice—*that voice!* It speared Ean. His chest constricted, and his breath suddenly refused to flow.

He knew that voice.

The woman led the group through a series of connected motions, extending her staff before her with one hand as she slowly crouched and twirled, twisted and spun, her arms working their own complicated adjoining pattern, and finally ended with her staff held in both hands above her head.

Ean realized he'd just seen the class do this sequence, yet something had been different as she'd led them through it a second time. The difference in the two versions had been so minor—Ean though it amazing she could've noticed any difference at all, much less how to observe such a thing while blindfolded.

"Who *is* she?" he asked breathlessly.

Julian glanced at him. "That's Isabel, Epiphany's Prophet."

Ean couldn't take his eyes off of her. "Isabel." Just the sound of her name called to him somehow.

"Isabel van Gelderan," Julian added significantly.

Ean gave him a startled look. His heart skipped a beat, and a lump formed in his throat. "Björn's…wife?" It would certainly be fitting for him to have a wife such as her.

Julian grinned—clearly Ean's reaction to Isabel wasn't lost on him. He shook his head, eyes sparkling with amusement. "His sister."

Ean's heart started beating again, and he exhaled forcefully in relief.

"Boy, you don't start small, do you?" Julian observed, still grinning. "Pinning your sights on Epiphany's Prophet?" He shook his head and let out a low whistle. "That's no small favor to win."

Isabel turned to speak with Markal while the class continued their chanting dance.

Ean shook his head, frowning as he gazed at her. His heart felt pinned to the end of a string looped around her finger, and every time she moved, the string tugged a painful desire in his chest. "I haven't..." he tried to say. "I just..."

Julian clapped him on the shoulder. "Hey—don't fret it, *mon ami*. Rest assured, whatever happens, *she* already knows how it will end. You can be certain of that."

Ean spun him a hard look. "What do you mean?"

Julian barked a laugh. "Haven't you heard a word I've said? Isabel van Gelderan is Epiphany's Prophet—she's a *real* prophet, not like that terrorist, Bethamin. Isabel *knows* things. She's special, Ean. She's..." he paused, frowned...shrugged. "Well, she's just not like anyone else in the world."

Ean knew that already. His palpitating heart told him so.

Julian joined him in gazing at Isabel. "They say she sees the future always," he advised in a low voice, as if loath to disturb her with even the whispers of gossip. "It's said that every path is laid bare before her eyes. She cannot help but know a man's ultimate end with a single look, so she wears the blindfold rather than gaze perpetually into infinity." He shuddered suddenly. "Imagine. It'd be enough to drive a man mad, I think."

"She's a Healer then?" Ean murmured, only half listening. "To have the Sight?"

"She's a lot of things. Come on," and he nudged Ean's elbow, "else we'll be here all day while you stare all moon-eyed at her."

With the greatest force of will, Ean tore himself away. "So...if everything is so peaceful here," he posed then, forcing thoughts of Isabel regretfully from mind, "if there will never be war and no one wears weapons, why build a wall with battlements?"

"So it's easy to see down into the gardens and the yards." Julian gave him such a look, like this reasoning was terribly obvious.

At the end of the Court Wall, they passed into a marble tunnel demarked by a carving of two rearing lions and emerged thirty paces later at the circular end of a great promenade.

In the middle of the turnabout, a majestic fountain sprayed water from myriad creatures, its mist glittering in the sun. A green-lawned park spread to either side of the promenade, which in turn was busy with strolling couples, children playing, peddlers tending to colorful carts, and men and women of varied races going about their day. The scene reminded Ean very much of his first sight of Cair Rethynnea, but without the sense of imminent disaster. Ean could just make out another fountain at the next circle, perhaps half a mile further down.

"This way." Julian grinned and tugged Ean after him.

They made their way down the Promenade and into the city, moving from park to piazza, from café to taverna to playhouse. Julian introduced Ean to everyone they met, from the barkeep at his favorite alehouse to the Mistress of Chambers at the *Teatro del Benedire Artista*, where Julian said the greatest musicians in T'khendar came to perform. In turn, everyone who met Ean steepled their palms, pressed fingertips to lips and bowed to him. He found it terribly disorienting.

While Ean appreciated Niyadbakir's beauty, he couldn't help but wonder how so many people came to be living in a realm that was supposedly barren of life—not just *living* there, but *making a living*. Niyadbakir was clearly a prosperous city, with flourishing commerce and a diverse population.

As they were heading across a wide plaza bordered on all sides by enormous buildings that Julian identified as the guild halls, a shadow passed before the sun, and Ean glanced up to see an enormous creature soaring across the sky. He stopped in his tracks.

"Dear Epiphany." All he could see of the dragon was its darkened underbelly in silhouette between him and the sun, but as the creature banked, its hide sparkled with bronze and gold. He turned an awestruck look to Julian. "Was that…?"

"One of the Sundragons." Julian gazed after it with a tiny frown furrowing his fair brow. "Rhakar, maybe? It's hard to tell the *drachwyr* apart when they're in the form."

Ean barely heard most of what he said. "What do you mean 'in the form?'"

"Well, they're fifth-strand." Julian shifted his gaze to Ean. "Like the zanthyrs. They have two forms."

"Oh…" Ean had forgotten all about the shapeshifting aspect of the fifth-strand's creatures. He didn't know anyone who'd ever seen a zanthyr in the form, but he was sure he'd never realized that the Sundragons were also shapeshifters.

"Sundragons," he repeated slowly, pondering what he knew of them. All he remembered was that they'd been banished by the Alorin Seat because they'd been sworn to Björn, and that more recently the Emir of the Akkad's Mage had recalled them from isolation. "But...I thought the Sundragons served the Emir's Mage."

Julian gave him a strange look. "Ean..."

And then it finally hit him. But before he had time to think through what it meant that Björn van Gelderan was posing as a Mage and involving himself in the war in M'Nador, Julian grabbed his arm.

"*Ean*—look! He's coming back!"

Ean followed Julian's awe-struck gaze to see a man approaching across the busy square. Even from that distance, Ean could tell he was very tall. He wore black boots and pants below a grey tunic and quilted vest, and the black hilt of a greatsword extended diagonally above one shoulder. As the man neared, Ean noted that the hilt of his sword was carved into the image of a dragon, with the cross-guard fashioned as the dragon's spread wings.

Everyone the man passed bent and bowed, hands steepled and fingertips pressed to lips, but it seemed the man had eyes only for...*him*.

Julian was looking positively exuberant.

As the man reached them, Julian pressed his hands together and bowed. "General," he murmured with excitement and awe coloring his tone.

The *drachwyr* only barely acknowledged him, for his dark eyes were pinned on Ean. His features reflected the same aristocratic perfection as the zanthyr's, although the two men looked nothing alike. The prince thought he saw a flash of confusion cross the other's gaze, but recognition quickly replaced it.

"You must be Ean," the man said in a voice that appeared used to command—indeed, he veritably exuded power through every pore, though his manner was entirely welcoming.

Ean felt the force of his presence like a furnace blast of heat. "Yes. But I'm sorry, I don't—"

"I am Ramu." The *drachwyr* introduced himself with a gracious nod.

Ramuhárihkamáth. Ean knew his famous name. *Dear Epiphany*, what a day this was turning out to be!

"Be welcome, Ean." Ramu glanced to the sky and offered, "When I first passed overhead, I confess I thought you might be your brother. I was confused, because it seemed too early for his arrival in T'khendar."

"My brother?" Ean gazed blankly at him. "You mean…Creighton?" It made no sense that the man would mistake him for a Shade.

Ramu's eyes widened slightly. "You don't know."

Seeing the look on Ramu's face, Ean had the dreadful premonition that the King's board was about to shift on him again.

Ramu took him by the arm. "Why don't we sit down?" He drew Ean towards the plaza's central fountain.

Ean's stomach lurched with desperate understanding. *My brother lives? Which brother? How?*

Ramu settled on Ean's right while Julian sank down on his left, looking concerned.

"More than three moons ago," Ramu explained then, "my brother Rhakar and I pulled a man from a well in the Kutsamak mountains. He was known to us as the commander of a company of the Emir's Converted—though he is not Converted himself. For five years he'd been serving the Emir, who looked upon him as an adopted son. Knowing this man's importance, we saved him from the well waters. The First Lord healed him of his injuries, and three days later he woke."

Ramu pinned Ean with a darkly compelling gaze. "We knew this soldier as Ama-Kai'alil, the Man of the Tides, but the First Lord knew his true identity. He is your brother, Trell."

Ean stared hard at the plaza stones and drew in a trembling breath.

"He doesn't know himself," Ramu continued gently. "He remembers nothing of his life before waking on a beach in the Akkad—his family, his kingdom…these memories are lost to him. But there are some things that do not hide in the shadows of his past: honor, enduring nobility, acts of true leadership, courage in command. You will be proud of the man your brother has become."

Ean pushed palms to his eyes and smiled so hard that his cheeks began to ache. That Trell lived changed so much—for everyone.

"I…can't believe it." He barely managed the words around his overwhelming happiness. *Trell lives!* The knowledge was too monumental, too impactful, to fully absorb.

Ramu placed a strong hand on Ean's shoulder, and the prince slowly looked to him. "The First Lord took steps to ensure Trell will find his way to those who will know him, who will help him reconnect with your family. While you cannot immediately seek him out, perhaps you can take reassurance in this knowledge."

Ean nodded. He'd known there was no chance of going after Trell.

"The First Lord will be relieved that I have told you this," Ramu added. "I'm certain he would've done so as soon as he felt you were capable of hearing it."

Ean just nodded. Admittedly there was no way he could've taken the news yesterday on top of what he'd learned about his Return.

"Oh, Shadow take me!" Julian suddenly jumped to his feet. "General, I beg your pardon, but we must go. Ean has an appointment with Monsieur L'Meppe to be fitted for his masquerade costume, and I fear we'll be late."

"Of course." Ramu stood and nodded farewell to Ean. Then he turned and strode away through the crowd, with the city dwellers bowing and murmuring in his wake.

Julian looked at the position of the sun in the sky. "Burn me, we'd better run."

They made it to the atelier of Monsieur L'Meppe in time to receive the sharp side of his tongue, but not so late that the man refused to do the fitting altogether. A narrow escape.

All the while the costumer taped and pinned and measured Ean, muttering under his breath, the prince felt in a daze. For so long his life had been a convoluted series of tragedies and mishaps, where treachery lurked at every turn and loss shadowed each waking moment with a perpetual overcast. Now, suddenly, he was getting answers to his most agonizing questions. He felt welcome, even...*wanted*, and he was surrounded by people who *knew* things.

And now...Trell lived.

When the Kings board of his life finally found its way back to solid ground, Ean saw that one of the priests had been righted along with it. He'd never imagined that treasured piece could ever find its place in his life again. But now, suddenly, he had *hope*. Hope that there could be peace for his father's kingdom, that his brother would have all that was rightfully his, that Ean might have his own future. But above all, hope surged from the one impossible truth:

My brother lives!

Monsieur L'Meppe gave him an odd look, Julian clapped him happily on the shoulder, and Ean realized he'd spoken the words aloud. He gave his friend a sheepish grin. The day seemed suddenly very bright.

When the costumer was done with the fitting but not with muttering under his breath about last minute demands, Julian and Ean made their way back to the White Forest with Ean in soaring spirits. He couldn't remember the last time he felt this happy. Quite probably it was before his brother Sebastian's death. That was when the light had faded in his mother's eyes, and he didn't doubt his had dimmed then as well.

Sebastian…it still hurt to remember him. Fynn liked to criticize Sebastian's dark sense of humor—mainly because it challenged his own— but growing up together, Ean had veritably worshipped his eldest brother, and Sebastian had rarely disappointed him. Yes, he'd been proud of his firstborn status, a confidence which had grated on certain personalities, but he'd been wonderfully knowledgeable about all manner of intriguing things and was never too busy to explain something to his inquisitive youngest sibling.

Then there was Trell…ever inventive, with his witty sense of humor and adventurous outlook. Trell had been Ean's confidant, always willing to dive into any misadventure at his side.

Ean wanted so much to be able to tell his queen mother of the incredible news that Trell lived, but he had to trust that the First Lord had Trell's interests in hand, as Ramu had said. Miraculously enough, Ean *was* willing to trust to this.

Until that moment, there had been but one man whom Ean trusted implicitly—despite Phaedor's admonishment not to. Now he'd found another. Ean wasn't yet ready to swear an oath into Björn's service, but he could see the first tendrils of the idea taking root.

And that felt *right*, too.

SIXTEEN

"We must be our own before we can be another's."

– Valentina van Gelderan, Empress of Agasan

OVER THE COURSE of the next week, Alyneri alternated Healing, resting and eating until one morning she woke and knew that she was fully restored. She felt for the bandages that bound her eyes, eager to be rid of them. Her fingers unworked the knot, and at last she felt the cool touch of air upon her eyelids, and then, finally, the light.

Opening her eyes, she blinked to focus on a bedroom much as she'd imagined it: small but tidy, with a bed, a table and a wardrobe built for function, not aesthetics. She saw his clothes hanging within the latter and realized only then that she'd been sleeping in his bed. Where had he been sleeping?

She slipped her arm free of the splint and stood up, then walked to the wardrobe and examined her head in the little mirror inside one door. The faintest scar showed along her hairline, just above her temple. She vaguely recalled being thrown from the coach. It must've been quite a blow to split her head so.

And now I've healed myself.

Who would've believed it? *She* barely believed it.

Alyneri was trying to get a comb through her hair when Yara came in and stopped short in the doorway.

Alyneri looked up with a smile. "*Sobh bekheir,* Yara." *Good morning.*

The old woman looked just as she'd imagined, with iron-grey hair and deep wrinkles lining her dark eyes. A heavy woolen sweater dwarfed her small but spry frame.

Yara arched her sparse eyebrows. "You look much improved. What magic is this?"

"I *am* a Healer," Alyneri reminded her.

Yara waved a hand at her. "*Pshaw*, and here I thought all this time the two of you were bonding. Who knew you both had it in you to be so crafty about such a thing as a Healer healing herself?"

"So you're not upset with me?"

She pinned her with a deliberate look. "Why? It worked, didn't it? We do what we must. Daughters of the sand are strong."

"Yes," Alyneri conceded, dropping her gaze. "Yes we are."

"Here," said the old woman, coming on into the room. "I brought you something."

Alyneri took the offered bundle and unwrapped it to find a dress of heavy silk taffeta in a deep sapphire blue, and a matching cloak lined in velvet. Her eyes went wide. "Oh, Yara, but I can't accept these! They're too beautiful!"

"To be certain you will. I've money to spare on account of that pirate, and as sure as Azerjaiman blows west, the dress isn't likely to fit me. Such fine silk can't go to waste."

Alyneri stared at her for a different reason than the dress. "On account of what pirate?"

"That vran Lea character. We had a bargain, and against all odds, he fulfilled his end of it."

"Do you mean...*could* you mean *Carian* vran Lea?" The pirate had been in service to the Vestal Raine D'Lacourte before Ean's accident at the villa in Rethynnea.

Yara arched a brow. "Know him, do you? Why am I not surprised?" Seemingly oblivious to Alyneri's stunned silence, Yara motioned her to put it on. Alyneri let the woman move her body with blank obedience.

Did such coincidences really exist?

What did it mean that Yara knew Carian? Surely the pirate had interactions with numerous folk, yet instinct told her there had to be a connection.

Yara did up the buttons on the back of the dress and then turned Alyneri around to look her over. "Well, your hair could do with help from fingers more deft than mine, but still, *soraya*, you're a sight to behold. A fitting gown for a prince's daughter."

Alyneri gave her a sharp look.

"Oh, yes." The old woman pinned her with a cunning gaze. "You look just like Jair, only blonde."

Alyneri caught her breath. "You *knew* my father?" What else had the old woman been hiding?

"Knew him well, I did, when he was near your age. My father was a scholar and advisor to the Haxamanis family. Prince Jair was a handful—as I'm sure his daughter is also, when she's not recovering from being nearly drowned."

Alyneri braced her cheeks with both hands, feeling them warm as her eyes filled with tears. "Will you tell me about him?" she asked in a small voice.

Yara gave her a big smile that brightened her wrinkled face and showed a reflection of the youthful beauty she'd once boasted herself. "Of course, *soraya*."

Alyneri threw her arms around the old woman and let her falling tears bear the weight of her happiness. "Thank you!" she whispered. "Thank you so much!"

Yara chuckled as she returned Alyneri's embrace, and she held her as any mother would, until the force of her emotion had calmed. Pulling away then, she took Alyneri by the shoulders and looked her over once more. "How about we see to breakfast, you and I. If that boy ever comes inside, we'll have something ready for him."

"That boy is here," came his cheerful reply from the other room a second before Alyneri heard the outside door closing.

"Well then." Yara moved to leave as Ama-Kai'alil was coming in, momentarily standing between Alyneri and preventing clear sight of him. But then—

Alyneri felt the world tilt and spin, and everything went black at the edges, all except her view of him.

Dear Epiphany!

Had her own mother been standing in the doorway, Alyneri couldn't have been more stunned. She felt the blood draining from her cheeks, staggered in place, saw him staring at her in shock and concern, and then, somehow found her feet again and drove herself across the space between them and fiercely into his arms.

"You're alive!" Tears fell freely down her face, while a boundless joy choked her. She hugged him tight, unable to bring him close enough to assure herself he wouldn't merely evaporate like the apparition he seemed. *"Epiphany bless you!"* she cried, not even knowing what she was saying, the words just spilling out of her. She pulled her face free of his shoulder long enough to look into his grey eyes, long enough to see his confusion and dismay, but in that moment caring only that he lived.

"Trell…" She barely believed the name was leaving her lips. "It's really you!" She took his face between trembling hands. *"Trell!"* She was laughing and weeping and totally hysterical but so full of joy that none of it mattered. "You're *alive!"*

Trell had risen before daybreak and spent the early dawn hours feeding the livestock and tending to Gendaia. Recovered from her injury, she was eager to roam, so he let her out to graze while he went about his other chores. Gendaia streaked away up the grassy hill the moment he released her harness, but by the time the sun cleared the mountains, she was back and nosing him for breakfast.

Now that Gendaia was well, there was no reason for him to linger in Veneisea. Yara had long told him she could survive just fine without him—in words not nearly as gentle—and he felt the weight of his agreement with the Mage coming to bear. He still had a message to deliver in the Cairs—never mind his own personal quest—yet…he wasn't eager to leave.

Alyneri was the issue. He still had not told her of Lord Brantley, and he didn't believe the man would've abandoned his search. While he felt reasonably sure Alyneri would be grateful that he'd kept her presence hidden from the earl, he wasn't certain of it. The longer he delayed telling her about the man, the more weight the encounter seemed to gather, such that he feared it would become a huge secret, a blight on their burgeoning path towards mutual trust.

It's cowardly and selfish to keep this from her, he scolded himself as he brushed Gendaia down, but Alyneri had become important to him, and he feared losing her.

More and more, he thought about the girl he remembered from the beach and Alyneri as being one and the same. He cursed himself for giving in to the temptation to romanticize their chance meeting into reunion, yet he felt connected to her in ways he couldn't explain.

Now he faced the issue of what to do with her. He dared not leave her where Lord Brantley could find her, but he hesitated to ask her to come with him to the Cairs. Oh, he desired her company, but what could he offer her? Not his name, certainly, nor even a place to call home—at least not right away. She had her own future to think of—didn't she say she held a Duchess's rank? And though she'd mentioned no other man in her life, a woman of her status wouldn't long remain unmarried.

Trell resolved to tell her immediately of Lord Brantley, as well as his intention to leave the farm, but still he hesitated…finding instead other chores to involve himself in. The idea of leaving her…it just didn't sit well with him.

Finally cleaning up from the morning's work, Trell took his blade and sheared off his growth of beard over a washbasin in the barn. He'd never really seen himself beneath it, and he didn't like the feeling that he wore yet another mask when he was already so tormented by the nameless countenance he faced every day.

Thus clean shaved, Trell stood just inside the barn doors with a heavy heart. He steeled himself to confront Alyneri, ducked his head as he made his way across the yard and headed inside the farmhouse.

Yara was saying, "…that boy ever comes inside, we'll have something ready for him."

"That boy is here," Trell answered, shutting the door. He mustered a cheerful demeanor he didn't feel.

"Well then." Yara emerged from the bedroom as he moved to go in, and something in the look she gave him caught his attention, so that he was slightly puzzled already when he turned to look upon Alyneri—and seemed to see her for the first time.

Without her bandages, without the bruises and contusions and swelling distorting her features… *It's her!*

She was unmistakably the girl from the beach.

And then he saw her face pale, and he saw her stagger, and confusion and concern overcame him. He wanted to reach out to her but felt pinned to inaction by the shocked expression she wore.

She reached a hand towards the wardrobe as if for support. Then, like a rising wave, she surged across the space between them and threw her arms around him, nearly knocking him over. "*You're alive!*"

Trell held her, feeling confused and anxious to understand. She clutched at him and murmured prayers of thanks. Then she pulled her face free of his shoulder and looked at him with wet lashes that framed lovely brown eyes.

She took his face between her hands. "*Trell*, it's really you!" His heart suddenly caught in his throat. "*Trell!*" She was laughing and weeping and completely beside herself. "You're *alive!*" She threw her arms around his neck again and laughed and cried.

The moment was so overwhelming, so unexpected, and yet this reunion was so obviously *true*. She'd known him the moment their eyes met. She'd called him by name, though he'd never said it in all their time together. But even had she discovered it from Yara, it didn't matter, for *he* knew her, too. Trell pressed his lips against Alyneri's hair and closed his eyes. "You *know* me."

"I know you." She pulled away and wiped joyful tears from her cheeks.

He took her hands in his and looked into her eyes. "I remember you, Alyneri," he confessed in a choked voice, for the first time trusting their reunion as truth. And though his joy abounded, he also felt somehow barren, like a canvas stretched too tightly. His emotions were scrabbling for a handhold in a cup already overflowing. "I have but one memory of you, but I *do* remember."

She smiled and wiped away more tears, for they flowed freely. "I thought you were dead—we *all* did—but your family…your mother, they…" she bit her lip to hold back a sob. "They never named you."

'*Is it a mercy to come back into their lives? If they've moved on, if they've grieved and named me and forgotten?*'

He remembered his words to Lily, what seemed a lifetime ago, and now he knew what they meant. His mother, his family…they'd thought him dead, yet they'd never named him.

Tears filled his eyes. His family hadn't forgotten him. They hadn't let him go.

Alyneri drew him to the bed and pulled him down to sit beside her. She pressed his hands between her own.

"More than five years ago, you left aboard the *Dawn Chaser* for Tal'Shira by the Sea with a contingent of the king's men and three crown Healers. My mother was among them." Her voice broke at this, and her grief drew him to focus. Hazy memories of a four-masted vessel floated at the edges of his vision.

"What happened?" he managed.

"No one knows. The ship never made it to port. None of her passengers were ever heard from again." She squeezed his hands and braved a smile. "Until now."

"Alyneri…" he whispered desperately.

She cupped his cheek. "You were lost, but now you're found."

"You found me."

She shook her head, smiled through her tears. "No…you found me."

Trell's chest burned and his throat felt tight. He knew that the monumental ache of so many years was over, but the collected emotion seemed to want to all flood out of him at once.

She was studying him with a compassionate gaze. She wiped tears from her face and smiled again, and then she wiped them from his. "Are you ready?"

"For what?" though he knew what she was asking.

"To know the truth?"

Trell gazed off and swallowed. He'd faced countless odds in battle; he'd been surrounded by death—had looked death in the eye many times himself—but he'd never known such apprehension as of the words she was about to say. A thousand fears raced through his mind, doubts and self-abnegation, words like *bastard, traitor, coward* echoing painfully in the recesses of his heart.

She took a deep breath, fixed her dark eyes upon him such that he couldn't look away, and said, "Your name is Trell val Lorian."

He knew she must've kept talking, for her mouth continued to move, but Trell heard nothing else but the name.

Trell val Lorian…val Lorian…val Lorian.

It couldn't be. Yet it was. He *knew* it was. The name—*his* name—resonated in a way nothing else ever had.

"Trell?" Alyneri pressed a hand to his cheek to recapture his attention. "You do know, don't you? You know that name?"

"Prince," he whispered.

"Prince Trell val Lorian," she confirmed with all the gravity the title deserved. "You are a royal prince of Dannym, the second son of Queen Errodan, often called her 'treasured middle son.' Your older brother was Sebastian, dead now these eight years."

"Sebastian." The name fit. It was right.

"And your younger brother is—"

"Ean," he gasped, and he drew in a shuddering breath. The elusive name—so long yearned for—had finally come. Trell covered his face with his hands.

"Trell…" Alyneri placed a hand on his knee, "you're next in line for the throne."

SEVENTEEN

"Self-delusion is the worst of all vices."

– The Adept wielder Arion Tavestra

RAINE DREAMED.

He stood in a library as great as the Citadel's had been before Tiern'aval fell. Thousands of works crammed the towering shelves, which vanished into dimness in the cavernous room. As he walked slowly among the stacks, he saw the titles of great and important works long lost to the realm. It crushed him to be reminded of the vast amount of knowledge that had been destroyed along with the island of Tiern'aval.

Even had the wealth of knowledge somehow survived, however, the gravest damage had come when Björn sacrificed the Hundred Mages. These peaceful, scholarly sages had spent their long lives in search of wisdom and understanding of the wielding of *elae*. They alone had performed the difficult testing for the many levels of Adept mastery that resulted in the gaining of the Sormitáge rings—a revered status for any Adept. Their slaying, beyond any other single act, had convinced Raine and Alshiba that Björn had finally succumbed to the same poisonous taint that had destroyed Malachai.

"Hello, brother."

Raine spun at the voice. It was unmistakable, even after three centuries.

Dagmar wore his characteristic black, though his blonde hair now hung to his shoulders and his green eyes harbored new lines to catalog the years behind him. He still wore the braided gold circlet of his family line, a tradition the Danes held to. Likewise he wore his oath-ring on the third finger of his right hand. The azure stone glittered in the muted light.

Raine stared at the ring. How could the color of the stone remain so true? How could Dagmar have survived in T'Khendar for three hundred years and *not* violated his Vestal oath?

But the stone appeared as true to color as Raine's own.

"It *cannot* be," Raine breathed explosively. The declaration embraced a number of recent experiences.

"Welcome to T'khendar, brother." Dagmar wore his reserve like a cloak, perhaps the better to mirror Raine's wild and varied reactions in comparison.

Raine searched his oath-brother's face but wished he might've been scouring his mind instead. What he would've given to pry into the vault of Dagmar's thoughts. Such skills were denied him in dreamscape; the latter was but a shadow of the waking world, a projection. Yet some things Raine knew remained true. Dagmar's ring, for example.

"It's been a long time, Dagmar." Raine gathered his composure, calling forth the decorum and manners that served him when all logic failed. "Alshiba and I thought perhaps the nature of the Vestal oath kept you from contacting us in dreamscape, but now I see it was simply a choice."

Dagmar grimaced. "A choice, yes," he agreed, but his expression betrayed the truth in Raine's accusation. Still, Raine saw a resolute determination in the other Vestal's gaze. "Everything in life is about the choices we make, is it not, brother?"

Raine shook his head and regarded Dagmar. Too much had come between them. Too much blame and denial—death and treachery long unpunished. There must be accountability, atonement. "Why did Björn bring me here?" The demand came with sudden heat. "Why are *you* here?"

"With a welcome, a gift, and a warning."

Raine's gaze hardened. "A warning?"

"Indeed," Dagmar replied, calm beneath Raine's ire, though he sensed a deep regret lacing Dagmar's tone. "But first the welcome. The First Lord, our oath-brother, is glad you've come. He knows you have questions, but before he will consider answering them, he requires something of you."

"He has no right to make demands of any of us!" Raine hissed. He felt anger flooding into him and fought to contain it. A battle in dreamscape would accomplish nothing—*though by Cephrael's Great Book, it might make me feel better to hit some*body.

"He presents you with this." Dagmar handed Raine a bronze coin. It was stamped on both sides with the same pattern, similar to an endless knot.

Raine accepted the coin with a force of will. "What's this?" he asked tightly.

"A reminder." Dagmar leveled pale green eyes upon him, his gaze unwavering. "That this effort has two sides, yet they are two sides of the same battle."

"No," Raine returned. "I do not accept that."

"Hence his warning." Dagmar gave him a rueful smile. "If you would find answers in Niyadbakir, you must face first the veils of your own failures."

Raine held his gaze hotly. "That sounds more like prophecy," he growled.

"Take it as you will, brother," Dagmar said by way of farewell, and the dream began to fade.

"You are sworn to *him* now?" Raine shouted after him, but the library was already gone.

He woke with his shout still echoing in the enclosed wooden wagon where he'd slept for the last many nights. His host slept soundly despite his outburst. Raine heard snoring coming from the bunk above and noted one hairy foot dangling from the same. Looking down to his clenched fist, he opened his fingers and saw Björn's coin resting on his palm.

Suddenly rage boiled inside him too hot to remain abed. Raine threw off his covers and stormed outside. The barest lightening of the eastern horizon heralded the coming dawn, while the moon rode low in the west. Unfamiliar stars twinkled in the heavens between—all, that is, save one familiar grouping.

Above him, midline to the zenith, Cephrael's Hand glowed. Raine stared at the constellation and tried to will his anger to drain away.

He remembered seeing those stars while in the company of Franco Rohre a month into their hunt for Björn...the night Ean val Lorian had been kidnapped by a Shade. He wasn't sure why he associated the constellation with Björn now—he certainly didn't ascribe such power to his oath-brother as to imagine him capable of influencing the stars—yet there seemed a connection.

Raine drew in a calming breath and let it out slowly, his gaze fixed upon the heavens.

'If you want answers in Niyadbakir, you must face first the veils of your own failures.' Dagmar's words, on behalf of another.

Raine grunted. *An appropriately cryptic remark, coming from Björn.*

He needed to walk, to let his heart find a purpose for racing, to let the intensity of his anger find balance in action. Shoving hands into his pockets, still gripping Björn's coin, Raine headed across the camp.

He didn't deny that he'd had his own failures, but he didn't think Björn was referencing a failing Raine had already identified. No, his oath-brother—ever audacious and unrepentantly exacting—would expect him to search deeper for those answers.

Shadow take the infernal man!

Raine had been gifted with a singular lack of ego—which he felt Björn more than made up for. But the idea that Björn might be justified in *anything*—surely the insinuation in Dagmar's words—was hard to swallow. Even if many recent events in Alorin must be pinned on the presence of Malorin'athgul, Björn still had the Citadel, T'Khendar, and the greater part of the Adept Wars to answer for.

As Raine was passing a red-painted wagon, its door opened and a man stepped out, already in the middle of a stretch.

"You're up...early..." Balearic noted through a yawn.

Raine lifted his gaze to the pirate-turned-gypsy and studied him as the latter scratched his beard and then tugged down his waistcoat.

"Good morning to you, Balearic." Raine turned and gazed eastward once more. The horizon had become a glowing line against shadow-black sands, while the heavens seemed a rim of pale gold that rapidly deepened to blue, stars now fading beneath the powerful coming of dawn.

Raine had been many days in T'khendar, traveling with the gypsy camp as they moved west. They were due to reach the city of Renato the following afternoon. While Raine wouldn't be sorry to say farewell to the Wyndlass Desert, he'd had little chance to speak with Balearic since the gypsy had rescued them. Much remained unclear to him about Björn's realm and those who dwelled within it.

"Nine years, you said." Raine watched Balearic descending the steps of his wagon. "That's how long you've lived here."

Balearic came to a halt at his side and joined him in observing the sunrise. "Aye, my lord."

"Then you know what they say in Alorin. You know the stories of this place...of my oath-brother."

"Aye," the gypsy admitted.

Raine settled him an inquiring look.

Balearic shrugged. "You can't believe everything you hear, Your Excellency. Fortune bite me, but you can't believe half of what you see, either." He headed over to his fire pit and stirred the coals back to life.

Raine followed him. "You knew the rumors, yet you came here."

Balearic squatted to put kindling on the burgeoning fire. "I wasn't in a position to care much about ancient history when I expatriated here, Your Excellency. What Carian said was true—I had the whole of the Agasi imperial navy searching for me. No matter what I did, my pirating days were over. I figured I'd make a new start in a place nobody knew me, somewhere even the Empress's long arm couldn't reach." Getting the fire back to life, Balearic settled an iron kettle on a hook over the flames and sat back, draping elbows over his knees.

Raine slowly lowered himself down beside the gypsy. "And?"

Balearic cast a thoughtful look at him. "Things are a bit unusual here. In many ways, life goes on the same, but in just as many it's completely different." He gave Raine an uncertain smile. "To tell you the truth, my lord, people here somewhat blame you and the other Vestals."

Raine drew back in surprise. "They blame *us?*"

"Through no fault of the First Lord's," Balearic was quick to declare. "No doubt he'd be the first to come to your defense, just because he's that way about things. But you know, in Alorin they're like to blame those who aren't around to defend their honor, and I suppose it's no different here."

Raine reflected it was an interesting concept to imagine himself the villain.

"No offense, Your Excellency..." Balearic fixed his attention on stoking the fire, "but there's some...well, *they* might've left you out in the Wyndlass to find your own way, if you know what I mean. I can't say for certain I would've made the trek myself if Carian hadn't been with you."

"I see." Raine regarded him quietly.

"Lots of us know the rumors circulating about the First Lord back in Alorin," Balearic continued, "and the people here don't like them overmuch."

Raine fixed his gaze upon the gypsy. "You're sworn to him?"

"I suppose of a fashion," Balearic admitted, "but not in the way you're likely thinking—nothing like an oath or any sort of magic—but people are loyal to the First Lord and the Lady."

"He's your ruler," Raine said equitably but with deep concern in his gaze. "It only follows."

"Oh no, the First Lord doesn't rule here." Balearic lifted his gaze to meet Raine's. "T'khendar is a realm of Free Cities. The governors are in charge of the cities, and they just report to the guilds."

Raine leaned back in surprise. "Björn doesn't rule?"

"Like I said," Balearic shot him a telling look. "Folks have a lot of wrong ideas back in Alorin."

Raine considered him for a moment and then observed, "You are quite forthcoming for a man of your background, Monsieur de Palma."

"Well…the general said we should be as truthful with you as we dared." Balearic focused on pushing at the fire with a long stick instead of looking at Raine. He shrugged. "You're as like to get ill stares from folks as you are to be greeted fairly. It's only fair you should understand why."

"I appreciate your candor more than you know," Raine told him. "Who is the general you speak of?"

"General Ramuhárikhamáth. He's the one who took note of you in the Wyndlass."

"Ah…" Raine arched brows. *So Björn maintains his allies in their same roles, but what of his other two generals? Arion Tavestra must certainly be dead…and Markal?*

Raine had been seeking Markal Morrelaine for centuries. The idea of perhaps finding him in T'khendar brought a sudden sense of hope. Then he inwardly laughed at the bitter irony, for what point in questioning Markal when Björn himself stood to answer?

"So you came here and you listened to different stories," Raine posed to Balearic then, "but you were a cynical man, if I'm not misreading you, Monsieur de Palma. What changed your mind?"

Balearic pitched his stick onto the flames and clasped hands before him.

He gave Raine an uncertain look. "People talk, like I said, but here they tell different stories. I suppose we're all wont to think the worst of others, my lord, but...well, there was something of these stories that just rang with truth to me." He gazed off over the fire and added quietly and with a sudden faraway look, "And then there was the lady. One can't see her but know she represents goodness in all its forms."

Raine looked at him in confusion. "What lady?"

"The Lady Isabel, his sister."

Raine stared at Balearic while reality came to an abrupt and staggering collision with the impossible. He knew he couldn't have heard the man correctly.

Isabel! Raine pinched the bridge of his nose and tried to breathe around the sudden tightness in his chest.

"I see you know her then."

Dear Epiphany—Isabel is alive?

Isabel van Gelderan had been the High Mage of the Citadel. She never would've condoned Björn's betrayal, so Raine and Alshiba had been certain Björn had killed her along with the other Mages.

He managed a swallow around a sudden pang of guilt. "Has she been here the whole time?"

Balearic regarded him solemnly. "Far as I know, my lord, she's been here since Tiern'aval fell."

Raine sank his head into his hands. "All this time...all this time, we thought—"

Balearic suddenly seemed to understand Raine's response. "Well, you didn't think he'd killed her! Not the lady, his own sister! Even *I* know the First Lord would sacrifice the realm he created with his own blood and tears before he would see harm come to the Lady Isabel."

Raine gave him a tormented look. "She was the High Mage of the Citadel, Balearic! The Citadel Mages were *sacrificed*. You know *that* story, certainly."

"Oh aye, I know it," the man said with a hard, uncompromising glint in his kohl-lined blue eyes. "But there's lots said of the Hundred Mages that isn't fact—why, the lady's not the only one as survived when all were said to have perished. There's the governors of the cities too—Governors Paledyne,

Tempest, val Kess, d'Norio and Ranner—all Mages once, and I hear Markal Morrelaine returned several moons ago, and others besides, I'm told."

Raine was reeling. "They're all alive? They're all *here?*"

"You shouldn't believe the stories, my lord." Balearic sounded highly disappointed.

"We saw the Mages' *heads,* man!" Raine threw out a hand towards Balearic in exasperation. "Malachai paraded them directly before us!"

Balearic picked up another stick to poke at the fire and posed quietly, "Did you count them?"

Raine stared at him. "*Count* them?" The remark roused a furious indignation, but then Raine saw the point of Balearic's question. Something within the obvious truth of it restored some semblance of order to his thoughts, and he suddenly deflated. "No." He exhaled a heavy sigh. "I suppose we did not *count* them."

"Wasn't a hundred, that's sure as silver," Balearic grumbled.

Raine pushed a hand through his hair. He wanted more than ever to strangle the life out of Björn van Gelderan.

"*By Cephrael's Great Book,*" Raine spun an exasperated look to Balearic, "if everything we know is a bloody lie, what *did* happen at the Citadel?"

Raine wasn't expecting an answer, but Balearic offered, "People don't even whisper about that night—not even the ones who lived through it. Someone comes along thinking to be smart, trying to make connections, conjecturing… the next thing he knows he's got a Shade asking questions at his door." He shoved his stick into the fire, sending sparks heavenward. "Ain't nobody wants that kind of attention."

Raine let out a forceful exhale and sank his forehead into one hand. Silence descended, a long stretch where only the fire crackled and the kettle boiled its low hum. Finally, Raine said quietly, "So far there hasn't been a single thing about this place that fits with anything I remembered or knew to be true."

"Aye," Balearic commiserated with a long sigh. "T'khendar will do that to you." Then he shook his head and muttered under his breath, "Thinking he'd let the Lady fall into harm…" he clucked his tongue. "Ye just don't know him at all."

No, Raine agreed, teeth clenched in frustration. *I clearly do not.*

'If you want answers in Niyadbakir, you must face first the veils of your own failure.'

Björn's words, but were they warning or prophecy? Raine was starting to believe that either way, the endeavor might prove more difficult than he'd imagined.

Franco Rohre stepped off the node into the glaring morning and was immediately assaulted by searing heat and the unforgiving brightness of the desert sands. In the distance, within the shadow of jutting basalt cliffs, Franco saw a splash of color and knew he'd found the Great Master.

He set off towards a green canvas tent, wondering why anyone in his right mind would purposefully create a desert. If you had the skill to birth a world from the womb of another realm, why not give it a temperate climate and cloak the hills in foliage? What was there to bloody appreciate about a furnace of stone and sand?

Dagmar was reclining in a hammock beneath the shelter of his canvas tent, whose sides were open to the breeze—not that the boiling wind did anything but cause a man to simultaneously bake and perspire—when Franco reached him.

The Second Vestal opened his eyes as Franco was trudging up in a shirt already soaked with sweat. "Ah, Franco." He twined hands behind his head. "Welcome to the Wyndlass."

"Thank you, my lord. I always wondered what hell felt like."

The Vestal chuckled. "It's been so long since I suffered from the heat that I forget how unpleasant it can be. Here, sit, have some *siri*," and he waved nebulously towards the other hammock and a table where a pitcher of *siri* stood, beaded with sweat. Franco willingly accepted the drink but forewent the hammock; the idea of anything else touching his body was abhorrent.

"I can teach you the patterns my oath-brother taught me so long ago, Franco," Dagmar offered. "That is, if you dare to work the fifth."

"No thank you, my lord. I'd rather endure a punishing heat than Balance's form of punishment."

Dagmar grinned. "It's true—the fifth should never be worked lightly. What's more, for those of us not born to the strand, working its patterns can feel much akin to baking in this desert." He swung his feet over the side of his hammock and stood to pour himself more *siri*. Then he turned and leaned against the table as he continued his thought, "But Franco, when you're spending weeks at a time in this heat, when the sun has stolen every ounce of energy and even your bones feel burned…in such times will you look upon the fifth as a blessing, no matter the threat of working it."

"Why were you spending so much time here, my lord?" Franco returned.

Dagmar arched resigned brows. "The Wyndlass is the outermost barrier to the end of the known realms, Franco. Beyond this desert lies the naked aether of unraveling space. The welds here must be unimaginably strong to resist the forces that pull against them. Björn and I spent months shoring up these aetheric places to keep *deyjiin* from seeping in. It's been my job to maintain the welds ever since."

Franco took a long swallow of the *siri* and wished he might've been drinking it somewhere he'd never heard of Björn van Gelderan. "I admit my confusion, my lord." He lowered his goblet and stared at the clear liquid. "From the way you said it just then…it sounded like you were speaking of the earliest days of T'khendar."

Dagmar gave him a strange look. "Franco…Björn's Council of Nine didn't understand what was happening in T'khendar in its nascent days. Even my oath-brother was confused in the beginning—something I hope never to again witness. He wanted my help…so he told me all."

Franco blinked at him. "*Before* the wars?"

Dagmar nodded.

Franco exhaled a low whistle. Raine and Alshiba were still tormented over Björn's motivations, and equally so over Dagmar's return to T'khendar after the wars had ended. It would be a considerable blow to them to learn that the Great Master had been Björn's ally all along.

But these were truths Franco would rather not know, so he didn't delve any deeper into them. "I've come at your calling, my lord. How can I assist you?"

Dagmar considered him quietly. "Long have I tended these welds, seeing to their welfare as a gardener nurses a delicate fruit to ripen on the vine, protecting it from dangers seen and unseen. The *drachwyr* are my silent watchmen. They observe from the air what only their immortal, fifth-strand eyes might witness, noting the tiniest snags in the fabric of the realm. Then do I tend to them. Now, I would have you here to help me, if you accept this role."

"Of course, my lord." Though Franco silently loathed the idea of spending even one more hour in the furnace that was the Wyndlass, much less an unknown number of weeks.

"But what of your other task?" Dagmar settled onto his hammock like a chair and sipped his *siri* as he swung gently. "What is your old friend Niko up to?"

"He plans to depose you, my lord," Franco reported with an appropriate underscore of acid in his tone.

Dagmar gave him a look of resigned acceptance. "I suspected something of the sort."

"You don't seem overly dismayed. I was ready to tear out his throat."

The Great Master rewarded his loyalty with a smile. "I know I have your support, Franco. You've always been true to your oaths. No," he said, sighing, "there are worse things than no longer being Alorin's Second Vestal."

"My lord!"

"Be at ease, Franco, and hear me out." Dagmar raised an imploring hand. "My brother's game far surpasses the mere politics of realms. I will not be changed if suddenly my ring is given to another. The Vestal oath is not just a ring to wear."

Franco clenched his teeth. *It is to Niko.* "He intends to take your place, you know."

Dagmar flashed a rueful grin. "That went without saying."

Franco felt protest and angst welling. He couldn't accept Dagmar's submission. "My lord, do you really intend to do nothing?"

Dagmar finished his *siri* and reclined back in his hammock. "The First Lord's advice is ever wise, Franco," he observed then, "and I have learned much of his philosophies in the last few centuries. We learn from the Esoterics of Patterning that the universe aligns towards our intentions. If we're focused on a single goal—that mountain in the distance, say," and he nodded towards a far basalt cliff jutting to scrape the sky, "then the more we continue towards that goal with singular focus, the more the universe aligns to bring it into being. However," and here he eyed Franco sagaciously, "if we're attacked along the way and we diverge from our path to meet each attack, we've stopped all progress towards the mountain. Our goal has been abandoned."

"So you're saying we have to ignore all attacks?" Franco challenged dubiously. "I cannot accept that."

"No, of course not. To ignore an attack merely brings it closer to your path. What Björn advises us is to accept that there will be attacks, and to solve them without diverging from the path towards our goal."

"And how do we do that?" Franco grumbled.

Dagmar leveled him a sardonic grin. "Therein lies the challenge of the game."

The game. That damnable grace-forsaken game!

Years ago, Franco had decided that he should've slit his own throat rather than take a role in the Fifth Vestal's blasted game—even as he knew he had no choice in the matter now, that in fact he'd made his choice long ago. This did not in any way soften the brutal reality that the game they were involved in was deadly beyond measure.

Even deadlier than working the fifth.

Grimacing, Franco poured himself more *siri*, feeling ill-humored. "I suppose I should learn some fifth-strand patterns then, my lord," he decided, turning to Dagmar with grim resignation. "At least that way, when the end comes, I'll meet it comfortably."

EIGHTEEN

"Take care when biting at the bait of mystery.
Always a hook lurks beneath its flesh."

— A joke among zanthyrs

RAINE AND THE gypsies reached the city of Renato in the late afternoon, emerging through arid foothills onto fertile plains where a sprawling walled city of stone and terracotta nestled between river and hillside.

The first day of Adendigaeth had arrived, and the city was abuzz with preparations for the twelve-day festival, which was set to begin that evening with the First Lord's Masquerade. Balearic had explained that the largest fête would be held at Björn's palace in Niyadbakir, but the governors became extensions of the First Lord's hospitality during Adendigaeth, and to launch the festivities, they hosted a masquerade in each of the realm's five cities.

As Raine and Carian arrived in Renato, the streets were jammed with people flooding in from the countryside to attend the fête. Many were already in costume, and revelers had begun spilling out of *tavernas* and cafés all over town, even as city crews still labored to string lanterns between rooftops or hang glass globes from trees and arbors.

The Iluminari had made camp on the outskirts of town at a site large enough for their wagons, so Balearic took Raine and Carian into the city on foot. As they reached the central piazza with its clover-shaped fountain, and the Governor's sun-gold palace rising four stories on the piazza's north side, Raine stopped suddenly. His diamondine gaze revealed his utter mystification.

Balearic came to a halt beside him, while the pirate swaggered over to the broad fountain, climbed in, and dunked his head under one of the downspouts.

"I just can't believe it," Raine said under his breath. The existence of so much, the commerce and prosperity, the masses of people living in a realm supposedly devoid of life—these truths dumbfounded him.

Raine found something eerily familiar about Renato. It had been bothering him since he entered the city through one of seven towering arches—said arcade reminding him uncomfortably of Tiern'aval's doomed seaport. "Where did it all come from?" Raine muttered, more to himself than Balearic. "Where did these *people* come from?"

"Renato was the first city in T'khendar built by human hands." Balearic was standing with his hands in his large pockets and grinning at the pirate, who was splashing around in the fountain as if trying to catch a frog. "From what I hear, the city was constructed by the inhabitants of Tiern'aval and was raised from its ruins."

Raine turned to him looking staggered. "What did you say?" he whispered.

"Tiern'aval." Balearic missed Raine's sudden change in manner, for his attention was fixed on the splashing pirate. "As the story goes, when Malachai twisted the weld between T'khendar and the Citadel on Tiern'aval, the city was ripped here. It lay in ruins, so the First Lord gave the inhabitants unlimited support in rebuilding it."

Raine felt ill. "You're telling me," he formed the words with difficulty around the disbelief lodged in his throat, "that we're standing on the rebuilt ruins of *Cair Tiern'aval?*"

"Aye." Balearic gave the Vestal a sideways look full of meaning.

Raine turned away from the gypsy, for he feared a certain lack of composure. He pushed hands into his pockets, clenched his jaw and tried to balance the forces of disbelief and horror that were assaulting him. After a moment, he set his mind upon a course of action. "Excuse me, Balearic," he murmured, and he set off across the square towards the Governor's Palace.

"Hey!" Carian leapt over the fountain's rim and sloshed across the plaza to catch up with Raine. "*Hey!*" The pirate snared him by the sleeve so that he had to stop and face him. "Just where're do you think you're going, poppet? I thought we were here to find a Healer for Birdie?"

Raine exhaled a long sigh. "No doubt Balearic will follow through on that promise. I have something I...need to do." He turned and headed on.

"So, we'll meet you back at camp then," Carian called after him, sounding annoyed.

Raine pushed on, barely cognizant of the pirate at all.

He had long suspected that Björn van Gelderan held all the answers—yea, he'd relentlessly accused the man of hoarding them like the proverbial jewels in a dragon's lair. Yet it was one thing to suspect such—for the accusation carried a heavy dose of remonstration and blame that felt righteous in the saying—and quite another to realize it had been entirely *true*.

All of the questions he'd been asking for so long...clearly there *were* answers. Somehow, Raine had fallen into an apathetic state about answers even existing. He'd just blamed Björn for having them without considering that he actually *did*. Meanwhile, many of the 'answers' he and Alshiba had decided upon had been naught but inventions, fabrications derived from their own failure to understand Björn's motivations and actions.

This latter realization brought to light an uncomfortable truth: so long as Raine could blame Björn for some problem or circumstance, he didn't himself have to be effective in addressing it. In essence, he could use his oath-brother's absence to justify all manner of his own failings. And had—*for three hundred years*.

That was a bitter pill, indeed.

It doesn't excuse what he's done. Yet this accusation was growing pale, weakened by truths that denied the integrity of Raine's invented explanations.

No, Raine was beginning to see—starting with Phaedor's cutting remarks before he was even willing to believe Malorin'athgul existed, and following through what he'd learned about Isabel and the other Mages—that there was a vast canyon of truth dividing what he and Alshiba didn't know and what Björn did.

Ruminating on these ill thoughts, Raine reached the palace and headed up the wide stairs leading to the entrance. The doors stood open, and men and women were flooding in and out, ostensibly setting up for the ball.

Raine made his way inside following four men who were laboring beneath an ice sculpture of a giant bird. He broke away as an imperious-looking woman in a black dress approached them.

Two corridors led to left and right, branching off the grand foyer. The left looked less crowded, so Raine headed that way and opened his mind to currents, listening, sifting…

Most people didn't realize their thoughts had force, or that the energy associated with the process of thought was naturally carried upon the currents of *elae*. They certainly didn't think about how an experienced *raedan* could glean their thoughts from the currents' flow, as like catching leaves in a net from the stream carrying them by. More often than not, Raine didn't need to use his truthreader's talent to delve into the minds of others, for they shouted their thoughts upon the tides of *elae*.

As he walked the long hall with his hands in his pockets and his eyes on the floor, Raine heard all of the myriad mental voices one might imagine on such a day: impatient thoughts, anxious thoughts, excited thoughts— *many* of these—but there were a select few mental voices he specifically listened for, voices he hadn't heard in centuries…voices he would know anywhere.

Eventually, one floated to him, though it was by far the last one he'd expected to hear.

Cristien Tagliaferro!

Cristien's mental voice was as unmistakable as the pain of hearing it was palpable, for Raine had shared minds with Cristien the way only two truthreaders might. Hearing Cristien's thoughts pierced Raine's heart. The bolt of recognition brought him to a breathless standstill in the middle of the corridor.

Cristien!

Of anyone, Raine had mourned Cristien's loss the hardest.

He swallowed against a sudden ill feeling in his stomach and pressed slowly on, following Cristien's energy up-current to the source, to the man.

He found him standing on the steps of a large gazebo, talking to a Shade. Cristien's curly brown hair hung in his eyes, as unkempt as ever, and his square jaw and cleft chin were in need of a shave, but he seemed otherwise unchanged. Every aspect of his lean form was as Raine remembered.

Behind Cristien, an orchestra was rehearsing while the conductor clapped the beat of a complicated rhythm that the flutists seemed to be having trouble keeping up with.

Cristien and the Shade both turned to Raine the instant he stepped out of the loggia into the sun. Cristien's colorless eyes pinned upon him, and Raine realized that his own troubled thoughts had likely been speaking louder than he'd intended.

For a moment Cristien stood transfixed. Then he launched towards Raine and grabbed him into an embrace.

"Epiphany bless the day!" Cristien laughed as he hugged Raine close and clapped him on the back with verve. "Have you *finally* seen the light?"

"Cristien," Raine said quietly, the hurt too plain in his tone.

Immediately the truthreader pulled away and took Raine by the shoulders instead. "Ah, *Cephrael*, no…" He searched Raine's eyes with his own, and gaining understanding, dropped his arms and took a step back. "My, what a hurricane of thoughts. What are you doing here then, Raine? After all this time?"

Raine shook his head. "I don't really know…yet."

"I see," Cristien said, though he clearly didn't.

Raine felt like he was staring at a ghost. A vast emptiness spread inside him where delight should've blossomed; rather than rejoicing in the certain knowledge that his dear friend lived, instead he only felt betrayed.

Cristien's brow furrowed, and his manner grew cool. "It was quite impossible, you know," he said, backing further off to stand his own ground, an invisible line now drawn between their loyalties, between the conflicting truths they each held inviolate.

Raine held his friend's gaze, two pairs of diamondine eyes pinned on each other from very different faces: one square and masculine, with deep-set eyes and a poet's sensuous mouth; the other softly handsome but tormented beyond measure. "What was impossible?" Raine inquired tightly.

"Contacting anyone." Cristien pressed his lips into a line. "In the early days the realm was too unstable for communication with Alorin. *Deyjiin* roamed freely here, wreaking havoc. It took the better part of half a century to cleanse the realm of it. And by then? What mercy to tell anyone, even had I the wherewithal to rejoin their lives? Things lost could never be regained. Everyone I'd known and loved had mourned me and moved on five decades in the past." He shook the hair from his eyes with a practiced toss of his head and implored Raine with his gaze. "It was a new world by then, a new time. Life moved on without me, Raine."

Some of us did not.

Cristien shot him a tormented look, too keen to Raine's mind for even unspoken thoughts to go unheard, even after all the time that separated their friendship.

Raine regarded him gravely. He had a thousand questions. Disappointingly, his pettiest one made it to the forefront first. "Were you always sworn to him, Cristien?" It sounded a bitter question, full of hurt.

"Raine, that's not fair."

"Cristien Tagliaferro sits upon the Council of Nine," said a voice from beside them, and Raine tore his eyes away from Cristien's to view the Shade standing there. "So has it always been, so will it always be."

Raine looked back to Cristien, who seemed dismayed.

"You don't recognize me, do you?" the Shade asked Raine.

Holding Cristien's gaze again, Raine said heatedly, "I confess my attention is fixed on another."

"I am Anglar."

That got Raine's attention. For a moment he stood in stunned silence, just staring, but then he recognized Anglar's features, albeit now encased in unearthly chrome. "*How?*" Raine was suddenly desperate to understand. "Anglar, they said you fell at the Citadel. Why…*this?*" and he waved nebulously at the man, wearing a horrified expression.

"There is much you don't know about the Battle of the Citadel," Anglar's Shade replied in that solemn, staid manner all Shades seemed to possess. "I made a choice then that cost me my life. The First Lord offered me a different path, and I took it."

"Anglar is the governor of Renato," Cristien advised quietly, still clearly as upset to see Raine as he was to see Cristien. "We…" He dropped his gaze for a moment and then lifted diamondine eyes back to Raine, suddenly resolute. "We both sit upon Björn's council. So has it been for longer than I care to recall."

"Even before the war." Raine felt bereft as he stared at his friend. That they had shared so much with one another, yet never this secret…it was a crushing blow.

"Why did you come here, Raine?" Cristien frowned with concern and consternation both. "Were you looking for me?"

"I didn't know you lived." Raine felt like the entire world was floating away, like there was nothing to hold onto, no truth to ground him. "I was just listening for a voice I recognized and I knew the governors were…" but he couldn't finish. Instead he fixed Cristien with an agonized look. "I never expected to hear your thoughts."

"*Raine…*"

Suddenly the numb disbelief vanished, replaced by fury. "*Damn it,* Cristien, *why?* Why did you side with him? Why then? Why *now?* What really happened at the Citadel?"

Cristien regarded him with sorrow and obligation equally consuming his thoughts; the force of these feelings cascaded into Raine's awareness such that he was required to confront them too. "I'm not the one you need to hear this from, Raine." Cristien shifted his gaze to his hands. "Truly, would you believe anything I told you?"

Raine clenched his jaw. Cristien was right. He wasn't likely to trust anything the man said now.

"Who would you believe?" Cristien looked back to him and beseeched Raine's understanding with his gaze, with the thoughts he willed the other to hear. They were two truthreaders, each viewing a different side of the same truth.

Raine looked away. He knew what Cristien expected. He just wasn't sure if he was willing to do it. He turned his diamondine gaze on the Shade instead. "Anglar, you were at the Citadel. Will you tell me nothing of what transpired?"

"It is not my truth to tell," the Shade said simply.

Raine looked back to his friend, disappointed but unsurprised. "Very well. Good-bye then, Cristien, Anglar." He turned to leave the way he'd come.

"Raine—*wait.*" Raine could feel the remorse in Cristien's thoughts; the truthreader pushed desperate memories towards him, that he might remember their years of camaraderie and trust.

"No…it is as you said, Cristien." Raine clenched his jaw and started off again. "Things lost can never be regained."

Raine took his time getting back to the gypsy camp, walking Renato's streets as twilight came and dimmed to dusk, as the city came alive in the night. He walked down boulevards crowded with masked revelers, with two-headed dragons and mythological gods, with fabled creatures and famous heroes—countless masks, each carrying their own tale, either imagined or true. Yet on that night, for the First Lord's Masquerade, all stories were real, each mask brought to brief but vivid life by the reveler who wore it, acting out the role it was meant to represent, a single face sometimes symbolic of much.

Raine walked with his shoulders hunched and his chin tucked towards his chest, hands in his pockets and Björn's coin clenched in his fist. And he thought of Cristien.

They might've been brothers they had once been so close. Their years in the Sormitáge had united them through trial and toil, as much as through the laughter of long nights and even longer examinations. Raine had always believed that Cristien was the stronger talent, though in truth they'd been well matched. But Cristien had been adventurous, *courageous*, willing to explore philosophies and ideas that Raine found uncomfortable—mainly because they were too afield of empirical truths, too close to the purity of faith. He recalled being startled when Björn had asked him to take the Vestal oath instead of Cristien. But now he understood better.

Since the beginning. Raine shook his head bitterly. Cristien had been Björn's since they left the Sormitáge together in search of their own paths.

But if Björn didn't trust me into his council even then, why ask me to Vestal the realm?

So much about Björn van Gelderan fell beyond Raine's ken.

Perhaps that's why. Because I never could understand Björn—not then, perhaps not ever.

But Dagmar and Alshiba? Why hadn't Björn trusted them?

Raine was still sifting through these painful questions when he reached the gypsy camp. The firelight drew him as truly as the music and cheering, and he passed through the ring of wagons to find the camp alive with dancing and merriment. The pirate seemed to be at the center of the frivolity, cavorting like a long-legged spider, his waist-length hair wild as he danced. Its wavy strands, floating on the wind, mimicked the smoke rising from the campfires.

For a moment as he watched Carian, Raine wished he might find such release himself. To be able to let go of these many threads, to find peace within, no matter what condition the world at large.

But he couldn't. The hundreds of threads he held in his mind connected a vast pattern that as yet remained unclear. He honestly feared if he released any one thread, the entire pattern would unravel, and everything he'd worked so hard to gather and understand would be lost.

"You are the Vestal?"

Raine turned to find a woman standing beside him. In the joyous noise of the night, he hadn't heard her approaching. "I am Raine D'Lacourte."

"I am Daria." She pulled her long grey braid across one shoulder and smiled. Deep wrinkles crinkled the corners of her blue eyes, while longer ones connected cheekbones to jaw, but her countenance held a certain purity. Raine imagined she might've been beautiful once—she still was, in truth, for beauty had many expressions of form. "The Islander said I should tell you what I saw of your companion," Daria said. "Would you come?" and she motioned him towards a wagon.

Raine realized she had to be the Healer that Carian had been seeking on Gwynnleth's behalf. "Of course—please, lead on."

He followed her inside the wagon and by the light of a hanging lantern saw Gwynnleth's sleeping form. She looked frail in her slumbering state, her harshly angular features seeming fragile, like a tiny bird lying helpless. So strangely out of character.

Raine suddenly welcomed the chance to be concerned about someone else, to ease off the clenching hold he had on his thoughts, dwelling on personal misfortune. It galled him to realize he'd been so self-absorbed. "What can you tell me of her condition?"

Daria knelt at Gwynnleth's bedside. She brushed a strand of fiery auburn hair from the avieth's brow and looked gently upon her. "She rests in an in-between. I have heard of it happening but have never before seen it—few third-stranders come to T'khendar, and those that do have often been warned."

"Warned? Of what?"

"That they cannot take the form here."

"Ah…" Suddenly an explanation began to take shape.

"The way it's been described to me is that the third strand is tied to Alorin differently from the other strands. That is, Gwynnleth's two forms are somehow supported by Alorin's pattern alone. Though T'khendar shares many of Alorin's formative patterns, it doesn't share the third strand's. Thus, when your avieth friend attempted to take the form, her consciousness had to reach all the way back to Alorin to find the necessary supportive pattern. The distance was too great—the forces between too powerful to overcome. That has created a limbo, where she remains."

Raine had surmised much of this from Daria's initial statement, but how to help Gwynnleth? He frowned at the avieth's sleeping form, thinking of all that she had done at his behest, risking herself on his order alone. "What can be done for her?"

Daria shook her head. "It is beyond my skill. I've shored up her pattern as best I could, and the Islander, your friend, has been seeing that she takes water and broth, but any help for her—if she can be helped at all, my lord—will only be found in Niyadbakir."

Niyadbakir.

The name remained always on the fringes of his thoughts. Niyadbakir, where Björn awaited. And Isabel. Where answers might be found if he was willing to pierce the veil of his own failures.

Well, he had certainly started that process, however unwillingly.

He yanked his thoughts back to the moment and gave the Healer a grateful look. "Thank you, Daria. I would offer you coin—"

"The Islander already compensated me, my lord," she told him kindly, making Raine wonder what that compensation could've entailed. Standing, she nodded to him and then to Gwynnleth. "The Lady's blessing upon her."

"Yes, thank you."

As Daria was leaving, Raine sat down on the bunk across from Gwynnleth. He was still sitting there resting elbows on his knees when the pirate came in several hours later.

"Oh," Carian said. "Hello, I guess."

Raine looked up. "You've been taking care of her," he said, feeling wretched and deplorably irresponsible.

Carian cast him a sooty look. "Well, one of us bloody had to. I reckoned it wasn't going to be you, seeing as how you vanished within minutes of arriving here and were gone all night, while I meanwhile tried all manner of resuscitation—in her best interests, mind."

"You're right to be wroth with me, Carian." Raine exhaled a heavy sigh. "I've been extraordinarily selfish since we arrived. I thank you deeply for caring for her when all I could think about was myself and my own troubles."

Carian looked a little caught off guard by this apology. He shook his hair out of his eyes and spied the Vestal suspiciously, as if waiting for some justification to follow. "You are awfully morose these days," he said then by way of cautious agreement.

Raine gave him a rueful look. "When we arrived here, I thought it might perhaps be the worst imaginable fate. I see now that assumption was a drastic understatement."

Carian snorted. He threw himself down onto the bunk, dislodging Raine from his position at the other end. "You know," he said, crossing his ankles. He slipped hands behind his head. "I know how you feel about the Fifth Vestal, but aside from whatever happened with the wars and so forth—which may or may not be Raine's truth, if you'll pardon the expression—what's your bloody oath-brother done since then that's so damned terrible?"

Raine gave him a pained look.

"No, I'm serious." Carian swung himself up to sitting and stared hard at the Vestal, who stood now in the shadows leaning against the wall. "Björn's got a bonny gig here, mate—maybe not as nice as a life on the account, but the people here are happy. The realm is at peace, and Adepts are training in Niyadbakir—did you know that?"

Raine shook his head, though it didn't surprise him. Björn would want an Adept army to replace the one Malachai's war had decimated. "You've been listening to Balearic's stories, I take it," he observed quietly.

"Hey, there's two sides to every coin," the pirate returned unrepentantly. He stretched out on his cot again. "And I ain't so sure the side everybody sees in Alorin is the right one."

Neither am I, Raine caught himself thinking—to his intense dismay.

He retrieved Björn's coin from his pocket and stared at it on his palm. Sometimes the coin seemed a foreign and intensely insulting object that had no right existing at all, but more often it was starting to encapsulate all that Björn was to him: an enigma, a closed door with no handle and no way to peer inside to glimpse what lay behind; an elliptical puzzle with neither entry nor exit to its logic, encouraging naught but one's own theories, most of them impossibly wrong.

And despite the many conjectures surrounding it, the coin lay remote, resolute, and utterly indifferent. The coin cared not if others maligned it or smothered it with praise; it simply remained inviolate, a steadfast representation throughout the ages, never altering from its original purpose even to defend that purpose to others. Nothing affected it. *Nothing* changed it!

Impossible! No man can be so immutable!

But Björn was.

The very recognition of this stabbed Raine with agonizing force, for this simplicity lay at the heart of a truth he could no longer deny: they had *presumed*, guessed, formed their own theories and declared them as fact. But they had never *known*.

Oh, to be sure, the evidence had implied one thing; yet their hearts had told them another—especially in the beginning. Raine and Alshiba had spent *eons* fighting with themselves and each other over what they would—what they *could*—bring themselves to believe about Björn. Raine knew that Alshiba still denied many of the 'truths' they'd supposedly agreed upon between them.

As the centuries had drawn endlessly on without answers, without solutions to the multitude of problems they faced in Alorin, Raine and Alshiba had lost faith—Raine had never had much to begin with—and they'd chosen to side with the bare facts, no matter how impossible they seemed. They couldn't be blamed for that...could they?

But Raine was starting to believe that they could.

The pirate snoring loudly drew the Vestal's gaze and offered a momentary respite from the agony of these thoughts. He pocketed Björn's coin and turned down the lamp as he left, envying the pirate his rest.

For he knew with certainty that he would find none of it that night.

NINETEEN

"Never ask a god for patience. He will teach it to you."
— Zafir bin Safwan al Abdul-Basir, Emir of the Akkad

T'KHENDAR'S FESTIVAL OF Adendigaeth began twelve days before the solstice, launching at sundown with the First Lord's Masquerade. As the sun was setting the heavens to flame, Ean stood beneath the towering arches of Björn's grand ballroom, looking out across a vast sea of masked revelers. It seemed the entire realm had convened there to celebrate, though Julian had told him that each city in T'khendar would hold its own celebration.

It took him the better part of an hour to find Julian—an unnerving hour spent inwardly grimacing as people he'd never met inexplicably pressed their hands together and bowed to him, just as Julian had bowed to Ramu.

"Ean!"

The prince turned with relief at the sound of Julian's voice. The lad came towards him wearing a deep crimson coat of velvet and matching pants. His fair hair had been tangled around sprigs of the darkest holly, and his mask was that of an older man with tiny horns extending from his forehead.

"Welcome, o Holly King." Ean recognized the familiar likeness at once. "And will you battle the Oak King tonight?"

"Not if I can help it. His name is Ferdinand, and he's a good deal stronger at swords than I am. Here—have some wine." Julian handed Ean a goblet. "Have you seen the First Lord yet?"

Ean shook his head.

"Raine's truth, his costume is creepy." At Ean's curious look, the lad nudged him. "Come, I'll show you."

The prince followed Julian through the crowd of masked faces, noting costumes that ranged from traditional—honoring the solstice theme—to extreme, representing impossible creatures or mythological gods. Here and there he took note of a particularly ornate headdress or costume, but mostly he just took in the scene in broad slashes of brilliant color.

Ean didn't know whose idea his own costume had been—he certainly wouldn't have picked it for himself.

Baldur. He knew the legend, which was a favorite of the Danes. He wondered if Dagmar had somehow arranged...but he couldn't see the Second Vestal choosing him to represent the handsome and much beloved son of two gods who was murdered by his brother and then resurrected by his father.

Still, the costume itself was gorgeous. Ean's black velvet doublet was worked all over with sparkling crystal spirals, and he wore a diamond-encrusted mask of similar black and silver swirls. In one hand, he carried a spear tipped in mistletoe, the weapon his godly brother Hodur had been tricked into using to slay him.

After trekking from one side of the vast ballroom to the other, Julian finally stopped Ean with a hand to his chest. "Look—there he is!"

The First Lord wore a jeweled sapphire coat and a silver mask similar in nature to his Shades. He stood talking to a man Ean identified from his silvering hair as Markal Morrelaine, though the fearsome horned mask he wore would otherwise have made it impossible to tell his identity. It wasn't until Björn turned to someone behind him that Ean realized the god he was portraying.

Ianus. The Two-Faced God.

Indeed, as Björn turned to speak to someone else, the silver face on the back of his head picked right up in conversation again with Markal.

Ean took half a step backwards.

"I know—it gets you right here, doesn't it!" A grinning Julian pushed a hand to his stomach, just below his ribcage.

Julian had the right of it. Seeing both faces talking at once was both disturbing and morbidly fascinating.

"Of course, it's the perfect costume." Julian veritably oozed that odd combination of awe mixed with disgust. "Ianus is the ancient Cyrenaic god of beginnings and endings—you know, their version of Cephrael. He's associated with doors and gates and the beginnings of a journey. In some legends, they speak of him as being able to see the past and the future, but the dominantly accepted view is that those concepts are part of Epiphany's domain. Still, a great costume, you must admit."

"Unquestionably." Ean found the two talking silver faces perversely mesmerizing. *How does he* do *that?*

Then a flash of fire caught his eye, and Ean forgot all about the two-faced god.

He saw a fiery, feathered crest cascading back from a crimson head as the Phoenix moved through the crowd, and beneath the mask... The Phoenix's beak extended down to a graceful point that hovered over Isabel's nose, just below a crimson blindfold. Rubies, citrines and garnets encrusted her silk gown—fire captured and bound to her will—and an ornate jeweled collar hung around her neck, sparkling in time with dazzling earrings of yellow diamonds.

Ean stood riveted by Isabel's presence. He had eyes for no one and nothing else.

"By Cephrael's Great Book," Julian murmured appreciatively. "She's something, isn't she?"

Isabel stopped about ten paces away from the staring boys to greet her brother. As she turned her back to Ean, he saw gilded feathers braided among her long chestnut hair.

"Why isn't she with anyone?" he asked Julian, even though the very idea of Isabel being with another man filled him with dread.

Julian cast him a sidelong look. "They say she's loved only one man in all her life."

Ean's breath stuck in his throat. "Who? Is he here?"

"That would be something, if he was." Julian seemed to be taking perverse amusement in the stricken look on Ean's face. "He died three hundred years ago. He's famous though. His name was Arion Tavestra. He was one of the First Lord's three generals."

Ean started breathing again. *If he's dead, then at least I have a chance.*

"Well, go on." Julian nudged Ean off. "Get it over with. She'll either love you or laugh at you. Might as well find out before you waste any more time pining over her."

Ean gave him a dark look. "I'm not pining."

"Drooling then," Julian corrected with a grin.

Fixing him with a sooty stare, Ean straightened his shoulders and headed purposefully towards the group that was Isabel, Markal and Björn. The First Lord saw him at once and held open one hand to receive him.

"Ah, Ean. Welcome. I applaud your choice in costumes. I trust our modest fête is to your liking."

Ean looked at the thousands of people eating, drinking and making merry and wondered what a fête that wasn't 'modest' would look like to the Vestal. "It is beyond words, First Lord."

Björn turned to his sister. "Isabel, have you had the pleasure of making the acquaintance of our newest arrival?"

She looked at Ean and yet did not, for clearly her eyes were covered with the crimson blindfold, but just the recognition of her attention came as a heady draught. "Ah yes," she murmured with the quirk of a smile, "he spent some time staring at me from the ramparts, I believe." Her voice was honey, liquid light; it had an ineffable tone that drew emotion in its wake.

"Well, that's nearly a meeting," Björn noted amiably. "Ean val Lorian, may I present my sister, Isabel."

Wearing the most devious shadow of a smile, Isabel extended her gloved fingers towards Ean.

He took them and pressed a chaste kiss upon the back of her hand. Though her eyes were tantalizingly veiled from him, he had the feeling she was watching him all the same.

"Excuse us but a moment," Björn said, and he and Markal moved away into the crowd.

"What may I offer you, my lady?" Ean asked.

One corner of her lips lifted in a delicious half-smile. "What have you to offer, my lord?"

My heart and soul in a vial to wear around your neck. "Would the lady like wine? Something to eat? Shall I escort you somewhere, or merely stand here within the shadow of your beauty and admire you?"

"Mmm," she murmured, thinking over her options. "Any of those sound delightful, but I think I must choose the first."

For half a second, Ean was sure she meant to reference his unspoken thought. "Wine then," he managed and began looking around for a steward. He was loath to leave her side even for a second; fortunately stewards were plentiful, and he quickly waved one over. "White or red, my lady?"

"Red is the lady's favorite," she murmured with her voice so throaty and inviting.

Ean chose a goblet for Isabel and placed it into her hand. Gently he closed her fingers around the stem.

"Thank you, my lord," she purred.

Mindful of her comfort, Ean looked around and spied a bench. What made it most ideal was that it was outside on the patio and away from the larger crowd. "There is a bench in the garden that seems to be waiting for us," he suggested. "Will you sit, my lady?"

"If you will but guide the way, my lord." She lifted her hand as he'd seen her do with Markal, and it was with immense pleasure that Ean placed his arm beneath her outstretched hand.

As they walked towards the towering doors, which stood open to admit the evening breeze, Ean felt so heady he might've been treading on starlight. He couldn't explain his emotional response to Isabel, and he didn't care to. He simply knew his place was at her side.

Finding the bench, Ean helped her sit upon it. "May I join you, my lady?"

"Please do, your Highness," she said with a secretive little smile.

Oh, to know what secret thoughts that crimson veil protects! "Please…don't call me that," the prince said as he lowered himself beside her.

"Then what shall I call you?"

Husband. "I am Ean."

"I am Isabel."

He still had her hand in his. She seemed willing to let him keep it, and since he was quite unwilling to let it go, the arrangement suited them both.

"Isabel," he said, gazing upon her, "you are a vision."

"As are you," she said. "A perfect Baldur."

"I doubt that very much," he disagreed with a smile.

She gave him a skeptical look by way of a delicately arched eyebrow—truly, even partly hidden by the crimson silk, her face was enormously expressive. "Have you met Baldur, Ean?"

"No, madam."

"Then it isn't fair to contradict me, is it?"

Ean chuckled. "I suppose not." As the night's quiet descended, he gazed upon her and a verse came to him. He spoke it as it came:

From the ashes of my heart
Rising sweetly stirs the sleeping dragon
The beast that roared unending,
Til fires extinguished
Now wakened by the Phoenix
Love reborn.

Ean flashed a sheepish grin. "I'm sorry," he laughed, feeling enormously foolish. "I don't know where that came from."

But Isabel smiled with delight. "I don't remember your being this charming the last time."

"I..." Caught slightly off guard by her comment, Ean offered quickly, "I suppose I...learned something in death."

"That is as it should be. Do we not celebrate this night the imminent opening of the Extian Doors and the renewal of all souls?"

"A myth, surely," he posed. "Parable at best."

"Yet all myths are symbolic of some truth," she pointed out, "else they would not endure the ages."

Ean gave her a soft smile. "Your wisdom humbles me, my lady."

Silence descended again as he gazed at her, but the silence was like a soundless caress. Ean might've let it last forever, with the night a blanket binding them together, but she said, "You may ask the question on your mind. I will answer if I can."

Ean hadn't realized he was desirous of anything beyond her attention, but the moment she said it, the question materialized. So he did as she bade him. "Why do you wear the blindfold, Isabel?"

"Because of a promise I made once," she answered, and though her tone remained light and gentle, he knew this was all she was going to say about it.

"Another question if I may?" He gave her fingers a squeeze, and she nodded for him to proceed. "Perhaps you can help me understand a most vexing problem."

"What problem is that?"

"One that occupies my consciousness more completely than any I've ever before encountered. I know not whence these feelings come, but they consume me. I cannot understand them."

"Hmm…" She pressed her goblet demurely to her lips and sipped her wine. "Would this be a question for Epiphany's Prophet or for the woman Isabel?" Her eyes were temptingly hidden, the crimson blindfold so provoking.

Yet there was something about her smile, something in the tilt of her head or perhaps in her presence alone, that made her expression clear to him. "This is a question most assuredly for Isabel."

"Then I must tell my lord that Isabel, being a mere woman, knows of a man's feelings only what he has confessed to her."

Ean lifted her satin-gloved hand and held it to his lips. "There is a woman…a devastatingly beautiful woman. She is the air I starve to breathe, the force that drives me forward. I cannot remove her from my thoughts. In the first moment I saw her, she reached in and claimed my heart for her own; and any time I'm parted from her, it feels that my heart is being torn in two."

"That sounds serious, my lord." She gave him a mischievous smile. "Perhaps we should seek the services of a Healer."

"Alas, I fear there is no cure for this ailment, my lady."

The quirk broadened to a grin that was unmistakably suggestive. "Surely we can find *something* that will do the trick." Her tone hinted of such lustful visions that Ean felt himself heat beneath them. The silence became hot, fervent even. She couldn't really be suggesting…

"Ah, Ean, there you are."

Ean looked up to see the First Lord approaching. Having doffed his two-faced mask for the moment, Björn took one look at a red-faced Ean and shifted his gaze to his sister. "Isabel, what have you done to the boy? He looks a bit…peaked."

She held out her hand blithely to him, and Björn obediently went to help her stand. "We were only talking," she said with an innocent smile.

Björn looked dubious. "Do not let the guise of innocence fool you,

Ean," he advised then, shifting his gaze to him. "My sister is as artful as they come."

"Yet never so artful as thee, dearest brother," she returned, but there was only adoration in her smile.

"Shall I—" Björn began, but she waved him off.

"I will find my own way. Until tomorrow, Ean." And then she passed gracefully through the doors to be enveloped by the crowd.

Björn gazed after her wearing a thoughtful frown. Ean felt strangely allied with him as they watched her departing.

"My sister," the Vestal mused. "She is predictably…unpredictable. Well, Ean," he looked back to the prince as Isabel's headdress moved out of sight, "there is someone else I'd like you to meet—if you think you're up for it."

Ean blushed slightly at Björn's dry tone. He tugged his jacket down and squared his shoulders. "Of course, First Lord."

Björn cast him a sidelong glance full of amusement. "So…what do you know of Markal Morrelaine?"

"Julian has told me a little of him, my lord."

"Markal is one of my generals," Björn explained as they moved back inside. "There is no finer wielder among us. He is *na'turna*, a non-Adept. When he began his training, he couldn't even sense the lifeforce. Over the years, through diligence and determination, he worked his way up the ranks. Now, as in his own day, his technique is unmatched." He glanced to Ean. "I know of no one better suited to instruct you in the complex art of Patterning."

Ean thought of Julian's lament over Master Morrelaine's weighty proverbs and laws of patterning learned in Old Alæic and somewhat dreaded meeting the man. That Ean had so often seen him escorting Isabel didn't help.

They found Markal among a collection of women dressed as nymphs, lecturing to them on the differences between the Wildling races of Alorin. "Markal," Björn said by way of greeting, then added to the others, "Do forgive my interruption, ladies, but I must speak with the general a moment."

"Of course, First Lord," several of them murmured, and they all bobbed curtsies and moved off together. Ean couldn't help but notice that they seemed a bit relieved.

Markal held his mask under one arm like a riding crop and looked less than enthusiastic about participating in the fête in any capacity. For all his silver-grey hair and weathered features, he remained undeniably robust, broad of chest and well-muscled beneath his gilded tunic. He immediately fixed a piercing gaze on Ean.

"Ah, if it isn't Baldur. So *you* were the one observing lessons from the Court Wall."

"Markal Morrelaine, may I present Ean val Lorian," Björn said pleasantly. He looked to Ean. "I will leave you two to make your plans together." He nodded to the both of them and left.

Ean felt unhappily abandoned. He looked back to Markal, who was frowning ponderously at him.

"Um…" Ean said.

"Dawn," Markal grunted. "In the practice yard where you wasted so much time ogling the Prophetess." He spun on his heel and vanished into the crowd.

Not wanting to get off on the wrong foot with a man renowned throughout the realm for legendary works of the fifth strand, Ean was waiting in the practice yard when the first rays of morning brightened the grey sky. Markal arrived only moments thereafter, as if riding the dawn tide.

He pitched Ean a coil of rope, which the prince caught out of the air. Markal also held a coil of rope. He took one end of it and slung the other towards Ean, and as the rope uncurled to its furthest point, it went taut. When Markal lowered it, he held a rowan staff. He set the staff at his sandaled feet and settled Ean a doleful look. "What are we doing here?"

Immediately puzzled by the question, Ean replied, "Learning to… pattern?"

"No!" Markal spiked the stone tiles with his staff.

Ean started at the resounding *clap*, which echoed in the empty court. "We're *not* learning to pattern?"

"One doesn't merely 'learn to pattern,'" Markal said imperiously. "So with the danger of repeating myself, I ask you again, why are we here?"

Ean frowned at him. "Am I supposed to know this already, because no one gave me any—"

"You are supposed to use that gelatinous mass of flesh you call a brain to *think* about the question, Ean val Lorian."

Holding Markal's gaze, Ean began shifting the rope through his hands, uncoiling and re-coiling. He recalled Julian's comments about Markal's many 'alabaster lessons,' as he'd come to think of them, and tried to distill his answer down to its most basic. "We're here…" he said after thinking for a moment, "because the realm is out of balance and someone has to do something about it."

"Not someone," Markal said, his brown-eyed gaze intense and not entirely friendly. "*You.*"

"Right," Ean said. "Me. And you're going to teach me how."

"No!" Markal pounded the stones again, and again the echo accosted Ean's ears. "You already *know* how," the wielder said disdainfully. "You have only to remember."

Ean was really trying hard to maintain his patience with the man. "Then you're going to…help me remember?"

"No!"

Ean rolled his eyes and sighed. "Might you just *tell* me what we're doing—"

Abruptly Markal lashed out with the staff, and the next thing Ean knew he was laid out on his back on the stones.

After he found his breath, he got up and leveled Markal a heated look while his backside smarted. "I get the idea we've been down this road before," Ean observed with admirable composure considering how desperately he wanted to wrap his hands around the man's throat.

Markal regarded Ean with all the joy of an opossum displaced from its den by a marauding bear.

Ean took his silence as affirmation. "So…" He leaned down and swept up the rope, coiling it in his hands again, allowing himself to imagine he would soon be using it to strangle his instructor. "Let's see if I'm catching on. Once upon a time, the great Markal Morrelaine was given the task of teaching one upstart young Adept who never studied, didn't know why he was there and ultimately failed—"

"Wrong *again*," Markal growled. "He was a brilliant student. He learned faster than any student I ever trained. He knew exactly what was needed of him, he studied within an inch of his life, and he still proceeded to go out and get himself killed."

"So you're being this asinine to protect me?"

Upon which utterance Ean found himself staring at the sky again. That time with a pounding headache.

When Ean had once more regained his feet, as well as a little more humility, Markal leaned on his staff, leveled the prince an incendiary stare and said, "You don't have to play the role you have played in the past."

"You don't have to treat me as though it's a foregone conclusion that I will!" Ean rubbed the knot forming on the back of his head and glared at the man under his eyebrows. "People can change."

"Not in this, not you," Markal lectured. "That aspect of your inherent nature which most goes against my inherent nature will never change. You are reckless, impetuous and foolhardy. You always have been and always will be. It's why she fell in love with you, though why that makes you so attractive to her I will never understand."

Ean got the idea Markal was no longer talking about him but about some long-ago dead version of him, which may or may not have any relevance to who he was now. Or at least, so he hoped.

Ean held his gaze. "Then where do we go from here?"

"You can keep landing on your back until something important breaks," Markal said, motioning at the stones with his staff, "or you can answer my question."

"Fine." Ean shoved both hands to his sides and tried to figure out what in Tiern'aval the man expected him to say.

"No!" Markal gave another ear-splitting slam of his staff. "Don't try to tell me what you think I want to hear!"

"You're no truthreader," Ean retorted with a black look. "How do you know what I'm thinking?"

"Because *I know you*." Markal emphasized each word by jabbing the end of his staff towards Ean. "*You* think we've just met. *You* think this is all new," and he opened one hand to the scene at large, "but who you were and who you are remain the same. One life to the next, all that changes are the *choices* you make. Your talents, your inherent flaws, even the skills you've mastered in one life—these you carry with you, Ean val Lorian. Sometimes you remember them and they become useful skills again. Sometimes they elude you and must be relearned, but *your basic nature* endures the centuries. *That is what is truly immortal.*"

Ean clenched his teeth and glared at the man. "Fine," he said again. He really did wish he remembered, because if what Markal said was true, then he was certain he must've known a really good way to knock Markal off *his* feet. "So I'm here to remember," he began thinking aloud, "but you're not here to help me do that. So *we* then must be *here* for a different purpose altogether." He glanced at Markal to see how he was doing, but the man just glared at him like a black-eyed badger.

'*...it means that no matter how complex things appear, there is a simple truth that, once found, will dissolve the complexity.*' Julian's explanation of the alabaster lesson seemed applicable.

The truth was, Ean didn't really know why he was there. He'd made a choice and that choice brought him to T'khendar. He believed he had a role to play in a larger conflict, but he wasn't sure what that role was, or even if he really understood the larger conflict.

"I don't know," he finally said.

Markal cast him a suspicious look. "You don't know what?"

Ean shrugged. "I guess I don't really know why I'm here. I could guess at the answer, but I don't really know." He expected another lambasting, but Markal merely grunted.

"At last, we reach the simplicity. And the subject of today's lesson. The First Law of Patterning: *KNOW the effect you intend to create.* Now..." and he pointed at Ean's hands. "You hold a rope."

Ean looked down at the braided coils. "So it would seem."

"Therein lies your defense."

It was all the warning Ean had. In the next moment, Markal's staff came sweeping for his feet. Ean jumped back. Markal swung again, on the advance. Ean skipped away.

Abruptly Markal straightened and settled his staff at his toes. "I did not say dodge and dart like a jackrabbit. You have a means of defending yourself. Use it." He swung his staff with sudden ferocity.

Ean veered back just in time to prevent its connecting with his chin. "*Shade and darkness!*" He glared hotly at the man. "Are you trying to kill me?"

Markal replied by swinging his staff low to catch the back of Ean's calves and knock him down. He finished with a lightning-swift jab between the prince's shoulder-blades, and Ean was licking the stones.

Smarting all over, and especially in the area of his pride, Ean pushed himself to hands and knees, calves throbbing, his spine burning. He cast Markal a black glare. "What in Tiern'aval am I supposed to *do* with the rope?"

"That is for you to decide," Markal informed him critically.

Ean climbed back to his feet and slung the rope out in front of him. He thought about Julian's admonition not to wear his sword and wondered blackly if it was to protect Markal from a horde of mistreated students hell-bent on killing him.

Holding the rope in both hands, he tried to get a sense of what to do with it. His talent had only ever appeared in the unworking of patterns, never in the conceiving of them. A great many people had told him, however, that the ability to work them lay dormant within him, that he simply had to wake it.

"KNOW the effect you wish to create," Markal said again, darting at him.

Ean slung the rope in defense but only managed to get it stuck around the staff. Markal had him down three seconds later.

The morning continued in this vein.

By midday, Ean was stripped to his britches and sweating. His torso bore the marks of Markal's teaching—long red welts, bruises that were circular and puffy, bluish shadows along his ribs on both sides.

As Ean pushed up from the ground yet again, wondering for the umpteenth time why he bothered getting back to his feet yet certain that he would, even if it was just to spite the older man, Markal said, "You must KNOW the rope will stop the staff, Ean."

"Yes, so you've been saying," Ean grumbled. He'd tried a thousand different ways of envisioning the rope stopping the staff, but none of them had any effect. "I've been trying to—"

"*Try,*" Markal muttered. "Don't *try. Try* isn't KNOW. Know is a state of being. It is the aggregate of *certainty* over energy, space, matter, time and form. It is the exact existence of a thing—the fullness of its complete concept. It is KNOW!"

"Yes, but I don't know the pattern!" Ean snapped.

"The First Law doesn't say 'know the *pattern*,'" Markal returned scornfully. "The First Law says nothing about patterns."

The First Law doesn't say anything about beating up students with your staff either, Ean thought resentfully, but he kept this sentiment to himself.

"Again." Markal brandished his staff, relentless in his expectation. "You have to KNOW that the rope will stop the staff."

Frustrated, Ean snarled, "It's just a rope!"

"It's whatever you want it to be," Markal returned resolutely.

Two hours and at least thirty bruises later, Ean was still no closer to knowing how to make the rope stop the staff, but he had definitely decided that little else was going to be learned by letting Markal beat him to a pulp.

He'd seen the man turn the rope into the staff. Ean reasoned that if there was a pattern holding the staff in that form, he could as easily unwork it as work some new pattern on his own rope.

He set to searching for the pattern as soon as he happened upon the idea, and he found it almost at once.

The next time Markal came at him with the staff, Ean snared the pattern and unworked it with ease. The staff collapsed harmlessly back to rope. Ean gave him a triumphant look.

Markal straightened and began coiling the rope in his hand, leveling Ean a quiet, contemptuous stare. "I see you haven't changed. You have ever only resorted to one skill to solve your problems—an indolent and shiftless approach to the Art. I'm only surprised you let me beat you up half of the day before you used it." With that, he walked across the yard. "Tomorrow. Dawn." And he left without looking back.

Ean found his way to his rooms, smarting on the inside as much as out. Markal's sharp words of censure had unexpectedly wounded him. He'd never imagined being compared against the standard of his own misdeeds—ones he couldn't even remember, no less! How could he but make the same mistakes if it was so impossible to change his basic nature? Did that mean he was doomed to die yet again, no matter what the First Lord said about Balance?

Worse, he had honestly been trying for most of the day to do what Markal asked of him. He didn't know what he was doing wrong. He didn't know why it wasn't working, and he was just as disappointed in himself as

Markal obviously was. Raine's truth, the man was impossible! Every bit as insufferable as the zanthyr…but at least the zanthyr had been sort of nice to him.

Quit feeling sorry for yourself. Ean chastised himself with gritted teeth; yet that innocent, selfless part of him that had been honestly trying now felt hopelessly wounded. As he reached his rooms in shame, it crawled beneath the sideboard and refused to come out again, leaving Ean with only his bitter, self-absorbed side for company.

He found a hot bath waiting for him, and after an hour's soak, he'd managed to relieve some of the stiffness, but he knew tomorrow would be a painful repeat of today if he didn't have some brilliant realization between now and then.

Just as he stood to exit the tub, there came a knock on his door. Ean glanced towards the robe folded on a chair far across the room. "Just a moment," he called, climbing out of the tub.

The door opened and Ean turned, dripping. Isabel stood framed in the portal. "Am I interrupting?"

Ean skipped forward, grabbed up his robe and wrapped himself in it. Blindfold or not, Isabel gave him the impression that she could see perfectly well. "If you were hoping to catch me naked and unawares, my lady," he returned with the slightest flush, "your timing was a little off."

She smiled. "Was it?" She moved slowly into the room, her black staff leading the way. She wore a green gown that afternoon, with belled sleeves embroidered in silver ivy. A black silk scarf embraced her eyes like a jealous lover, its long folds left free to mingle with her lustrous chestnut hair.

"Markal mentioned you might be in need of a Healer," she said as she made her slow approach.

Gazing upon her, Ean felt suddenly as if a lost part of himself had returned. He no more understood these feelings of connection to Isabel than he could deny them. He simply stood still, letting the feelings wash over him, and drank in the sight of her.

Isabel stopped mere inches away. She set her staff on end on the floor and left it to stand freely in midair. Then she placed her palm on his damp chest. He tingled at her touch.

"Your pattern is definitely frayed. Shall I smooth it for you?"

"What would that entail?" Ean inquired breathlessly.

Isabel placed her other hand on his chest, and heat flooded Ean. "Isabel…" he whispered, closing his eyes.

"Shh…" She moved even closer, so they stood nearly in an embrace; only the width of her hands separated them. Ean watched his own chest rising and falling with his quickening breath. He wanted to rip off her blindfold and gaze into her eyes, but he also wanted to bed her with the blindfold on—*Dear Epiphany*, the things he envisioned them doing together…

"The healing goes faster when the subject's mind is less active," Isabel advised with a half-smile hinting on her lips.

"Whyever would I want that?"

She chuckled. "You do not fear the consequences of courting Epiphany's Prophet?"

"There is no fear I wouldn't face to stay forever at your side, Isabel." He startled himself in the pronouncement, but it startled him more to know he'd meant it.

"Hmm…" Her teasing smile was a delightful torment.

A heartbeat later, Ean felt the last of his pain easing and knew she'd completed her Healing. He grabbed her hands before she could remove them, pinning them instead against his skin, that he might know her touch just a few moments more.

She stood and let him maintain their silent contact. Finally, when the desire to seal his mouth upon hers and carry her to his bed was more than he could bear, Ean released her hands and exhaled a forceful breath, stepping back.

She gave him her smile as a parting kiss.

"When—" he asked with sudden desperation.

"Dinner," she murmured as she turned and took up her staff.

He watched her leave and close the door. Then he sagged into a near chair and pushed palms to his forehead. *Epiphany preserve me from this woman!*

For despite how baffling it seemed, what he'd said had been completely true. He knew there was no evil in the world he wouldn't face to spend his eternity with Isabel van Gelderan.

TWENTY

*"No move is made as doesn't affect every other. The game is played
upon the lake of time, casting ripples through the ages."*
— Ramuhárikhamáth, Lord of the Heavens

JUST AS EAN was about to put on his boots and head out to dinner,
another knock on his door disturbed the silence of his thoughts.
Hoping it was Isabel again, he opened the door instead to face a
Shade. It took him a precious few heartbeats to recognize Creighton.

"Ean!" the Shade grabbed him into a hug.

Ean was so startled to see him, and so disappointed in the same
moment that he hadn't been Isabel, that he stiffened within Creighton's
embrace.

The Shade withdrew from him at once. "I beg your pardon..." His
silver face betrayed his injury at Ean's unintended rebuff. "I shouldn't have
presumed, Ean. I just thought..."

His expression tore at Ean's heart. "Creighton, I didn't mean—"

But the Shade was already fading.

Ean stood in the threshold for a long time, cursing himself.

When he finally made it to dinner, his heart felt as heavy as
a stone lodged in his chest. While his rejection of Creighton had
been unintentional, he admitted he was still uncomfortable around
Creighton's Shade and couldn't bring himself to think of this...unearthly
representation as truly being his blood-brother.

They took dinner that evening in Björn's private garden, a lush habitat of soaring acacia trees, coconut palms and tropical flowers. The First Lord stood to receive Ean as a servant was showing him out onto the marble-paved patio. Ean noted that the table had been set for three.

"Welcome, Ean. Thank you for joining me tonight."

"I'm honored, First Lord," Ean replied, taking Björn's indicated seat. He cast an admiring gaze around. "This is a marvelous place."

"Thank you. This part of the mountain protects natural hot springs. The elms we'd planted were dying, but these tropicals, as you can see, have flourished." He sat back in his chair and gestured with his goblet, noting philosophically, "All living things cannot be forced into the same mold, regardless of how similar they appear. Creation is frenzied and diverse." He eyed Ean inquisitively then. "And how did your training go with Markal?"

"The man has it in for me," Ean muttered tactlessly, only to immediately regret his outburst. "Forgive me." He dropped his eyes with embarrassment. "That was churlish and uncalled for. My day has been... difficult."

Björn gave him a tolerant look. "No doubt this *is* exactly how it seems to you," he admitted. "Yet if that were true, if Markal cared but little, he would merely teach you as he does the others. They have an infinity of time in which to learn—lifetimes of study yet before them. You—*we*— don't have that luxury. You must relearn or remember as much as you can in the time allowed us, and unfortunately, such forgotten lessons are rarely recovered to our consciousness except out of dire necessity."

Björn settled him an even look, but there was no way to diminish the seriousness of his words. "Markal does what he does, Ean, because if there is a way for us to prevail in this endeavor—if there is a way for you to do this without sacrificing your life in the bargain—*this* training will lie at the base of it."

Ean heard these words and knew he spoke the truth, yet he still didn't know what 'this endeavor' actually encompassed. And he was too embarrassed—too certain that he *ought* to know this above all—to ask. He rested elbows on the marble table and sank his head into his hands. "There's so much I don't remember," he lamented miserably. "Why can't I remember?"

"The veil of death occludes your past," Björn said compassionately. "It was meant to be a mercy, this amnesia, to give us each a new start in the Returning. Most organisms learn through the process of death—their evolution through death and rebirth gives them sharper claws, tougher skin, stronger poison. But for the gift of immortal souls, humanity merely carries forward. We remain tied to the deeds of our past, still the unconditional effect of mistakes made ages ago. *We* haven't evolved, you see, and we cannot escape our choices, in this life or in the next."

Ean looked up at him with his head still resting in his hands. "*Can* we remember?"

"Certainly."

"How?"

"One merely must take ownership of—must claim, in effect—every action he has ever caused."

"Oh, is that all?" Ean grunted derisively and rested his forehead in his palms again. *Might as well say I should just decide to spontaneously combust. That would be easier to manage.*

"I did not say it would be easy," Björn advised, blue eyes twinkling, "only that it is not impossible."

Isabel arrived on the heels of this pronouncement, much to Ean's immense pleasure and relief. That night she wore a satin gown of the darkest sapphire, with a wide neckline that extended from shoulder to shoulder and revealed an enticing portion of her décolletage. Her lush hair was embellished with twisting braids and caught up with sapphire pins.

As always, the black silk blindfold separated her from Ean in a way that was deeply profound to him. Though he didn't understand how or why, he knew it represented an intimate connection—*their* connection. He knew this in the same way he'd known Björn was telling him the truth about having lived and died before...in the same way he'd recognized the Extian Doors. Yet he didn't know *how* he knew this, and it wasn't a subject he was ready to discuss with Isabel. The topic felt too tender, their budding relationship too new.

Ean and Björn both stood to receive Isabel, and the latter kissed her on both cheeks in welcome. "Sister," Björn murmured as he took her hand and guided her to her chair. "A ravishing choice of gowns. You do us great honor."

Isabel settled into her seat and smiled up at him as he released her hand. She looked to Ean, though how she knew so precisely where he

was—how she saw at all with the blindfold constantly across her eyes—
remained a mystery. "Feeling better, my lord?"

"Much, thanks to you," Ean replied, feeling a warm flush suffusing
him, the product of her attention.

Björn raised his goblet. "To my sister," he said, "a woman of many
talents."

Ean clinked glasses with him as Isabel decorously received their
admiration.

Björn waved an airy hand then, and servants appeared carrying trays
emitting a tantalizing combination of spicy fragrances.

Sensitive to Ean's troubled state of mind, Isabel kept the dinner
conversation light, chatting amiably of her work with Markal's students or
the ongoing Adendigaeth festival in the cities. The courses were prepared
and served perfectly, and Ean felt much restored by them.

When the table had been cleared and everyone was well sated, Isabel
stood, and both men rose with her. "Thank you for the lovely dinner,
brother of my heart."

Björn nodded, "As always, dear sister, your presence makes it more
than remarkable."

She smiled for his pleasure and announced then, "I wonder if I might
have an escort through the gardens? It is too nice an evening to forego
admiring them."

Ean jumped at the opportunity to fulfill her need. "It would be my
greatest pleasure, my lady."

"Why thank you, my lord." Isabel held out her hand in that delicate
way, and Ean moved swiftly around the table to place his arm beneath her
fingers.

Down into the garden they walked, passing among towering acacia and
their smaller counterparts, royal flame-trees with their brilliant orange-red
flowers. The night was balmy, a warmth aided by the presence of the near
hot springs, and the air came soft and fragrant with camellia, liliko'i fruit,
and jasmine. Stars peeked here and there through the high canopy, but for
Ean, nothing in the garden approached the glory of Isabel's smile.

"You are thoughtful tonight, my lord," she noted as they were walking
a path overgrown with tiny white flowers, each footstep releasing a flush
of fragrance.

"I felt very...inadequate today." It surprised him how easily he confessed to her. He couldn't have admitted such to Alyneri.

"In what way could you ever be inadequate?" she returned with a smile.

"No, I was quite a disappointment, even to myself. I knew what Markal wanted me to do, but I...I couldn't make *anything* happen. In the end...well, in the end, I gave up." He shook his head. "A poor showing all around."

"You were working with the First Law?"

"KNOW the effect you intend to create," he said despondently. "I tried so many different ways to make the rope stop the staff. Nothing worked. I don't know the pattern—"

"The pattern is not the issue."

"So Markal pointed out."

"Patterns are but one way, Ean," she advised then, her tone gentle but firm. "An Adept of a particular strand rarely needs to 'know' the pattern because he inherently *knows* the pattern. As in *knowing*—a conceptual understanding of *all* that it is: its energy, its material composition, its exact form, even its placement in space and time. Do you understand? Adepts *think in the patterns of their strand*. When you have no inherent connection to a particular strand of *elae*, *then* you must learn the pattern in order to compel that thing." She stopped and turned to him, placing her hand to cup his cheek tenderly. "But this is not the case for you."

He desired so much to press his lips into her palm, to take her in his arms, but he stood as stone and breathed in the scent of her and let her touch be enough...almost.

"Take the chemists of the Iluminari," she said by way of example. "They work with complicated mathematical formulae to achieve the perfect combination of powders to create the Fire Candles we will see exploding on the Longest Night. Without those equations to guide the chemists, the powders would not ignite. Yet the *drachwyr* might cause the same explosions by merely envisioning their occurrence as a child daydreams."

She placed her hand on Ean's chest, and he covered it tightly with his own. "If you were like Markal, with no inherent connection to *elae's* fifth strand, then yes, what he demands would be impossible without envisioning a pattern. But Ean...*you* work the fifth as an *Adept,* like the *drachwyr.* Fifth-strand patterns are ingrained in how you think. You need only remember how to think with them." She put both hands to his face and chided tenderly, "You must let yourself remember this."

Ean knew he couldn't remain there with her like that and not try to kiss her. Tension pulsed through him, wakening and heightening every sense so that he felt too alive, as though his very skin was aflame.

Letting out a measured breath, Ean took Isabel's hands from his face and held them between his own. Gazing at her hidden eyes, he confessed gravely, "Perhaps now that you have commanded it of me, Isabel, I can do so."

Her lips curled in a smile. "I don't remember you being this compliant the last time."

Ean released her hands but returned one to his arm and started them walking again. "Me either," he replied grimly. *For I remember nothing at all!*

Isabel chuckled. "So morose! I do remember this dramatic display of emotion being an enduring aspect of your nature. But see now, I believe you're going about it the wrong way," she added, returning them to the first topic and the source of Ean's angst. "The effect isn't the rope stopping the staff. That's the outcome. These are not interchangeable terms in Patterning."

Ean gave her a curious look. "Then what is the effect?"

"It is simpler than you have imagined. The effect is what you must do to the rope to make it *capable* of stopping the staff. *That* is the effect you're creating. The rope then has its own effect of stopping the staff. One concept, one cause, one effect. Balance takes care of the rest."

Her words stopped him in his tracks. He *had* been thinking about it the wrong way!

He imagined the game of Kings he'd been using so often to compare his experiences against. *Moving one piece can create a ripple effect.* A player makes one effect on his piece—moving it. But the piece thereafter has numerous effects on other pieces—one play that sets into motion an entirely new sequence of events, and even potentially changes the balance of the game.

He settled her an intense look. His very being was vibrating with the magnitude of his realization. "This is about making me into a Player, isn't it?"

Isabel nodded solemnly.

Ean felt his world shift, the resounding impact of which shuddered through him. "I know why I'm here," he breathed aloud, heady with the discovery. He leveled Isabel a look that conveyed the force of his gratitude and fastened his mouth upon hers, pulling her close. The kiss felt infinitely divine...a moment at once passionate and delicious with promise.

Too soon it ended, yet Ean felt he'd shared an eternity in that brief joining. He pulled back just far enough to look upon her face.

TWENTY-ONE

"Beware the locked door isn't keeping the dog inside."

– Bemothi proverb

TRELL NEEDED TIME. Time to process what he'd learned, to fit the pieces into their proper order. Time to restore his sense of self within the framework of a new name.

Trell val Lorian, Prince of Dannym.

Yet as much as he needed time, it was the one thing he didn't have.

He was still sitting on the bed beside Alyneri when Yara came in, took one look at them, and assessed from their expressions what had transpired in her absence. "So…" She leveled each of them a shrewd eye. "It's time."

Alyneri looked up at her. "Time for what?"

"A story. Come *khortdad, soraya,* we must talk."

Trell frowned at Yara, beset by the premonition that what was about to come might be nearly as startling as all that had come before. He gave Alyneri a reassuring look and took her hand, and they followed Yara into the other room.

She poured *czai* for them, then sat down in her chair at the head of the table and fixed her dark eyes upon Trell. "I told you that I would speak to you someday of how I came to possess a weldmap."

Trell pulled out Alyneri's chair for her and then took his own. "Yes, I remember the moment."

"Here then is the story: When I was a young woman not much older than you, *soraya,*" and Yara nodded to Alyneri, "my father and I met a blind woman traveling on the road to Baiz. These were turbulent years in M'Nador, before the War of the Lakes, and Saldaria was already rising against the Hadorin princes. It wasn't safe to travel the roads alone, even in Kandori—and especially for a woman. And *this* woman..."

Yara's wily gaze grew wistful, as if remembering a dream. "Well...she was young and beautiful for all that she was blind, and we feared for her safety. I asked my father to stop, and I offered her my horse."

Trell arched brows. "You offered to *give* your horse to a strange blind woman—just like that?"

Yara flashed a grin, and for a moment Trell saw her in her youth—a wild and beautiful girl with a wide smile and eyes dark as loam. "There was something about this woman, Trell of the Tides," she said, shaking her head with a rueful look. "You would've done anything for her too, I'll wager. My father was just as surprised to hear my offer as you were just now, but he was just as affected by her spell, and he congratulated me for my generosity. The woman accepted the gift of my horse but begged me to ride with her into Baiz."

Yara sipped at her tea and eyed the two of them over the rim. Trell held Alyneri's hand in his own.

After a moment, Yara set down her tea and continued her story. "While we rode together on the long road to Baiz, the blind woman told us stories. She was a fine storyteller—one of the best I have ever heard. And oh, but her tales were compelling! One of them I passed along to you," she added, nodding at Trell.

"Which one?"

"The legend of the Kandori fortune."

"Ah..." He well remembered the tale of the dragon and his mortal lover, and how the story had somehow made him think of Naiir.

"When we reached Baiz," Yara said then, "we parted ways. My father, a Scholar, had come there for a meeting with Prince Sabahi—one of your great-uncles, *soraya*, though Inithiya has long since claimed his spirit—and we were to stay for at least three nights. So the blind woman asked if I would come to her inn on the following night, and I readily agreed." Yara smiled quietly again, wistfully. "You see, I was captivated by her."

"So you went to see her?" Alyneri asked.

"Of course." Yara took up her tea again and drank it, and there was so much unspoken in her dark-eyed gaze. Silence settled upon the table, for Yara seemed lost in her memories. Suddenly she roused from them with a start and eyed Trell and Alyneri sharply. "So...I went to see the lady. She greeted me in her hotel, and we shared a cup of tea in her rooms. She had money this woman—for all she had been on foot on a lonely road that day—and her room was as opulent as any in the prince's palace." Yara drew in a deep breath and let it out slowly. Her lined dark eyes captured first Trell's gaze and then Alyneri's. "After the tea, she read my future."

Trell blinked at her. "A fortuneteller?"

"This was no charlatan soothsayer," Yara remarked tartly. "She was an Adept Seer. She took my hands and looked into my eyes—though how she saw me at all through the blindfold she wore, I vow I shall never understand—and she told me what my life would bring."

Trell felt Alyneri tense beside him. "Was it...true?" she asked haltingly.

Yara leveled her a piercing look. "All of it."

Trell shook his head. He was increasingly amazed by the things that no longer amazed him. "What did she tell you, Yara?"

"My life," she said, waving him to silence. "She told me of the man I would marry and the daughters I would bear, and how my grandchildren would bring me boundless joy. But she told me other things," Yara said then, eyeing them both in a way that indicated she approached the important part of the tale. "Once she'd assured me I would live a long and healthy life, she asked a boon of me. I've already told you I would've given her anything. I accepted without question."

Yara sat back in her chair and crossed her arms. She seemed dwarfed by her bulky woolen sweater, but as she looked up at them beneath wispy grey brows, her dark gaze was surely as compelling as the Seer's had been so long ago.

"That's when she walked to a chest—I've never seen such a chest as this, so ornately carved—and withdrew the map."

Trell sat back in surprise. "Carian's map?"

"The very same. She told me many things then, things I must do and how to know it was time to take the next step on my path. In the end, she told me I would travel to Veneisea and make my home near L'Aubernay. And then..." Yara settled them both an unsettling look. "Then she told me of the two of you."

Trell felt chills sprout down his arms and legs. He exchanged a look with Alyneri, who seemed equally startled.

"I will never forget her words," Yara said, adopting that far-away tone once more. "She told me, *'In Veneisea, you will meet a man who doesn't know himself, and he will stay with you for a time. He will soon be joined by another, and once they have found each other,'*" and Yara eyed the both of them critically again, "she told me, *'once they have found each other, no matter the time of day of this happy reunion—Yara, before nightfall, all of you must be gone from that place.'*"

Trell held her gaze, feeling the weight of prophecy suddenly hanging upon him. It felt uncomfortably akin to his interactions with Naiadithine.

"Or...?" Alyneri meanwhile asked.

Yara shook her head. "There was no *or*, no ultimatum. Simply the information."

"But..." Alyneri shook her head. "But why?"

"I think I know." Trell looked to Alyneri. "While you slept in a fever, I took a trip to L'Aubernay, where I crossed paths with a man who was looking for you. He announced himself as Lord Brantley."

Alyneri caught her breath and clapped a hand across her mouth.

Relieved that his instinct not to trust Lord Brantley had been justified, Trell squeezed Alyneri's hand and reassured her, "He struck me as an unsavory fellow, so I told him nothing of you."

Her face flooded with relief, and she threw her arms around his neck. "Oh, bless you for being so clever!"

"But," Trell gently extracting himself from her embrace and captured her eyes with his own, "but I think he recognized me—or at least my sword."

"Your *sword*?"

"More than one person seems to have recognized me by it." He stood and went to where his cloak hung on a hook by the door and retrieved his sword from underneath. He brought it around to her and pulled the blade free with a ring of steel. "Perhaps you can tell me why, Alyneri."

Her eyes widened, and tears came into them as she blinked up at him. "You kept your sword? All this time?"

"It was my only possession," he told her simply, "the only connection to my past."

Alyneri looked back to the blade and wiped a tear from her eye. "It's a

Kingdom Blade," she told him, using the familiar—if still meaningless—name. "These swords are only worn by members of the royal family of Dannym or their liegemen, and yours, with that sapphire pommel stone…" She looked up at him again with her brown eyes quite large. "Anyone who knows anything about the royal family knows that stone, Trell. It pronounces your birthright as much as your family name."

Trell looked down at the sword in his hands. *All this time…* He'd had a card of calling with him all along. No wonder the Lord Commander in Tregarion had treated him thusly, and Indora's truthreader had advised the man to tread carefully. No wonder the Veneiseans had called in the Magisteré, who in turn had begged him to stay.

Alyneri put a hand upon his. "Are you all right?"

He nodded, but words failed him.

"*Soraya*," Yara asked Alyneri then, "could this Lord Brantley be the threat the Seer intimated so many years ago?"

Alyneri exhaled a forceful breath. "Assuredly—Trell is right. Lord Brantley is an unscrupulous man, and the lord he serves is worse." Her fair brow furrowed with a sudden memory, and her gaze grew even more troubled. "I…" She dropped her eyes to her lap and confessed then, "The coach I was traveling in belonged to the Duke of Morwyk, Brantley's liege lord. Morwyk had…kidnapped me. When the storm came and our coach faltered, I thought it was Epiphany's blessing."

Yara's gaze grew darker, and she remarked to herself, "So…it would seem this story shall close as the Lady predicted."

"And what did she predict?" An ill apprehension colored Alyneri's tone.

Yara turned her a swift look, sharp and shrewd. "Ah, but that is *my* future, *soraya*, not yours." The old woman gentled her words with a faint smile. She looked to Trell but included both of them as she asked, "Where will you go?"

Alyneri and Trell both answered at once, "The Cairs." Then they gave each other startled looks. Trell motioned for Alyneri to explain, to which she offered, "Ean is there, and your cousin Fynnlar."

Ean…

Trell shook his head wondrously. Had the Mage known his brother was in the Cairs? Was that why he'd sent him there, to ensure that he somehow regained his family? But…why would the man care?

Because you are a celebrated commander in the Emir's army.

Because you are the son of a king…his enemy?

Neither of these answers seemed to fit.

"Trell?" Alyneri asked.

He focused back upon her and shook his head. "Sorry…" Smiling, he reached a hand to brush her cheek and marveled that she could've become so dear to him already. "Much on my mind today."

Alyneri looked troubled. "Trell, I realized something. Carian vran Lea—"

"He knew me." Trell captured a lock of her hair between his fingers and watched the streaming sunlight from the window turn it a pale, silken gold. "I know. I was meant to leave with him just days before you came, but Gendaia fell lame, and I wouldn't risk her." He glanced to Yara. "I suspected that Naiadithine had her hand in that occurrence. Now I *know* she did."

"So it would seem," Yara agreed.

"Naiadithine?" Alyneri gave him a puzzled look.

"The River Goddess and I have a history," Trell murmured.

Yara laid both palms on the table. "So…let us make our preparations," and she shooed the both of them into action.

TWENTY-TWO

"The best revenge in life is living."

– Yara, an old Kandori woman

AS TRELL HURRIED to prepare for departure from Yara's farm, a thousand thoughts were battling for his attention. While he rejoiced in knowing his name after so long, in many ways the knowledge came as a blow. His was no simple title. It signified a royal lineage and succession to the Eagle Throne—a throne the Duke of Morwyk was apparently seeking with bold declaration. More troubling to Trell in particular, Gydryn val Lorian had allied with Radov abin Hadorin, and Trell could never support that alliance.

He pushed a hand through his hair, pausing upon this thought. What a tangled mire he'd landed in. He'd always expected his name would tie together pieces of his past; he'd never imagined it would rope him into the politics of kings.

Time enough to worry about these things in the Cairs, he thought—he hoped—for he really didn't know what his future held now.

Trell saddled Gendaia and then hitched up Yara's wagon. Then he swung into his saddle and rode Gendaia over the hill to the neighboring farmstead. He found the boy Deon in the fields with his sheep and gave him the news that they were leaving. They had already settled Yara's accounts with Deon's father, Yara's landlord. Deon and his brother would come later to retrieve the animals left behind. But as he said goodbye to the lad, Trell made one last request.

"A horse?" Deon said. "But of course my Da can spare a horse for you, Trell of the Tides."

"I will pay him fairly."

Deon squinted up at him. "With everything you've done for us, I'm sure he won't ask much."

So it was that Trell procured a horse for Alyneri and was soon making his way back to Yara's. He was deep in thought when he came to the river and focused on his surroundings, only to realize it was the same crossing where Gendaia gone lame. The moment seemed significant in a way that touched him deeply.

He dismounted and knelt by the edge, letting the river's chill waters rush across his hand while he opened his heart to Naiadithine's song.

I'm sorry I doubted you, my Goddess.

She had brought him Alyneri. She'd brought him his name. She'd carried him full circle, from the moment when he'd lost everything in the deep waters of the Fire Sea to this day, when it had all been restored to him. Or at least the parts that mattered most.

I'm forever in your debt, my lady.

He sat in silence, letting the cold waters chill his flesh, until at last he heard her whisper.

Follow the water, Trell of the Tides...

Trell stood and looked upriver to where the water tumbled over dark rocks not unlike those that studded the Cry. He reached inside his shirt and withdrew Lily's tiny silver flask. It was time to open it now, and though he already suspected what it would say, he still felt a thrill of anticipation as he unrolled the note to read the words written in her tidy hand:

You are Trell val Lorian, Prince of Dannym

Trell swallowed. *Thank you, Lily.*

She'd known him by his blade, by his story, but she'd told him she'd known him in truth by the nobility he'd displayed; by his courage and generosity and honor. Trell hoped he would find these traits in his family, in his father and brother. He prayed for this as he'd once prayed to know his past.

Exhaling a sigh that was as much a release of his lingering doubts as hope for the future, Trell let the ornate little flask fall in the water, a token offering before beginning yet another important journey. He believed Naiadithine would be pleased. Lily's vial was meaningful to him in a way that only Graeme's dagger had been.

Trell recalled the moment he'd first heard Naiadithine's whisper. Now her words seemed to define him as much as his name.

He gave the river one last parting smile, and then he led Gendaia and Alyneri's new gelding across the shallow fording and back to the farmstead.

As Alyneri hurried to help Yara pack the last of her things into the wagon, her head felt too full. The ramifications of Trell's survival were vast, and as each new idea dropped into the cup of her mind, it displaced the whole, until she was struggling to keep all her thoughts from spilling over the sides and being lost.

And what about Yara's startling story of the blind Seer? Had it not so obviously been divine intervention that brought her and Trell together, Alyneri never would've believed it. Despite the romantic stories, the idea that a god would take such an interest in a man was simply outrageous—the very idea of gods existing at all seemed far-fetched to her. But Alyneri couldn't deny the inexplicable coincidences in their lives. She felt touched by grace, and it scared her.

The women finished the house quickly, for much of the work had already been done in preparation for this day. Alyneri couldn't quite get her head around the idea that all of this time Yara had been packing for a journey foreordained decades ago. Was there a difference between destiny and fate if all of your choices were already made for you? If you weren't free to live your life by your own choosing?

As she was loading the last of Yara's supplies into a crate, Alyneri paused and looked up at the old woman. "Yara...did you ever discover anything about the Seer? Her name? Where she was from?"

"No, *soraya*." The old woman kept at her task of stuffing apples into a sack. "I knew that if she'd wanted me to know such things, she would've told me."

Alyneri shook her head in wonder. "I don't think I could stand it."

"Stand what?"

"Living my life as if my entire path was predestined."

Yara paused in her packing to settle Alyneri a shrewd eye. "Every once in a while, *soraya*, someone comes into your life and you're forever changed by the encounter. Meeting the blind woman was like that for me." She dropped her eyes and gazed at the little winter apple in her hand as if it held all the mysteries of the universe beneath its ruddy flesh, as if eating it would open the door to secrets unknown by mortal man.

"I never felt that I lived my life by design of another," she admitted then. "I simply felt that…well, that she'd looked into the future and had seen the outcome of choices I'd already made—that it was *my* future she was seeing, not some predestined path laid out for me. As each new thing came to be—even though it aligned with what the Lady had told me—I saw that it was indeed *my* choice that had brought me to that place, and I knew I would make the same choice again, if given the chance."

Yara gave Alyneri a wistful look that somehow encompassed her choices far and vast and the many trials and joys she'd experienced. Then she smiled sadly. "Even if I've faced tragedies in my life, I cannot blame the Lady for them. I only feel blessed for having met her."

Alyneri dropped her eyes to her hands. "Your wisdom humbles me, Yara."

"*Pshaw*," grunted the old woman, waving off her regard. "We live and we learn. What else would be the point of life?"

Yara returned to her packing, but Alyneri remained, thinking of someone she felt blessed for having met.

On that night spent with the zanthyr working to heal Ean, she'd seen into Phaedor's soul, and it had been brilliant to behold. In all her many healings, she'd never seen a spirit so ablaze. Whatever source fueled Phaedor was something far beyond her understanding.

She knew she'd been forever changed by that encounter. Moreover, it hadn't been the circumstances of their healing Ean together that had changed her, but rather the intimate contact with Phaedor. She felt like one of those mortals from a story where the gods interfered in the lives of men and left again, leaving everyone akimbo.

Alyneri saw how one's entire life could turn in an instant. For good or ill, through tragedy or triumph, a single moment could define the path of one's future. Alyneri wondered at what point she'd arrived on her current path. Was it when she'd met Sandrine in the apothecary? Was it when she'd decided to go into the city instead of sitting at Ean's beside? Was it when she'd agreed to accompany Ean on his quest—or even earlier than this? Had she always been on this path?

"Let it go, *soraya*," Yara murmured without looking up from putting jars in the crate. "You'll never come to any conclusion that seems to fit, and it won't matter anyway."

Alyneri turned her a swift look. "How did you know what I was thinking?"

"Because I know that look." She glanced up under wispy grey brows. "I've seen it in my own eyes far too many times. The Kandori say every step ahead is a stone behind."

Alyneri let out a slow breath. "What does it mean?"

"That the past cannot be altered. Only the future is open to change."

Alyneri saw the truth in this. Her future was certainly in motion—in fact, it bordered on chaotic—but she saw so much promise mixed into the chaos that she felt more hope than fear.

Trell lived.

There was nothing she might not now do, when such miracles were possible.

When Trell finally returned with the horses, Yara emerged from the farmhouse brushing her hands on her skirts. "Well, it's about time," she grumbled, but she had a smile in her dark eyes. "We were about to set off without you."

"I thought it prudent for the Lady Alyneri to have her own horse." Trell took the horse by the bit and led him over to Alyneri. "His name is Baiard."

Alyneri broke into a surprised smile. "From the romance?"

Trell grinned.

"What's this?" Yara glanced up at them while checking her things in the wagon.

"It's a famous Veneisean legend from the *Chansons de Geste*," Trell supplied, still marveling that he could remember entire books he'd read as an adolescent but not where or when he'd read them. "Baiard was the name of a magic horse that belonged to the four sons of Aymon. The stallion had the ability to grow larger or smaller depending on which one of the sons mounted him." He looked to Alyneri. "Deon's father assured me he's steady and strong. We'll need to ride fast."

Yara stomped up the stairs and shut the farmhouse door. Then she turned and settled hands on her hips. "Well…that's the end of it."

It was barely midday and already time for goodbye.

"Come now." Yara opened her arms to receive them both. "One day you children shall come to see me in Agasan, and I will rejoice in the reunion. Until then, fare thee well. May Jai'Gar watch over you."

"And you also, Yara," Trell and Alyneri said together.

Trell helped Yara onto her wagon and Alyneri into her saddle, and then they were all heading up the hill together. At the road, they parted ways. Yara turned west, towards Tregarion and a ship to Agasan, and Trell and Alyneri headed south, towards Rethynnea. Trell's last sight of the old woman was of her iron-grey head dwarfed by her bulky wool sweater.

He looked to Alyneri. She smiled in return. He found much in her gaze that was intriguing to him. Alyneri seemed to be everything he might've wanted in a friend, a companion…or a wife. Odd to think it, though now within his right.

But he dared not get ahead of himself.

He nodded towards the road before them, and together they set off.

They made good time while their horses were fresh, and during the afternoon they crossed from Veneisea into Xanthe. They spent little time in conversation that day, for they were absorbed in their thoughts, but one moment from that ride made an indelible impression on Trell's memory.

Early in the day they'd come upon a long stretch of road that ran flat between high hills. Alyneri's mount, Baiard, had been itching to stretch his legs beyond the steady trot they'd been keeping. She'd cast Trell an inquiring look, and then, laughing, had given Baiard his head.

The horse shot into a hard gallop, only too happy to work out his energy, and Gendaia of course had been obliged to follow. They ran them in the race then, letting the horses have their moment, the riders as exhilarated as their animals. Trell sensed that Gendaia wasn't keen to take second, and he let her off the bit to find her own pace. She was rapidly gaining on Baiard's flank when Trell lifted his gaze to Alyneri…

She spun him a challenging look over her shoulder. Her brown eyes were bright beneath her long pale hair, which the wind had lifted and wrapped about her face, and with her silken cloak floating behind her and that exuberant smile, Trell was stricken by her beauty enough that he straightened in the saddle.

Gendaia sensed his change both of position and of mental state, and hesitated. Baiard pulled free and won the chase by a length.

Alyneri slowed to a trot and reined Baiard in a circle. The wind caught her pale hair again, lifting it wildly about her face and shoulders as if it had a life of its own, and her sapphire cloak rippled and ballooned around her. Trell thought he'd never seen anyone so simply beautiful.

"What is it?" she'd asked, lighthearted and rosy-cheeked from the run.

Smiling, Trell shook his head. "Nothing. You took the race, my lady."

She gave him a long look in unconvinced response, but the moment remained fair. Soon they were off into a canter that stole away further conversation. But the moment stayed with Trell, as did that vision of Alyneri.

They stopped for the night in the hamlet of Lenth. By tacit agreement, Trell acquired a room in the hamlet's only inn, giving their names as a married couple from Tal'Shira by the Sea and speaking only halting Common to do it. Alyneri kept her hood up and her eyes downcast, and Trell kept his sword hidden beneath his cloak. So it was that they gained a room and had a meal sent up to them, and felt moderately secure in their lodging for the night.

Which was well and good, for Trell felt little certainty in much else.

Their room barely fit a bed and small table, but the linen smelled clean, and the one window seat boasted room enough for both of them to sit and enjoy the night air. They took their dinner together there as the sun was setting, looking out over the dark strip of mountains that bound the eastern horizon—the Assifiyahs in all their majesty. A storm was rolling in from the southwest, and its dark clouds eventually obscured the stars.

After the meal, they sat leaning against opposite walls of the window alcove, sipping on watered wine. Alyneri pulled her knees to her chest and gave him a look he'd been expecting for quite some time. He liked knowing he could read her expressions so readily—he surely must've known her in his past, for she'd become wonderfully familiar to him in important ways.

"Trell," she said with her fair brow furrowed in a way that was entirely too endearing, "there is much you need to know."

Trell leaned his head back against the wall and let his grey eyes stray beyond the open window, out into the deep night. The air held the promise of rain. "Then I suppose you must tell me, Duchess," he answered quietly. He could almost see them together under different circumstances—pleasant ones, and—

"It's very likely that your life is in danger."

Trell shifted his gaze to her at this unexpected statement. "Why?"

"Dannym is embroiled in a political struggle, one made worse by the king's continued support of M'Nador. The Duke of Morwyk is outspoken against our part in the war, and many nobles agree with him. He's powerful and has aims upon the Eagle Throne, but there are...others, too, who have conspired against the val Lorian reign. I'm not privy to details known by your brother and your cousin Fynnlar, but Morin d'Hain—your father's Spymaster—did tell me some things. Enough to indicate that the treachery extends beyond seditious men within a single kingdom, and that both your life—as we thought at the time—and your eldest brother Sebastian's, had fallen prey to their design."

Trell gazed hard at her, his mind awhirl. "You mean to say you think my ship was attacked? Purposefully sunk? That *I* was the target?"

She held his gaze with her large brown eyes.

Trell drew in a deep breath and let it out again, frowning. "So this Lord Brantley who seeks you," he mused, "a man sworn to the Duke of Morwyk. Do you think he might be seeking me now as well?"

"If he recognized you, it's possible. But more than this, Trell—" She stopped and caught her lower lip between her teeth, looking uncertain. "It's just that...well, assassins have been hunting Ean ever since he returned to the mainland and have several times nearly succeeded in killing him. Morwyk was certainly behind a few of these attacks, but..."

When she seemed reluctant to say more, he leaned to capture her gaze. "But?"

She shook her head ruefully. "It will be very hard to believe this."

Trell gave her a wry grin and sat back again. "You'd be surprised at the things that no longer surprise me, Alyneri."

Holding his gaze, she let out a slow exhale. "Very well..."

Alyneri told him then of his brother Ean. Starting from what she knew of his kidnapping by the Shade and ending with his near death in Rethynnea.

Trell sat in stunned silence when she was finished. To have come this far, to finally learn he had a brother, only to discover his life was in mortal danger...that indeed, he may not recover? Fate had never twisted a crueler thorn in his heart.

Alyneri reached a hand to rest upon his, where he gripped one bent knee close to his chest. "Trell." She drew his gaze back to her. "I want you to know something, and I hope you can believe as I believe—that you can trust in what I'm about to tell you."

"I do trust you, Alyneri."

She blushed slightly and dropped her gaze. "I have no way of proving this to you, nor can I explain how I know it so completely, but I assure you, there is no way...absolutely *no way* that the zanthyr will let Ean come to lasting harm." She looked back to him. "If he must tread the paths of the dead to retrieve Ean, I assure you, he will. I don't know why he's so sworn to Ean's well-being, but I know that he most assuredly is, and—" Here she halted and closed her eyes, as if praying upon the words. When she met his gaze once more, it held an immutable glint of certainty. "And when the zanthyr is upon a mission," she finished determinedly, "there is *nothing* he cannot do."

Trell regarded her as he worked to make sense of all that she'd told him. He felt dazed. Odd pieces of his life seemed connected with Ean's. "Who is this zanthyr?"

"His name is Phaedor—" Again, she stopped herself, biting off the words even as she dropped her eyes. It seemed Alyneri struggled with many aspects of his brother Ean's activities.

Trell took her hand, enjoying the feel of their simple contact, of her skin against his. "We *must* trust each other," he said quietly. "There is no other way to do this, Alyneri. As certain as you are of this zanthyr's loyalty to Ean, I am certain that without trust between us, we won't survive whatever is to come."

Alyneri's brown eyes were wide as she looked up at him, but she nodded. "Phaedor," she said somewhat weakly, "is sworn to Björn van Gelderan. We know the Vestal has returned from T'khendar—he sent a Shade in search of Ean—and the zanthyr serves Björn, though he tries to be vague and ambiguous about it."

Trell frowned at this news. He knew he was missing something important.

Alyneri hastened to fill in the rest. "You see, Ean has Returned—Returned and *Awakened*," she added wondrously, "as impossible as it seems…"

Yet Trell no longer heard her, for he recalled another's words…

'…*so different in temperament, yet they are brothers to the core. One has the mind of a master tactician… The other has Returned, and has been long awaited… The time has come to hone them both, these, my Kingdom Blades. They can no longer go on being mere pieces; they must become players.*'

"The Emir's Mage," Trell whispered. A chill striped him.

Alyneri absently brushed a lock of hair out of her face. "Yes, Fynn thinks Björn van Gelderan is masquerading as the Emir's Mage—*oh!*" She clapped a hand across her mouth and stared at him.

He leveled her a telling look. "The Emir's Mage…the First Lord…Björn van Gelderan." He said each name slowly, significantly. "The same man."

Her eyes grew very large.

Thunder sounded, followed by the sudden patter of rainfall. A rising breeze brought a damp mist to wash over them, but neither moved to close the windows.

"What do you know of him?" Trell asked, echoing his own question to Ware from so long ago.

She shook her head, wide-eyed. "I know only the stories, and I trust them not."

Trell arched brows. "Even so? I would've thought…well, most people repeat the stories as truth."

Alyneri exhaled a troubled sigh. "I did too, once, but now…"

"Yes?"

Her eyes flew to his. "Now I don't know." She sighed dispiritedly. "Trell, I've seen Phaedor's soul!" She dropped her eyes and confessed in a bare whisper, "It is the closest I've ever come to gazing upon divinity."

For some reason, Trell recalled Vaile and Jaya's conversation about the First Lord's zanthyr being older than the sun.

Alyneri meanwhile shook her head. She seemed close to tears, obviously deeply troubled by the matter. He could feel her tension through the connection of their hands, and he wanted only to comfort and reassure her. "Come," he tugged gently on her hand.

At first hesitant, she moved into his embrace, turning to sit between his legs and leaning back against his chest. Wrapping his arms around her and drawing her close, he rested his cheek against her head and they gazed out at the storm together.

"Things are rarely as they seem, Alyneri," he noted quietly. Then he added with a chuckle, "The more obvious they seem, the less true they are, I think. I, too, know fifth-strand creatures sworn to the First Lord—your Björn van Gelderan, my Emir's Mage. They're powerful beings of great wisdom and purity. I cannot see them giving their oaths to a man unworthy of their loyalty."

"No." Alyneri relaxed a little in his arms. "Phaedor wouldn't either—I just know that he wouldn't."

"So we agree that the Fifth Vestal is not what people say of him. We will base our conclusions not upon rumors but upon the verisimilitude of those who serve his cause."

She gave a little laugh at this, a release of the tension she'd been holding back. "Trell," she whispered, brushing a tear from her eye as she gazed out into the rain, "you are such a gift to me."

He would've kissed her in that moment except it was entirely too perfect already. The rain fell quietly outside their window, and for a time the song of the rain and the accompanying thunder were all they heard. They just sat and listened, content to rest in each other's arms and have that be enough… almost.

After a long time where they kept their own thoughts, Alyneri lifted her head to look at him, and something in her gaze warned him of her words. "Trell…the Emir had to know who you are."

"I realize that, Alyneri." It made sense out of the mystery of why the Emir would've treated Trell as if he were his own son.

"For the longest time," she told him quietly, "we thought the Emir stood behind your death. Many still blame him for Sebastian's, but…" she exhaled a troubled sigh. "But it mustn't be true. It can't be, can it?"

"No, I think it can't."

"But if it wasn't the Emir…who?"

Neither of them had an answer to this.

They let the silence come again, and Trell retreated to his thoughts while he enjoyed Alyneri's closeness. Pieces of him remembered her, but they were young memories, full of the green eagerness of adolescence. What he felt for her now was somehow much stronger. It wasn't the fiery passion he'd had for Fhionna, which burned hot enough to scald him in unexpected moments. Rather than singeing and expiring capriciously, his feelings for Alyneri infused him. He felt a deep connection to her in a way that was quite profound to him, and he knew, above all, that this was a gift from Naiadithine too.

The thunder of horses preceded the five men as they stormed to a dusty halt at the top of a hill overlooking a modest farm. The sun hung low on the horizon, burning beneath a building storm that cast long shadows over the little valley.

The neat farmstead looked abandoned. The pens stood empty, the barn closed up, and though it would've been time for an evening meal, no smoke rose from the chimney.

"Looks like they've gone, Earl," one of the five men remarked in the Common Tongue. "You sure this is the place?"

Lord Brantley, Earl of Pent, smoothed his longish moustache and beard several times as he frowned down the hill. "It has to be," he said after a moment. "For all that tavern keeper is daft as a goat, he knew the man by description and was certain he'd been staying here."

"You want us to check it out?"

The earl gave him a bland look. "No, I would like us all to mill abjectly about wondering whether or not they have gone."

The man shrugged and nudged his horse down the hill, and the others followed.

The earl observed that sarcasm was generally wasted on the witless. "Langdon," he called to the last of the men. "Scout around. See what you can find."

The man named Langdon reined his horse in a circle and headed back up the road.

The earl stroked his moustache again. He lamented the episodes of ill-luck which had befallen him. No doubt had he come but one day earlier...

Of course he'd been suspicious of the bearded man he met in town that day, and especially after noticing that he carried a Kingdom Blade. Brantley couldn't be certain of the stone in the pommel—such stones told of the lord a man served, if one was well-versed in the stones and their associations—but Brantley hadn't gotten a decent look at the stone.

The same afternoon he'd encountered the kingdom man, they'd finally uncovered the whereabouts of Lord Everly, who'd been charged with bringing Alyneri d'Giverny to Morwyk, and Brantley necessarily had to leave town. Two days wasted on the road only to discover that the man had been dead a week! It did not serve to improve the earl's disposition.

And now that mongrel desert bitch and her nameless knight had eluded him yet again. How had they known?

Lord Brantley considered himself a man of quality and vision. It was, for example, only good business to deal with Bethamin. The Prophet was on the up and up, and his following was growing exponentially. He would become a powerful force—anyone with vision could see that. That's why his lord, the Duke of Morwyk, was dealing with the man, despite his being a low-blood primitive. It wasn't as though the duke intended to socialize with the barbarian, but Bethamin had his uses.

This was also why the duke wanted Alyneri d'Giverny on a short leash before he launched his coup on Calgaryn. Having an heir to the Kandori fortune within his retinue would ensure the financial backing he needed to move his plans forward in a timely fashion. Likewise it would keep those Kandori savages in their place in the unlikely event they found the balls to rise against him.

Morwyk would be displeased if Brantley failed to retrieve the duchess. In fact, if he failed, Lord Brantley knew he'd best not return to Dannym at all.

Lord Brantley often bemoaned his plight in life—to be constantly surrounded by men of low intelligence and breeding seemed an unjustified punishment. However could he be expected to accomplish acts of greatness when saddled with incompetent underlings?

The sun had nearly set by the time his men reconvened upon the rise. The scout Langdon was the first to return.

"Well?" Brantley demanded irritably of him. If Langdon saw anything beyond the tip of his overly large nose it would be a fair miracle.

"Tracks look recent heading away from the farm, milord," Langdon reported. "Heavy wagon heading west."

"Any others?"

Langdon shrugged. "Hard to say. The road's fair packed and lots of traffic along it."

The other men soon returned, and the foremost of them reported, "It's abandoned, milord. Recent though, even in the last day. Earlier today there were horses in the stalls; the manure is fresh."

Brantley wrinkled his nose, making his longish moustache tremble and twitch, and frowned at the farmstead. Could any one of these middling men have escaped the clutches of that insufferable Captain Gerard back in Acacia? Could *they* have so long outwitted old Duke Thane val Torlen? The impotent old fool never knew how many of his men were aching for strong leadership, or how easy it had been for Brantley to turn them to Morwyk's cause. And now here he, Brantley, Earl of Pent, was relegated to chasing down a damned heathen bitch like he was naught but a barnyard goon and her a prized pig gone astray.

"Where to, milord?" Langdon asked.

Brantley stroked his moustache and looked to the south. "The Cairs. We found her there once, we'll find her there again." Suddenly he smiled, certain now that his choice was the correct one—as all of his choices were. He added with a sneer at Langdon, "I have an idea who can tell us exactly where we'll find her."

TWENTY-THREE

"The only dependable virtue a man possesses is greed."
– Radov abin Hadorin, Ruling Prince of M'Nador

TANIS AND PELAS walked the harbor road past wharves and docks and an untold forest of sailboat masts. Tanis didn't know where they'd come, but the water was amazingly blue.

Pelas still had his bundle of swords over one shoulder, and though it had to be heavy, he carried it as effortlessly as a bag of down. Tanis regarded him fretfully. He could see the blood soaking one side of Pelas's fine shirt.

"Sir, you're hurt."

Pelas eyed his side and the long gash peeking through the knife-slit in the silk. "I suppose I am. It would've been worse if not for your miraculously reappearing dagger," and he gave the boy a look that was both alarming and amused.

Tanis dropped his gaze to his hands. "I don't know how the dagger came back to me, sir."

"Indeed?" Pelas eyed him quietly. "Well, I can't remonstrate you for it too forcefully, being that its presence saved our lives."

"Yes, sir," Tanis said by way of *you're welcome*.

Pelas caught the inflection in his tone and chuckled. Then he looked ahead to the marina, and his smile broadened. "Ah but look—we're here."

They turned down one of the smaller jetties and made their way past numerous sailboats to a sleek vessel a bit over thirty feet long. Pelas pitched his bag of weapons onto the deck, hopped the distance from dock to boat, and began immediately tending the lines to be away.

At Pelas's instruction, Tanis unwound the mooring lines from the cleats secured to the quay and then found his way a bit more carefully across the watery chasm, only to then rush around following Pelas's orders until they were ready to shove off.

Pelas got the sail up and had them underway quickly, and once they were free of the marina, they had quiet seas and a steady headwind to keep them cool.

Tanis couldn't stand seeing the man just bleeding all over the place, so while Pelas had the helm, the lad made him strip off his shirt, and he did his best to tend the wound. It was not very deep, but it looked gruesome. Tanis bound Pelas's side with strips cut from his ruined shirt, and then took what comfort he could in knowing he'd done all that he might for him.

But it left him feeling frayed—both because he honestly cared, and because he felt that perhaps he shouldn't care so much. It didn't help that he'd been jostled about the realm like flotsam on a stormy sea, flicked from morning to night to afternoon. Tanis wasn't sure if he should feel tired because his body thought it was midnight, or hungry because they'd missed an important meal.

Feeling generally disgruntled, Tanis settled down on a bench built into the side of the stern. "You know, sir," he pointed out while hugging his knees to his chest, "if you saw fit to use the services of a Healer instead of cutting them into little pieces, she could've mended your side much better than me."

Pelas cast him a dry grin as he manned the wheel, holding them on their tack. "I didn't know you cared for me so, little spy."

"Neither did I," Tanis muttered.

"Fret thee not." Pelas glanced once more to the lad. "I am not so different from you. I heal quickly. And I fear a Healer's craft would be wielded in vain upon me."

"Why?"

"I'm not like you, little one. *Elae* doesn't flow in my veins."

"How do you know?"

Pelas gave him a strange look.

"I mean, you could be of the fifth, you know." It had only just occurred to Tanis, but he thought his logic was sound.

Pelas shook his head. "Our power corrupts and destroys. Your frail shells cannot contain it, much less channel it, without soon deteriorating."

"That's not true. Adepts of the fifth can wield it."

Now Pelas really stared at him. "How do you know such a thing?"

"I know…people—fifth-strand Adepts—who can work both powers."

Pelas blinked. "Truly?"

"You know I cannot speak a patent untruth, sir," Tanis pointed out, "and you'd know if I was holding back or offering only a half-truth."

Pelas admitted that was so.

"How do you know that you're not of the fifth?" Tanis persisted. "How do you know that it isn't possible for you to wield *elae*? I'm certain that you've never tried."

Pelas looked shocked and…intrigued at the idea. "It would be something to experience, wouldn't it?" Then he shook his head as if to clear his thoughts and turned to the lad. "Here, little spy. Take the wheel while I tend the sheets."

Tanis took over at the helm, and Pelas moved around adjusting the ropes that controlled the mainsail and the smaller triangular sail at the bow, called a jib, tightening them with winches so the sails stayed taut in the wind. When he was assured of the sails' trim and a promise of steady progress, he threw himself down in the stern and extended long legs towards Tanis. The lad reflected that Pelas seemed very at ease on the sailboat, barefoot and barechested and with his pant legs rolled up.

He set to braiding two sections of his long black hair, one on each side of his temple, and then joined the two at the back of his head, taking the plait all the way to the end. The braid kept his thick hair pinned in place and out of his eyes, but it also made him look more like a pirate.

"You know," he remarked as he extended his arms along the sides of the boat, reclining in fair humor, "it is an interesting experience having my own truthreader."

Tanis cast him a sooty look. "Is it?"

Pelas's expression turned quite serious. "I've never in my long life held acquaintance with a man I could trust."

Tanis frowned. "That's sad, sir."

"Perhaps. I don't know, but it's an interesting truth to note. Yet you changed that, little spy."

"I did?"

Pelas eyed him quizzically. "I can trust you to tell me the truth, which isn't to say that I can trust you unequivocally, but in the former, at least, I believe that I can. It's more than I've ever been able to say before."

Tanis didn't quite know how to answer him. He was grateful that he needed to keep his attention on their heading, which spared him the necessity of meeting Pelas's gaze. It wasn't that he disagreed. He just...

"I think...we're becoming friends." Tanis managed a little smile.

"Friends." Pelas looked amazed. "There's a word I never thought I'd use. *Friends,*" he said again thoughtfully. He lifted copper eyes to Tanis. "I wouldn't have thought it possible even a week ago. I never thought such a thing was real, but...I believe you're right."

"I kind of wish I wasn't," Tanis muttered.

Pelas laughed gently at his tone. "No doubt. I am not an easy man to appreciate, as might be required in a friend. That *is* what this feels like, isn't it?" he added musingly, truly seeming to grasp the idea as true for him. "There is some kind of bond between us, yet we made no agreement, no contract to fulfill. We aren't bound together here by quest or command."

"Does that mean you'd let me leave if I chose to?" Tanis braved.

Pelas frowned. "I...don't know." Then he shook his head and frowned harder. "If this is friendship, I suppose I must. How intriguing." Abruptly he pinned Tanis with a fervent gaze, his manner suddenly alert. "Do you intend to leave?"

"We're kind of far from land right now," Tanis pointed out with a grin. "It would be a long swim."

Assured Tanis wasn't planning to abandon him in the middle of the ocean, Pelas idly scratched his bare chest with long fingers while he gazed toward the bow and the open sea. "There is merit in this," he remarked quietly, intently, his brow furrowed from the force of his concentration. "There is merit in this connection, in this experience." His gaze found Tanis again and lingered upon the boy. "I am strangely drawn to you, little spy."

Tanis gave him a frightened look.

"Not in the way you're thinking." Pelas reassured him with a wink. "This is...different. I cannot explain it."

"Then..." A wave of relief washed across Tanis. "Then you didn't enchant me like the others?"

"Enchant you? Like what others?"

"But..." *Could it be?* Could it be that the man was honestly just so charismatic that he didn't see the effect he had on others?

As Tanis thought carefully on what he knew of Pelas, he realized it could be true. Pelas collected experiences like marbles on a board. He didn't mean for this pastime to be in any way harmful, though it became so when the darkness took him. Tanis saw Pelas standing at the center of a great wheel, spinning...spinning, gazing wondrously at the vast and varied scenes flashing endlessly by as if they'd been placed there for his sole enjoyment, yet utterly disconnected from every part of it, from life. His ideology, so thoroughly indoctrinated, prevented him from ever actually *participating*.

It was tragic and sad. Tanis could only imagine the joy Pelas might actually find in life if he decided to involve himself in the race instead of being a mere spectator intent upon its eventual destruction. If he actually *cared*...what a force he could be!

No wonder his brothers were terrified of him.

Which raised the question...

But before Tanis could ask it, Pelas jumped happily to his feet and pointed. "Look, little spy, there is the point. Round that to windward and we'll find safe harbor and dinner if we're lucky."

They were too busy then for deep conversation. They worked the lines and the helm to maneuver the ship through the choppy seas around the point. Just beyond, they turned into a cove where high cliffs rose above a sandy beach shaded by coconut palms. Pelas guided them into the cove and dropped anchor while still in deep water, but it was so clear that Tanis could see the sunlight glinting off the sandy bottom.

"How deep do you think that water is, sir?" Tanis asked as he hung over the side.

Pelas joined him in peering into the crystal-clear depths. "Couple fathoms. Not more than three. You can tell from the color of the water. See there," and he pointed out to sea where the water's shade darkened. "It's at least five fathoms out there, and just beyond, the sea floor falls out from under you very fast."

Tanis turned to sit back against the side and looked up at him. "How do you know so much about sailing?"

Pelas walked across the boat and stared up at the near cliffs with hands braced on his hips. "I told you," he said absently, "experiences can be worthwhile." He spun Tanis an adventurous look over his shoulder. "Do you swim well?"

"Moderately."

A grin split his face. "Come, then!" and before Tanis could say a word, Pelas had stripped out of his pants and was diving off the side of the boat. He swam easily towards the cliffs, seeming wholly indifferent to his earlier injury.

The lad could do no less than follow, though he reckoned he struck nowhere near the specimen of manhood as Pelas.

Leaving his clothing behind, Tanis dove in and followed. The water was that perfect temperature of cool without being cold, and the sun, though falling now towards the west, was still hot enough to warm his back. Tanis caught up with Pelas as he was treading water beneath the cliffs.

The waves were at mid-tide and not too heavy, but they had enough swell that they required timing if one wanted to safely gain the rocks. Pelas went first, riding the rising wave to a jutting precipice he'd determined as the best point of access, and when the waves were right again, Tanis followed.

Pelas hauled him out of the water effortlessly and turned to assess the cliff while the lad found his footing.

"Um, sir…" Tanis flipped wet hair from his eyes. "What are we doing?"

"We're going to climb that cliff and dive off."

"But it's got to be twenty paces high."

"Yes, perfect for diving."

"Perfect for dying," Tanis muttered.

"Nonsense." Pelas clapped a frosty hand on the lad's bare shoulder and grinned. "The bottom is sand and three fathoms deep." He gave him a chastising look. "You'll have to be more adventurous if you hope to keep your position, little spy."

"My position as what?" Tanis challenged. "Your truthreader or your friend?"

"Just now I was thinking 'accomplice.'"

Pelas showed Tanis how to find handholds on the cliff face, and then they started climbing. Tanis struggled while Pelas shimmied up the steep side faster than a mountain goat. By the time the lad reached the top, Tanis was starting to resent Pelas his nature—whatever that was. Then, when he looked down, Tanis decided the man was verifiably insane.

Pelas grinned at him. "Looks a lot higher from up here, doesn't it?"

Tanis gave him a baleful stare.

"Just follow me." He gave the lad a swat of encouragement. "Dive or jump, but if you jump," and here he grinned broadly, "best...you know... keep everything pulled in tight." Then he laughed uproariously and dove off.

Tanis watched him vanish beneath a splash and surface again soon thereafter.

Well, here goes...

He dove in after him.

The force of the water against the top of his head felt like a tree had just bounced off his skull, and even though he forcefully exhaled, saltwater still shot up his nose. He came up coughing and sputtering and with all the fair humor of a wet cat.

Pelas grinned from where he was treading water about five feet away. "That was an experience, no?"

"You could say that," Tanis gasped.

Pelas laughed at him and headed back over to do it again, but Tanis decided one experience was enough and swam back to the boat.

The Malorin'athgul turned out to be good at more than sailing and diving off cliffs. After he'd had his fill of head-bashing against the waves, Pelas snared two blades from his stash—Tanis was quite sure one of them was his dagger—and speared a skate for their dinner.

This they took on the beach by a fire that Pelas started the old-fashioned way—with magic. Tanis had no idea how he'd done it, since he claimed he didn't use *elae*. Pelas tried explaining the negative properties of fire, but Tanis got lost the moment he said 'meridian transference.'

When they were well fed and Pelas was enjoying feeding dry brush to the fire and watching it blaze heavenward, Tanis finally asked him, "Sir, why do you think your brothers tried to kill you?"

"Probably because they feared I might turn against them." He pitched another branch onto the flames. "You know, switch sides." Then he winked at the boy.

Tanis frowned. There was truth hidden beneath Pelas's flippant grin. The lad pressed seriously, "Why would they think that, sir?"

Pelas leaned back on one elbow to regard Tanis, and for a moment he was silent, just gazing at him. Then he said, "I was the first, you see." He scratched idly at the scruff on his neck, extending his chin like a cat as long fingers slowly roughed up the sandpaper of the day's growth of beard. "When I first arrived, I just wanted to taste every moment, experience everything I could possibly imagine." Pelas brightened considerably upon recalling these memories, and Tanis saw such a lightness of spirit within him that it startled the boy. "When my brothers arrived a…long number of years after me, they were disappointed with my progress along our objectives." He eyed Tanis pensively. "Our eldest brother, Rinokh, claimed I had betrayed them all."

"Why?" Tanis whispered.

Pelas sighed, shrugged. "I suppose because I hadn't *done* anything as far as he could see. But what I'd done was experience much of this realm…there is so much to observe and do here, Tanis!"

It was the first time the man had called him by his name, and there was something perilously intimate in hearing him use it.

"Darshan showed me how wrong I was," Pelas added after a moment. Tanis heard true bitterness in his tone for the first time. With mention of his brother, a darkness descended upon his thoughts. "Ironic," all the light faded from Pelas's countenance, "one night with my brother showed me the error of a century of life in this realm."

Tanis heard this tragic statement and knew that he verged on an important understanding. Suddenly that sense of duty resonated strongly—indeed, it veritably hummed.

But Tanis didn't yet comprehend its melody. He didn't know what he was meant to do, and eventually the moment passed. The night lingered, warm and sweet, but the fire died down.

They swam back to the boat and slept in the lee of the wind, and when the sun rose to golden the heavens and gild the waters, Pelas took them back to sea, and home.

TWENTY-FOUR

"Experience is the name men give to their mistakes."

— The Espial Franco Rohre

D AWN FOUND EAN on the practice yard with high hopes for the day. His talk with Isabel had been enlightening, and he stood to face Markal's formidable lessons with a renewed sense of purpose.

But of his night with Isabel, the kiss remained most predominately in his thoughts, a pleasurable torment, for he only wanted more of her. All night, visions of Isabel had dominated his dreams, and he woke feeling agonized for want of her body entwined with his own.

Markal arrived as the clouds above were shedding their rosy cast, once again with a rope in each hand. As on the previous day, he pitched one to Ean and simultaneously slung the other into a staff. Settling its tip on the stones, he leaned upon it and cast Ean a challenging look. "I half expected to find you missing this morning, nursing wounds in your room."

Ean held his dark gaze. "I'm not the man you knew before—no matter what you say."

"Oh, you've somehow evolved in death? The one exception?"

"No, but I've had about eighteen years to learn some new things since then. I don't have to make the same choices."

"You did yesterday," Markal pointed out, but his tone was slightly less hostile.

"And I learned from it."

"We'll see." Markal lashed out with his staff, and Ean envisioned the rope becoming as stone as he swung to block it—that is until Markal swept his feet out from under him.

Ean bit back a curse and rolled to his feet, leveling Markal a heated look as he stood. "What am I doing wrong?"

"At this point I wonder if there is anything you're doing right."

Ean thought of punching him but decided it would set a poor precedent for the day. "Look," he said, forcing patience, "if you were instructing someone who knew nothing about how to do this, what would you tell them?"

"To KNOW the effect they intend to create."

"Yes, beyond that," Ean grumbled. "What specifically?"

Markal cast him a wondering look. "You really remember nothing at all."

"*You* try dying three times for the First Lord and see how well you fare at remembering the Logics and Esoterics!" Ean snapped heatedly.

Markal arched a black brow at him. "So you do remember some things."

Ean shook his head, frustrated with his own ineptitude. He had no idea whence the words had come or even what they meant. "Things come and go." He waved vexedly at his head. "My mind is a god-forsaken sieve. What things I manage to accomplish, more than half the time I do them without understanding."

Perhaps taking pity on him for once, Markal leaned on his staff and deigned to reply, "Every wielder works the lifeforce differently, Ean. Even amongst Adepts, there may be some agreement as to how to identify and tap into their talent, but that's as far as the commonality goes. It is because of the Fifth Law."

As if to prove his own point, the law came to Ean without warning, such that he answered automatically, "*A wielder is limited by what he can envision.*"

Markal eyed him circumspectly.

Ean opened palms to the sky with a helpless glare.

"A wielder is limited by what he can envision," Markal repeated the Fifth Law of Patterning, still regarding Ean through a veil of suspicion. "A Healer can teach another Healer to find a man's personal pattern, and may even describe how she goes about repairing it, but to do so potentially limits the vision of the student. It may prove workable as a means of teaching the precise craft of Healing, but it's a poor way to instruct Patterning."

Ean could see how this would prove true: the limits of the teacher become the limits of the student. He also had a sense that this fact had challenged instructors of Patterning for some time. "Then how do you teach it?"

Markal straightened. "To do it correctly takes time. Trial and error. The student's personal exploration of basic concepts within a field that cannot harm him or others. Those that excel—those with the most potential—grasp the concepts quickly and advance to more difficult ideas. Those who don't...well, those who cannot easily master the basics learn for themselves that Patterning is a poor occupation for them."

"So proper instruction also weeds out the weak and the inept."

"Unquestionably. Patterning is not for the dilettante."

Ean considered him and his explanation. "Time then," he surmised. "That's really my problem isn't it? We don't have time to allow an orderly revival of skill and knowledge through experimentation and exploration, as you said."

"Just so." Markal pinned his almost-black eyes on Ean compellingly.

"But this isn't working either." Ean's tone betrayed his aggravation. He wasn't looking forward to another day of beating and bruising to no avail.

"Perhaps the stakes are not high enough," came a chiming observation from behind Ean.

He turned at Isabel's voice. She emerged from the loggia into the courtyard wearing a flowing linen dress. Her black staff shone dully as she walked, absorbing the morning light without reflecting it back, and Ean realized for the first time that the staff was Merdanti—the same enchanted black stone that the zanthyrs used to craft their infamous blades.

"My lady," Markal said gravely, nodding to her.

"Good morning, my lords," Isabel greeted. With her black blindfold and simple linen dress, she reminded Ean uncomfortably of a sacrificial virgin. She stopped midway between Ean and Markal and rested her staff lightly upon the stones.

"I know your methods are the most effective, General," she began, nodding towards Markal, "and I know he is trying with everything that he is," she added, nodding towards Ean, "yet the efforts pass unawares of each other, two ships in the mist."

She approached Ean and explained, "It is *need* that drives the Awakening, necessity that overcomes the veil of death. It must be more than mere desire to know. There must be a need so critical to survival that it evokes the strength to pierce the veil."

Stopping in front of Ean, she smiled up at him for the sweetest breath of a moment and released her staff. It remained standing on end at his side. "Therefore," she said, turning back to Markal, "*I* shall provide this need."

Markal's expression immediately darkened, even as Ean declared, "Absolutely not!" They'd both perceived the intent of Isabel's plan, and neither wanted anything to do with it.

Patently disregarding their protests, Isabel said, "Markal knows unequivocally that Ean possesses the knowledge to alter the rope, while Ean judges unquestionably that Markal will do as I require of him," and she smiled at Markal at this. "To this end, we are all agreed on the danger inherent in this endeavor."

"Isabel—" Ean said wretchedly, "I don't *know* that I can—"

"What you must know, my darling, is the effect you intend to create," and the smile she gave him was so beautiful that Ean felt his soul rending itself in homage. Isabel added serenely, "I think you know quite well what effect that needs to be." She turned to Markal. "So…let us waste no more time with delays. Face your fears, gentlemen."

"Isabel…" Markal growled, glaring at her fiercely from under his brows, "sometimes I deplore you for the things you make me do."

"I forgive you, Markal," she returned solemnly. Then she lifted her chin and stood at the ready, and Ean's instincts screamed so loudly in protest he thought his eardrums would burst.

Markal shifted his gaze to Ean. The deadly warning in his glare was clear. Ean only stared helplessly back at him—for what else could he do? He would lose his own life before seeing Isabel come to harm!

Markal inhaled, drew himself tall, and let out his breath in a slow hiss, his eyes piercing Ean with their determination. He lifted his staff slowly, measuring the necessary force.

Mentally, the prince felt frantic. He stood with his rope in hand, torn by uncertainty and despair. His mind was blank, frozen. His eyes locked onto Markal's with the same desperate protest in which he'd watched Reyd slaying Creighton.

Markal drew back his staff—

Ean searched vainly in the blackness of his mind for any flicker of memory, even the slightest notion of how to prevent—

Markal swung—

The moment shocked Ean with pain and dread, fear of loss, anger, vivid protest—myriad emotions balled into one overpowering burst united within a single intent: *NO!*

Into the void flooded the knowledge.

Ean spun the rope overhead, hand to hand, whipping it fiercely as he launched forward. He slammed it down before Isabel with a thunderous *clap*, the stones cracking beneath it an instant before Markal's wooden staff shattered across its beam.

In the silence that followed, both men stood with chests heaving, their eyes locked heatedly upon one another. Between them stood Ean's granite staff, hovering an inch in front of Isabel's nose, and Isabel herself, smiling beatifically.

She waited long enough for the men to calm, for the fiercely protective instinct roused in each of them to settle its wolfish nose once more upon its paws and retreat to watchful silence. Then she said, "Ean, restore your staff to rope."

Ean did it easily, unworking the pattern he'd so unwittingly impelled upon it. The staff withered into rope again and fell impotently across his clenched fist.

"A perfect example of the First and Fifth Laws at work," Isabel complimented as she turned to retrieve her own staff from its quiet respite. "Had Markal specified a pattern to use, it would've been merely *his* vision, his concept. You would only have used the pattern he chose, Ean, instead of creating your own." She settled her Merdanti staff at her feet. "As you saw, the patterns each of you picked were different, but the effect was essentially the same."

Ean watched her with a confusing mixture of emotions. On the one hand, he was relieved beyond measure that her ruse had worked, and he wanted only to cradle her safely to his chest and exhale his relief. On the other, he was quite desirous of forcefully strangling her for risking herself so readily.

Markal glared like a wolf cornered by a bear, resentful and determinedly unforgiving. "Thank you for that abject lesson, Isabel," he grated. "Epiphany willing, we can find our own way from here."

Isabel nodded to him, curtsied slightly by way of farewell, and made her stately way out of the yard. Ean suspected she was smiling the whole way.

Feeling the aftereffects of plunging adrenaline, that shaking sensation of what had *almost* been, Ean looked to Markal and swallowed. "I would rather slit my own throat than go through that again."

Markal nodded at him as he took up his broken staff and rejoined it with a look—the split-second firing of intense concentration, a connection of concept and intent forced into a single pulse of *become*.

"Then let that be the driving force of your need, Ean val Lorian," he said as he held the staff before him again at the ready, "and spare us both the dire contemplation of such deed as might've occurred this day."

Thus in agreement did Ean continue the morning's training.

The remainder of the day went much better. They continued their practice creating similar effects, working the First Law until it had become second nature for Ean.

As they were breaking their fast at midday, Markal being satisfied with their progress thus far, the wielder set Ean upon the Second Law. "*What applies to one applies to all*," Markal explained as they sat beneath the loggia overlooking the practice yard where a table had been placed for their meal, their view framed by draping boughs of bougainvillea. "The pattern that will change a rope to stone—or water, or wood—will equally change stone to sand or seawater to volcanic glass."

"But not pure glass?" Ean asked as he ate a tart of roasted duck and cherries redolent with tarragon.

"No," Markal confirmed. "The pattern we work changes the elemental construction of a thing—what it's made of—but it doesn't change its *form*. To change its form, to reorder the exact arrangement of its parts...that is a very different and far more complex working requiring the simultaneous compulsion of potentially many different patterns at once."

"Tomorrow's lesson then," Ean quipped.

Markal arched a black brow at him. "The Esoterics you so blithely mentioned earlier deal with the form of things," he advised. "This topic is not even contained in the Laws of Patterning."

"I get it. It's difficult." Ean drank some wine and leveled Markal a thoughtful look. "So the patterns we're using might change the elemental composition of a thing but not the arrangement of its parts—not its shape or form," he summarized. "The rope can easily become a staff because the essential arrangement of its parts is already in that shape. Sand and water and stone can easily assume any shape. But blown glass, cloth I suspect— things crafted by human hands require the use of Form to change them, which patterns are far more difficult to master and..." he added, as the memory resurfaced, "are therefore advanced concepts discussed in the Esoterics instead of the Laws."

Markal eyed him critically over his empty plate. "I confess, I am relieved to see that you haven't lost all your wits in the intervening centuries since our lessons."

"Did you think dying would make me stupid?"

"You have given me reason to think so, yes," and when Ean opened his mouth to demand indignantly to know when, Markal preempted him by answering, "*Many* times."

The next day Markal introduced Ean to the Ninth Law.

Ean met the wielder in one of the larger gardens. When he arrived, Markal was waiting for him beside a reflecting pool a hundred paces long and twenty wide. Eyeing the pool curiously, Ean walked around it to where Markal stood leaning on his staff. "Is one of us going to get wet today?" he asked suspiciously.

Markal gave him a look that implied he could answer this question himself.

Ean looked down at his clothes and sighed. "Should I just undress now, do you think?"

Markal arched a brow. "O ye of little faith."

"You're the one who said I couldn't change."

"I never questioned your ability," the wielder remarked critically, "just your intelligence in applying it."

Ean let that one go—the man might have a point. "So what's with the pool?"

Markal drew himself tall. "The Ninth Law."

"Which is?"

"What, no instant recitation?"

Ean gave him a sooty look. "I told you, the knowledge comes and goes."

"Encourage it to linger, won't you?" He motioned with his staff for Ean to go to one end of the pool and himself headed towards the other. As he walked, he used *elae* to enhance his voice to carry across the distance. "The Ninth Law states: *Do not counter force with force; channel it.*"

"That seems far too simple," Ean muttered as he took his position at the narrow end of the pool. If he'd come to know one thing thus far about the Laws of Patterning, they were none of them as simple in application as they seemed in theory.

Markal took his position at the other end of the long pool, which gleamed aqua-clear in the bright sunlight. Then he swept his staff before him, and the water surged into a twenty-foot wave.

The sight of the massive wall of water rushing towards him was enough to pierce the veil of Ean's memory. The knowledge appeared as it had in Dannym, as it had in Rethynnea, and he forced the fifth to comply with his intent. The air solidified around him just as the wave crashed across its protective dome.

Ean's heart raced as he watched the wave breaking around his shield. He couldn't help cringing slightly as the water pounded down, though there was no way for it to reach him. Then it was over. Breathing hard, Ean released *elae*, straightened, and turned to Markal.

The wielder looked immensely unimpressed.

"What?" Ean shot him an injured glare.

"In what way," remarked Markal, "did you apply the Ninth Law?"

"I didn't counter it with force," Ean pointed out petulantly.

"Nor did you channel it! You stood to be the *effect* of my force, *my* cause. You caused *nothing* in return. Even should you have cast the water back towards me in violation of the law, t'would have been preferable to such cowardly abdication of cause."

His words stung. "It wasn't like you gave me any time to think about it!" Ean retorted.

Markal took but one step and was suddenly standing before him—truly, Ean barely saw him move before he was simply there, nose to nose and glaring fiercely. *"What do you think we are playing at here?"* he hissed with eyes like fiery coals. "You expect the Malorin'athgul will *warn* you before they claim your life? That they'll not take advantage of any ineptitude, *any* weakness, *any* hesitation? Think you, perhaps, to find *mercy* in their blade?"

Ean held Markal's gaze with his own hot glare, though the wielder's words shamed him with a painful truth. He forced back the protest raging to escape him, that desperate instinct towards battle—towards *survival*—that roused itself at mention of the Malorin'athgul. Too many times he'd fallen prey to them, and instinct had become a vicious animal that stood ready to attack at the least provocation.

Perhaps sensing the disparate and tormented emotions warring for purchase in Ean's consciousness, Markal said with slightly less criticism, "If I coddle you, if I demand anything less than that which I *know* you're capable of, do you think that will help you succeed?" He shook his head and turned away, stating resolutely and with grievous regret, "This game is vicious and unyielding, and only the fiercest players survive."

Ean watched him as he walked back to his end of the pool and took up his position once more. "Again."

And onward came the wave.

That time it crashed over Ean and pummeled him into the grass. He pushed up on hands and knees, coughing and sputtering, but he didn't cast any looks towards the wielder, no flippant remarks. He just got back on his feet and tried again. And again.

And again.

Around the fifth time of being pounded by the wave, an idea at last came to him. Ean pushed to his feet, dripping and winded but still determined. When Markal again sent the crushing wave, Ean focused a pattern in response. The water met with a wall of force that sent it cascading back towards Markal.

Well, at least it didn't flatten him.

"You are still thinking of this the wrong way, Ean," Markal observed after the water had settled back into the pool.

Ean pushed wet hair out of his eyes and took off his dripping shirt, slinging it to the side. The sun felt good on his chilled skin, warming, renewing. "How?"

"You persist in attempting only to think with patterns."

"Because *you're* sending patterns at me!" Ean immediately argued, his frustration evident.

Markal smiled ferociously. "Exactly. You are continuously *violating* the Ninth Law."

"What?" Ean protested, indignant now. "How?" But then he saw it. "No—never mind," he grumbled. *Shadow take the insufferable man, but he's right.* Markal was sending patterns at Ean, and he was only responding with similar patterns—not channeling the force towards his own use. They were just batting a ball of *elae* back and forth between them.

As Ean looked upon their practice thus far, he saw that Markal's 'force' actually could be thought of as the *intention*—the *idea* being channeled to produce an effect. In Patterning, first one conceived of the effect he wanted to create—*KNOW the effect,* as stated by the First Law. *Then,* if he was an Adept like Ean, he simply created a pattern with his *intent.* He didn't need to know the pattern that compelled the water. He only needed to know what he wanted the water to do, and his mind would form the pattern automatically as he focused his intent.

As this understanding came to him, Ean applied it towards the Ninth Law: *Do not counter force with force; channel it.* Ean had been countering Markal's effect—his force—with his own effect: another pattern. What he should have been doing was taking over the energy that Markal had summoned and rechanneling *elae's* energy to his own purposes.

He exhaled a heavy sigh and nodded, acknowledging Markal's point. He still didn't exactly understand how to channel the force to his own aims, but he understood that merely countering it with a similar pattern was just applying force against force. There had to be another way.

"Again," said Markal, relentless and unyielding.

And the wave came on.

By midday Ean felt utterly spent.

Markal called a halt, and they broke their fast beneath a stone gazebo covered in flowering jasmine, its fragrance heady and sweet. Ean's persistent failure had given him a morose outlook, and now he saw only the reasons why this course of action was doomed to fail. He feared he'd never be able to summon an appropriate response to Markal's working and bombarded himself with excuses and untruths, justifications for his failings.

Barely aware of what he was eating, only knowing that he would need his strength to keep from drowning, Ean roused from the mud of self-abnegation long enough to notice two figures walking among the trees on the far side of the clearing, beyond the pool. Isabel's form called to his heart.

That day she wore a dress of jade, and she walked arm in arm with another woman who wore a fiery gown fashioned in the desert style. As the ladies passed from shade into sunlight, Ean saw citrine stones sparkling in the other woman's flame-gold hair.

"She walks with the Sundragon Jayachándranáptra," Markal supplied, mistaking the interest of Ean's focused gaze.

Ean tore his eyes from Isabel, having barely even noticed the other woman. "What? Oh…yes. I met Ramu a few days ago." He looked back to his plate and was relieved to discover that he'd managed to eat most of his food. "I suppose we should try again…" but his gaze strayed wistfully back towards Isabel. The ladies were just heading down a promenade of stately oak trees and out of view.

Markal eyed him speculatively.

They took up their places as the sun was arcing westward. Ean felt somewhat restored—more by sight of Isabel than the food he'd managed to consume. His thoughts kept straying to her now, remembering their few conversations together, imagining moments to come. More than anything, he wanted to chase after her, to find her and be with her, even if it meant simply walking at her side as she spoke with her friend. It wasn't long before thoughts of Isabel consumed him, such that he didn't even see the wall of water until it was too late.

The force catapulted him off his feet and through the air to land in a sprawl while the crushing wave battered him relentlessly into the grass. He lay there choking for a good three minutes afterwards, just trying to manage a painful gasp.

The second time he wasn't so lucky, and he truly thought he might drown before the water relented—Markal worked the fifth to fill the pool with an endless supply. Ean was sure Markal had somehow sent extra water in that wave, and as he got back to his feet, he shot the man a baleful glare.

Markal leaned on his staff. "If you don't get that woman out of your head, Ean val Lorian, you're going to die again before you have a chance to live your life with her. Worse, you'll likely take the rest of us down with you in the bargain."

Ean growled the most uncomplimentary thing he could think of, to which Markal replied, "And when you retreat in shame to the Extian Doors for a *fourth* time to await your Returning, I think *I* will claim Isabel for myself."

Even knowing he meant it as a taunt, Ean stiffened. The idea of Isabel with any other man enraged him beyond reason.

"Yes," Markal remarked thoughtfully, "I shall take Isabel to *my* bed." He swept his staff before him, calling up the waters even as he declared in an *elae*-enhanced voice, "Isabel shall lie naked before me, wanton and lustful for my loins, and she shall beg—"

The water rushed towards Ean—

"—for a release that I shall deny her—"

Ean lashed out. The force of the water coming towards him spun into a towering vortex of whipping sand that speared back towards Markal. The wielder raised his staff, and the sand turned to wind, a gale that drove him backwards towards the trees until at last the pattern exhausted itself.

Dislodged leaves floated idly down upon the settling tides of *elae*, but Ean stood in a battle stance, his shoulders taut, fists clenched, ready to launch towards the man in a fury.

Markal tugged his tunic straight and smoothed his silver-white hair, which Ean's wind had displaced. "A mite touchy, aren't we?" His dark eyes gleamed with triumph.

It took the greatest force of will for Ean to allow himself to release the intent he harbored so dangerously within, an intent that had already gathered unto itself a deadly quantity of *elae*. The power hummed within his consciousness, just waiting to assume some shape, some form…waiting for his will to mold it.

Exhaling through clenched teeth, Ean let *elae* ooze out of him to reassume its natural channels. He wondered if Markal had any idea how close he'd come to being annihilated. He suspected that he did. That was probably why he was smiling.

"Let us explore the reasoning behind the Ninth Law," the wielder said then. "This time, counter my pattern with the same pattern." He sent a smaller wave towards Ean.

Ean easily copied the pattern and sent an identical wave back towards Markal. Both forces met in a geyser of whitewater.

Once the patterns had exhausted their force and the pool had stilled, Markal said, "This time, let us re-direct our force, repel it."

He lifted his staff, and the water rose at his command and shot towards Ean. Ean threw up a pattern that channeled the same force back towards Markal, rerouting the water in a stream the opposite way. Markal added his own layer to the same pattern, casting the water back towards Ean, who again countered, until a looping tunnel of water churned between them.

Abruptly Markal dropped his arms, and the water dove back into the pool with a violent splash. As the water stilled, Ean stared at the pool, feeling dazed. He realized just how much of his own lifeforce he'd exhausted with the last few workings, and it occurred to him that while he could call *elae* to him in abundance, the actual use of it—the *channeling* of the lifeforce to comply with his intention—was exhausting all out of proportion to how much of it he could summon.

Markal pinned Ean with an incendiary look. "Explain what you have just experienced."

Ean finally felt sedate enough to find his voice. In truth, it disturbed him how violently he'd reacted to the wielder's taunts about Isabel; yet the ache in his heart remained a palpable thing.

Markal approached steadily with his gaze fixed on Ean, clearly awaiting his reply. Ean decided he'd rather not get drenched again, so he focused on the wielder's demand: an explanation of the day's lesson.

He pushed damp hair out of his eyes. "The most effective way of countering an effort coming against you is to use the power already being channeled. You re-align the power another has summoned to suit your own will."

"Just so," Markal confirmed.

"You can take someone's effort and pit your effort against it," Ean continued slowly, thinking through what he'd just observed with the geysering water, "but then you have two opposing efforts pushing against each other, forming a ridge of energy, like the geyser of water. It doesn't accomplish much. Likewise, sending the same effort back towards its origins just causes the cycle to repeat. Both of these approaches waste your energy."

"Ah, good," Markal commented, "so you noticed."

"I noticed." Ean exhaled a sigh and moved to sit on the edge of the stone pool, resting elbows on his knees. "I don't exactly understand it. I mean…" he pushed a hand through his hair again and glanced up under his brows at the older man. "I was holding so much *elae* just then—" He dropped his gaze and shook his head. "You have no idea."

"I have an idea," the wielder remarked with shadowy amusement. He walked to stand in front of Ean. "Take a deep breath—as deep as you can possibly draw."

Gazing curiously at him, Ean did so.

"Now keep it in."

Ean held his breath and stared at Markal while his chest grew tight and hot, blood vessels constricting.

"Blow it out—hard."

Ean forced a powerful exhale.

"Now do it again."

Ean followed his directions. Five more times did he draw breath as deeply as his lungs would allow and forcefully exhale. By the end, he felt lightheaded and drained.

"It is the same with *elae*," Markal explained then, taking note of Ean's physical response. "Like air, there is more *elae* in the world than you will ever be able to hold within you. The lifeforce is boundless and inexhaustible. *You* are not. Your lifeforce is but one tiny spark of this immense whole."

He leaned on his staff and fixed Ean with his piercing gaze. "Your body's innate energy can be expended until it cannot itself contain *elae* within it any longer. No amount of drawing upon the lifeforce will restore a body which has become a sieve."

Ean thought this over carefully. "So the lesson of the Ninth Law is also a lesson on survival."

Markal eyed him gravely. "They are *all* lessons in survival."

TWENTY-FIVE

"Take the road less traveled. Bandits prefer more bountiful pickings."

– Dareios, Prince of Kandori

ALYNERI WOKE IN Trell's arms, comfortable beneath a cool morning breeze blowing in through the open windows. She vaguely recalled Trell carrying her to the bed in the wee hours of the night, after they'd both fallen asleep in the window seat. The sound of his soft breathing, his arm around her waist, holding her close through the night; they were small things, yet they served to deepen her affection. She'd never felt so safe as she felt in his arms.

Trell lives!

The miracle of it still shocked her at odd times and sent a thrill fluttering through her chest. These moments where she realized anew that this was *Trell* beside her, speaking with her, guiding her…they brought indescribable happiness. Trell was a tonic to her soul.

Such happiness imbued her just being in his company—a stark contrast to her travels with Ean. With Trell, she felt protected, confident that whatever came to bear upon them might be weathered in the lee of his leadership. Her time with Ean, by comparison, had always been characterized by angst, anxiety and a sense of desperation.

"*Sobh be kheyr*," Trell murmured into her ear. *Good morning*. When they were alone, they spoke almost exclusively in the desert tongue. Trell pulled her closer and pressed his nose against her neck.

Alyneri had never felt so blissful. Even Trell's voice roused heady thoughts…dreams from private moments. She blushed to think of them now. "Good morning to you also," she returned in the desert tongue.

"It looks like dawn is calling us."

Her heart was beating faster for his nearness, for his touch…for wishing it was more. "Yes."

He tightened his hold on her again. "We should be off, but…"

Alyneri knew his mind; it mirrored her own. "Yes, we should go." She turned in his arms, and her eyes promised there would be other times. His gaze in return assured her there most certainly would.

Alyneri laughed, and he smiled and winked at her. Thus did they separate, but the powerful sense of connection remained.

"I realized last night that I really have no idea how to find the others," Alyneri admitted as they sat up towards opposite sides of the bed. "I think maybe I could find my way to the villa if we started on Faring East—"

Trell glanced over with a smile. "I have a feeling Fate will lend a hand."

She arched a brow at him.

He cocked his in turn and straightened to stand.

As Alyneri looked up at him, so tall and broad of shoulder, and with his black hair and wolf-grey eyes, he reminded her almost painfully of King Gydryn. She nearly lost her breath for admiring him.

Trell's smile turned to a grin. "Come." He extended his hand to her. "On the road, I have another story to tell you."

They headed out as the sun was just clearing the Assifiyahs. It gave a golden cast to the world and sent long shadows westward towards Rethynnea, marking their path. They broke their fast on horseback, content to eat as they rode.

Alyneri couldn't stop thinking about Trell and what it would mean to the kingdom—and to her—that he was alive. They'd been betrothed, after all. Yet though she had every right to nurture her growing feelings for Trell, she still felt odd glimmers of guilt and unease. She'd love Ean for so long…

Trell noted her thoughtful expression, which had brought a little furrow to her brow, and he gave her a wry grin. "Deep thoughts, Duchess?"

She blushed beneath his gaze. "Oh," she dropped her eyes with a soft smile, "I was just thinking about how different you are from Ean."

"Really? In what way? I remember so little about him, but I long to know more."

She glanced up at him and then turned forward again. "You look like brothers, though your jaw is slightly more squared, like the king's. You and Ean have the same eyes, but Ean has your mother's coloring—again, you take after the king." She smiled. "You are very much your father's son."

"I see," he said. Then he frowned.

"Ean is reckless," she pushed on. "Headstrong. Impetuous. But there is something wonderful about him, too. He's brave and adventurous—the other sides of those traits. You both have a sense about you…" She glanced to him again and confessed quietly, "You both make people want to follow you."

He gave her a soft look of thanks.

"But weren't you going to tell me a story?"

"Yes." He gave her an intense look. "Yes, I was." So did he proceed to tell her of his visit to Naiadithine's shrine in the Kutsamak and his subsequent near drowning; of his rescue and healing by the Emir's Mage, and of his interactions with the mysterious and compelling *drachwyr*.

Alyneri stared in amazement. "You *met* Sundragons?"

Trell grinned at her. "You would like Ramu. He's incredibly gracious for all he could probably annihilate both of us with a simple thought."

Alyneri laughed with sheer incredulity. After a thoughtful moment, she remarked, "You know, the Mage did more than heal you."

His brow furrowed. "How do you mean?"

"I noticed when we three were linked while healing Gendaia. He made your pattern stronger somehow; he restructured it without altering its basic form. It was like…it was like he *remade* you with new material—better stuff, stronger stuff. I haven't the least idea how he did it," she added with a wondrous look on her face, "though the fact that the *Fifth Vestal* healed you at least makes sense of what I saw."

"I'm not sure I understand."

She looked seriously to him. "Björn van Gelderan is rumored to have translated the *Sobra I'ternin* in full. His knowledge of Patterning is unmatched. If anyone could remake your inherent composition with better stuff than the Maker saw fit to start with, he could."

Trell turned his gaze forward, frowning. "Why would he do that? It baffles me why this man has taken such interest in my welfare. Vaile said it was good luck to have the blessing of the Mage." He cast Alyneri a rueful grin. "I'm still not sure if I agree with her."

A sudden surge of inexplicable jealously pricked Alyneri upon hearing of the woman named Vaile who'd had the blessing of Trell's company and was obviously a friend. Then she chastised herself for such ridiculous insecurities.

"The Mage is the reason I'm heading to Rethynnea," Trell added then. "As I was preparing to leave the sa'reyth, Balaji—one of the Sundragons—presented Gendaia to me." The horse nickered upon hearing her name, and Trell leaned to rub her neck. "The Mage gave her to me as a gift, along with new clothes and a fortune in Agasi silver."

He turned Alyneri an unreadable look. "Balaji also gave me a letter to take to the Mage's contact in the Cairs. I'd already decided to go to Xanthe—not for any reason I can explain, I think it just seemed as good as place as any to start looking for my past—but the Mage made sure I would go to Rethynnea by requesting that I deliver his message."

"Trell…he must've known who you are."

"Undoubtedly." Trell grunted and shook his head. "Balaji asked me once what I thought the Mage did for the Emir. At the time I understood him to imply that the Mage had many talents. Now I think he hinted at something else entirely."

Alyneri gazed at him, not understanding.

Her turned her a look. "I don't think the Mage serves the Emir. I think it's the other way around."

Alyneri's stomach fluttered.

"Everything changed when Björn van Gelderan appeared," Trell remarked, pensive now. He gazed unseeing at the road ahead. "The entire balance of a six-year war shifted within days of his arrival."

Alyneri hugged her cloak closer, though the sun was shining strongly on her back. Yet it was a chilling contemplation to think that the Fifth Vestal had a grand plan encompassing kingdoms. Certainly all the stories spoke of him as some evil mastermind. But until that moment, she'd never imagined *herself* being somehow involved.

"Do you think the Emir knows the Mage's true identity?" she asked in a small voice.

Trell gave her a telling look. "Without question, and I think it's safe to say the Mage means for me to have a role in his game."

Alyneri looked uneasily to him. The zanthyr's loyalties notwithstanding, she had no proof that the Fifth Vestal meant well, for certainly nothing of the sort was ever attributed to him. The idea that the wielder had plans for Trell frightened her. "Why do you think that?"

"He mentioned me in one of his journals. Ean and I both. But I needn't disturb you with these thoughts, my lady," he added with a smile to lighten the mood. "Things will be as they will. We can only walk the path ahead of us and see where it leads."

As she continued to gaze at him, Alyneri realized that even with all her burgeoning fears, she would willingly walk that path—so long as Trell walked it beside her.

The royal cousin Fynnlar val Lorian knew Fate was punishing him. It remained a mystery which one of his many misdemeanors had finally drawn Cephrael's loathsome and merciless eye, but Fynn was certain that even the most egregious of them should not have required *this* penance.

He sat nursing his wine in the company of Seth Silverbow, Third Vestal of Alorin; Rhys val Kincaide, Captain of the King's Own Guard; and Björn van Gelderan's personal zanthyr.

Since the night Creighton's Shade had claimed Ean and all of the others had vanished, Fynn felt he'd been somehow transported to purgatory. That Seth put himself in charge only rubbed salt in the wound. Fynn would rather have taken orders from the zanthyr than get bossed around by an overgrown pigeon with an ego complex. Not that he actually *did* anything Seth told him to do. He just felt irritated about it on principle.

Which didn't mean he wasn't doing anything about the fact that Tanis and Alyneri had vanished, or that Franco Rohre and Creighton's Shade had dragged Ean across a node that Carian, Gwynnleth and Raine later vanished across, or that the Temple of the Vestals had been magically disintegrated overnight... However, there wasn't much he *could* do.

It galled him that he hadn't been there to see it all himself—that he'd only the word of two immortals to explain what had happened. That the zanthyr and Seth were in agreement on the facts didn't exactly prove their verisimilitude, but he was willing to give them the benefit of the doubt, under the circumstances.

As if any of them cared what he thought.

"...no information of any kind," Rhys was saying when Fynn tuned back into the conversation. They'd all gathered that day to pool their recent discoveries and any progress on the tasks assigned to each of them, but so far the soup of news was pretty damned thin. The Captain finished, "Cayal and Dorin have now inquired in every store along three miles of the Thoroughfare and only the one barmaid remembered seeing anything of Tanis."

"The boy cannot have simply vanished," Seth grumbled. For some reason he'd taken Tanis's disappearance as a personal affront.

"Pretty much looks like that's what he did," Fynn pointed out. He was tired of the same argument day after day—he could be drinking at the Villa D'Antoinette right now instead of listening to Seth's grumbling.

The avieth shot him a fiery glare. "You don't seem overly concerned about the welfare of your companion, Fynnlar val Lorian. Perhaps you were complicit in the boy's disappearance. A traitor in our midst would certainly explain some things."

The royal cousin belched loudly. "Phaedor already told us what happened to the lad." Not that Fynn believed him outright, but it was always convenient to blame things on the zanthyr.

Seth glowered at Fynn and then shifted his gaze and glowered instead at Phaedor, who stood like a shadow leaning against the wall, coolly disinterested, as if he couldn't be bothered even to yawn. When it became clear to Seth that Phaedor wasn't going to speak simply because he was glaring at him, the avieth demanded, "Well?"

"Well what?" replied the shadow that was the zanthyr. Only his green eyes glowed from beneath his raven curls, bright among the darkness that hovered around him.

"What news of the boy?" Seth snapped.

"If I had any news of Tanis, Vestal, I would've told you already."

"You're the one who claims some kind of connection to the boy," Rhys pointed out—he always sided with Seth if it pitted him against the zanthyr.

Phaedor flipped his dagger and caught it by the point. "Tanis lives."

"How very new and insightful," Seth noted blackly.

Fynn often wondered…if the zanthyr didn't intend to give them any information or be helpful in any way, why did he bother coming to the meetings? Then he realized it was probably because Phaedor wanted to keep an eye on the rest of them.

Shadow take the insufferable creature.

"What do you hope to hear from me, Vestal?" Phaedor meanwhile remarked. "I've already told you Tanis won't be found until he's ready."

"You imply he's purposefully hiding from us," Rhys growled, "that the lad went off willingly."

The zanthyr arched a raven brow and spun his dagger by its point on his middle fingertip. It whirled like a top, deadly and straight.

"I just can't believe that of him," Rhys continued. "What would make him wander off in the middle of the city and never return?"

"Finally, a question worthy of consideration."

Fynn regarded the zanthyr sourly. There really was no question as to who actually led their motley group—Fynn would be the first to admit this, so long as he didn't have to admit it out loud. He knew that as soon as the zanthyr declared something to be done, they would all spring into action. Fynn just wished the pretense of it all could be put behind them so he could get back to the Villa D'Antoinette and Ghislain's excellent wine.

Except…he'd been spending so much time at the Villa D'Antoinette of late that Ghislain was starting to drop not so subtle hints about his playing Kings with her. As no game with Ghislain could ever end pleasantly, and since Fynn was attached both to his coin and his pride, he had long ago vowed to never—*ever*—become involved with Ghislain D'Launier over a Kings board. Which left him in an uncomfortable limbo with none of his prospects appearing exactly desirable.

"What's that supposed to mean?" Seth meanwhile demanded of Phaedor.

As if Seth hadn't spoken at all, the zanthyr said, "Tanis is beyond your reach, Captain. You would better serve your prince by searching for his brother."

Rhys gave him a belligerent look.

Despite Fynn's insistence, the obstinate man refused to believe Trell was alive. Not that Fynn cared what Rhys thought.

Fynn had his own people working to find Trell, and he was fairly sure that if *they* couldn't find any trace of him, the Captain certainly wasn't going to. Fynn was also certain that Carian vran Lea knew perfectly well where Trell was hiding. Fynn would've happily strangled the truth out of the pirate, if only Carian hadn't taken it upon himself to permanently vacate the realm.

"No," Rhys muttered, looking uncertain and sounding completely lost. "We need to stay here in case Her Grace or the boy turn up."

"An effective use of your time," the zanthyr remarked darkly.

Seth glowered in reply to Phaedor's sarcasm. "Well, what would *you* have us do?"

But the zanthyr steadfastly refused to advise them—as usual. Fynn half expected he would blame his reticence on Balance—if he ever deigned to explain himself at all—or some other such obscure excuse that none of them might understand anyway.

As if in response to this thought, the zanthyr shifted his emerald eyes to Fynn, and the decidedly telling look in his gaze made Fynn sprout gooseflesh from head to toe. *Belloth take the bloody creature!* He suppressed a shudder and violently wished he could be anywhere else—or at least that the zanthyr might be.

Seth turned to Fynn and demanded churlishly, "What about you, Fynnlar val Lorian? What of your tasks?"

Feeling slightly sick to his stomach—mainly from contemplating the zanthyr's reading of his mind and what this might mean to his immediate future—Fynn drank the last of his wine and pushed out of his chair. "I've already requisitioned two Nodefinders and the Guild Master of Rethynnea to look at the temple node." He walked to pour himself more wine from the sideboard. "I'm not going to chase down another one willing to brave those crumbling ruins just so he can tell us *again* that the bloody thing can't be traveled."

The Temple of the Vestals had been destroyed, and all of Rethynnea was up in arms over it. Only those in this room had any idea what had caused the destruction, and the zanthyr had made Fynn swear an oath to silence on the matter.

Even his reluctant oath hadn't been enough for the creature, though—which fact would've rankled if it hadn't been so justified. Phaedor had done something while Fynn gave his oath—worked some kind of pattern on him.

He could feel it sitting there any time he put attention on the thought. If he so much as conceived of the idea of speaking about what had happened at the temple, he got the abominable sensation of live worms squirming in his stomach. Fynn didn't dare push to see how much worse the feeling could become. He liked his wine inside his body.

"But it *can* be traveled!" Seth retaliated. "I *saw* them cross it! I almost had Gwynnleth—"

"Raine was all about how that node had been tampered with." Fynn turned back to Seth as he poured more wine. "Whatever Franco Rohre did to the node, he obviously constructed it to self-destruct or something, once they were across. If the Guild Master of Rethynnea himself says it can't be traveled, *it can't be traveled,* Seth."

Seth turned and glowered at the zanthyr as if he was somehow to blame, whereupon Fynn noted that the zanthyr's eyes were still fixed unerringly on himself.

Fynn shot back his wine in one a gulp and set his goblet somewhat ungently down on the sideboard. "I'll be at the Villa D'Antoinette."

Raine's truth, he'd rather endure Ghislain's ridicule than spend another moment as the focus of the zanthyr's omniscient gaze.

Alyneri and Trell reached Rethynnea in the early afternoon. Their route brought them into the city from the surrounding hills, and they soon joined the thronging crowds along the Avenue of the Gods, which overlooked the city from a high and winding vantage. Alyneri gazed wondrously at the many temples on the long boulevard. She'd always wanted to visit the Temple of the Vestals, and might've had the chance to do so if not for that untimely meeting with Sandrine du Préc. As they were passing the black marble temple of the Wind God Azerjaiman, Alyneri straightened in her saddle in anticipation of finally seeing the Vestal temple—and gasped.

A great giant seemed to have stepped down and crushed the vast structure that had been the Temple of the Vestals, leaving only shards of crumbling white marble, piles of sand and shattered glass. A constant crowd of people ogled the destruction. Some of them had ventured up onto the edge of the rubble to look down upon the lower levels within, but most stayed prudently distant, letting their eyes and whispers do the exploring instead.

Trell looked to her when he heard her intake of breath. "What is this place?"

"It *was* the Temple of the Vestals," she whispered, turning to him wide-eyed.

"I take it the place was still standing when you left."

She nodded.

"Any idea what happened here?"

Alyneri felt a little sick to her stomach. "I have an idea."

Trell looked back to the ruined temple, and his brow furrowed. "Let's push on. Perhaps the Mage's emissary can tell us something."

They made their way to the Rue de la Mer, a long road that wound along the highest hill at the west end of the city. It commanded impressive views and played host to some of the most luxurious and exclusive homes in Rethynnea.

Their destination was a pink marble mansion. A groom ran up to take their horses before they'd even dismounted in the circular drive. Trell pulled a leather case from his satchel, took Alyneri's hand, and headed up the steps.

The double doors opened to reveal a lovely brunette in a gown of shimmering silk. "Welcome to the Villa D'Antoinette, my lord and lady," she said with a Bemothi accent exotically lacing the inflection of her words.

Alyneri stood somewhat in awe of her.

Trell nodded in greeting. "I bear a missive for the Lady Ghislain D'Launier. Is she present, madam?"

"But of course. Come inside."

As they moved within, the brunette looked Trell over appreciatively with her lips curved in a suggestive smile. Then she led them through the mansion's luxurious rooms, where men and women of varied races were talking and drinking wine.

"Is your mistress throwing a party?" Alyneri asked the woman.

The brunette gave Alyneri a look that reminded her uncomfortably of Sandrine but quickened her pulse all the same. "Always, my lady."

Alyneri cleared her throat. "I hope we're not intruding."

"There are no intruders at the Villa D'Antoinette," the woman replied in her exotically throaty voice. "Only the most interesting people to make acquaintance with."

"Sounds like another place I know," Trell murmured.

Alyneri looked at him strangely.

The brunette led them up a grand, curving staircase to the second level and down a long corridor that opened upon more rooms. Alyneri wondered what Madam D'Launier did to host so many people at all hours of the day.

When they reached her, Ghislain was reclining upon a divan, before which sat three men at three different Kings boards. They were all hunched over the boards and wore similarly dark expressions.

Ghislain straightened from her languorous repose. "And who do we have here, Riselle?"

"An emissary, my lady," answered the brunette. She gave Alyneri a nod, Trell a shameless look, and took her leave.

"An emissary." Ghislain eyed Trell curiously. "Well then." She stood, revealing a voluptuous figure in a fuchsia gown, and motioned them to come along.

They followed her into a salon paneled in chestnut-hued velvet. Ghislain seated herself in an armchair and extended her hand to Trell. "Let's see what you have for me."

Trell handed her the leather case.

She broke the seal on the parchment and read the contents with a swift pass of her dark eyes. Then she settled the missive in her lap and looked upon Trell more carefully. "Have you some idea what this contains?"

"Yes, madam."

Ghislain's shrewd gaze swept Trell, appearing to note every detail, from Kingdom Blade to wolf-grey eyes. "And what is your name, sir—your true name?"

"I am Trell val Lorian."

"Ahh…" she broke into a smile. Her enigmatic, dark-eyed gaze flicked to Alyneri. "And who might you be, dear girl?"

"Alyneri d'Giverny." She cringed at how young and unworldly her voice sounded by comparison to Ghislain's.

Ghislain sat back in her chair and looked over the both of them with an expression of sardonic amusement. "Incredible. Half the city seems to be looking for you, dear," she said to Alyneri. Then her eyes shifted back to Trell. "And the spy networks of three kingdoms are on the hunt for you, Prince of Dannym."

"We—I…" Alyneri cleared her throat. "I've been separated from my companions. We were hoping you could help us."

"To be certain, you've come to the right place." Her eyes had never left Trell, and both challenge and the hint of amusement gleamed in her gaze. She waved the missive enticingly. "Would you like to read it?"

Trell's expression flickered through a host of emotions. "Perhaps…yes," he answered at last.

Smiling sublimely, Ghislain handed him the paper.

Alyneri read it over Trell's arm. The words were written in a flowing hand.

Please see that he reaches his family, Ghislain.

Alyneri's eyes filled with tears.

Jaw clenched, Trell handed the parchment back to Ghislain. "Why?" he asked tightly.

Ghislain shrugged. "Who knows the inner workings of a Mage's mind?"

Trell held her gaze. "Do you know who he is?"

Ghislain gave an elliptical smile. "He is a great man with many names."

Trell dropped his chin towards his chest, and Alyneri sensed a certain tension bleeding out of him. "He is that," he admitted, his tone intense though the words had been softly spoken.

"Come, darling ones." Ghislain stood in a rustle of silk. "I have something to show you."

She led them from the room without waiting for a reply. Alyneri followed, somewhat in awe. Ghislain reminded her in some ways both of Queen Errodan and the Fire Princess Ysolde—also women of authority who bore their power lightly.

Ghislain led them through her mansion and into a salon that opened upon a small balcony. Outside, near a railing covered in bougainvillea, a man sat in profile to them. His shaggy dark hair obscured his face as he gripped a goblet of wine and scowled down at a King's board.

"Have you made your move yet, my lord?" Ghislain asked as she neared.

The man turned her a sudden scowl, and Alyneri gasped. "Fynn!"

Seeing Alyneri, Fynn leapt from of his chair—*dropping* his wine—and threw his arms around her as if she'd just rescued him from a hurricane sea.

Alyneri laughed and hugged him tightly in return. "I never imagined I'd be so happy to see you, Fynn!"

"Your Grace, you have saved me from a fate worse than death!" He clutched her close. "Ghislain has already taken my coin and my pride. I was beginning to fear she'd set her sights upon my very soul."

"You pawned that trinket long ago, my lord," Ghislain murmured with dark amusement.

Fynn flickered a baleful look at Ghislain. Then he drew back and took Alyneri firmly by the shoulders. "Where in thirteen bloody hells have you been?"

"Retrieving me, I think," Trell offered.

Only then did Fynn take notice of the man standing just behind Alyneri. He stood back to better view him. Then he stared, and then he laughed boldly. "By all the bloody fortune in the thousand realms!" Fynn bounded three steps and threw his arms around Trell, shrugging him roughly from side to side. "I never thought I'd see the day! Welcome back, cousin!"

Trell modestly received Fynn's affections. "I think I remember something of you, cousin," he observed as Fynn continued his mobbing of him with affection. "Something about…mud pies?"

"No, no—the pies were entirely Sebastian's idea." Fynn grabbed Trell by the shoulders and laughed again. "I knew it!" He shot Ghislain a telling look. "I told you it was true!"

His comment gave Alyneri pause. "What do you mean, Fynn?" She touched Fynn's arm to gain his attention. "You knew Trell lived?"

He released Trell and went to pour himself more wine from a near credenza. "I'd gone to investigate rumors out of Veneisea, you may recall—after the attack on Ean. I returned with news of Trell the same night the rest of that bloody mess happened."

Alyneri went cold. "What…bloody mess?"

"Oh, Fortune curse us all—you don't know?" Fynn looked from her to Trell and back again. Then he looked to Ghislain, the quiet observer of their reunion. "It'll have to wait," he remarked with an accusatory glare at their host. "Some things aren't safe to discuss, even in the Villa D'Antoinette."

"And I was so looking forward to finishing our game, my lord." Ghislain cast him a somewhat predatory smile. "You must return soon, that we may complete our accord."

Fynn murmured something noncommittal and dragged Alyneri and Trell from the room.

There followed a tense half hour spent mostly in silence as they rode back to Fynn's rented villa. When Alyneri arrived in the villa's drive to find the place looking abandoned, her trepidation grew immensely. "Fynn, where is everyone?"

"Rhys and Brody are probably off searching the lower city again," Fynn grumbled. He somewhat threw himself off his horse and motioned Alyneri and Trell off theirs. Then he handed off his reins to a stable boy, who came up to them looking as if he'd just woken from a nap.

"Bastian sailed north with the *Tungsten* three days ago to deliver news of you, cousin," he said, nodding at Trell, "to my dear auntie, your queen mother. Seth got tired of being ignored by the zanthyr and left at the same time I did this morning. I don't know where Phaedor is." He glowered around at the bushes and trees and the high walls and added under his breath, "Probably just waiting for the opportune time to appear and scare the thirteen hells out of us."

"And everyone else?" Alyneri's unease was reaching alarming proportions. "What of the Fourth Vestal and Tanis and Ean? Carian vran Lea?"

"Yeah," Fynn muttered darkly, "we'll get to them."

He led them inside the manse, which seemed disturbingly dark and empty to Alyneri, and into the closest room that hosted a bar. He poured three glasses of wine, and as he handed Alyneri's to her, he said gravely, "Your Grace, you'd better sit down." Then he looked to Trell. "You might as well sit down too, cousin."

They sat. Trell reached over and took Alyneri's hand. She squeezed it gratefully.

Fynn settled into an armchair across from them. "The night you disappeared, Your Grace, everything went to hell. Brody and arrived back from Veneisea to report to the Vestal on what we'd learned of Trell." He looked to him. "You apparently made quite an impression on the Lord Commander of the Tivaricum, as well as Indora's Magisteré. I'm glad to know you take after your old cousin Fynn." He winked and gave Trell an approving nod.

"But as I was saying," he went on then, abruptly exchanging his grin for a gloomy expression, "Raine D'Lacourte was up in arms about having learned something important about the Fifth Vestal's plans, all certain of a sudden that he had the upper hand—a lot of shite and nonsense that turned out to be." He looked sternly to Trell. "Never believe a Vestal when he says the game is up. Raine told me he was planning to take Ean to Illume Belliel, because he believed the Fifth Vestal intended to claim Ean as he'd claimed Franco Rohre—"

"He *what?*" Alyneri gasped. "Fynn, for Epiphany's sake—"

"But that's not even the worst part," Fynn continued dourly. "Vran Lea returned from Belloth-knows-where to tell us that Franco Rohre had been seen in the Temple of the Vestals, and then the zanthyr appeared with news that Ean had awoken."

Alyneri pushed hands to her cheeks. "Was he—?"

"As witless as ever," Fynn grumbled. "I was on my way to tell him that you lived, cousin," he said, looking to Trell, "but I was too late. He took off with Creighton's Shade—"

"Creighton's *Shade?*" Alyneri very nearly shrieked. "Fynn, have you gone mad?"

Fynn pushed a palm to forehead and rested his head back against the chair. "If only."

"Creighton," Trell meanwhile mused. "I know that name…"

"He was Ean's blood-brother," Fynn said with eyes still closed. Then he dropped his palm and looked despondently back to Trell. "The son of a powerful Agasi nobleman."

"And now he's a Shade?" Trell inquired, as if the man had simply become a knight and not a specter of fell magic and shadow.

"The damnable creature left me frozen in Ean's rooms for the better part of two hours, curse him."

Alyneri gaped at Fynn in utter disbelief.

"And then?" Trell prodded.

"Raine called for the pirate and left with the avieths and his army of mercenaries, and the zanthyr leaped over Ean's railing claiming he was off to avert disaster but I've no proof it wasn't him who destroyed the Temple of the Vestals."

"How *was* the temple destroyed?" Trell asked.

Fynn darted his gaze around the room. The he looked back to Trell and swallowed uncomfortably. "...*Deyjiin*," he somewhat gasped out.

"Which is what?"

"A dark power." Sudden understanding chilled Alyneri. "What happened to him, Fynn?" She felt a desperation welling, along with a sick feeling, which she often and unfortunately associated with Ean.

"Ean lives," Fynn reassured her, though he looked oddly green himself, "but from everything we can tell, he's joined Björn van Gelderan in T'khendar. Seth claims..." He paused to force a swallow—he was looking truly unwell. "The avieth says Franco Rohre took Ean across a node... and the pirate followed with Raine...and Gwynnleth...there at the end." He took a deep breath and whispered sickly, "Everything I know of what happened at the temple came from the zanthyr or Seth. Their stories match, so I suppose they must be true—Epiphany knows they wouldn't have collaborated on them. Now if you'll excuse me, I have to go throw up," and he rushed from the room.

Alyneri followed him with her eyes, feeling numb.

Trell drank his wine in silence.

Fynn came back before too long, but he didn't seem much better. He didn't even reach to fill his wine, just slumped down in his chair across from them looking morose. "If you don't mind, Your Grace," Fynn muttered then, "maybe you can ask the zanthyr if you've any more questions about... the temple."

But Alyneri didn't care about the temple. "Where is Tanis? Is he with the captain?"

Fynn slapped a palm to his forehead. "Belloth's bloody balls—you mean you don't know about that either?" He swore an oath under his breath. "Tanis vanished the same day you did—apparently just up and left the café where he'd been waiting for you with not a word to Rhys or anyone. We were hoping maybe you knew something about it."

Alyneri felt a faint hysteria, and her wine started rippling in her goblet. She realized in that detached sort of way that it was because her hand was shaking.

Trell took her cup gently from her hand while asking Fynn, "Who is Tanis?"

"A young truthreader," the royal cousin answered at the same time that

Alyneri whispered, "He's like a brother to me." Her eyes shifted back to Fynn. "*Shade and darkness,* Fynnlar—have you no idea? What if he's hurt somewhere?" Her voice rose sharply with her distress. "What if he—"

"Tanis lives," came a deep voice from the shadows

Alyneri pushed from her chair and spun to face the zanthyr, who was entering through the open patio doors. "How could you *lose* him?" Her voice broke, and tears welled in her eyes.

"As a point of fact, Your Grace," the zanthyr returned stoically, "*you* are the one who lost him. He went missing while you were in the apothecary."

"Being *kidnapped!*" she protested incredulously.

"Belloth's bloody balls," Fynn growled, for he had yet to hear Alyneri's story, and this was the first he'd learned of it. "Are we all cursed, or is it just a spell of increasingly ill luck?" He glared at the zanthyr as if Phaedor was somehow to blame for their combined misfortunes. "Who took Your Grace? Or do you know?"

She turned to him but didn't seem able to find her voice.

"Morwyk," Trell supplied in her stead.

"Ah, yes," Fynn sat back in his chair. "Our favorite Duke of the Apocalypse. Would that his mother had seen fit to drown him at birth." His gaze shifted back to the zanthyr, and from the look in his eyes, he was clearly wishing the same fate upon him.

Alyneri took hold of her chair. "If something happens to Tanis, I shall never forgive myself." The zanthyr moved on across the room, always availing himself of the shadows instead of the light. "But you...you say he lives?" She followed Phaedor with a desperate gaze. "He's safe then?"

"I did not say he was safe."

"Please, Phaedor!" Forgetting herself completely, Alyneri chased after him.

Once she might've held her ground, tried to show he couldn't intimidate her, but she'd shared a night of healing with Phaedor. She knew the light he harbored in his soul—the others be damned if they couldn't see it too!

She took his hand in both of hers and pressed his palm to her heart. "Please," she whispered, unable to look into his eyes but feeling his powerful gaze upon her all the same. "Won't you tell me what you can? Is he in danger?" When the zanthyr didn't immediately answer, Alyneri leaned forward and pressed her forehead to his chest. "*Please...I beg you.*"

"There is nothing I can say to ease your fears, Duchess." Phaedor stood as resolute as a statue beneath her entreaty, though his tone conveyed a gentle understanding. "I don't know where the lad is, only that he's upon a mission he feels duty-bound to complete."

"And how do you know this?" came an iron voice from the balcony.

It seemed Seth had returned.

"Yes, I'm quite interested to hear that answer myself," Fynn grumbled. He seemed to have recovered somewhat from his earlier affliction, for he got up and poured himself another goblet of wine.

Alyneri lifted her head and gazed into Phaedor's emerald eyes. She kept the zanthyr's hand pressed over her heart, refusing to release it until he gave her some hope to hold onto instead.

Coming closer, Seth commented hotly, "I know of no working that would reveal such knowledge unless you'd bound the boy to you—" Suddenly he stopped and stared, and the room filled with silent accusation while he found uncharacteristic restraint for his anger. "You *bound* the boy to you!"

"I wouldn't put it past him." Fynn leaned against the sideboard and glared daggers at Phaedor over the rim of his goblet.

"I should call Illume Belliel's Paladin Knights to claim your head!" Seth hissed. "Binding a child against his will? You're no better than that bastard you serve!" He spun on his heel and stalked out again, leaving a wake of contempt to stain the air.

Fynn opened his mouth to contribute, but Trell, whose gaze had never left the zanthyr's face, murmured quickly, "Cousin, not now."

Alyneri felt tears coming to her eyes, felt them well and brim and fall, warm and then cool upon her checks. For she understood what had truly happened.

A babe brought to them in mystery and secret...

Phaedor would never have bound Tanis without his consent, which left only one explanation. "You bound yourself to him," she whispered, barely managing the words, for their ramifications were so profound and devastating, "for forever and all time? *Dear Epiphany,* Phaedor!" Tears streamed down her cheeks as she stared at him in awe. "He was a babe of two...and you gave him everything that you are."

The zanthyr just gazed at her, his silence admission enough.

"Why?" she whispered weakly, though she knew he wouldn't answer. After a moment she released his hand and wiped the tears from her face. "What should I do?"

"Nothing. Tanis walks his own path now."

"But you're watching for him," she said, knowing it was true whether or not Phaedor deigned to admit it. *Ean and Tanis both…*

She now understood: the zanthyr would keep them moving upon their paths no matter what it took.

Giving him a look of understanding, willing that he might see as deeply into her soul as she'd seen into his, Alyneri nodded her agreement and returned to her chair, albeit unsteadily.

Fynn meanwhile sat down again looking gloomy, perhaps because his hopes to condemn the zanthyr outright had once again been frustratingly thwarted by the truth. After a moment, his gaze found Trell. "So…what in Tiern'aval happened to you, cousin? We all thought you were fish food. You…Sebastian." Fynn grunted and drank his wine. "Shadow take me if *he* didn't end up as fodder for that damned Basi's dragons."

Trell gave him an amused look. "I have met those dragons you mention so blithely, cousin. Trust me, they wouldn't deign to eat men, no matter how princely the sacrifice."

Fynn arched a brow over his goblet in unconvinced response.

"And how did you come to know the *drachwyr*, Prince of Dannym?" asked the zanthyr.

Trell lifted grey eyes to meet Phaedor's. "The First Lord saved my life— that is, after Ramu and Rhakar pulled me half-drowned from a well. Balaji welcomed me to the First Lord's sa'reyth, and Vaile took pity on me and invited me to dine at her side. I star-gazed with Loghain, lost too many games of Kings to Náiir, and witnessed the imminent destruction of those who refused to give their oaths."

The zanthyr arched brows at all of this. The hint of a shadowy smile played across his lips. "You have witnessed much it would seem. What did you learn from the experience?"

Trell thought on that for a moment. "That the Mage is a man of many names and even greater aims…that few things are truly as they appear; and that there is often more to be achieved in the journey than in the destination."

Phaedor held Trell's eyes with his piercing gaze, but there was appreciation in it. "He will be pleased to know you have gained so much." Then he flipped his dagger, flashed a grin and vanished.

Fynn jerked so hard that he nearly spilled his wine. He swung a sooty glare at the place where the zanthyr had last stood and grumbled acidly, "He does that just to spite me."

"Well, you sort of deserved it," Alyneri told him.

"What's that supposed to mean? I vow he's got you under some kind of spell." He pointed emphatically at her. "He can *do* that, you know. *I* have first-hand knowledge."

Trell meanwhile smiled softly. "That was the First Lord's zanthyr." He looked highly pleased by something.

Fynn cast him a flat look. "I think you've both gone loopy, trusting that creature."

Trell arched brows at him. "You mean you don't? I would've thought you a better judge of character."

"Oh, cousin, you have no idea what a bad judge of character I am," Fynn returned, shaking his head resolutely. "No idea at all."

TWENTY-SIX

"Do not seek to know thyself. Seek to know my will, for I alone of this world am divine."

– The Prophet Bethamin

KJIERAN WAITED IN the vestry feeling raw and even more unnerved than usual. That morning he'd sent off a hastily scribed message to the Fourth Vestal reporting on everything he'd heard since Dore Madden returned to the temple. The man claimed he'd finally found the pattern he needed for the Prophet to turn even simple men into wielders of Bethamin's Fire and effectively build the Prophet's army of would-be Shades. The mere thought was so horrific to Kjieran that he'd taken particular risks to relay the message. Now he waited uneasily for Dore to arrive with his 'proof.'

When Dore did appear, he was leading four Ascendants, who carried a litter between them. At first glance, Kjieran thought the litter bore a life-sized ebony statue, but as the group neared, he realized to his horror that they were actually carrying a man.

Dore led the Ascendants through the nave into the north transept, which culminated in an apse whose dome hosted ornate fan vaulting, such that the walls and ceiling seemed to be made of bleached bones. An identical apse crowned the south transept. Each time he entered the apse, Kjieran felt like he was intruding on the lair of a great spider. He avoided looking up whenever possible.

Dore was instructing the Ascendants in placing the dead man atop a stone altar when the Prophet arrived. He came striding down the transept in white pants and a flowing robe that revealed his muscled chest. "What have you for me, Dore Madden?"

"A triumph, my lord." Dore pushed his hair back from his forehead and licked his lips, giving the Prophet an unctuous smile. "One of many more to come in your name."

Kjieran hovered at the edge of the apse, ostensibly waiting to serve his lord. The vantage gave him a clear view of everyone now standing on the dais.

"What is this then?" The Prophet flicked a long finger at the man lying atop the altar.

"This is the future of your army, my lord. I've uncovered the secret Malachai ap'Kalien and Björn van Gelderan were hiding about their Shades—the reason the creatures can wield the dark power *deyjiin*. I theorized that Malachai had used first and fifth-strand patterns to alter the basic composition of the men who were to become his Shades. Following this theory, I found a pattern similar to the one Malachai may have used. I fear it's not the same pattern, yet using the pattern I've found, a mortal body can withstand your superior Fire."

The Prophet looked over the man upon the altar. "This one does not seem to be alive."

"Regrettably, he died during the conversion process—but had he first been *bound to you*, my lord," Dore added pointedly, "his lifeforce tied to yours, pinning his soul to his body, his sight subject to your every inspection...*then* such a man might become a true weapon, even an extension of your divine will."

The Prophet looked at him sharply. "What is this? A new binding?"

"There are many types of binding patterns, my lord. Each engenders a different level of awareness between the subjects being bound. They all require mutual fluids—blood or semen are best—to seal the bond. A blood-binding allows one to know another's mind...to see what he sees."

The Prophet arched a brow. "To hear his thoughts?"

"That's the beauty of it, my lord." He licked his lips. "Establishing telepathy within a binding is very difficult. It is rarely achieved except with Adepts of the fourth strand. However, the binding of which I speak would achieve it. As the subject's body changes from living flesh into a powerful weapon of your Fire—yet with his soul pinned to you such that death is unable to claim his soul—it's conceivable that you would eventually rule such a one completely."

"How long would this process take?"

"The Pattern of Changing takes some weeks, my lord. During the conversion, your control over the subject will vary. But once the conversion is complete..." Here he licked his lips again, eyes wild, his voice rising and words coming faster with his excitement, "My lord...you would have the freedom to move into and out of any member of your army at any time, taking over their body to carry out your will! In this way, we would bind your army to you, but you would not be bound to them, my lord. No, *no*— they would not know your mind unless you willed it."

Kjieran's trepidation grew with each new piece of information, for Dore's logic was sound. *He could really do this!* The very thought made Kjieran shudder. Even without knowing the exact patterns Dore intended to use, it was conceivable in theory to accomplish everything the madman claimed.

The Prophet stroked his chin thoughtfully.

"Perhaps a demonstration, my lord?" Dore rubbed his hands together excitedly. At the Prophet's nod to continue, the wielder explained, "If you were to send your Fire into this man," and he drummed spindly fingers upon the dead man's leg, "enough to destroy a mortal body, I would that you might see the result."

The Prophet arched a skeptical brow, but he laid his hand upon the man all the same. Kjieran felt the room grow colder—so instantly cold that his next exhale frosted in the air. He hugged his arms and watched with growing alarm as a grey miasma spread beneath the dead man into the altar. It had consumed only half of the supporting pedestal before the entire altar erupted in a geyser of marble dust. Billowing clouds enveloped the entire apse. Kjieran threw one arm across his nose and spun away.

When the dust had finally settled and the spasms of choking from those present had subsided, the altar was gone but the dead man remained, lying haphazardly across broken stones beneath long sunrays that filtered down through the chalk-stained air. A dusting of pale powder enshrouded apse and men, yet the Prophet stood untouched, his black braids gleaming in vibrant contrast.

Bethamin turned his piercing gaze on Dore. "I must think on this." Then he left.

Kjieran left, too, fleeing to his chambers to send yet another desperate report to the Fourth Vestal.

He'd just finished sealing the bottom of the pillar candle when a pounding on his door startled him enough that he nearly dropped it. His heart was racing as he set the candle behind all the others on his shelf and went to open his door.

An Ascendant stood on the threshold.

Seeing him, Kjieran's stomach turned.

No. Oh no!

With a sinking feeling of dread, he managed, "Yes, Ascendant?"

"The Prophet calls you to attend him, acolyte."

"Of course," Kjieran answered, though he could barely breathe.

He followed the Ascendant to the Prophet's chambers with fear like an anvil crushing his chest. Everything about this meeting felt wrong. Instinct told him that he should be more afraid still.

He found the prophet waiting in a stone-paved cloister, where a central tiered fountain made quiet music. Bethamin was facing away from Kjieran with his hands clasped behind his back, but he turned as the truthreader approached. Kjieran fell to his knees and bowed his head. "My lord."

The Prophet took Kjieran's face in his hands and drew him to his feet. "I would look into your eyes again, Kjieran."

Kjieran dutifully raised his head to meet the Prophet's dark gaze. Bethamin's hands were warm upon his face, but his eyes were so very cold...

His thumb brushed across Kjieran's lips, once...twice while those eyes assessed him. "You heard Dore's good news." He dropped his hands and motioned for Kjieran to walk with him.

Kjieran cringed at the descriptive. *Good news?* "Yes, my lord."

"It is timely, for our ally, Prince Radov, goes to parley with the leader of the desert tribes, his enemy. I'm told the King of Dannym will also be there." He turned Kjieran an intense look. "It suits our purposes for Dannym to fall."

Kjieran nearly missed a step. He felt a sudden pit of apprehension open in his stomach. "How...is that, my lord?"

The Prophet stopped at the end of a courtyard framed in fig trees, where four marble thrones were arranged in a circle. He turned to Kjieran. "You have served me loyally, Kjieran, and for this, I shall reward you."

Kjieran stiffened. Bethamin had twisted ideas of reward and punishment. Terror reared within the quiet court and grabbed Kjieran in its clutches.

Bethamin's eyes as he held Kjieran's gaze were utterly without feeling, as devoid of emotion as the icy edges of the cosmos, yet Kjieran understood that the Prophet felt *something* for him.

"Dannym is a bastion that must crumble if my brothers and I are to accomplish our objectives, if my faith is to prevail in the hearts and minds of men. Without Gydryn val Lorian—without any of his sons to carry forward his line—this northern kingdom, which has so long stood against me, will falter. Without a strong king, the people of Dannym will embrace me wholly."

The Prophet came and settled both hands on Kjieran's shoulders. "This great honor do I bestow upon you, Kjieran. To become my hand in Tal'Shira and destroy this king."

Kjieran stopped breathing.

"I know that he denied you, turned you away from his service. Is it not fitting, this reward? Are you not grateful for the chance to serve me in eliminating Gydryn val Lorian and gaining your due retribution?"

"I live for your s-service, my lord," Kjieran stammered.

"I would that you should kill the king during this parley. It is the opportune time, when the fault may be laid at the feet of any number of others."

"But..." Kjieran searched desperately for some counter to this plan. "But King Gydryn is Radov's ally, my lord. Would not such an act against the prince's allies endanger your relationship with M'Nador?"

"Radov's duplicity has taken royal blood before on behalf of the Duke of Morwyk," the Prophet remarked dismissively. "Mention not the task you are upon for me, yet trust that none in Tal'Shira shall prevent you from its accomplishment."

Kjieran knew he couldn't have heard him correctly. Had the Prophet really just intimated that *Radov* was behind the deaths of Prince Sebastian and Prince Trell on behalf of the Duke of Morwyk?

Dear Epiphany! Radov claimed to be the king's ally!

The Prophet cupped Kjieran's face with one hand. Had Kjieran not known him so well, he might've imagined there was tenderness in the gesture. Bethamin's eyes seared into him, pinning him with their force, snaring his attention to the exclusion of all else. "In you I have discovered new ideas," the Prophet confessed, rousing Kjieran's foreboding to alarming levels, "concepts as yet untried and untested. You have alerted me to bold new areas where I might venture…and you've engendered something I have never known before."

Abruptly he leaned and captured Kjieran's mouth with his own in a fierce kiss. Bethamin held Kjieran's face with both hands and took of him what he would. His mouth was demanding, his tongue a flame that stole Kjieran's breath, and suffusing every part of his kiss was the Prophet's hunger for him.

When Bethamin finally released him, it was only to rest his forehead against Kjieran's, as if the kiss had been an intimate connection and not a brutal rape. "I find that what I desire, Kjieran," he told him quietly, "is to give you what you desire."

Kjieran was reeling. He didn't know where this was going, only that it was nowhere he wanted to be. "How?" he whispered, agonized and terrified.

"The greatest reward: to serve me as the first of your kind. Bound to me, that I might truly know your mind—"

Kjieran tore away from the Prophet and staggered backwards into a marble throne, his entire being railing against such horror.

Mistaking his reaction, the Prophet came after him and collected him back into his embrace. "You desired freedom, and I am giving it to you. This is what you wanted, is it not?"

Kjieran's mind was in a panic. He couldn't think of a single way out, and fear pierced him so wholly that he could barely breathe.

"As my newest servant, you will be bound to me body and soul. Dore assures me the only end for such as you will become is immolation." He ran his hand down Kjieran's face, blending in his tears, and murmured ominously, "You shall be mine forever more."

Kjieran gasped, "*This* is freedom?"

The Prophet laid his forehead against Kjieran's again, his powerful arms still holding him, already binding him to his will. "I do not wish to compel you, Kjieran." He said the words as if speaking an intimate troth. "I know you're strong enough—brave enough—to give me honesty in return for these graces I'm bestowing upon you. You've proven this to me. It is still true, is it not?"

Sucking in a shuddering breath, Kjieran nodded.

"But if I must compel you, I will do so," the Prophet warned. "Dore assures me the bond will facilitate compulsion once the conversion is complete."

With this ominous caution, a promise and a farewell, the Prophet grazed his lips across Kjieran's forehead and then stepped back. Abruptly rough hands grabbed Kjieran's arms and hauled him backwards into the stone chair, and ropes were slung about his body, binding him to it.

Dore arrived then, coming into the yard from an angle out of Kjieran's sight—he only heard the wielder's voice as he advised, "You will need some of his blood, my lord. It must be within your energy as you form the binding."

"How much blood?"

"Half a teaspoon is enough."

The Prophet leaned to claim another kiss, and Kjieran shut his eyes. Bethamin's mouth scalded him, and then the Prophet bit hard into his lip. Kjieran mumbled a muted cry but it was lost within the Prophet's seal upon his mouth. He sucked on Kjieran's lip until it flamed and throbbed, and then, finally, he withdrew.

Kjieran had always promised himself he would meet his fate with dignity and a stoic resolve, but this fear was too intense, too severe. He trembled and shook—he may have even wept, so lost did he feel in those dreadful moments. Yet he knew what he must do.

He had prepared for this day, though it was a day he'd also prayed would never come. Raine had laid in patterns of protection over Kjieran's mind and had taught Kjieran—ingrained in him—how to survive Bethamin's Fire. While Kjieran imagined this binding would be a thousand seasons worse, he had to hope that somehow he might survive it. He *had* to. Otherwise the Prophet would merely send another in his place to Tal'Shira. Kjieran stood as his king's only hope.

He heard Raine's voice in memory '...*return to your core, shelter within the deepest levels of your mind where I have built a refuge for you, protect yourself...'*

He barely heard Dore explaining, "...ensure he survives the change, we must bind him to you first. Here, I will show you the patterns..."

Time passed, and Kjieran sank deeper into himself, sealing away all perceptions of the world, losing touch with his arms pulled so painfully taught against the marble chair and the abrasive ropes that cut into his ankles. Finding shelter behind Raine's patterns, even forgetting for a moment what was to come until he heard Dore say, "You must bind him to you now with the pattern I've just shown you, and then I will work the Pattern of Changing..."

Kjieran squeezed shut his eyes. He felt Bethamin's hands resting upon his head, felt the man's cold power seeping into him. The pattern of binding came at him then, thunderous and violent, roaring through his mind in a hurricane of scalding power that vaporized thought and seared memory, setting his soul to flame.

Kjieran screamed without knowing it, for the part of him that was still himself sheltered like a shadow in the deepest recesses of Raine's refuge. He had no idea how long he screamed, how long the working took to take hold, but he knew the moment Dore's hand found his head to work his own fell pattern.

For no matter how he cowered in fear and pain, no matter how he trembled like a tiny creature trapped at the bottom of a deep, dark well, he could not shield any part of himself from Dore's Pattern of Changing.

Into the vacuum of life Dore murmured, "Now you will die and be reborn."

And Kjieran was.

TWENTY-SEVEN

"If life be art then paint me in vivid color. Let no shade hide from my ken."

— The painter Immanuel di Nostri

I
N THE DAYS following their sailing expedition, Pelas took Tanis
on a whirlwind tour of the realm that the lad might come to know
just a smattering of the infinite experiences to be observed—from
the bullfights of Vaalden, to the violent ball courts of Ma'hrkit, to the
Wyr'Umjai Crater on the Agasi island of Palma-Lai, where a host of strange
and exotic animals thrived. He took Tanis to the ruins of Cyrene near the
city of Sakkalaah, then across the Fire Sea to view the vast crystal caves
of Vest. He even showed him the smoldering deserts of Avatar and their
spontaneous smokeless fires that covered miles and sometimes burned for
years on end.

Even had every day not been wondrous and fascinating and somewhat
manic at times, still Tanis would have willingly gone, for each day that Pelas
spent entertaining him was a day he didn't torture and kill another of the
realm's Healers. Tanis lived in fear of this, for he knew Pelas's darker side
must eventually resurface. Every time he thought of the round-faced Healer
at the party in Bemoth, who'd seemed so kind and so unaware of the deadly
creature that lusted after her, he felt somehow burdened with her protection.

So he did his best to keep Pelas interested in showing him things,
and to challenge him to question his doctrines. Tanis felt terribly small
and inadequate to the task of changing a Malorin'athgul's point of view.
He learned enough of Pelas by then to understand that the man had lived

for eons. How could a mere boy of fourteen teach an immortal creature anything of the truths of their realm? Yet if Tanis did not, who would?

The Fhorgs were certainly of no help. If anything, they exacerbated the issue—they were always drawing their own blood in grim ways for different rituals that were somehow vitally necessary for the sun's rising and setting, or something equally ridiculous. Never mind that most people lived perfectly adequate lives without slicing themselves up on a daily basis. Try to explain that to a Fhorg, and he'd look at you like you were the most uneducated imbecile ever to walk the realm.

Tanis had several times wondered if the Fhorgs fueled Pelas's obsession or if his fed into theirs. Whichever was truth, Pelas's relationship with the Fhorgs sustained each in their mutual delusions.

They'd only recently returned to Pelas's home when Tanis woke on an overcast morning to find Pelas gone. None of the Fhorgs knew where he'd gone or when he'd left, and Tanis feared the worst.

All day he moped about the manse with a sick feeling of dread, starting at the least little noise and jumping at shadows. Phaedor's dagger had found its way back to him again, and he thumbed the blade all during the day's idle exercise, though the cold black stone offered little by way of emotional support.

Not much for conversation to begin with, the Fhorgs eyed him uncertainly and kept their distance. Tanis knew enough from their thoughts to know they suspected him of being some kind of witch because he was immune to Pelas's power. They also thought he'd cast a spell on Pelas due to the close relationship the two of them were forming, and they were *certain* he was a spy.

Another day passed without word from Pelas, and Tanis grew ever more uneasy, only now he feared for Pelas as much as he for the Healer. Had something happened to him? Had one of his brothers caught up with him? Had an assassin's Merdanti dagger found its mark? These and many more fears accosted the lad repeatedly, interrupted only by his own self-ridicule.

The man's managed to keep himself alive for centuries without your help, Tanis! But with all of the incredibly dangerous and reckless things Pelas did, Tanis felt it was sheer dumb luck that the man survived at all.

On the third day after Pelas's disappearance, Tanis woke to find the house completely empty and knew Pelas had returned.

On the one hand, this alleviated his fears for the Malorin'athgul's welfare. On the other, intuition told him that Pelas had returned with a Healer, and the knowledge made him so sick of heart that he couldn't eat a thing all day.

A storm was battering the manse, and the rains only grew worse as the day drew on. Tanis fretted in each moment about Pelas's activities, and he wandered nervously from room to room trying to make up his mind what to do.

He had to stop him.

That much he knew, even without the painful urging of that sense of duty, which grew so tremendous during the afternoon that Tanis was near to tears over it. He couldn't bear feeling so inadequate, but he'd wracked his mind trying to think of some way to help Pelas, or at least the Healer, and…nothing. Even should he envision some elaborate plan, he had no idea where Pelas or the Fhorgs even were—certainly they were nowhere in the house, and naught but empty cliffs spread for miles in both directions.

Tanis was leaning his forehead despondently against one of the large windows overlooking the cliffs to the north when lightning split the sky and he saw five small, dark shapes making their way back to the manse, the last of them emerging from beyond the cliff's edge even as he watched.

Instantly, the lad bolted off—even before that sense of duty started screaming. Even before a desperate panic overtook him.

Tanis sprinted through the rain, his booted feet eating up the distance across the moors, until he came upon the Fhorgs as they were rounding a rise. The one called Jain was in the lead.

Tanis knew all of their names now, though they didn't like it when he used them and only really tolerated Pelas doing it because he could annihilate them with one finger. Fhorgs were weird about names.

Tanis came to a skidding halt in front of Jain, who lifted his woad-stained face and pinned the lad with a look as storm-ridden as the day. "What happened?" Tanis gasped. He bent and pushed hands to his knees to catch his breath.

"Pelas went to confront his brother." The Fhorg looked him over circumspectly, as if reluctant to have said even that much. "It did nae go well. Now he's in a rage as we've ne'er seen. Been at it all night w'th' Healer, but really he's only just begun—" he was interrupted by one of his brethren shouting at him irately in their own language, and the two of them went at each other while Tanis waited with desperate impatience.

Finally, Jain punched the other one into sullen submission, looked back to Tanis and finished, "Pelas sent us away, I'l spy. We did nae e'n inspect the Healer's blood."

The other Fhorgs grumbled fiercely about this in two languages. Tanis didn't catch all of it, but he gleaned enough from their thoughts to realize there might still be a chance to help the Healer and Pelas both.

"Which brother did Pelas see?" he hastened to ask, thinking it might be important.

Jain shrugged. "He does nae confide in us as 'e confides in ye, I'l spy," he answered loudly over the storm. "Perhaps ye can help him find himself again, for I think his brother sent him o'er the edge."

"Where is he?" Tanis looked desperately around.

"In the caves," and Jain jerked his head back the way they'd come.

Tanis took off in a dead run.

"*Ye take yer life in yer hands goin' down there!*" Jain called after him. Tanis couldn't be sure, for he was running so hard, but he thought he heard him shout, "But maybe ye should...for his sake!"

In the flash of a moment, Tanis realized that while their ideologies might lead them to draw very different conclusions about what is morally acceptable, this did not necessarily make the Fhorgs inherently evil men. That Jain understood Pelas was in need of help...clearly he cared for him, even as Tanis did.

The lad almost missed the stairs leading down the cliff face, for the trail opening onto them could barely be discerned among the black rocks. He had to slow as he took the stairs, for they were treacherous indeed, cut right into the side of the cliff with no handholds and nothing to prevent a fall of several hundred feet onto razor-sharp rocks should his foot slide on the perilously wet stone.

The cave opening came into view when Tanis was halfway down the cliff face, but the lad was cringing even before he reached it, for Pelas's thoughts came tumbling up to him—wave upon wave of malevolent fury. He had to concentrate as much on trying to close his mind against Pelas's anger as upon setting each foot safely on the wet steps.

He paused just shy of the cave's entrance to catch his breath, but the force of Pelas's anger made it a worthless effort. Fury blasted out like heat from a forge, repelling Tanis mentally as well as physically, pummeling into him with palpable force.

Shivering now from the pelting rain as much as from his fear, Tanis managed a shaky inhale and braved a look into the cave.

He recognized the Healer, Merida, naked and spread-eagled between two wooden posts. Her flesh had been marked in many places. Tanis knew it would be too dangerous to open his mind to her thoughts to better assess her condition, for he would then become equally subject to Pelas's onslaught, and he didn't think he could experience that and keep his wits about him.

But he didn't have to know the Healer's mind to know she wished for death. The look on her face communicated that clearly enough.

Further back in the cave, closer to the torches, Pelas stood with his back to Tanis assessing a table of knives. Tanis knew it might be his only chance to act.

Moving as quickly as he dared, Tanis stole into the cave. At one point Pelas selected a blade and almost turned, and Tanis dropped to his knees, holding his breath, but a different knife caught the Malorin'athgul's eye instead, and he set to sharpening it.

Tanis crawled the last few paces on hands and knees. He was shaking so desperately when he reached the Healer that he could barely grasp his dagger to get it out of his boot.

He blessed Phaedor a thousand times for the dagger's ever-returning nature...for its being Merdanti. The *goracrosta* ropes that bound the Healer parted with ease beneath the dagger's razor edge.

Tanis had just released Merida's final limb when Pelas turned.

The look on his face would haunt the boy's dreams for weeks to come.

The man he knew was gone. In his place scowled a vicious creature whose features were so twisted with pain and fury that they seemed a mummer's mask. The darkness consumed Pelas wholly.

The monster that had Pelas in thrall threw his hand out, fingers splayed. Tanis felt an invisible force crash into his chest, thunder without sound. It ripped the breath from his lungs and flung him and the healer into the air. The lad's head hit hard against the cave wall with a blinding flash of pain, and then he fell helplessly forward, sucking in dry gasps around lungs that refused to fill.

As he lay dazed on the cave floor, with his skull pounding and his vision nearly black, he saw Merida dragging herself towards the cave mouth.

Then Pelas was upon him.

He grabbed the boy up by his throat in a choking hold. "Where did you get this dagger?" Pelas shook the lad and ripped said dagger from his fingers.

Tanis knew something was dreadfully wrong. He couldn't move one arm, and his head felt fuzzy yet throbbed violently at the same time.

"*Tell me who gave you this weapon!*"

Tanis felt Pelas's dark power wrapping around his mind. He tried to meet his gaze, but he couldn't make his eyes focus. It took everything he had in him to manage a choked whisper, "*...no.*"

Pelas shouted a cry of rage and threw the dagger so furiously that it sailed out of the cave to be swallowed by the storm. He shoved Tanis backwards and slammed his body into the cave wall, the Healer all but forgotten. "*Tell me!*"

The force of his intent was so powerful that Tanis felt the words rattle through his chest. His face was flaming, his head was screaming, and he worried he was going to throw up. He managed weakly, dizzily, in a tiny voice yet fueled with the power of his love for Phaedor, "You can't...have it, sir."

Pelas's eyes were scalding and merciless. "I will have it out of you in your blood then, stupid boy!" Pelas forced him towards the poles where Merida had been bound.

Tanis realized he was crying, though he couldn't remember when the tears had started. "You'll not have it...even if...if you kill me."

Pelas's fiery eyes flashed. "'Tis not death you should be fearing right now." He threw the lad roughly to the floor.

Tanis closed his eyes and lay shivering in pain, just barely holding unconsciousness at bay. It occurred to him that Phaedor wouldn't care in the least if Pelas knew his name, but Pelas had bled so many other confessions from him, Tanis vowed he would not get this one. *The zanthyr is sacred... and you cannot have his memory.*

Pelas snatched him up, stood him unsteadily on his feet, and started binding his wrist to the post—

In that moment, Merida reached the cave mouth. Weeping, she struggled to her feet and turned to look back at them. Even with the raging storm, Tanis heard her say through lips bloodied and broken, "Death…is only…the beginning."

Then she threw herself off the cliff.

Pelas roared in outrage. He slung Tanis to the floor and surged after her, but there was no retrieving Merida for his dark pleasure. She was free.

The explosion of fury that followed was beyond description. Tanis lay on his side trying not to throw up as wave after wave of thunderous rage battered him, crushing his chest, so that with each passing surge, the lad couldn't breathe. He managed only little gasps between the crests, while his head exploded with pain and his stomach turned inside out.

Until…at last, it faded.

Tanis might have blacked out. He couldn't be certain, but he thought he probably had, because he recalled a point where he'd felt no pain, but then it seemed to detonate everywhere at once. When he opened his eyes, Pelas was standing over him.

That time, he wore a mask of horror.

Suddenly he was on his knees and cradling Tanis's head in his lap. The lad heard him swearing darkly, furiously.

The Healer's blood was cold, the Healer herself was gone, the darkness had retreated, and now a different pain consumed Pelas. "*No, no, little spy.*" Pelas caressed Tanis's cheek, looking tormented. "You shouldn't have come here. You should *not* have interrupted me!"

Tanis couldn't be sure, because he really couldn't focus his gaze, but he thought Pelas was actually crying.

It took a long time for Tanis to make the thoughts in his head form into words, and longer still, it seemed, for his tongue to utter them. "…*no choice.*"

"No *choice?*" Pelas very nearly shouted at him. "You could've stayed where you were safe!"

"But *you* weren't safe, sir," Tanis murmured.

With a groan of guilt, Pelas drew Tanis closer into his arms and cradled the lad's body against his own. He said nothing; it seemed words failed him.

Tanis blacked out again.

When he came to, Pelas was still holding him, but now they were beside a fire and he felt warmer and slightly less nauseated, though his body still inadvertently trembled.

"Sir?" Tanis found he could focus his eyes a bit better.

Pelas looked down at him, and his gaze was tragically tender. "You will live," he said, "and I will have your hide for this tomorrow."

Tanis managed a weak smile that quickly faded beneath his concern. "You left," he managed through a swollen and painful throat. "What happened?"

Pelas drew Tanis closer to him, cradled like his own child. He said in a low voice, his tone intense and shadowed, "I went to confront Darshan on some of my recent theories, formulated as a result of our conversations." He added through clenched teeth, "It did not go well."

"You…" Tanis was amazed—a mite dull-headed still and perhaps a little slow in forming his thoughts, but amazed all the same. "All those times… you really were thinking on all of the things you said you must think on?"

"Of course."

Tanis felt such a rush of unexpected tenderness for him. In the back of his mind, he'd suspected that Pelas's remarks were glibly spoken as a means of moving the conversation along. Yet all this time he had been honestly considering everything Tanis said.

The lad realized something else. He wasn't sure if he came to the conclusion on his own, or if Pelas unwittingly spoke to him through the force of his own thoughts, but it occurred to Tanis with a pang of compassion that Pelas wasn't reveling in the darkness.

He was trapped by it.

"I should not have gone to him." His fury at himself was all too apparent in his tone. "I should have trusted my own reasoning, but I couldn't…I wanted confirmation."

"Of what, sir?"

Pelas shook his head. "It doesn't matter."

"I think it does."

Pelas gave him an agonized look.

"Sir, you don't have to be this way…no matter what you think." Concern for rang through him, and that sense of duty sang stronger than ever. "You don't have to forever battle these forces that tear you in two."

Clearly not trusting himself with a reply, Pelas shifted Tanis off his lap to lie closer to the fire and looked away with his jaw clenched so tightly…as if to draw back all of the fury he'd unleashed that night. "Yes, I do."

Tanis watched him from an awkward position, loath to move his head for his brain throbbing so violently. "You can decide to walk a different path, just as I might have."

Pelas turned him a fiery glare. "It's not the same! *You* had a choice. For me there is *none.*"

"Why not?"

Pelas shot him a desperate look. "The choice has already been made."

"Who made it, if not you?"

He looked away again, and after a moment he answered bitterly, "There never was any choice. I am what I am."

"If that is truly so, then change what you are."

Pelas spun his gaze back to him and asked despairingly, "*How?*"

Tanis had no real wisdom to offer, only what seemed obvious to him. "Decide to."

Pelas exhaled a growl and fell backwards onto the floor. He shifted his body to align his head so it rested near Tanis's own, so that they both gazed towards a ceiling lost in shadows, their shoulders almost touching.

A long silence followed wherein the only sound was the fire's crackling song and the crashing of the distant surf, and then Pelas said quietly, "When I realized that I'd hurt you, Tanis…when I finally surfaced through the blood haze of rage that had clouded my vision…" He drew in a deep breath, let it out slowly, and confessed in a raw voice, "In that moment I questioned everything that I thought to be true—all of my brother's doctrines, everything he's ever taught us."

Swallowing, Tanis gingerly turned his head to look into Pelas's eyes, their bodies so close that their foreheads nearly touched. "Why, sir?"

Pelas gave him a tragic smile. "Because I did not want you to die."

Tanis stared at him. He could barely image what the confession must've cost him.

Pelas grunted despondently and looked away to stare upwards into darkness. "It is so strange…I sense something of our Maker in you, little spy. You make me feel as if there could be something else for me, even though I know such is impossible." He managed a soft smile, infinitely sad. "I don't know if that is a good thing to feel…but it *is* interesting. It's an experience. I

like experiencing new things. This whole world was a new experience, once."
Tanis heard the anguished longing in his tone, even as he felt the shards of
shattered hope as Pelas finished, "And then my brothers came here, and I
realized there was nothing for us but to be that which we are."

That sense of duty rang like tower bells inside Tanis's head. The lad
finally knew what he was meant to say to help him. "*Then*," he whispered,
"but not before?"

"No," Pelas sighed. "Before Darshan took me in hand, everything was
different."

"Then perhaps that explains why he truly fears you, sir."

Tanis suddenly felt impossibly tired. Before he could receive Pelas's
response, sleep claimed him.

TWENTY-EIGHT

"The forgiveness that most often eludes us is
that which we grant to ourselves."

— The First Vestal Alshiba Torinin

E AN SOUGHT OUT Björn one night with a question—the first
he'd managed to craft into an inquiry that didn't also sound an
accusation.

He found the First Lord in his library in counsel with Ramu. The
Sundragon waved off Ean's apologies for interrupting with an explanation
that he'd already concluded his business, and he bade them both good
evening. Ean watched him leave, feeling an immense affinity and respect for
the *drachwyr*.

Björn received Ean with equal grace. He poured wine for them both
and asked as he handed Ean a glass, "So, what have you come to ask me
tonight? I would tell you anything you wish to know."

Caught off guard by this candid inquiry, Ean stumbled to formulate the
simple query he'd spent at least half an hour crafting in his rooms.

"First Lord…" Odd how natural the term of respect felt crossing his
tongue. "What role do you mean for me to play? You've known me from the
beginning, while I—Raine's truth, I recall hardly a fraction of who or what
I've been. I know I'm to be a Player in your game, but I don't really know
what game we're playing, or…even exactly what we're trying to do."

Björn considered him, and Ean tried to hold his gaze in return. Bearing
in mind everything else he'd recently endured, holding Björn's gaze should

have been rather effortless. But it was one of the more difficult moments of his day.

One could not stand before Björn van Gelderan without feeling the emanation of his presence. It radiated, as palpable as the sun on one's skin. The fact that Björn seemed so humbly unaware of his own power and yet so obviously confident in it was a compelling contradiction.

"Walk with me." Björn finally released Ean from the force of his gaze, and the prince visibly exhaled, relieved to find his breath returned to him instead of held in the thrall of the Fifth Vestal's potent consideration.

The Vestal walked with a purposeful stride. He cast the fifth before him to open two tall, mullioned doors and led Ean out onto a grand balcony.

Sunset bathed the world in crimson and gold. The clear sky seemed a sheet of flame, while the city and countryside undulated beneath variegated waves of gold-limned shadow. The high mountains across the valley loomed darkly, their peaks a great swath of jagged basalt towers, while lush hanging valleys collected the night as water by trees greedy with thirst. High, thin waterfalls split the darkness in silver-gold streaks, like moonlight dripping down from the veil of clouds. And nearer, just below their high balcony, the alabaster city glowed rose-hued and brilliant, seeming reborn as the day died.

The beauty was just so astonishing that Ean blurted, "This must be paradise."

Björn glanced his way. The First Lord had his own sort of beauty, one that seemed somehow reflective of the magical light that existed in the moonlit waterfalls and the gilded air.

"Paradise...this concept conveys an ideal, yet one that's ultimately unattainable." He arched a dark brow. "Perhaps paradise could exist on some plane. Yet, there would be no game in it." He cast Ean a compelling look. "Do you see my meaning, Ean? Games require obstacles—challenges, barriers—while perfection necessarily excludes the presence of such things. The Laws of Patterning tell us there are no absolutes, but that there is Balance in all things."

He looked back to the view. "T'khendar wasn't meant as a paradise. But there *is* a reason to introduce beauty into the world, Ean." He turned the prince a smile. "Revolution may be fueled by the worst sort of vice, but beauty is the driving force of any evolution with the potential to bring about higher states of being."

"And this is our objective?"

Björn's cobalt eyes danced. "It would be a worthwhile aim, don't you think?"

Ean was really trying to understand, but these philosophical explorations just confused him. What could fighting Malorin'athgul possibly have to do with evolution to higher states of being? He shook his head, frustrated with himself. "What am I missing?"

Björn placed a hand on his shoulder and guided his gaze to the heavens, where the first stars were just then appearing. "Look...watch...wait."

They stood in silence together then. Ean expected a somewhat torturous wait beneath the sheer number of unanswered questions he was shouldering, yet he found instead a surprising contentment merely standing at Björn's side.

As they watched the sky, drinking their wine, the last glow of sunlight vanished beneath the rim of the world, and a wind blew in the stars, scattering them like diamond dust across the heavens.

"The Avataren Fire Kings believe the stars are the souls of their loved-ones watching over them," Björn observed with quiet contemplation. "The Kandori name each star—many for the immortal *drachwyr*, one of whom you've met. Ramuhárikhamáth, Lord of the Heavens." He took another contemplative sip of wine. "Agasan's Sormitáge Scholars would tell us each star is the gateway to another world, perhaps one of each of the thousand realms represented in Illume Belliel." Casting Ean a brief smile, he offered, "I like to think that T'khendar now appears to other distant worlds this way, a sudden flare that materialized three centuries ago and remains brilliant to this day."

Ean continued listening, but couldn't keep his attention from straying to the seven stars that had just appeared, hovering at eye level above the dark swath of mountains. "Cephrael's Hand," he murmured. He felt a personal and highly unsettling connection to the constellation.

Björn cast him a sidelong look. "Cephrael had but one task assigned him by his father. Would you like to know what it was?"

Ean turned to him. "Of course."

"He is the caretaker of this realm." Björn gestured with his goblet, moving it in an expansive arc. "He cares for all of the realms of Light, in fact, though the blessed son is known by different names in each. Balance is Cephrael's governance. But look out there, Ean." Björn lifted a finger off his goblet to point above the distant mountains. "Beyond the protection of this world, beyond Alorin's enveloping shield, what lies there?"

Ean shook his head. He felt heady—not from wine, but from the sure knowledge that everything being spoken there was vitally important. "I don't really know."

"No one does for certain," Björn murmured with a shrug. He leaned forearms on the railing and held the brim of his goblet between long fingers. "But I will tell you this: beyond the veil of the known worlds, between a protective shield woven of light and *elae*, chaos lurks. Chaos—formless, frenzied, boundless."

His gaze surveyed the realm he'd made. Beneath him, the city lights, like stars of the earth, seemed a mirror of the heavens. "The *Sobra I'ternin* tells us the Creator formed our worlds within a spiral. At the core of this spiral lies the raw power of creation, and at the far unraveling edges, just beyond *this* world—the spiral's last world—destruction thrives. This is how it was meant to be, this balance of beginnings and endings. There is no natural cycle in which the pattern of creation isn't found. That cycle is Balance in its purest form."

"Yet Alorin is dying."

Björn turned and leaned one hip against the railing. He regarded Ean gravely. "Indeed."

"But that can't be right—not if there is Balance in all things."

"This, too, is true."

Ean shook his head, missing the connection. "Then…what?"

Björn lifted his gaze to the hovering stars. "I suppose we could say Cephrael must correct the imbalance," the Vestal mused. Then he added wryly as he looked back to Ean, "But I've never been one to lay responsibility at the feet of another."

Ean gave him a long look.

The First Lord finished his wine in one swallow and clapped Ean on the shoulder. "Tomorrow my sister will show you what it is we're doing here." He moved them back inside.

Ean set his goblet down on a table. "Thank you, First Lord." He made to depart, but Björn took his arm.

"We were friends once, Ean." Björn held the prince's gaze with a startling sincerity. "I hope we can be so again."

Ean felt the power of his invitation resonating inside him. "That is my hope as well, my lord," he surprised himself by saying.

Björn smiled. "Good. I will see you in a few days then. Safe journey."

And with that, Ean said goodnight to the Fifth Vestal, his thoughts already turning to the morning, and Isabel.

He dreamed of her that night.

Yet in his dream, he knew her by another name, a name he somehow couldn't recall. They stood upon a rocky beach where the waves crashed just steps from their feet. The rush and ebb of the powerful waters echoed the steady beat of Ean's heart.

He stood with Isabel enfolded in his arms, his lips pressed to her hair, their gazes aimed at the sea. Her hair was different than he remembered, highlighted by long days beneath a strong sun, though still long and very soft. The wind made vines of it around his arms, around his back, doubly binding them together in a moment that would define the rest of their days—these things Ean knew the way one knows things in a dream, though he didn't understand them.

"Are you certain?" he asked her with desperation riding the crest of his uncertainty, an imminent sense of loss as a terrible ache. "How can you be sure? You've told me always the future is framed by the choices we make."

"But you have already made these choices, my lord," she returned softly. "The path is set. You will not veer from it any more than I would leave your side because of it."

"If I'd known it would mean I would lose you—"

"You will never *lose me," and Ean felt* the truth *of her words. He knew then that he and Isabel were threads bound into a pattern that could never be unraveled. Where his threads ended, hers began, and vice versa, the bond of their troth an endless knot, forever entwined. "And it would not have changed anything," she added quietly. "This, you also know."*

"Yet I would wish it so." Despair and duty entwined confusingly within him. He pressed his lips into her hair, smelling of its sweet depths, smelling of the sea, so long a part of both of them. "Do you think...is this punishment?"

Their position kept him from seeing her face, but he sensed her smile. "Punishment? From whom?"

"Fate? Your father?"

"My father!" she laughed.

"I'm serious."

She pressed herself closer to him, and he tightened his arms around her. "We make our own fate by our choices in this life and those that came before...by the agreements we make with our own conscience, those we keep or break. Fate is the entwining of the paths of our lives, the aggregate of misdeeds and conclusions, of promises made and broken, the choices that bring us to now."

"The path of honor," he heard himself say, though he didn't understand why he said it.

"Sometimes," she agreed with a sigh.

"I will never see you again—" His voice broke in the saying. Ean wanted to scream from the unbearable pain of this truth.

Isabel turned in his arms and took his face in her hands. She kissed him deeply, a kiss to linger through the ages. Her eyes were closed as she pulled away and murmured close, her breath a whisper across his lips, "Not in this life—"

Ean gasped and shot up in bed, his heart racing in a panic, fists clenching the sheets into hard knots. Beyond his windows, a silver-grey dawn made the air luminous with promise, but he still felt caught in the horror of the dream. He turned and—

For a moment, seeing her sitting on the edge of his bed confused him. Then he realized she was actually there, and he grabbed her into his arms, choking back his relief with a muffled exclamation. She held him as she had in his dream, unhurriedly, with her cheek resting on his bare chest. The dream faded, and his heart calmed. He reluctantly released Isabel.

She straightened to hover slightly above him with the hint of a smile on her lovely lips. "Happy to see me, I take it."

"My lady, you have no idea." Yet Ean wondered if indeed she understood too well. One thing he could say about Epiphany's Prophet, her timing was unmatched.

He let her warmth melt away the last vestiges of the disturbing dream. "And how may I serve you today, my lady?"

She pushed up to sitting again. "Today we travel. Three days will be sufficient, if you would like to pack some things."

Ean contemplated three days alone with Isabel and thought he'd found paradise despite the Fifth Vestal's insistence that such places couldn't exist. He made to throw back the covers but reconsidered—suddenly aware of his nakedness and determined to protect her honor. He gave her a chastising look. "A lady should turn away."

"I wear a blindfold, my lord," she protested innocently.

Indeed she did, the black one that so immediately and intensely aroused him. "My lady, if I thought your sight was even remotely hindered by that piece of cloth, I wouldn't let you take a step without me at your side."

"Perhaps my lord should then think of me thusly," she reasoned.

"Isabel…" He managed a grin while battling the longing and desire that were such wonderful torments. "Unless you're ready to let me bed you here and now, I'm honor-bound to protect your reputation."

With a tolerant sigh, Isabel dutifully pressed palms to her eyes.

"Not good enough."

Laughing, she kept her eyes covered *and* turned her head away.

Ean rose from the bed and donned his britches. A kiss, gentle and soft, released her from her bondage. She dropped her hands and murmured in her silken voice, "Thank you, my lord, for your discretion. Now your arousal and my sight are equally veiled, a fitting resolution."

Ean resisted the urge to take her into his arms again, but just barely.

They took breakfast together on his balcony, and then she led him out into the palace.

Ean walked at her side, never prouder than to have her hand upon his arm. She wore a dress of bronze silk that day but in a heavy weave, nubby and raw and styled for travel. She carried her staff in her right hand, and the tap of its base rapped a steady accompaniment to their steps.

"Where did you get the staff, my lady?" he asked as they were walking down a long hallway interspersed with regular alcoves housing statues of varied design.

"Phaedor made it for me," she answered as if this was the most ordinary of events.

"Oh, of course." Ean flashed a sardonic grin. "And how might I get one of those?"

She arched a brow at him. "Did not the zanthyr remake your blade for you?"

Ean came to a sudden standstill. He stared at her. He remembered too well the moment the Shade had driven his sword into his chest in an eruption of ash, and as well the sight of the blade restored after his first wild ride with the zanthyr. The remaking of his sword suddenly claimed a profound new meaning. "But it's not Merdanti..." Yet even as he said it, he wondered.

"What is Merdanti?" Isabel cast him a subtle smile. "Is it the stone, quarried and wrought by mortal men? Or is it the magic used to craft a weapon into a sentient thing?"

Ean stared at her, marveling at the zanthyr's impossible foresight. But then he pushed aside memories of Phaedor, for they brought feelings of guilt that would shed a maudlin cast to the day. Ean cleared his throat and started them walking again, affecting a light manner as he inquired, "I suppose he taught you how to use the staff?"

"Well, certainly. One does not carry a Merdanti weapon and have no idea how to use it. That would be inviting of trouble."

Funnily enough, the comment reminded him of Alyneri and her chastising of Tanis for carrying the zanthyr's dagger, conversations overheard from horseback as they rode through the meadows of Veneisea with the Assifiyahs scraping the eastern sky. It seemed so long ago now.

A pang of regret filled him as he thought of his friends. Memories of Tanis especially made him regretful. The lad had become so special to him. More than with anyone else, the idea that Tanis might think Ean had betrayed him was enormously hard to bear.

Embroiled in these sudden memories, Ean barely noticed the man approaching down the long corridor until he was nearly upon them and Isabel was gently tugging his arm. Ean did stop then.

Dagmar Ranneskjöld pressed his hands together, his fingertips to lips, and bowed in greeting. "My lady, Your Highness."

"Dagmar," Isabel greeted with a smile and a nod.

The Vestal shifted pale green eyes to Ean and extended his hand. "At last in the flesh we meet, Ean. Be welcome. I'm relieved you chose the path that led to us."

Knowing what he now knew of himself, Ean wondered if he'd ever had any choice. He regarded Dagmar amid a confusing mixture of emotions. Their last conversation had not gone well, though as it turned out, Ean had been furious for all the wrong reasons.

He clasped wrists with the Vestal. "My lord." He heard the contrition in his greeting, his embarrassment and regret. He hoped Dagmar heard it too, for he didn't know how any apology would make up for the things he'd said.

"*Cóir taisteal,* Dagmar," Isabel called his attention back to her. "Events progress. I trust you're pleased so far."

"I begin the preparations for their arrival as we speak," Dagmar said by way of acknowledgement. "My lady, your advice is ever apt."

"One does try to be of some value," Isabel murmured modestly.

Dagmar shifted his gaze to Ean, and there was something in it that reminded him of someone...the briefest ghost of a countenance that he couldn't place. "Ean," the Vestal said warmly, "I rest easy knowing our great lady travels in the best of company. Do not let her be too reckless."

"I am never reckless," Isabel returned with a prim lift of her chin.

"I won't, my lord," Ean assured him, believing whole-heartedly that Isabel was even more reckless than he was.

Just then a shimmering behind Dagmar drew Ean's eye, and a second later a Shade materialized, coalescing out of the shadows. Dagmar turned when he felt the creature behind him, but Ean's heart sank to realize it was Creighton. Here was another soul he'd wounded deeply, another for which any apology seemed inadequate.

"The First Lord requires you, my lord," Creighton told Dagmar. "He awaits in the map room."

"I'll come at once, certainly."

Creighton shifted his obsidian gaze to Isabel and Ean. "My lady," he said, nodding, and to Ean, he pressed hands together, fingertips to lips and bowed. "My lord..."

"Creighton—" Ean reached out a hand to him, but he was already fading.

Dagmar also departed with a nod of farewell, leaving Ean watching the vapor of Creighton's passing with a heavy heart.

"What happened between you?" Isabel asked into the silence that remained.

"I wronged him." Ean bowed his head, suddenly bombarded by guilt.

The most depressing part was that this conflict was as yet unresolved; to think otherwise would merely be duplicitous. "I owe him my life," he murmured, "but when he thought to embrace me as the brothers we were… are…I rejected him."

"Don't let appearances fool you," Isabel advised gently. "We are none of us the shells we wear." Ean gave her a stricken look, and she returned a reassuring smile. "Come," she said after a moment's pause, time enough to let him brood over mistakes and misdeeds. "The sun lengthens, Ean."

Feeling suddenly heavy-hearted, the prince walked with Isabel until they came to a set of towering doors similar in height to the Extian Doors but enameled in crimson, their facing edge deeply adzed to mirror the design of the arch above them. Isabel traced a pattern in the air, Ean heard a click, and the doors swung inward.

Before them spread the torturously long hallway Ean remembered from his first moment of arrival in T'khendar. Black-lacquered doors lined the endless corridor on both sides. The passage truly seemed to go on forever.

"What is this place?"

Isabel nudged him through, and the doors swung silently shut behind them. "We call it the Nodes," she replied as she led away down the corridor, with her staff setting the meter of their pace. "It is a creation of the Second Vestal, one of many improvements he's put in place since *elae* was restored to T'khendar."

There was another mystery Ean had never gotten answered. "About that…Raine D'Lacourte told me *elae* didn't exist here."

"In the beginning it did not," she confirmed.

"Then how did *elae* come to be?"

"What is *elae* but the force of life? The entire population of Cair Tiern'aval became stranded here when the island's weld was twisted—the force of that working tore the city from Alorin's fabric into ours. Those people are the original inhabitants of T'khendar. Through them…through the others of us who remained, *elae* began to flow. In time, T'khendar's population flourished, and *elae* became powerful. Now the lifeforce has settled into natural currents."

Ean shook his head. It made perfect sense if one just took the time to examine natural laws.

Isabel stopped before a door. "Now we must travel. Come—take my hand."

Ean happily obliged, and she opened the door and led them into darkness. A heartbeat later they emerged through another door as if merely exiting from a lightless wardrobe into the bright of day.

They stood at the edge of a farmstead. To the south spread fields of corn, still productive though the Winter Solstice approached, while to the west, fields of wheat were shooting up green sprouts. Ean looked behind him to see a simple door built into a stone casing. Glancing around the frame, he found nothing behind it but grass.

"Isa! Isa!"

Ean turned at the sound of children calling excitedly, *ee-sah! ee-sah!* in joyous voices. Moments later, a bevy of children came hurtling out of the cornfield, emerging like a flock of birds disturbed from their midday meal. A rotund woman followed in their wake, brandishing a straw broom that seemed an appropriate tool for managing such a gaggle of younglings.

The children swarmed around Isabel emitting joyous exclamations, a dozen or so in all, each wearing simple linen tunics and woolen leggings. None of them looked especially clean, but they seemed well cared for and wore only the normal amount of dirt for children of such an active age.

"Ah, Lady, 'tis a pleasure to see you, as always," said the wide woman as she neared. "Settle ducklings, settle!" she shushed, motioning to the children who were clinging to Isabel. "They've been watching for ye all morning, of course, ever since General Ramu stopped to tell us to expect ye."

"*Céad míle beannachta*, Treva," Isabel greeted, and somehow Ean knew these words, foreign though they were to him. *A hundred thousand blessings.*

"All right, all right." Isabel opened her arms to embrace as many children as could crowd around her. "I may have something in my bag for each of you. Who's been good since I was last here?"

"Me!" came the staggered chorus of replies, accompanied by a multitude of jumping beans with upraised hands. Isabel glanced at Ean, and he got the sense her eyes were smiling at him through the blindfold. Then she let the children pull her to the side where she might better retrieve their presents from her own pack.

"Blessings upon your house, General." The woman Treva bowed to Ean with steepled fingers pressed to her lips.

Ean turned to her with a frown. "I'm no general. I'm Ean val Lorian."

"Of course ye are," she replied, eyeing him in that way women have, as if he'd be expected to say naught but foolish things. "And I'm Treva. The Lady told us a fortnight ago that ye'd be arriving in T'khendar soon. We're so glad ye've made it at last." Treva shook her head and lamented on Isabel's behalf, "Epiphany knows, the Lady's been missing ye something fierce these long years, though she'd never say it aloud."

Ean considered her fretfully. Her candid words fell upon a truth that speared him with sharp insistence.

"Might as well come up to the house." Treva gave a contented sigh. "They'll be about this for a while. She has nae even seen the older brood. They'll be wantin' to talk to her. Well, come on then," and she gave Ean's sleeve a friendly tug.

Not wanting to leave Isabel but recognizing that she had her own relationship with these children, Ean allowed Treva to pull him away. "Where are we?" he asked as they headed into the cornfield. The tall stalks quickly muffled the children's excited voices and brought only echoes on the breeze.

"The nearest town is Roth's Crossing," Treva answered. Then she frowned. "But ye probably aren't familiar with T'khendar, are ye, milord?"

"Not really."

"We're a few hours southwest of Niyadbakir by horse, but closer to Legacine, one of the Five Cities."

"The Five Cities?"

"That's right," she said. "Renato, Legacine, Torian, Dumarre and Premeira. These are the Five Cities of T'khendar, and of course Niyadbakir, but the Prime City isn't on the river route."

"You're losing me, Treva."

She cast him a wry look. "No matter, General. This is Sionym House where you've come, and that's the important part."

They emerged into an open yard that fronted a stone manor and outbuildings, the workings of a healthy farmstead. Children of all ages buzzed about like bees, taking no note of them. Towering eucalyptus trees cooled the farmstead and formed a barrier between the fields and the jutting mountains beyond. "We're an orphanage under the Lady's care." She settled hands onto her hips with a look of proud satisfaction.

"An orphanage." Ean looked to her in surprise.

But of course, what other explanation could there be for so many children? Ean observed the many youngsters buzzing about, some light-skinned, some so dark as to be carved of ebony, some with hair like fire and others as pale as moonlight.

"Where do the children come from?"

"Here and there." Treva waved nebulously. "Few enough are from T'khendar. Mostly Djurik collects them from his travels."

"Collects them from where?" Ean gave her a confused look. "Who is Djurik?"

"Djurik Nagraed," said a dark-skinned man, who was just then emerging from a near stone barn. He brushed the hay from his overalls and flashed a brilliant white smile. From his ebony skin and pale blue eyes, Ean guessed he was descended from one of the southern jungle tribes.

Djurik stopped in front of Ean and bowed as Treva had done—as so many had bowed to him since arriving in T'khendar.

"Be welcome, General," Djurik said. "It is our greatest honor to host you and the Lady."

"I'm Ean," he insisted lamely, suspecting it would make no difference.

"May I show you the farm, General?" Djurik offered, proving Ean's suspicions correct.

For lack of any reason not to, only wishing they'd stop calling him *General*, Ean agreed. Djurik showed him the outbuildings and paddocks, pastures and fields. Ean saw easily four score children of varying ages, from the youngest tending the goats and chickens to the oldest working the wheat.

"Are they all orphans?" Ean asked as they were walking between a fenced-in vegetable garden, ripe with gourds and cabbages, and a smokehouse, outside of which two older boys were chopping wood.

"Aye," Djurik exhaled a dramatic sigh. "The Lady found me herself when I was naught but trouble with a stick. She set me to task helping to build this place and then to fill it."

"So you're an Adept." As soon as Ean said it, he realizing Djurik had to be a Nodefinder—or at least one of the Wildling tribes of the third-strand, who often shared this second-strand trait. Though how Djurik was traveling outside of T'khendar defied explanation. "Are the children Adepts as well?"

He didn't like the sudden idea that came to him, that Djurik might be taking Alorin's adepts away when all were so desperately needed.

"A few," Djurik admitted to Ean's first question, "but these younglings are mainly just innocents without hope—homeless, parentless. Adepts like us…we make a way for ourselves even in the worst of circumstances." His pale blue eyes searched Ean's, and his gaze said much more than his words alone conveyed. "We're born with a gift, whether we use it for good or ill. These children had nothing, no one."

Recognizing his concern had been for naught, Ean chastised himself for ever doubting Isabel.

"But how are you traveling between the realms?" he asked the Adept then. "I thought the nodes to and from T'khendar were hopelessly twisted." He recalled the zanthyr chastising Carian for that very fact.

"Aye." Djurik eyed Ean surreptitiously. "And how deep does the alabaster go?"

Ean did a double-take on the man.

Djurik just grinned at him, his straight white teeth bright against his ebony skin.

Uncomfortable with where the discussion was heading, Ean returned them to safer waters. "Where do the children go from here?"

"Once they finish their schooling, they're free to return to their own lands—or stay in T'khendar and join the First Lord's crusade." He rested hands inside the flap of his overalls and exhaled a thoughtful sigh. "I'm proud to say most choose to stay."

A hubbub of excited shouting interrupted further talk—Isabel's arrival at the farmstead.

Still surrounded by a froth of children all clearly beneath the age of seven, Isabel was soon bombarded with two dozen more coming at her with shouts of surprise and welcome. Ean watched with a wide smile as Isabel allowed the youngest children to take her hands and guide her towards the manor, while the oldest boy claimed her satchel and two of the adolescent boys—all long legs and lean-muscled arms, so like Tanis these days—carried her staff between them.

"You know," Djurik mused, gazing at Isabel just as entranced as Ean, "there's a lot of folks as say they stayed in T'khendar 'cause of the First Lord, to serve him and do their part. I reckon that's true enough. But I warrant there's just as many of us are here to serve the Lady. Not that there's some competition," he added, glancing at Ean, "but this world is their world. We all know that."

Ean considered Djurik. Outwardly the Adept seemed a simple man, with his tattered work clothes and sweat-stained neckerchief, but he wondered...

'We are none of us the shells we wear.' Isabel's admonishment. Ean was beginning to see the truth of it.

TWENTY-NINE

"They never seem to sleep like respectable people."
— The Lord Captain Rhys val Kinkaide, on zanthyrs

TRELL DRESSED FOR dinner with his head spinning. In the last forty-eight hours, he'd learned that he was a prince; that his family still loved and mourned him; that his brother Sebastian had been sacrificed as part of a plot to gain the Eagle Throne; that *he* might be in danger as a result of the same plot; that his brother Ean was also being targeted, but was in more danger for being involved in a some vast game masterminded by the Fifth Vestal; that the same man held an unexplained interest in him; and that he was falling in love with Alyneri d'Giverny.

All things told, it had been a busy two days.

These experiences fell on the brighter side of his life. On the darker side, he knew now that the Emir had kept his name a secret from him for five years, even knowing how it had tormented him. He knew he was next in line for the Eagle Throne, which was a precarious position to occupy at present; and he knew that his father was the sworn ally of Radov abin Hadorin, whom Trell could never support.

What he didn't know was what he intended to do about any of it.

He'd touched upon this fear even while still in the Akkad. He'd wondered if he might be forced to reassess his own loyalties once he learned his name. Now the truth had become a very real obstacle to accepting any part of his birthright. His *name* alone, he supposed, was his to claim, but beyond that…well, he had much to think on.

Having washed and dressed, Trell stood staring at himself in the mirror, at his angular features and raven hair, at his grey eyes, always so intense. '*You are your father's son...*' Alyneri's words, spoken with admiration. But what did it really mean to be the son of Gydryn val Lorian? What kind of man was Dannym's king?

Though he now knew his name, Trell felt like his journey had only just begun.

He was somber as he headed down to dinner, finding Alyneri, Fynn and four others assembled in the dining room when he entered. The tallest of the strangers had stormy grey eyes, a thin, flaring nose, and dark brown hair held in place by an earl's bronze circlet. With his reddish beard and broad frame, he reminded Trell somewhat of a lion.

But he didn't seem the least bit fearsome when he turned to Trell and their eyes met. Trell saw a flash of raw emotion cross the older man's face, and then he abruptly bent his knee, pressed his fist to his chest and bowed his head. The other three men followed, looking equally stricken.

"My prince," said the first man, his voice gruff with emotion.

Trell felt dismayed.

"Trell, this is Rhys val Kincaide." Alyneri came to his rescue. "He is the captain of the King's Own Guard and has been a faithful member of our company since we left Calgaryn. His men are Dorin and Cayal."

"Well met, Captain." Trell wished that they might stand instead of remain so bowed, which only heightened his discomfort. "Please...I would that we might not keep these formalities." He gazed uncertainly at Rhys. "I've been long from my father's kingdom...long from such titles."

"Through treachery alone, my prince," Rhys returned as he and his men reclaimed their feet. "Surely no fault of yours."

"Be that as it may, I would rather we stood as equals in this company."

From the affronted look on his face, Rhys clearly discounted this idea as folly, but he blessedly didn't argue it. Trell supposed that was as much as he could hope for, under the circumstances.

"And this is Brody the Bull," Alyneri introduced the last man among them, who seemed aptly named. "He is Fynnlar's traveling companion."

"Not for much longer if I can help it." Fynn shot Brody a dark stare.

"He can't," Brody returned stoically. "I serve his father, Prince Ryan."

"Just because I haven't figured out how to be rid of you yet doesn't mean

I won't eventually." Fynn looked to Trell and suddenly brightened. "Now we're all buddies again, cousin, let's eat." He moved to the table without waiting for anyone's leave and started attacking the roasted turkey.

"Have you somewhere to be this evening, Fynnlar?" Alyneri suppressed a smile at the royal cousin. She let Trell help her into her chair, eyeing Fynn the while.

"As a matter of fact I do, your Grace," Fynn replied around a mouthful of poultry. "It's anywhere other than where I'm expected."

"I see," she said, though she clearly didn't.

"It's because of the pirate." Brody took a seat at the head of the table, the better to keep an eye on Fynn.

"That bloody pirate is the bane of my existence." The royal cousin drowned his mouthful of turkey with a long drink of wine, belched, and explained to Trell between bites, "Carian's got a cousin named Haddrick, who I've never gotten on with particularly well, being that he and I like the same sort of plunder."

"The easy kind," Brody noted.

Fynn shot him a sooty look. "Anyway...Haddrick is in town while his ship, the *Ransom*, takes some minor repairs. It seems our esteemed friend Carian vran Lea missed a meeting with his cousin at the Nugget down on Faring West, and the man has been hounding *me* relentlessly for news of Carian ever since—as if *I'm* somehow to blame for his bloody cousin being a Nodefinder and going wherever in Belloth's thirteen hells he wants to go."

"Can't you just tell him you don't know where Carian went?" Alyneri asked.

"That's sort of the crux of the problem," Fynn complained into his wine.

"Haddrick is a truthreader," Brody explained.

Alyneri looked shocked. "A *pirate* truthreader?"

"Jamaii has a right to its Adepts the same as any other kingdom," Fynn retorted. Then he frowned again. "But because I *do* have an idea of Carian's whereabouts..."

Trell was beginning to see the problem. "Have you taken some sort of oath that prevents you from speaking of what happened at the temple, cousin?"

Fynn gave him a grateful look. "See, I knew you were more than just a pretty face."

"Yes, I get that a lot."

"But forget Haddrick." Fynn looked Trell over. "I'm more interested in what we're to do with you."

Trell exchanged a look with Alyneri. They hadn't made it that far in their own discussions. "I would like to meet my father," Trell admitted, looking back to Fynn.

"His Majesty would want that too," Rhys said.

Fynn arched a brow. "Might be just as well. The king's gone to the parley in Tal'Shira, which would appear to be quite a bit safer for you than good ole Dannym these days."

"Why?"

Fynn gave him a long-suffering look.

"Don't tell me." Trell eyed him sardonically. "*Another* oath requiring your silence?"

Fynn drank his wine, apparently unable even to comment.

Alyneri gazed at him in astonishment. "Fynnlar, did the Fourth Vestal truthbind you?"

He shot her a frustrated glare. "As if I could *answer* that!"

"He did," Brody confirmed. "Otherwise Lord Fynnlar would've blabbed to everyone."

"I know how to keep a secret!" Fynn protested indignantly.

"So long as it's bound with the fourth," Brody agreed.

Trell felt the strangest flutter in his chest at this phrase. He took a drink of wine to settle it—though it didn't seem to help much. "What does it mean to be truthbound?"

"The fourth strand of *elae* compels the energies associated with thought," Alyneri said. "Tanis spoke to me in depth as he was learning of these workings. Truthreaders have the knowledge to bind men's thoughts behind veils of compulsion that prevent their speaking of certain events. Truthbindings can span memories that may encompass many years."

"Years?" Trell repeated uneasily.

"Fourth-strand bindings are tricky, vicious things," Fynn said grimly. It seemed he was able to talk about the subject in general, so long as it didn't concern him specifically.

"How are they vicious?" Trell asked, though he had the uncomfortable feeling that he already knew the answer quite intimately.

"They lay these things on you," Fynn grumbled, clearly speaking from experience now, "in such a way that they can make you forget entirely the thing they're binding you against in order to protect the information during a possible interrogation. If someone were to question you the wrong way, you could forget *years* of your life—"

The idea dawned on all of them at once.

Everyone turned and stared at Trell.

He barely noticed their appalled looks, however, for he was hovering at the edge of a dangerous truth. He could almost see it...but it lay blurred behind a volatile cloud of energy. Just looking at the cloud made him ill.

"*Oh gods,*" Alyneri whispered. She took his hand and stared at him.

"Mayhap my uncle, your father, can shed some light on the mystery." Fynn sounded uncharacteristically sober.

Trell wasn't sure what he thought about any of it—about seeking answers from the king, about going to Tal'Shira, right into the heart of the enemy's stronghold. But if he meant to reestablish any sort of relationship with his father, what choice did he have?

"We'll need the services of a Nodefinder to get to Tal'Shira by the Sea," Fynn noted, oblivious to Trell's dismay and indecision. "Being that tomorrow is the start of three weeks of Carnivále—during which the whole damned city shuts down to better drink themselves into a stupor—it may take me a few days to find one willing to take us there."

"I think we could do with a few days," Alyneri murmured, to which sentiment Trell heartily concurred.

After dinner, Alyneri walked with Trell back to her rooms. She felt strange returning there, where the memories of the night of Ean's accident still lingered so vividly, as if painted on the walls.

Alyneri led outside, thinking the night air would clear the cloying memories from her consciousness, yet walking out onto her balcony immediately brought images of the zanthyr scooping her off her feet to fly through the air...of Ean lying broken in the earth—a vision that still brought a latent shudder—and later, of the zanthyr healing her...of the tingling feeling of his lips on hers...

Trell placed his hands on the railing and gazed out over the gardens. "It's lovely here," he said in the desert tongue.

Alyneri came to stand beside him. She knew the gardens were the last thing truly on his mind. "I would help ease your troubles if I could," she offered, using the same tongue. It was starting to feel like their private language.

He gave her a grateful smile. "Thank you. I believe that." He leaned elbows on the railing, his grey eyes intense as he gazed into the night. "My mind is overfull these days." He shot her a rueful look. "If a *djinn* offered to magically alleviate my most troubling concern, it would be a challenge to select just one."

Alyneri realized she'd been staring at him, her gaze drawn to the angular line of his jaw, and the way his lips always seemed just on the edge of a smile.

How incredible that *Trell val Lorian* was actually standing beside her. She had to pinch herself for the heady excitement that accompanied the recurring realization.

"Trell…" Alyneri forcing her gaze away out of common decency. "Why do you think the Emir kept your identity from you?"

He turned her a quiet look. "A good question. I've been thinking on it also. I have a feeling he must've known my life was in danger."

"From the accident?"

"Maybe. I don't know. The Emir's Spymaster is a formidable man with a vast network at his disposal. Very little occurs in the realm that he's not aware of. If anyone were to know the details behind the sinking of the *Dawn Chaser,* t'would be him."

Alyneri gazed at him in wonder. "You think the Emir felt you would be safer at war than returned to your own family?"

Trell gave her a grim look. "That is my suspicion, yes."

Alyneri hugged her wrap closer about her shoulders. "It's so strange to try to think of him as an ally." Upon noting Trell's concerned frown, she added, "though I believe he was certainly an ally to you."

Trell shook his head. His gaze was deeply troubled. "My father allies with Radov abin Hadorin. I cannot begin to tell you of that man's crimes."

"I don't think the king willingly maintains the alliance," Alyneri admitted. "The kingdom is quite divided over it."

He latched onto this information with sudden interest. "Truly?"

She shrugged. "No one likes the idea of sending brothers, fathers or sons to a war in a kingdom of heathens," and then she grimaced at the bigoted beliefs evident in such a statement.

He considered her gravely. "Heathens…like you? Like your father?"

She nodded, feeling the sting of barbs sunk too deeply to extract.

Trell exhaled a slow breath. "Radov…" he shook his head and pressed his lips together tightly. "The man sent monsters after his own daughter because she dared to love a boy without his consent. He allies with the Prophet and lets Saldarian mercenaries commit horrific crimes against his own people. I can't support a man like that under any circumstances."

Alyneri drew back. "Trell, are you saying…" She stared at him. "Radov is *allied* with the Prophet Bethamin? Surely not!"

He gave her a long look.

"But…are you certain?"

"Unequivocally."

Alyneri felt a welling sense of alarm. "Trell…" she held his gaze significantly, "his Majesty would never support Radov if he knew he was allied with the Prophet. Your father has forbidden Bethamin's supporters from even entering the kingdom," whereupon she added darkly, "though they certainly seem to snake their way in somehow."

"If he heads to a parley in Tal'Shira, my father will no doubt discover the truth soon enough," Trell replied darkly.

Alyneri let out a tremulous sigh. "Such troubling times."

He wrapped an arm absently around her shoulders and pulled her close.

Alyneri looked out over the darkly gleaming bay. "While traveling with Ean, it felt like it was just us against this evil force out to get him, but I see now that entire kingdoms are reverberating with discord. It's like a great gong has been rung, trembling the world, sending angry ripples everywhere."

He exhaled a contemplative sigh. "The realm is out of Balance, and magic is dying."

She turned to him, startled. "What do you know of Balance?"

"Little enough personally, but those who are in a position to know of it have spoken to me. Balaji said Balance often requires great subterfuge, and Vaile and the others were very concerned about the Adept race dying. They said this is what the Mage worked to correct."

Alyneri's heart fluttered at this news. "Do you think it's true? It would mean—Trell, it would mean the Fifth Vestal works in our best interests still." She bit her lip and gazed at her hands. "I don't know why the idea gives me so much hope...I really want to believe he's a good man, even though everything I've heard says otherwise."

Trell turned her to face him, and when their eyes met, she saw a confusing mix of desires in his stormy eyes—so like and yet so different from Ean's. He drew her into his embrace, and she rested her head against his chest while a wondrous tension quickened.

"Alyneri, *azizam*..." his breath felt warm in her hair. "I'm grateful it was you I found that day."

Her heart beat faster simply upon hearing him say her name. "So am I." How could he have become so important to her when she'd known him for such a short time?

But you've known him all your life!

Yet this truth didn't fully explain her feelings. She sensed his own desire through their contact, through the way he held her, so strong and yet so carefully; through the sound of his breath coming faster and deeper. She felt him lift his head from hers, and when she dared look up, he was gazing intently at her.

Her heart fluttered, and she caught her lip between her teeth. He closed his eyes and exhaled, letting his breath alleviate the tension that ostensibly bound him, too. She almost wished he wouldn't control himself so completely...but at the same time, she was grateful that he could. They were so new to her, these heady feelings that thrilled and terrified equally.

Trell laid his forehead against hers and let their noses touch, the slightest caress. "I find you very beautiful, Alyneri. I'm drawn to you in a way that speaks deeply to me."

"I..." She caught her lower lip between her teeth. "I feel the same."

He drew back to look at her again, and that feeling of connection grew exponentially. He ran the back of one finger down her cheek and gazed into her eyes. Heat flooded Alyneri.

He must've seen her blushing even in the darkness, for he dropped his hand and took a step back. A gentle formality filled the space between them, but Alyneri found it a welcome respite from the tumultuous feelings spawned by his closeness.

"I will see you in the morning then, Duchess," he said, switching back to the common tongue. He gave her a dazzling smile. "Good night, my lady."

"Your Highness," she managed, breathless and dizzy and alive in ways she'd never imagined.

Trell was wound too tightly for rest as he left Alyneri's rooms, so he found his way into the gardens to work off the restless energy that had him in thrall. After roaming aimlessly for an hour or so, he emerged from a sculpture garden onto a wide span of lawn that fell away towards a cliff and the dark swath of moonlit sea beyond. Tiny bulbs glowed among the endless waves, the running lights of ships leaving with the evening tide.

Likewise beckoned by the open space of the ocean and the vast starlit sky, Trell headed towards the water. His head felt tangled. A jumble of confusions and questions had been energized by his sudden desire for Alyneri, the latter of which had to remain unsatisfied. She was a lady, and still a girl for all she was ten and eight—and though girls her age or younger were often married off, that didn't make them any less frightened by the prospect of a coupling with a man. He'd sensed Alyneri's desire, but he'd also sensed that it had startled and confused her...that she wasn't ready to give in to those desires.

Never mind that their social statuses made any coupling impossible without also involving the politics of kings. That was a problem for another day.

Reaching the edge of the cliff, Trell found a staircase leading down to a swath of beach far below. As he descended, the sound of the crashing sea became louder, and the salt air smelled strangely familiar...

The sudden image of that same beach where he'd remembered seeing Alyneri flashed to mind, only this time he and his brothers raced on pale horses at the edge of the crashing surf. His older brother had the lead, black hair flying on the wind, while his younger brother's horse inched nose to nose with Trell's mount. The boys' hair was damp from spray, and sand clung to their boots and the wet, snapping hems of their cloaks. All were laughing.

A terrible longing and loneliness accompanied this vision. Trell paused just off the stair and suddenly recalled another day, when he'd sat at the ocean's edge and stared in anger at the sea, his chest clenched in a vise of grief.

"You are very like him," came a deeply resonant voice from out of the darkness.

Trell spun with a sharp intake of breath, and his hand went automatically to his sword, but it was only the zanthyr who stood at the water's edge. He'd been so still, Trell had barely noticed him.

Exhaling the tension that had risen with his alarm, Trell rested one hand on his sword hilt and walked towards the zanthyr. "Like who? My father, or Ean?"

"Like the First Lord." The zanthyr turned, and his green eyes seemed to glow in the deep night, luminous like the stars.

The zanthyr's intense gaze caught Trell so off guard that it took him a heartbeat to process his words. But then he shoved all other thoughts aside. "I am like the First Lord?" Felt both deeply complimented and intrigued. "How?"

"You're both thoughtful men," the zanthyr replied, "careful and considerate. You spend too much time in your heads."

Trell smiled at this, knowing the latter statement was true for him at least. He moved closer to Phaedor, close enough that he could make out the sculpted lines of his face limned by the moonlight. "How well do you know the First Lord?"

The zanthyr arched a brow. "Your single question of the *djinn* and this is the one you choose to ask?"

Trell did a double-take. He'd mentioned the desert genies to Alyneri only an hour before, but how did the zanthyr know of their conversation? Moreover, they'd been speaking in the desert tongue! Yet Trell didn't for a moment believe that Phaedor had produced the same analogy out of coincidence.

"Very well," he said, attempting to cover his surprise. "Since you're offering, I am curious about something." He exhaled and frowned off towards the glittering lights of the distant city. "Why does the Mage allow so many lies to be spread about him? Why does he let them continue when surely he could set the record straight?"

"What would be the point in such an effort? Men will believe what they will."

"But…" Trell frowned.

"You don't win a game by focusing on things you cannot control. You win it by focusing on those things that you can."

"A game," Trell mused, struck again by the familiar analogy. His eyes flew back to the zanthyr's as he added significantly, "Pieces and Players. The Mage wrote of such terms. What do you know of them?"

"I know much."

"What will you tell me of them then?" Trell amended with a smile.

The zanthyr pinned him with one green eye, the other being partly obscured by his raven hair as it tossed on the sea breeze. Trell expected the man to artfully deny him, even as Balaji had so often managed, so he was happily surprised when Phaedor replied instead, "What would you know?"

Trell barely needed to think on it, for a question remained ever on the edge of his thoughts. "Why does the Mage want me to be a Player in his game?"

The zanthyr regarded him quietly. "I don't know his plans for you. I do know that the First Lord's game requires thinking men to act with foresight and conscience if we're to succeed, and I needn't tell you there is a vast shortage of such men in the realm."

Trell frowned out to sea, towards the ship nearly vanished in the west. "I have this sense that the path I would choose is the same one the Mage needs me to walk." He shifted his gaze back to the zanthyr. "I'd always imagined my journey would end with the discovery of my name, but it seems it's only just begun."

The zanthyr regarded him steadily.

"And the path before me," Trell added with a measured exhale, "I often wonder if it will lead me back to him, to your First Lord."

"You can do no less than walk your path," Phaedor advised, neither confirming nor denying the possibility, "wherever it leads."

Trell managed a rueful smile. "Is it strange that I hardly know your First Lord, nor even truly the game he plays, yet…I believe I would give him my oath?"

"He would have it, Trell val Lorian, if you offered."

Trell felt oddly gratified in hearing this. He gazed at the zanthyr in thoughtful silence. "Alyneri told me you saved my brother's life," he said after a moment. "I want to thank you for that."

Phaedor cast him an unreadable look. "I did not do it for Ean's sake."

"Still," Trell wasn't quite sure how to take the comment, "in the end, the result is the same. So, thank you."

Phaedor gave him a barely perceptible nod, accepting of his gratitude, and looked back out to the sea. "Goodnight, Prince of Dannym."

Trell smiled, nodded and made his way back towards the stair. Strangely, as with the ending of his conversation with Ramu, he didn't resent at all being dismissed like a child.

As Trell returned to the villa, he considered the zanthyr. Phaedor's presence had gripped him, tenaciously and exactingly, such that the only thing that felt real in that moment was the zanthyr's gaze holding his. The man was easily as compelling as Ramu, though far less accessible.

The others he'd met—Rhakar, Naiir, Loghain, even Vaile, with all he'd seen her do—they cast only a pale shadow of Phaedor.

'He is the closest I have ever come to gazing upon divinity...' Alyneri's heartfelt words, her vision of the zanthyr.

As he made his way back to his rooms, at last ready for his bed and sleep, Trell decided that Alyneri definitely had the right of it.

THIRTY

"Suspicion haunts the guilty. The killer sees assassins in every shadow."
— Errodan val Lorian, Queen of Dannym and the Shoring Isles

THE INFAMOUS COURTESAN Ghislain D'Launier strode into her third-floor salon to find a man waiting for her.

Ghislain could tell much from looking at a man. For instance, she knew that this man thought highly of himself, for he wore a longish moustache and pointed beard despite the style being out of fashion. This told her that he tried to show himself above courtly trends—or at least above the trends of the court to which he was supposedly sworn.

From the state of his clothing, Ghislain knew he'd been traveling for the better part of a month and that he'd spent much of that time ahorse. This same observation showed her that the man had little regard for others, or for himself, for he hadn't bothered to change his clothing before visiting the home of a famous courtesan. This could also mean he was in a hurry and possibly feared for his life.

Finally, she read from his brazen stance before a lady unknown to him that he was a man of dishonest temperament and likely harbored an ignoble nature.

"Lord Brantley, I presume," Ghislain said as her assistant, the buxom Riselle, shut the door behind her.

"Indeed," he clucked, puffing up his chest like a rooster. "I am Lord Brantley, Earl of Pent."

"And how may I help you, Lord Brantley, Earl of Pent? It is not every day that visiting lords whose acquaintance I've never made request to meet me in private."

"I'm told you are a woman of information, madam."

"Among other things." She walked to the sideboard. "Will you share a drink with me, my lord? Perhaps you could use some refreshment after such a long ride."

"I certainly could—" Brantley bit back his words as she turned with goblets in hand. His expression harbored a deep suspicion and a darkness that told her much about his temperament. "Who told you I was coming?" he somewhat hissed. "How did you know where I've been—what did they say about me?"

"My sources are inviolate, I'm afraid." Ghislain calmly handed him the goblet. She took a sip, eyed him over the rim, and then added with a smile, "But of course, you know that."

Despite his mistrustful stare, Brantley accepted the wine and drank deeply of it. He seemed to have the manners of a stable hand and smelled similarly fragrant. "I'm searching for a woman," he told her once he'd drained most of his goblet.

Ghislain settled demurely into her armchair. "Would this woman have a name? There are many women in our fair Free Cities."

"Her name is Alyneri d'Giverny. She is the Duchess of Aracine."

"I see. And what do you want with her?"

"That's none of your concern." Brantley's moustache twitched with irritation.

"Oh, but it *is*, my lord," Ghislain corrected with a smile. "How else shall I gauge the value of the information on her whereabouts?"

Brantley stared at her for a moment, drank the last dregs of his wine, and finally cleared his throat. "Well…she is desirable to my lord."

"And who would be this great lord?"

"His Grace, Stefan val Tryst."

Ghislain fixed her dark eyes upon the Earl of Pent. "I am most interested to know what the Duke of Morwyk hopes to gain by apprehending the Duchess of Aracine. Did he not already attempt to kidnap her once?"

Brantley went pale.

Ghislain gazed evenly at him. The man was entirely out of his element.

"I'm not...privy to the details of the Duke's interest in the Duchess," the earl hedged uncomfortably.

Ghislain took another sip of wine. "What then have you to offer me, Brantley, Earl of Pent? The whereabouts of the Healer Alyneri d'Giverny will not come cheap."

Brantley took a step towards her. "I have coin—"

"The only coins exchanging hands within these walls, my lord, are gifts from my patrons, and I don't believe your pockets are nearly deep enough to contract for that service."

Brantley pulled uncomfortably at his doublet. "Then what...?"

"As you well noted, my lord, I'm a woman of information. *This* is the currency I expect in exchange. Now..." she settled more comfortably into her chair, "I will know why the Duke wants the Duchess so desperately. And while we're about it, you can fill me in on his other plans. I'm most interested to know when he expects his army to march on Calgaryn."

Brantley went whiter than a winter hare. "I couldn't...couldn't possibly—"

"Now, now, Earl," she cautioned. "You need this information. You know it, and I know it. That's your first error in coming to me, for you've no leverage with which to wage your bargain. If I'm not mistaken, you need not return to Dannym at all if not in the company of Alyneri d'Giverny. So...which is more important to you, Lord Brantley, Earl of Pent? The girl, or the information I require in payment?" Ghislain blessed the earl with a lovely smile, reminiscent of her younger years, but he was looking entirely too ill to appreciate its glory.

Not much later, Ghislain stood in the deep shadows of the balcony outside her salon overlooking the Villa D'Antoinette's moonlit yard, where Lord Brantley and his men were imprudently discussing their plans. Their words carried upon the evening breeze as if shouted in an amphitheater, floating up to her ears with crystal clarity. She had often used the vantage to learn secrets too delicate to be spoken even within her walls. Unfortunately, on this night, the knowledge would be of little use to anyone.

"You told them where to find her, my lady?" asked the exotic Riselle, who stood just behind Ghislain in the shadows.

"Of course." Ghislain's voice carried to Riselle's ears alone. "The price was right. I have many contacts who will pay handsomely to know when Morwyk marches on Calgaryn—especially Morin d'Hain."

"But what of the Mage's missive?"

"The Mage mentioned nothing of the duchess. She'll have to make her own way."

More voices floated to them from below as Lord Brantley issued his commands, sending men to watch the villa where the duchess was staying.

"My lady," Riselle said quietly then, "don't you think the Mage would want you to protect the prince *and* his lady love?"

Ghislain sighed. "You know I cannot be seen to take sides, Riselle. And who am I to presume what complex twists drive the Mage's game? Perhaps whatever happens with this Lord Brantley is important to the greater whole. One never knows such things." She turned and headed back inside.

Riselle's dark eyes remained troubled as she followed and closed the door.

Noting her companion's unease, Ghislain cupped Riselle's face tenderly with one hand. "We walk the paths we are upon, Riselle, taking things as they come. Seeking to know what lies around each bend only brings regret, as Epiphany's Prophet has long advised. Trust to the river that carries us all—that is the best we can do."

Riselle dropped her eyes. "Yes, my lady."

"Now come. You have guests to greet, and I have patrons waiting to be embarrassingly schooled in a game of Kings."

And so did the ladies depart to their mutual entertainments.

THIRTY-ONE

"Destiny is a pleasant fiction. Choice determines our fate, not the gods."
— Isabel van Gelderan, Epiphany's Prophet

ALYNERI D'GIVERNY REGARDED herself in the standing mirror with a tiny crease furrowing her fair brow. She didn't know what she thought about the dress she wore that morning. It was not her usual style. In fact, she never would've had the courage to wear the style in Dannym.

Finding the gown had been a welcome surprise upon rising that morning. Ironically, it had been delivered to the villa on the day she'd been kidnapped. When she'd ordered it and two others soon after Ean's accident…even then, she hadn't been sure if she'd ever find the gumption to wear the dresses.

But she had changed.

The zanthyr had begun this transformation. Ever since her first confrontation with Phaedor, Alyneri had started seeing herself changing; the northern ropes that had long bound her began fraying as she reached towards her own truth. Shrugging off the attempt to be someone she wasn't felt uniquely liberating, and her disposition had generally improved as a result.

Even her feelings for Ean had been affected. That she cared for him went without question, but even before his accident, she'd begun to accept their diverging paths. She no longer suffered from a perpetual longing for his affections; and though she hadn't spotted it at the time, somewhere on their travels south, she'd finally forgiven him for not loving her.

And then, somewhere between being kidnapped, nearly killed by a mudslide, and learning to heal herself, Alyneri had embraced her desert heritage in a way that felt...well, it felt *right*. Respectful of her father and all that he'd given her, of her family name and relatives who cared for her. She felt more honest and authentically *herself*.

She'd tried living among her mother's northern friends, but without the Lady Melisande to dignify Alyneri's presence, they'd looked upon her like a rather exotic and unusual daisy: idly interesting, a topic of speculation to be certain, but still, ultimately, a weed.

The teal desert gown Alyneri now wore was crafted from heavy silk and felt incredibly soft against her skin. The wide collar arched gracefully from shoulder to shoulder to reveal the lovely line of her collarbone, and the gown clung to her breasts in ways that made her blush. Fitted through her torso and hips, the skirt flowed seamlessly to her feet. She especially loved the tiny hook-and-eye closures along the hidden placket on one side, which allowed her to dress herself. The gown was elegant, refined, simple yet very beautiful, and it startled her to see herself in it.

It startled her more to realize she looked alluring.

Her dress wasn't all that she'd altered, though the second change proved slightly less dramatic. Northern ladies wore their hair in braids or sculpted curls like crowns upon their head, but daughters of the sand left their hair long and free, at the most held with a net of precious stones.

So Alyneri had ordered a net of tiny garnets, which had always brought out the color in her dark eyes. She wore the cap now. She liked the way it held her flaxen hair out of her eyes while letting her long locks fall free, and she liked how it framed her heart-shaped face, making her eyes look larger...

A knock came upon her bedroom door, and she automatically called for entry. Trell came in looking upbeat, but he stopped in his tracks when he saw her.

He pushed palms to his temples. "*Alyneri*," he moaned good-naturedly, "what are you *doing* to me?"

She turned to face him and immediately blushed, for she couldn't help but notice the way his eyes were hungrily exploring her body. "I—I had it made before everything happened."

He approached her slowly, his grey eyes pinning her in place while her heart tried to race away with her breath in tow. "I've known many women who wore such gowns," he murmured in the desert tongue; the words were all the more intimate for having been spoken thusly. He carefully lifted a strand of hair from her shoulder and gazed into her eyes. "None of them were as beautiful as you."

Alyneri's stomach did a little flip. She felt trapped by the heat of his gaze and by her own longing for his touch. "*Trell...I—*"

He captured her mouth with his own. When his tongue found hers, a thrill coursed through her. He slipped one hand into her hair while his other found the small of her back. Gentle pressure brought her body close against his. She felt him powerfully then, felt his own strength and his rising need. A current of desire woke every waking sense.

When he released her, she stood exhilarated and blushing fiercely.

He rested his forehead against hers while his thumb captured her bottom lip. "You mustn't wear such alluring things, Duchess, if you don't want this reaction out of me."

I shall never wear anything else!

Alyneri finally found her voice, though it sounded very young when she spoke. "I...I shall take your advice under consideration, Your Highness."

His lips spread in a slow smile. Then he stepped back from her and assumed that polite formality he was so good at, his mind easily moving on while she gazed at him in wonder, still enraptured by his kiss.

"Fynnlar has gone to see about acquiring a Nodefinder to take us to Tal'Shira." He pushed hands in his pockets and smiled at her. "What would you do in the meantime, Your Grace?"

Only be with you, she thought, but she said, "It's Carnivále. Do you think we could go?"

Trell considered the idea. "It could be dangerous. Brantley might still be looking for you."

"I thought perhaps if we wore masks..."

Trell took up her hand, but he didn't pin her breathlessly that time, only moved his thumb slowly across her skin. "I've never lived in fear of losing my life," he remarked, holding her gaze with thoughtful regard, "but I wouldn't endanger yours needlessly."

"I don't want to live my life carefully, Trell." Perhaps it was the dress that emboldened her, but she felt herself standing taller, her shoulders straighter. "I want to live it bravely. Ean was impulsive and reckless with his life, and… well, I don't mean that we should be so cavalier, but I…" She paused and gave him a little frown. "I have a feeling that adventure will find us, no matter how careful we might be."

She truly meant it. She wasn't sure if the sudden feeling was the shadow of a Seeing, but it certainly resonated within her in a way that defied explanation.

Trell regarded her intently. "Whatever path we're upon, we have to walk it?"

"Something like that."

He released her hand and ran the back of his fingers down her arm. She held her breath and tried to keep her imagination in check, but she couldn't stop the flush that sprouted on her cheeks.

Trell grinned at her—she couldn't be certain if his humor came at her response to his words or to his touch. "Very well, Duchess. We'll walk the path together and face whatever it brings."

Whereupon Alyneri wondered if she could ever love anyone more.

The sun hung low above the Bay of Jewels as Alyneri and Trell's coach drove towards the Rue Royale, a broad boulevard that ran through the center of the city, and where the largest of the parades and fêtes were being held.

Carnivále in the Cairs was an extravagant affair, a combination of traditions as celebrated by the disparate races and faiths that populated the city. The men and women from Rimaldi celebrated Carnivále with the reversal of traditional roles, where men dressed as women, women dressed as men, lords dressed as slaves…and rather more bizarre interpretations.

Other traditions were represented in the vast party in the streets, in costumes or with toasts, in rituals by candlelit ceremonies or processions of singing and chanting celebrants. At one point Alyneri watched in baffled wonder as a host of dark-skinned maidens ostensibly bathed in a fountain. Trell explained that the Solstice was the time when the Wind God collected the prayers of the people and delivered them to Jai'Gar. In Duan'Bai, this was a time of corporal purification, fasting and contemplation, but in the Cairs, where frivolity reigned, it seemed the ritual cleansing had been uniquely reinterpreted.

The sun had nearly set by the time they arrived at the Rue Royale to find the party in full swing. A parade celebrating the Bemothi Festival of the Sun was just passing, and she exited the coach in mesmerized awe at the majestic creations moving past. Puppets ten paces tall were animated by puppeteers, who wore their stilt creations upon their backs like inverse marionettes. The puppets dove and danced, spun and cavorted while their puppeteers moved in lively unison below. Both puppets and puppeteers wore coordinated costumes, so that together they seemed dancing giants.

Trell held Alyneri's hand firmly in his, and as the parade moved past, he tugged her on. The two of them wore matching velvet masks, which Fynn had reluctantly acquired from one of his many contacts—lovely, feathered things tied on with long silk ribbons. Trell's grey eyes seemed unearthly behind his sapphire mask, while her dark eyes looked molten against sanguine velvet.

Into the crowd Trell pulled her. Music and laughter surrounded them, as much a part of the harmony of celebration as the sound of tambourines and drums, or cheers made in toast. Trell pulled them to a halt as a long line of running girls went streaming past, laughing and shouting, all of them wearing sheer silk shifts, their long hair tangled with flowers.

"Would you rather see me in that?" Alyneri asked with a tart smile once the girls were gone.

He leveled her a telling look. "I would rather see you in nothing."

That brought a bright flush to her cheeks, and she buried her head in his shoulder and giggled helplessly.

He squeezed her hand. "Come. I hear music."

They headed into a square where a troupe of acrobats were doing flips on a canvas trampoline held by their counterparts. Alyneri watched one of the lithe men spin, flip and corkscrew his way back onto his feet just in time to be thrown up into the air to perform yet another twisting combination, that one met by a cacophony of cheers.

Trell dragged her towards a café, and he bought them each a drink served in a painted wooden cup. At their next stop, Trell bought sweet cakes drenched in orange water and honey, followed by minced lamb pies from a street vendor, and then pheasant tarts from a woman with a tray standing outside a *taverna* whose street-side tables were packed to bursting with masked revelers.

On and on they walked and ate and drank, mixing with the celebration and taking of it what they would. Night fell and the stars appeared, barely visible beneath the haze of torches and the smoke of fire candles, which had started going off almost as soon as the sun dipped to the horizon. At one point, Trell bought Alyneri a sparkler stick that utterly captivated her. The long, taut wick sprayed light from its tip in a slow burning coal that left one end desiccated while the flame continued its brilliant expiration.

While it burned, Trell stood behind her with his arms tight around her waist, watching over her shoulder as she gazed in excited fascination. "That's you," he murmured in her ear, nodding to the brilliant sparkle. Then he pointed to the ashen end. "That's me."

She elbowed him and he chuckled.

Shortly they found themselves in a small square off the main boulevard where musicians played upon a stage and masses of people danced with no particular rhythm.

Trell pulled Alyneri into the fray and spun her to the pulsing beat of bongos and tambourines. Lutes picked up the melody as the pipe-players released it, and their fevered strumming seemed to mimic the beating of Alyneri's heart. Her face hurt from smiling, and she was lightheaded from the wine and sweets, from Trell's nearness, from his smoldering gaze and his smile.

As the musicians joined together and the music crescendoed, Trell spun Alyneri into a twirling dance. Laughing, Alyneri held his gaze so as not to become dizzy. Thus she saw the flash of movement behind him and knew the moment his eyes went blank. Alyneri screamed.

Someone grabbed hold of her even as Trell was falling in a daze. They dragged her into the shifting crowd with a hand hard over her mouth. She screamed and struggled against her captors, but no one took notice of her; she appeared to be just another overzealous partygoer being carted off through the throng.

Just beyond the small square, Alyneri's captors shoved her into a waiting coach. Rough hands grabbed her and pinned her down in darkness, while others tied her hands behind her back. She kicked and shouted—that is until they pushed a foul-smelling rag inside it.

It was dark in the coach, and the men kept Alyneri on the floor between three sets of boots. One set demonstrated its willingness to kick as she attempted to sit up. After that she stayed down.

He'll come. Somehow he'll come.

Lying in the darkness, Alyneri alternated between cursing her own stupidity and chastising herself for 'daring to live bravely.' That the odious Lord Brantley hadn't yet shown his face in no way prevented her from blaming him, for this new affront to her person reeked of his methods.

Trell will come, she assured herself again, and though the coach cleared the Rue Royale and turned downhill, heading for the harbor, Alyneri didn't cry.

Trell came to as rough hands were dragging him into an alley. He could still hear the musicians playing, so he knew he couldn't have been unconscious for long. Their first mistake was in not killing him in the square. Their second was in not relieving him of his sword.

He felt it securely at his side as the two men dragged him by his arms. He could hear the footsteps of others following behind. As yet, none of them knew he'd woken. By rights, as hard as they'd hit him, he probably shouldn't have woken at all. Doubtless, if not for the Mage having 'shored up his pattern' as Alyneri had phrased it, this alley would've likely been his final resting place.

For a split second as he gathered his wits, Trell thought of these things, and how he owed his life to the Mage yet again. By the time this adventure was over, he would no doubt owe the man three lifetimes of service in exchange.

The pounding in his head offered a powerful antidote to unconsciousness. As soon as he was sure of himself, he shoved his left foot forward to anchor himself and swept his other leg in front of the man to his right, making him stumble. The man on Trell's left jerked and cursed his companion's clumsiness. Trell used the momentum to wrench free of their hold.

He spun away and drew his sword, and finished the turn by plunging his blade into the closest man's chest. The other man cursed and grabbed for him, but Trell sidestepped and sliced his blade down across the other's back, opening his flesh. He elbowed a third man in the nose as he came rushing up behind him, and he kicked away a fourth, who tumbled backwards over one of the fallen and cracked his head with a dull clap on the stone wall.

It was a close and fervent battle to dispatch the last two. Trell was a skilled swordsman, while the men who'd been sent for him were naught but thick-necked ruffians willing to kill for coin. Trell felled them dispassionately, his only concern being Alyneri.

One he left alive for this purpose. As the man lay on the ground moaning around the hole in his gut, Trell grabbed him up by his jerkin and pulled his face close. "Where did they take her?"

The man choked and sputtered.

Trell shook him, but when that seemed to send him towards unconsciousness, Trell hit him in the jaw instead. "*Where?*"

The man seemed to focus somewhat, his dark eyes looking up, glazed with pain.

"Your wound isn't mortal," Trell hissed remorselessly, "but I can fix that readily enough."

The man coughed again, but he was listening.

"Where are they taking her?"

"…Olivia…danae," he gasped. Then he passed out.

Trell dropped him and ran.

Alyneri boarded the *Olivia D'ne* bound and gagged, dragged between burly men with heavy boots and sour breath. Hairy hands pitched her aboard with all the ceremony of a bag of cabbages, and she fell to her knees and had trouble getting up again until a man's hand slipped beneath her arm to steady her.

She would've preferred the Earl of Pent had left her on the decks.

"How nice to see Your Grace again," he crooned.

Alyneri pulled her skirts out from beneath her feet and straightened to face him. Thank Epiphany her mask had come off during the struggle, for it would've diminished the effect of her baleful stare.

Brantley looked her over boldly. "It is with profound relief that I find you in such a healthy state. Alas, Lord Everly did not fare so well in the accident in Veneisea. We finally found him dead in a town several miles downriver."

A fitting end for the man, she thought ungraciously. *I hope they found him stuck head-first in the mud.*

Lord Brantley untied her gag, and she somewhat spit the foul rag at him. He seemed to be waiting for some kind of thanks, but when she merely returned a level gaze, he frowned at her, grabbed her upper arm and said poisonously, "I had a late meal prepared for your arrival. We shouldn't let it grow cold."

She went stiffly with him into the captain's cabin—not that she had any choice. He shoved her inside, slammed the door behind them, and walked to a round table in the middle of the large room.

"Now then. Come…sit," and he pulled out a chair for her. "There's no need to make our voyage unpleasant. We have two long weeks ahead of us, and we might enjoy such time in conversation…or even dalliance."

When Alyneri merely stood rigidly by the door, Lord Brantley's expression darkened. "Or, if you prefer, I can pitch you below decks to entertain the crew. They mislike having women aboard on principle, but I'm sure a lovely thing like you can find ways to make it worth their while."

Alyneri wondered if he would dare make good on this threat; she wouldn't put such a crime past a man who would sell truthreaders to Bethamin's Ascendants. So she walked stiffly over to the chair and sat down, radiating immense indignation.

"Excellent," Lord Brantley murmured. He took a chair across the table and draped a linen napkin across his knees, proceeding then to uncover the many plates of food that the ship's cook had prepared.

Alyneri admitted the food smelled wonderful, but she'd take her chances with the crew before she ate anything dispensed by the Earl of Pent. He didn't seem to mind her reluctance to eat, clucking at her about nervous stomachs and women of delicate dispositions while he gluttonized himself.

Throughout the meal, Alyneri stared at Lord Brantley and thought of Tanis and what would've become of him if not for Epiphany's blessing, which somehow had made him immune to Bethamin's Fire. She thought of the Marquiin who'd died in Tanis's arms, and the boy Piper, who was probably dead by now, a victim of the Prophet's corruptive Fire.

For each of these crimes, she blamed Lord Brantley, and the flames of her condemnation warmed her stomach better than any wine.

When the earl had sated himself, he sat back in his chair, wiped his longish moustache with his napkin, and regarded Alyneri. The man seemed naught but an overgrown rodent, with his long nose and the way his moustache twitched when his lips moved.

"Morwyk is anxious to make your acquaintance, Your Grace." Brantley settled the greasy linen back in his lap. "Imagine our dismay when we parted in Acacia, only to shortly thereafter learn of your impressive connections."

Alyneri just stared at him.

Brantley rose from his chair and walked around to her. He perched a leg on the edge of the table and took up a lock of her hair, rubbing the strands between his fingers while he considered her. "I never would've taken you for an heiress."

She shifted her gaze to meet his. "Do you know what the Kandori do to men who try to ransom the heirs to their fortune, Lord Brantley?"

He settled hands in his lap and gazed eagerly at her. "Do tell, Your Grace."

"They open up the bowels of such men and tie them by their intestines to the branch of a tree. If the men survive this punishment, the Kandori set smoke to drive out the carrion ants, which feast upon their organs. It is said the men take many days to die in this fashion. By the time their hearts give out, such men are hardly recognizable as men any longer."

"A fitting end, no doubt," Lord Brantley said with a wan smile. "I think His Grace has other plans for you than ransom, my dear. A virgin such as yourself, as yet unwed, would make a fitting gift for one of his sons."

"I understood his sons to have wives already."

"Wives are easily dispensed with." The earl gave her a sharp sort of smile. Just when Alyneri was deciding this meant she was safe from the crew, Lord Brantley continued, "That being said, if you were no longer in a condition befitting one of his sons, the Duke has mentioned other uses for an Adept of your talents."

Alyneri could only imagine what the corrupt and amoral Duke of Morwyk might do with his own personal Healer.

First-strand patterns could be used to harm men as easily as heal them.

She knew many patterns that might be repurposed to cause pain or even death.

She must've paled at these thoughts, for Lord Brantley smiled with satisfaction. He reached a hand to touch her face, and Alyneri impulsively jerked away from him. This angered him, and he grabbed her by the back of the head, pulling tightly upon her hair to force her to look up at him. "The sooner you come to understand who your masters are, *duchess*, the smoother this will go for you."

His fingers hurt her, and she feared him and his threats, but Alyneri was determined not to succumb as easily to the earl as she had in Acacia. There were worse things than having one's body raped. The rape of the mind would be infinitely worse, a torment easily accomplished by a depraved truthreader or wielder.

There were patterns for just about every debased and dreadful thing a man could dream up.

Whether or not the Duke of Morwyk had the means, fourth-strand compulsion at least was something Lord Brantley could not manage. "He will come for me, you know." Alyneri gasped. Her throat felt tight, her breath strained from the way Brantley held her head at such an awkward angle. She was working hard to hold back tears.

Brantley stared at her for a moment longer, and then he released her with a jerk. "Who will come?" He pushed off the table. "Your knight from the city? I think not."

He doesn't know him, she realized with a painful swallow. She took some small solace in knowing Trell's identity at least remained safe from the earl.

Brantley walked to pour more wine. "No...your bonnie knight was easily dispensed with, I'm told. By now he's lying in an alley somewhere. The sooner you realize I'm your last hope, Your Grace, the better this will go for you." He came back to her holding his goblet and boldly ran his fingers down her cheek. His gaze hungered for her in a way that made Alyneri cringe.

She dared not openly defy him again, not for something so benign, but his touch sent chills of revulsion coursing through her.

She couldn't let herself believe that he'd spoken the truth about Trell. If Epiphany allowed her one grace in this disaster, it was the sure belief that Lord Brantley had underestimated him.

"See, that wasn't so hard, was it?" He stroked her face while his hot gaze seared across her bosom. "I can even make things pleasant for you."

"I seriously doubt that, Lord Brantley," Alyneri answered tightly, fighting back tears. Her heart beat a frantic pace, and her stomach was so twisted with loathing and anxiety that she felt sick. The man was absolutely vile. The idea of him touching her more intimately…

"You say that now," the earl remarked, his expression stony, "but you may reconsider before this is through."

Alyneri merely stared hatefully at him.

He frowned at her while his moustache twitched, clearly deliberating on a tactic for swaying her affections. Then he seemed to decide something. "Look here," and he pulled a dagger from a sheath behind his back, "if you promise to behave, I'll cut those bonds of yours. You would like that, wouldn't you?"

Alyneri nodded in spite of herself.

He cut her free and then sat there smiling at her, as if this simple act of kindness should entitle him to great rewards.

A knock upon the door spared her his lascivious consideration. Brantley opened the door to reveal a sailor. The latter murmured something too low for Alyneri to overhear.

"Very well," said Lord Brantley, sounding annoyed. "The drunkards likely got sidetracked. Leave them—we sail with the tide."

The man muttered something else, and Lord Brantley closed the door. She saw him lock it and pocket the key. Turning to her then, the earl leveled her a hungry sort of smile. "Now then, where were we?"

THIRTY-TWO

"Your gods are fickle, impotent creatures thriving
on the inane worship of deluded men."

– Shailabhanáchtran, Maker of Storms

EAN AND ISABEL left Sionym House in the early afternoon along a path that quickly became a mountain trail. For several hours they climbed in silence, hearing only the sounds of the breath, their steady footfalls and the wind sighing in the trees. Isabel led the way with smooth strides, her staff finding an unerring place along the rough trail, never mind that she walked blindfolded.

Ean had spent the hours brooding on what he'd learned at Sionym House. As they gained the top of a forested ridge and the trail leveled out, Ean asked, "Isabel, why did you take me to Sionym House?"

She glanced over her shoulder at him with a brow aching gracefully above her blindfold. Then she looked back to the path ahead. "There is much to know about my brother's game, Ean. Much to recall—too much to explain. You must see something of what we've created here, of the people who chose a life in T'khendar. You must make your own connections, form your own conclusions. My brother will not have your oath unless it is in full knowledge of what you swear."

My oath.

The words made Ean uneasy. He looked away from her and exhaled a troubled breath, pushing a hand through his hair. Of course he'd known it would be expected, he just…well…

But that was her point, wasn't it? She knew he wasn't ready to give his oath, that he didn't understand nearly enough about what they were doing. He wandered the formless midlands between the two sides, unable to choose either, for the objectives of both were obscured beneath a haze of falsehoods and unknowns.

Only Isabel was clear.

Ean decided to change the subject. "I haven't asked you, because it hasn't mattered," *because I would follow you anywhere,* "but…where are we going?"

She cast him a brief look, frowning over pursed lips. Then she turned back to the path. "To see him."

"Who?"

"Rinokhálpeşumar."

Ean stopped abruptly. "*Rinokh.*" He stared after her. A dry-throated panic welled at the idea of confronting the creature again. "But I thought…" Ean adjusted the straps of his pack and tried to calm down. "I thought he was…undone."

Isabel halted several paces ahead and turned her blindfolded gaze over her shoulder. "Malorin'athgul cannot be unmade. Only the shells they've chosen to wear in this realm might be stripped away—and even that isn't easily accomplished. Come, Ean," she reached back for his hand. "You must understand what it is we fight."

Ean thought he had a fair idea of that already, but he took her hand and allowed her to lead him on, for he could refuse her nothing.

Yet as they started walking again, Ean kept seeing that dreadful confrontation with Rinokh superimposed over the path before him, and the persistent memory started an ill roiling in his stomach. He thought he almost felt again the man's chilling power crushing him into the earth, and either this or the increasingly steep climb soon had him sweating beneath his tunic.

With a swallow, Ean tried to push the disturbingly vivid vision of his near-death from mind and focused on his surroundings, which made him wonder… "Why do we not travel on the nodes?"

"There are no nodes leading to this place. It would be too dangerous."

The path grew steeper until they were using hands as well as feet to climb from boulder to boulder. Isabel tied up her skirts around her knees and used her staff for support, climbing sure-footed in suede boots. Ean shouldered her pack as well as his own, and in this fashion did they progress up the mountainside.

It was nearly sundown when they emerged into a clearing where a waterfall had carved a grotto out of the stone. Above them, the bare rock face angled up and out of sight, while to their right, a lush valley spread hundreds of feet beneath them.

Seeming close enough to touch, the deeply ribbed walls of the adjacent ridge soared to impossible heights, temples of the earth. Their emerald sides were softened by a lush canopy of trees that somehow clung to the near-vertical walls. More waterfalls fell from on high in long lines of silver-white, gleaming against the granite face. It was a magnificent and unearthly vista.

Standing amidst such majesty, Ean felt an inexplicable sense of expansion, as if some part of him was being stretched, his awareness extending to the peaks of the mountains and beyond, the rest of him filling the valley, becoming the water of its bountiful cup.

Staring at the vista, Ean suddenly saw another picture superimposed over the lush canopy of trees—a scene of barren basalt mountains and scalded red sands. The two images were part of the same circle of time, the same view separated by hundreds of years.

Isabel called his attention with a light brush of fingers across his arm, and then she led him further down the path. It narrowed as it hugged the mountainside, tracing the edge of a sheer drop to the valley canopy, but finally it broadened again onto another clearing, this one wider, grassy, and framing an even larger waterfall, which charged hundreds of feet down from the very lip of the mountaintop. Bathed in the waterfall's mighty mist, a stone cottage gleamed.

"Ah," Ean said as a welcome understanding dawned. He'd been wondering how they planned to overnight with no bedding to shelter them from the chill of the earth.

Isabel cast him a smile over her shoulder, and then she led him into the cottage. Inside, he found a table and chairs, a large butcher's block over which hung an assortment of pots, and a wide featherbed standing near a generous fireplace.

They prepared dinner together, working in quiet tandem, their actions as effortlessly coordinated as if they'd lived lifetimes thusly. And perhaps they had. Ean certainly felt at ease with her in a way he'd never experienced with anyone before.

The result was a tasty stew concocted from vegetables and lamb, which Treva and the children had provided. Isabel made a tea of lemongrass and mint, and afterwards they sat across the table from each other, which arrangement suited Ean—the better to admire her beauty.

"I asked Djurik Nagraed about the paths to T'khendar," he said as they sipped their tea. He watched her expression carefully to gauge her reaction.

"Mmm," she murmured into her cup.

"He implied the nodes to T'khendar are not as twisted as people of Alorin might believe."

"How deep does the alabaster go?" she echoed with a smile.

Ean looked at her intently. "Is it so?"

Isabel set her mug on the table and aimed her blindfolded gaze at it in thoughtful silence. One finger explored the smooth rim. "Conventional wisdom," she said after a moment, then added drily, "—said wisdom most often being the testimony of the First and Fourth Vestals—declares the nodes to T'khendar were twisted when Malachai opened the weld into the Citadel on Tiern'aval."

"So I've heard." This was the only information ever given about T'khendar's nodes, yet it occurred to him that it couldn't be entirely true, for not only had he traveled to T'khendar across a node with Franco, but Carian vran Lea had also supposedly been to Niyadbakir and returned to speak of it—though admittedly with the help of the zanthyr. Ean lifted his gaze back to Isabel. "And the truth?"

Isabel sat back in her chair. "The making of T'khendar was monumental. Nothing like it had ever been done. With the assistance of the Council of Nine, Malachai and my brother grew the world from within the womb of Alorin's own aether. This process stretched the nodes and welds that formed the woof and warp of Alorin's fabric. Some of these nodes splintered and had to be closed off. Others were purposefully twisted."

"Intentionally?" Ean asked. "Why?"

"To protect Alorin from *deyjiin*," she answered. "The consumptive power roamed freely here at first. It took my brother too long to reason out how *deyjiin* had seeped into the realm, and many died because of this failing. We both failed the others in this—the greatest of tragedies."

"*Deyjiin*," Ean murmured. He was too intimately familiar with that power to take any reference to it lightly. "How did *deyjiin* get here? Was it always here?"

"No." She shook her head. "Deyjiin exists in the chaos beyond the Realms of Light. T'khendar sits on this boundary, one side opening to Alorin, the other to the unraveling fringes of the cosmos."

She traced the rim of her cup with her finger again, a contemplative gesture. "Eventually we learned that when my brother stretched Alorin's fabric to create T'khendar, the fabric became so thin in places that *deyjiin* seeped in, like water through cheesecloth. After the last weld into our sacred realm had been safely closed—consequently ripping Tiern'aval from Alorin into T'khendar—my brother and Dagmar labored tirelessly to shore up those aetheric places in T'khendar's fabric where *deyjiin* was entering. Once this was done, *elae* flourished."

Ean suspected there was much more to this story, more than Isabel could explain to him in a single night—or in a month of such nights. "So the nodes were twisted to protect Alorin from *deyjiin*," he summarized. "Which means..." Already hints of the truth were pushing at him—whether by intuition or some barely perceived ghost of a memory, he couldn't say. "If they twisted the nodes, they could just as easily untwist them, once the threat of *deyjiin* was gone."

"Aptly deduced, my lord."

He felt her praise unjustified, for the answer was too simple. The stories of Malachai making a pact with supposed 'dark gods' seemed utterly laughable now.

Yet T'khendar's truth awakened strange stirrings within him, vague and distant memories that held an acute apprehension, memories as yet formless, save for the glimmers of feelings that were their heralds.

"All my life I've been told untruths compounded by fabrications." Ean was trying his best to fit the various pieces into their proper place, simultaneously dislodging the lies that had so inadequately been filling them. "It's difficult to reconcile where real truth begins and ends. Everything just feels...upended, the full deck of Trumps scattered."

She gave him a compassionate smile. "You cannot simply jump into the middle of a game in play and expect to understand it. So much has come before—too much to tell it all. But what we can explain, what we can show you, we will—always with the hope that each new idea may reawaken others." She placed a hand over his. "We need your help in this game, Ean. But more than this, *you* are important, to my brother...and to me."

He stared at her in silence upon this pronouncement, feeling suddenly scraped by her words. "Isabel," he dropped his eyes to the table. "Julian told me a tale of the man you were said to have loved. One of the First Lord's generals—Arion Tavestra." He looked up at her under his brow. "Is it him to whom you made your promise? Do you wear the blindfold for him?" *Am I fighting him for your love?*

"I think you know," she replied softly.

But Ean couldn't claim this knowledge from beyond the veil of death, no matter how much he desired to know it. There were truths behind that door as yet too painful to recall.

He cursed his own cowardice, yet he feared what he would find behind the veils of memory...truths far surpassing mere knowledge of the man Isabel professed to love. Instinct told him that waking those memories would somehow signal the end of the bond he was building with a woman he already couldn't bear to live without. Ean stared hard at the table, working the muscles of his jaw.

Isabel rose from her chair and walked to Ean's side. He looked up at her wishing he knew the secret to claiming her heart as thoroughly as she'd claimed his. He could sense a distance between them, one he felt should not exist. Yet he didn't know how to correct it, how to bring Isabel closer to him, and it was agonizing, that separation.

Isabel took his hand and drew him up, and they stood facing each other with Ean painfully aware of her closeness. His skin ached for want of her touch, and equally his soul for a bond he sensed should exist but didn't. Silence bound them as Isabel wrapped her arms around Ean's waist and moved into his embrace, resting her head against his chest.

Ean enfolded her in his arms and let out a shuddering exhale. He remembered too nearly the dream where he'd last said goodbye to her. In acknowledging it's remembered truth, he suddenly had to choke back powerful emotions.

It might've been five minutes or the better part of the night that they stood this way, but finally Isabel slipped from his arms and took his hand in silence. She led him to the bed and motioned for him to lie down. Then she settled her body in the curve of his.

Long after he knew she was asleep, Ean stared at the reflection of the firelight on the rafters recalling his conversation with Björn.

"Can we remember?"

"Certainly."

"How?"

"One merely must take ownership over every action he has ever caused."

But no matter how hard he *wanted* to do it, no matter how desperately he sought to rejoin Isabel—and it *was* a rejoining, Ean knew this somehow…knew that *his* distance, *his* unwillingness to remember was all that was keeping them apart—no matter this understanding, he couldn't open that door.

He woke to the smell of frying ham. Ean rolled onto his side and found Isabel already at work in the kitchen. Sleeping all night by Isabel's side had restored his body and much of his spirit.

"My lady," he sighed happily, settling his head onto one hand, "you look positively domestic."

She shot him a grin over her shoulder. "Why thank you, my lord. Would you like to join me? We could use more wood for the fire and some fresh water also."

Ean rolled from the bed to do as she'd bidden him.

Housekeeping with Isabel felt intimate and familiar. He couldn't help but wonder, as he went about his tasks, if they'd lived together before. He dared not ask, however, for fear she would answer him.

When they'd eaten, Isabel donned a cloak from her pack and took up her staff. Ean followed wearing a navy cloak edged in silver, which was eerily like the one he'd worn that fateful night on a lonesome beach when his whole life had changed.

Together, they found the trail once more.

It eventually led to a cave, where Isabel took up a torch from an iron sconce in the wall. Ean offered to recall the working for summoning fire— he was quite sure he could remember the pattern if she commanded it of him—but Isabel just struck the provided flint against her staff and a spark caught on the torch at once. As it flamed to life, Ean saw a narrow, arched corridor, smooth as black glass, vanishing into darkness.

Ean frowned into the gloom. For some reason, he recalled suddenly another conversation, another dream that wasn't a dream.

"Will you cross this bridge with me, my friend?" Björn had invited him.

"Why should I?"

"To regain your future and your past."

"Where does the bridge lead?" Ean had asked.

"To pain," Björn had answered with honest regret.

"What will I find on the other side?"

Björn had smiled. *"Yourself."*

Even then, while standing on death's moors, Ean had suspected that the pain Björn was speaking still awaited him, that he'd only had the barest taste of it. Now he was certain that the First Lord had been speaking of more than one moment, more than one life or one untimely mistake.

When Ean had accepted Björn's invitation to return across the bridge, he hadn't been accepting an offer to regain the painful knowledge of the errors of one life and death, but of *three* of them.

The tunnel was long, and Isabel kept her own silent council during the hours it took to traverse it, giving Ean time with his thoughts. He knew she held a deep awareness of him, in the same way he knew she was leading him towards more than just Rinokh; that this tunnel, like Björn's bridge, would eventually end in pain.

The smallest light at the far end gradually brightened, widened, until they emerged into daylight.

But it was a strange daylight, a harsh light beneath a grey-green overcast. The sky crackled with lightning that flared in huge sheets, blasting the turbulent clouds into sere white brilliance and then retreating defiantly, leaving a sickly greenish hue. The canyon before them lay barren, while the basalt towers of the surrounding mountains stood in black silhouette against the sky.

A rough stairway led down to the canyon floor, and Isabel kept her torch as she led Ean down. The soft thud of her staff tapped a reassuring comfort, something normal among this place that twitched with unmaking.

Their descent took the better part of an hour, until at last Ean stepped off the final stair and set both feet somewhat reluctantly upon the canyon floor. A million stones rattled every time the lightning cracked overhead. There found no bare earth upon which to safely tread, only the molting rocks.

Isabel turned them to their right, where the towering basalt walls narrowed as they angled further into the canyon. Into this chasm they strode, unevenly, taking care on the volatile stones.

The further they went, the more charged the air became. Isabel's hair floated away from her head in spidery strands, and Ean felt the hairs rising on his arms and realized his own hair was doing the same. The air crackled with static, which simply gathered there, building and amassing in voluminous clouds until the lightning released it into the upper atmosphere.

Finally they reached the narrowest point, where the sheer sides of the canyon met at a soaring wall of black volcanic glass. It jutted in a smooth sheet from molting stones to the sky, where it disappeared into the overcast far above.

"Obsidian," Ean murmured, noting the glass's telltale dark gleam.

Isabel set down her staff and took his hand in hers, sparking his fingers with her first touch. "This place is the furthest edge of the known Realms of Light. The veil between worlds is very thin. Beyond this wall," and she indicated the darkly translucent obsidian before them with her pointing staff, "we look into the outer chaotic fringe of the cosmos itself. That chaos is the place of unraveling where the Malorin'athgul reside, working their consumptive power to dissolve the edges of the ever-expanding universe," and she added solemnly, as if part of a ritual prayer, "...for there is Balance in all things."

"What *are* the Malorin'athgul?" Ean felt a sudden desperate need to understand his enemy.

"They were made in the Genesis along with the *angiel*," she explained as they stared at the volcanic glass wall while the world crackled and shuddered around them. "They are as much the Maker's children as Cephrael and Epiphany."

Ean gaped at her. "But—" Why would their Maker knowingly bring such evil creatures as Rinokh into being?

"They are the balance to creation, Ean," she tried to tell him as lightning flared and thunder rumbled the stones beneath their feet, rippling the air even within their chests. "They are...complicated creatures."

A static wind charged down from the overcast and whipped Isabel's hair into a frenzy of wild strands. She pulled up the hood of her cloak to contain it and continued, shouting to be heard above the din, "The Malorin'athgul were never meant to know of our world at all! Their only purpose for being is to unmake the unraveling fringes of our universe, while at its core it is continuously self-creating."

"Then *how*—"

"A truth for another day!" She was shouting now, though they stood side by side.

Ean stared into the madness surrounding him and wondered not for the first time why they were there. "Then...where is Rinokh?"

"We must hold the light to the wall!"

She moved towards it, holding her torch high while the wind tried to tear her cloak from her shoulders. Confused, Ean staggered after her.

The static wind sent the heavy cloth of Ean's cloak snapping tautly behind him as he struggled forward, yet the light of Isabel's torch remained steady. *So there is a little magic in it after all.*

Not understanding why, only trusting Isabel, Ean watched as she held the fire to the depthless glass. The obsidian seemed to absorb the flame, to draw it deeply inside and magnify it. He saw a blossoming gold reflection spreading far through the deep, dense wall, widening as if a light-tower beacon, when suddenly—

Ean leapt back, stumbling on the uneven stones. A great eye pressed against the other side of the volcanic glass, magnified in turn from an immense, unknowable distance by the wall that was more than a wall. As Ean stared, the eye vanished, to be replaced by the reptilian face of a monster.

Ean stared at the wall, chest heaving, uncomprehending of what he saw.

"He is trapped now!" Isabel shouted Ean through the raging static wind. "Trapped beyond the veil of this world. His original means of entrance to the realms of light is now denied him, and he knows it, but still he searches, hovering at T'khendar's edge, hoping..."

"It's...he's...." Ean pointed hard at the glass. "He's a *dragon!*"

"He is Malorin'athgul."

Swallowing, Ean looked back to the creature. He could see it swimming beyond the obsidian wall that separated the worlds. Here a spiked tail raked the volcanic glass, there a great eye peered intently, maliciously, inward. A head appeared in full, turning from side to side, displaying double rows of teeth, and then the mouth opened violently, and Ean wondered if Rinokh played some fell power upon the wall, trying to unravel it as he had so nearly undone him. The thought brought a latent shudder.

"They cannot be unmade, Ean!" Isabel called over the roaring thunder and the shuddering rocks and the crackling, electric wind, "but they must not be allowed to unwork the living realms. *This* is our enemy! This is who we are sworn to fight!"

Much later, Ean sat in silence at the table in the cottage, his mind still dwelling in that heavily charged canyon that so throbbed with unmaking. He'd barely said a word in hours, but he didn't need to. Isabel knew his mind.

Though the encounter with Rinokh in his true form had been unsettling, what had disturbed Ean more was learning, as they were leaving the valley, that three more of these creatures dwelled within Alorin, unmaking it by the malevolent force of their presence as much as by the dark mischief they were most certainly about.

"Am I meant to face them? Is this what he needs of me?" he'd asked her somewhat desperately.

But Isabel would not answer him in this.

She made dinner for them, and they ate in silence while Ean struggled with his new understanding. Three times he'd battled these creatures and died—failing not merely himself but all who'd been counting on him.

She'd told him that the Malorin'athgul need do nothing but exist within the realm and Alorin would eventually wither and die. *They* were the reason Alorin was out of Balance, why the Adept race was dying.

No wonder Markal had treated Ean's incompetency with such vehement disdain. Every moment such creatures were allowed to remain in Alorin, the realm itself moved one step closer to death. And each time Ean confronted them and failed, he only prolonged their tenancy. He was as much to blame for the realm's dying as the Malorin'athgul.

Ean felt a black and explosive self-loathing.

Might as well invite them to stay at their leisure for all the good I've done!

"Ean..." Isabel called his attention.

He looked up to find her sitting across from him with hands clasped on the table. The dishes were gone, cleaned. He didn't even remember eating the meal.

"My brother thought it would be better if we kept this knowledge from you a little longer," she said. "He feared that if you knew the threat we faced—if you knew how critical our position and how volatile their presence in our world, if you knew what failure meant to our future—you would take these failures upon your own shoulders as a weight that only you might bear, as if you and you alone had failed the entire world."

Ean stared at her with red-rimmed eyes, tearless but burning. "I...never imagined he knew me so completely."

Isabel arched a brow. "*I* told my brother you would never be so ridiculous as to imagine yourself the sole cause of the realm's misfortune."

Ean frowned at her.

"Whose game are we playing? Yours?"

Her abrupt tone injured his already raw sensitivities. "I...but—"

"Did *you* craft the rules, Ean? Did you choose the players? Is the game board of your design? Did *you* establish what parameters would be used to measure success or failure? Was *any* of this your creation, Ean?"

"No," he admitted bitterly, "but—"

"And did *you* invite the damnable creatures into Alorin? Did you open a window into our realm that they might partake of the view and *desire* it?"

"No!" he hissed.

She arched an imperious chestnut brow and sat back in her chair. "Well then. Like I told my brother, I cannot imagine any man I love being so foolish—so absurdly unintelligent—as to suppose himself the sole cause of the realm's misfortune and subsequent foundering."

Ean stared at her. All thoughts of the Malorin'athgul had vanished the moment she'd said the words.

...the man I love...

"*Isabel*," He nearly choked over her name, his gaze hot upon her face. "You...love me?"

Her lips twitched with the shadow of a smile. "Is that what I said?"

"I'm certain that you did," he told her seriously.

She gave an inconsequential shrug. "Then I suppose it must be true. Epiphany's Prophet never lies."

"Isabel!" He grabbed her hand and gazed imploringly at her. The blindfold was meaningless to him—arousing admittedly—but clearly no barrier to her vision. He knew she saw him, and he imagined he saw her behind its silken folds. "Don't torment me with simple teasing, I beg you. Not about this."

"If I meant to torment you with teasing, my lord," she returned in that velvet voice that nearly drove him insane with wanting her, "I assure you I would find better ways of doing so."

In a heartbeat, Ean stood and swept the table out from between them. He grabbed her up into his arms, bound and close, and pressed his mouth just inches from hers, their gazes locked as if the blindfold did not exist.

"I have never loved anyone but you," he confessed hoarsely. He ran his lips along the graceful arch of her neck, feeling her shiver and wanting her all the more.

"Prove it," she purred, sending a thrill of pleasure through him.

"How?" He could barely breathe for want of her.

"Bind yourself to me."

"I am already bound to you, heart and soul!"

"Not in this life. You know the pattern," she murmured, and her velvet voice was an exquisite torture. "If you would have me in this life, my lord, *bind us now.*"

He had no thought but to comply. Guided by his need, by her command and his longing to please her, by the desire they so clearly shared, he looked, and the knowledge appeared.

He called forth a pattern of the fifth layered with patterns of Form from the first strand and the fourth—called the working into being with a desperation driven by his craving to possess Isabel, and by the understanding that she wanted nothing less than the same. Into this matrix of patterns, he channeled his intention.

The binding was irreversible—this he also knew. It would link him to Isabel in a way that would become devastating should either of them fall into harm. But these latter ramifications paled next to her keen demand. He wanted only to prove his love to her.

The moment he had the pattern fully conceived, Isabel whispered, "*Yes.* Now we seal it...*take me,* my lord."

He didn't need to be told twice.

Ean swept her into his arms and carried her to the bed. He pressed her down, his mouth sealed upon hers, his hands reaching to release her clothing. She worked in turn the laces of his pants.

"You must hold the pattern in place," she breathed into his ear. Then she gasped as he penetrated her, himself uttering a charged exhalation, sweet ecstasy entwined with painful need. She clung to him as he drove into her, this their first union, an impassioned reunion propelled by wild desire.

At her command, he held the pattern ready. This in itself was a thrilling torment, for the pattern kept trying to explode out of him, so charged it had become with power. He felt her adding her own layers to the pattern, again of the fourth, the first, even—unexpectedly—the third. And when he could hold the pattern no longer, when he'd driven into her almost beyond his own endurance, sealing symbolically what he captured within the tides of *elae*... When they were both gasping, Isabel cried out and trembled deep inside, and Ean shuddered with his own release. In that moment, he forced the pattern into being along with his seed, the entire coupling carried now upon the tides of *elae*, inextricably united within the binding itself.

Ean collapsed atop Isabel, breathless and spent, weighed down by the binding lying heavy upon them now. Never had he known such a feeling. Ean could sense it, almost as if tensing against a supportive membrane. The binding linked them, forging an awareness of her as acute as his knowledge of himself—in some ways more so.

Finally he understood why he'd felt that distance between them—this was the connection he'd been missing.

Isabel found his mouth once more. Her lips were satin, her tongue as sweet as any wine. Desire reignited in his core.

Laughing as she sensed him rousing again, she pulled gently away and sat up on the bed. A sweep of her arm gathered her luscious hair, and she tormented him with that hidden gaze. "Undress me, my lord."

Ean dutifully sat up and examined the buttons along the back of her dress. "I believe I see the problem. They must be undone, each with a kiss."

Her lips curled in a smile. "Is that so?"

His answer was the first of many kisses, long and deep. As his hands made their way down the buttons, she slipped her arms free and then the rest of her, each limb appearing long, lovely and perfect in his estimation. Ean pressed her backwards onto the bed. He trailed his fingers down each arm, feeling her shiver with pleasure and promise, and suddenly he could wait no longer. He grabbed her and rolled so she rose atop him, the perfect hourglass of her body as tantalizing as the feel of himself trapped beneath her.

Her long hair draped around her shoulders, and the blindfold…he found it even more arousing to see her straddling him and know there was still some part of her that remained beyond his reach. It made him want to possess her all the more.

"Isabel," he moaned happily. Her smile concealed every secret he sought, her love the map to his soul. He lifted himself to capture her mouth with his, and suddenly they were caught once more in the force of their need, as if passion alone might expunge the years that had stretched between them.

That time their release was longer in coming, a powerful deliverance for each of them. Isabel lay atop Ean when they were finished, their skin forming a seal between their bodies even as the magical bond connected their minds.

"I love you, Isabel," Ean whispered with desperate conviction. He'd never known any truth so fervent as this.

"I know," she murmured, and though Ean's eyes were closed, he could still see her smile.

THIRTY-THREE

"The well of his conviction is inexhaustible."
— The Adept truthreader Cristien Tagliaferro,
on Björn van Gelderan

RAINE AND CARIAN finally came in view of the alabaster city of Niyadbakir on the eve of the Solstice. For the longest time, Raine stood on the wide cobbled road that led down to the city just staring at the view, his throat strangely tight and his chest tense with emotion.

Niyadbakir.

It had been naught but hostile basalt when last he'd seen it, the city's hundreds of towers and spires scraping a red sky. Even knowing T'khendar had changed, Raine still somehow expected to see the same darkly menacing creation in Niyadbakir, a fitting representation of Malachai's twisted end.

Instead, he found a city of surpassing beauty.

Crowning the mountainside and flowing down into an emerald valley, the white city of bridges and towers seemed to radiate light. Waterfalls fell like shafts of sunlight in the surrounding mountains, while east of the city, fertile farmland spread, a chequerboard dotted with farmsteads and manor homes.

"I cannot believe it," Raine muttered.

"Ah…the Alabaster City." Balearic wore an appreciative smile as he joined Raine in gazing at the view while the rest of the Iluminari wagons ambled by.

"How?" Raine turned him a desperate look, though he knew too well the *how* and *who*.

Balearic shoved hands in his pockets and rocked back on his heels. "Some stories proclaim the First Lord changed the city to alabaster during the weeks of Adendigaeth two centuries ago, while others claim it happened in a single night." The gypsy shook his head and grinned at the truthreader, his blue eyes bright within their lining of kohl. "Changing the essential makeup of an entire city…it must've been the longest day of his life."

"I don't know," Raine muttered miserably, thinking of the creation of T'khendar itself and all that had followed. "I think he's probably had longer ones."

They said farewell to their Iluminari hosts just inside the majestic gates of the sprawling city. The gypsies had been generous beyond measure. Raine wished he'd had more to offer them than his gratitude. He said as much to Balearic as they shook hands in parting.

In return, the pirate-turned-gypsy held fast to his hand and called Raine's gaze to meet his own. "Not for me, Your Excellency…not for any of us," and he glanced towards the pirate, who was just then adjusting Gwynnleth's unconscious form in the litter they'd procured to carry her. "But for Alorin, my lord, for those whose lives hang in the balance. For *them*," he said, holding Raine's gaze, "won't you please try to see his side? I think something important is happening—you live long enough in T'khendar and the sense of it just permeates you—and I think he might be the only one who knows what to do about it."

Raine held his gaze. "I would that we don't make the same mistakes twice, Balearic," he agreed, realizing the phrase might refer to any number of situations. It wasn't much in the way of a promise, but it was the best he could offer.

Balearic seemed to understand, and he nodded. "Farewell, Your Excellency. The Lady's blessing upon you."

Raine exhaled a measured breath as he watched him go. Balearic was taking his wagon to a predestined location to set up for the fire-candle display later that night. In some ways, Raine was sad to part, for he felt that he hadn't done the gypsy justice in exchange for his hospitality…or for his words of wisdom. Yet while Balearic took his leave, the gypsy's reminder of 'the Lady' stayed with Raine.

Isabel. He suspected she was somewhere in this city, and the thought of seeing her both uplifted and terrified him—mostly the latter.

For three centuries—ever since Raine and the others had found themselves on a lonely beach wondering where the island of Tiern'aval had gone—Raine had assumed Isabel must be dead. He and Alshiba both suspected Björn had killed all of the Mages in order to get to her alone, for there was no hiding one's intentions from Epiphany's Prophet. Björn would've *had* to have killed her, they reasoned, to work the evil that they blamed him for.

*But now…*to have learned instead that Isabel stood firmly behind her brother's actions…that she was in fact working at his side—and everyone in T'khendar spoke of them as one, 'the First Lord and the Lady'—was a fact Raine could not ignore, no matter how the knowledge tore at him.

Unless she has somehow been subverted, too…

But it seemed utterly impossible. There was no one in the Thousand Realms like Isabel van Gelderan. In all of his life, this was the one and only truth Raine had ever taken on faith.

"You gonna stand there mooning all night, or help me with this?" Carian complained.

Raine stirred from his deep introspection to see the pirate had his hands on the front end of Gwynnleth's litter and was waiting for Raine to take the other. The Vestal moved to do so. "Sorry."

Carian shook his head with a rueful grin. "Oh man, I certainly wouldn't want to be your conscience these days."

Raine cast him a dark look. "Thank you, Carian."

"Any time."

They joined the masses moving down the Rue Montague, one of the major thoroughfares through the city. After walking for a while, Raine looked around with a puzzled frown. "Where are we going anyway?"

He realized he'd been fairly useless as a traveling companion. If not for the pirate, he'd probably still be sitting on a mountain of sand back in the Wyndlass, blistered and miserable and praying for death.

"Balearic says there's a hotel on the Rue Caravaggio that might still have rooms." Carian looked at him pointedly. "You do realize this is the last day of Adendigaeth, don't you?"

Raine nodded. *The Longest Night.* The day when, according to the *Sobra*

I'ternin, the *angiel* opened the Extian Doors to allow the waiting souls to pass through Annwn and learn the secrets of death and life so they could Return. The significance was not lost on Raine...nor the timing of it.

Raine had noted this fact some time ago.

Franco had been operating on some kind of timeline when Raine had faced off against him and Ean that night in Rethynnea. Was it outrageous to think that Björn's plan for their journey through T'khendar might've been part of that timeline?

Not if Isabel had anything to do with it.

Factoring Isabel into the equation changed a lot of things.

No, it changed everything.

With the sun falling low in the west and Carian at his side, Raine once again made his way through a city in celebration. He had to admit a humbling sense in seeing so many people united in observation of the sacred rite. The Empress and her people still rigorously observed the old ways, but the Agasi Empire was such a blending of cultures and beliefs, you would never see the entire city of Faroqhar celebrating the solstice with the same traditions. Yet Niyadbakir seemed every bit as vast as the Sacred City, and Raine was hard-pressed to find anyone not involved in or preparing for the evening's fête.

As Raine and Carian were crossing a large piazza, where a series of fountains spewed jets of water back and forth, a shadow befell them. They both looked up at the same time.

"Belloth suck me sideways!" Carian hissed as he observed the *drachwyr* flying low over the city. "There's *six* of the bloody things!"

Raine noted that each dragon took a second or more to pass overhead, yet their immense forms soared with majestic grace. The angle of the sun perfectly caught the fire of their hides, and the Sundragons shimmered with gold and bronze, dark crimson and even hints of violet. They were perhaps the most beautifully fearsome creatures Raine had ever seen.

For a tense moment he recalled his battle with Rhakar on the plains of Gimlalai. That had been at sunset as well; but in his human form, Şrivas'rhakárakek was not nearly so elegant—indeed, he fought with a feral brutality. Raine had been wielding a Merdanti weapon, shielding with the fifth, *and* sending *elae* into his blade, and still the man had dominated the fight. The stories liked to draw out their battle, but in truth, Rhakar had made short work of him.

Şrivas'rhakárakek, The Shadow of the Light. There was a story to that name—there were stories behind all of their names—though Raine didn't know them.

As he watched the last of the *drachwyr* passing overhead, Raine wondered which of them was Rhakar and then decided he'd rather not know.

"Didn't you fight one of them once?" Carian craned his neck to watch the dragons until they'd vanished from view.

"Yes," Raine muttered.

"Yeah?" Carian turned to him brightly. "How'd that go for you?"

Raine gave him a peevish look. "I ended up here."

"Oh, right." Carian grinned impudently. The he shrugged his eyebrows, hefted Gwynnleth's litter higher, and they set off together once more. "You know, poppet, I fought the zanthyr once." He shot Raine a rakish look over his shoulder.

"Yeah? How did that work out for you?"

"Got a bruise on my arse that lasted a fortnight and a vow of silence that still gives me indigestion."

Raine felt a smile touch his lips. Epiphany knew he could use a little levity—he especially needed it once he saw the man approaching across the plaza.

Masses of people stood between them and the oncoming man. They all moved busily about their own affairs, whether that be watching a near troupe of performers, buying solstice candles or trinkets from the hundreds of vendors dotting the square, eating or drinking, or just talking or lounging with friends in anticipation of the fête. Yet everyone stepped aside as *he* neared. Even those who didn't see him, who had their backs turned to him, inexplicably moved out of his way; those who did see him pressed their hands together, fingertips to lips, and bowed deeply.

"Belloth lick *my* salty balls!" Carian stared in amazement. "Is that—?" He turned to Raine and asked in a low voice full of mischievous delight, "Is that your nemesis coming right now?"

Raine gave him a long-suffering look.

In point of fact, it was not Rhakar who crossed the plaza, though

Epiphany knew Ramuhárikhamáth was almost worse. At least Rhakar made it easy to dislike him. The Lord of the Heavens was entirely too…amiable.

As Ramu neared, Raine noticed the dragon-hilted greatsword strapped diagonally across the *drachwyr's* back and grimaced. He would happily have never seen such a sword again.

Ramu came towards him parting the crowd like the prow of a ship. He held out his hand as he reached them. "Raine D'Lacourte."

Raine solemnly clasped wrists with the *drachwyr*. "Ramuhárikhamáth." Raine nodded soberly to him, then gestured to Carian. "May I present the Nodefinder Carian vran Lea."

"Ah, yes," Ramu's dark eyes swept the pirate. "The intrepid explorer who would free the Great Master from the Fifth Vestal's basalt prison." Ramu's tone held a decided undertone of sardonic humor. "You are he?"

Carian grinned like a wench who'd just been heartily propositioned. "Who knew you were so tall?" He looked Ramu up and down. "Are all of you that tall? I mean, I thought *I* was tall." He ambled closer to Ramu and stood up straight, eyeing their respective shoulders critically.

"Carian has trouble with authority," Raine murmured in response to Ramu's inquisitive look.

"Perhaps I should introduce you to my brother Rhakar," Ramu suggested to Carian. "He also lacks a certain perspective."

"But can he drink an entire bottle of rum while banging a Vaalden barmaid?" Carian demanded with one arched eyebrow.

"You must pose that question to him tonight, Carian vran Lea. I am most interested to know how he responds."

"You haven't come to cart us off to prison then?" Carian sounded disappointed.

"Sadly not." Raine sensed the utter amusement behind Ramu's composed demeanor. "Though no doubt you may wish by the end of the evening that I had."

Carian leveled him a suspicious glare. "How's that?"

Ramu looked to Raine. "The First Lord has asked us to host you for the Solstice celebration. Of course, we are more than pleased to do so."

"I see," Raine said quietly.

"Do you accept our invitation?"

"Do I have a choice?"

Ramu regarded him with his piercing dark eyes. "You always have a choice, Vestal."

"*What?* Of course we'll go!" Carian shot Raine an annoyed look. "Lead on, Your Majesticness."

"Please, call me Ramu," the *drachwyr* replied. "That particular term of endearment is only used by a certain zanthyr whose memory I would rather not invoke this evening."

"Oh," Carian sounded uncharacteristically contrite—as if united suddenly with Ramu against zanthyrs in general. "Sorry about that."

Ramu nodded in gracious acceptance of his apology. "Follow me, gentlemen, if you please." He turned and headed off across the plaza, and once again the crowds parted for him like waves. Raine and Carian followed in the *drachwyr's* wake.

"I've a question for you, my handsome," Carian posed to Ramu, who arched a brow at the appellation. "If your First Lord always intended to receive us so equitably, why couldn't he have grabbed us in the Wyndlass?"

"I did send someone to your aid, if memory serves," Ramu noted.

"Yes, and many thanks for letting us walk all damned day first," Carian complained sourly. "I needed to work out a few kinks in my back."

"If you like, I can return you to the Wyndlass."

"But we've already made the journey now. Doesn't that mean we've seen what he brought us here to see?"

"It appears there may be more to be gained." Ramu turned an arch look at Carian.

"Carian is new to my oath-brother's philosophies, Ramu." Raine wished that he might have less experiential understanding himself. "He may not realize that in Björn's view, the journey is as important as the destination."

Carian snorted. "Tell that to Gregoire nach Kugghen."

"Who is?" Ramu asked.

"*Who is?*" Carian threw up his arms indignantly. "Only the first man to sail the West Agasi Sea to the far edge of the known realm! Six months aboard the *Kuggenhainen*, surviving storms and scurvy and a near mutiny to finally land at Kugghen Rock in 489aF."

"And during which part of this exploration did Gregoire learn the most, do you suppose?" Ramu inquired without turning. "The journey, or the landfall?"

Carian cast a sooty glare at the *drachwyr's* back.

Raine might've told the pirate it was pointless to argue philosophy with a Sundragon, but he decided he'd let Carian discover that painful truth for himself.

They traded the wide city square for a smaller lane that wound uphill among storefronts and tall city homes. Just when Carian was opening his mouth to lodge a complaint—presumably about the torturous incline—Ramu halted before a stone edifice housing a single black-lacquered door. He traced a pattern in the air and then opened the door.

"You might gather your companion," he advised then, to which Carian collected Gwynnleth into his arms, but not before shooting Raine an incendiary glare full of blameful annoyance. They followed Ramu through the dark portal and emerged on the other side into an endless hallway.

"Belloth take me for his *bitch*!" Carian swung his head to look from one end of the passage to the other, his face completely transformed by astonishment.

"No doubt, you comprehend the laddering effect of the nodes," Ramu noted as he closed the door behind them.

Carian abruptly shoved Gwynnleth into Raine's arms, who scrambled to accept her before the pirate dropped her completely.

"This is incredible!" Carian shoved both hands into his wild black hair and swung to stare from end to end. Suddenly he spun to Ramu. "This is the Great Master's work!"

"But of course."

Carian let out an excited whoop and ran to the nearest door, which he yanked open, peered into, and then slammed shut before rushing across the corridor to the next closest door and repeating the process.

Ramu frowned as Carian headed for the third door. "I fear he could be about this for some time."

"Undoubtedly, if allowed." Raine regarded Carian with a pained expression. "Is it safe to leave him?"

Ramu considered this for a moment. Then his gaze swept Gwynnleth's form, heavy in Raine's arms, and he seemed to make up his mind. "Yes, come. I shall send Rhakar to ensure the pirate doesn't fall into trouble."

Raine wondered how much trouble the pirate could really discover there.

As if in answer to this thought, the Lord of the Heavens offered, "The First Lord's Shades mislike renegade Nodefinders running rampant about the realm. Some of them display a less than tolerant temperament on the matter."

Right then Raine realized Carian could get into quite a lot of trouble and was glad Ramu thought to send Rhakar to watch over him.

He rather enjoyed imagining that pairing—the volatile Rhakar matched against the irrepressible pirate; a little insouciance was all Rhakar needed to rouse his ire to wildfire proportions. The entire scene became a heady contemplation. Raine almost wished he could be there to witness it.

Several paces down the long hallway, Ramu stopped before another door and led Raine through. They exited into an elegant marble hallway and crossed to another room, which was dark inside save for a pair of lamps burning low to either side of a large canopy bed.

"Leave the avieth here," Ramu advised from the doorway. "The First Lord will see to her welfare."

Raine accordingly laid Gwynnleth on the bed and then stood frowning down at her.

'...any help for her—if she can be helped at all, my lord—will only be found in Niyadbakir...' Daria's advice.

Well, he'd done all he could to this end, but he regretted leaving Gwynnleth in that condition. Raine smoothed a strand of hair from the avieth's face and looked to Ramu.

The drachwyr nodded them on.

They were soon walking the endless corridor again, with the node doors passing by in a repetitive blur. "What of your journey, Vestal?" Ramu asked during a moment of silence—every twenty seconds or so, they'd hear another door open and close from far down the corridor as Carian continued his enthusiastic inspection. "What have you learned?"

"Is this a test?" Raine glanced at him.

"It is merely my own curiosity. You need not share your thoughts with me."

Raine sighed. "I'm sure your First Lord would be pleased to know the extent of my discoveries and subsequent foundering, but he will have to ask me himself if he wishes to know my thoughts."

"You mistake me for a Shade, Raine D'Lacourte." Ramu eyed him sagaciously. "The First Lord doesn't know my every thought, nor am I bound to him. But one cannot come to T'khendar after being so long in Alorin and not face certain truths that shake the foundations of what one believes." He gave him a knowing look and a little smile. "The tempest inherent in your answer is enough. I see that you've been giving it an honest look. It is all any of us could ask of you."

In that moment, Raine wished very much to be an ostrich that might hide his head, and his embarrassment, in the sand.

It's not such a terrible thing to be humbled by an immortal creature, he reasoned.

But his own churlish remark now rankled him.

Raine endured the silence that followed as his own form of self-imposed chastisement, well knowing the *drachwyr* was perceptive to his discomfiture. They reached the end of the torturously long passage, and Raine followed Ramu through a pair of tall doors into the palace.

They passed many inhabitants and guests already elegantly dressed for the evening's celebration. Raine thought he might've recognized a few of the faces they met in passing. To be certain, he would know others among the faceless masses, for certain thoughts reached his truthreader's mental ears with a familiar chord.

Both to his relief and subsequent disappointment, however, Isabel's mental voice was not among the music of the fourth that night. He thought of inquiring of Ramu as to her whereabouts but changed his mind when he realized the *drachwyr* would probably tell him.

Isabel.

She'd never expressed an interest in Raine that was anything beyond platonic, her heart having long been claimed by Arion Tavestra, but that hadn't discouraged Raine from dreaming of her often. Allowing himself a rare memory from happier days, before Malachai's war, Raine remembered Arion Tavestra as the most universally envied man alive.

He cringed slightly then at other memories of Arion, who like Cristien, had been a friend once. Arion had been a force to be reckoned with, whether facing off publicly in Sormitáge trials beneath Markal Morrelaine's critical dark gaze, or intimately, across a King's board.

Though he'd been sworn to Björn wholly even before the wars and therefore became Raine's enemy, Arion was one of the few who Raine honestly missed—and certainly the realm was diminished for want of his talent. The best and most brilliant of them had fallen to Malachai's madness, in one form or another.

Raine wondered how Isabel was faring with Arion so long vanquished. It surprised him to feel the slightest glimmering of hope—however unlikely—that with the wielder gone, she might entertain thoughts of himself instead.

It wasn't hard to become obsessed with Isabel van Gelderan. The challenge was in not being so.

"Ah, here we are," Ramu said pleasantly. He cast the fifth before him to open two towering doors, but not before Raine realized what doors they were copies of.

And beyond the Extian Doors, a great game room awaited, already packed with revelers. Raine immediately noted many silver faces of Björn's Shades scattered among the partygoers. Realizing that some of those Shades might be the ghosts of men he'd once known brought a new perspective to his concept of their being.

"*Raine?*" someone called. And then shouted: "It's Raine D'Lacourte!"

Suddenly countless people were rushing mobbing him with excited shouts of surprise. The next many minutes became a blur of faces and thoughts—all of them pleasant and full of hope—of hugs and hands and warm kisses of welcome. Behind him all the while stood Ramu, whose presence remained a grounding force among the whirlwind of strangers and once-friends alike.

When the hubbub had finally calmed, Ramu touched Raine's elbow, and they continued crossing the vast room. Everywhere Raine looked people smiled, nodded, waved. In a room full of strangers, he felt like everyone *knew* him. Certainly as a Vestal he was used to being recognized, used to being welcomed by kings and queens, used to a certain level of homage even—but this welcome was somehow much more profound.

Ramu led him out onto an expansive balcony that overlooked the city glowing in splendor all around them. Once again, its unexpected beauty took his breath away—even the cityworld of Illume Belliel could not hold a candle to the brilliance that was Niyadbakir.

But then...Björn had spent centuries in Illume Belliel, plenty of time to plan and design his own city and make improvements, which was something he certainly would've done.

At the far end of the balcony, several figures stood apart from the other celebrants. They were all dressed in elaborate desert-styled garments typical of the Kandori. Raine would've known them immediately, even had he not perceived the quiet force of their presence, which was equally reflected on the currents.

As Raine and Ramu joined the other *drachwyr*, the Lord of the Heavens said, "Rhakar, you are needed in the Nodes. Keep an eye on the pirate Carian vran Lea or bring him here, as you wish, but see that he doesn't fall into harm." Raine was amused to note the undertone in Ramu's words, which clearly implied that Carian mustn't meet harm from Rhakar, either.

Dressed in an elaborate kurta of crimson silk embroidered with gold, and matching thread-of-gold desert pants, Rhakar actually looked... attractive. His yellow eyes were as fierce as ever, however, and his disposition certainly had not improved in the three centuries since Raine had last confronted him.

Rhakar took one look at Raine, arched a critical brow and shoved his empty goblet into the truthreader's hands before stalking off. Raine imagined he could see the dragon-hilted greatsword strapped to Rhakar's back, though this was only an impression...he hoped.

"Welcome, Raine D'Lacourte."

Raine tore his gaze from Rhakar's retreating figure to find Naiir extending a hand. Raine took it, feeling unbalanced. "Náiir." They'd met only once, long ago. Raine had been too new to his talent and too awestruck to notice much detail about the *drachwyr* at the time. Now, however, he saw Naiir as the currents revealed him: a brilliant force of power and courage with a deeply introspective mind.

"Ah...'tis well that you join us this evening, Vestal," said Balaji, who approached carrying two goblets. Raine had never before met Dhábu'balaji'şridanaí, but He Who Walks the Edge of the World was unmistakable, if yet as enigmatic, as Björn's zanthyr.

Balaji handed a goblet to Raine in exchange for Rhakar's empty one. He flashed a smile of pearly white teeth, bright against his caramel skin; yet though his manner was amiable, for all he seemed a youth of ten and six, there was something decidedly feral about Balaji.

"The Solstice is upon us," Balaji continued, eyeing Raine quietly, "a new year, a new life, a new Return. One might say the same of you in many ways, might they not?"

"I…" Raine blinked at him, for he hadn't realized that his own journey was so intimately connected with the Solstice until that moment.

The two females approached then, and the darkly exotic one, dressed in a gown of blue, said gently, "Welcome, Raine D'Lacourte."

Raine nodded to her. "My lady," he managed in reply.

"You've had a difficult journey, I think," observed the female dressed in opaline silk, a startlingly lovely woman with golden hair and eyes like citrines, brightly sparkling.

"Raine, may I present my sisters," Balaji offered. "Amithaíya'geshwen," and he indicated the dark-haired woman in blue, "and Jayachándranáptra."

Raine bowed, and to Jaya, he couldn't help himself observing, "My lady, the brilliance of your beauty indeed rivals the sun," for this was the meaning of her name.

"Yes, so I keep telling her," Naiir noted in amusement, "yet she insists her beauty is not the reason she is so named. Being that she is my oldest sister, I am forced to disagree with her."

Ramu rejoined Raine's side and oddly handed him a goblet of wine in exchange for the one Balaji had just given him. He smiled and said, "Jaya would have us all believe her name is but a forewarning of the power our father bestowed upon her."

"It is how she keeps us in line," Naiir noted.

Taking all of this in with his head already slightly spinning, Raine sipped his wine and found it excellent. "A very nice Volga," he complimented, to which Ramu turned Balaji a sublimely superior smile.

And yet, the look Jaya cast her brothers was somehow even more so. She extended her arm to Raine, inviting of his escort. "I would partake of the view. Will you accompany me, Vestal?"

"It would be my honor, my lady." Raine wrapped Jaya's hand around his arm, and together they strolled along the balcony railing. Far and wide the city lights glowed. Even the stars paled in splendor, dimmed by the city's brilliance.

After a time wherein they merely absorbed the many sounds of revelry from near and far, Jaya said, "You have been here…what, a fortnight?"

"Or so," Raine said.

"I envy you." She cast him a solemn look. "Ramu and Rhakar move between the realms at will, but the rest of us are granted but brief respites from our duties."

Raine recalled then what she must be speaking of when mentioning said duties—those mounting stories of Sundragons recalled from isolation by the 'Emir's Mage.' It was yet one more mystery within his oath-brother's vast web.

He turned Jaya a troubled look. "Why is Björn involving himself in a war between mortal kings?" Never mind that his own affairs brought him perilously close to the same.

She turned her oddly beautiful tangerine eyes upon him with one gilded eyebrow raised. "Is that what he does? I thought you better learned, Vestal."

"I find myself increasingly ignorant of obvious truths," Raine grumbled with no small measure of angst, knowing it neither behooved him nor complimented him to dissemble amongst this ancient race.

Jaya laughed gently. "What is it you think we're about here, Raine D'Lacourte? Making a game of confusing the brightest minds? Merely taking idle pleasure in observing the decline of the Adept race, laughing like indifferent gods from high in the clouds?" She considered him beneath one delicately arched brow. "Playing at being important, perhaps?"

Raine cast her a pained look, for the tragedy was that he *didn't have a clue* what they were about. He stopped walking and turned to lay hands on the balcony railing, looking out over the dark valley lit with streams of bright gold, pathways of revelry.

When it was obvious he had no answer, Jaya joined him in admiring the view. "Malorin'athgul," she told him then, her gaze becoming sharp and piercing. "Therein lies your answer."

"I faced the one who called himself Rinokh," he admitted quietly, feeling simultaneously tense and furious again, feelings from that night immediately resurrected. His failure there rankled, his mistakes still un-reconciled. "Until that moment, I didn't believe. I still don't know how to believe it...or how I didn't see them before."

"You forget the Fifth Law," Jaya advised.

"*A wielder is limited by what he can envision,*" Raine spoke the painful truth.

She leveling him a telling look. "The First Lord's vision has no limits, Vestal. Remember you that."

"Jaya, look—it is time." Naiir joined them at the railing and pointed to the east, where the first explosions of color were gracing the sky. The Iluminari at work.

The other *drachwyr* filled in around them, such that Raine stood between Jaya and Naiir, with Ramu's tall form just behind, easily watching the display over and between their heads.

"They do good work this year," Balaji said approvingly. He stood on Jaya's left, between her and Mithaiya.

"The Iluminari are a boon to us," Jaya told Raine while the fire-candles blossomed in fabulous explosions below them. "Otherwise the people would expect *us* to provide this entertainment." At Raine's curious look, she sighed and muttered, "The males enjoy evoking such violent displays of the fifth, but I find the exercise tedious."

"Jaya would prefer we had *no* excitement," Naiir complained. He leaned around Raine to view his sister. "There is no miraculous edification to be gained in sitting on your tail for eons, contemplating infinity."

"Nor in bedding every female that comes within ken of your seed," Jaya remarked imperiously.

"But one is certainly more fun," Naiir returned with a sharp grin.

To which Balaji interjected, "Jaya, that's unfair. Naiir may have loved many women in his long life, but he *loved* each of them as surely and deeply as you have delved into your own search for infinity."

"Thank you, brother," Naiir remarked, sounding vindicated. He told Raine then, "Jaya is just jealous that nine Kandori princedoms trace back to my loins. She would have us all celibate or impotent, or both."

"Perhaps if you didn't take such perverse pleasure in recounting all of your escapades in excruciating detail!"

"Jaya, I *am* the paterfamilias."

"Bastardizing an entire race of humanity can hardly be considered *familial*," she retorted.

"This is hardly an appropriate conversation for the Solstice," Ramu muttered.

"Do you hear this, Balaji?" Naiir threw out one hand. "You and Ramu destroyed the entire city of Nab Kaleer in an argument over your precious wine-making skills and received naught but a raised eyebrow from her, but I sire a few princedoms and suddenly I'm anathema." He gave Jaya a frustrated glare. "I *provided* for them all."

"They don't seem to mind being princes, Jaya," Mithaiya offered in Naiir's defense.

"You always take his side, Mithaiya," Jaya grumbled. "I cannot believe you are my sister sometimes."

Raine was beginning to feel trapped within a den of wolves who by stroke of grace hadn't yet noticed him, but which provident condition he feared might be reversed at any moment. Luckily Carian arrived just in time.

"Winds blow me proper!" the pirate declared loudly from further down the balcony. Following behind the pirate, Rhakar emanated malcontent—his decidedly unfriendly thoughts preceded him on the currents.

"Ah, here is our pirate friend now." Ramu sounded pleased. "And still in one piece. I am most impressed with Rhakar."

Jaya sighed. "You never give him the benefit of the doubt, Ramu."

"Of course I do, Jaya. Otherwise I would never have entrusted him with the pirate's safety."

Said pirate having availed himself of the spectacular view, Carian swaggered over to the group. His eye immediately caught upon the dark-haired and exotically beautiful Mithaiya. "My aren't you a lovely chase." He looked her up and down with a wanton grin. "And what would your name be, poppet?"

"Amithaíya'geshwen," she returned, eyeing him dubiously.

"Amithaíya'geshwen." Carian repeated the complicated name with perfect precision, letting it roll off his tongue like a fine wine. "I could enjoy saying that name if I had you pinned beneath me at the time."

Mithaiya regarded him narrowly. "I have eaten men like you."

"Even so?" He gave her a lustful grin. "I'm sure I've never eaten a woman like you."

Raine couldn't be sure, but Mithaiya may have actually blushed.

"Which one were you?" The pirate stepped closer to her, brushed a lock of dark hair from one lovely shoulder and trailed his fingers down her bare arm. "Were you the one with the really long tail? Because that could be interesting…"

The Iluminari show was yet ongoing, but the others began to disperse, with Naiir and Jaya still bickering. Raine remained acutely aware of the power wielded by his current companions.

He thought he understood why Ramu had told Carian he might regret spending the evening with the *drachwyr*. It wasn't due to their sibling banter; it was because these vastly powerful creatures were throwing around thoughts at each other, and every thought landed with force.

Raine could see the currents stirring in the wake of their communication like a still pool ruptured by a shower of pebbles—myriad ripples expanding outward.

And the stories themselves...

Naiir had sired *nine* Kandori princedoms? Ramu and Balaji were behind the destruction of Nab Kaleer? The city had been a treasured center of learning before the last cataclysm—which facts now placed that incidence itself into question.

"Vestal, a word if I may?"

Raine turned at Ramu's voice to find the Lord of the Heavens extending another glass of wine for him. He accepted it and arched a brow inquiringly. "I take it this is one of your vintages?"

Ramu settled him a slightly pained look. "Naiir often trivializes our endeavor, but the crafting of a fine wine is a noble undertaking requiring skill and concentration. A fitting use for our talents."

Raine regarded him in wonder.

Ramu indicated they might walk a little, and they wandered away from the others towards the far end of the balcony.

"We *drachwyr* speak freely amongst ourselves," Ramu noted as they walked side by side. He stood easily a head taller than Raine, but his imposing build was the least of his qualities, for one couldn't stand near the Lord of the Heavens without feeling his radiating power. "I would that you know we're not without remorse for the mistakes we've made...though they may be mentioned blithely in this company."

"I am hardly one to judge."

Ramu cast him a sage look. "We all make mistakes. It seems the longer we live, the more mistakes we have to live with. One would think wisdom brings one to err less, but logic dictates that wisdom is more often gained through our errors than through those choices which meet with simple conclusions."

Raine didn't make the mistaking of thinking that Ramu was telling him this to justify anything the *drachwyr* had done. No, he was opening the door for Raine to accept his own mistakes. But what Ramu didn't understand was that Raine had made so many unforgivable mistakes, each one a drop into an ever growing sea...he was sure he would drown before he swam to the other side of them.

Raine was silent for a long time, and Ramu didn't intrude on his thoughts. Finally, the truthreader confessed, "I'm not sure I have the fortitude to swim that ocean."

Ramu exhaled a slow sigh. "The First Lord likes to say there are different kinds of courage. There is courage on the battlefield. There is courage in facing known opponents, and a different kind in facing unknown ones. There is courage in trusting to faith, and courage in persisting on a given course despite all odds." He cast Raine a look of grave sincerity. "But the First Lord says there is also courage in accepting one's own wrongness—and often this is the deepest and most difficult form of courage to muster, for laying claim to one's own misdeeds is to confront the accumulated pain not only of one life, but often of many."

Far below, streams of gold flowed along the city streets as revelers prepared their candles for the symbolic opening of the Extian Doors. Raine knew Ramu only told him the truth, but he also knew that there was a canyon of difference between knowing the truth and accepting it.

Ramu placed a heavy hand on Raine's shoulder. The man was showing him uncommon compassion, and Raine was both grateful and appalled by it—appalled that he needed it so desperately...appalled that his past actions gave cause for it at all.

"Facing your own wrongness without letting the knowledge of it destroy your character," Ramu advised as Raine stared with clenched jaw out over the sparkling city, "...without deciding that it is now the wrongness that must ultimately define you...this is courage in its purest sense."

Raine closed his eyes.

All across the city, bells began to ring and a joyous cheer erupted, carrying to them even so high above. Finally, as the gathered masses below began their chant—'*Epiphany show us the way! Cephrael show us the way!*'— Raine gathered himself enough to respond.

His voice sounded a hoarse whisper to his own ears as he forced out a naked and painful truth. "I do not know if I have such courage, Ramu."

"If you did not," the Lord of the Heavens replied solemnly, "the First Lord never would have brought you here."

THIRTY-FOUR

"Tis not our deeds but our decisions that haunt us through the ages."
— The Adept wielder Marius di L'Arlesé,
High Lord of Agasan

EAN AND ISABEL returned to Niyadbakir just in time to make
ready and join Björn for an intimate Solstice dinner. The last night
of Adendigaeth was upon them, and across the realm, people were
rejoicing.

Having dressed for the celebration in a garnet-hued jacket worked in
gold, a companion to the gown Isabel was wearing, Ean headed uneasily to
dinner with Isabel at his side. He was anticipating any number of gruesome
reprisals from the First Lord for his utterly reckless and impetuous working
back in the cottage.

It wasn't just that he'd slept with Björn's sister out of wedlock. Ean had
enough sense to suspect that the First Lord might not appreciate his having
worked a complicated, dangerous and irreversible pattern upon his sister—
especially without so much as a 'by your leave…' Especially being so newly
returned to his talent.

They were to meet and dine that evening on one of the many bridges
that connected the varied halls, libraries and galleries of Björn's personal
apartments. This particular bridge connected two towers that overlooked
the city, hundreds of paces below. Wide enough for four horses to walk
abreast, the lovely white bridge appeared even more magical that night due
to the hundreds of tea candles that had been upon it in celebration of the

Solstice. The tiny lights covered every spare inch of the alabaster bridge, as well as the walkways beyond, and the area glowed as brightly as the moon.

Björn awaited them on the bridge. He received them warmly and gave his sister a kiss on both cheeks. "May we meet in the Returning, Isabel." Björn blessed her with a smile and the traditional Solstice greeting.

"And know each other by Epiphany's grace, dearest brother."

Björn took Ean by the shoulders and hugged him warmly. "May we meet in the Returning, Ean."

The words had never been so meaningful to the prince as they felt that night. "And know each other by Epiphany's grace, my lord," Ean finished solemnly. He met the man's gaze as they pulled away, holding his breath in anticipation of the chastisement surely to follow, but Björn merely nodded, smiled and bade Ean to take a seat at his velvet-draped table.

The First Lord was a most amiable and gracious host, but Ean wasn't fooled into thinking the man ignorant of his and Isabel's tryst. The anticipation of certain reprimand made the prince as jumpy as a long-tailed cat in a pen of wild horses. His apprehension welled as the meal continued, such that during the soup course, Ean dropped his spoon twice and nearly knocked over his wine.

Isabel responded to these mistakes with a secretive little smile, while Björn acted as though Ean's clumsiness was completely natural and to be expected after having visited the near edge of the known universe.

Ean rather thought the wind at the unraveling fringe of existence felt a quaint summer breeze compared to the force of the Fifth Vestal's omniscient gaze leveled in forbearance. Indeed, every time Ean's eyes met Björn's, he knew—*knew*—that the Vestal was purposefully tormenting him with his tolerance, patience and understanding.

They'd just finished a course of roasted duck stuffed with figs and apricots when full night descended and the stars suddenly seemed to spark into brilliant life. "Ah...perfect timing." Björn dabbed his mouth and placed his napkin on the table. He stood and motioned them to join him at the wide stone railing. "Come, see—the celebration begins."

Ean took his place between Bjorn and Isabel and looked down upon the city. The streets seemed rushing rivers of torches, candlelight and revelry, like a multicolored, multi-faceted serpent undulating throughout Niyadbakir.

"The Solstice is upon us." Björn turned Ean a smile. "Rebirth and renewal. That's what we celebrate tonight. Both are concepts you're becoming more familiar with, I believe."

Ean stifled a grimace. "Intimately so, my lord."

"So much of our game is founded upon these beliefs," the First Lord observed as he returned his gaze to the revelers below. "The Solstice is the death of the old year and the birth of a new one, even as it represents the death of the winter sun, to be reborn anew with the warmth of spring. It's a celebration symbolic of passing through the darkness that is death's veil of amnesia into the rebirth of knowledge on the other side. The Returning itself is the rebirth of an old soul into a new lifetime, just as the Awakening is another rebirth, this one of Adept talent. And when the realm is restored and Adepts are once more Returning *and* Awakening, then will we have a rebirth of Alorin itself."

"There is Balance in all things," Isabel murmured reverently.

Björn cast her an adoring smile. "Ah, look…" A sudden blossoming of colorful stars exploded over the city—fire candles of gold, violet, crimson and silver-white. The First Lord's eyes sparkled as he watched the skilled Iluminari setting off their rockets filled with explosive powders, which created such a brilliant display of airborne fire.

"The Iluminari have outdone themselves this year."

"Indeed so." Isabel's face seemed full of light.

After they'd seen their fill of colorful explosions, they made their way back to the table, where the dessert course had been set during their absence.

"By the by," Björn mentioned as he was taking his seat and settling his napkin back on his lap, "I noticed an interesting working on the currents this morning."

Ean reached urgently for his wine.

Isabel lifted her spoon and dabbed delicately at her pudding. "Even so?"

Björn eyed her benignly. "A pattern of binding, as you know, is quite telling on the currents. You can read nearly everything that was done to seal it. It was almost as if I'd been there to witness it myself."

Ean choked into his wine.

Isabel took a languorous bite of pudding. "A binding, you say?"

Björn cast them both a droll look. "There are but few men in the realm who could've produced that working, Isabel. Even if Ean's seed hadn't been all over it to announce his culpability, being that neither Markal nor I were likely to bind ourselves to you in this fashion, it required little intelligence to determine what had been done and by whom."

Isabel was licking her dessert spoon in a most alluring way. She turned to her brother and murmured sweetly, "One does try to make things simple."

Björn cast her a sardonic look before turning fully to face the prince. "Ean, I must say, I'm pleased to discover that my sister has encouraged you to recall more of your former skill. The working was perfectly managed. I noticed that it was layered with Form and released with *precise* timing. I made a point of mentioning your renewed ability to Markal, so he's aware of your readiness to move forward into more esoteric practices."

Ean inwardly groaned.

"Good progress overall, I would say."

Isabel blessed her brother with a beatific smile.

Björn leaned forward and kissed her on the cheek. "I am happy for you, you know that. This reunion is long deserved."

He looked to the prince as he sat back in his chair. "Ean, now that you will no doubt be regularly bedding my sister, and knowing how difficult it can be to think of anything else, it's my hope that you'll find the clarity needed to continue advancing quickly—that you won't let Isabel become a distraction. We have a short window in which to achieve so much."

Ean managed, "No, my lord. Of course not," even while wondering how in Tiern'aval he was going to accomplish that. How could being in love with Isabel van Gelderan be anything *but* unbearably distracting?

Isabel pushed back from the table, and Ean and Björn both stood to attend her. "I wish to spend some time in the city. I've asked Dagmar to accompany me."

As if on cue—or possibly because she already knew he was approaching—Dagmar's pale head appeared over the rim of the arching bridge. Grinning broadly, the Second Vestal came forward and greeted his oath-brother with a fierce hug. "May we meet in the Returning, brother!" Dagmar clapped Björn on the back and then withdrew to take him by both shoulders instead.

"And know each other by Epiphany's grace." Björn placed his hands on Dagmar's shoulders in return, and they shared a long, knowing look.

Dagmar then greeting Isabel and Ean in like manner. Once the Solstice had been properly observed, the Second Vestal extended his arm to Isabel.

She walked around the table and planted a kiss upon Ean's mouth that was so deep and languorous it would've shamed the boldest courtesan. Casting her brother what could only have been an imperious look beneath her blindfold, she accepted Dagmar's offered escort and departed.

Ean watched her go feeling electrified and slightly confused.

Björn retook his seat, settled back in his chair and crossed booted ankle over knee. "My sister…" the First Lord took up his wine and sipped it contemplatively. "Once…a *very* long time ago, I had the audacity to doubt her. She likes to remind me of this failing when the opportunity presents itself."

"Thank you for the warning," Ean said, feeling dazed as he retook his chair.

Björn sighed. "Isabel has a long memory."

He considered Ean for a moment in silence then, leveling a penetrating gaze upon the prince all the while. Ean's anxiety grew to alarming levels in anticipation of the host of reprisals he expected, now that Isabel had gone. He dropped his gaze to his wine.

"Ean…" Björn called the prince's eyes to meet his. His tone had touched Ean with a compelling power, yet his gaze reflected only affection. "My sister has waited a long time for you to rejoin her. I cannot possibly convey to you my joy in knowing that your love has been restored."

Ean never knew what possessed him to confess desperately in return, "My lord, I worked a fifth-strand binding of Form upon your sister without a second thought! If anything had gone wrong, she could've—"

Björn waved off his haphazard apology. "I suspect there was little chance of anything going wrong. This isn't the first time you've bound yourselves to each other, nor even the first time she's required me to witness it."

Ean looked back to his wine, feeling dismayed and unnerved. It was one thing to perform the working in private and quite another to discover that your almost brother-in-law knew all of the intimate details.

"It's difficult for you, I know," Björn observed quietly. "Your successive lives are layered like Form in a pattern."

Ean shot him a stricken look. His words could not have been truer, nor pierced him deeper, though they'd been kindly spoken.

"I feel the *rightness* in everything I've learned since coming here," the prince confessed, relieved on some level to be able to voice his thoughts, "but it's hard to assimilate it all." He pushed a hand through his hair and swallowed. His brow furrowed as he stared hard at the table. "It's as if I have two very different lives…and they don't exactly reconcile. I don't *doubt* the memories from my other life—truly I don't," and he cast the First Lord a determined look, "but…I don't know how to incorporate them into *this* life."

Björn regarded him gently. "How easy it would be if we lived but once. One life, one set of choices, one path, winding though it may seem at the time. The truest simplicity. Alas, 'tis not so." He held Ean's gaze with his incredibly blue eyes. "We are the accumulation of eons of choices, mistakes…tragedies. Most of us never know that so many of our decisions are made without our true volition, but rather as the slaves of decisions made in some earlier life—decisions which affect us still."

Ean thought of the curtain that concealed his previous life with Isabel.

"Until we accept our choices and decisions," Björn advised, "until we are willing to confront them and declare them our own—for good or ill—we will remain the unwitting prisoners of them."

Something in this explanation reminded Ean of Raine and the Fourth Vestal's frustration at his own inability to understand his oath-brother.

"My lord," Ean lifted his gaze to meet Björn's, "why is there such conflict between you and the other Vestals? I've seen the obsidian wall. I know what it is we fight—insomuch as I can understand it—but I can't understand why the other Vestals don't see the truth of what you're doing. For me, everything just…resonates."

Björn considered him for a long moment of silence, his gaze intense. Just when apprehension was beginning to flutter inside Ean again, Björn roused from his contemplation. "Time is a factor in many aspects of our existence…" He considered Ean again—intently, piercingly—as though the prince held a deep secret that Björn felt compelled to draw forth. "Time is the deciding factor ultimately in what is right."

Ean frowned. "I'm not sure what you mean."

Björn took up his wine and leaned back in his chair. "When determining the right course of action, do we determine what is right for one life, here, today, now? Do we save one life today? Do we save a hundred lives a year from now? Do we save a million lives three hundred years in the future by what we do here today? And are those millions of lives worth the sacrifice of thousands?"

Björn eyed him inquisitively, posing this question for Ean's consideration. "And if you had the ability to envision such a grand scope of events far into the future—moreover, if you had the fortitude to endure the ages, the tragedies, the terrible sacrifices, and still persist on your given course, if your conviction is strong enough to carry you through all of this, well…" and here he shrugged. "If that is the game you've chosen to play, it only follows that the things you may be doing will seem *utterly* inexplicable to those who live only for one game, one life, here, now."

Ean tried earnestly to grasp the far-reaching implications of this statement. The part of him that had been playing Björn's game for eons knew that this was not merely one man's stubborn rationalization of why others didn't understand him. This was at the core of everything they had been doing—*were* doing. The revelation hit with that soul-vibrating truth that Ean had come to know so well.

Suddenly he had no doubt but that he'd known this truth many times, that he'd accepted it many times, that indeed, at one time—perhaps for a long time—*this* was the truth that had defined him completely.

Ean forced a dry swallow. "But Raine…" he managed then, "why couldn't *he* understand?" For all that the Fourth Vestal had misused him, Ean knew him to be a good man with only the best intentions.

Björn exhaled regretfully. "Raine has ever been limited by a strict adherence to empirical thought. Everything must be explained, and all of the pieces have to form a perfect pattern in his experiential whole. If some of these pieces are not empirical facts, Raine chooses instead ones that are—even if these latter facts don't mesh as well; even if the less empirical facts provide a *better* explanation. Yet he cannot accept them, because they lie outside the limits of his rationale."

Björn pushed back from the table and got to his feet. Ean followed him over to the railing and joined him in gazing out over the world that he and Malachai had created. "You have to take *some* things on faith, Ean." The First Lord cast him a tragic sort of smile. "Everything cannot always be explained or even fully quantified. For example, how would you explain these feelings you have, where you just *know* something to be true?" He arched brows at Ean in inquiry.

The prince shook his head. "There is no way I could adequately explain them to anyone. I barely understand them myself."

"Yet you *know*."

"I know," Ean whispered, feeling that sudden constricting guilt welling once more.

Björn opened his hands and seemed to address the world at large. "There has to come a point in your logic where you say, 'all right, I've seen A to be true, and I've seen B to be true, and while I haven't seen C to be true, it yet follows in line with A and B and therefore it must also be true.'" He turned to Ean, looking grave. "Raine can't make that leap."

Björn pushed hands into his pockets and exhaled a measured breath. "It has forever limited Raine as a wielder, and it has been his greatest disability as a Vestal." He turned and leaned sideways against the railing and added with a tragic arch of his brow, "I wonder sometimes if this entire game wasn't played out in part to give Raine the empirical facts he needed."

When Ean looked startled by this, the Fifth Vestal shook his head and cast him a reassuring smile. "Of course it was not, yet it has served the same purpose. Raine at last will have his empirical proof. Would that events had not needed to progress so far for him to gain it."

Ean didn't know what to say. The tragedy of it was beyond words.

"But these are grim thoughts for so joyous a night." Björn clapped Ean on the shoulder. "Go now. Be merry. Use your restored bond to find my sister and enjoy this night of rebirth together. The Solstice must be *strictly* observed," he finished with a wink, leaving Ean to wonder what other Solstice traditions he might be referring to.

Ean bowed his head. "Thank you, my lord." He felt immensely indebted to him now that he better understood all that he had done—all that he continued to do: for being willing to be hated and feared, for taking on such a staggering responsibility, because no one else would have.

Björn smiled and nodded once, a simple acknowledgement that yet conveyed so much.

Overwhelmed with gratitude, Ean left. To keep from tumbling into the despairing hole of guilt he could sense looming on his horizon, he quickly focused his thoughts on Isabel. No sooner did he think of her than he could feel her, confident in her presence within the pattern that bound them.

Gratefully single-minded on his mission then, Ean headed into the city, becoming just one more of thousands who were already celebrating there. Isabel's presence beat a steady pulse, drawing him forth; he never erred in choosing his direction, for he knew instinctively what roads to follow. Indeed, he walked the jammed streets as Ramu so often did, clearing a path for himself by the force of his intention alone.

He found her by the fountain where Ramu had told him of Trell. She stood watching a troop of acrobats performing a wild display of skill and strength. When Ean joined her side, nine men had formed a pyramid by standing on each other's shoulders. Most of them were juggling flaming torches.

Isabel turned to greet him, looking joyous and serene, and extended her hand. He pressed her fingers to his lips as he drew her into his arms and gazed miraculously at her. "My lady, you take my breath away."

"'Tis only fitting, since you have my heart."

Ean shook his head and wondered what he could've done to so please the gods to have Isabel as his reward. "Where is Dagmar?" he murmured after a moment, for he realized the man had left her side.

"There." She pointed to the acrobats. Ean followed her gaze to find Dagmar at the base of the pyramid of men, himself helping to balance three others. "He couldn't resist." Isabel aimed endearing smile at the Vestal.

A crowd of revelers rushed behind them suddenly, knocking them off balance. Isabel clung closely to Ean and laughed. Overhead the stars glowed brightly, and all around the world seemed in motion.

"My lord, my lady!" A girl rushed up to them holding two candles. "'Tis almost the hour!" She pushed the candles into their hands and then ran back to her partner, a large man who was carrying a tray of small tin buckets jammed with candlesticks.

Isabel pressed closer to Ean and turned her face to the candles in their hands. Both wicks suddenly flamed to life. She lifted her head as if to gaze deeply into his eyes, and Ean imagined he could see her adoring expression beneath her blindfold as she whispered, "To reunion."

He touched his candle to hers, too blissful to speak. The onlookers burst into applause as the acrobats finished their act—and just in time, for across the city, bells began ringing, resounding through streets, echoing off towers and spires and in the hearts of all who heard them.

The crowd erupted into cheering. Isabel looked up at Ean, expectant of his kiss. He captured her mouth with his own and pulled her tightly against him, drinking in the feel of her in his arms as the people shouted and the bells rang and the city resounded with celebration.

The chanting began moments later, sounding in time with the bells.

Epiphany show us the way!

Cephrael show us the way!

Ean reluctantly released Isabel from his kiss. She turned in his arms and leaned back against him, letting her head rest upon his chest while he enfolded her, her own gaze lifted to the heavens where Cephrael's Hand glowed brightly.

Epiphany show us the way!

Cephrael show us the way!

On and on, the chanting continued, growing in volume until the Alabaster City reverberated with voice.

Knowing only Isabel in his arms, Ean gazed at Cephrael's constellation and murmured in her ear, "*Are* they with us still? The *angiel* Epiphany and Cephrael?"

Isabel sighed contentedly in his arms. "Is this a question for the woman Isabel or for Epiphany's Prophet?"

"I think this is most assuredly a question for Epiphany's Prophet."

"Mmm…" She turned him a shadowy smile. "Then Epiphany's Prophet would like to point out that she would be out of a job if they were not."

Ean wrapped his arms tighter around her. He loved her so desperately in that moment he could barely breathe. "And Cephrael? What does Epiphany's Prophet say of him?"

"Cephrael…" Isabel looked back to the stars wearing a contemplative smile. "I can tell you this much, my lord: if Cephrael were here…he would have his hand in this game."

THIRTY-FIVE

"Truth may walk through the world unarmed."

– A desert proverb

AFTER HIS ORDEAL in the cave, Tanis slept all the next day. When he woke, a brilliant morning was bathing the coast in golden light. It was the first time he'd seen the sun since coming to Pelas's home. As if the blue sky heralded fairer days to come, Tanis opened his eyes feeling felt hale…and hungry.

And the zanthyr's dagger was lying in the palm of his hand.

Pelas seemed to have an uncanny sense for knowing when Tanis was awake, for he came into his room just as the lad was getting out of bed. Tanis heard a tap upon his bedroom door, and then the man's head slipped through the parting. "Ah, good," Pelas said pleasantly, his copper eyes bright. "You're up."

He came inside carrying several packages, but Tanis barely noticed them, for his attention was riveted to the man instead.

Pelas looked resplendent in a violet coat cut in his usual flared style, the silk worked all over with spiraling arabesques stitched in black and gold thread. His long, thick hair was pulled back with a black ribbon edged in gold, and several longer strands fell free, framing his face. He looked… softer somehow, less severe. Or maybe it was just that he was himself again, with no hint of the terrible monster that slept within the heart of his desires.

Pelas unwrapped one of his bundles and held up a coat for Tanis. The lad's eyes went wide.

"Do you like it then?" Pelas's copper eyes sparkled.

Tanis came and took the garment from him. "It's marvelous!" He ran a hand over the thick silk, but it was the coat's color that truly amazed him. Neither grey, nor lavender, nor pale blue, nor even the iridescent fire of opal, yet it somehow encompassed all of these. "However did you find such a magical cloth?"

"I had it made." Pelas leaned against a chest of drawers and crossed his arms. He looked pleased. "Your eyes inspired the color, little spy."

Tanis lifted said eyes to the man, suddenly wider. "Really?"

"They look just like that, you know. Sometimes any one of those colors might reflect within your eyes, and sometimes they're just...open— not empty," he assured the boy, his tone taking on a whimsical and yet introspective quality, "not truly colorless, just waiting...as if to show a man the color of his own thoughts."

Tanis gazed wondrously at him. "My eyes do all of that?"

Pelas came over and smiled down at him, and in their meeting of gazes, Tanis felt an intimacy that he'd never experienced with anyone. "All that and more." Pelas confirmed ruffled the lad's hair. "But come—get dressed and let us break our fast. We have such a day ahead, little spy!"

"We do?"

Pelas walked to the windows and gazed out over the cerulean sea. "Do you know what today is?"

"No, sir."

Pelas turned him a look over his shoulder. "The Longest Night. The Solstice. Adendigaeth. *Carnivále!* Across the realm, people are celebrating. Some have already been at it for weeks. Have you ever been to the Rimaldi Coast for *Carnivále*, Tanis?"

"No, sir. But I've heard stories about the fêtes there."

"After tonight, you will have your own stories to share," Pelas assured him with a wink. He nodded for Tanis to dress and then left him to ready himself.

Tanis sank down on the edge of his bed, still holding the impossibly colored, elegantly fashioned coat. He wasn't sure why he found it so beautiful. Perhaps he too saw his own eyes reflected in its iridescent sheen.

As he sat staring at the garment, his throat constricted and his chest grew tight. He hugged the coat close and closed his eyes. There was much more in this gift than the presentation of a mere garment. Tanis knew that. What he didn't know was how to tell Pelas it was time for him to go.

Just as he'd known in the café that he must follow, so did he know now that it was time to leave. He still didn't understand that sense of duty, or even what he'd been meant to do when the hand of Fate had guided him to follow Pelas; whatever the intent, Tanis no longer regretted heeding that call.

His time with Pelas had been frightening and terrible and…wonderful and enriching, and in the end, Pelas had needed his help. Whatever else he'd managed, Tanis believed he had at least encouraged the man a little bit towards the light.

Exhaling a tremulous sigh, the lad finally pushed off the grief that gripped him at the thought of leaving Pelas and got washed and dressed. Not that he had any idea how he was going to leave anyway. It was hard enough just thinking about it, much less figuring out a means of accomplishing it.

He found Pelas on the patio where he'd first seen him, only now the day was bright and clear, and the chill in the air came as a pleasant embellishment to the morning. The Fhorg called Jain was just leaving Pelas as Tanis arrived. For the first time, the Wildling actually grinned at him as he passed. The moment was surreal.

Pelas turned and gave Tanis a winsome smile that drew an anguished pang of regret through the boy. When Pelas was himself, he was…dazzling. Tanis still saw the unearthly creature he'd glimpsed on that first day, when Pelas had stood much in the same position as he was now; but now Tanis understood all that he was seeing in him—the enthusiasm, the irrepressible interest, the excitement for things large and small; and the darkness that hungered, seeking as much to dominate its host as the doomed Healers it forced Pelas to consume on its behalf.

Tanis smiled in return, though he felt heartsick, and they broke their fast together at a table at the patio's end, where the cliffs fell away. Tanis remained pensive as they ate, his mind consumed by that same sense of duty, which was now urging him to leave. It was much in conflict with his personal feelings…as ever it had been.

Pelas mistook his thoughtful silence. "Do you harbor ill thoughts of me, little spy?" he asked with such anguished concern that Tanis's eyes flew to his.

"No, sir!" Indeed, Tanis loved him now even as he loved the zanthyr, and he could find no ill will in his heart for him. "I was just…thinking."

"About?"

Tanis frowned. "Choices?"

"Ah, that inexhaustible conflict. It has become the bane of my thoughts of late as well."

Tanis was relieved to know that he was at least thinking about the topic. But now that he'd brought the matter up, the lad couldn't help himself saying, "Sir, at some point, you have to accept that if you can make a choice about one thing, you can make a choice about something else."

Pelas gave him an endearing look, with a half-smile teasing the corner of his mouth. "I do, do I?"

"Yes," Tanis declared, holding his gaze firmly. "If you can choose not to destroy this world right now, if you can choose to find joy in something, if you can choose to see the world differently from your brothers, then those *are* choices and *you* are making them and you can't deny the existence of choice while yet obviously making choices that are real!"

Pelas regarded him solemnly. "These are all fair points, little spy."

Emboldened by his agreement, Tanis pressed on, "And…and it only follows that if you can make one choice, you can make other choices, too. A choice is simply a decision. Some are harder than others, but they are all within your power. Unless you give something the power to control you, it cannot truly do so. And that, too, is a choice."

Pelas held his gaze, saying nothing.

Tanis dropped his eyes to stare at his plate, feeling frustrated and even a little desperate. It just seemed so simple to him. Why couldn't Pelas understand that he was the one complicating it? Tanis looked up to find Pelas still regarding him quietly. The lad met his dark copper gaze. "Sir…if you can choose to see joy, you can choose to be not as you are."

"Yes," Pelas gave Tanis a smile that did nothing to lighten the anguish in his gaze, "so you have told me."

They retreated to the silence of their thoughts then, and Tanis imagined the day had almost imperceptibly darkened, but then Pelas finished his wine and spun out of his chair and swept a hand before him, bowing low. "Our carriage awaits, little spy."

Tanis pushed out of his chair uncertainly. "Our carriage?"

Pelas straightened, and his eyes danced.

Tanis frowned at him. "It would seem our carriage is sorely lacking for seats."

"Seats!" Pelas waved indignantly at the offensive idea. "Seats would only be a nuisance when navigating Shadow." He held out his elbow to the boy. "Come."

Tanis approached and took hold of his arm. "Shadow?"

"The carriage of our particular travels," Pelas murmured while concentrating upon calling his portal. The silvery line split down through the air, and arm in arm, they walked into the darkness.

Moments later they stepped out into a cloister connecting two buildings. Tanis heard the quiet music of a fountain nearby, but the ivy-bound columns of the walkway obstructed much of his view into the garden.

"I would be misleading you if I said Shadow was truly a place," Pelas noted as he led off down the covered walkway at a leisurely pace. "It is a dimension, not a realm. It's only location is in time."

Tanis felt lost already.

Pelas chuckled at his baffled expression. "Our power tears the fabric of the realm. It is what this power was created to do—to dissolve and destroy, to unwork what has been woven, to rend that which was whole."

Tanis gave him a troubled look.

Pelas shrugged. "Argue what you like about my nature, little spy, but *this* truth is incontrovertible."

Tanis decided not to take up the point. "And Shadow?"

"Shadow lies between. It is the buffer between the realms and is therefore everywhere and nowhere. There is no such *place* as Shadow, for it only exists in the time between, in the measurement of change, of what was and is and will be. It is *time* that connects the realms together, *time* that binds the universe."

Tanis shook his head and gave Pelas a rueful grin. "I don't think you need worry about me passing along this secret, sir. I don't understand a word of what you're saying."

Pelas chucked. "It's just as well. Navigating Shadow is far more complicated than a Nodefinder's simple travels. There are no paths into and out of Shadow, no nodes, no pattern to travel across. We must create the nodepoints ourselves, using time."

"But you can go anywhere by traveling through Shadow?"

"There are limitations, but the places you and I have traveled are ones I know well."

"And that makes a difference?"

"An important one," Pelas said, winking.

They made their way through the next building, seeing no one, and exited through tall doors that opened onto a crescent of descending steps. The moment Tanis emerged into the world, he was assaulted by scents and noises and the heady perception of thousands of minds shouting exited thoughts loudly into the aether. The streets seemed one undulating mass of people, many already in costume for the night's revelry—although to look at some of them, Tanis rather wondered if perhaps they'd simply been wearing the costumes for days.

The lad had never been to the Rimaldi Coast, but the city where they'd arrived was not unlike Cair Rethynnea, if perhaps older and with larger, more ornately imposing buildings. Yet he noted just as many races as in the Cairs, and the architecture itself held similarities.

Pelas blended right in with the affluent crowd that jammed the streets in that part of the city, yet in no way did this make him invisible among their number. Everywhere Pelas walked he drew attention, for he was just so very *interesting* to look upon. Tanis noted that when Pelas was truly himself—as he was that day—one couldn't help but stare.

It wasn't that his coat was so fine—though it was; or that he was so handsome—which he was; rather, it was that Pelas's genuine interest in everything around him seemed to attract the interest of others, as a crowd of people staring at something will draw others to investigate.

Tanis had never had so much fun just walking with someone, though he imagined walking with the zanthyr would have been a similarly thrilling experience.

Pelas took them through the city, pointing out his favorite places so that Tanis might admire them also, and as the sun was nearing its zenith, they turned down an avenue toward a majestic marble building of soaring heights. A huge glass dome glittered splendidly at its crown, almost too sparkling to look upon in the midday sun.

Rather than walking up the long flight of wide steps leading to its entrance, Pelas cast Tanis a conspiratorial grin and led him into the park that bordered the building's southern face. A slender path led away from the park's main walkway, winding down through lush undergrowth and eventually ending back at the building and a shadowed side door. Glancing left, then right, Pelas pulled Tanis over to this door and tried the handle. It was locked.

"Give me that dagger of yours, little spy."

Tanis gave him a suspicious look.

"I'll give it back!" he laughed. "Come now," and he held out his hand. "I know you must have it."

Reluctantly, Tanis withdrew Phaedor's dagger from his boot and handed it over.

Pelas considered the Merdanti weapon with renewed appreciation. "A truly marvelous treasure," he commented with a wistful sigh. Then he grinned at Tanis and proceeded to use his prized dagger for the lowly task of jiggering the lock. Tanis heard a click, Pelas flashed him a triumphant grin, and the door swung inward. He handed him back his dagger with a wink.

"Couldn't you just have used your power to dissolve the lock, sir?" Tanis asked as he slipped the dagger back into its sheath—no point trying to hide it now—which he was wearing on his belt.

Pelas gave him a lightly chastising look. "Of course, but where would be the fun in that?" He led Tanis through the heavy door into a dim corridor.

"Where are we, sir?"

"The Nodefinder's Guild Hall." Pelas cast him a mischievous grin and led away down the passage. "They're fussy about intruders, so walk quietly, and if anyone notices us, try to look important."

Tanis thought that would be no trouble at all for Pelas and quite a challenge for him. Fortunately, all the guild's members and administrators seemed to be out enjoying Carnivále, for he and Pelas encountered no one as they moved through the wide halls and up a grand curving staircase to the second floor. Down another long hallway past what appeared to be libraries or archives of some kind, they reached an open gallery located beneath the crystal dome Tanis had noticed from the street.

The dome opened over an atrium five floors below. Great works of art adorned the walls of the circular walkways at each level. Pelas took Tanis up a flight of stairs to the third level and stopped before an oil painting at least twenty paces across. It was so immense that Tanis had to step back all the way to railing to appreciate its scope.

The base of the painting was full of vibrant color and light and even sound—if such could be said of the impression of its ebullient motion. The story in that part of the painting depicted a party, but it was so much more than this. Within each vignette, each collaboration of faces and people, Tanis saw a new revelation—something discovered, something new, something expressed or admired. Some people danced, some ate and drank, some talked or argued, conspired or laughed. Every detail of their lives in that moment had been captured in paint; each jewel in a woman's necklace or a man's ring fashioned with its own particular and unique sparkle.

The brilliance of the painting's main focus was remarkable, but especially in contrast to the darkness that hovered above. The artist had expertly blended the colors of his fête into the blanket of a starry night, color sweeping upwards to be captured by the heavens and reflected ever so subtly in the stars. But it was *above* the stars, in the darkness of cosmic clouds, that Tanis saw them hovering. Watching. They were but shadows with eyes—more impression than fact. Their eyes were sentient stars, celestial bodies of a different, darker nature.

When he saw them, he knew.

Tanis turned Pelas a swift look. "You painted this!"

Pelas grinned at him. "I hoped you would see. I thought you might." He looked back to the painting and assessed it critically, as only its own creator could. "There are many who do not notice us at all."

The painting frightened Tanis more than he cared to admit. "Is it…is that what it's like…for all of you?"

Pelas cast him a sidelong look that hinted at a smile. "Never fear. We're not gods hovering in the clouds, little spy. This is just a metaphor for how I feel…felt… about your world."

"Why is it here? I mean…" Tanis looked around and then whispered, "Do they know you painted it?"

"It was painted by an imminently respectable artist named Immanuel di Nostri. *My* name, once." He gave the boy a conspiratorial smile. "I've had many identities, but Immanuel was always my favorite."

Tanis looked back to the painting. "It's…incredible."

"Thank you." Pelas smiled at him. "But you needn't praise it. I only wanted to show you, because I thought you would appreciate its message. And I see that you do. That is enough, truly."

Tanis gazed at him in wonder and not a little awe. Cliff diver, sailor, courtier, interrogator, intrepid explorer and artist. He wondered how many other skills the man had mastered.

"But come," Pelas said brightly then. "There is much still to see."

He led Tanis through the gallery, explaining that it was actually an archive of masterworks from around the realm. He also told him that Immanuel di Nostri had many paintings in the Sormitáge.

"Have you ever seen the Sormitáge, little spy?" he asked as they were walking past a series of paintings depicting famous bridges of the realm.

"No sir."

"The Sormitáge's great museum, the *Primär Insamling*, is five times the size of this guild hall. The Sormitáge encompasses countless buildings this size or larger and is nearly a city unto itself. It is worth seeing, if you should find yourself in Faroqhar."

Tanis noted the passion with which Pelas spoke of the famous university and wondered why it hadn't been on their visiting list early on. He was savvy enough, however, to recognize there was probably a reason they'd stayed away, one Pelas clearly didn't want to discuss.

Afternoon had come by the time they rejoined the festivities out in the streets of Rimaldi, and Tanis was famished. Pelas was ever amused at the capacity of the lad's stomach, but he humored him and miraculously procured seats at a crowded café along one side of a square.

The large central fountain was jammed with people splashing in its waters, while further across the square a Kings tournament was being held, with men and women hovering intently over the black and white boards in three long rows, while crowds of supporters watched and joked and drank and generally disrupted concentration for all involved. The rest of the square saw all manner of activity, from lovers to acrobats to good-natured brawlers.

The table Pelas had found for them was shaded by trees studded with tiny oranges, the limbs trained over a sprawling arbor that ran all along one side of the square. Pelas ordered food for Tanis in the Rimaldian dialect, and wine for both of them, and they sat for hours just observing the expansive variety of revelry all around.

"Tell me of your life, Tanis," Pelas said at one point. He was sitting crosswise in his chair with long legs extended, one arm draped over the back and idly holding his goblet of wine. "What do you do when you're not following incredibly dangerous men about the realm?"

"I was training as a truthreader before my lady and I left Calgaryn," the lad said. "We'd been traveling lately with Prince Ean, as I told you."

"Upon a perilous quest as he ran for his life," Pelas supplied.

Tanis gave him a wary look, because he'd never said such as that.

Pelas held his gaze. "I asked my brother Shail about Ean val Lorian." Then he added darkly, "He had much to say."

Tanis was suddenly dry-mouthed and apprehensive.

Pelas laughed at his frightened expression and reached over to muss his hair. "Fear not!" he declared, still laughing. "If any of my brothers speak vehemently against a man, he is most certainly one I want to meet."

Tanis looked at his hands, still feeling unnerved. "I think it was one of your brothers who came to our camp. We saw him, but...he didn't see us."

Pelas arched brows. "That would be something indeed. However did your prince accomplish such a feat?"

Tanis grimaced. "He had...help."

"Ah..." Pelas gave him a curious look, but there was also something deeply knowing in his gaze. Tanis worried he was beginning to suspect Phaedor's nature, and then he wondered why that worried him.

"So what does one study as a truthreader?" Pelas returned them to safer waters.

"A lot of endless rules," Tanis grumbled. Then he grinned sheepishly. "I've only been studying for a year or so. I've learned my Truths and the basics of our craft, how to do Readings and Tellings and such."

"Which are?"

"When you enter rapport with another's mind and...well, you look for stuff—memories and the like."

"I see." He smiled. "Anything else you've learned, oh truthreader-in-training?"

"Well...Master o'Reith had begun training me in Truth-bindings."

Pelas latched onto this. "What bindings are these?"

"Fourth-strand patterns that can be used to keep a man from speaking about certain things."

"These fourth-strand patterns," Pelas mused, "they compel the energy of thought, do they not?"

"Yes, sir. From everything I understand about them."

"Are these the same kind of patterns you mentioned in use upon the Marquiin?"

"They could be, I suppose. I really understood so little about what happened to him—but the fourth *can* be used to compel people against their will. It's…" he dropped his gaze, suddenly embarrassed.

Pelas leaned forward wearing an amused half-smile. "It's what?"

Tanis looked back to him. "Well…it's just that I think you work the fourth yourself sometimes and just don't know it."

Pelas sat back in his chair, looking amazed. "You think *I* work the fourth?"

"The feeling is the same, sir. I've been under compulsion many times from Master o'Reith as part of my training, and I've…well, I've been under compulsion from you. It felt the same, except…"

Pelas waved at him, grinning. "Go on then. You can't stop now."

Tanis managed a sheepish look. "Well, yours was somehow…darker."

Pelas shook his head thoughtfully. "How very, *very* interesting." He sipped his wine in pensive silence for a while. Tanis was just beginning to think he'd escaped the conversation when Pelas leaned towards him again and placed a hand over his. "Tanis," he used the intimacy of his name to draw the lad's gaze to meet his own, "might you be able to work a Telling upon me?"

Tanis naturally found this idea dismaying, for he knew the deadly power lurking in Pelas's mind; yet how could he deny him something which clearly took such courage to ask? "I could try, sir," he managed weakly.

"And within this Telling," Pelas continued intently, pinning the lad with his coppery gaze, "might you be able to see if someone had worked a compulsion pattern upon me?"

Tanis went cold, and not because of Pelas's icy hand holding so tightly to his.

"Yes…" Pelas murmured, and their eyes locked upon one another, even as their minds met upon a single thought.

Tanis forced a swallow, for in that moment, two things became clear:

first, he *had* to do this for Pelas; and second, this kind of a working would cause a shift in the currents of *elae,* and as soon as he did that…

He didn't know why he hadn't thought of it before. Yet…the duplicity in this action made the boy heartsick—even though Pelas had asked it of him, even though Tanis *had* to do it, it would also act as his card of calling upon the currents of *elae,* shouting his location to the zanthyr.

Suddenly overcome with sorrow, Tanis murmured, "Close your eyes, sir."

Pelas did.

Tanis lifted his hand to find the truthreader's hold, but for a moment he just froze. Here was this being—this magical, magnificent and decidedly deadly immortal—who was submitting wholly to his will, who was trusting to him so completely as to place his entire mind within Tanis's full control.

The lad felt such a weight of responsibility in that moment that for a brief time he didn't know if he could go through with it. But then he reminded himself of all of the good that was in Pelas and how important this was, and he placed his fingers across the man's face and temples as he'd been taught.

It was surprisingly simple to find rapport with Pelas, and not merely because the man was so easily and willingly allowing him into his mind. No, it was like…like they were somehow of the same cloth—as outrageous as that seemed, for Tanis knew they were not even of the same race. Yet there it was.

Sinking deeper into rapport, Tanis was about to tell Pelas what to look for when he felt his mind opening yet again.

He heard me, the boy realized, startled that they were already so connected as to share their thoughts.

But when Pelas opened his mind fully to Tanis…

The boy started as if a static shock had just thrilled through him, for he saw what he knew had been true all along. There was no other way to describe the way *elae* collected around Pelas's mental energy, around his thoughts, ready to comply to his intent. He *was* able to use the fourth strand, and that could only mean one thing.

The lad shuttered his excitement at this discovery, however, for he'd yet to do as Pelas had so humbly asked of him. Though it still frightened him immensely, Tanis mentally told Pelas where to direct his attention.

No sooner did he have the thought than the man obediently looked there, and—

It was as though the night opened up, and huge billowing clouds of darkness came gushing out. It was so akin to the storm in Piper's mind that Tanis had to grit his teeth and forcibly make himself stay in rapport to explore the darkness. He soon shook with the effort, and his head began to pound painfully, but though he tried as hard as he could, he couldn't penetrate it.

Finally he withdrew.

Pelas opened his eyes, and their gazes locked again.

"Did you see what I saw?" Tanis asked weakly. He was startled and excited, terrified, anguished and heartbroken.

"Yes…but you will have to explain to me what I saw."

Tanis pushed palms to his eyes. "You saw the energy collecting."

"Is that what it was?"

"What it was," Tanis said, dropping his hands and leveling Pelas a tormented look, "was the fourth."

Pelas sat back and regarded him. "The fourth," he mused, frowning ponderously. His gaze flicked back to Tanis. "What was it doing?"

"Waiting," Tanis groaned, for the knowledge nearly made him weep. "Pelas—sir…" Tears came to Tanis's eyes, much against his will, for he understood too well now. "You can work the fourth, and you *have* worked it, and that means you are like the zanthyr. You're *fifth-strand*. You're…" but he couldn't say it, for it was too monumental to him.

"We are…like you?" Pelas asked gently.

Tanis nodded.

Wearing an unreadable expression, Pelas leaned across the table and held a finger to Tanis's cheek to capture a single tear. "Little spy," he stared marvelously at the boy, "I think perhaps you cannot be human."

"I'm as human as you are," Tanis protested without thinking—the words just tumbled out of him, he was so overwhelmed. But once he'd said it, the lad wondered how he could've made such a claim. Moreover, what did it actually meant that he *could* say it? Everyone knew truthreaders were incapable of lying.

"And what of the patterns you spoke of?" Pelas sat back in his chair and fingered his goblet.

Tanis swallowed and shook his head. "I couldn't see any patterns, but that darkness…did you see it?"

He frowned. "No, I sensed you moving on through my thoughts, but I was somehow unable to follow."

"I don't know if this will make sense to you, but the dark storm I saw was very close to what I witnessed when I worked a Telling upon a boy who'd been tested for Bethamin's Fire." Tanis dropped his gaze to his hands. "Piper went mad from the Fire, so there was much more of his own insanity clouding his mind, but…but they *were* similar. I don't know if that helps you at all."

When Tanis lifted his eyes again, he found Pelas staring compellingly at him. "More than you could ever know, Tanis," he replied quietly after a moment.

The silence stretched until Tanis could no longer stand the secret he harbored. When he looked back to Pelas, the other's gaze was still focused on him.

"Sir," the lad whispered, terribly disheartened and fretful now, "I… think I'm going to be leaving soon."

But Pelas merely smiled at him. "Then I suppose we shouldn't keep sitting here, or we'll miss all of the fun." He pushed out of his chair and spun with a flourish, extending his hand towards the city at large. "Shall we away?"

Looking at Pelas frozen in such an extravagant bow, with his sparkling eyes and devastating smile, Tanis decided he really loved this man.

Thus they headed off together, with Pelas in surprisingly good spirits considering all they they'd just witnessed of each other's minds. But Pelas wasn't wont to dwell on things—this much Tanis knew of him—so he wasted no time on emotions that did not contribute to the gaiety he intended them to share that night.

As ever, he was a force to be reckoned with as they headed down the streets, for people were ever attracted to him, such that he was always being stopped to greet someone new or pausing to clasp wrists with a man who thought somehow they'd met before.

He was veritably accosted by anyone with something to sell, from street vendors to restaurateurs, courtesans to fortune-tellers. He did stop to buy a handful of lovely flowers from a woman on a corner, and because she blushed so prettily and smiled so chastely though she was clearly no maiden, he blessed her with a piece of Agasi silver that would've bought her entire wagonload and more besides.

By the time night fell, Tanis had become heady from the sights and experiences, as much as from the steady supply of wine that Pelas kept feeding him. Eventually they reached the central city square where the largest celebration was ongoing. A huge orchestra played atop a stage lit by iron braziers, and the entire plaza was alive with people dancing. Pelas laughed at Tanis's marveling expression and pulled him across the pavement towards the center of the fabulous melee. The musicians finished a song, and as they were preparing for the next, everyone broke into four lines. Pelas pulled Tanis into line with him, and they faced two rosy-cheeked maidens across the way.

"Do you dance, little spy?" Pelas asked into his ear, for it was quite loud in the square even without the musicians playing.

"It's a little late to ask me that, isn't it?" Tanis protested, but he was giddy and excited and had all but forgotten that the zanthyr was very probably coming for him even then.

As if by some unspoken command, the line of men walked forward and bowed to the women. As Pelas was bowing to the two girls across from him and Tanis, he conjured flowers out of nowhere and handed one to each lass before their line retreated.

The girls beamed at him.

Tanis cast him a wondrous look. "Where did those come from?" he laughed. "You weren't holding any flowers!"

Pelas cast him a sideways grin. "The flower-seller. Remember?"

"Yes, but I don't recall your pushing flowers up your sleeve."

Pelas gave him a peculiar look. "Why in heaven above would I put flowers up my sleeve?"

Then the music started and the dance began, and Tanis added magician to Pelas's ever-growing list of talents.

The men skipped forward and back, then the women. The next time they met in the middle and linked arms, and so did the courtship of the dance begin. Forward and back, spinning and turning, linking arms and swapping air kisses, on and on. And when that dance was done, another began.

Pelas knew all of the dances.

Whenever Tanis faltered upon a step, Pelas was there to encourage him on, and when the orchestra moved to playing music for partnered dances, he taught Tanis the steps with laughter and patience.

So did they spend the Longest Night, and always when the dance led them to new partners, Pelas produced new flowers, each seemingly more lovely than the last. Tanis suspected that more than half the females in the plaza had a flower from him by the time the moon was falling in the west. He also imagined any one of them would have offered more than their hands for a dance had Pelas shown the least interest; but he only had eyes for dancing—and for keeping Tanis at his side whilst they did.

The boy was happily struggling through the fairly difficult steps of a partnered jig when a flash of raven hair snared his eye. Tanis caught his breath and spun a look around, but the plaza was awash with dancers in an undulating sea—heads bobbing, twisting, turning...

Pelas had spun his most recent partner off onto a fast-turning caper that had the girl giggling hysterically as she tried to keep up. He was gazing kindly into her eyes but was relentlessly turning, turning...

"Is something wrong, milord?" Tanis's partner asked him. She was a sweet-tempered girl, and it was their second dance.

"I'm sorry," he told her as he gazed over her shoulder. His heart was racing for a different reason than the dance. He knew he hadn't imagined what he saw. Tanis met her gaze and squeezed her hands. "I'm so sorry, but I have to go."

She gave him a shy smile and then stood on tiptoes to plant a feather-light kiss on his cheek. She blushed demurely as she withdrew. "Thank you, milord, for the dance."

Tanis nodded to her, but then he was pushing through the crowd, chasing after a raven-haired shadow. It was almost as if Phaedor's near presence pulled Tanis unerringly forth, for he couldn't be averted from his path, even if it meant breaking through the middle of a dancing pair.

When the lad at last cleared the main celebration, he stood with his back to the sea of dancers and looked hurriedly around. A courtyard branched off the plaza, and somehow Tanis knew this was where he must go. He ran then, his excitement growing, until he was sprinting to reach the courtyard, and when he did...

The zanthyr stood beside a gazebo in its center, an imposing shadow with emerald eyes.

Tanis flew into his arms. "You came!" He was so impossibly elated to see Phaedor that all other thoughts and emotions were like the flat shadows of midday beneath the dazzling sun.

The zanthyr's chuckle was the rumble of a lion's purr, echoic of a growl. "I was just waiting for your call, lad," he murmured, holding the boy close.

Tanis was suddenly laughing and crying. He'd never known such impossible joy as this reunion. Though they'd spent but a few weeks apart, it felt like years.

But when the zanthyr patted him on the back in a certain meaningful way, Tanis felt the crushing weight of a hundred other emotions come barreling in upon him.

He turned to find Pelas standing at the courtyard's entrance.

"Ah, so…" The Malorin'athgul slowed his approach, and his copper eyes were pinned unerringly on the zanthyr. "Some things at last become clear."

Seeing him, knowing it was time to leave him, Tanis felt his heart tearing in two. He cast a tentative mental probe that he might know the other man's mind in that moment, but Pelas's thoughts were suddenly closed to him.

Pelas stopped about ten paces away. Tanis wanted so much to go to him, to try to explain…

Pelas's gaze was fixed on the zanthyr. "The lad is yours then?" he asked, and Tanis could read nothing in his tone. It was agonizing to be shut out of his thoughts after sharing the space of his mind for so very long.

"No," replied the zanthyr in his deeply compelling voice. "I am his."

"Ah," Pelas returned, thoughtful now. "Yes…that makes sense."

What? thought Tanis, *how does that make any sense at all?*

"Then he *is*—"

"Pelasommáyurek," the zanthyr growled in sudden warning, shaking his head. "Not here. Not like this."

Pelas looked taken aback. "I'm…I didn't…" His gaze locked with the zanthyr's, and they exchanged a long moment of silence, wherein much was communicated beyond Tanis's understanding.

Finally Pelas tore his eyes from Phaedor's to give Tanis a troubled frown. "This then is our farewell, eh, little spy?" For all that he'd closed his mind to the lad, Tanis heard the heartbreak in his voice.

The lad left the comfort of Phaedor's warm and heavy hand upon his shoulder to join Pelas. He stopped before him and looked up into his copper eyes, so different from the zanthyr's and yet just as beautiful in their way. "I have to leave you," he said, hearing his own voice break with the confession.

Pelas gave him a gentle look. "I know."

Tanis understood now why he had to go. Pelas had to make a choice, and Tanis was somehow connected to that choice. The lad knew Pelas couldn't make that choice if he stayed with him.

He reached into his coat and withdrew his dagger. "Here." He handed it to him.

Pelas took the dagger, but he lifted his gaze to observe the zanthyr as he did. Looking back to Tanis then, he asked in confusion, "Why are you giving this to me?"

"You have to make a choice, sir." Tanis pushed a tear roughly from one eye. "Maybe the dagger will help you find me once you've decided—that is, if...if you want to find me. I mean...if that's the choice you make."

Holding his gaze intently, Pelas spun the dagger through his fingers and made it disappear.

Tanis couldn't stand his distance anymore. He threw his arms around him in a fierce hug. "Please," he whispered. "Please..."

"I know, Tanis." Pelas's breath felt a cool breeze across his cheek.

Then Tanis pulled away and rejoined the zanthyr, feeling wretched and miserable. When he turned a last parting glance over his shoulder, Pelas had gone.

Phaedor looked down upon him with his emerald eyes aglow. He was so impressive. *So* imposing. Taller than Pelas and broader still.

Next to the brilliant force that was the zanthyr, even giants became as men.

Tanis let out a tremulous sigh and hugged him again, but it was not joy that drove him into the zanthyr's embrace that time.

"He's not like the others," Tanis whispered with his face pressed against the zanthyr's strong chest, his arms wrapped tightly around him. He felt choked with loss. He didn't know how Pelas would choose, and the idea of never seeing him again was like losing a part of himself.

"Do not be disheartened, Tanis," Phaedor advised gently. "Your paths do not end here. For good or ill, they will cross again."

"What will happen when they do?"

"That depends upon his choice."

Tanis pulled away and wiped his eyes. "I don't understand how I can feel for him so. He's done…monstrous things."

"Love takes many forms," the zanthyr consoled. "Sometimes is it the truest expression of compassion."

Tanis sniffed and dabbed at his nose with his sleeve. "I do love him…" *Like I love you.* "He is the brother I never had."

The zanthyr took the lad tenderly by the back of the head and drew him into the circle of his arms once more. He held him until Tanis felt a measure of hope restored.

When the lad next pulled away, his outlook had become a little brighter. Phaedor kept his arm around Tanis's shoulder and called a portal. Tanis had never seen the zanthyr travel this way, but he'd known Phaedor could work *deyjiin* and was somehow not surprised.

The silver line split down, and then they were walking through Shadow and out onto a midnight field where two horses waited in the luminous fall of moonlight, one black, one silver-pale.

"Caldar?" Tanis shot the zanthyr a startled look.

"A distant cousin," he answered with a smile. "This is Draanil, sire of his own line of noble Hallovian steeds. He will carry you, I think, if you will have him."

"Of—of course!" Tanis stroked Draanil's neck and murmured, "I'm honored, Draanil."

Phaedor took the leads of his midnight stallion, and they walked the horses side by side along the crest of a grassy hill. Tanis could see the golden lights of a city sparkling in the distance, but he didn't think it was Rimaldi. Nor did he care. He was with the zanthyr, and that was all that mattered now.

"My lord," he looked to Phaedor as the zanthyr was turning them towards a dark swath of mountains. "Why did you say you were mine back there?"

Phaedor settled him one of his decidedly disturbing gazes, the kind that always drew chills out of the boy. "Because I am bound to you, Tanis."

Tanis stopped dead in his tracks. "You *are?*" he croaked. "How? *When?*"

"When I made a promise to your mother to keep you safe," he answered as if this wasn't the most earth-shattering statement of Tanis's entire existence.

"You *what?*" the lad veritably shrieked.

Phaedor cast him a sidelong look full of shadowy amusement.

"And you didn't think to tell me this until now?" Tanis protested shrilly.

"You didn't ask."

Over the course of the next few minutes, Tanis muttered a steady stream of inhospitable things under his breath. He wondered if perhaps Fynnlar might be occasionally right about the zanthyr; sometimes he really could be insufferable.

Then something else occurred to him that cheered him somewhat. "So, if you're bound to me, my lord," Tanis observed the zanthyr with an imperious tilt to his chin, "does that mean you have to do what I tell you?"

The zanthyr eyed him dangerously. "Try it and find out, Truthreader."

Tanis went a little pale.

Phaedor grinned and flipped his dagger.

Far across the realm, in the Prophet's temple of Tambarré in Saldaria, Kjieran van Stone fell through the doorway of his room onto hands and knees, shaking uncontrollably. The Ascendants who'd carried him back from Bethamin's courtyard dared say nothing to him, but he could feel their disgust radiating as they made their way off down the hall. They didn't know the torture he'd just endured, but they wouldn't have cared more for him if they had.

He kicked at the door until it slammed closed and then crawled on his elbows and belly towards the chest against the far wall.

He felt violently ill.

Kjieran had never imagined such pain could exist within the realm of human perception, or that his mind might share as much agony as the rest of his body and still be sane. Whimpering with every motion, Kjieran dragged himself across the room and collapsed. His head was swimming. Suddenly he felt vertigo rushing up, and he rolled onto his side and vomited, though nothing remained in his stomach. Still he couldn't stop retching.

His organs felt ruptured, his lungs burned, and every vein in his body seemed to run with fire instead of blood. He was sweating profusely yet felt uncommonly cold—infinitely cold—cold like death long settled into his bones.

Think of your king!

It was all he could manage, this one thought, all that had kept him holding to sanity throughout the torture of Dore's interminable working. It was what drove him to press on, to crawl, elbow before elbow, dragging unresponsive legs towards that chest and his last star of hope.

Reaching the chest, he collapsed with a shuddering sob and almost lost his resolve, almost gave in to the swarming darkness and the pain, but he knew he had to contain his despair a little longer.

He could feel the Prophet's binding heavy upon him, but without compulsion to guide it, the pattern lay dormant. If he could just get to Raine's talisman…

Kjieran struggled up, fighting vertigo and near unconsciousness at every stage. He knew he took a chance working the trace-seal, for Bethamin might be watching even then through Kjieran's own eyes, subverted now to become extensions of the Prophet's.

In the air before the chest, he traced the pattern he'd memorized so long ago, and—

Nothing happened.

He tried again to equal lack of effect. After the fourth agonized attempt, Kjieran finally realized that his hand was shaking too badly to form the pattern properly. He used one hand to hold the other steady and traced the seal again. On the second attempt of this nature, he heard a nearly imperceptible click.

Kjieran tore out the drawer at the bottom of the trunk and grabbed the little amulet Raine had constructed for him. It was naught but a small silver disk inscribed with the *iederal'a*, the sign of the Adept race, a circle crossed by three lines forming an A; but the entire chain and amulet were a talisman, a focal point for *elae*. Drenched in patterns, the talisman protected the wearer from subversive fourth-strand workings. The talisman had been crafted to stave off the deleterious effects of Bethamin's dark power—as best the Fourth Vestal could provide, which was not inconsiderable by any means.

Kjieran shoved the amulet over his head and fell onto his side, sucking in wheezing gasps around the overwhelming pain and grief that gripped him. He wept then, letting the world spin, praying the talisman would have some power against the terrible things that had been to done to him.

He must've slept, for he woke in darkness with a scream. Bethamin's bond lay foremost in his mind, a cold and heavy weight of presence. When Kjieran realized his last many hours hadn't been just a horrible dream, he broke down again, and a desperate sob escaped him before he found the courage to hold the rest back.

Everything was not lost.

He still had hold of his mind—for now. He could still act upon his own direction, so long as he did not seem to be working against the Prophet's desires.

And he was being sent south to kill his king.

He knew Dore's pattern had begun to change him already, but he felt slightly less overwhelmed by the knowledge, as if perhaps Raine's talisman was at least slowing the process. The idea gave him hope. Perhaps something could be salvaged.

He was immensely relieved that he had written his last report before being claimed. Even so, there was more to add—*Morwyk and Radov and a secret alliance!* He would have to be very careful writing such a truth, careful that the Prophet wasn't watching, but he could still leave it for others to pass on.

He would be departing soon for Tal'Shira—Dore was taking him there upon the nodes—but with Raine's talisman staving off the ultimate end, perhaps there was some chance...some *slight* chance that he could salvage something of this disaster, even if nothing might be salvaged of him.

PART TWO

THIRTY-SIX

"It has often seemed to me we might all reach untold heights if each expected greatness of the other."

— The Fifth Vestal Björn van Gelderan

...OLIVIA DANAE...

TRELL HEARD THE words like a chant as he pushed through the crowds on the Rue Royale. Who was Olivia Danae, and what did she have to do with Alyneri? Was she a noblewoman? And if so, did she reside in Rethynnea? Was she behind Alyneri's kidnapping, in league with Brantley and the Duke of Morwyk?

Or was Olivia Danae a place? A villa?

Or a ship?

Even as he thought it, he realized this had to be the answer. *A ship. They've taken her aboard a ship.*

Trell stopped in the middle of the road. The crowd surged around him, bumping and jostling him amid laughter and general merriment, but he hardly noticed.

He'd been known for thinking on his feet—praised for it by the Emir, among many others. The skill had never felt so vital as in that moment.

He knew he'd never make it back to where their coach awaited them— too well, Trell remembered the ship he'd seen sailing with the evening's tide just the night before. It was already past midnight; the tide would be departing and taking Alyneri with it. He needed a fast horse and an even faster ship.

Trell went for the first horse he saw that wasn't hitched to coach or wagon. The animal's owner stood talking to a woman wearing a winged mask. Trell approached the owner with quick strides.

"I need your horse." He shoved two pieces of Agasi silver into the startled man's hand, grabbed the animal's reins without waiting for his approval and jumped into the saddle. "You'll find him at The Nugget if you want him back!" He heeled the animal into a canter.

The horse was fast for all he was an older gelding. Trell steered him off the Rue Royale and onto a smaller avenue that wasn't as crowded. He had a vague idea of his destination, and he guided the horse in a wild race down the cobbled streets, shouting people out of his path, the horse's hooves clattering loudly upon the stones.

The columns of the Thoroughfare soon came into view above and between the near buildings, their bands of cobalt, garnet and silver glowing with torchlight. Trell steered the horse down a flight of wide steps running beneath the columns, yelling people out of his way, but he had to slow when he reached the crowds jamming the Thoroughfare.

The place he sought lay along Faring West—Fynn had said as much— and Carian had told him that pirates never strayed far from their ships. But the Thoroughfare ran for miles. As Trell passed tavern upon tavern—none of them the one he sought—he was beginning to fall prey to the first shadows of despair.

And then Fortune's eye fell upon him, as if beneath the benevolent moon, and he came in view of the tavern named The Nugget.

Trell was off the horse before the animal even came to a full stop, and he threw open the door as if charging through an infantry press. The door slammed against the wall, and everyone inside turned with a sudden descending hush.

The Nugget was a pirate establishment, and its patrons formed a motley assortment of swarthy, long-haired men. Trell saw more piercings than in an entire village of Shi'ma.

"I'm looking for Haddrick," he announced, breathing hard as he stood framed in the portal.

"And you'd be...?" asked one of the pirates who was sitting with his back to the far wall.

"Trell val Lorian."

They laughed at him, of course.

That is, until they realized he was serious. Perhaps it was the trickle of blood dripping down his temple, or maybe it was just that he was clearly not a man to be taken lightly, even by pirates.

"Aren't you supposed to be dead?" asked the same man.

Trell assumed he was Haddrick. "So they tell me." He kicked the door closed behind him and walked purposefully towards the man. "I need to hire your ship. Tonight—*now*."

Haddrick scratched at the violet scarf he wore over his long and tangled black hair. "And what would be in it for me?"

"A ship called the *Olivia Danae* and anything she carries—save for the girl who belongs to me—and the answer to what happened to your cousin, Carian. And this." He dumped half the contents of one of the Mage's bags of Agasi silver onto the table. Instinct alone had driven him to grab the entire bag when he'd left his rooms that afternoon. Thalma was still watching out for him.

Haddrick's colorless eyes widened appreciatively, and he reached for the silver, only to draw back again as the end of Trell's kingdom blade suddenly appeared beneath his chin.

The other pirates jumped to their feet, and Trell found himself at the end of sabers and cutlasses aplenty, but his eyes remained leveled on Haddrick, along with his weapon.

"First the accord: rescue and delivery back to Rethynnea within a reasonable span of days. You'll get half the money now, and the other half when my girl and I are safely aboard the *Ransom*."

Haddrick broke into a grin, displaying a slightly crooked gold cap over one front tooth. "I like you, Trell val Lorian. You've got balls for all you're a pretty chase. Carian told me about you...though he called you something else, if I recall."

"Trell of the Tides."

"That would be the name." Haddrick lustfully eyed the fortune in Agasi silver that Trell had just dumped onto the table. "And Carian?"

"On the way to your ship," Trell pressed.

"How do I know you can provide the information you claim?"

"Because I wrung it out of my cousin Fynnlar despite his being bound with the fourth." It wasn't exactly true, and Haddrick would likely sense the half-truth, but Trell knew better than to show any weakness before a pirate at the bargaining table, even when he was a truthreader.

Haddrick barked a laugh. "You wrung it out of him, did you! I would've liked to have seen that!" He waved for his brethren to put away their swords and pushed to his feet. "Very well, Trell *val Lorian*," he said amid the sounds of sheathing steel. He extended his hand while eyeing him circumspectly. "We have an accord."

Trell sheathed his blade and clasped wrists with the man.

Haddrick lifted his colorless gaze to the rest of his crew. "Now I've had the best of *two* val Lorian princes!" He scooped up his money with a lusty grin and began looking over each piece.

"Haddrick," Trell said. "I'm in a hurry."

Pocketing the coin, Haddrick pushed the table aside and wrapped his arm around Trell's shoulders, turning him towards the door. "Never you fear, Trell of the Tides." Then he looked Trell in the eye and asked, "You don't mind if I call you that? It has such an adventuresome ring to it."

"Call me anything you like so long as we catch the *Danae*."

"The *Olivia D'ne*," Haddrick shouted to his mates, who were following them out of the tavern. "Who knows her?"

"She hails from Kroth but flies a noble flag," one of the pirates said.

"And she sails tonight with the tide, eh?" Haddrick turned them onto Faring West and headed towards the docks. "Never you fear, my handsome. The *Ransom* is the fastest ship this side of the island. We'll catch the *D'ne* before dawn or you'll keep that silver of yours."

Trell eyed him steadily, waiting for the rest of it.

"Do you perhaps care to wager on my claim?" Haddrick asked when Trell didn't automatically rise to the challenge.

"No need. There's a reason I sought the best."

Haddrick gave him a sour look. "Carian trained you too well in our ways. He always did talk too much. Where then is my dear cousin? He missed our meeting, as you may've heard."

"He's in T'khendar."

Haddrick came to a standstill and turned to stare at Trell. Then he barked a hearty laugh. But when Trell kept regarding him steadily, Haddrick cleared his throat. "Balls of Belloth, you're serious. I can hear it in your thoughts."

"Travel to T'khendar is no joking matter," Trell said, as if he knew deeply of such things.

Haddrick looked uncharacteristically dismayed. "Well...what's he doing in T'khendar?"

This was the tricky part. Trell didn't want to compromise Fynn by speaking of the Temple of the Vestals, but he knew the pirate truthreader would know him for a liar if he attempted anything less than the truth. "Carian spoke to me of rescuing his Great Master, the Second Vestal Dagmar Ranneskjöld."

"Oh...well then." Haddrick looked relieved, which only made Trell wonder what else the man might've worried Carian went to T'khendar to do.

Haddrick's mates were already readying the *Ransom* for departure when Trell and the pirate captain reached his ship. She was a sleek vessel, for all she'd seen her share of battle, square rigged and armed for heavy seas. Haddrick was barking orders long before he set foot on the deck, and in short order the massive ship was inching away from the dock.

Trell stood in the forecastle with the wind whipping his raven hair and watched the *Ransom* eating up the waves. For the smallest span as he gripped the railing, he allowed himself a moment of worry, a moment of regret, a moment of fear. Then he put these things behind him and concentrated on what he would do to the Earl of Pent when they met again.

Alyneri stood at the cabin window hugging her arms and staring into the dark night. The earl had been called away to attend the ship's captain, leaving her a moment's peace, but she didn't know how she was going to survive two weeks aboard ship with him. The man constantly vacillated between giving due regard to her station and threatening her with whoredom and a life of bondage. She couldn't tell if his threats held water, and her own indecision about how to respond to him had resulted in his making greater and more forceful attempts to violate her.

So far she'd kept her composure. She hadn't cried, even when he spoke

in detail of the horrors he would bring to bear upon her if she denied him...
even when he bragged about how his men had killed Trell.

She'd feared in those moments, but her heart told her Trell lived, that he
would come for her somehow. In the early hours of the night, she'd believed
this wholly, but now that they'd set sail beneath a lonely moon, it was more
difficult to find that conviction.

*Am I just fooling myself with hope? Embracing denial when I should be
facing the truth?* Yet she worried that denial might be the only way to keep
her sanity, for surely a life as what awaited her under the Duke of Morwyk's
hand would not be worth living.

And the facts *were* against her: she sailed on a nameless vessel towards
an uncertain fate; and once again, no one knew where she'd gone. It was
laughable in a way. Alyneri did laugh out loud a little, but it was a humorless
sound, tinged with fear.

She drew courage from the hatred she felt for Brantley and his lord,
Stefan val Tryst. What gave them the right to physically lay hands upon her
person and cart her away like chattel? *Twice!*

It infuriated her beyond measure; yet she faced an ever-threatening
sense of panic in the knowledge she could do nothing to stop it. She had no
weapon, and even if she did somehow overwhelm or incapacitate the earl,
where then was she to go? She'd nowhere to run but overboard.

It's not true that you have no weapon.

Alyneri hugged her chest tightly, but the very idea chilled her more than
the breeze coming through the open cabin windows. She closed her eyes and
let the cold night air calm her thoughts and settle her tremulous stomach.
It wouldn't do to head so rapidly towards desperation. Was there already *no*
hope, that she must imagine such a dreadful compromise of everything she
held inviolate?

Yet she couldn't push the idea from her mind.

There were first-strand patterns that could be used to maim and injure,
but they were so antipathetic to a Healer's basic nature that only the most
debased of Adepts used them. Healers formed a deep rapport while Healing,
but the wielding of destructive patterns could not be done while in rapport
or one ran the risk of damaging oneself in the process. She wasn't sure she
could even wield such a pattern—or that she *would* do it, even if she could.

But if it means escape?

Lord Brantley returned a long while later, long enough that the room had grown icy and Alyneri had moved away from the open windows to sit in a warmer corner.

"So, Your Grace," Brantley entered and locked the door behind himself again. "I've been thinking it's time you and I got better acquainted."

Alyneri stared miserably ahead—for truly, it mattered not what she chose to do or say. The foul man would speak his mind regardless. She tried not to think on his words, tried not to envision the scenes he was likely imagining for his own cruel pleasure.

Brantley came to stand in front of her, his eyes lustful and his cheeks flushed with drink. He ran his hand across her head, down her hair. "You know...I could be persuaded to look after you."

Raine's truth, the man was naught but a fount of blackmail and extortion. Alyneri suppressed a shudder and refused to look him in the eye.

"You seem a bright enough girl. You could probably be taught how to please me." He caught her chin with his hand and jerked her head painfully up to meet his gaze. "Please me enough, and I can put in a good word with His Grace, that he might deal kindly with you."

"You are an astonishing man, Lord Brantley," Alyneri replied tonelessly. She felt cold inside—cold with fear of him, with anger towards him, with wondering if she would indeed find the courage to debase herself in defense against him.

Brantley's moustached lip lifted in a sneer, but he released her chin. "You still hold to hope—I can see it in your eyes. You think somehow you'll emerge unscathed, but you won't. You won't."

Alyneri clenched her teeth and forced a swallow. "The Duke will know," she whispered.

Brantley laughed at her. "The Duke thinks all you desert bitches are whores and sluts after good men's hearts! He'll not bother to ask how many men have used you, or when or where." Abruptly he grabbed Alyneri's shoulders and pulled her into his arms. "I'll have my way with you and likewise my men—those deserving of reward—and no one will be the wiser for it!"

She could feel him hard inside his britches, smell his sour breath hot across her neck. His hand found her breast and squeezed painfully, and she struggled, managing to free one hand. She struck him without thinking but succeeded only in turning his face from her throat.

He looked slowly back to her as her handprint flamed on his cheek. "So you like it rough, do you?" His eyes veritably glowed.

When he struck her in return, she saw stars. Had he not been holding her so tightly against his own body, she would've fallen. As it was, blackness dimmed the edges of her vision, and she stared dizzily while he buried his whiskered face in her neck and fondled her breasts again.

Being in such close proximity, Alyneri found Brantley's life pattern within moments. She knew he would deserve any pain she caused him. She just didn't know if she'd be willing to do it, even to save herself.

Brantley took hold of her arm, swung her around and shoved her towards the bed. She stumbled and fell to her knees with a gasp, but he just grabbed her around the waist and hauled her up again. Alyneri kicked and struggled against him, crying out, but he was far stronger for all he boasted a modest stature.

He threw her onto the bed and pinned her down before she could escape. One hand caught and thrust both of hers over her head, while his other hand fumbled with his britches, releasing himself. Then to her horror, he threw up her skirts.

No! Not like this!

He mounted her, and Alyneri, desperate now and feeling her fear too close, took hold of his pattern in the way Sandrine had taught her—

"Earl!" an urgent call accompanied a persistent pounding on the door.

Alyneri nearly wept with relief.

The earl hissed a curse and rolled off of her, holding up his pants with one hand as he stalked to the door. Unlocking it hastily—with the man beating upon it all the while—he threw it open. "*What?*"

But in the next moment he'd thrown shut the door again and turned with a wild look, and then Alyneri heard the crash, and a thunderous explosion, and the pounding of running feet and men shouting. She hastened to cover herself again, barely daring to hope.

Brantley rushed across the room and threw open a chest. He rummaged roughly through it and came out with a vial of black liquid. This he poured hastily on his dagger and sheathed it behind his back just as the door crashed open. Pirates poured into the room, fierce and formidable, and in their wake…

Trell.

"Get her to safety," the prince ordered, and two pirates came towards Alyneri while others searched the cabin.

As they were veritably hauling her up off the bed, Alyneri finally found her voice. "He's got—" but then they were sweeping her out of the room into fire and flames, and acrid black smoke choked off any hope of warning him.

"Lord Brantley, Earl of Pent." Trell leveled his sword at the man, but it was not so deadly as his gaze.

The earl sniffed, making his longish moustache waggle and twitch. "You know my name, sir, but I confess I don't know yours."

"Do you not?" Trell approached him steadily. "I thought surely you'd recognized me in L'Aubernay."

"Your Kingdom Blade, yes. There are many carried in Dannym, sported by men despoiled by service to a withered king."

"And Morwyk will change all of that," Trell remarked dubiously.

"The Duke of Morwyk is a man of vision."

"I'm afraid I don't share his vision." Trell motioned with his sword for the earl to make his way out of the cabin.

"You don't intend to kill me then?" Brantley began edging along the cabin, keeping his front to Trell.

"I thought I'd let the sharks do it."

Brantley sneered. "Afraid of drawing noble blood?"

"Your blood would sully my blade, Earl of Pent."

Brantley looked to the burning decks beyond the cabin, to the billowing smoke and glowing fires. "All this for the little desert whore?" he remarked in honest astonishment. "Or are you after her fortune, too?"

His remark caught Trell off guard.

Brantley noted his expression. "Didn't you know? The little bitch is an heir to the Kandori fortune. Why do you think my lord wants her so badly? Certainly not for his own pleasure. He'd never pollute his seed in a heathen's cunt."

Trell decided he'd heard quite enough from the mouthy earl. He suspected the man was stalling for some reason.

Just as the earl rushed at him brandishing a dagger, the *Ransom* broadsided the *Olivia D'ne*, and both Trell and Brantley staggered in the concussion. The earl's dagger caught him through the fleshy part of his side, a minor contusion. Trell easily disarmed the earl and cast him to the floor, once again pinned at the point of his blade.

"You'll have to kill me," the earl gasped. He looked wild about the eyes now, a feral creature cornered and caught. "Or pay me. That's the only way your secret will ever be safe."

"What secret would that be, Lord Brantley?"

"The stone of your sword," the earl said hastily, a last attempt to extort his safety. "It gives you away. See, I do recognize you after all…Prince of Dannym."

"My name is no secret. Soon the world will know it."

Brantley fixed him with a hot gaze. "You'll be sorry if they do."

Haddrick stuck his head through the door. "You going to kill this wastrel, Trell of the Tides, or should I?"

Trell considered Brantley for the space of an indrawn breath. "Be my guest," and he turned his back on the man.

Haddrick grinned and slipped inside the door. As Trell was leaving, he admitted a certain satisfaction in hearing Lord Brantley's gurgling cry.

The pirates soon had the *Olivia D'ne* in hand. Trell crossed the gangplank back to the *Ransom* while the pirates rushed about preparing to get both vessels back under way.

But as he jumped down onto the Ransom's deck, he swooned.

He'd felt the dagger pass cleanly through his side and knew the wound shouldn't have been enough to cause such a response. Trell summed it up to the earlier injury to his head, followed by a very long night.

Regaining his footing on the deck, he headed to Haddrick's cabin and threw open the door, his mind consumed with thoughts of one person only.

Alyneri spun as he entered.

Three steps and he had her in his arms.

"I *knew* you'd come!" She clung to him desperately. "I thought I was deluding myself…" Tears fell from her brown eyes, but they were relieved tears, bright against her skin.

Trell allowed himself to relax for the first time since they'd been separated. During those intervening hours, he'd been as focused on regaining her as in any battle, with no patience for any thought that didn't contribute to his goal. Now that she was in his arms again, he could…

The deck seemed to rock beneath him, and he staggered unevenly, suddenly dizzy. His hand went to his side, which had started to burn.

Alyneri took his face between her hands and looked into his eyes. "Trell, did he cut you? Did Brantley mark you with his dagger?"

Her words sounded strange to him, hollow and with an echo that made them so slow he struggled to understand. "My…side," he managed.

Alyneri's expression became as stone, and she pushed him forcefully to the bed. He fell back with a muted exhale, and the world spun violently. He thought he might be sick and tried to find something to focus on.

Alyneri had her hands on the wound at his side and was doing something. He could tell this from her intense look of concentration—that is, when he could see her face at all. Mostly it was a blur passing back and forth before his eyes.

Soon the burning in his side began to abate, and ever so slowly, the nausea and vertigo faded, until seemingly all at once he gazed clearly upon the nubby ceiling. "I think…I think you fixed it." He managed a grin that she didn't note, being so focused on her Healing. He lifted his head to better gaze at her.

Her brown eyes were glazed, and she had that little furrow between her brows that was so endearing to him. In such moments, Alyneri reminded him of a wild creature—a gentle creature—but wild and free. She had spirit and fire but also compassion, and her sensitivity made her fragile in the most endearing of ways.

Every part of her nature called to an equal—and sometimes opposite—part of his. Where Alyneri needed protection, Trell desired to offer it. Where she wanted to explore, he sought to lead her. He had only to determine if this compatibility extended to more…carnal pleasures.

And he didn't mean to wait much longer to find out. He wasn't sure he could endure it. He'd almost lost this woman who had so quickly become immensely important to him, and it wasn't a situation he intended to allow to happen twice.

Alyneri struggled to hold Sandrine's pattern against poison in place while simultaneously working her Healing on Trell's side. It was challenging, but between what she'd learned from Sandrine and what she'd learned from observing the zanthyr, she managed both. She felt immense relief when she saw the poison seeping outwards from Trell's wound back into his clothes.

This immediate danger addressed, Alyneri moved her attentions to Trell's head. Upon first inspection, this wound was much more grievous. The gash in his skull had been bleeding all night. He'd never even thought to bind it.

You fool man! What were you thinking?

Despite the brutal nature of the wound, Trell's pattern remained strong. The Mage had accomplished a near miracle, and Trell survived because of it. Alyneri tended the minor, outlying threads that healed the skin of Trell's head, but the most she needed to do within his core pattern was mend a tiny splinter.

It was truly astonishing.

If she'd ever doubted the innate goodness of Björn van Gelderan, Alyneri doubted no longer. There was no need for him to do what he'd done for Trell—she'd no idea *how* he'd done it at all. Changing a person's innate pattern would be an immensely complicated working requiring incredible skill and understanding of Patterning, yet the Fifth Vestal had done it apparently out of simple kindness.

At last feeling satisfied that Trell was well and whole, Alyneri withdrew from rapport and sank down on the bed beside him, exhaling a sigh.

Trell turned his head to better look up at her. "*Azizam*," he murmured in the desert tongue, giving her a soft smile. "Did you miss me?"

"Brantley almost didn't," she told him flatly in the same tongue. She was more than a little miffed at his disregard for his own wellbeing and it unsettled her after the fact.

"But I knew I had you to heal me." He ran a hand gently along her arm.

His touch awakened such sensations in her…she couldn't possibly be vexed with him. Still, she gave him a troubled look. "It wasn't just your side or Brantley's poisoned blade. Your *head*, Trell—"

"It's all fine now, isn't it?"

She gave him a long look.

"Did you not ask for adventure, Duchess?"

The words stung her, and she dropped her eyes. "Not like this," she whispered.

Trell pushed up and took her chin with forefinger and thumb, turning her gaze back to him. His face was close, his grey eyes intense as they held hers. "All adventures have some cost, Alyneri. It's the reward at the end that makes them worth it."

She held his gaze, feeling entirely too desperate for words. "And what is your reward?" she whispered.

"You." Then he kissed her.

The entire night's pent-up emotion flowed into that kiss—all of Alyneri's fears of Brantley, of Morwyk...all of her fears for Trell, every emotion that had plagued her since they were separated suddenly found its release. She clutched him, in her desperation wanting only that he might claim her so that no other man could.

When he pulled away just far enough to gaze into her eyes, letting his thumb caress her lips, she thought she must tell him—that she really *should* tell him—but then his mouth was on hers again, and he had her bound in his arms, and she forgot about everything else for a very, *very* long time.

THIRTY-SEVEN

"Violent hatred of one's neighbors gives a man
a permanent sense of purpose."

– The Adept Nodefinder Cassius of Doane

THE KARAKURT SAT behind her screen listening to the men conversing in the room beyond, their argument heated and brewing naught but conjecture. What *had* happened at the Temple of the Vestals?

She though it unlikely that her people would discover anything new about the destruction of Rethynnea's temple, no matter how many survivors they questioned. Raine D'Lacourte had been involved in that catastrophe—this much the Karakurt had ascertained—and involvement of the Fourth Vestal usually signaled truth-bindings that even she could not unwork.

Especially now…

It came as an unwelcome thought, bitter with the vitriol of hindsight.

The Karakurt shifted in her chair, and the tiny bells on her headdress jingled with her malcontent. She found it hard to focus on the rough deliberations of Pearl and the men arguing beyond her screen, for a prickling disquiet troubled her, one that waxed as her confidence waned.

The Karakurt was no stranger to the workings of *elae*. Rumors about her origins abounded, and this suited her, for anonymity was her greatest ally. Yet she'd studied at Agasan's famous Sormitáge. She'd even gained her first truthreader's ring—that much-admired accolade that announced an Adept had attained a level of mastery at their craft. It was untrue, the popular rumor that only the van Gelderan line spawned female truthreaders. The Karakurt was proof of this.

Only...

Pressing two fingers to the bridge of her nose, she exhaled a long breath and pushed away swarming fears, reminders of a truth she no longer dared avoid. When one's entire existence involved the bartering of deceptions—patterned, layered, shallow or vast—it never suited to attempt to deceive oneself in the bargain.

Oh...she'd known from the beginning that taking up with the Lord Abanachtran would be dangerous—*incredibly* dangerous, *yes*, but also immensely intriguing! Everything her spies had learned of him warned that dealing with him would either be disastrous or remunerative beyond compare. But there was always risk in any game, and the game of espionage was the riskiest of all. She hadn't masterminded a network infiltrating multiple kingdoms by taking no chances.

Still...upon reflection, the price of working with the Lord Abanachtran was greater even than she had envisioned.

Her talent was dying.

At first it had manifested in little things—a missed falsehood, a violent thought that seemed somehow...blurred. Finally, after recurring episodes, she'd recognized the terrible truth: every time she came into contact with the Lord Abanachtran, a small part of her talent died.

A deep part of her most elemental self was withering—she could sense it if not understand it—and as the pestilence the Lord Abanachtran had implanted within her spread, her connection to *elae* had begun to wither.

In the intervening weeks since she'd first recognized something wrong, she'd grown increasingly less able to sense *elae,* and now...now she suspected with miserable foreboding that her talent was failing entirely.

She could hold out yet, for such moments were intermittent, the nuisance of a recurring headache that came and went. But she dared not try any working that required too much handling of the lifeforce, and she dared no working openly for fear of others witnessing one of those untimely moments of disruption.

So she didn't interrupt the conversation beyond her screen, and she didn't attempt to unwork the patterns that truth-bound those mercenaries of the Fourth Vestal's recent employ that they'd managed to round up for interrogation. The catastrophe at the temple no longer interested her.

Her thoughts traveled instead to the man called Işak'getirmek.

He was a fascinating enigma.

The Lord Abanachtran had sent word ahead of Işak's arrival requiring her to assist the man to the limits of her ability. Being that their purposes were aligned towards capturing Ean val Lorian, who had proven far too resilient against her efforts alone; and being that the Lord Abanachtran's punishment for failure was severe, the Karakurt looked upon collaboration as a boon.

When the man arrived, however, she'd found a new enigma to occupy her considerable mental talents, for the mystery of Işak's origins and background intrigued her greatly.

Işak'getirmek was not his real name. This she knew, for she spoke the desert tongue and understood his name to mean 'light-bringer.' *Ironic...* for a darkness clouded his mind which she'd rarely witnessed outside of the Prophet's horrific Marquiin.

Oh, she well knew the signs of compulsion patterns laid upon a man—certainly she was no stranger to their use—and the symptoms of compulsion were especially evident when a man such as Işak attempted to fight the pattern's domination.

But in the several chances she'd had to explore Işak's mind—tentatively, gently, so as not to rouse his awareness of her probing—she'd seen oddities even she didn't understand.

The Karakurt had a keen sense of people. Much of this, she admitted, was drawn from her nature as a truthreader, which gave her an innate perception of a multitude of human conditions. A truthreader's early training was more about honing these innate instincts and perceptions than ever it was about learning the Truths or working Tellings. The Karakurt could sit within a room of hundreds and read each individual man's mind—providing their thoughts were loud enough, and what *na'turna* ever learned to guard his thoughts?

Yet Işak was *na'turna* and a wielder—a rare combination but one with a robust precedent set by Markal Morrelaine. She wanted to know more of Işak's training, but the man guarded his thoughts as rigorously as if he harbored the map to the Kandori fortune within his ken. This secrecy intrigued her greatly.

Though ostensibly in charge, Işak in no way resembled the cold-eyed leader of the Saldarian mercenaries who accompanied him, a man named Raliax, whom she trusted not at all. Yet she would've hired Raliax—and might still, if he lived through the coming conflict—for he was an efficient and merciless killer who harbored no illusions about honor; such men were a boon to her, for they negotiated easily and had no qualms about dealing death to the innocent.

But Işak was not Raliax. Whereas the latter had clearly never known a shadow of nobility, she perceived that Işak had somehow fallen from grace—*no, not fallen*, she corrected herself. *Rather… it is as though grace has been stripped from him.*

She wondered who Işak had been before he became *Işak'getirmek,* before he drew swords within the ranks of the Lord Abanachtran—for everyone came away changed by the Lord Abanachtran's touch. A part of them permanently lost contact with the light.

Upon this thought, the Karakurt closed her eyes and exhaled a fluttering sigh. She knew too well that beneath the Lord Abanachtran's burning gaze, even the halest of souls shriveled like weeds in the Avataren sun. Yet for all her lord's fierce intensity, the man left her feeling cold inside. *So very, very cold.* Oft times after he left her company, she would lie before a roaring fire letting the flames sear her bare skin and still feel naught but the chill of his touch worming eternally within.

She caught sight of Işak passing suddenly outside her window. Her colorless eyes followed him as he walked the long balcony of her borrowed manse in Rethynnea's exclusive hills. He'd just returned from a task in the city, one of many such expeditions he took upon himself without seeking counsel or assistance. The man was a lone wolf among a pack of hyenas whom he sought neither to lead nor to dominate, yet who followed him just the same.

Upon sight of Işak, inspiration struck. Just that morning she'd received interesting news. Now she would put it to brilliant use.

The Karakurt removed her headdress and veil and rose to join Işak on the balcony.

Işak'getirmek was a handsome man despite the scar that marred his face and the slight limp that bespoke of hardship in a foreign land, or possibly at sea...some place Healers were scarce. There was a story behind these tarnishments, and the Karakurt wished to have that tale—indeed, she craved Işak's story more than any other she'd come across in recent months.

For she collected men's stories as her own sort of jewels. Within each man's story lay a key, the secret to manipulating him, to shaping him to her will. This was a specific talent of hers—discovering and then catering to a man's deepest desires, twisting his objectives to align with her ends. It was her particular strand of unique poison, and she had yet to find a man immune to it.

Her namesake, the actual karakurt, was a desert spider in her homeland; bulbous, spindly-legged, noxious, capable of killing a camel with a single bite. She fashioned herself more potent still.

She and Işak had spoken but few times since his arrival at her borrowed mansion, and never in private, for often wherever Işak stood, Raliax hovered. Now the two of them would be alone, a flawless opportunity.

The Karakurt flowed towards Işak in diaphanous crimson silks and with her thick black hair bound in golden bands. She knew men found her womanly curves attractive, and she took great pleasure in knowing how few might resist her charms. So also was it a great privilege to gaze upon her face without her headdress and veil. This much she suspected Işak understood.

As she neared, he was resting muscled forearms on the limestone balustrade and gazing out over the city and the glimmering azure bay. His long fingers were occupied with a length of string, absently tying it into elaborate knots.

"Işak'getirmek," she murmured in her low, husky voice.

"Madam," he replied without turning his gaze from the view, his voice distant and cold.

She leaned back against the railing to better look upon his face, upon his wavy black hair sweeping back from a strong brow—at his piercing eyes that shifted between blue and grey. The scar that marred his cheek had been neither stitched nor Healed but rather left alone to become a constant pale flame of reminder. He might've grown a beard to hide it, but apparently he chose to ignore its existence, shaving instead whenever the fancy struck him. It had not for many days, for a dark scruff shadowed his jaw.

When she said nothing more, merely watched him with the ghost of a smile hinting upon her lips, his eyes flicked to her and away again. "What do you want?"

*A great many things…*she thought as she considered him appreciatively, but she replied, "How proceeds your hunt for the prince?"

His eyes tightened, and she inwardly smiled. How could he know that she might read so much in a glance?

"I know no more than you at present."

Nothing in his manner invited further questioning—indeed, each answer seemed to conclude the conversation with brusque finality. It was a manner oft adopted by princes and kings, though she perceived that Işak used it instinctively to widen the moat between himself and any who might seek to know his mind. Yet she sensed no fear of her within him, no matter that she was a truthreader. This, also, told her much.

Who are you really, Işak'getirmek, and what truth do you hide so desperately from the world?

She turned and joined him in gazing out across the mansion grounds towards the Bay of Jewels in the far distance, a brilliant expanse gleaming in the strong sunlight. "Ean val Lorian," she said then, musingly, allowing her voice to reveal the smallest hint of her own annoyance, that they might bond in sharing this mutual frustration. "He is but a boy, for all I've heard of him, not even twenty years."

"I hear he is a wielder."

"One hears many things. Certainly he has the help of wielders."

This drew his eye to her—fierce eyes, pale-blue just then in the bright sunlight. "You do not think it so? He broke the bond between the Prophet and one of his Marquiin. How was this done if not with the lifeforce?"

"A particularly intriguing question," she noted agreeably. Her gaze drifted past his shoulder into the room where her servant Pearl deliberated with Raliax. She didn't think their ideas of value. "You are a wielder, yourself," she said to Işak, arching an ebony brow in challenge. "Surely you have no fears of facing this northern prince. He cannot have been trained except in the most basic of patterns, but you…" and here she gave him a smile suggestive of admiration, "you have trained for many years."

He gave her another piercing look at this. "You know nothing of me."

"I would know more, to be certain," she admitted. "The Lord

Abanachtran informed me I'm to work with you." She let a small, derisive laugh escape her. "I work alone."

"As do I," he growled.

"Yet here we are," she said equitably, opening her palms to the sky. He had not moved once save for the hand that absently wove its knots, save to shift his gaze to her. This, too, told her much. Her lips parted in a smile. "What shall we do, Işak?"

She could see him deliberating. Oh, he was an intelligent man. He could see as well as she that they were getting nowhere on their current tack—weeks of searching for Ean val Lorian had delivered nothing save the location of the villa where he'd once stayed. There was speculation, and even the hint of possibility that he'd been involved in the disaster at the Temple of the Vestals, yet this could not be confirmed despite ardent attempts. For all intents and purposes, the prince had vanished from the realm.

Which was not, in itself, an impossibility.

This avenue was also being investigated, for the Karakurt left no idea unexplored. She had well-paid contacts within the Espial's Guild who had just that morning proven more than useful. That the information they delivered had not directly concerned Ean val Lorian's whereabouts by no means made it dross.

The Karakurt knew there were avenues open to them beyond sitting and waiting—which Pearl and Raliax were far too content to do—but she wanted to see if Işak would come to the same conclusions which she had already reached.

It was infinitely better to have someone else do her work for her.

"I need your information," he growled finally—all the admission she was likely to get out of such a man. He straightened and turned to her, pocketing his string, and added with narrowed gaze, "And you want the protection of my name upon the act...when it comes."

She broke into an appreciative smile. *Bravo!* "Indeed." She gave him a look of admiration.

He still held her gaze, and she admitted there was force within those grey-blue eyes, enough to make even such as her wary of crossing him. Here was a man who inherently commanded power, more perhaps than he knew himself. His tall form contributed to his strength of presence. "Where do we go from here?" he asked tightly.

"Your men think there is nothing to be done until Ean val Lorian is found," she noted. "Mine seem unfortunately to agree."

"*My* men," he growled, casting her a deliberate stare. "The best of them are naught but cutthroats and spies."

"Then what does that make you, their leader?" she inquired with an amused look.

He turned away from her. "I don't lead them."

"Yet they follow you."

This drew his gaze again, fast and stinging with sharp scrutiny. "Speak your terms or leave me be."

The best Ma'hrkit toreadors knew when to bait the bull and when to step aside. She backed down, the better to draw him closer. Bowing her head slightly, a subtle nod to his superiority—or at least a feigned implication of her submission to it—she moved away from the railing. "Might we adjourn somewhere more private to discuss the details of our accord?"

He followed.

She could feel his eyes hot upon her back as she led him to her personal chambers, windowless and bare-walled, the only place where she could be certain none of Raliax's men might overhear and where even her own people left her alone.

There she served him rare and expensive wine. They sat beside a giant fireplace that dominated the room, though the hearth was gaping and cold on that overly warm winter day.

Settling into an armchair, she looked him over quietly. "An accord with the Karakurt is sealed with truths. From me to you, from you to me. If we are to understand each other—if we are to work together—this is how it must be."

His eyes looked wolfish in the room's muted light, their mystery made more so by the shadow of his black hair falling across his brow. Always it was the wolf, cornered and fierce, that lurked within Işak's gaze; never the solitary wanderer. This told her much of the hardships he'd faced. Işak never let down his guard.

He shifted in his chair as if uncomfortable in civilized surroundings, though they seemed more fitting to his person than the rough company of 'cutthroats and thieves.'

"Well…" He glared up at her under his brow. "What do you offer?"

Her lips spread in a slow smile. "New information. A way to flush out Ean val Lorian no matter where he hides—to bring him to us."

She could tell that he held her in suspicious regard, but this didn't discourage her. If a camel could fall from a single tiny bite, so could her unique poison seduce a man into foolishly trusting once again, even a man so clearly abused as Işak'getirmek.

He watched her narrowly, mistrustfully, too careful to be drawn into her web with ease. "What do you require of me?"

"A sharing of knowledge, Işak. You're looking upon my unveiled face, into my eyes. You know then that I cannot lie. You know also that *I* will know if you attempt to lie to me. Thus do we stand on even ground."

His expression darkened. She caught but the barest shards of fractured thoughts slipping beyond his vigilant control. He guarded his secrets carefully and well—as was to be expected from a man of his craft—but the Karakurt could read a man's expressions as easily as his thoughts, and she knew she was making progress.

"I've given you much already." She took a sip of wine and regarded him over the rim of her goblet. "You know me now to be a truthreader. This fact alone might be traded with my enemies to grave result. Surely you understand why."

"There are not so many female truthreaders in the land," he answered, holding her gaze intently, "and fewer still with their first Sormitáge ring," and his eyes strayed to the thin gold band she wore on her ring-finger.

So you noticed that, too—my, my! Her truthreader's ring was but one of many she wore—the least of them in weighted worth, though the engravings upon the slender gold band were elegant work. That he'd noted the ring at all among the many others that graced her fingers told her he knew how to spot a Sormitáge ring. Indeed, it told her much about his other acquaintances.

"So you see what I have given you already, Işak," she returned quietly, a tiny offering to coax the wolf into the open. "What will you give me in kind?"

She could see him begin an internal struggle at this question. Here was a man who shared no secret willingly, for so much had clearly been stripped from him already.

This she knew unequivocally.

There was a specific feeling to a man's mind when he built walls to keep prying minds out. Such often seemed a thick and impenetrable fog that molded and reformed around an intruder, never revealing the hidden secrets. But Işak's mental shield ran much deeper. Beneath the usual obscuring mists erected by any wielder trained in the art, Işak's walls stood rigid, as dense and impervious as the moss-eaten battlements of the ancient fortress of Kjvngherad. Yet the Karakurt sensed that Işak's shields had been erected not to keep others out so much as to keep his own memories within.

So tormented…but what secrets haunt you?

That he agreed to answer her at all was impressive. That he did so without a hint of anguish crossing his features or shadowing his tone was more impressive still, for surely the anguish lurked there among the gnarled and bloodied roots of his past. Yet his gaze remained hard and cold. "What would you know?"

The Karakurt set her goblet on the table and fixed her colorless truthreader's eyes upon him. She was enjoying this immensely. "Tell me, Işak," and she laced her words with the barest touch of the fourth strand, "what vendetta do you harbor against the val Lorian line?"

His expression twisted at the question—hurt, betrayal and hatred flashed in one fierce glare. Her accusation had speared him deeply, and in turbulent thoughts burst forth, revealing much. The Karakurt was pleased with her efforts, yet she needed more of the story to make sense of this explosion. She *would* have the secret out of him, but not by compelling it—*no, no*, he knew too intimately the twisted dagger of compulsion. Much better to coerce and coddle.

"Shall I tell you what I know of you already?" she offered while he battled his demons amid a dense cloud of fury. She draped an elbow on her crossed knee and leaned forward. "A truthreader learns the tell-tale signs of a man who is under compulsion—especially one *who is trying with his every breath to fight it.*"

He stared balefully at her, the wolf brought to bay.

"I don't know the extent of the compulsion upon you, but perhaps… with the right encouragement, I could help you…modify it."

Işak gritted his teeth and looked away. After a long, brittle silence, he pushed from his chair and stalked awkwardly across the floor to stand in the archway between her drawing room and bed chamber. His hands clenched at his sides, and his shoulders hunched forward as if to contain an explosion of emotion. Finally, he murmured with dark conviction, "There is nothing you can do."

She was aware that he now held *elae*—an instinctive response for one who was ever under attack from within. She must tread carefully. She didn't esteem him a violent man by disposition, but the compulsion patterns he fought were volatile indeed.

"Patterns can be altered—"

He spun to her, snarling, "*Can you work the fifth?*"

The Karakurt drew back, astonished by this truth.

Who could've worked the fifth upon him?

"I...cannot." She stared at him in open disbelief, for he deserved that much honesty from her. She was more determined than ever to know his story in its fullness, but she'd clearly underestimated the task.

He seemed to gather himself while she gazed in wonder, and he returned to claim his wine. A long drink saw the cup emptied, whereupon he stared into the bowl and told her in a voice like gravel, "The vendetta you required from me? Gydryn val Lorian sent me to N'ghorra. A death sentence."

She sat back in her chair, allowing him to note her surprise. "The salt mines of N'ghorra," she repeated with the proper amount of compassion, sympathy and horror mixed in her tone. "Why?"

Işak turned her a bitter smile, full of anguish and snarling hate. "He blamed me for the death of his sons."

One of whom apparently lives despite someone's best efforts, she thought as her curiosity achieved perilous heights. "And you would slay the last of them in retribution. A fitting revenge."

He opened arms in submission to this truth, but his smile was acrimonious and his eyes deeply shadowed by grief.

You are a complicated man, Işak'getirmek, the Karakurt decided. There was much more going on here than she'd anticipated, and the mystery couldn't have been more compelling. *Who were you before N'ghorra...before the compulsion patterns of a mysterious wielder stole away your will?*

She stood and walked to him, for he was hurting deeply now. His thoughts spilled out in waves, and she gleaned much of his inner torment, if not the reasons for it.

She knew how to comfort a man though, and Işak was handsome for all he was clearly broken. A man such as he would not be unwelcome in her bed.

She came up behind him and slipped the goblet from his hand. "I cannot rectify your plight," she murmured in his ear, letting him know from her tone and inflection that he might take of her what he would. "I cannot repair your suffering…but I might offer *some* release." She reached a hand to touch his cheek, and he grabbed it and spun her into his arms.

His kiss was heated, his mouth fastened hard upon hers, but she didn't mind. Işak was alive and warm, and though his need was impassioned and his lovemaking fierce and without joy, he didn't leave her feeling cold inside.

THIRTY-EIGHT

"How does a man respond to pain? How does it change his will, his drive, his urges, his obedience? These are questions worth pursuing."
— The Adept Healer Taliah hal'Jaitar

KJIERAN VAN STONE stood upon a long balcony of Radov's palace in Tal'Shira by the Sea, searching the horizon for signs of a ship. He dressed as the locals did, wearing a beaded *kameez* tunic and loose *shalwar* pants bound at the ankle, both garments sewn from a shimmering silk that migrated from blue to lavender to grey. The color accentuated his dark hair and pale skin and made his colorless eyes seem as diamonds in the sunlight.

His hands were shaking.

Kjieran couldn't stop them shaking anymore. His hands had begun to represent a no-man's land, that ephemeral boundary between the living and the dead where the doomed souls wandered. His hands demarked a battleground of biological forces that met and clashed and exploded in violent antipathy. They twitched with the Prophet's chilling, consumptive power, and they shook with *elae's* life-giving, fiery warmth. Dore's Pattern of Changing was working its fell magic upon him, and Kjieran was helpless to stop its progression.

It had taken days to recover from the initial working, days of fevered torment while his body raged against the malfeasance waged against it. During those days, he surely lingered in this life only because the Prophet's will bound him there—for the sickness and horrors he endured would've driven even the most stalwart to seek the Returning. Now, part of him walked on the other side of death. Though his body outwardly yet seemed human, Kjieran knew it had crossed a threshold.

As yet, *elae* remained with him, but he didn't know how long this would last. This impending loss frightened him the most. Death claimed all men in the end, but to be cut off from *elae*…even the evils already perpetrated against him paled next to this horrible thought.

That his mind was still his own, that the Pattern of Changing was so slow to claim him fully…for these graces he thanked Raine's amulet. The tiny disc lay snug against his chest, and its influence remained strong. The amulet served as Kjieran's sole source of warmth, for he could no longer feel his own heartbeat, so frail and intermittent was its rhythm. He didn't hold out hope that the amulet would save him—he knew it merely slowed the inevitable end—but he prayed the amulet would give him enough time to do what he'd come there to do.

Kjieran's hands twitched on the balustrade.

From his vantage, the city of Tal'Shira spread like the wings of a butterfly to either side of Radov's palace, which crowned a massive hill at the butterfly's oblong head. A crenellated limestone wall built upon a rough sandstone base enclosed the entire palace complex. Another great wall surrounding the city itself protected from invading Khurds as much as sandstorms, which were infrequent this far east but still a threat.

Tal'Shira was a bustling city, a thriving sea port, and the home of sultans and rich merchant princes alike. People went about their business as if the princedom hadn't been at war for eons, effectively ignoring the ever-growing sea of refugees amassing outside the city walls. But this façade of normalcy was but a mass illusion mutually agreed-upon by the city's elite. In truth, Tal'Shira was the sweet reflection upon a still pond, concealing the slime beneath.

Everyone blamed Radov for the city's decline. Kjieran had recently learned that during the course of the last many moons, Radov's infamous paranoia had crested perilous heights, and now the prince was rumored to be descending into madness. His advisors were cowed, the Congress of Princes was growing ever more fractious, and Saldarians were running rampant and unchecked, gleefully marauding in Radov's own city—not to mention elsewhere in the kingdom.

Without Radov's leadership—which while militant had at least been effective—the plug of lawfulness had been yanked from the city, and now Tal'Shira swirled lazily down the drain towards anarchy.

Adding insult to injury, a host of Ascendants—ever the Prophet's spies—had descended on Tal'Shira. They watched over Radov on their master's behalf, reporting to Bethamin on the Nadori prince's every order. They walked freely about the palace, often accompanied by one of the Marquiin, and the people of Tal'Shira shied away at their passing. These Ascendants fashioned themselves as kings, thriving in the shadow of Radov's disgusted indifference, and they meted punishment as readily as commands to all who fell under their notice.

They'd thought to order Kjieran as well when he'd first arrived, accosting him with threats and demands for explanation of his presence. No sooner did they take him in hand, however, than a dark haze spread across Kjieran's vision, and the Prophet's viscous presence flooded into his mind, suffocating all thought but awareness of *him*.

"DO NOT SEEK TO KNOW MY PURPOSE HERE." Kjieran felt his tongue form the powerful words, heard the Prophet's own resonant voice booming out of his chest, rumbling like thunder through the palace passage.

The Ascendants went white.

"BOW TO ME!"

They prostrated themselves at Kjieran's feet in a scramble of clinking gold.

"WHEN YOU SEE THIS SHELL, KNOW *ME*, AND ACT ACCORDINGLY, OR KNOW MY WRATH."

The Prophet left Kjieran then. Heavy, slippery tentacles withdrew from his consciousness, freeing his thoughts. As their cold weight receded, warmth spilled in, but it was the thin warmth of the winter sun upon a meadow many moons encased in frost. Kjieran's sight was the last to return, and as that nimbus of shadows gradually withdrew, light was restored to the day.

He blinked painfully in the sudden brightness and looked around, feeling dazed and shocked and utterly violated. The Ascendants were still prostrate at his feet, while a crowd had begun to gather down the passage. Their whispers floated languidly across the distance, but their thoughts rolled in as pounding waves, shouting to his truthreader's sensitive mind.

News that the Ascendants bowed to Kjieran had crossed every tongue in the palace that day. Ripples of the news spread outwards through the city, until it seemed everyone he encountered had heard the tale. Not that anyone would speak of it to him, but their thoughts were loud enough.

Kjieran's hands twitched on the balustrade, possessed of jumping beans, of a rampaging ill-mannered spirit…possessed.

He had not yet seen Radov, not that he expected to. The prince was notoriously wary of truthreaders and refused to allow them in his presence. Kjieran wondered if Radov really harbored so many wretched secrets that just the company of a truthreader enflamed him, or if this paranoia was just one more facet of his ever-growing madness.

In either case, Radov had only just arrived back in Tal'Shira. The prince and his advisors had been investigating the site where the parley with the Akkadian Emir was to be held. Tents were being erected in the midst of the Sand Sea, miles from the lines of either side, the proverbial middle ground. Radov and the others had returned from the desert only the night before, ostensibly to welcome Gydryn val Lorian, whose ship was expected any day.

Kjieran still did not know what he was going to do.

That he held out hope stood as testimony to his nature as a truthreader, for there was an incorruptible innocence and goodness in all such Adepts—at least, those who hadn't been touched by Bethamin's Fire. Kjieran suspected that even the Marquiin harbored a kernel of it in the depths of their blackened souls, even if it manifested as a secret dream that one day a man would succeed in putting a blade through their hearts and ending their eternal torture.

The most twisted part of it was that even were the Marquiin to confess a desire for death to the Prophet, he would only believe it proof of his doctrine, evidence that all men craved their inevitable end. In the Prophet's view, hope and denial were two sides of the same coin.

"Envoy van Stone?"

Kjieran turned to find a palace servant facing him, his eyes and skin very dark in contrast to his turban of orange silk. He, too, wore the traditional Nadori *shalwar-kameez*, but Kjieran couldn't immediately place his position within the hierarchy of serving staff. Kjieran was still learning the differences in status among the palace servants, which the color and style of their embroidered finery told.

"My lord, you are needed." The man gave him a deferential bow.

The palace staff were uncertain of Kjieran's position in the court, and until Radov declared otherwise, they treated him with at least as much deference and discomfort as they would a Marquiin, and possibly a bit more.

This did not bode well for Kjieran's *actual* mission—that is, learning who was really behind the assassinations of Trell and Sebastian val Lorian. The Prophet had told him that Radov's 'duplicity had spilled royal blood,' hinting that Radov may have played a role in the treacheries leveled against the Eagle throne's heirs. But Kjieran needed proof for his king. Someone in Tal'Shira knew the truth of Sebastian's death, and possibly Trell's as well.

He'd hoped the servants would see him as an equal, and that he might earn their trust, but Bethamin had crushed any hope of that. People hardly dared look at him, much less divulge secrets to him. Yet if he couldn't develop any alliances, how would he gain the knowledge he sought?

Ever battling a disheartening and hopeless gloom, Kjieran nodded for the servant to lead the way, wondering who had called for him. He followed the servant through the sprawling palace, aware of the eyes that shied from his passing, of the looks and glances and whispers that stirred in his wake. Oaths fluttered as moths mingling in the night, speculation as the hiss of pale wings singed by fire. Each thought collected upon Kjieran until he felt smothered by gossamer, battered by each feather-light touch of minds.

The Palace of Tal'Shira had been fashioned after the Sacred City of Faroqhar—which encapsulated the seats of Agasan's government, the vast Sormitáge University and the Empress's palace, not to mention parks and plazas beyond compare. Yet Radov's palace was a collection of immense, empty courts and ornate temples; of impressive buildings for a government barely allowed to function; of fifty-two royal mini-palaces not a single prince would deign to occupy. It was a pretentious display of wealth and grandeur without a shred of taste.

Kjieran was at last escorted into a grand, circular room. Mosaic tiles lined the outer walls, while inner columns supported a soapstone dome. Both columns and dome were elaborately carved with intricate arabesques. Vaulted windows along the base of the dome shed light through artful wooden screens, casting complex shadows upon the dizzyingly colorful walls.

There was but one vast door, whose multitude of panels were carved with interlocking flowers, and the servant closed it behind Kjieran. In the room's center, down five rings of pale travertine steps, two low-backed couches curved towards one another across an iron-footed table of etched glass.

Kjieran was still standing just inside the door when the servant returned with a tray bearing a curving silver teapot and tulip-shaped glass cups rimmed in gold. Kjieran caught the scent of mint as the man descended the steps. He set the service upon the table, bowed to Kjieran once more, and left him.

A meeting room... Kjieran walked down the steps and looked up at the carved dome, *but who comes to meet me?*

The Prophet had assured him Radov would not stand in his way, but this hardly meant he was safe in Tal'Shira. Kjieran had overheard too much whispering, too many thoughts shouting of the internal power struggles between the Radov and the other Nadori princes; angry accusations of increasing taxes to support a stagnated war; bitter hatreds and prejudices for the Prophet's minions as much as for the Saldarian mercenaries 'infesting the city'...a laundry list of complaints against Radov's leadership, and a festering malcontent.

"Deep thoughts, truthreader?" asked a male voice suddenly from behind.

Kjieran turned with a start, for he'd heard no one enter through the massive door.

A dark-eyed Nadoriin faced him. Tall and gaunt, he wore silk desert robes in wielder's black with the folds of an ebon *keffiyeh* draping around his shoulders. His long face sported a goatee peppered with grey, while deep shadows carved from lean cheeks to jaw. His face displayed a smile, but his dark eyes, lined by years and the unforgiving desert sun, were coldly calculating.

A flash of gold on his hands drew Kjieran's eye, whereupon a brief glance revealed eight Sormitáge rings—one thin gold band worn on each of his fingers, leaving only his thumbs empty. The rings pronounced that he'd twice mastered each of the first four strands of *elae*. An uncommon accomplishment even before the wars. Though they'd never met before, Kjieran could not mistake him.

"You are Viernan hal'Jaitar," he said, swallowing despite himself.

"And you are Kjieran van Stone," hal'Jaitar returned, "but what else are you, I wonder?" The smile deepened, the dark eyes scalding in their curiosity.

Kjieran was justifiably wary of Radov's wielder and Prime Consul, for he was known to be cunning and extremely intelligent. Viernan was one of the few Adepts who had survived the Adept Wars, a member of the famous Fifty Companions. He'd continued his study at the Sormitáge after the wars, gaining a formidable reputation as one of the most powerful wielders to arise since the fall. He reportedly consorted with all sorts of disreputable Wildlings—even zanthyrs, as the need arose—and though he did not work the fifth, he was still as deadly as they came.

Seeing Viernan himself come to meet him, Kjieran had no doubt that a secret door opened from this room into the bowels of the palace, a tunnel for shuttling men unseen and unwilling from place to place.

Kjieran shoved his twitching hands behind his back and regarded the wielder with veiled concern. He felt suddenly ill-prepared to face off against this new enemy. Viernan guarded his thoughts well—as any trained wielder would—and Kjieran could read nothing from his eyes, so he was forced to ask the older man, "How may I be of service, Consul?"

Hal'Jaitar came slowly down the steps towards him. "The prince is curious as to the nature of your presence in his kingdom, truthreader." He looked Kjieran over sharply, his gaze penetrating. "You are neither Marquiin nor Ascendant, yet they bow to you. I had heard the Prophet was antipathetic to truthreaders in their, shall we say, *native* state. Unsullied, as it were," and here he smiled wider, revealing straight teeth yellowed with age and an unbridled contempt for the Prophet's work. Kjieran shared in this contempt, but he could never let hal'Jaitar know it. "Yet here *you* stand, apparently...unspoiled."

"If you wish to test my talent with the lifeforce, Consul, I am at your disposal," Kjieran replied. "A reading on yourself, perhaps?"

"Tempting," said hal'Jaitar flatly, "but I am interested more in *why*. Why were you spared Bethamin's Fire?"

"It is a great honor to be chosen to receive the Prophet's kiss and become cleansed," Kjieran said uneasily, careful to ensure his answers offered the least amount of information at the greatest level of truth.

"You give me schooled responses without conviction," the wielder returned in disapproval, his dark eyes hot with accusation.

Kjieran struggled to form a reply. He should've realized that Radov and hal'Jaitar wouldn't trust him merely because he carried a letter from the Prophet. These were highly secretive men, renowned for their dislike of foreigners—never mind truthreaders.

Kjieran felt unprepared for this confrontation. Tell the wielder too much, and he was doomed; not enough, and his steps would be ever dogged by Viernan's spies.

Kjieran dropped his gaze and fought to still his shaking hands. "I don't know why I wasn't chosen to receive Bethamin's Fire, Consul," he murmured at last, which was the blessed truth.

Hal'Jaitar's eyes were like black stones. "We are told you came to attend the parley in Bethamin's name," the wielder offered after an uncomfortable moment of considering Kjieran. "The prince would know why."

"I but carry out the Prophet's will, Consul."

"Ah yes, again the failsafe response, so obvious, so expected. But you are not Marquiin, forced into Bethamin's mental mold…nor, I believe…one of his true disciples."

This accusation chilled Kjieran. What could hal'Jaitar possibly know? *How* could he know anything at all? Perhaps it was just another test to throw him off his guard, to see what he might reveal? Yet Kjieran's insides wormed with sudden fear.

Kjieran was no stranger to the double-speak perfected by politicians and truthreaders alike, nor unused to compartmentalizing his emotions, but hal'Jaitar was a deadly and unpredictable enemy, and Kjieran didn't know enough of him to retain solid footing in this sort of sparring.

"I don't know what you mean, Consul." He let his gaze harden, his shoulders straighten, his tone convey his displeasure at the wrongful implication.

"Don't you?" Hal'Jaitar smiled again, sharply suggestive. When Kjieran didn't answer, his smile faded. "Here's a question then, *truthreader.* How did you come to serve Bethamin when your allegiance lay with Gydryn val Lorian?"

Ever conscious of the wielder across from him, who was far more suspicious than Bethamin—for the Prophet felt all men should bow to his will and accepted any that passed his Ascendants' slipshod screening—Kjieran told hal'Jaitar the tale he and Raine had arranged as truth, that Kjieran might have no trouble in the retelling. The Ascendant who'd found him in Veneisea half a year ago had accepted his story without question, but hal'Jaitar's trust was not so easily gained.

"I heard nothing of this so-called falling out between you and Gydryn val Lorian, our ally," the wielder murmured when Kjieran finished his story, his gaze pinning Kjieran so fast that his twitching hands were all that dared move. "It hardly seems like the King of Dannym to cast a valued Adept from his service."

"His Majesty was most distraught at my failure," Kjieran replied with downcast eyes. It was true enough, though the king blamed himself as much as his advisors for their failure to unearth all of Morwyk's deep-rooted, pernicious conspiracy to gain the Eagle Throne.

Hal'Jaitar arched a brow, took a step down and brushed past Kjieran, idly walking the lowest ring of circular steps with hands clasped behind his silk robes. Kjieran turned as the wielder passed, keeping his eyes on hal'Jaitar and his body as a shield for his ever-twitching hands.

"Truthreaders are notoriously loyal," hal'Jaitar eyed Kjieran critically from beneath furrowed brows, "especially those Sormitáge-trained and sworn into service by the Fourth Vestal," and he pinned Kjieran with a telling look upon this accusation. "Since you claim you now serve Bethamin instead of your king, Kjieran van Stone, have you also then forsworn your allegiance to Raine D'Lacourte?"

Kjieran felt a shock of fear course through him. In the same moment, he became aware that Viernan now worked the fourth. He could feel the change in the currents of *elae,* though Raine's truth, the pattern was artfully done.

He dared not try to persuade hal'Jaitar, only answering as truthfully as he could, "I was sent away from Dannym, Consul. The Prophet's Ascendants found me and brought me to Bethamin. He did not see fit to make me Marquiin, only allowing me to serve as an acolyte in his temple." He let the fear that was his constant companion bleed into his voice as he added, "I believe you gravely underestimate the Prophet's power if you think a man might serve as a spy beneath his gaze and emerge unscathed."

"Is that what you are?" Viernan's dark eyes scraped him up and down. "Unscathed?"

Kjieran could not have managed words in that moment, even had he been able to think of an answer.

Hal'Jaitar observed him with a cold half-smile. "I am told you are one of the Prophet's favored acolytes." He came to sit on the low couch across from where Kjieran stood, adding as he settled down and crossed one knee, "oft visiting his chambers in the night." There was much that his tone implied—disgust and contempt not the least of them.

Kjieran inwardly groaned. *Shade and darkness! What else does the man know?*

How naïve he'd been. Logic dictated that hal'Jaitar would have his own spies in Bethamin's temple. Worse was realizing that Viernan hal'Jaitar might've actually learned of his mission for Raine D'Lacourte—certainly he hinted at such knowledge. Had one of the Brotherhood's contacts been compromised? Or could it be possible that Kjieran's nameless contact served two masters?

Viernan was obviously enjoying his discomfiture. "Tell me, *Envoy* van Stone," he posed, "what is the Prophet's mind towards our parley with the Emir? Towards our Prince Radov?"

With growing dismay, Kjieran managed, "The Prophet does not reveal his mind to his servants, Consul…even favored ones."

"Nor, it would seem, to his allies," hal'Jaitar replied. The smile was back, disarming to anyone who'd heard nothing of his reputation and an outright threat to those who had.

Kjieran knew he faced the rearing king cobra in Viernan hal'Jaitar, and he feared making any motion to draw its deadly strike.

"Please," hal'Jaitar indicated the tea service with long fingers. "Let us drink and know one another, as is the custom in my land."

Kjieran swallowed, eyeing the tea uncomfortably. It was the height of folly to take tea with a wielder of such unscrupulous repute, and a death sentence if he did not. Feeling increasingly overmatched, Kjieran took the offered seat across from Viernan and shoved his twitching hands partly beneath his legs to pin them still.

Viernan filled four glasses with amber tea, notably letting Kjieran choose one. Then he sat back on the couch and regarded Kjieran coolly, crossing one knee over the other once more. Kjieran settled the glass cup in his lap for fear of his shaking hands spilling it, and returned the wielder's gaze. Only his truthreader's court training kept his expression from revealing the anxiety that gripped him so thoroughly.

"Now then," said the wielder, "let us speak candidly, as befits Adepts of our mutual training."

"Go on, Consul," Kjieran returned, liking this less and less.

"Let it not be said I gave you inadequate opportunity to divulge the truth," Viernan posed with a smile that was all fangs. "We *know* your true motivations, Kjieran van Stone."

Kjieran tried to breathe normally. If Viernan hal'Jaitar suspected that he was actually seeking the truth of the Trell and Sebastian's deaths and Radov's complicity in them, Kjieran knew he would not walk out of that room alive.

"Just so?" Kjieran forced an innocuous smile. "What would those motivations be, Consul?"

"We know you are here to kill your sworn liege, *truthreader*," Viernan sneered with contempt, his dark eyes flashing. "Dare not deny it."

With the fourth rolling so tumultuously in the room, Kjieran certainly would not, but nor could he confirm such a truth when the Prophet had forbidden him to speak of his assignment—never mind what it might mean to his future should the words ever leave his mouth in Viernan's company.

When Kjieran said nothing, hal'Jaitar continued, "Since Gydryn val Lorian's demise equally suits the purposes of others who will be left unnamed, I will not prevent you from this task, but you must not act unsanctioned."

"Assuming there is any truth to this claim," Kjieran replied quietly, trying to maintain his footing on such a slippery slope, "whose sanction must I seek, and how?"

"That the missive will come from me is all you need know."

"And how will you convey this sanction, Consul?" Kjieran inquired with a twitch of a derisive smile. "Shall I be on the lookout for a note penned in disappearing ink? Or perhaps a cipher, the code slipped to me within a steaming pot of tea?"

Viernan glowered, making Kjieran reconsider the wisdom in baiting him. "When the time is right, you will be instructed to act."

Kjieran did not like where this was heading. As the Prophet had intimated, Radov apparently also wanted King Gydryn eliminated, and clearly hal'Jaitar intended Kjieran to bear the blame for the deed. "What if I refuse, Consul?"

The wielder smiled humorlessly, his eyes icy ebony orbs. "We both know that you won't."

Kjieran squeezed the glass cup in his lap as anger warmed him. Hal'Jaitar's certainty troubled him. How could the man be *so* sure of Kjieran's mission? This implied spies deep in the Prophet's inner sanctum. More frightening still, if hal'Jaitar could know such secrets as these, what information had he gained about Kjieran's other clandestine activities?

Hal'Jaitar was still smiling at him, the cat admiring the pinned canary, knowing it could have its snack any time. His dark eyes drifted to the cup in Kjieran's lap, and Kjieran knew the man was waiting for him to drink, that there was no way he was leaving that room without doing so.

The better to get it over with, Kjieran thought, and drank the tea. It was steeped of mint and sweet with honey. Unsurprisingly, hal'Jaitar did not share it with him.

Kjieran downed the tea, hoping the action would at least buy his freedom, but hal'Jaitar seemed in no hurry to release him from his gaze. Kjieran wondered what poison was in the tea that the man was clearly waiting for it to take effect. It was some comfort that at least hal'Jaitar knew nothing of his changed nature—or perhaps he did and was merely testing the information he'd been given. In any case, the tea was impotent—how could anything trouble him when his body was already dying, his spirit merely pinned to its shell by force of a working of such ghastly malfeasance that none but a lunatic could have conceived of it?

Eventually the wielder's dark eyes narrowed. He stood in a billow of ebon silk. "Until we meet again, *truthreader.*"

THIRTY-NINE

"An idea is not made great merely because great men die in defense of it."
– Loran val Whitney, Duke of Marion

THE PIRATE SHIP *Ransom* returned Trell and Alyneri to Cair Xerses three days later. As Trell and Alyneri were disembarking, Hadrian had shaken the bag of Agasi silver tied to his belt, winked at Trell and bidden him call again any time.

They spent that night at a nearby inn, and the next morning they hired a coach to return them to Rethynnea. After a long day's ride, they now finally neared the villa. To Alyneri, it seemed a lifetime since they'd left—so much had happened in a few short days.

It amazed her that they were returning after surviving life-threatening jeopardy, and… nothing had changed. Alyneri still faced the same troubling future as before, and so did Trell.

The path before them almost seemed predestined to her now. Had they not encountered a multitude of alternate possible futures in the past few days, their road splitting again and again towards varying conclusions, only to arrive back upon the same demarcation point? Returned, as it were, to the doorstep of their initial future?

Reunion should've brightened that horizon, yet going to M'Nador to meet King Gydryn somehow seemed no less perilous to Alyneri than the danger they'd just averted.

What *would* happen when they reached Tal'Shira by the Sea?

Alyneri turned her gaze to Trell beside her and saw a reflection of her trepidation in his features. Alyneri placed her hand over his. "He loves you, Trell," she said in the desert tongue, calling his gaze to hers. "He will embrace you and name you as his heir. Be assured of it."

Trell arched brows. "I wish I could be, Alyneri."

"You are his son. He won't care what you did in unknowingly, in support of the man who gave you refuge—no matter the Emir was his enemy. If you'd been responsible for Sebastian's death personally, still he would accept you back with open arms. I know him. You must believe me."

Giving her a soft look, he leaned to kiss her forehead and murmured, "I believe you believe it."

Alyneri arched a brow at him, dissatisfied with his lack of accord.

He smiled and took up her hand to kiss her palm, giving her a potent look.

She was still a little pink in the cheeks when the coach turned inside the villa gates and pulled to a halt in the yard. Alyneri stepped out to find Rhys rushing up in a fury.

"Damn us all thirteen hells, woman, what were you *thinking*—running off into the city with half of Morwyk's men in search of you?"

Alyneri grimaced. "I always admire your candor, Lord Captain, even if it's lacking somewhat in gentility to sweeten its sting."

"To the contrary, Captain," Trell remarked as he climbed out behind Alyneri, "the Duchess envisioned a brilliant ruse to lure Morwyk's men into the open." He stepped down beside her and wrapped an arm around Alyneri's slim shoulders. "It didn't go off exactly as planned, but all's well that ends well, as they say."

"I…suppose, your Highness," Rhys muttered by way of reluctant acquiescence. Alyneri noted that the captain acted far more subserviently towards Trell than he ever had towards Ean. But Trell commanded respect from everyone he met—even, it would seem, pirates.

"But how did you know about our little excursion?" Trell inquired as they headed across the drive while the wrought-iron gates were closing behind them.

"Hadrian sent a message," Fynn said from the villa steps. Then he belched.

Alyneri hadn't seen him standing there, though he seemed firmly ensconced, leaning against a pillar with the ever-present goblet in his hand.

She wondered if Fynn didn't actually sleep with that goblet and marveled that his flesh hadn't grown over and around it.

"That's…considerate."

"I suspect he hoped to ransom us," Trell told her. Then he shoot a knowing look at the royal cousin.

"Fortunately I had no coin," Fynn said by way of confirmation. "Ghislain took all of it and my soul besides."

"More likely you expended your fortune on refilling that bottomless goblet," Alyneri murmured.

"I don't criticize your religion, Your Grace. Don't spit on mine."

"What religion is that? The Church of Inebriation?"

"Actually, *Dissipation* is the preferred term," Fynn corrected with an airy wave of his goblet. "It's the newest of the Veneisean Virtues—elected in just last week by the Council of Cardinals along with Lust, Lewdness and Profanity."

"I though we were talking about virtues," Trell said with a hint of a smile.

Fynn gave him disapproving look. "Let's not bandy semantics, cousin. It's what we hold in our hearts that counts."

They'd moved inside the villa by this time, and Alyneri saw Brody, Cayal and Dorin coming down the staircase with bags in hand. She turned to Fynn. "Are you going somewhere?"

"We all are." Rhys pushed past her to help his men.

"With Seth and the zanthyr gone," Fynn said, "never mind everyone else, we've no cause to linger here." He threw himself onto a velvet settee to watch the others carry out the bags.

Alyneri felt a little flutter. "The zanthyr's gone?"

"When?" asked Trell.

"The same night you two decided to double-date with Hadrian." He gave Trell a sour look. "Was it Brantley? I hope you gutted the rat-faced bastard."

"I believe he met with a fitting end."

"Then—" Alyneri dared to hope. "Has Phaedor gone for Tanis?"

Fynn gave her a frightful look. "As if the damnable creature reports to me!"

"Have you found us a Nodefinder, Fynn?" Trell asked.

"See…" Fynn waved at him with an appreciative flourish of his goblet. "That's why you're the right man for the job."

"What job would that be?"

Fynn belched gratuitously. "Sebastian was an insufferable ass," he continued talking over Trell's question, "firstborn, proud…always preening publicly in front of mummy and daddy—the perfect son. And Ean is far too impetuous—as like to give away half the kingdom out of guilt or compassion or else single-handedly attack an army thinking he alone can save the world, but you…" he eyed Trell sagaciously and saluted with his goblet, "you're on the money, cousin."

"Thank you, Fynn," Trell remarked with a wry look. "It's a relief to know you stand firmly behind me in the unlikely event my father gives me the Eagle Throne."

"No," Fynn leaned towards him, swaying a little. "Thank *you*."

Alyneri frowned at him. He was more than his usual degree of sloshed. "Fynn, did something else happen?"

"He's rushing out of town for some reason," the soldier Cayal remarked with a grin as he passed on his way back upstairs, "but he won't say why."

"It's none of your bloody damned business, that's why!" Fynn shouted after him. He sprang to his feet and opened his arms to the room at large. "I'm a *free* man! I come and go as I please!"

"For the moment," an entering Brody muttered. He came over and stood beside Fynn expectantly.

"What do *you* want?" The royal cousin swayed, swinging overly close to Brody and then drawing precipitously back.

The Bull just looked at him.

"I really don't—" Fynn swooned.

Brody caught him as he fell and swooped him up over one shoulder. He seemed to have much practice in the maneuver. "He'll be ready at first light, your Highness," the Bull told an amused Trell.

"Put me down…" Fynn slurred. As Brody was carrying him up the stairs like a sack of flour, Fynn lifted his head and grinned at Alyneri and Trell. "You know, it's only right about you two…I mean…your being betrothed and all…" Then his eyes rolled back, his head fell forward and he started snoring loudly, still miraculously holding his cup.

Alyneri stood in startled silence, her heart in a panic. The room seemed far too quiet suddenly.

"Betrothed?" Trell asked in a low voice.

Alyneri closed her eyes. She had honestly forgotten—well, not entirely forgotten, but mostly so, in the way one pushes an uncomfortable thought from one's mind as long as possible and thereafter can often ignore that it's there, hovering at the edge of awareness. She'd thought of telling him recently more than once, but always something had stopped her.

"I...told you," she said in a small voice, not looking at him. "Remember?"

"In a frightfully different context," he returned tightly.

She could tell he was angry, or hurt...both. She'd kept it from him, yes, but not for lack of love for him...only because she feared so greatly being tied to a throne. He walked away from her, hands in his pockets.

"Trell..." she turned hesitantly to him.

He spun her a tense look. "Ean?" he said with sudden accusation, having just connected the story to the truth. "The boy you were in love with—my *brother?*"

Alyneri flinched beneath his ire.

"And the one you were betrothed to 'however unwillingly,'" he posed in a cool voice that was terrible for its sudden dispassion, his gaze upon her severe. "Me?"

"It was *years* ago—" she said desperately.

"And so unimportant that you simply forgot to mention it."

"Trell, forgive me, *please*—I didn't mean—"

"Are you ashamed of me, Alyneri?"

She recoiled from the idea. "How could you *think*—"

"Ashamed of a man who willingly served his father's enemy? Or are you still in love with my brother?" and the hurt in his voice was horrible to hear. "Is that why you didn't want me to know we're betrothed? Do you find the idea so repellant?"

"I—" she blanched beneath the severity of his accusations. "It was just so long ago, and it shouldn't—it doesn't *matter.*"

"It matters, Alyneri," he said. Then he turned and took the stairs two at a time, leaving her alone with her guilt.

Morning brought stormy seas and charcoal skies and a foreboding sense to the day. Trell stood at the window feeling a prickling sensation in the base of his spine. It was as untimely as it was unwelcome, but unfortunately he knew it well. He'd felt the same sensation more than once, the last time being the day of the unexpected battle that had claimed Graeme's life.

'We are all just glass globes bobbing upon the seas of time, willing chance and luck to cast us upon a friendly shore…'

Trell clenched his jaw at Fhionna's words, whispered while they made love on their parting night. It had been many weeks since Trell thought of the *nymphae*—her presence in his mind had been decreasing since Alyneri had come into his life—but he found himself thinking of her now.

Mostly because he wanted to *stop* thinking about Alyneri.

Perhaps it was wrong of him to feel betrayed. The truth of their betrothal may have been difficult to voice. He could see that she might've been seeking the right time to tell him. But he didn't entirely trust the reassurances she'd thrust upon him yesterday. Was there some other truth she wasn't telling him out of compassion or fear?

Did she really still love his brother?

Unfortunately, her keeping this secret from him had escalated a minor misunderstanding into something sharper, for it had pierced into deeper concerns: would his father accept him, knowing he'd served the Emir, knowing the many battles he was responsible for winning on the Emir's behalf, knowing how many kingdom men had died at Trell's hand? And if his father did miraculously accept him back, would there be conditions attached to his return to good standing? What would the king require from Trell?

And what of the accident itself, the foundering of the *Dawn Chaser* that had stranded Trell on the shores of the Akkad? Many men and Healers—Alyneri's own mother—were also lost in the disaster, which may or may not have been directly caused by Trell's presence on the ship. Would his father blame him for this?

Trell already felt responsible, even with what little he knew of what had transpired.

Then there was the Triad pact itself. Alyneri had assured him the king would not honor his pact with Radov once he learned the Nadori prince had joined forces with the Prophet Bethamin, but was that really true? And if not, what would he do if his father required *him* to honor the kingdom's commitment to Radov?

'We are all just glass globes bobbing upon the seas of time, willing chance and luck to cast us upon a friendly shore…'

Trell had never felt so a like a fisherman's floating ball of glass, tossing and bobbing in an uncertain sea.

Disturbed by the formless premonition that was hounding him, as well as by his lingering upset with Alyneri, Trell joined the others as they were gathering in the yard.

Cayal and Dorin looked eager to be off, and even the Lord Captain seemed in uncommon fair humor. No doubt for a soldier like Rhys val Kincaide, sitting at a villa in Cair Rethynnea with nothing to do but wait for something to happen was about as close to a living hell as could be devised.

Alyneri came down the steps wearing a cerulean desert gown and matching cloak, her long hair capped with a net of garnets. The more Trell looked upon her in such desert finery, the more beautiful she seemed.

Their eyes met as she reached the last step, her expression attentive to his mood, her gaze conveying an eager desire to explain, but this was neither the time nor the place.

He shook his head slightly. *Not now.*

She dropped her gaze and moved off to her horse, and in the turn of her shoulder, an unexpected wall formed between them. Suddenly Alyneri seemed as inaccessible as the stars.

He turned to Gendaia with his jaw clenched.

Fynn and Brody joined them at the last, the latter coming out with a sack over his shoulder that clinked and clanked with the sound of glass. "Be careful with that!" Fynn hissed as Brody slung the bag over the back of Fynn's horse. "You've got all the grace of a bloody ogre!"

"An ogre would as soon eat you as carry out the bag of wine you're still too drunk to manage yourself," Brody pointed out.

Fynn gave him a sooty look. "I might be better off if it did."

"Is your conscience speaking too loudly this morning, Fynnlar?" Alyneri affected a cheerful demeanor, but Trell saw the hurt lingering behind her gaze.

"Your Grace, I thought we ascertained long ago that I have no conscience to speak of," Fynn remarked while trying to mount his horse. He managed it awkwardly on the third attempt.

"I haven't given up hoping that your soul might yet be salvaged."

"A conscience is hardly a guarantee of salvation, your Grace," Fynn pointed out as he finally gained his saddle. "In fact, I rather think it's our consciences that do us in. What need have we of salvation unless we have a conscience to begin with? A free man is one who cares for nothing."

"Yes, I've met many such men in his majesty's prison," Rhys remarked.

Fynn gave the captain a look of rancorous indignation.

Alyneri's gaze took in all of the horses and pack animals, and she turned a frown to Rhys. "Lord Captain...where is Ean's horse?"

Rhys harrumphed disagreeably, whereupon Cayal answered, "We think the zanthyr took him, Your Grace. The horse vanished from his stall the same night Phaedor left."

"I see."

So did Trell. He was beginning to wonder if the First Lord's zanthyr might've had the same prescient foreknowledge as Balaji—ever gazing at things to come.

They soon set off through the still-reveling city towards the Espial's Guild Hall on Faring East. Two hours later they reached the massive building, which dominated an entire city block. Fynn led them into a large court bordered by four arched tunnels, each of which branched into further courtyards.

The Guild Master soon emerged to greet them. A rotund, bearded man of middle years, he wore an elaborate chain draped from shoulder to shoulder but seemed most proud of the two thin gold rings cinching the fat pointer finger on his right hand.

"He's an espial of the second degree," Alyneri murmured as the man was greeting Fynn. Trell turned to her inquiringly. "The two gold rings mean he trained at the Sormitáge and achieved the second level of mastery in his craft—quite an accomplishment."

Trell noted the rings as much as Alyneri's wistful tone, which he found puzzling. He tried to remember if he'd ever seen anyone else wearing such rings. The *drachwyr's* only accoutrements had been ebon-enameled nails, and certainly Carian hadn't worn one. But then, Trell recalled that the pirate had frowned upon an espial's life, talking about them as 'kept pets,' and he'd scoffed at training at the Sormitáge.

Just then Fynn waved Trell over to join them, whereupon the royal cousin introduced, "Trell, this is D'Varre, Guild Master of Rethynnea. D'Varre, may I present my cousin, Trell."

As their gazes met, the Guild Master connected Fynn's introduction with Trell's name, and his pudgy eyes widened. "*You*—but I thought you were dead!"

"Yes," Trell muttered, "I get that a lot."

D'Varre turned to Fynn. "You said it was just the duchess traveling with you and your men."

"Trell *is* one of my men." Fynn waved nebulously at Trell. "He's a *man*, isn't he?"

D'Varre looked inordinately discomfited. Trell wondered why the news of his identity so troubled the Adept. He regarded the Guild Master with a narrowed gaze.

D'Varre signaled to a man standing in the shadows next to a horse, waving him over. Then he patted his brow with a kerchief. "Regarding the terms of your contract, my lord…"

"What? What?" Fynn pressed impatiently.

"As I explained to you upon our initial meeting, it's too dangerous to travel the nodes directly into Tal'Shira. Radov is terrified of invasion from the Khurds and has set Saldarians to guarding the known nodes. The ruffians shoot on sight without bothering to ascertain friend from foe. The guild has suffered some losses and will not risk the node again."

"Yes, you told me all of this already. What's your plan—just spit it out, D'Varre."

D'Varre tugged at his waistcoat, which was straining around gilded buttons. "Gerard here," and he indicated the man who'd just joined them, "must take you across three nodes to bring you within a day's ride of Tal'Shira." He pinned Fynn with a highly significant look. "Two of these nodes are in Akkad-held lands. Very dangerous."

"If this is about upping your fee—"

"I mean only to think of your welfare, my lord." D'Varre dabbed at his brow again and aimed a confusing glance at Trell. "Are you *certain* you will not reconsider traveling via the weld in Tregarion instead? This would bring you into Kandori and—"

"Cost half the Kandori fortune to do it!" Fynn objected shrilly. "No, we'll take the route you've planned for us. Give me the bloody paper to sign. The sooner we get moving the better."

Which statement Trell interpreted to mean, *the sooner I get out of here, the safer I'll be.*

D'varre mopped his brow with his handkerchief again and motioned for a clerk, who trotted forward with parchment and quill. Scowling, Fynn placed his incomprehensible scrawl across it.

"You will note upon the contract that I have advised them of the danger in choosing this route," D'Varre said to the clerk, who made the appropriate notation and rushed off again.

The Guild Master looked to Fynn and then to Trell and forced a smile. "Very well, my lords. I leave you in Gerard's capable hands." With that, he bowed and left them as hastily as his bulk allowed, leaving Trell to wonder what secret he'd escaped with back into the dim recesses of his Hall.

Gerard meanwhile scanned the assembled group as if counting heads. He was a thin fellow with a nose that seemed to have been endowed with the face's full complement of prominence and a chin that had received none. Trell noted the single, etched gold band on his right pointer finger and made a mental note to start noticing such rings, now that he knew their significance.

"Very well," the espial said in a deeply resonant tenor that belied his understated build and generally unimpressive countenance. "Let us be off."

The node lay at the center of another courtyard, its exact location marked by a banded circle of cobalt, silver and garnet tiles. Trell noted that the colors mirrored the famous columns along Rethynnea's harbor Thoroughfare, but he couldn't help comparing the great circle to a bull's-eye. His gaze strayed to the rooftops, for the seasoned soldier in him remained too wary of archers to make an obvious target of himself.

The espial led his horse to the middle of the garnet circle. "I stand here," Gerard spread his hands to indicate his current position, "holding open the node. You cross there," and he pointed to the red tiles in the center of the bull's-eye, "and keep walking towards the edge. There are many of you who need to cross, so please do not merely stop the moment you emerge on the other side."

"What do you mean walk towards the edge?" Rhys asked.

"You will know it," Gerard assured him in his booming voice. "Do not continue past the edge."

"Duly noted," Fynn muttered. "Stop before you walk off The Edge. Can we go now?"

Gerard cast him a censorious look. "A moment, please, to prepare the node. Cyrene was not built in a day, my lord."

"No, but it fell in one," Fynn pointed out disagreeably.

"Once everyone is through," Gerard told the group, patently ignoring Fynn now, "we will proceed to our next nodepoint. Do not proceed into the near city until I have joined you. The lands are perilous for unwary travelers." With that, the espial closed his eyes and ostensibly set to 'preparing the node.'

"As if we'd leave without him," Fynn muttered.

"What has you so worked up, Fynn?" Alyneri finally asked.

But Trell remembered a comment Carian had made about traveling on nodes controlled by the Guild and thought he understood. "Just how much is this endeavor costing us, cousin?"

Alyneri turned the royal cousin a swift look as understanding dawned. "Fynn—where did you get the money for us to travel this way?"

"He borrowed it from Ghislain," Brody the Bull rumbled.

"*Traitor*," Fynn hissed spectacularly at him.

"No wonder you're fleeing the kingdom," Trell chuckled.

"I am a free man to go where I please!" Fynn declared shrilly.

"Until Ghislain gets her hands on you," Brody pointed out.

Fynn spun him a heated glare. "Whose side are you on?"

"I serve my lord, Prince Ryan."

"Who would rather not see his only son in the clutches of that conniving black-widow of a siren!"

"But surely she would hold nothing against you once you repay her," Alyneri protested.

"Yes, I think that's the essence of the problem," Trell noted with a quirk of a grin. "Fynn obviously has no intention of repaying her."

"The money was *mine* to begin with!" Fynn protested indignantly.

"I don't recall anyone forcing you to spend all your waking hours drinking her wine and playing Kings," Rhys remarked.

Fynn settled him a long-suffering look. "Little do you know, Captain. Might as well say, 'so we're going to drown you now, and if you survive the drowning, we'll let you live.'"

While Rhys was pondering that logic, the Espial Gerard opened his eyes and announced, "The node is prepared." He indicated the garnet circle with one hand. "If it please my lords to cross."

Having traveled across many nodes in recent months, Trell somewhat expected the transition of placing one foot upon the vibrant red tiles and the next elsewhere in the realm—he hardly even noticed the momentary disorientation—but the view that spread before him as he emerged from the Pattern of the World onto a grassy slope surprised him greatly.

They stood upon a high mountainside overlooking a great walled limestone. In the center of the city, two towering jade pillars stood higher than any other structure, dwarfing even the glittering gold dome of the sultan's central palace.

Recognizing too well the skyline of that city, Trell spun a look behind him, but he knew what he would find.

The Assifiyah mountains reared startlingly close. Their craggy, snowbound peaks were just then shredding a bank of clouds into cotton-like strips. Turning back, Trell saw that the hill the stood upon ended in a cliff. He knew what lay at the bottom of that chasm, too: Naiadithine and the Cry.

"It's very beautiful here." Alyneri led Draanil to a halt beside Gendaia. "Have you any idea where we might be?"

"I have an idea," Trell said tightly. His grey eyes drank in the view, and it tasted strongly of foreboding with a heavy dose of unwanted nostalgia stirred in.

Sakkalaah.

To think, he might've managed a several week journey in a single hour had he known of such things as nodes and espials for hire, but then he would never have met Carian vran Lea, or Yara, and who knows where he would've been?

Trell supposed he still would've delivered the Mage's missive, ensuring a similar inevitable end, but he couldn't help thinking that the journey truly had been as important as his destination—perhaps more so.

"*Trell…*" Alyneri reached out to him again with her eyes and her tone.

"Not here, Alyneri." He mounted Gendaia and trotted over to join the espial, who had just come through.

"Our next node is found in the Guild Hall in the city," Gerard announced. "Please follow me." He mounted up and led them away.

FORTY

"A bird in the hand is safer than one overhead."

– A popular pirate saying

"**W**AKEY, WAKEY."

Raine opened his eyes to find Carian vran Lea's unshaven face hovering nose to nose with his own.

"Oh, good, you're up," the pirate noted cheerily. His looming face vanished abruptly, only to be replaced with a steaming mug of Akkadian *kaffe*, which Raine was obliged to take from him.

As the Vestal sat up to a grey morning, Carian held up his own mug of *kaffe* to his nose, leaned against Raine's bedpost and remarked, "I don't know how they get all this stuff. Do you know how hard it is to come by Akkadian *kaffe* beans? I've made the trip to Hazak myself dozens of times, and I can tell you these are as fresh as they come."

Raine pressed palms to his eyes to extract the lingering sand of sleep from them. "They probably grow the beans here, Carian."

"Oh." The pirate scratched his head. Clearly this solution had been too simple to have occurred to him.

"Carian," Raine called the pirate's gaze to his. "Why are you in my bed chamber?"

"Oh, yeah, that. We've been summoned, poppet."

Raine set his *kaffe* on a chest by the bed. "By whom? To where?"

"You think they tell me these things? I'm the one with a dragon for a nursemaid."

"Rhakar is still with you?"

The pirate grinned. "Well...not exactly." He made a point of loudly thinking about his bedroom escapades with Mithaiya.

"Ugh! Go think those things somewhere else!" Raine waved the pirate away in disgust.

"I am very into lizards right now." Carian obligingly wandered to the far side of the vast bed chamber.

Raine climbed from his bed, feeling molested by the suspicion that this day was going to be difficult.

And why shouldn't it be? You've only yet to reunite with Dagmar, Isabel, Björn and about a hundred other people you either thought were dead or who you'll surely learn have betrayed you.

As he threw on some clothes and secured his belt, Raine reflected that cynicism was probably not one of his more admirable attributes. He donned his cloak and looked to the pirate.

Carian grinned. "Yeah, so...this way."

He led out into the hall, where Raine unsurprisingly found Mithaiya waiting.

"Mademoiselle." He gave Mithaiya a nod of greeting.

Mithaiya smiled. "Good morning, Vestal. I hope you slept well."

"That I slept at all is an improvement, my lady."

"Alas, I cannot say the same," she remarked with a telling smile.

Carian shrugged his eyebrows at her. "So I told Mithaiya," he said, clapping Raine on the shoulder, "that I would be more than pleased to help her mother an entirely new line of Kandori princes. Lo and behold, she took me up on my offer."

Raine didn't tell him that he'd already seen far too many details of their lovemaking due to Carian's very *loud* recollection of it.

"The pirate made extraordinary claims which I felt obligated to disprove," Mithaiya added with her gaze pinned on Carian.

Carian shot her a saucy grin and ambled closer to her, loins in the lead. "And did you?" He wrapped arms around her waist and drew her hips against his.

"Do I need to be here for this?" Raine asked somewhat desperately.

Carian growled and buried his face in Mithaiya's neck. She eyed

Raine while the pirate gobbled at her ear but finally took pity on him and murmured, "I believe your presence is required elsewhere, Islander."

Carian drew back looking disappointed. "Oh well. There's always tonight."

"Perhaps. If I am still interested. I cannot imagine there is much else to learn of you."

"Oh, poppet," he sighed, settling her a wanton grin, "you haven't even begun to experience the benefits of my expertise."

"Isn't there somewhere we're supposed to be?" Raine remarked pointedly.

Mithaiya seemed to enjoy tormenting him, for she leveled him a predatory smile while the pirate fondled her breasts and growled lascivious promises into her ear. Finally she pushed him off, spun lightly and led away down the hall.

As they followed the exotic *drachwyr*, Carian sighed dramatically and elbowed Raine. "Hey, did you know they can breathe fire even in their human form?"

"*Yes*, Carian," Raine replied through gritted teeth, "as a matter of fact I *did*."

Mithaiya led them on a long walk through the sprawling palace, but eventually they reached a door guarded by a Shade. He bowed at their approach and stepped aside. "The Vestal awaits within."

Raine felt an icy hollow open in his chest. He was in no condition to confront Björn.

But then the Shade opened the door, and Raine raw that the Second Vestal, not the Fifth, awaited them within. As he entered, he recognized the bedroom where he'd left Gwynnleth.

Dagmar was standing at the window when they came in. Carian immediately fell to one knee and bowed his head. "*Great Master.*"

Dagmar turned. His pale green eyes fastened first on Raine. Then he came over and placed a hand on Carian's shoulder. "Welcome, Carian vran Lea." He smiled down at the pirate. "It's a pleasure to at last greet you in the flesh."

Feeling incredibly disconnected from reality, Raine studied Dagmar as the Vestal motioned Carian back to his feet and greeted him with a brotherly hug. The Second Vestal looked much the same as he had when Raine had last seen him in Alorin, on the day Dagmar had turned his back on them to seek out Björn.

Had he known then he would never return? Had it been courage and honor that drove him after Björn, as they'd suspected, or had he always been secretly sworn to the Fifth Vestal, even as had Cristien?

Dagmar released Carian and looked to Raine, and his green eyes carried within them a recognition of all that had come between them. They did not greet each other, for no greeting could bridge the distance.

Raine retrieved the coin from his pocket. "I believe this is yours." He opened his hand to reveal the circle of bronze lying on his palm.

Dagmar took the coin and pocketed it. Perhaps he knew it had served its purpose. He motioned to the bed. "Your avieth friend," he moved to Gwynnleth's side, "our Healers have seen to her welfare. While she sleeps, she is sustained. You need not fear for her wellbeing in this regard."

"What about in the other regard?" Carian asked.

Dagmar cast him a look of concern. "As to the other, I've done all I can."

"In dreamscape," Raine supplied, understanding now why Dagmar had met them there.

"Indeed, brother. I looked for Gwynnleth in the world of dreams, but she's traveled a great distance. I worry that she may have passed onto the paths of the dead. If she has ventured there…"

"Then what?"

Dagmar shook his head, holding the pirate's gaze. "There is grave danger of becoming lost among those moors, for their melancholy draw is powerful. Even I dare not follow her there. I lit a beacon for her in Dreamscape. Now we must wait and hope that she finds her way back to it."

Carian stood frowning over the avieth's sleeping form. After a moment, he spun to Dagmar. "What if I went in after her?"

Dagmar considered him. "I…could bring you into dreamscape with me, but what reason have you to think it would make a difference?"

Carian turned an irritable glare back to Gwynnleth's sleeping form. "She despises me enough that she might return just for the opportunity of pointing out my faults in front of you, my lord."

Morning dawned, and Ean dreamed.

He stood on a balcony overlooking a moonlit sea. The waves of high tide crashed against and around sturdy pillars beneath him, close enough he could feel the salt spray when the wind shifted. The heavens were miraculous above him, millions of stars so brilliant in the clear night that to gaze upon them was to lose oneself in infinity.

And before him spread the mercuric sea. It called to him as well.

He didn't want to leave this life. He didn't want to leave her. Yet he knew that he would. Duty called to him as strongly as the bond he shared with her. These opposing desires tore at his heart and sundered his soul, soiling all that was bright.

She joined him on the balcony in silence, yet he could always feel when she was near. The bond of their love had connected them long before magic sealed it permanently. Coming up behind him, she wrapped her arms around his bare chest and pulled herself close. The breeze tossed her long hair around them both, and it clung to his damp skin.

"I cannot bear to leave you."

"Arion, this path has long been set. We cannot but walk it now. Why do you let this guilt torment you so? It is but a sullen child lacking understanding of the world, and you cater to its petulance."

He clenched his teeth, because he knew she was right. "But why won't you tell me how long it must be?"

After a long silence, she answered, "Because I do not want to frighten you."

He turned into her arms and drew her close. The grief of losing her felt suffocating. His throat grew tight with protest against a future he couldn't prevent. "Death holds no sway over me," he whispered. "It is only the years without you that threaten my resolve."

"The better your courage may inspire us, my lord."

He pulled away just enough to take her face in his hands. "It is you who inspires me. Always."

The moon leached the color from the world, and her pale eyes looked like diamonds in the night. She was so beautiful and so infinitely special. In the entire universe, there was no one like her.

Feeling overwhelmed by the future he faced, he pulled her close once more and pressed his cheek against her head. "I am so afraid of losing you for all time."

"That's because you are lacking faith," she teased gently.

"I've seen too much to trust to faith," he heard himself reply. Regret anchored his soul in overpowering seas, and he was drowning from it.

Ean understood then, in the way one suddenly knows things in dreams, that while they shared these moments of stolen peace, in fact a war was raging all around them.

"But you know love," she replied, "and they are of the same cloth."

He sighed. "I would that these were not the moments I'll remember." Though somehow he knew they would be.

"Then love me—love us," she laughed, bringing joy to lighten the space between their hearts. "Never let your doubts obfuscate the truth, my lord," and she pulled away to cup his face with her hand. "That there is hope. That my brother guides us as truly as Polaris calls her sailors home. That these sacrifices will not be for naught."

She lifted herself to kiss him, long and deep. There was no divinity more pure than her kiss. "Stay the course," she whispered then, their lips close, her advice a lover's sweet promise. "Be our inspiration. Lead us, my General. We are all looking to you."

Ean opened his eyes to a grey dawn. Beyond his windows, night yet lingered, clinging heavily to the world, the moon's devoted lover disinclined to depart.

Isabel lay in his arms. Her chestnut hair draped across the pillow they shared, and her eyes were closed beneath the ever-present blindfold. The strip of black silk seemed a torment to him after that dream, a punishment. His soul felt bruised.

A name weighed heavily upon his heart.

Arion Tavestra.

It had been his name, once.

'They say she's loved only one man in all her life.' Julian's words, haunting him now. *'His name was Arion Tavestra. He was one of the First Lord's generals.'*

Ean knew that these were just the first of many memories to surface, sieving through the holes in the veil of death—holes made by other memories already speared forth. But Ean didn't want these memories. They were too painful, too layered with grief. There was an enormous feeling of guilt associated with them, and Ean feared their truth.

Later, as they rose together to greet the day, Isabel sensed Ean's mood but didn't question him on it, only kissed him deeply before she departed. Ean expected she knew his struggles better than he did.

As soon as he could break away from his lessons with Markal, Ean sought out Julian. He hadn't seen the lad since the First Lord's Masquerade, and he missed Julian's effortless company and lightness of spirit.

Ean found him in between lectures—the First Lord was running a veritable Citadel in the lower levels of the palace, with blue-robed Masters, many of them Shades, leading classes and taking on students in advanced studies.

Julian emerged from the lecture to find Ean waiting for him in the back of the hall. His face lit with enthusiasm. "Ean, I'm thrilled to see you!" Julian grabbed him into a hug. "We've just been learning about the Twelfth Law."

"Which one is that?"

Julian quoted at once, "*A pattern need not be perfect, but the wielder's concept of it must be.*"

"Interesting."

"But tell me…" Julian adopted a conspiratorial manner and spun about to ensure they were alone. "Is it true?" He pulled Ean towards an alcove and the hall's tall windows and then launched into a dramatic recounting of everything he'd heard of Ean's relationship with Isabel.

The prince sighed at the stories already circulating—it didn't seem to matter in what realm he dwelled; rumors about him spread like wildfire.

"So it's true," Julian surmised from his pained expression. "You worked a binding of the fifth layered with Form on Epiphany's Prophet."

Ean grimaced, nodded.

Julian's face lit with awe. "Brilliant!"

"Julian," Ean hoped to get them off the topic of his and Isabel's romance. "I wonder if I could call upon your vast knowledge of Adept history,"

"Anything," the lad agreed with a smile.

"What do you know of Arion Tavestra?"

Julian gave him an odd look, but he answered, "He was one of the First Lord's closest friends and a general during the Adept Wars. He sat on the Council of Nine."

The familiar name rang a chord in Ean's memory. "Isabel mentioned them once. What's this council?"

Julian frowned at him, looking genuinely concerned. "They really don't tell you anything, do they?"

Ean gave him a rueful look. "It is important that I remember what I can on my own—which isn't to say you can't offer some aid to that end."

The lad leaned back against the wall and crossed his ankles. "Well…" he regarded Ean uncertainly, "the Council of Nine is the First Lord's war council, but it's more than that. It comprises his closest advisors, those who have been with him since the beginning."

"The beginning of what?"

"I think since they first learned of the threat to Alorin and began planning what to do about it."

Ean frowned. "How long ago was that?"

Julian gave him a wide-eyed look. "A *long* time ago."

"Who sits on the council now?"

Julian scratched at his head and dislodged a tuft of blonde hair to stand on end. "The Council hasn't changed, Ean. Only…"

"Only what?"

"Well…some of the chairs are empty."

"I see." Ean felt that weight descend upon his heart again. "Like Arion Tavestra's?"

"And Malachai's."

Ean held his gaze. "What else? About Arion, I mean."

Julian shifted and crossed arms, narrowing his gaze in thought. "Arion led several of the important battles: Köhentaal, Gimlalai. He was responsible for apprehending the other Vestals and bringing them to T'khendar. And he was at the Citadel when it fell."

Ean's throat felt tight. "How did…he die?"

Julian shook his head. "No one knows—at least, the ones who do know aren't telling. The Battle of the Citadel is shrouded in mystery. As far as the people of Alorin are concerned, the only survivors were the Fifty Companions, and they've been truthbound not to speak of that night. Those of us in T'khendar know that others survived the fall, but they're equally as mum about the whole thing." He frowned suddenly. "But Ean, wouldn't—wouldn't the First Lord just tell you if you asked him?"

"I'm sure he would," Ean muttered grimly. Hearing the truth from the First Lord would be more than he could bear. He gave the lad a weak smile. "Thanks…for answering my questions."

Julian looked concerned. "Ean…" He reached a tentative hand to brush his arm. "You know, it can't be as bad as you think."

Ean grimaced. "How not?"

Julian held his gaze. "It's just…whatever is tormenting you…it's not like they don't already know about it, you know? I mean…whatever it was you think you did, *they* remember. Obviously they've forgiven you."

Ean admitted he had a point. He turned to look out the window and worked the muscles of his jaw. "I think, Julian," he confessed after a long and depressing silence, "I think the problem is that I can't forgive myself."

After leaving Julian, Ean walked aimlessly through the palace, head down and shoulders hunched, hands shoved in his pockets. Seeking answers from another hadn't been such a great idea; the truth was painful no matter how he learned of it.

Eventually his feet brought him to the yard where he most often practiced with Markal. Ean picked up a stick he'd been using as a wand during an earlier lesson and twirled it absently through his fingers.

In their recent training, Markal had been working with him on the use of talismans, as covered in the Seventeenth Law: *The use of talismans must focus force without limiting scope.*

Ean preferred to use his hands when any focal point was required at all, but Markal constantly tried to disabuse him of this inclination, saying it was dangerous.

'*Talismans of themselves may have no power,*' the wielder had explained. '*They merely become a focal point for the channeling of the force. Rather than summoning all of this force and holding it within a nebulous concept of one's own sphere, a wielder channels the force through his talisman.*'

'*But why can't I just be the talisman?*' Ean had argued.

To which Markal had replied critically, '*Because then all of the force of your working has to channel through* you.'

Ean still didn't understand why it was such a problem. Looking at the stick in his hand, he pointed it at the empty air and channeled the second strand through it. The air started spinning in front of him. He altered his intention, layering a pattern of the fifth, and the air became sand. He channeled more energy into the layered pattern, and the vortex tripled in speed, skyrocketing upwards until it was easily a hundred feet high and towering above the courtyard walls.

He changed the concept of his intent, and the sand became a surging geyser of water and cascading spray. *Higher*, he thought with gritted teeth. *Faster.*

Elae flowed into him, focused through his intention into the stick, his talisman, and shot forth to alter the patterns at work. The geyser grew, it spun faster, spraying water across the entire courtyard so that Ean was soon drenched and dripping, and still he forced it to continue.

His head started pounding, and he knew he should stop, but focusing his will required all of his concentration, which meant he had no room for guilt and regret. He deemed a pounding headache was probably worth a few moments of peace.

And then he heard a voice behind him.

"*Ean.*"

The prince released the patterns, letting them expend themselves. A momentary shower of rain pelted him as he turned to face Creighton, dripping and cold and immediately anxious.

"Creighton." He bowed his head, remembering their last encounter and the way he'd so unforgivably slighted his closest friend. "I'm so sorry."

The Shade remained untouched by the water pouring down. "Ean…" Creighton called the prince's gaze back to meet his. "There is nothing you could do that I wouldn't forgive. You're right to feel as you do. I'm not the same man I once was…no matter how we might both wish it so."

Ean heard the regret in his blood-brother's voice, and he realized that they were united in that wish.

"You might not believe me," the Shade said then, managing a slip of a smile, "but I chose this path."

Ean grunted. "You're right—I find that hard to believe."

"Yet I *was* given a choice," Creighton insisted. "It didn't seem like much of one at the time, but as I look back on it now, I see that it was a fair one. I *did* choose to become a Shade when I agreed to keep this form rather than fade from the world. I chose to give my oath freely, and I'm proud of that decision."

Ean gazed at him with profound admiration. "You are where I want very much to be, but I…just can't seem to get there."

Perhaps they were not so different, after all. Both of them had come through death and emerged again, and they'd both had been irrevocably changed by the encounter.

We are none of us the shells we wear.

Suddenly making a decision, Ean reached for his friend. "I'm trying very hard to see *you* beneath the shell you wear," the prince murmured as he held him, feeling agonized by the truth of it. "I beg you be patient with me, my brother."

Creighton hugged Ean in return. "Would you prefer an illusion? I... could work the same illusion I worked in your dreams."

"No, I want to come to know you again in this form. I want only truth."

The Shade in Ean's arms smiled, and for a moment, the man that was Creighton shone brilliantly through. "Take as long as you need, Ean," the words felt a gentle absolution. "There is only eternity before us."

After a moment more, Ean nodded and released Creighton. "Thank you."

The Shade murmured dryly, "Don't mention it." His obsidian gaze swept Ean. Noting his drenched clothing, he arched a silver brow. "Would you like to talk about it?"

"Not especially." Then Ean added with remorse, "But I will...if you want me to."

Creighton motioned for them to walk, and Ean fell in beside him as they traded the courtyard for an arcade of sculpted columns, each one supporting an elaborate arch. "You're battling demons of your own devising," the Shade observed as they walked.

"Very probably," Ean admitted.

Creighton glanced at him out of the corner of his eye. "So much of everything that we deal with is simply happening within ourselves." Seeing Ean's surprise at this wisdom, he explained, "When you share a mind with immortals, you are privy to an immortal's understanding."

Ean admitted the obvious truth in that.

"The First Lord says we limit ourselves by our viewpoints," Creighton said then, "by what we are willing to experience, by what we are willing to let others experience, and by what we are willing to let ourselves believe."

"Belief isn't my problem," the prince muttered.

"Then what is?"

He grimaced. "Courage, perhaps?"

Creighton gave him a curious look. "What is there to fear in your memory, Ean? What's done is done. Nothing you can do will change that. Why not just accept it?"

Ean shook his head. "It's…complicated."

"Is it? Or are you just making it seem so? Regret is just our effort to change the past, but all we're really doing is trying to exert control *now* to make up for our failure to control it at a time when we might've made a difference."

Ean gave his friend a rueful grin. "If only I might've become a Shade, I could be wise like you."

"Don't tease. You have your life. Live it, don't waste it."

"I will if you will promise to do the same."

The Shade turned him a startled look. "And what do you mean by that?"

Ean eyed him speculatively. "I think you know."

"Ahh…" Creighton did not sound pleased.

"If I can see past the shell, Creighton, so can she."

"Katerine," the Shade murmured. He turned Ean a grave look. "Do you really think so?"

"I do."

The Shade sighed wistfully. "I would like to believe it."

"I know this much," the prince offered. "If the situation were reversed, and it was Isabel who waited in Calgaryn for news of me, I wouldn't hesitate. So long as there was breath in me, I would seek to be at her side."

"Wise words," Creighton said, smiling. "Then we have a pact? We shall live our lives and not waste any more time on fear or regret."

Ean turned and extended his hand to the Shade, and they shook on it. But as he took leave of his friend to seek out Isabel, whose presence ever called to him, Ean only hoped the oath would help him find the courage to follow through with his promise.

Raine left Dagmar and Carian to their working, exiting back into the hallway to find the Shade still waiting there—or else newly reappeared. It was hard to know for certain.

"Your Excellency," the Shade greeted him with a bow.

Raine gave him an odd look as he closed the door to Gwynnleth's room. There was something in his face perhaps, or at least in his presence, that called for recognition. "Do I…know you?"

"My name is Creighton," the Shade replied. "Creighton Khelspath, once."

Raine did a double-take. He remembered Prince Ean's letter describing his blood-brother's death, as well as Morin d'Hain's report of his missing body. "You're...Ean val Lorian's *blood-brother*?" The words sounded pathetically shrill.

"I was, once."

Raine still had hold of the door handle and was suddenly grateful for it's sturdy support. He leaned back against the wood as the ramifications of this realization settled into a new pattern. "Björn's Shade didn't slay you as Ean thought," he surmised, reaching the logical conclusion.

"No. The Geishaiwyn assassin did. I was nearly dead when Reyd's power called me forth. My body obeyed his command."

"And there on the plain he made you into a Shade?"

"He claimed my soul for the First Lord," Creighton corrected, "but the later choice to keep this form was my own."

"You are bound to my oath-brother now." It wasn't a question, yet he hoped the Shade would answer him all the same.

"The bond with the First Lord anchors me to this body—my body, though its form has been altered with the fifth to resist the corrosive effects of *deyjiin*."

Raine was fascinated. "Why not heal you?"

"It was too late for healing. There was no one there to heal me, in any case, only Reyd, and we Shades cannot work the first strand. There was no other choice available to my mentor if he meant to save my life. I'm glad he acted as he did. I wasn't ready to move on, to pass through the Extian Doors and take my chances in the Returning."

Raine pushed off the door and started walking down the hallway, and Creighton moved silently at his side. "But why *deyjiin*?" he asked, deep in thought now. Raine was intensely curious to know why Björn had used *deyjiin* to create his Shades—those he'd created since the fall of Tiern'aval— Shades like Anglar.

But for that matter, why had Malachai made them in the first place? Once, Raine had believed there was naught but evil motive behind the deed, but now he suspected else.

No, he suspected *better.* Was he finally finding faith in his oath-brother after all these years, after all that had come before?

It was strange to think so.

Suddenly rousing from this stream of thought, which had occupied him for quite some time, Raine looked to the Shade who was walking patiently at his side. "Were you waiting for me back there?"

"Indeed, Your Excellency. I was asked to accompany you, but you seem already to know where to go."

Raine looked around and saw a pair of carved doors he'd never seen before. Odd that his feet had found their own way to this place. He felt a pang of anxiety, a premonition of what lay beyond. He thought of Ramu's speech on courage and steeled himself for whatever Fate was holding in store for him.

The Shade opened the doors on his behalf and stood aside to let Raine pass. He noted that the creature did not follow him. He could feel the doors closing behind as he made his way down a vaulted corridor. Passing a few other people, who nodded a silent hello, he emerged upon a cloistered garden.

He saw her then, sitting on a bench with her back to him. Waiting.

Raine's heart was suddenly beating too quickly, his breath coming shallowly.

Isabel.

Raine inhaled a deep breath and walked into the courtyard. The grass was soft under his boots, and the roses were still in bloom though midwinter had now passed. Raine imagined roses would bloom for Isabel no matter what time of year it was.

"Come and sit beside me, Raine."

He was still far behind her and walking silently, but there was no hiding from Isabel. He noticed she wore a blindfold, black as night against her fair skin and chestnut hair, and he wondered at it. But he also did as she'd bidden him and sank down onto the bench beside her.

She took his hand, and Raine turned to her. His heart beat faster as he looked upon her face for the first time in three centuries. "Can you see me, Isabel?"

"Of course," she said, smiling. "One does not go blithely blindfolded into the world."

He smiled at her words, but the anguish he felt inside was unmatched. "Isabel..." He dropped his eyes. "When Malachai brought us to T'khendar and we learned about Arion's death, and then when we witnessed that gruesome parade of heads, I thought..." but he couldn't bring himself to say the words now.

It didn't matter, for she knew his mind. "You thought I might've willingly embraced my end to join Arion in the Returning."

His eyes flew to her. "Yes."

"You knew me better than that, I thought."

Raine again dropped his gaze; there was no way he could look at her and give his next confession. "Worse was what we thought of your brother."

"I thought you knew him better than that as well," she chided gently.

"I thought I did, too," he managed a hoarse reply. After a moment, he lifted his eyes to look upon her, though it pained him greatly to do it.

"All this time..." he was appalled by the desperation his tone betrayed. "You've been here helping Björn...since Tiern'aval fell?"

"It has ever been so." She squeezed his hand, which she still held. "We are bound to the same cause for all eternity, my brother and I. There can be no other game for me but my brother's game, wherever it leads."

Raine looked away and clenched his jaw. Hearing it from her lips...he could ill deny how wrong they'd been—about everything. "Alshiba mourned you more than any other," he said after a moment, too weak-hearted to take up deeper matters.

"Wasted tears. Better they were shed over the years lost between what has been and what must be, or not shed at all and her attentions put to proper focus. My brother has not denied himself her company for three centuries that she might spend them mourning those who were neither lost nor in need of her compassion."

"Then why has he?"

Her eyes were bound, yet still her gaze chastised him. "Because it was necessary, Raine."

"For the good of the realm?" He heard the cynicism in his tone and inwardly cringed at it.

"If you deny still that my brother works for the good of all, then there is little hope for you." She cupped his cheek with her hand and adding more kindly, "But I do not think that is so."

Raine stared into her blindfolded eyes, knowing she saw him clearly, that the cloth was no barrier to their connection, and he tried to rein in the imminent sense of doom that had him in thrall.

Raine D'Lacourte considered himself a good man. He tried to be fair and just, honest in his dealings. He tried to consider more than the good of a few. But what truly speared him—what had shaken him to the core and kept him lying awake in the bitter hours each night since coming to T'khendar— was wondering if he was a good enough man to admit that the Fifth Vestal was a better man still.

A groan escaped him. "Isabel," her name sounded like a fiercely whispered prayer, "when you believed a man had betrayed everything that you shared between you, and when you consequently vilified him for three hundred years..." He squeezed her hand tightly, drawing strength from her touch, took a deep breath and continued, "How do you reconcile such a thing once you learn it was..." —*gods above* it was so hard to say!— "... wrongfully done?"

She cupped his hand with both of hers then and leaned to plant a tender kiss upon his cheek. "With a little faith, all else shall become clear."

"Faith," he growled as she sat back again. "It has never been my strong suit."

"Yes, we've noticed that about you."

"Isabel—" but he cut off his own words, for the force of another man's thoughts suddenly silenced him.

In the same moment, Isabel's lips spread in an exquisite smile that brought such a radiance to her face, it alone might have silenced Raine. "Come join us, Ean," she said into the garden at large.

Raine turned on the bench just as a man stepped around a column. The Vestal recoiled at both recognizing Ean val Lorian and realizing it was he who was exuding such fierce thoughts of protection and possessiveness towards Isabel.

More startling still was seeing how the fifth-strand currents surged and collected around Ean, awaiting his command. These perceptions defied Raine's comprehension. He could not be facing a youth newly born to his gift. These were the workings of a wielder in the prime of his understanding.

Raine stared, trying desperately to make sense of what he was seeing, and that's when it registered...

"Oh gods above." The knowledge sent him to his feet.

Suddenly it all made perfect sense. Björn sending a Shade and his zanthyr to protect an inconsequential prince was incomprehensible, but to do so in order to protect one of his generals newly Returned...

Of course he'd had to keep a long arm for the sake of Balance, but Björn would go to any lengths to reclaim one of his generals, and especially Arion Tavestra, the eternal soulmate of his sister Isabel.

Raine pushed both hands to his hair and stared at Ean.

As the tensely charged moment seemed likely to draw out indefinitely, Isabel rose and extended her hand to Ean. He came to her side and offered his arm that she might rest her hand upon it.

"Ean, I believe you know Raine D'Lacourte," Isabel murmured with benign amusement, all but laughing at the both of them. "Raine," she said then, "I believe you know Ean as well. Perhaps I should leave the two of you to—"

"No!" they both exclaimed with equal heat.

Isabel attempted to suppress her smile and failed miserably, though Raine suspected she didn't try very hard. "Hmm..." she turned from one to the other of them. "This is...intriguing."

Raine summoned his composure. "Ean, it is good to see you well," he managed, meaning it—much to his own surprise. "I see that you've reunited with Isabel, and...and I'm happy for you."

Ean seemed to relax somewhat, but the currents still surged around him.

After a moment, Isabel murmured, "Perhaps you might release the fifth, my darling, as a show of faith in Raine's veracity."

Ean looked to her blankly, and Raine realized then just how much danger he was in. Ean was so enwrapped in the fifth that he might've snuffed Raine like a candle with the least provocation, at the slightest misstep towards Isabel.

And if Ean feels thusly towards her, imagine what her own brother must feel!

Suddenly the idea of Björn allowing any harm to come to Isabel became utterly unimaginable. How could he and Alshiba have been so deceived, so misled by their own hurt and confusion? How could they have let themselves forget everything they knew to be true about these dear friends, whom they'd once respected so deeply?

Raine resurfaced from these thoughts to notice with some relief that Ean had finally released the fifth.

"I'm...sorry," Ean said then, clearly meaning it.

Raine shook his head, his diamondine gaze serious and thoughtful. "We have both come through a long journey to reach this moment, I suspect. But we're not at odds, Ean. Not anymore."

Ean nodded, and Raine saw a darkness leave his gaze. "I'm relieved to know that. It has been...difficult, this feeling that I betrayed everyone."

Raine regarded him soberly. "I suspect the others will have to work through their own confusions, even as we continue to do." He looked to Isabel and gave her a grateful look. As painful as it had been, there was edification in confessing one's heart to Epiphany's Prophet.

Isabel preempted his next statement by saying, "You must go to him, Raine."

"I know." Raine shifted his gaze, jaw clenched. "I have an idea where I might find him."

"I expect that you do."

Thus did Raine take his leave of Isabel van Gelderan and her true love, and although the encounter had been shocking and painful and altogether uncomfortable, as he left the cloister, Raine felt a lightness of spirit that he hadn't known since before Tiern'aval fell.

Carian walked in dreamscape. Somewhere on the vast distant plain, Dagmar worked his talent, weaving the pirate into the blank canvas of the realm of dreams. Now that he'd arrived, however, Carian wasn't sure what to do. Dagmar had explained that the closer Carian got to Gwynnleth's dreams, the more the world would assume focus, but right now Carian saw only formless mist.

"Birdie!" he called for lack of anything better to say. "Oh, birdie!"

In the silence that followed, Carian tried not to feel the fool. It wasn't that he had any great love of the avieth—or so he told himself—but she was...well, special. Anyone could see that. She didn't deserve an end like this. The avieth was a warrior—Carian had seen that in her from the moment of their first meeting—and no warrior should be left to wither and die in their dreams.

Plus she was courageous, and passable smart…and she had a *really* nice ass.

"Birdie!" he called again, smiling at the appellation he'd created for her. He thought it entirely apt, though she seemed to deplore it vehemently, which only made him use it all the more. "Come, my captivating canary!"

The mist drifted endlessly before his vision, revealing nothing.

Carian took a break from calling her to snarl a few curses. This improved his mood considerably, so he tried again. "Birdie! Now listen up, little bird, my cock-loving cockatiel…I know you're desirous of my loins now. Don't be shy! You can watch me banging the lizard tonight if you come now, little lovebird."

Silence again, but Carian thought he could just make out a mountain in the distance. He took it as a good sign and tried again. And again.

And again.

Though time lengthened, gradually Carian began to see shapes in the fog, and it heartened him, emboldened him—as if he needed such encouragement—so he persisted through the endless hours despite feeling utterly foolish shouting into the mist.

"Birdie!" Carian called for the thousandth time as if it was the first. "Oh, Biiirdeee! Where are you, chickadee? Come to your master now, sweet parakeet. Biiirdeee! Oh biiiiiir-deeeee…"

"Hello, Islander."

Carian spun, and the world exploded into vivid color and shape.

Gwynnleth stood before him with one ginger brow arched.

The pirate let out a whoop and grabbed her up, pinning her arms at her sides and swung her around, ignoring utterly her raging, indignant protests.

As Raine made his way to the Hall of Games, he reflected on the irony of all that had come to pass. This was far from the reunion he'd so often imagined, where he overcame Björn through strategy and righteousness and Balance chose his side for once; where he brought the Fifth Vestal in shackles before the Council of Realms to answer for all of the crimes Raine and Alshiba had attributed to him. Raine pushed a hand through his hair and shook his head. How far he'd come on this journey…how far he'd yet to travel.

But that he'd traveled any distance at all was largely thanks to Isabel.

Ironic, Raine thought again. He did know faith after all. He knew faith in Isabel, and recognizing faith in any form had somehow allowed him to know other sides of it, too.

He still didn't understand why Björn and Malachai had created T'khendar, but he was willing now, much to his own amazement, to trust that small bit to faith—that Björn *did* have a reason for creating this world, and it was nothing so petty as having his own realm to rule. Nor had he done it simply to show he could—two of the many suppositions Raine and Alshiba had entertained.

No, whatever the reason for T'khendar's creation, it had to have been essential to Alorin's survival.

The truth seemed so simply grasped now. Why couldn't he have seen it three centuries ago? What a bitter pill to swallow, that while he could easily sense the truth in others, this one had eluded him completely.

The recurring irony galled him.

Absorbed with self-abasements, Raine walked through the Hall of Games, barely noticing anyone else in the vast room, and headed out onto the balcony where he'd spent the Solstice with the *drachwyr*.

That had been an unexpected kindness on Björn's part, though to be sure there had been purpose in it too. Björn never did anything without purpose stacked nine layers thick.

The day was uncommonly warm and humid, the air heavy and saturated with the promise of rain. Laying his hands upon the railing and gazing out over the deep valley, Raine saw a storm building in the south—a massive wall of charcoal clouds was pouring over the near mountains and heading their way. For the first time, Raine observed the world through a different pair of eyes, seeing it for an incredible accomplishment instead of a shocking affront.

Still...it only followed that such a display of power and skill would frighten the very souls out of people.

"*Why...?*" Raine whispered desperately to the world. "Why did he create you?"

But T'khendar kept Björn's secret close.

"This is my favorite view." Björn came to stand beside Raine.

Even having expected he would come, Raine still started at his arrival.

The Fifth Vestal settled hands on the carved stone railing, and Raine noted his oath-ring sparkling in the muted light of the rising storm. He wondered if it might be more pure of color than his own.

His eyes moved upwards from the ring, past Björn's sky blue jacket to his face in profile, to his patrician features, strong lines framing straight nose, cheekbone and jaw...and finally to his eyes, cobalt blue and gazing earnestly upon the world he had created—for there was no doubt in Raine's mind but that T'khendar was wholly Björn's creation, despite Malachai's being blamed for it.

His oath-brother felt a quiet force beside him, focused and still, harboring all the latent power of a calm ocean at dawn. Raine was surprised to realize he'd missed the familiar—if intimidating—feel of his oath-brother's presence. He hadn't looked upon the Fifth Vestal in three hundred years, yet Björn didn't seem to have changed at all. There was something profound to Raine in that realization.

Things were changing for him...shifting...realigning seemingly without his consent. Some of the threads of the pattern he'd held so inviolate had unraveled all the way back to their origins.

Raine turned back to the view, swallowed. He clenched his jaw against the force of his own feelings, for centuries of thoughts, confusions, frustrations and betrayals churned in the cauldron of his conscience.

That he could stand shoulder to shoulder with his oath-brother at all and honestly not want to kill him was incredible. That he could be there willingly wearing the mantle of his own guilt was beyond the impossible. Yet there they both stood.

Words failed him.

"The mountains were Cristien's idea." Björn glanced at Raine, who met his gaze but for the flash of a moment and still felt pierced by it. "Malachai didn't have an artistic eye."

Raine forced himself to take a deep breath and let it out slowly. Then he asked with careful regard, "Was it all of you, this creation? Everyone on the Council of Nine?"

"It would be unfair to say otherwise. Certainly one man alone couldn't have harnessed the necessary forces, nor conceived of so many disparate and vast patterns within his own single consciousness. It took all of us, and it was still far from perfect."

"It looks fairly perfect now," Raine startled himself by saying.

Björn turned him a smile, and their eyes met again. Met and held, and more passed between them than ever might've been spoken aloud. "That must've been hard to say," Björn offered gently.

Raine grunted and looked back to the view. "You cannot be surprised to know your plan accomplished its purpose. I'm not the same man who passed through the node a fortnight ago."

"If you were, I would be supremely disappointed. But I can't take credit for bringing you here. Isabel demanded it."

Raine blinked in surprise.

"Not much escapes my sister. I am too often praised—or vilified—for what is only her brilliance."

These words touched closely upon a painful truth, and Raine looked back to the view with deep feelings of regret battling to claim him now. "Why didn't you trust me?" The question came out quite against his own volition, colored by hurt and anger, spurred by bitter confusion.

Björn gave him a look of grave apology. "It was never a matter of trust, Raine. It was a matter of understanding you, of knowing what *you* could believe. It was simply application of the Fifth Law." He gripped the railing and turned Raine a concerned frown. "How long did it take you to accept that Malorin'athgul had come into Alorin?"

"Too long," Raine admitted grimly.

"And how willing would you have been to accept it when they were but a shadow darkening the horizon?"

He didn't have to answer that; it was obvious.

Jaya had the right of it. Raine hated himself for his own evident shortcomings, for his failure to take a view broad enough that he might've gained Björn's trust before now.

"But it's also application of the Eleventh Esoteric," Björn added. "A wielder is limited by what he can envision *himself* envisioning—so says the Eleventh Esoteric. This Esoteric should never be confused with the Fifth Law, for they are very different. *A wielder is limited by what he can envision...* applying the Fifth Law, a wielder might envision any manner of things and be great in his application, but he will yet be limited in his *scope* if he considers that any effect lies outside of his ability...if he considers the reach of his power to be *limited* in some way."

Björn turned to face Raine and leaned his hip against the railing. "Take Malachai." He opened his palms to the view and the storm now blowing in over them, while his blue eyes held Raine's gaze captive. "Malachai was not limited in what he could envision. He could envision an entire world, could he not? And make no mistake of it, Raine, Malachai was the focal point for this working—through him, we channeled it all. Yet he was limited in what he could envision *himself* envisioning. He could see a great city, but he could only imagine it formed of the bedrock of the world. He could see a great sky, but it was boiling with the ash of volcanoes newborn. What reason not to raise Niyadbakir already formed of alabaster? If he could create it at all, it follows that he could create it of any stone, does it not?"

Raine nodded, holding his gaze, hearing more than just this story—an entire undercurrent of explanation, of reasoning, of belief.

"Malachai was limited only by what he could envision *himself* envisioning. He was limited in that he thought the scope of his ability was limited. This is the true message of the Eleventh Esoteric."

Raine drew in a deep breath and let it out slowly. Here was a man whom he'd vilified for three hundred years, and instead of laying blame, instead of requiring Raine's contrition...instead, here Björn was trying to help him understand that Raine hadn't failed him at all.

He looked out over the valley and clenched his jaw. Tears came unbidden, brimmed and fell, the first drops of the coming storm.

He thought of the thousands of times he'd spoken out against Björn, of the heinous things he'd accused him of. He thought of all the people who believed Björn van Gelderan was a traitor—in no small part due to Raine's own account of but one side of that coin. Truly—Björn had told them nothing, and perhaps he had some culpability in his lack of explanation—but the bulk of the defamatory content had been created by Raine and Alshiba in their attempts to craft explanation out of the inexplicable—and of course, they'd supposed the worst.

Even though their conscience had been whispering otherwise for three hundred years.

Who then was the traitor here in truth? Björn, who continued his courageous work in care of the realm, or Raine D'Lacourte, who was undermining his every step with seditious rumors and false claims?

"What makes a good man, Raine?" Björn was gazing up at the clouds with a slight furrow between his brows. "Is it in the way he treats others? Is it his generosity or compassion? Is it his good work? You're a truthreader; you know men's minds. Do these things make men good?"

Raine brusquely wiped his eyes. "I don't know." He felt only the heavy weight of guilt suffocating him.

"I believe such traits do comprise a good man," Björn observed, "but in my view, a *great* man needs but one truly notable attribute."

Raine fought back the clenching feeling in his chest to ask hoarsely, "Which is?"

"The willingness to claim responsibility for things he didn't cause."

For some reason, this made Raine have to work even harder to hold back his grief. "Brother..." he whispered wretchedly, lifting his eyes in the last to meet Björn's, "I have wronged you so."

"No more than I wronged you, Raine."

But Raine knew this was untrue. He bowed his head and clenched his jaw, feeling threadbare and tawdry beneath the Fifth Vestal's observation.

"This contrition is unnecessary, Raine." Björn took him by the shoulders and drew him into an embrace. "Don't you think I have regrets? I can't begin to list them all." He squeezed Raine's shoulders and drew away, capturing his tormented gaze. "But we simply haven't the time for regret. Every day is a new day, a new choice, a new beginning. This is the essence of Adendigaeth, which we've just observed. This idea that tomorrow brings another chance to live life anew, no matter what has come before."

"Yes," Raine whispered. "That is true."

Thunder sounded above them, deep and hollow, the cracking open of the very heavens to emit the rain. It started as a downpour and quickly deepened to a deluge, and before they'd even raised their eyes, they were drenched.

"What say you to this game, brother?" Björn asked as the rain pelted them and thunder sounded again, close overhead. "Will you join me in it?"

Raine never imagined in all his life that he would've said yes.

But he did.

FORTY-ONE

"Neighboring kings, like truthreaders and spies, cannot be trusted."
– Radov abin Hadorin, Ruling Prince of M'Nador

GYDRYN VAL LORIAN, King of Dannym, stood at the edge of a marble table staring at the vellum in his hand. He was alone in his chambers in Radov's palace—as alone as he could be with fifty knights surrounding his rooms—but he dared take no chances, not since the bird from Morin d'Hain had found them aboard the *Sea Eagle* a day north of Tal'Shira.

Gydryn looked at the letter from Morin one last time, recalling fully the words scribed upon it. Dangerous words, laying waste to a litany of lies. Yet they'd been few words, in truth: the whisper of a long-standing alliance between Morwyk and Radov had reached Morin's ears as a result of Kjieran van Stone's efforts in Tambarré. Morin hadn't conclusive proof, and the information had come second-hand, funneled through intermediaries loyal to Raine D'Lacourte, but Morin believed it.

In his heart, Gydryn did as well.

Morin's missive had eschewed the usual deductions for purposes of brevity, but Gydryn didn't need an exhaustive summary to reach the same conclusions as his Spymaster. And if the information Morin had given him was accurate, then only one conclusion truly mattered: the Akkadian Emir Zafir bin Safwan al Abdul-Basir was not his enemy.

Radov was.

It was an acerbic truth, one that brought a foul turbulence to his stomach and a lingering ache to his heart. Perhaps he'd known it all along. His wife, Errodan, had often cautioned him that good men shied away from seeing the evil in others. Gydryn knew he was culpable in this failing, guilty of being too lenient, too merciful towards those who sought power; guilty of the hubris inherent in believing that treason and betrayal were not the bywords of *his* noble houses.

But there was no doubting that Radov needed Dannym's army. If his deductions were correct, and Gydryn believed they were, then Radov had gone to great lengths to bolster his war with Dannym's forces. Gydryn was not so foolish as to imagine that the ruling prince would now just let them all leave.

Steps would have to be taken, necessary sacrifices. He wouldn't allow Radov to take control of his army, and he most certainly was not going to let Stephan val Tryst have his kingdom—for whatever else was certain, should the Duke of Morwyk march to power, the Prophet Bethamin would be riding on his train.

Lowering his hand with Morin's dangerous missive crumpled within it, Gydryn walked towards a wall of screen doors carved of honey-hued wood, which opened upon a balcony and the sea. The water reflected a strange color in this far southern princedom, a startling turquoise that rapidly faded to azure blue, so different from the charcoal seas of his home. The king leaned against the doorframe, his grey-eyed gaze deeply troubled as he looked to the east, his thoughts snared by the Prophet...even as an alarming number of his subjects had been.

Dannym's peoples embraced many faiths. The Highlanders of Iverness worshipped a panoply of earth gods and goddesses, spirits and sprites, paying homage to trees and rivers and standing stones. They always seemed about some festival or another that involved dancing half-naked and burning boughs of stinking herbs for who knew what purpose. Gydryn didn't understand their faith, but it seemed to keep them happy.

His wife's people believed strongly in the Storm God and his Concubine, and the peoples of the southlands followed the Veneisean Virtues as often as their own Lord of Crows and Sparrows. In Calgaryn and its surrounding duchies, the folk mainly followed the old ways of their Agasi forefathers who'd founded the kingdom centuries ago, a faith closest to the Adept religion espoused in the *Sobra I'ternin*.

All of these faiths and more besides, disparate though they were, had somehow coexisted harmoniously in his kingdom, its peoples tolerating each other, often laughing at the others' 'odd' rituals, but never condemning them. Until now.

Bethamin was a scourge upon the realm. His religion seemed antipathetic to faiths of all kinds, appealing instead to men's baser instincts, and his doctrine sowed distrust and malcontent among all who followed it. Gydryn wouldn't condone such filth in his kingdom.

Returning to his marble desk, the king set one corner of Morin's missive over a low-burning candle and watched the flame take. Holding the paper while it burned, his grey eyes observed the inked letters as they spread and vanished, overtaken by wings of blackening flame. If only the lies those words indicated might be so easily dispelled.

Gydryn set the charred paper onto a silver dish, poured a clear liquor upon it, and set the candle to the spirit. Flames seared upwards, and heat washed the pepper-grey hair of his beard as the charred paper burned to ash. When only a tarry sludge remained, the king wiped the dish clean with a scrap of linen and tossed the latter onto the smoldering coals in the hearth.

Gydryn saw his own kingdom facing such a charred and blackened end if Morwyk took power. He'd lain awake long hours into the night, every night as they'd sailed south, the steady rush of waves past the hull too often seeming the muted roar of burning flames, the creaking of masts and rigging the steady disintegration of his kingdom.

Before Morin's missive reached him, he and Loran val Whitney had spent long hours behind locked doors—hours spent, in the main, arguing. The Duke of Marion had strong views, and their decades-long friendship made him bold in declaring them.

"I do nae like it, Sire," Loran had protested. He was a big man, like most of his Highland brethren, broad of chest, with a mane of black hair striped through with grey, and fierce blue eyes that often flashed as sharply as the kingdom blade that was ever present at his hip. He seemed a caged bear even in the generous space of the *Sea Eagle's* royal cabin. "We shouldna' be goin' back there—should nae be sacrificin' our brothers to the insatiable greed of a craven bastard like Radov abin Hadorin."

"What would you have me do?" Gydryn had repeatedly growled in return, so often sunk into a low-slung armchair, the vantage giving him a view of the Fire Sea beyond the cabin's mullioned windows. It was that or watch Loran pace restlessly back and forth until his head began to ache. "*Shade and darkness*, Loran, would you have me break a pact that has held three kingdoms together for centuries?"

"Yea, Sire, if ye must."

"I'm not prepared to do that."

"By the bloodless horns of Herne, ye'll lose yer kingdom if ye can't find some compromise with yer honor! It'll drag ye down to the depths and the rest of us w'ye—cause ye know we shan't be abandonin' ye, even to the ends of the realm!"

"A king with no honor is a stain upon his kingdom, Loran."

"A kingdom with no rightful king stands a barren shore, Sire."

And so it had gone, round and round, neither of them gaining purchase against the other's views. All day in argument with his General of the East, all night in conference with his conscience. He found no peace in any quarter.

And then, after a month of these contentious deliberations, Morin's bird had found them, and all of those hours, all of those words, became moot.

He'd told Loran nothing of the letter—the Duke of Marion was already raring to leave M'Nador, and Gydryn dared not give him room or reason to make a press. No, they couldn't just withdraw their forces from the princedom, withdraw their support of Radov—not without more bloodshed. Gydryn understood this too well.

Resting one hand on the carved limestone mantel in Radov's palace, the king chose an ivory-handled poker and nudged the piece of linen back onto the coals.

How had his life come to this?

Once he'd had three strong sons, a loving wife and queen who held his heart in thrall, a kingdom at peace. What sinister spirit had plucked the thread of his life from its pleasant pattern and rewoven it elsewhere among the strands of iniquitous men? What crossroad had he chosen that his path became so darkly treacherous, so full of treason and dishonor that he lost two of his beloved sons upon it and must needs sacrifice the companionship of his wife to protect his third? What gods had he angered that they exacted such vengeance upon his house?

The questions were endless, but the answers…well, there were no answers to the questions of why. There was only the *what*. What he would do. What he could do. What he must do.

Gydryn replaced the poker in its place and returned to the marble desk. Another letter remained there, blotted and dry. His personal seal pressed in wax beneath his signature marked the letter as an authentic statement in his own hand.

He'd written some strange things upon that page, unexpected things… the kind of things a man writes when he anticipates death over the next rise. He'd addressed the letter to a man he'd met only once, but he trusted the captain to do his duty.

A knock sounded on his door. Gydryn looked up as two soldiers entered. The first wore the red livery of his personal guard and stood crisply at attention. The second wore a short-sleeved hauberk over linen and looked travel-worn and battle-stained. Baldric and belt displayed the val Lorian eagle engraved in the leather, while the man's tanned skin bespoke long hours beneath the relentless Nadori sun.

"The Captain Jasper val Renly, Sire," announced the king's personal guard, "at your request."

"Thank you, Daniel. Please send for Loran now."

Daniel bowed and left, closing the door.

The king observed the captain's exhausted state. "Come, Jasper, break your fast with me." He motioned the soldier into a sunlit room. A meal waited his pleasure on a table draped in fine linen, but Gydryn's appetite had abandoned him in the Fire Sea. He offered the meal to his captain instead. "You rode through the night?" he asked as he indicated Jasper to take a chair.

"Yes, Sire. As soon as your missive reached me." He seemed at first reluctant to sit and eat and shifted on his feet, but hunger proved more insistent than propriety. He moved his sword aside with the familiarity of a man long used to its companionship and sat down.

The king rested one hand on the back of a chair across from the captain. "How far is it to your camp, Jasper?"

"Twenty miles or so, Sire, as the crow flies." Having yielded to his urges, he shoveled food onto his plate now with a sort of desperate eagerness. "But the mountains never let a man keep a straight line."

Gydryn noted the bright creases at Jasper's eyes, the result of long days spent squinting into the sun. "Loran says you've been a strong leader in his name and a great support to the men."

"Thank you, Sire."

"He said also that you've traveled to every stronghold east of Kandori and know these lands well."

"Aye, Sire, as well as any of us can. His Grace sent me often to relay his orders to our outposts, and I've traveled with Radov's scouts to learn the lay of the land. The prince's army is spread thin, and his hold over Abu'dhan is ever threatened. The duke has deployed certain battalions in support of strategic positions, but our army ranges along the entire front."

"Indeed," Gydryn murmured while quietly watching the captain eat. "Loran outlined to me the deployment of our forces. They seem well scattered."

"Aye, that's Raine's truth, Sire," Jasper mumbled through a mouthful. "We've men all along the Qar'imali augmenting Radov's main army, as well at Dar'ibu and Chamaal. We've a sizable force in Taj al'Jahanna, though they're naught but baking their heads waiting for someone to put an arrow in those bloody dragons and break the impasse. Or, I suppose, if something comes of this parley..."

Gydryn arched a raven brow. "You are not hopeful, Captain?"

Jasper grimaced. He sat back in his chair and settled hands in his lap. "Forgive me, Sire. I forget my place."

"I would know your thoughts."

Jasper lifted his gaze to his king, eyes brown beneath a shock of sun-streaked hair. He reminded Gydryn very much of his younger brother, the Lieutenant Bastian val Renly, another trusted soldier who was even then risking his life to protect Gydryn's last surviving son.

Epiphany watch over you in the Cairs, Ean.

"'Tis a strange war, Sire, if you require my mind upon the matter," Jasper offered reluctantly. "We've all heard stories from our fathers of the wars of the past, wars fought in defense of king and kingdom..." He ran a finger absently along the linen scarf lining the top edge of his hauberk, the skin beneath it chafed and sunburned. It seemed the absent gesture of a man long inured to inconsequential discomforts. "Mayhap I'm far off the mark, but it seems ill policy for a ruling prince to let men pillage and plunder in his own kingdom."

Gydryn exhaled a slow breath. "You speak of the Saldarian mercenary forces." This was but one of many troubling details he'd learned upon arrival in Tal'Shira.

"Aye. My men and I...we've seen horrors to be sure, Sire—a soldier learns to bear witness and still take his evening meal when it comes—but there's rightful pillage and then there's delight in the killing, and Belloth take me if I'm wrong, but these Saldarians..." He shook his head. "They respect nothing."

The king considered him quietly. "And the men...how is their morale?"

"They remain loyal to you, Sire, but not a one would choose to fight this war."

Gydryn exhaled resignedly. "That might be said of any war, Captain, even those bearing the standard of righteous motive." He gave Jasper a sage look of resignation. "Once the novelty of retribution wears thin, war is just what it seems: a brutal and ugly stain upon the consciences of men."

"Yes, Sire." Jasper dropped his gaze.

The king walked towards the open balcony doors, trailing one hand along the tabletop. "Tell me, Jasper...what outpost might you know of, something far away and no longer in use, yet it would have a defensible position?" He glanced at the captain over his shoulder. "Is there such a place?"

Jasper furrowed brows and chewed absently through an almond-flour biscuit as he considered the king's question. After a moment, he brightened. "I believe there is a place, Sire. Nahavand. It lies in the mountains northwest of Taj al'Jahanna. The Nadori forces abandoned it many moons ago."

"Abandoned, yet it remains defensible?"

"Very much so, Sire. There just wasn't any point in maintaining Nahavand, because the Sundragons made it useless as an outpost—'tis too easy for the damnable creatures to pick off soldiers and supply lines coming to and from the fortress."

The king considered him. "In the northwest. Is it close to Taj al'Jahanna?"

"No, Sire. The only way to reach it is straight north through the Pass of Ryohim and then head due west. It lies deadly close to the western lines."

"Just so?"

"Aye, that's part of the problem with its location, Sire. After the Emir's forces gained Raku, they forged north, ousting errant Nadoriin. The Nadori consider the fortress lost behind the lines, but to my knowledge the Basi haven't claimed the outpost."

"Is it well known by the men? Would Loran know it?"

"I don't think so, Sire. We've never had men stationed there."

"Can you draw me a map to Nahavand, Jasper?"

"Certainly, Sire." He pushed back from the table.

"No, no," Gydryn raised a hand to stay him. "Finish your meal."

He walked to the other room and retrieved paper, ink and quill. Returning and laying these next to the captain, Gydryn nodded to the materials. "The map now, Jasper...be as detailed as you can."

Jasper drew the map as requested, taking care with important landmarks and making meticulous notations. Looking over the map when the captain had finished, the king found it quite suitable. "This is well drawn, captain." He glanced up under raven brows. "You've a nice hand and a good eye for detail."

"Thank you, Sire." Jasper looked a bit uncomfortable with the praise.

The king folded the map and slipped it inside his vest. "Come," he said gravely then. "I have new orders for you." He returned to the other room and the missive waiting upon the marble desk. This he extended to the soldier.

Arching a curious brow, Jasper took the parchment and looked it over. Immediately his eyes widened and his tanned face went slack. When he'd finished reading all of it, he lifted uncertain brown eyes to his king. "Sire?"

"We shall seal it now." Gydryn took the parchment back from Jasper, folded the letter carefully, and then used the little candle to melt another blot of dark blue wax over the joining, pressing his signet ring in the last to seal it. This done, he extended the letter back to the solider. "Your orders, Captain."

To his credit, Jasper pulled himself together smartly. "Sire!" He pushed his fist hard across his chest and bowed his head. Then he spun on his heel and departed to his task.

"Godspeed, Captain," the king murmured as another guard was closing the door behind the soldier.

It wasn't long before Loran val Whitney arrived. Time enough for the king to pen orders for the Duke of Marion and prepare his thoughts for the storm ahead.

The guardsman Daniel escorted Gydryn's General of the East into his chambers with the announcement, "The Duke of Marion, your Majesty."

"Sire," said the duke as Daniel was closing the door behind him. "Hell of a morning."

"Trouble, General?"

"The usual mischief from men too long idle." Loran spied the table in the other room and cast Gydryn an inquiring look.

"By all means." The king held out a hand in offering of his table.

Loran stalked over eagerly. He shrugged out of his baldric and the kingdom blade it held and hooked it on the back of his chair. Then he slung one leg over the seat and planted himself upon it.

As Loran was dishing food onto his plate, the king reflected on the challenge inherent in sharing a room with him—the duke's imposing frame claimed more than its share of space, and his personality took up the rest.

"I'm relieved to hear the men are anxious for action," the king said as Loran set to attacking his plate full of food, "for I've a task for them, and you."

"Milk of the Mother!" Loran shoved a pastry brown with cinnamon and sticky with honey into his mouth and washed it down with steaming tea. "Have they called the parley at last?"

Gydryn settled into a chair at the table's head and murmured, "Jasper val Renly came to see me earlier this morning."

"Thirteen bloody hells, fer what possible purpose? The man knows to find me with any report."

"No, I asked to see him, to hear from a soldier on the state of our men."

"Their state is bloody damned ready to leave this hot-as-Belloth's-fiery-black-arse desert."

"I gather that is evidently your state of mind, Loran."

"Ye'r damned right it is." Loran banging a fist on the table, making the china chink. "Say the word, Sire, and we're right behind you."

The king eyed him soberly. He'd known Loran since childhood, and he trusted no man more, but he dared not share his plans even with the duke. As he spoke his next words, he reflected how easily lies crossed the tongue when a man thought them justified.

"Jasper told me there have been recent skirmishes at Nahavand."

"Nahavand…" Loran repeated, frowning. "Nahavand. Not sure I know it."

"It's an important stronghold against the Basi incursion in the northwest. Jasper told me the Akkadian forces have been pushing north from Raku. Radov can't lose Nahavand, Loran. It would be disastrous—an opening right into Kandori."

Loran wiped his bearded mouth and tossed his napkin onto the table. "All right. We can redeploy—"

"No, my old friend. The importance of this stronghold needs your hand upon its defense. I need you to go to Nahavand personally, take command of the forces there and fortify the outpost. You must make it defensible, Loran, and fortify it well. It will play a vital role in the coming conflict."

The king leaned elbows upon the table and clasped hands before him. Val Lorian grey eyes pinned the duke intently as Gydryn added with grave certainty, "I trust no one but you with this task."

Loran sat back in his chair and frowned at his king. He seemed to be waiting for more, expecting more, for he had a suspicious glint in his sharp blue eyes.

He was right to expect so, for Gydryn then laid the final straw. "You will take forty of my knights—"

Loran exploded out of his chair. "Begging Yer Majesty's pardon, but are ye out of yer bloody mind!"

"Ten knights should prove sufficient protection for me," the king returned evenly, his position firm against the onrush of Loran's protest. "Or perhaps you think the Emir's reach so vast as to strike me down even here, deep in the Palace of Tal'Shira?"

Loran flung out an arm towards the nebulous west, growling, "Tis nae the damned Basi I'm concerned with!"

Gydryn sat back in his chair. "Who then?"

Loran leaned both hands on the table to pin his king with a fiery look. "Sire, ye can't trust Radov." He dropped his voice suddenly, smoldering and low. "And you *certainly* can't trust hal'Jaitar. There's Bethamins everywhere in Tal'Shira, Saldarians picking their teeth with the bones of Radov's own people…" Abruptly he spun away and stalked about the room, spinning the king a heated glare as he snarled under his breath, "In the three moons I've been away, it's grown worse than when I left!"

Gydryn settled hands in his lap and considered the duke. He would've liked to tell him how right he was, to validate the man's keen perceptions with what little truth they possessed, and he longed to share with him what he planned.

But he knew that should he do so, the man would never go through with the plan. Such was the lonesome province of kings: keeping secrets even from those whose loyalty would never be in question.

"An honest man requires proof before he declares his allies enemies, Loran," Gydryn remarked with furrowed brow.

"An yer honest man dies with a knife in his back the same as a dishonest one," the duke returned brusquely.

"I will not forsake my honor, Loran, nor the honor of my kingdom."

"Is it honor?" The pacing duke cast the king a caustic eye. "Cause it stinks more like pride."

Gydryn's expression darkened. "Loran, you go too far."

"Not nearly far enough!" The duke flung a hand in a southerly direction. "Loyal men are fightin' and dyin' in this wretched place fer sake of yer honor—fer Raine's truth, 'tis nae other righteous purpose that keeps us here!"

"Be that as it may—"

"Tell me ye don't see it!" Loran turned back and slammed his palms down on the table. He dropped his voice again and growled with a desperate plea in his gaze, "It's nae just the palace, Gydryn. The whole bloomin' city reeks of wrongness."

"I claim no disagreement with you, Loran." He had to give the duke that much, and it was evident to anyone with an eye to the truth that a darkness had descended upon Tal'Shira.

The king's agreement seemed to mollify Loran somewhat. He turned away again, and his pacing became calmer. "It's like we're livin' in a bloody den of vipers!" He shot the king a glare expressing his grave dissatisfaction.

Gydryn knew Loran would be unsatisfied with anything less than a decision to vacate M'Nador completely. He settled the pacing duke a firm look. "I would that you leave tonight, Loran."

"Tonight!"

"Tonight," the king stressed, leaning forward to rest forearms on the table again. "Without fail."

"Aye, I see it now," the duke grumbled. "This is yer way of punishin' me fer tryin' to make ye see some sense."

"It becomes crueler still," the king returned. He suppressed the twitch of a smile at the duke's indignant glare. Gydryn stood and approached his general. "There are rumors of Basi spies in the city—never mind the flood of Saldarians. Let no one see you leave tonight, and take all measures to ensure you're not followed."

All pretense of complaint vanished from Loran's manner. He drew up short and stared hard at his king. "That's a tall order with forty men and horse."

The king placed a hand on the duke's shoulder. "Which is why I can entrust it to no one but you, Loran."

"Aye, Sire," said the Duke of Marion resolutely. He placed a hand on Gydryn's shoulder in return and held his king's gaze. "Your will be done."

FORTY-TWO

"There is no standard large enough to cover the shame of war."
– Gydryn val Lorian, King of Dannym

I T TOOK THE greater part of two hours for Trell's party to descend from the foothills, but at last they gained a busy road leading to the limestone-walled city of Sakkalaah. They fell in among dark-eyed Khurds riding camels, and merchant caravans whose turbaned guards walked with hands perched readily on the scimitars at their belts. Before they even reached the gates, Trell smelled the familiar scents of the city: the pungent aroma of spices, the acrid tang of livestock and unwashed men, and that ever-present scent of sand, which permeated all who made their lives among the lands of the Seventeen Tribes.

Trell noticed Rhys looking twitchy, his stormy gaze alighting on everyone with suspicion, and he suppressed a smile. To the Lord Captain, no doubt anyone in a turban seemed an enemy.

As they headed beneath the city walls, Trell thought of his last visit to Sakkalaah. He wondered if Lily and Korin had yet made their way east to Duan'Bai, or if Krystos had left on his next great expedition. He would've liked to have seen his friend again, that he might tell him how right he'd been about his origins, but his own path was still too uncertain.

The espial led them through the winding streets, past crowded, colorful markets and the high-walled gardens of city homes, until they turned upon a sandstone-paved avenue and found the Guild Hall. Trell had never seen the building before, though its staunch limestone walls and elaborate, aging mosaics clearly bespoke a centuries-long hold upon the location.

Two men in blue and grey turbans admitted through the main gates. Trell knew from these colors that the men were members of the al-Haduik tribe, which was well-respected among the seventeen united tribes.

In the entry yard, Gerard called them to a halt, and they all dismounted. "We shall rest here for a few hours and then proceed across the next node," he announced. "You may take refreshment within."

Then he handed off his reins to a groom and departed.

"Terribly chatty fellow, isn't he," Fynn observed, but he seemed in better humor now that they were far from Rethynnea. He grabbed a bottle from his sack and leaned an elbow on his saddle, pinning val Lorian grey eyes upon Trell. "I'll bet you know where we are," he noted before tearing at the cork with his teeth. "Raine's truth," he spit out the cork and eyed the bottle mouth before taking a swig, "I'll bet you even know what everyone's bloody saying."

"They're saying we should go into the shade where it's cooler," Alyneri offered as she handed off her reins to another groom.

Fynn gave her a flat look, to which Trell chuckled. "That's actually what the groom just said, Fynn."

Fynn eyed Alyneri narrowly. "Did I know you spoke the desert tongue? No, I believe I did not."

"Forgetfulness is a sure sign of alcohol poisoning," she told him sweetly.

"Which would only be a fitting end for me," Fynn observed with a flourish of his bottle, "you must admit."

With everyone dismounted, they followed a young steward in a white turban through an archway and into a *sahn*, a traditional courtyard bordered by a four-sided arcade. The Guild Hall's *sahn* had been made into a garden and was shaded by date palms and orange trees. A nearby fountain gave the illusion of moisture.

"We'll all be prunes after an hour more of this heat," the soldier Cayal remarked. They found seats beneath the shade of the vaulted arcade.

"It takes some getting used to," Trell admitted. After the temperate climate of the Cairs, the relatively dry air of Sakkalaah seemed intolerably arid, but it was balmy compared to the Kutsamak and Duan'Bai. "That's why we're stopping now, in the heat of the day. If our next nodepoint is further east, we're likely to endure a harsher climate still."

"And if it's hard on us, imagine the horses," Dorin noted.

Trell agreed. "We'll likely be advised to pack a lot of water, for there is little enough of it between Sakkalaah and the Fire Sea."

"Sakkalaah," Fynn murmured. "So that's where we are. I've heard of Sakkalaah." He looked around more appreciatively. "A man might find a good living in a place like this."

Rhys gave him a stony glare. "I've heard the Khurds don't take kindly to thieves."

"For the hundredth time, Captain," Fynn drawled, turning him a bland eye, "I'm an *agent* for thieves. I don't do the thieving *myself*."

"I don't know that the Seventeen Tribes make such distinctions, Fynn," Trell said with a smile. "I'm not sure there's even a word for 'agent of thieves' in the desert tongue."

"I think the word you're looking for is criminal," the Bull rumbled.

Fynn sighed despondently. "I am *so* misunderstood…"

As Fynn continued his lamentations loudly to anyone who seemed to be listening, Alyneri approached Trell. Her brown eyes revealed the fullness of her contrition. He nodded wordlessly at her and motioned her to follow him into the garden.

Though paling in comparison to the splendor of those at Krystos' Inn of the Four Faces, the Guild Hall's garden was lovely and comparatively cool. Trell walked beside Alyneri along a limestone path towards the sound of the distant fountain.

"Trell, I'm so sorry," she said in the desert tongue when they were deep among the foliage.

Trell took her hand and pressed his lips to the backs of her fingers, wishing they walked in different gardens under entirely different circumstances. "I don't want to talk about it, Alyneri." He liked none of what he was feeling that day—the ache of distance between them, the sure sense that the Guild Master D'Varre had been hiding something, and that feeling of apprehension that both dominated and clouded his thoughts.

"But—"

"What's done is done," he said, immediately wishing the words hadn't sounded so cold in their accusation.

He felt her wither beside him. "Can you not…forgive me?"

Trell glanced at her and frowned. He seemed ill able to say anything productive. Shaking his head, he arched a brow and remarked derisively, "Your betrayal pales compared to my own."

"Oh, Trell, *no*…"

But Trell didn't want to speak on the subject when he was as likely to hurt her again as repair the links already broken. Turning away, he brushed his lips across her fingers again and asked, keeping to the desert tongue, "Did you notice how uncomfortable the Guild Master D'Varre looked?"

She blinked at his abrupt change of subject. "No…I…" She shook her head. "No. Was he?"

Trell exhaled in frustration. "I don't know. I thought so."

Her dark eyes seemed large in contrast to her hair, and she gazed at him with worry furrowing her brow. "Trell…is something else bothering you?"

He would've liked to confess his thoughts, but he hesitated to share his apprehensions with Alyneri. *He* understood too well that troubling over what the future held was as close to doing nothing as sitting and watching the arrow coming at you. Alyneri, on the other hand, would chew on the bitter berries of worry until they turned to mush and then only go and gather more.

So he shook his head and gave her a look he hoped was softer than the one before. "Just thinking about the path ahead."

She sighed. "It seems ever clouded."

Exhaling his own agreement, he gripped her hand tighter. "The clouds cannot last forever, I suppose."

"Can they not?"

Though he only felt bombarded by that unwelcome premonition, he hoped to give her some reassurance. "Somewhere in the world the sun is shining."

"Let's go there then," she said with sudden fervor, and for a moment Trell felt the wall between them thin, that he might almost gaze again into her heart. "I would live with the sun and the sea in a place where the sky is always blue," she whispered. "Does such a place exist?"

He kissed her hand again, thinking of a bit of land along an isolated coastline that he knew quite well. "I think it may indeed, Your Grace."

As the midday hours passed and they prepared to be off again, Fynn regaled them with a story about Carian vran Lea and a Vaalden barmaid. The story had Trell laughing in spite of his mood, it set Alyneri to blushing, and it even managed to draw the quirk of a grin from the Lord Captain. When all were readied in the guild hall's nodecourt, the laconic Espial Gerard began instructing them on the next leg of their journey.

"Once we cross this node, our next nodepoint lies to the east, behind Akkad-held lines. We must travel overland for two days to reach it." He settled a steely eye upon the assembled group. "I will do my best to keep you out of harm's way."

"How close to the lines will we be?" Trell asked.

"I'm not certain. The node lies deep in the mountains, far from any settlements."

"In the Kutsamak?"

"Just so."

"The Akkadian forces are centered in Raku."

"The node is several days this side of Raku, in my estimation. There is no other way than upon this route, my lord. Do you wish to continue?"

"Yes, yes," Fynn waved impatiently at him. "Get on with it, man. If I'm to be forced to endure this heat, I want to be moving eastward at least."

"Worried Ghislain is coming after you already, Fynnlar?" Alyneri teased.

The royal cousin gave her a round-eyed look. "You have no idea the intensity of that woman's desire for me, Your Grace."

"Desire to see you drawn and quartered, perhaps," Rhys muttered.

Fynn waved airily. "I don't profess to approve of Ghislain's vast and varied entertainments...only to have participated in many of them."

"You are a truly dissolute man, Fynnlar," Alyneri noted with a sigh. Then she smiled at him.

"One cannot but walk the path before one," Fynn remarked philosophically. "Isn't that what you always say, cousin?" and his gaze alighted upon Trell.

"I don't think I placed the sentiment in quite the same context," Trell murmured with the ghost of a smile.

"My lords," Gerard opened his eyes at last, "the node is prepared. Please proceed as before."

And so they did, trading the Guild Hall in Sakkalaah for a vast, arid plain that seemed the barren delta of a once-great river. To their left and north, ochre mountains challenged the sky to wash the brilliant color from their slopes, while the single wall of a vast escarpment reared several miles to the south.

Looking across the dry delta towards that high ridge, Trell saw a caravan line of tiny men and camels backlit by the angle of the equally westbound sun. Suddenly he knew exactly where they were. "That's the Ruby Road," he said under his breath, feeling ever more ill at ease.

"Is that bad?" Alyneri asked.

"Not necessarily, it's just—"

"Come." Gerard trotted his horse to the front of the group. "This way."

He led off eastward, towards a distant point in the delta where the northern mountains seemed to join the southern ridge. Trell had his eye out for a particular peak.

By late afternoon, their route had moved them deep into the mountains. Trell had taken a different path on his journey towards the Cairs, but he knew they couldn't be too far from the winding trail that led back to the Mage and his strangely wonderful guests.

A part of him wished he and Alyneri might tear away and find again the path to the Mage's distant sa'reyth, though he remembered Balaji's comment that he hoped Trell need never return there.

"What is it?" Alyneri asked in the desert tongue just as the horses were rounding a rise and they gained a distant view of the arid mountains ahead of them. "Don't tell me nothing is wrong. You've not been yourself at all today, and you keep searching the sky for I don't know what."

He regarded her pensively. He'd never had such a strong feeling of unease with no logical reason to account for it. Instinct pushed him to turn them around, to abandon this path and even perhaps the goal of Tal'Shira altogether. Yet Trell couldn't be certain that his instincts weren't colored by his own uncertainties and fears, and he refused to succumb to the shadows of cowardice. After too long with these thoughts turning a circle in his head, he finally answered, "We're close to the trail I followed westward from the First Lord's sa'reyth."

Her brows lifted, and she looked around, frowning at the vast mountain range now in view. As far as the eye could see, the Kutsamak spread, its labyrinthine ridges deeply shadowed by the falling sun. "However would you know it?" she murmured in wonder. "Everything looks the same to me."

"Because of Jar'iman Point," he answered, though the truth in her comment brought a smile. The Khurds often said the Kutsamak had been designed by the desert god Ha'viv, who was known for his mocking trickery.

"I've been looking for the pinnacle they call Jar'iman Point," he explained, wishing he'd had more time to mend their bond, to ease the jagged distance between them. "You can't miss it—it's a sandstone spire that looks like a dagger. The trail to the sa'reyth lies in its shadow."

He remembered crossing the node in the early morning on the day he'd begun his journey west, remembered finding himself in the shadow of the mountain as the sun had been climbing out of the east. "If you walk towards the Point, staying in its early morning shadow, you can't but cross the trail to the sa'reyth."

Alyneri looked out over the miles of barren mountains, mottled just then with shadows cast by distant clouds carrying no promise of rain. "Would that we could just break away and go there," she mused. "You made it sound like a wonderful place."

He gave her a culpable look. "I can't say I haven't entertained the notion myself a few times this afternoon."

"Especially after the second hour of Fynn's incessant belching," Alyneri noted plaintively, switching back to the common tongue. She shot the royal cousin a pained look over her shoulder. "It was like unto a camel attempting to sing."

To which said royal cousin belched gratuitously, a long, wavering note somehow reminiscent of a dirge.

This time he succeeded in drawing the Espial Gerard's eye; he wrinkled his substantial nose in disgust and turned away again, shaking his head.

"No one appreciates my many talents," Fynn complained to Brody.

"Perhaps if you ever displayed any," the Bull suggested.

Fynn lifted his chin. "We criticize what we do not understand."

"*No one* understands you."

"My point exactly!"

To the hum of Fynn's continued protests, they found their way deeper into the mountains and eventually lost the view—but not before Trell caught sight of the tip of Jar'iman Point off to the southeast.

The sun fell low and the air grew chill as night spread its blanket across the Kutsamak. They were all donning their cloaks, and Gerard and Trell had begun looking for a place to camp, when Gendaia nickered in the same moment that Trell stiffened in his saddle.

He turned to Rhys, who was riding several lengths behind him. "Something's wrong."

The captain heeled his mount forward at once. "What is it, Your Highness?"

Trell looked up at the high ridges surrounding them, his gaze narrowed, waiting... and then he smelled it again. *Smoke.*

He cursed himself for not bringing additional guards. The Kutsamak held a vast array of dangers—bandits being the least of them—yet even bandits knew better than to burn wood in this land; the commodity was scarce, but more importantly, its smell carried too far on the wind. That meant Nadoriin...or worse.

"Someone's burning wood," Trell told the captain in a low voice. "I caught the barest whiff, so their camp can't be in this canyon—"

Gerard let out a cry and pitched forward over his mount with a black bolt extending from one shoulder. Alyneri screamed.

Trell felt a bolt whiz by his own ear. He heeled Gendaia forward, snatched the reins from the barely-conscious Gerard and turned them all in a retreat, shouting for the others. Fynn cursed and Rhys barked orders to the men, and they all made a fast exodus back down the ravine.

The pounding of their horses' hooves mingled with yells from behind and above as the bandits roused in chase. Trell recognized the language of their pursuers with a grim clench of his jaw.

Saldarians.

More bolts whizzed past as Trell reined Gendaia towards a narrow ravine, but the shadows of horses were already rising up from within its depths.

He swore an oath and urged Gendaia on, but then men and horses were pouring in from all directions. Trell tossed the espial's reins to a startled Alyneri, drew his sword and charged into the advancing line, with Rhys close on Gendaia's flank.

The clash of swords echoed against the arid hills as the men of Trell's party joined in the battle. Ever true, Gendaia seemed always to know when to rear and when to sidestep, dodge or bolt, and Trell felled many a man in those early minutes with the help of her talent.

The battle raged fast and desperate. Trell did his best to keep an eye on his companions, to know who stood and who faltered, to be of aid when possible. But the Saldarians outnumbered them, and Trell had the distinct impression this was only the first wave. When he saw Dorin tumble from his horse and then heard crossbow bolts beginning to fly again, he knew they had to retreat and regroup.

He yelled as much to Fynn, just as Gendaia reared against an oncoming Saldarian. The man toppled backwards from his horse, and the mount shied away, giving Trell the opening he needed.

He yelled his companions through the broken line of Saldarians, back towards the little ravine, sadly abandoning Gerard and Dorin that he might save the rest. Turning into the ravine, they galloped along a dry creek bed furred with muddied grass, close between high sandy ridges.

The Saldarians didn't chase them into the ravine. Trell suspected the mercenaries were regrouping, that they thought the ravine would provide no escape, but Trell knew these mountains. East and west-facing gullies almost always dead-ended, but the north-south ravines, like the one they were following, more often than not led to tributaries that fed into the main channels.

His hopes for quick escape were crushed when the ravine narrowed to a slot canyon just wide enough for a single horse and rider. Frustrated, Trell reined Gendaia in a circle, thinking fast of other options, while Rhys, Cayal and the others reined in. The moment his horse slowed, Fynn started listing to the side.

"Fynn!" Alyneri reached for him even as Brody heeled his mount forward to catch him before he fell.

"I'm...fine," Fynn whispered, but he clearly was not. He gingerly opened his cloak to reveal a dark stain spreading across his shirt.

"*Dear Epiphany,*" Alyneri breathed. "Is that—?"

"Shuriken," Trell pronounced grimly. Three dark spikes were protruding from Fynn's abdomen, just below his ribcage.

"Belloth take me," Fynn managed a sickly swallow. "That looks...bad."

Trell heard the Saldarians coming in pursuit. They had little time.

He knew what he had to do.

He reined Gendaia around to Alyneri's side and leaned to capture her mouth with a sudden rough kiss.

She drew back in alarm. "Trell, *what—?*"

"Alyneri, you have to take Fynn and get to safety." He kept his voice low, but his tone was commanding. They didn't have time for explanations. "Follow this ravine. If I'm right, it will eventually take you to another canyon."

"But can't we all—"

"There's barely room for one horse at a time!" he growled, but he was only furious with himself. "We'll never make it together—their archers can follow along the rim and pluck us off like fish in a barrel." Shooting a fierce look at a listing Fynn, he asked, "Can you heal him?"

Tears brimmed in her dark eyes. "I don't know. I don't want to leave you—"

He took her face in his hands and fastened another kiss upon her mouth, this one lasting and deep. If only they'd had a little more time together… if only he'd been willing to mend the rift that still wounded both of them.

"Hurry," he urged as he drew away. "Get Fynn to safety. I'll join you when I can."

"*Gods, Trell!* Where do I even go?"

In that moment, Trell understood.

It was as if he could see the Mage's plan from the outset, now finally come to fruition. Chills striped his arms, even as a sudden sense of peace flooded him.

Abruptly Trell swung off Gendaia and grabbed hold of Draanil's bridle. Looking up at Alyneri, he ordered, "Switch horses."

Uncomprehending but not daring to question him, Alyneri climbed from her mount onto Gendaia's back. Trell pulled off his sword and scabbard and shoved it into her hands, drawing an even greater look of alarm.

"The sa'reyth," he held her gaze, willing her understanding. "Remember everything I told you about it, and follow Gendaia's lead. I will try to meet you there." Then he took Gendaia's head in his hands, looked into her eyes and whispered in the desert tongue, "Get her safely to the Mage, *please*, Daybreak, for me…because I love her."

Gendaia nickered and tossed her head.

Trell looked to a listing Fynnlar. "Can you ride, Fynn?"

Wordless and grim, the royal cousin managed a nod.

"Away then!" He slapped Gendaia's flank with the urgent command. Then he watched grimly as Alyneri cantered off into the narrow crevasse, trailing Fynn close behind.

For a fleeting moment, Trell felt a desperate sense of loss. Then he pushed off the feeling and sought instead that cold place of focus, the place where his own sort of power resided: that determined and steadfast will which had seen him through circumstances even more hopeless than what he now faced.

He turned resolutely to Rhys. With Brody and Cayal, they made four… against how many? The odds were dismal and the outcome nearly assured, but Trell had lived through too many battles to bother with the odds. He swung into Draanil's saddle. "This is as good a place as any to make our stand, wouldn't you agree, Captain?"

"Yes, Highness," Rhys replied with a hurricane of a frown. He handed Trell a spare blade.

And the Saldarians stormed into the ravine.

Trell and the others felled the first wave with luck on their side, but eventually Thalma's eye turned to other interests, and Trell floundered in the midst of a mercenary sea. A dozen hands pulled him from Draanil. The horse reared and fled while Trell struggled to tear free.

Then Rhys was charging to his side again, and Brody and Cayal, and suddenly they were all back to back and holding off the Saldarian force. Trell knew only the steady pace of his heart, the dull ache in his arms, the sound of his blade clashing with another's, and that sense of purpose that ever drove him on.

And then, confusingly, he knew fear.

It infused him like a noxious cloud, a tainted vapor inhaled with every labored breath, and the more of it he drew within, the deeper the fear spread through his consciousness. Cayal first fell prey to its malaise, crying out and shying from a blade as like as any other. The Saldarians grabbed him.

Rhys and Brody began to stumble beneath fear's weight, whereupon Trell realized a bleak enchantment was at work. "Fight it!" he growled. "It's not real!"

Just speaking the words helped him shake off the clinging miasma, but then a shapeless force pounced upon him, equally suffocating and unassailable. It compelled him down…down…

He gasped and doubled over as the working accosted his mind with twisting, flickering images of gruesome death. Abject emotions flooded him, battering his composure with wretched torments.

He found his face pressed to the earth, his sword being lifted from limp fingers, and still all he could do was suck in a shuddering breath, while his mind endured brutal visions and his head throbbed from their wake.

He saw a pair of boots stop before his blurred eyes, their edges brushed by the hem of a black cloak. A wielder's cloak.

"Bind him," a distant voice ordered.

To which the wielder standing above Trell remarked humorlessly, "He is bound already. Just get him on a horse."

FORTY-THREE

"It's better to have bad luck than none at all."

– A saying among the Iluminari

KJIERAN VAN STONE walked shirtless along the seaward-facing wall of Radov's palace, letting the strong Nadori sun bake his pale skin, desperately wishing he felt its warmth.

There, on the palace's high eastern wall, the ever-present desert wind met and battled the incoming ocean breeze. The clash of forces tossed Kjieran's shoulder-length dark hair into wild designs, even as his hands twitched erratically at his sides.

Kjieran liked walking the wall. Because of the strong, shifting winds that battered anyone brave enough to explore that boundary, he rarely encountered a soul beyond the palace guards on regular patrol, their crimson *keffiyehs* wrapped into turbans, mouths and noses protected by a hanging drape of cloth. They'd watched him suspiciously at first, dark eyes narrowed and piercing, but now they merely nodded slightly as they passed, and their thoughts never whispered of him.

Kjieran had first taken to walking the wall to escape the constant circumspection of Viernan hal'Jaitar's spies, who kept their dark eyes close upon him and doubtless reported back to the wielder on every person he came into contact with. As Kjieran had feared, their vigilance was greatly hindering his attempts at investigation.

Understanding Radov's paranoia about truthreaders, Kjieran might've come to Tal'Shira better prepared had he been given time to think upon it. A

Marquiin, though loathsome, might be tolerated, for they retained any but the merest grasp of the lifeforce; but a truthreader *with all of his faculties…*

Viernan hal'Jaitar was Sormitáge trained. He knew how easily truthreaders might pluck secrets from unsuspecting minds, and for a court with so many secrets…no wonder Radov refused to share a room with truthreaders of any sort. That Kjieran was unspoiled…this made him immensely dangerous in hal'Jaitar's view—on top of being a supposed spy. Never mind what else the wielder suspected of him.

Yet, had Kjieran not been forced to walk the wall to find isolation from Viernan's spies, he might never have stumbled upon the idea that drove him to walk it that afternoon…might never have heard of a man named Yveric.

He'd first seen him several days ago, on the afternoon of King Gydryn's arrival. They'd both been enduring the battering winds while watching the *Sea Eagle* make anchor in the bay. Like Kjieran, Yveric had seemed glued to the moment, as if fearing a terrible explosion or some other imminent destruction of the ship.

Kjieran's had derived much of his perception of the man from Yveric's turbulent thoughts—which was no small feat, considering Yveric was a Marquiin and his mind was ever a torrent. But Kjieran had experience sifting through the raving madness in a Marquiin's skull. He felt reasonably certain of his assessment of the man.

The next afternoon, Kjieran had again walked the wall, and again he passed Yveric, who'd been standing as a statue draped in billowing grey silk, staring east. Yveric reminded Kjieran very much of himself back in Tambarré; he'd often gazed wistfully, longingly, at the jutting peaks of the Iverness range of southeastern Dannym, wishing he might one day walk again as a free man and serve in the court of his king.

An idea had begun to form that day as Kjieran watched Yveric. He realized the Marquiin might prove a bountiful source of information, if he could manage to gain his confidence. Over the next two days, he followed Yveric in his daily routine, being careful to keep out of sight while staying within mental contact of his mind and the minds of those around him. He learned much.

Yveric had been the first of the Prophet's Marquiin to arrive in Tal'Shira, and was the oldest among them. He'd once been a prime questioner for the Prophet, but now his health was failing. That he'd lingered as long as he had was a fair miracle, for the Marquiin were notoriously short-lived. Yveric was Avataren; most auspiciously, he was rumored to share a distant connection to the Fire Princess Ysolde Remalkhen, lifelong Companion to Queen Errodan of Dannym.

Kjieran became convinced that if ever he was likely to find a kindred spirit in one of the Marquiin, it must be Yveric—and with no time to spare, for King Gydryn's arrival had pushed up Kjieran's timetable considerably.

He still had no idea how he was going to save his king, or even how to contact him. Gydryn remained sequestered among his knights in a distant wing of the palace where Kjieran was most certainly not welcome.

And then there was Dore's Pattern of Changing, the effects of which were finally starting to show. The night before, Kjieran had awoken to a terrible itching in his feet and a painful tingling that had radiated up his legs like a swarm of fire ants feasting on his flesh. He'd scratched desperately in the darkness for hours and finally had stumbled out of bed to turn up the lamp. Then, to his horror, did he see the results of his efforts—a sight which had sent him staggering to his chamber pot, retching.

He'd pulled off what was left of his toenails the following morning. They'd become as a yellowish fungus and had detached with a sickening sound, like the sucking of a rock plunked into a stinking bog.

Kjieran hadn't known what to expect from Dore's working, but looking at the strips of withered skin still resolutely clinging to his shins, he began to better understand what it was doing to him.

The skin of his legs had begun to slough away; he was a snake shedding a thick husk to reveal the new scales beneath. What remained was all muscle, and it was as cold, hard and black as a Merdanti dagger.

That's probably the fundamental spell Dore patterned the rest of his working on.

A violent, hopeless laugh escaped him. He was turning into a Merdanti blade.

Now he walked the eastern wall on fleshless legs of stone, glad for the dark silk pants that hid what he was becoming, grateful he could still bare his chest to the sun.

Kjieran saw Yveric from afar and spent the intervening minutes reviewing again what he would say to him, how he might convince a man who could very well be insane to help him.

He passed the usual guard patrol about ten paces before he reached Yveric. The guards nodded to Kjieran as they passed, their thoughts too quiet for him to overhear. The two soldiers were good men, a rare pair among the ever-growing hordes of rough-and-tumble cutthroats that swarmed Radov's court.

Ahead of him, the Marquiin's form stood tall and still beneath his billowing silk. Kjieran came to a halt near Yveric and joined him in gazing out to sea.

The man turned to assess him. Though Kjieran could see nothing of his features beneath his veil, he seemed to be looking Kjieran over. Then he returned his attention to the panoramic city, the crescent-shaped bay, and the distant sea.

"What do you see, Marquiin?" Kjieran asked after a moment, making his voice just loud enough to be heard over the blustery wind, the whisk of his tossing hair, and the snapping of Yveric's veil.

"I see death, truthreader." His voice was like dry gravel and echoed with the clipped tones of his mother language. "Is that not what the Prophet teaches awaits us all?" When Kjieran made no reply, Yveric looked to him, and the wind pressed the veil to conform to his features.

Kjieran could make out the strong lines of his face, an aquiline nose and one edge of a squared jaw.

"You were his paramour—the one who survived," Yveric observed brutally. "I heard tales of you." Looking back to the sea, he hissed with sudden acrimony, "You have a pretty look about you. Is that why he spared you this fate?"

Despite Yveric's sharp words, Kjieran felt only sympathy for the man. He knew that Yveric struggled with each moment to think his own thoughts, to fight the raging inferno of Bethamin's eternal Fire, a constant mental storm. Kjieran was becoming his own sort of monster, but at least his mind remained his own—most of the time.

"We all have our roads." He grimaced at the hopelessness he heard in his own voice.

This response drew the Marquiin's swift attention. He snatched Kjieran's upper arm, leaned close and growled under his breath, "*Who* told you to say that to me?"

Kjieran felt the power that was the Marquiin's particular poison, a gift from their master, shoot out to envelop him, compelling an answer. But this same power also coursed through his own life-pattern now, and the formless compulsion had no effect.

"No one." He wondered at the intensity of the man's unexpected response. Glancing at the Marquiin's hand on his arm, he noted for the first time that he was wearing gloves. *Odd in this heat.* "It merely occurred to me as a truth worth sharing."

"Did it?" Yveric dropped his hand and turned away again. The sun was falling behind them now, casting golden rays upon the azure bay. "You sought me out," Yveric said then. "What do you want?"

"I require your aid."

"I am beyond helping anyone, *Envoy.* You should understand that. Even the Prophet has washed his hands of me." Abruptly he barked a harsh laugh, acrimonious and bitter. "The irony!" His rumbling laughter continued to brew, growing louder, harder, until its rancor resounded as the breaking of stone upon stone.

Upon the peak of this crescendo, however, his voice abruptly cracked. He sucked in his breath with an abrasive wheeze and his laughter devolved into a fit of desperate gasping that lasted several frightening minutes.

Kjieran stood mute, unable even to conceive of a way to ease his pain, though his concern was evident upon his clean features and in the shock in his colorless gaze.

When Yveric had finally recovered enough to fill his lungs with shallow breath, he turned his shrouded face to Kjieran. "I am dying…do you see," and then he added in a raw whisper, "…at long last."

They found their way to Yveric's chambers. He occupied a single room in the west wing of the palace. A wall of carved screen doors overlooked a small garden. It was a low floor where the wind barely stirred and the sun made a furnace of the stones. Still, it was nice quarters considering what Radov thought of the Marquiin—a token gesture, no doubt, in support of the prince's alliance with Bethamin. Kjieran was quick to note in comparison, however, that his own quarters were centrally located and overlooked the sea—the better to keep an easy eye on him.

Yveric staggered past the open screen doors towards a sideboard on the far side of the room. He ripped off his veil and left it to drift down in his wake. He leaned heavily on the cabinet with one hand while he poured them both wine from a dewy pewter pitcher. He downed his first dose even as Kjieran was approaching and instantly sloshed out another. "Take it," he gasped, still leaning hard on one hand, his back to Kjieran. He indicated the other pewter goblet with a tilt of his shaved and tattooed head.

As Kjieran came up slowly beside him and reached for the chilled wine, the Marquiin turned to look at him.

Kjieran's hand stilled on the goblet.

"Yes," Yveric said brokenly, a humorless smile gracing his lips. "It's something to see, isn't it?"

Kjieran forced himself to lift the goblet of wine as he held Yveric's gaze. Once colorless, the man's eyes had now turned a solid black. Worse was the flesh that surrounded them—grim, violet-dark swaths of necrotic tissue that extended like tentacles across his brows and temples, spider-veining along his shaved skull. Once, the man had likely worn the typical Marquiin tattoos around his eyes, but the flesh was now too devoured. It was the mask of a monster imposed upon the face of a man.

Kjieran saw then that similar blotches of violet-black flesh webbed Yveric's throat beneath the edge of a worn woolen tunic. Doubtless the rest of Yveric's body looked much the same.

"They say death comes soon after your eyes go black," Yveric told him in a gravel wheeze. Then he added acidly, "They know nothing."

Kjieran remembered the wine and managed to drink a few swallows without sloshing too much out of the cup, but his hands were twitching like dry branches snapping in a fire. Giving up, he set the mug down and looked back to find the Marquiin's black eyes considering him intently.

"What did he do to you then?"

Kjieran shook his head, too overcome by the truth to speak of it, even if he dared.

"So your road is no different from mine…in the end." Yveric shook his head, downed his wine and poured a third. "Mayhap he's right," he said as some color seemed to return to his gaunt face. "The Prophet, I mean. Perhaps all there is for any of us is death. I certainly crave it."

"He made it seem so." Kjieran felt himself on the edge of a perilous cliff to speak such words aloud. The Prophet had not sought to invade his mind again since that first day, but Kjieran had several times felt his awareness open on the other end of the bond and had known Bethamin was watching through his eyes.

He could tell that the Prophet's attention was turned away from him in that moment, but there was no way of knowing when it would come back— the great eye of Bethamin's awareness cycling around in the light-tower of his mind to once again fall upon Kjieran's activities. Nor did he know what other torments might now be possible through the growing strength of their bond. It kept Kjieran alert in every moment.

Yveric staggered over to the doors and stood between them, square in the boiling afternoon sun. "I'm cold, truthreader," he whispered, listing unsteadily. "I'm always cold." When Kjieran didn't answer him, Yveric turned his head and pinned those ghastly eyes on him again. Kjieran could barely look at him, for it horrified him to wonder if his own face would soon become a similar horror.

Yveric barked a humorless laugh. "Ha! I know what you're thinking—"

"I seriously doubt that," Kjieran muttered.

"Just tell me this," he said, swaying like a drunkard, "did she come to you too?"

Kjieran shook his head. "She? Who?"

"Just tell me if it's so!"

Kjieran held up his hands in a placating manner. "Peace, Yveric. I swear to you in Epiphany's name, no one came to me."

The Marquiin grunted. "Then it's true." He closed his eyes and swayed like a young pine in a stiff wind.

Mystified, Kjieran picked up his goblet with both hands and slowly crossed the room towards him. "I'll tell you what I was thinking."

"What?" asked the man through closed lids.

"I was thinking you seem impossibly...sane...for a Marquiin."

This drew another gravelly laugh from the man. "Among my kind, there is a rumor that the end for the Prophet's *blessed chosen*," and the words came out in a venomous snarl, "comes in one of two ways." Eyes still closed, he lifted his appalling face to the sun. "Either you go out stark raving mad... or you suddenly turn lucid, that you might know *every moment* of the horror that awaits you at the end." He swayed dangerously in place. "Seems I picked the short straw again."

"I'm...sorry."

"Ha! You're one to talk!" Yveric opened his necrotic eyes and looked at Kjieran, leaning close as he observed, "Something gives me the idea your fate will be worse, Envoy."

Kjieran looked down at the goblet, which he was gripping so tightly that his hands had gone white. Even with all his effort of concentration, still his fingers inadvertently jumped off the goblet. The muscles in his arms and hands twitched beneath his skin as the battle between *elae* and Bethamin's fell power continued.

He shook his head grimly. "I believe you may be right."

Yveric turned in the doorway and leaned his other shoulder against the portal, letting the sun bake his backside instead. "So…" He looked haggard. "What is it you want from me?" Before Kjieran could answer, he added, "You needn't fear confession. The Prophet hasn't haunted my dreams in many moons. He sees my infirmity and loathes me for it."

Kjieran blinked at him. "Your dreams? The Prophet treads the path of your dreams?"

Yveric grunted sourly. "Dore Madden taught our master all manner of torments—I thought you must surely know."

Kjieran shook his head, immensely grateful that his dreams, so far at least, had been his own. Yet now that he knew the Prophet cavorted in his subjects' dreams, he suspected such grace couldn't last.

"No matter," Yveric meanwhile muttered, "you're safe enough speaking to me. Epiphany be kind, I shall not wake tomorrow." With this oath, his kissed his gloved thumb and held it to the sky.

Kjieran drew in a deep breath and let it out slowly. "I seek…" He pressed lips together and trusted to the moment, to this doomed man, and to Epiphany, that she would not forsake him entirely just yet. "I seek the truth behind the deaths of Sebastian and Trell val Lorian."

Yveric stared at him for a long time with those unsettling eyes. Finally he said, "Then you seek the Shamshir'im."

FORTY-FOUR

"A free mind is infinitely more powerful than a captive one."
– The Fourth Vestal Raine D'Lacourte

I ŞAK'GETIRMEK BRUSHED PAST the Saldarian mercenary as the latter threw the prisoner down near the fire. Işak still had the man bound with the fourth, and he lay limply, his eyes unseeing. Işak's fourth-strand working used the man's own mind against him, claiming it as an unwilling participant, binding him with his own thoughts.

The Saldarian leader, Raliax, joined Işak's side as the other prisoners were being dropped beside the first, their feet and hands bound with stout rope. Raliax assessed the line, frowning beneath heavy black brows, while Işak in turn assessed him.

An impatient man, and unforgiving, Raliax had flashing dark eyes and an insincere smile. He delighted in the spilling of blood, during which times he often caught his bottom lip between his teeth in a smile. Yet he fashioned himself as a nobleman. He kept his jaw clean-shaven, and he wore his black hair in an intricate braided club, as was the fashion among the Nadori nobility. But his nails were dirty, and his breath reeked of sour drink, and Işak wasn't deluded by any part of his charade.

Among all of this pretense, something in Raliax whispered to Işak…a distant memory that quivered with warning. But its message was gossamer thin and too frail to convey any clear meaning. Still, he had not a breath of trust for the man, and liked him even less.

Having looked over the assembled prisoners, Raliax demanded of his hirelings, "Where's the cousin?"

"Isn't he one of these?" a man named Joss returned.

"If he was, I wouldn't have asked!" Abruptly Raliax hissed a curse and shouted, "Find Fynnlar val Lorian!"

"I put three darts in 'im," said a man Işak knew only as Sharpe. Raliax's men hailed from Saldaria, but the province's mountainous borders with Dannym were vague, and Sharpe spoke the Saldarian dialect with a harsh northern accent. "He willn't get far w'my nails in 'is belly."

"Get after him," Raliax growled, "lest I claim his value in your blood."

"No," said Işak in a low voice, commanding silence and stillness from the group. They knew him as a wielder and were suspicious and wary of him, but they listened when he spoke. "Are you certain you marked him, Sharpe?"

"Sure as silver."

"Fine. He won't get far, and in this darkness Joss would be as likely to walk past him as trip over his body. Better to search in the morning."

"He'll be dead by morning," Sharpe pointed out.

"Then he'll be especially easy to find." Işak assessed the assembled prisoners from beneath the deep cowl of his cloak. He liked the sense of anonymity his hood gave. "So who *do* we have?"

Joss grabbed the prisoners, one by one, and yanked them to their knees. Işak was pleased to note the last one, the one he still had bound with the fourth, was by far the most docile of the group—though to be certain he'd fought the fiercest from what Işak had seen of him back in the canyon.

"You heard him." Joss kicked at the one on the end. "Give the man your name."

When none of them immediately replied, Raliax sighed dramatically. "You can give us your names and live, or keep them and die. Dead men are less trouble, so I hope you choose the latter."

Joss kicked the first man in the gut.

He doubled over and snarled through gritted teeth, "Cayal val Oren."

Joss kicked at the next man. He spun a defiant glare at Joss and earned a fist to his jaw in reward. "Lots more where that came from if you're hungry for it. Give the man your name." When the prisoner didn't respond, Joss slammed his boot into his back and sent him sprawling, face down, into the dirt. Joss hauled him up again with a sigh. "Your *name*."

"Brody," he said in a voice like gravel.

"And you?" Joss addressed a fierce looking man who sat taller than the other two. Işak had noticed him fighting and was impressed with his competence with a blade.

The man said nothing, so Joss battered him into the dirt and hauled him up again. This continued twice more until the last man, the one Işak had under compulsion, said in a quiet voice, tightly controlled, "Rhys...do what he asks. They have our names already."

Işak arched a brow. He knew his prisoner must be suffering beneath the working he held over him, and it suited him to continue it—the better to keep him docile, as Dore had so viciously taught him—but he would not have imagined the man capable of thought with such compulsion capturing his consciousness.

His intelligence shone equally through, for he'd accurately estimated their situation.

The soldier named Rhys shot the other prisoner a sideways glance. Işak could see him deliberating, but he finally growled, "Lord Captain Rhys val Kincaide."

"Excellent." Raliax rubbed his hands together. "We've the Nodefinder and the other injured soldier, and the dead cousin, once found, makes seven. They will provide a fine incentive to draw out our missing prince." He spun away and headed to his tent, calling upon another of his men to follow him.

"But who is the last?" Işak asked then, his curiosity piqued. He peered intently down upon his prisoner from the depths of his hood.

With an obvious force of will, the man lifted grey eyes to look up at Işak. "Trell...val Lorian."

Trell val Lorian!

Işak stumbled back. "Im...possible..." His mouth had gone suddenly dry. "Trell val Lorian died... years ago." Strange that he could not now remember how many years that was supposed to have been, but his days since N'ghorra seemed naught but a solid span of living hell. Was it truly surprising that time had lost all meaning to him?

Trell dropped his head back into the dirt, succumbing perhaps to Işak's compulsion once more. Işak stared at him...something did seem familiar about his face. If it really *was* Trell, he would've been but a teen when Işak had last seen him.

Yet if Trell val Lorian wasn't dead, then *why*—

Something wormed inside Işak at this question. It leaped from the deep darkness of Dore's web of spells to entangle Işak with shards of memory.

His head burst with a pain so violent as to momentarily blind him, so powerful that Işak nearly lost his hold on the patterns binding Trell, but he retained them at the last and gritted his teeth against the inexplicable explosion in his skull.

What is happening to me?

He felt as if a door had been cleaved, one he never knew existed, but now he gaped in horror at the filth seeping out through the cracks—filth that he realized had been thriving in his mind. Only as he recovered from this attack did Işak note the avid whispering among Raliax's men.

The man himself emerged from his tent just moments later. He came stalking across the camp, grabbed Trell up by his hair and stared into his face, searching his features. "It *is* you!" he hissed after a breath of time. He slung the prince back into the dirt and shouted madly, "I watched you die! *I saw you die!*"

Işak had never seen the man so insane with fury. He stalked around an incapacitated Trell, snarling and spitting curses, mad as a cornered cobra. After a few savage moments of this, he kicked the prince several times and screamed, "*I put* you into the Fire Sea five years ago roped to an accursed *trunk*! You could *not* have survived!"

This wild, unadvised outburst earned the fury of the other prisoners, who had to be forcefully subdued—the Lord Captain alone needed two men to hold him down whilst a third made a pulp of his face.

Still lying on his side in the throes of Işak's compulsion, Trell gave Raliax a humorless smile reminiscent of torments unknown. "It seemed Fate had...a different end...in mind for me."

Raliax roared in fury and stalked off, hissing and cursing foully. Joss and several others rushed after him, and a heated argument soon erupted at the edge of camp.

The enormous implications of Raliax's confession had Işak reeling.

"I put you into the Fire Sea five years ago..."

If Raliax had been responsible for Trell's purported death, why would his king have blamed *him* for it? What's more, how could the king have blamed him if he was already in N'ghorra?

For as long as Işak could remember, he'd believed that King Gydryn held him responsible for the death of his *two* sons, but now he realized that couldn't be true.

And why couldn't he remember the moment of his actual banishment, when they'd surely laid the dreadful sentence upon him? When he tried to think that far into his past, he saw only a formless curtain of fog.

Something isn't right.

For years Işak had been certain of the vendetta he held against King Gydryn. Now the memories were bleeding into streaks of painful color. Işak felt unglued, unhinged.

Things no longer fit. He *knew* this. He just didn't know what pieces had fallen away.

As Işak stared uncomprehendingly at the prince, Trell slowly pushed back to his knees and pinned his grey eyes upon him in return. Even possessed by compulsion, the prince's gaze speared Işak. "Why are you... trying to...find...my brother?"

What power of concentration he had to form thought around such treacherous patterns as Işak had thrust upon him! Yet Işak was hardly faring better, for he battled his own demons now.

Ironic, he thought as he stared at Trell, that while he bound Trell's mind, the prince had somehow found a way of binding his in return.

"Ean val Lorian owes a debt to the Prophet," Işak answered tightly.

He looked to the Lord Captain, who seemed slightly more pliable now that he'd been effectively bloodied, while his mind continued that desperate search for the missing piece of the puzzle called his past. "So, Captain, your middle prince survived Raliax's best efforts, it would seem." Işak was relieved to note his voice carrying such cool dispassion, for surely he was straining to accomplish it. "And we shall soon have the youngest in our grasp. But what of your king's firstborn?"

Rhys spat blood onto the earth. "Dead, of course," he grated through swollen lips. "Our Prince Sebastian was killed by Basi assassins eight years ago—"

Killed by Basi assassins?

With the thought, Işak's entire consciousness exploded with pain.

The pattern he wielded against Trell instantly dissolved, for Işak couldn't hold onto it beneath the blinding force that ripped through his mind. He staggered away, unable to think, unable even to breathe…

"Get him!" someone yelled at the same time that another man shouted, "Raliax!"

Işak could only grab for a near tent pole and cling to it, gasping, as a suddenly freed Trell stole a sword and attacked Raliax at the camp's shadowed edge. To Işak's ravaged consciousness, they seemed demons battling in the night.

The two fought fiercely while the Saldarians stood stunned, apparently wondering whether or not to interrupt. The prince was winning, and might've claimed Raliax if the latter hadn't shouted urgently for someone to grab the damnable man and pull him off.

In fact, it took five Saldarians to subdue the prince. The smartest of the bunch finally knocked him unconscious with the hilt of his sword. They dragged him back to the fire and bound him with stout rope that time.

The Lord Captain was laughing in a low gurgling wheeze when Raliax stomped back into camp. "Would've killed you," he rumbled happily.

Joss went over and kicked him, but Işak could still hear the Lord Captain laughing even as he bled into the dirt.

…killed by Basi assassins eight years ago…

Why had those words so shaken him? What untold working upon his consciousness had the words disturbed?

Raliax stalked up to where Işak clung to the pole, pushed his nose inches away and snarled, "You gimp-legged bastard! What were you bloody thinking, letting him at me like that?"

Işak collected himself out of necessity. "Your tone is somewhat lacking for respect, Raliax." Recalling the pattern he'd just used on Trell, he released it onto Raliax instead.

The Saldarian swore an oath and grabbed Işak by the collar of his cloak. "Get it off me!"

"Or what?" Işak whispered, low and dangerous. He made the pattern more solid, and Raliax cried out. He clutched at Işak as he fell to his knees, but the pattern had him firmly. "You forget your place." Işak looked coldly upon the man, whose expression was twisted with pain as he writhed on the earth. "Shall I leave you to consider our varying roles, or can you behave?"

After a moment, Raliax's hand twitched, which Işak took as an affirmation. He allowed the pattern to dissipate, letting the collected energies of *elae* gradually exhaust themselves. Raliax sucked in a shuddering breath.

"Come inside," Işak growled. "We need to talk." He turned to the men and ordered in a voice loud enough to be heard by all, "Secure the prisoners and break camp! At dawn we ride."

Işak ducked inside his tent, roughly pushed back his hood and walked to pour himself a drink. It appalled him to see his hand shaking upon the task. *What is happening to me?*

"Do that again in front of my men and I'll gut you in your sleep."

Işak glanced over his shoulder to find Raliax standing at the tent's entrance. "Give me a reason to think you might, and I'll bind you to my will with the fifth."

It was a lie, of course. Dore would never have taught him such powerful patterns, but Raliax didn't know that.

Işak looked back to his hands and willed them to stop shaking. "Tell me…" He laid a fourth-strand truth pattern upon the Saldarian—for he wouldn't believe anything Raliax offered willingly. "What is the story behind your failed assassination of Trell val Lorian?"

Raliax glared at him.

Işak moved to sit in a folding camp chair near a glowing brazier. He'd hoped its warmth would soothe the ice that had hold of him, yet he barely felt the fire's heat. "The real story now," he said as he settled in, "if you please."

The Saldarian moved slowly inside the tent and let the flap close behind him, pinning Işak all the while with a razor-edged stare. "I don't know why they wanted the prince killed," he finally answered, resentful and belligerent. "I only know hal'Jaitar hired me to take care of it."

"Viernan hal'Jaitar? Wielder to Radov?"

Raliax nodded confirmation, albeit unwillingly.

Işak drank wine from his pewter cup, grateful that he'd finally gotten his hands under control, even if his insides still writhed. He eyed the Saldarian leader over the rim. "What else?"

Raliax shrugged. "There wasn't much to it. Board the *Dawn Chaser* off the coast of M'Nador. Question the prince to see what he knew. Kill him.

Fire the ship…we did all of that. The royal family assumed the *Dawn Chaser* had foundered in a storm."

Işak stared wordlessly at him. There was just no questioning it: Gydryn val Lorian could not have blamed him for Trell's death. Işak was already in N'ghorra when Raliax did the deed. Where then had such an idea come from?

Işak pushed away these confusing truths, which seemed to be accompanied by a blinding pain in his head and an ill feeling of foreboding in his stomach, and refocused on Raliax. "Where has the prince been all this time?"

Raliax shrugged. "Where he's been ain't as important as where he's going to be. I'll make sure he's dead this time."

Işak arched a brow. "I rather think that a mistake of grave proportion."

"*You* think—" Raliax exploded on him. "*You* can barely ride a horse with that gimp leg! What do you know of a man's work? I'd like to see you in a real battle—I'll bet you can't even swing a blade!" He looked Işak over with malice in his dark eyes and hissed, "*You're* naught but a madman's plaything. What makes you think you're better than me?"

Işak leveled Raliax a chilling gaze, for his words had sheared close and cut deeply. "The prince has been *somewhere* for the past five years," he pointed out to the fractious man. "Who has he told, and what has he told them? How many others know Prince Trell val Lorian walks among the living? An assassin whose marks mysteriously return from the dead is not long for this world."

"So I should kill him now!" Raliax declared as if to prove his own point.

"You could, you could," Işak agreed, marveling at the man's unusual rancor. "But how many of Radov's enemies know Trell val Lorian lives? And what will Radov say when he inevitably learns of it? I hear the ruling prince is not a trusting man. Think he'll believe you when you claim you killed the prince a second time?"

Raliax frowned. It would seem even a man such as he could see this truth. Or perhaps his fear of Radov's infamous paranoia was enough to give him pause. "So you're saying what? I should take him to Radov?"

"I would think so, yes, and in somewhat of a condition to answer the ruling prince's questions."

Raliax glowered at him. "You mean alive."

"I mean alive and *unharmed*. It's not up to you or I to decide the fate of Trell val Lorian now. That boon lies in your master's hands."

Raliax clearly saw the benefit in this notion; laying blame at the feet of another was ever the coward's comfort. The Saldarian shoved hands in pockets and paced, muttering for a while. Then he stopped and glared at Işak again. "What will you do?"

"Continue on as planned."

"So I travel hundreds of leagues overland while our Nodefinder takes you north in a matter of days?"

"There was a Nodefinder among their party," Işak pointed out. "If he lives, he could be of use to you. I recommend sending a man with him to Tal'Shira that they might gain the capital before the captured Adept dies. Radov will surely send another Nodefinder back for the rest of you in order to claim such a prize as your miraculous prince." When Raliax said nothing, Işak offered, "Or if you would prefer our roles are reversed and I take Trell val Lorian to present to Prince Radov instead—"

"I'm not saying that!"

Işak opened palms placatingly.

"Should've left you to rot…" the man muttered acidly under his breath.

"What was that?"

He shot him a venomous glare. "I *said* Dore Madden should've left you to rot in…wherever he found you." He spun on his heel and stormed from the tent.

Would that he had, Işak thought as he sat in his chair feeling worms crawling through the tattered remains of his consciousness. In N'ghorra, he'd at least been his own man—or so he liked to believe. The truth was he remembered too nearly those punishing years and too distantly the man who had endured them.

N'ghorra was but the first level of hell, Işak lamented as he stared at his empty goblet, *and I have since come to know them all.*

Dawn saw clear skies and the illicit troop ready to be off.

Most of the prisoners had spent the night tied to stakes near the horses, but Raliax had ordered the prince kept at the edge of camp under constant watch. When Işak emerged from his tent, pulling the cowl of his cloak low over his eyes, he saw the prince sleeping with his back to his guards.

Trell compelled his interest. Işak had barely been able to get his mind off of him. Leaving the Saldarians to break down his tent, Işak approached the prince. As he neared, he grew certain that the prince was alert, though for all purposes he seemed soundly asleep. "Go find Joss," Işak told the two mercenaries guarding Trell.

They headed off without a backwards glance.

When they were alone, Işak told the prince, "You're being taken to Radov."

After a moment of silence, Trell asked, "Why? Because he tried to have me killed?"

Feeling unusually ill at ease, Işak murmured, "So it would seem." He peered at the prince intently then, but in the dim shadows of dawn, his eyes merely saw a man sleeping. He laid a fourth-strand truth pattern upon him and asked, "Tell me...how did you survive?"

After a moment's pause, the prince answered, "A god took pity on me."

Though it was an outrageous claim, Işak believed him—even had the fourth-strand pattern not resonated, there was an element of such naked honesty in the blunt, if improbable, answer that he had to trust to it.

Would that your benevolent god had seen fit to spare me as well, prince of Dannym.

It was a strange thought that came so suddenly...another man's thought. He had been another man once, before N'ghorra, but he no more remembered that man than he understood why Gydryn val Lorian had sent him to the mines—

Immediately that shattering headache burst through his consciousness again, bringing a painful sharpness to his thoughts.

Why?

What could be happening to him that such pain accompanied certain thoughts? Was the pain meant to ward him away from following these memories too deeply? From tracing them to their true origin?

If not for his sure certainty that bindings of the fifth could never be broken, Işak might've speculated that Dore's patterns were coming undone.

But hope had long abandoned Işak, and he never wondered.

Joss's scuffing boot-steps preceded him through the quiet dawn. "You wanted me, Işak?"

Işak kept his eyes pinned on Trell and ordered, "Take five men and find Fynnlar val Lorian. I want to be well on our way to Saldaria by nightfall."

Joss nodded and headed off.

"Saldaria," Trell murmured. "Where you plan to lay a trap for my brother?"

Işak wondered why he felt so compelled to interact with this prince, his prisoner, a man who should already be dead and likely would be very soon.

When Işak said nothing, Trell turned his head to look up at him.

In holding the man's gaze—even from the shadows of his hood—Işak became acutely aware of the scar that marred his features and did not want Trell to look on it. He was glad for the deep cowl of his cloak to collect and contain the concealing darkness.

Trell looked at him with serious eyes, his brow furrowed as his gaze took in Işak's hooded face, his form. He paused when he noted Işak's left hand, half-concealed by the long fall of his cloak, working its string into silent knots, and his frown deepened. After a moment of consideration, Trell lifted eyes to stare up at him again.

"Why do you serve such men as Radov abin Hadorin and the Prophet Bethamin? You're not like them."

"You know nothing of me." Işak felt scalded by the prince's perceptions and confusingly wished they could be true.

"No," Trell agreed, frowning slightly. "I don't, do I...and yet..."

Işak's heart hung painfully upon that pause.

"...I feel as if I should."

Işak turned away from him, feeling unbalanced. He noticed that his hands were shaking again and cursed his own foolishness.

But the truth was...he felt the same way about Trell.

Işak left the prince in haste then, walking purposefully through the camp to disguise the ill feelings that haunted him. But he wondered, *why did a god spare your life, Trell val Lorian? What made you so special?* And behind these thoughts, so faint as to be nearly nonexistent, repeated another whispering plea, *why did He not see fit to spare me as well?*

A part of Işak wished he could take the prince back to Tal'Shira himself, but he knew the compulsion patterns laid upon him would never let him diverge from his assigned task, and a passing interest in a northern prince was not worth the incapacitating infirmity that resulted from attempts to fight Dore's will.

Still…

It was full daylight before Joss returned, and his expression, plus the lack of a seventh member in their party, did not bode well for his success. He jumped from his horse and stalked over to where Trell lay.

"*You!*" He grabbed him by the hair and hauled him up to his knees. "Where's your damnable cousin?"

The commotion drew Işak's attention, and he closed upon the scene to find Trell sitting on his heels regarding Joss with an unyielding storm-grey gaze. Işak saw great strength in the prince for all he could hardly be twenty and three.

"Your man put three darts into my cousin," Trell told him coolly. "That's the last I saw of him."

Joss spun to Işak. "Make him tell the truth!"

"I believe he just did," Işak replied. "The problem seems to be your dull-witted questioning."

While Joss glowered, Işak inquired from safely within the shadows of his hood, "And after Sharpe damaged your cousin, what did you do? Did you help him in some way?" He made sure his compulsion pattern was fully upon the prince before he finished this question.

Işak could see Trell fighting the compulsion—amazingly, it took the entire force of his own will to hold the pattern upon him! But in the end, Trell gasped out through gritted teeth, "*Fled*—with—a Healer."

"Ah yes, the *Healer*." Işak had forgotten about her—they all had—so focused they'd been on gaining the royal cousin. But Rethynnea's Guild Master had reported to the Karakurt that a Healer would also be traveling with Fynnlar val Lorian.

"Shite!" Joss shoved Trell and set to stomping and cursing. That's when Raliax finally joined them, looking ill-humored and unkempt, as if the harlot Sleep had been arousing and denying him all night. "A bloody Healer took Fynnlar val Lorian away!" Joss shouted to Raliax.

Işak meanwhile looked to Trell. Disbelief colored his tone as he said slowly, "So you…*heir* to the Eagle Throne, *you* stayed with your men to divert us so that your wounded cousin and a simple Healer might escape? How terribly…noble."

Raliax spouted a stream of curses. "We'll never find them now! Should've been after them last night!" He cast Işak a glare of venomous accusation.

"Yes, no doubt last night in the pitch dark you and your men would've proven more effective at capturing your quarry than you have in the past." Işak pinned the man with his shadowed gaze. "Tell me, how many other princes have you slain who will soon be coming back to life?"

Though Işak had meant it only as a slight, Raliax recoiled at the words.

Joss's gaze flicked between Raliax and Işak. "We'll just tell Ean val Lorian we have the cousin."

"If we say we have the cousin when we don't," Işak replied, "and by some good fortune, or perhaps the Healer's skill, the cousin survives Sharpe's darts and turns up elsewhere, this will call into question the validity of our hand."

"Afraid of a lie?" Raliax sneered. "Worried it will sully that ego of yours?"

Işak looked to him curiously. His strange barbs seemed better aimed at another man. Işak perceived a simmering resentment in Raliax that seemed to have come from nowhere, yet it must've been building for years.

"When wielded properly, a lie can find its mark truer than any blade," Işak replied to Raliax, "but when used improperly, it's about as useful as a spoon in a swordfight."

Raliax rounded on him. "You think you're so high and mighty," he hissed, nose to nose with Işak, his breath foul and reeking of drink. "But when it comes down to the end of things, you're no better than me."

"No...I am far worse."

Raliax growled in frustration. "Do what you like." He waved a brusque hand. "Ean val Lorian is your problem now." He looked to the assembled men who were going with him. "Bring a horse for our remarkable Prince Trell, back from the dead—and make ready! We head for Tal'Shira."

"And us for Saldaria," Işak told Joss. "Get the other prisoners. We'll leave the cousin to Fate."

As the men were dispersing, Trell lifted his gaze back to Işak. Even dirtied and bound, he displayed a grave dignity. "Why do you hide your face from me?" he asked quietly, the slightest tightening of his grey-eyed gaze the only hint that the question troubled him.

Why do you know so completely that I do?

"Farewell, prince of Dannym," Işak said, turning away. He could no longer bear conversing with the man; the prince's presence filled him with an uncommon ache. "I do not think we shall meet again."

"I wouldn't be so sure of that," Trell murmured, and when Işak swung a sharp look over his shoulder, he saw that the prince was smiling.

FORTY-FIVE

"Give me wine or give me death—I prefer the wine."

– The royal cousin Fynnlar val Lorian

ALYNERI RODE WITH fear as her closest companion. Fynnlar was hanging on by a thread, and she had to stop frequently during the interminable night to see to his welfare. Each time, Alyneri repaired what she could of Fynn's life pattern and forced him to drink some water, but she dared not remove the pronged darts that impaled his flesh. She was ever casting an eye over her shoulder, hoping at every new junction, turn, or trail that Trell would be there, hale and smiling, racing to catch them.

Gendaia seemed to sense unerringly which direction to take among the labyrinthine canyons—indeed, the horse refused to follow any of Alyneri's commands if they involved changing from her own course. In time, Alyneri began to trust that the horse actually knew where she was going. It gave her hope that perhaps she would find help…that she hadn't lost Trell forever.

When dawn finally came, Gendaia was treading a high road out of the gorge. All around, the Kutsamak spread, a mottled, forbidding maze of shadowed canyons and stark, jagged ridges, their crumbling edges illuminated in the glaring morning light. Alyneri had no idea where they were and no idea how long they would have to keep going, and she feared with every breath that Trell wouldn't come.

Between the strain of gnawing fears and pouring everything she had into strengthening Fynn's pattern all night, Alyneri could barely keep her eyes open. It seemed that each new footfall of sunlight across the mountains stole away a second more of Fynn's life. Only her regular ministrations were keeping his heart beating.

Alyneri spared another glance at him. He looked bad. Blood made a dark stain of his clothes and soaked down his horse's flank.

Pulling gently for Gendaia to halt, Alyneri slipped out of the saddle intending to check on Fynn again, but as her foot touched the earth, a great dizziness cast blackness across her vision and brought a threatening nausea. She daren't try another healing then, not without food or rest, but one look at Fynn told her that he wouldn't live to see another sunrise.

Alyneri gripped her saddle until the world no longer spun dangerously. Then she took her canteen over to Fynn. She hadn't thought him conscious, but he whispered, "…fine…" as she reached his side.

"You are not fine."

"Just…a scratch."

Alyneri gave him a sip of water while regarding him with gratitude and admiration. "I think all that wine you've consumed must be acting as an embalming agent. Anyone else would've given up seven canyons ago."

"Want…see…dragon." He took another sip of the water she offered but pushed her hand away after that.

As if on cue, the sun cleared the rim of the mountains in a spearing glare, and the heat came riding on its tide. Squinting in the suddenly over-bright morning, Alyneri stripped Fynn of his cloak and sorted through his pack until she found a linen tunic the right size for her needs. With a bit of rope tied in a rose knot—the specific knot used in the traditional Kandori *agal* circlets—she fashioned Fynn a *keffiyeh* to protect his head and neck.

Then she did the same for herself using a long scarf she'd found among Trell's packs. With nothing else to be done to help Fynn, Alyneri took up her reins. But as she placed her hands on her saddle, she dropped her chin to her chest and forced a shuddering inhale, trying desperately not to cry. Her hands were shaking terribly. She was exhausted and frightened. There seemed no hope of a favorable outcome.

It took a few agonizing minutes to pull herself together—minutes Fynn probably didn't have, and which she berated herself about afterwards—but eventually she swallowed her despair, set her foot into the stirrup and remounted.

Alyneri shook out her hands as if to disperse the fear that gripped her and took up her reins. Them she looked grimly to Fynn. "We have to keep going."

He made the barest of nods in acknowledgment, and they set off again.

It was a very long day.

They rested for a time during in the shade of an overhanging rock. When not resting, Alyneri tried to travel in the shadows as much as possible. But this was the Kutsamak—the ochre walls were formed of shale and crumbling sandstone, and their sheer sides offered little relief from the relentless sun.

Still, she did what she could, and whenever she came upon a stream that still flowed, she rested there to let the horses drink and tried to put a little life back into Fynn with whatever of her own she could spare. When Fynn started drifting in and out of consciousness, she tied him to his saddle with a combination of rope from their packs and torn strips of cloth and took up his reins herself, looping them about her own pommel.

And ever she pressed back a continuous thrumming fear and a standing wave of grief. The enemy of exhaustion required constant vigilance, but her own mind posed a bigger adversary still.

Who were those men? What had they wanted? Had they been coming for Trell or another of their company? And had anyone lived through it?

Alyneri didn't know how she survived that second night still in her saddle. The hours of darkness blurred together until, with the paling of dawn, she looked up to find Gendaia standing in the unmistakable shadow of Jar'iman Point.

Abruptly she jerked awake.

She spun a look at Fynn and grabbed for his wrist. She detected a faint and feeble pulse, as well as the barest rise and fall of his chest.

Somehow they'd both made it through the night.

Alyneri looked around, trying to get her bearings, trying to focus and think through her exhaustion…trying to understand why Gendaia had inexplicably stopped.

The trail looked much like any other they'd followed thus far: an arid expanse of sun-baked rocks and dry earth. Her eyes were scanning an outcropping of rock when a shadow fell across it. Alyneri shaded her eyes with one hand and lifted her gaze to the eastern sky.

An immense dragon flew between her and the sun—she wagered it must've boasted a hundred feet from nose to tail. Bathed in the backlight of dawn, the outline of its hide flamed a brilliant gold nearly too bright to look upon.

Abruptly Alyneri understood why Trell had given her his horse, his weapon. He'd told her that the *drachwyr* could see the smallest details from great distances. She dove for Trell's blade and then used both hands to wave the sword back and forth in the air. "Please..." she begged, "*oh, please...*"

At last the dragon turned and began coming towards her. Soaring overhead, it buffeted her with the rising tide of heat from its wings, banked in solitary silence out over the canyon, and began heading back the way it had come.

Alyneri lowered Trell's blade to her lap and exhaled a shuddering breath. A host of new fears sprouted as she watched the Sundragon flying away. Yet, what had she expected would happen? That the creature would relinquish the form, perhaps in a geyser of light, as Gwynnleth was wont to do, and come to her immediate rescue?

Well...yes. That's apparently what she'd been hoping for.

It was agonizing watching the dragon disappearing into the distance without knowing if she'd accomplished anything at all. A lump caught in her throat, and her chest constricted with breath that refused to come...

"...dragon..." Fynn murmured.

Alyneri turned him a startled look.

Beneath a grimace of pain, Fynn was grinning.

Ever grateful for Fynn's remarkable spirit, Alyneri pulled out her flagon and leaned to give him another sip of water. Then she laid her hand on his knee and closed her eyes, seeking rapport.

But *elae* felt slippery in her grasp. Every time she reached for it, stinging nettles speared her eyes and needles pierced her brain. She ignored these warning signs through sheer obstinacy and finally held *elae* again.

Once she had hold of the lifeforce, she did what she could to smooth the frayed edges of Fynn's pattern. As she released *elae* again, her head exploded with a viselike throbbing, and she sucked in a desperate gasp and swooned. She caught both hands on the pommel of her saddle and sat, hunched over, until the violent, swimming blackness before her vision cleared and Gendaia's mane came back into focus. It was a frightening moment while her heart raced and her mind fought frantically to remain conscious.

Alyneri knew she was nearing a deadly boundary. If crossed, it would mean her sure end, as well as Fynn's.

Alyneri swallowed back a sick feeling and the taste of bile and slowly looked up again.

A tall woman was approaching.

Lithe and shapely in form-fitting black leather, she wore her raven hair in a long braid and walked with dual swords strapped to her back, the hilts extending above each shoulder. Alyneri knew at once who she must be. She searched through the fog of exhaustion and finally came up with a name.

"Vaile." Alyneri's voice sounded a desperate gasp. She summoned her strength and her courage in equal measure. "You *are* Vaile, aren't you? Please tell me you are!"

Vaile's green eyes took in Alyneri, Gendaia, and Fynn all in one sweep, and her gaze tightened. "Where is Trell of the Tides?"

Alyneri burst into tears.

It all came out in a rush then—hysterically, disjointed, the story following as a flock of frenzied birds, flying everywhere and nowhere in the telling. Yet she managed the most fearful points: the attack, their urgent flight, Trell's promise to meet her at the sa'reyth, Fynn's desperate state...

The air felt charged when she was finished, as in the moments before a thunderstorm breaks, when the storm is yet rising and the world has gone dark. Alyneri realized it was the fifth strand she sensed, that Vaile had summoned it with her fury, and now it hummed in static impatience. She turned on her heel. "Come with me."

Alyneri followed in numb silence. The one time she thought to say something to the zanthyr, Vaile silenced her with a sharp look.

Then they crossed a node.

Alyneri felt a momentary disorientation, and the landscape changed abruptly. Arid hills changed to a rolling meadow of deep green grass bordered by violet-hued mountains.

In the haze of exhaustion, Alyneri found herself wondering if all zanthyrs could travel the nodes while fretting over Fynn's condition and fearing what it meant that Trell hadn't come. All of these worries seemed to swirl in her brain, a poisonous mix that refused to blend.

They rounded a rise and came in view of a large compound of conjoined coppery tents lower on the hillside. Two men were walking through the long grass up the hill to meet them.

"Vaile, what have you?" asked the taller and older-looking of the two.

"This is the Healer Alyneri d'Giverny," Vaile replied, "betrothed of Trell of the Tides, and Trell's cousin Fynnlar, also a friend of the pirate Carian vran Lea—and in dire need of Healing." Then she added with some heat, "Náiir, they have taken Trell."

Alyneri was amazed Vaile had gleaned all of that information from her hysterical ramblings, for she remembered saying little of it.

Náiir's expression darkened as if a cloud had overtaken the sun. *No— not a cloud, a hurricane.* "*Who* has taken Trell?" he asked, ominous and low.

"Saldarians, I gather."

This came as news to Alyneri. She had no idea how Vaile could've reached this conclusion when she herself had known nothing of it.

Náiir gave Vaile a telling stare. "I will notify Rhakar to search for them." He spun and rushed away.

Vaile looked to the other male then, whose sapphire tunic stood out brilliantly against his youthful caramel skin. "Balaji, the cousin is in desperate need of Healing, and I must see what I can do to help him. Take Alyneri to Jaya, who will be of better comfort to her than you or I. And someone had best contact the Mage."

Balaji gave her a quiet look in return. Alyneri saw much of wisdom in his gaze, for all he seemed barely ten and six. "Are you certain of this course, Vaile? If you take it upon yourself to heal this man—"

Vaile's eyes flashed. "He is *Trell's* cousin, Balaji. That makes him one of us!"

Balaji's gaze hinted of warning and amusement in one. "You know what it is you declare?"

Vaile snarled her reply in a language that sounded as old as the bedrock of the realm in a tone that reminded Alyneri uncannily of the affronted growl of a cat. Then she spun and stalked off, leading Fynn's horse.

Gazing after her, Balaji smiled faintly. "Apparently you do." He looked to Alyneri then, and his expression fell into concern. "Come, *soraya*."

Thus, Alyneri followed the youth named Balaji, and the next hour became a blur. She remembered being handed over to a lovely woman with citrine-colored eyes and given something hot and spicy to drink. She remembered weeping desperately on a sofa while the lovely woman comforted her with kind words, and then…nothing else for a long time.

FORTY-SIX

"I do not believe in failure. The supreme test of
a man is his ability to persevere."

– The Adept wielder Arion Tavestra

LONG AFTER NIGHT had claimed Tal'Shira and sleep had claimed the Marquiin Yveric, Kjieran stood in the shadows of an arcade that opened onto one of the many stone-paved courtyards in Radov's palace complex.

This plaza, called the Court of Fifty-Two Arches, had been built in honor of the original fifty-two Nadori princes who'd paid tribute to the Hadorin rule, centuries past. The coat of arms of each prince had been carved into one of the plaza's pillars.

Kjieran couldn't imagine living life in a kingdom of fifty-two princes who each believed himself of equal right to rule. No wonder M'Nador was always at war.

Draped in shadows, Kjieran watched all who came and went and listened to the thoughts of careless passersby who didn't know how to think in whispers. To any who glanced his way, he would've seemed but one more shadow, for he had mastered fourth-strand illusion patterns in the Sormitáge, and as yet, *elae* remained his to command.

The vast courtyard bustled even at that late hour, for it was a gathering place for anyone with legal business inside Radov's walls. But Kjieran watched the square because it held the only node in Tal'Shira not guarded by Saldarians.

Dore had used this node to bring Kjieran from the Prophet's temple in Tambarré to Tal'Shira. His own travel notwithstanding, the node otherwise boasted exclusive use by men upon business for Radov or Viernan hal'Jaitar. If ever Kjieran hoped to cross paths with one of the Shamshir'im, it would be in the Court of Fifty-Two Arches.

The Shamshir'im were hal'Jaitar's men. Wielders, assassins, spies… capable of any manner of treachery in the name of princedom or by mere warrant of their leader's will—for hal'Jaitar needed no more justification to order men upon perfidious deeds than because it suited his aims. Yveric had assured him: if a secret was to be found in Tal'Shira, it would be found among the Shamshir'im.

Not that Kjieran expected anyone to confess culpability in Sebastian or Trell's death, yet there were ways of encouraging men upon a subject. A truthreader might use any manner of subtle mental prodding to bring a topic to light. How many times had his own Sormitáge master elicited whispering among a group of malcontents that he might learn of their allegiances? Or introduced a revolutionary idea into a meeting of young idealists by the merest thought placed within the aether and made to linger, floating among them like a bright candle, until one of them picked it up, thinking it his own?

A trained truthreader knew a host of subtle, delicate ways to elicit information without anyone becoming aware of it. Tellings and Readings were the blunt mallets of brutes compared to this fine craft.

Such mastery might be observed in a truthreader who had his second Sormitáge ring. Before the Adept Wars, hundreds of Adepts had boasted multiple rings—even as hal'Jaitar wore, and more besides.

Swapping tales of the ringed wielders of the Fourth Age was a favorite pastime of Sormitáge students—especially tales of Markal Morrelaine and his most famous pupil, Arion Tavestra, both of whom were rumored to have worn two rows of rings on all ten fingers. Such investiture claimed an advanced understanding of the Laws of Patterning as well as expert application of the Esoterics.

Of course, the Fifth Vestal was said to have worn five such "rows"—ten fingers, five rings upon each—but Kjieran had always believed those tales laughably exaggerated.

How far they had fallen when most trained Adepts claimed but a single ring.

As fears for his dying race were accosting him like bats flapping blindly in a brightly lit room, Kjieran saw two men suddenly appear in the middle of the court. One looked injured and clung to the other as they stepped off the node into the Tal'Shira night. Even as Kjieran watched, the taller, haler man turned to his damaged companion. Kjieran saw steel flash in the moonlight, and the slouching man fell backwards onto the stones, his throat severed.

Kjieran reached quickly for their thoughts. He gleaned but little from the dying man, who had been mostly dead before he crossed the node. The other set off purposefully, but not before Kjieran plucked a whispered name from his thoughts.

Kjieran latched onto the other's mind and slipped through the shadows in silent pursuit.

But oh, he had to be careful!

Hal'Jaitar was a known *raedan*, and the pattern Kjieran worked to hide himself from view would leave its mark upon the tides of *elae*. If hal'Jaitar traced the working back to him, it would mean his certain end—yet Kjieran could ill afford to be *seen* following one of Viernan's spies.

To minimize his risk, he used real shadows to conceal himself when he could, created the illusion of them when he could not, and allowed himself to be openly seen when he believed the danger not too great. He hoped the pattern he was using would appear in such brief flashes upon the currents that it would be difficult to trace it back to him. But he also knew *hope* was as likely to betray him as Fate already had. In truth, only duty drove him on.

The lower half of his legs felt strange as he walked, heavy yet empty, solid but with the sensation of nothingness. From the odd feeling, he might've considered he had no legs at all—

Suddenly he felt the Prophet's attention open upon him. Bethamin's presence suddenly flooded into Kjieran's mind amid a deluge of chill power and webbed heat, electrifying the bond in a fiery seal between them.

Kjieran gasped and released his pattern just an instant before the Prophet flayed his mind with the dagger of his attention, baring its tender places to his least inspection.

Kjieran forced himself to keep moving, to act as if nothing had changed in his own actions or thoughts. The Prophet had warned him that he might compel Kjieran at any moment, even as he had done upon his first arrival in Tal'Shira, and he was loath to give the man cause to do so again.

Bethamin gazed through his eyes for a time—a frightful few minutes. Eventually Bethamin must've concluded that Kjieran was merely out for a walk and left him to it. He withdrew his presence like leviathan tentacles sliding back into a lightless lair.

Kjieran exhaled a tumultuous gasp. Immediately he summoned his pattern of shadows, only feeling safe when he again felt *elae* infusing him, once he knew no one could see his twitching hands.

For the space of an indrawn breath, Kjieran clutched Raine's amulet hidden beneath his tunic and squeezed shut his eyes. Desperation seized him.

Then the feeling passed, and Kjieran opened his eyes. His quarry had gained a wide lead while he'd been despairing, so he ran to close the distance.

Heading into a narrow, arched tunnel, Kjieran nearly collided with a man coming from the opposite direction. He wore a black chequered *keffiyeh* wrapped by a red *agal*, a fringe of small tassels declaring his minor sheikdom amid the vast wealth of the Nadori princehoods—the larger the tassel, the greater the fortune; the nobility spoke of Radov's grandiose tassels as boasting wealth in outrageous proportion, though it was whispered among less esteemed company that the unending war had drained the prince's coffers, and now he merely boasted.

The sheik stopped between Kjieran and his quarry, barring access through the narrow tunnel, and Kjieran plastered himself against the wall with growing animosity while the sheik relit his stub of a *siyar* with a spark of flint and steel. Exhaling a cloud of bluish smoke, he pushed past Kjieran, never noticing him. Kjieran was tempted to plant within him the idea that he no longer liked the taste of *siyar* leaves but dared not risk such a working merely to assuage his annoyance.

Emerging from the tunnel into the Court of the Winds, he cast his mind in a fan of perception. He picked up the thoughts of hal'Jaitar's spy on the far side of the square, just before he disappeared into another arched passage. Kjieran wouldn't have recognized him by sight alone, for he now wore a red chequered *keffiyeh* and seemed one of a hundred others. Only the specific feel of his mind radiating his urgency to find hal'Jaitar made him visible to Kjieran.

Kjieran pinned his attention on the man more directly and sprinted across the courtyard, dangerously making his pattern solid that none might notice him running in chase.

He dove into the tunnel after the man but came to an abrupt halt. A single lamp lit the arched passage, and the spy had stopped beneath it to search through the purse at his belt. Kjieran drew shadows as a cloak around him and slipped into the deeper darkness to watch and observe.

The man counted his coin idly for a while, though Kjieran read from his thoughts that he was waiting until he was sure he was alone. Then he spun to the wall beneath the iron sconce and worked a trace-seal in the air with both forefingers, a complex pattern that spiraled in opposite directions. Kjieran rejoiced in seeing it, for only a wielder such as hal'Jaitar might've crafted a trace-seal of such complexity, and surely none but his Shamshir'im would've known it.

The stone wall swung inward with a nearly inaudible click, and the man slipped through the parting into the darkness. Kjieran darted after him before the seal reactivated and the portal closed.

The doorway opened into a narrow stone corridor. Wielder's lamps, called 'brighteyes,' were set into sconces every twenty paces. The iron lamps depended upon the touch of *elae* to spring to light, but they were usually calibrated to recognize the lifeforce inherent in all living men, wielder or no. The brighteyes lit up like chimes struck by a passing hand the moment their pattern touched a living man's, and they winked out again when a man moved beyond reach of the patterns that bound each lamp.

Kjieran's spy had already reached the second brighteye, which blinked on just as the first extinguished, casting Kjieran into darkness. He rushed to close the distance, lest the lights blink on and off again and alert the spy to his presence.

Had he been less focused upon following the man, Kjieran might've wondered why the brighteye blinked to darkness at all, considering he was standing so near to it. But Kjieran's mind was too occupied with other worries, and the thought never occurred to him.

They descended a set of narrow, twisting stairs that had Kjieran feeling lightheaded by the time he reached the landing. At the end of another corridor stood a wooden door bound in iron. The spy opened this door with another trace seal.

Kjieran followed him into a vaulted antechamber, obviously subterranean. Looking around, he saw additional doors opening into the room, while one long wall sported hundreds of pegs upon which hung black hoods cut with narrow eye slots. The spy grabbed a hood and shoved it over his head before walking towards a pair of massive double doors at the chamber's far end.

Draped in shadows, Kjieran stole a hood and followed.

The final portal stood at least thirty paces high and was carved with the raging face of the Wind God, Azerjaiman. The doors opened with a single touch of the spy's finger upon a stylized golden plate. Kjieran made sure to slip through before the doors shut, for he'd seen such plates in use in Agasan. They were attuned to each spy's life pattern, and no amount of Adept craft could impersonate it.

Just inside, Kjieran drew up short.

He stood within a massive stone chamber, whose vaulted ceiling disappeared in shadows. Two rows of square stone columns supported the ceiling beams, and every side of every column sported a different banner, each five times the length of a man. Gigantic hearths on the four walls warmed the subterranean room, while ringed chandeliers illuminated the length of the great chamber.

Between each column, along the walls, faceless statues twice as tall as a man wore stylized, oversized armor representing a host of countries and kingdoms. Each one sported a different weapon frozen in a killing blow.

Closest to him, Kjieran saw a knight in gold plate armor with a red axe embedded in his helmet. Further down, a statue wearing a hauberk and surcoat emblazed with a kingly crest stood with a black-feathered bolt through his blank eye; while a statue resplendent in a gold lamellar cuirass under a violet desert robe stood with arms thrown back and three wicked, seven-pointed stars buried in its chest. Countless other suits of armor stood forever trapped in their own dramatic moment of death.

Then Kjieran's eyes fell upon the tapestry at the end of the room, and he lost all interest in the gruesome statues.

Hanging from ceiling to floor, the tapestry covered the entire rear wall. Fifty horses might've stood upon its midnight-black wool with room to spare. In the center of the tapestry, sewn with thousands of spools of thread-of-silver, shone the three-daggered crest of the Assassin's Guild.

Kjieran managed a dry swallow.

Hooded men crowded the room. Notably, none of them wore weapons—at least none that could be seen—though Kjieran felt this only made the men more dangerous. He released his pattern of illusion in favor of the simple hood, lest hal'Jaitar note the working upon the currents. But as he secured the hood around his face, it occurred to him for the first time that Dore had irrevocably changed his life pattern. With a grim smile, Kjieran realized he might not even *have* a life pattern any longer.

At least two hundred guild members strolled the vast room, milling and talking in small groups as they drank wine, perhaps making alliances...or breaking them. For so many people, the hall remained eerily quiet.

Kjieran kept one eye pinned on his spy, whose chequered *keffiyeh* peeked out from beneath his black hood, and followed as the man walked through the crowd intently, his thoughts a jumble of fractious censure.

Kjieran walked behind him, listening to the room at large with ears and mind. Many had walled their thoughts behind strong patterns of protection, and Kjieran marked these men as wielders. Such were trained to keep one eye on their back and another on the currents, that they might perceive when someone was working *elae* nearby. Kjieran gave them a wide berth.

Blue-robed servants in half-masks of dazzling silver carried trays offering an array of varied refreshments. One such bowed to him, and he felt obliged to take the goblet of wine the man offered. But he didn't drink from it, and he set it down again at the first opportunity, lest his twitching hands rouse the curiosity of this sharp-eyed congregation.

And then, with a sudden sinking feeling, Kjieran realized he would *have* to work some illusion; a truthreader would never be admitted into this company, and his eyes would give him away the moment he met another's gaze.

Just then the spy stopped to watch a man approaching from across the room. It took a moment before Kjieran realized it was hal'Jaitar, for the wielder was equally hooded. Yet his was a distinctive walk, the gait of a man who believed he owned the world.

Kjieran needed to get closer to overhear their conversation, but they stood in the middle of the hall. Quickly summoning a different pattern,

Kjieran joined a group of four men who were standing within earshot of hal'Jaitar and his spy. The fourth-strand pattern he used made each of the men think Kjieran was one of the others, while never noticing a fifth had actually joined their number. Kjieran hadn't worked the illusion in many years and had never been very good at it to begin with, but he could think of no better way to conceal his presence from hal'Jaitar's piercing observation.

Kjieran concentrated on holding the pattern and shifted closer to the spy, whereupon he heard hal'Jaitar hiss, "What are you doing here? Why aren't you in Tambarré?"

"Events move quickly," the spy answered in a low voice. Kjieran couldn't quite place his accent, though it sounded eastern—perhaps of Vest. "Dore sent his puppet wielder, Işak—the one you told me to watch—on a hunt for Ean val Lorian."

"He *what?*" Hal'Jaitar hissed a curse in the desert tongue, a vicious oath full of rancor. "*What was he thinking*, putting the two of them together? By the foul testicles of Belloth, I vow that lunatic cannot tell the difference between fortune and folly. What if the puppet remembers something of his former life? No patterns are so foolproof they cannot be unraveled by a wielder of greater power!"

"There's more," remarked the spy significantly.

Hal'Jaitar drew back. "More," he repeated. "*What* more?"

"Raliax and Işak'getirmek took some of Prince Ean's men hostage. They were aiming for the royal cousin Fynnlar, son of Prince Ryan, but they found another instead."

Suspicion darkened hal'Jaitar's gaze. "Who?"

"Trell val Lorian."

Trell!

Kjieran nearly lost hold of his pattern; he grappled mentally to reclaim it before it flew out of his control. The infraction made just the slightest hitch in the currents, yet it was enough to catch the attention of hal'Jaitar, who turned and looked directly at Kjieran's group.

Kjieran went still. He knew he would seem but one more hood among the many, yet his heart was racing. Hal'Jaitar stared in his direction for a harrowing few breaths more. Then his own business ostensibly became more pressing, for he looked back to his spy. "You're certain it was the prince?"

"I wouldn't have come otherwise. I'm expected to bring a Nodefinder back to the camp to retrieve Raliax and the prince. 'Getirmek and the rest continued on, following the original plan."

Hal'Jaitar grabbed the spy by both shoulders. "Raliax is bringing Trell val Lorian to the palace—*with Gydryn val Lorian veritably in the next room?*"

"'Getirmek said Radov would want to know what the prince knows, where's he's been, who else knows he lives."

"Far too many!" hal'Jaitar snapped. Then he abruptly collected himself. "Of course—of course, he must bring the prince to us…but this poses new complications." He pinned his spy with a vituperative glare. "What did the prince say? Where has he been all this time?"

"'Getirmek questioned him. I didn't hear his answers."

"Unfortunate…but we shall have our chance. And Işak'getirmek himself?" Hal'Jaitar searched the spy's eyes with his own icy onyx gaze. "How did he react to the news?"

"He seemed a little…off after learning the prince's name, but the man is always off." He shrugged.

"Yes…he has too much of Dore Madden in his head." Hal'Jaitar brow furrowed deeply, and his attention momentarily strayed, as if with thought. "It seems at least the fourth-strand patterns are holding. Well and good." He cast a piercing gaze once again across Kjieran's group, who were just then dispersing. Kjieran decided he was pushing his luck and moved off at an appropriate pace.

Inside he was reeling.

Trell lives?

Kjieran quietly sought the safety of the shadows and then headed towards the doors. He kept his eyes downcast and his twitching hands hidden within his cloak. If only his heart had still functioned, it would've been beating furiously. As it was, he felt as if every hair upon his body stood on end, the news had so electrified him.

"I don't believe we've met," said a man suddenly from behind. "Or have we?"

Kjieran nearly missed a step upon hearing Viernan hal'Jaitar's voice so close in his ear. He had no idea of the protocol among this group, how they acknowledged each other or knew friend from foe. The door and escape seemed suddenly miles away.

"I asked you a *question*." The wielder grabbed for Kjieran's wrist.

Kjieran felt his hand twitch reflexively, felt the Prophet's chill power leap out of his palm—leap for hal'Jaitar as lightning seeks the highest point.

The wielder hissed a curse and drew back with a violent jerk.

Kjieran urgently called the shadows around him and bolted for the doors. He careened through a group who were just then departing, thrusting several ungently out of his path, and heard hal'Jaitar shouting from behind. He had but a few precious seconds to escape, for once the wielders in the crowd were alerted to him, his simple patterns would be shattered as easily as glass upon a rock.

He pushed clear of the group at the doors and stumbled into the antechamber. Two men were just then leaving through one of the portals. Kjieran drew heavily upon *elae,* as much of the lifeforce as he could hold. He made his illusion pattern completely solid and rushed towards them—

And the Prophet's eye opened upon him.

Perhaps his use of *elae* had resonated through the bond back to the Prophet and alerted him, or perhaps it was just ill chance, but Kjieran felt Bethamin's awareness awakening powerfully within him. He staggered—just paces from the portal and escape—conscious only of the agony of the Prophet's scalding attention.

KJIERAN, WHAT IS THIS YOU DO?

For a moment, the world went white with pain. As focus returned, Kjieran realized he'd lost *elae* completely…that others were staring at him.

Danger, my lord! Still reeling, Kjieran careened into a wall and nearly fell, for the Prophet's presence in his mind was all-possessing, a blazing force that eradicated independent thought.

In the main chamber, men were yelling.

My lord, I'm in terrible danger!

The Prophet's awareness flooded into Kjieran's mind and took control, seeing what Kjieran saw, understanding…calculating.

The chamber doors burst open. Kjieran spun to see hal'Jaitar leading a band of others. The Prophet read Kjieran's frantic thoughts and understood the approaching men were enemies.

A great blast of power burst forth, thunder without sound. Kjieran barely recognized that the power had come from him. He was the resounding gong of the Prophet's mallet, sending waves of energy rebounding against the cavern walls. The men nearest him fell beneath the onslaught, but hal'Jaitar and his wielders must've shielded themselves, for they stood their ground—if with difficulty.

Wearing Kjieran's body as if his own, the Prophet turned to the nearest door and splintered it with a look. He thrust Kjieran towards it like a marionette.

Kjieran stumbled into the tunnel, and the Prophet drove his body onward, sprinting through the dark. Rock shattered around him as he ran; lamps exploded, and every step left a dent in the stones beneath his feet.

Kjieran ran for a very long time.

Finally seeing a door, Bethamin splintered it with another bolt of soundless thunder and charged Kjieran's body through the opening. He stumbled out into a dark alley.

WHERE?

Kjieran could barely think, but he managed a vague picture of the ocean. Tal'Shira's cliffs would be the safest place to hide, for the elemental forces of sea and wind diffused *elae's* currents.

The Prophet turned him east and drove him on.

Kjieran finally collapsed inside a sea cave. The Prophet had been controlling Kjieran's body with the abandon of an immortal who stood unquestioned by the elements; accordingly, he'd swum through a raging surf, been tumbled in battering waves and all but shattered against the rocks.

Finally, as Kjieran was lying there upon the damp and clinging sand, the Prophet withdrew from his mind, leaving Kjieran ragged and spent, his will broken.

He'd felt violated all during the Prophet's possession and then horribly vacant once the man had gone. For all that Kjieran despised his lord in so many ways, yet the Prophet's force of being was godlike. No mortal might commune intimately with a god and not be left lacking upon separation.

Kjieran lay for a long time staring dully into the darkness. He realized with a latent sense of horror that his body needed neither breath nor sustenance; it seemed a grim irony that he couldn't even shed a tear over all that had been taken from him.

He was still lying there, numb with hopelessness, when—

He found himself lying within the Prophet's torch-lit chambers. He blinked to focus on the vastly cold and impersonal rooms where he'd so often been called in the dark of night. He pushed up on his hands, dumbfounded, trying to understand what had just happened. Had the Prophet *actually* moved him so instantaneously, or was this some kind of illusion?

"Kjieran." The Prophet's deep voice thundered through him, bringing ice to his veins, setting his pulse alive. Bethamin paused in the portal between two chambers. His muscled chest and legs were bare, his loins draped with a rectangle of silk held with a gold chain caught low around his hips. The vastness of his presence filled every inch of the room and still could not be contained.

Kjieran scrambled to his knees and pressed his forehead to the floor in reverent greeting. "My lord," he whispered, feeling his warm breath between his lips and the cold marble floor.

No, this was definitely not real, for his breath no longer came at all in life. But what then was it?

The Prophet approached. Kjieran felt the heat of his fury as the sun upon his back. Yet Bethamin's anger equally mingled with desire and uncertainty, intertwining without combining, a rotating flask of incompatible emotions.

"I have found it difficult to gain your dreams," the Prophet informed him. "Dore explained the nature of the bond may now prevent this medium but has instead engendered another."

Kjieran sat back on his heels, for he somehow knew the Prophet desired to look upon his face, yet he kept his colorless eyes downcast. "My lord." He watched the Prophet's black-enameled toes come to a halt before him. "Where are we?"

"We stand in the antechamber of my mind."

Kjieran closed his eyes upon hearing this. T'was little wonder the Prophet's thoughts and emotions were so clear to him. Yet the realization left him trembling, for there could be no escape from whatever nightmare the Prophet now dreamed, no release until Bethamin desired it.

Kjieran wanted to cry, but tears were denied him now in life, and he doubted very much he would find them there, in the mind of the Prophet Bethamin.

"I don't approve of what occurred tonight, Kjieran."

Kjieran felt the cold wave of Bethamin's displeasure crash over him, colder than the waves that had battered his real body only hours before. He trembled beneath their chill censure. "My lord," he murmured wretchedly, "I can explain—"

"Dore says I should take you in hand, Kjieran. He warns that without compulsion, you cannot be trusted."

"No, my lord!" Kjieran gasped, more horrified than ever by the threat. "I am your servant!"

"How were you serving me tonight?"

Kjieran stared hard at the marble floor. His eyes and throat burned with unshed tears. "Hal'Jaitar," he managed weakly, "he works against you."

"Indeed," murmured the Prophet, sounding dubious.

"He has already tried to kill me once and was attempting to do so again when you...when you came to me. I didn't know how to defend myself—"

"I felt you draw upon a foreign power." Thunderous censure accompanied these words. "I did not know *elae* was still yours to command."

Kjieran saw but one chance to save himself from the oblivion of compulsion. "Only...I think only because it bends to your will, my lord," he whispered. "I do not understand how it has come to me." It was a bold lie, yet Kjieran had no trouble saying it. He couldn't bear to contemplate the fact, for this was a devastating truth to confront about his new existence.

The Prophet stood silent for a moment, considering him. "You may be correct in this conclusion," he finally replied, and some of the threat dissipated from his manner. "No power in this realm is denied me, and I am just beginning to explore the limits of our bond."

"Yes, my lord," Kjieran whispered, repentant and contrite.

How strange to find that there, in the Prophet's mind, his heart still beat, his breath still came quickly in his chest, and he still felt the sting of unshed tears. Did the Prophet not understand that all of these experiences were now denied him? That the very pulse of life had been stripped away as like the withered flesh of his calves? Or did Bethamin merely choose to ignore this truth, perhaps enjoying more the fantasy of his own creation?

The Prophet placed one hand beneath Kjieran's chin and bade him rise upon his knees. "Kjieran, look at me."

Kjieran lifted his eyes, craning his neck as far back as it would go to meet his master's gaze. The Prophet's eyes were fixed upon him darkly, lustfully. They scalded him with their desire—in the man's own mind, there was no dissembling how he felt about Kjieran, or what he wanted of him.

Kjieran forced breath, forced himself to let the Prophet drink in the sight of his colorless eyes, yet all too aware of their mutual positions and the Prophet's arousal before him.

Bethamin slipped his cold hand along Kjieran's jaw and brought him to his feet with gentle urging. Kjieran swallowed as he complied.

"It is like you are truly here." The Prophet's dark eyes speared Kjieran with their hunger. "Yet I know you are not." His fingers found Kjieran's lips and explored their shape, a sculptor caressing his creation. "This is an interesting experience."

"Yes, my lord," Kjieran whispered. His heart was racing and his breath felt as sand in his lungs. He wasn't certain he could bear these torments, or even how he was feeling them at all.

"I must mention it to my brother, Pelas," the Prophet continued. "He has an… unusual view on the value of experience."

Kjieran did not value *any* experience if it happened within the confines of Bethamin's mind.

The Prophet frowned. His fingers paused in their minute inspection of his face. "Yet it is not the same, your being here."

"The same as what, my lord?" Kjieran whispered.

The Prophet's eyes were so terribly dark. "As having you before my person in the flesh."

Kjieran didn't know what to say to that. Being within the confines of Bethamin's mind, he understood what the Prophet wanted him to feel. That he was still free to experience anything of his own volition was surprising. More startling was the understanding that the Prophet wanted Kjieran to desire him *without* compulsion.

He dropped his eyes and swallowed. "I'm sorry, my lord."

If anything, his contrition only deepened the Prophet's hunger. Kjieran could feel Bethamin's mind pulsating with it, as if the very room throbbed in synchronicity with his lust. The Prophet pushed his thumb into the hollow of Kjieran's throat and then along his collarbone. "No one has ever intrigued me as you do, Kjieran. What will it take for you to desire me as I desire you?"

It was nearly more than he could bear, this entreaty, this offered temptation. Kjieran didn't *want* to like this man, yet the Prophet was courting him as strongly as any paramour, courting him with hope, with possibility, with trust…

It might be his only chance to save his king.

Kjieran knew what he would be forsaking in the moment he offered the bargain, but he laid it upon the table in trade nonetheless.

"You've granted me freedom, my lord," he managed a threadbare voice, for the Prophet's hand was still gripping his throat, "but is it freedom if you're watching my every action, my every step? If you're always there in my mind influencing my thoughts, is any decision really my own? And if my decisions are not my own, am I truly free?"

Hearing this, the Prophet dropped his hand sharply and gazed down at Kjieran, looking fierce and unearthly. He was frowning, yet Kjieran knew he wasn't entirely displeased with the question.

"Normally I would say choice is but an illusion, but you…" and his dark eyes considered Kjieran newly, "*you*, I have made more than you were. That you are seeking choice…this intrigues me. It is a consequence I hadn't explored—indeed, I hadn't thought it possible, though surely it is my imprint upon you that engenders this concept. Still…I must ask my brother Pelas what he thinks of this. No doubt he never imagined such a thing could become."

The Prophet turned away from Kjieran and moved towards the portal in which he'd first appeared. "Very well, Kjieran. I will grant you my trust. I shall not invade your thoughts unless you call for me." He turned in the portal and pinned Kjieran with his gaze, ever as cold and unfathomable as the endless night sky. "But I will call you regularly here to attend me," he noted significantly then, "and when I do, I hope to see the freedom I have sown begin to reap bountiful rewards."

FORTY-SEVEN

"The years were long and sometimes lonely,

but I was busy. I was busy living."

– Isabel van Gelderan, Epiphany's Prophet

E AN DREAMED OF another man's life, yet in that half-awareness one sometimes has in dreams, he knew that it had been his life... once.

He held a bloody sword and stood in a cavernous hall beneath a shattered dome. The crumbled debris of once-great vaults now supported the dead and dying. The marble floor was a littered wasteland, and all around him, the sounds of battle raged. There were other sounds as well: the abrasive roar of a distant, hungry fire; the unwholesome cries of the fallen as death sank in its spiny claws; and worst of all, the crackle of deyjiin on the tides of elae.

His hands and vambraces were slick with blood. Though none of it was his own, he felt as if much of the blood shed that night had belonged to him personally, so dear to him were those who had already fallen.

He looked down upon the man dying at his feet: a Paladin Knight in shimmering, elae-enhanced armor. He came from Illume Belliel along with thousands of his brethren, come to claim Malachai ap'Kalien in the name of the Council of Realms...in the name of the new Alorin Seat. This would have been a very different battle if not for the Knights' untimely arrival. And while the Paladins fell beneath his Merdanti blade the same as mortal men, yet he felt he fueled the wrath of entire worlds against their cause each time one died at his hand.

Ean sensed his lord approaching—indeed, the very force of his being preceded his arrival in waves. The First Lord's presence was powerful in peacetime, but that evening's dire events had made a gale force of his wrath. No man possessed such innocence as to stand unaffected before him.

Ean bowed his head as Björn neared, feeling an immense weight descend upon his consciousness. He realized he'd been shouldering this burden for many months, perhaps years. "My lord," he murmured wretchedly.

Björn placed a gauntleted hand upon his shoulder, a simple acknowledgement that yet said all that must be declared between them.

Ean looked to him. The First Lord wore a high-collared black coat and carried his Merdanti sword, and his eyes might've swirled with the elemental force of a nascent galaxy for the fury that shone in them. "Anglar fell. I have offered him another path."

At this news, the man whose body Ean wore was suddenly overcome with an anguish too acute, and he drew in a shuddering breath that seemed to convey the enormity of all they had endured...of the blood-drenched path that still sprawled in front of them, winding into a future too agonizing to contemplate.

Clenching his jaw, Ean turned and settled his gaze upon two massive gilded doors on the far side of the hall. They were barred from the inside and bound with the fifth, but still they wouldn't stop his coming. "Somewhere in there," he said tightly, nodding towards the doors, "the traitor cowers."

"Do not think of him thusly," Björn cautioned as his own cobalt gaze pierced the doors. Perhaps the First Lord could see through them to where the traitor lurked. It would be a minor feat compared to all Ean had seen the man accomplish that day alone. "He looks with the eyes of our enemy, and as such, we dare not underestimate him."

Ean felt his anger welling, felt elae pooling obediently around him, and he knew that all that had come on this eve had been as a result of the man he was about to face.

"How will I know him? How will I know the traitors from the true?"

"By those who stand against you," Björn replied with deep regret. "Isabel has taken all those she could be sure of with her already. As to the rest...I fear the wheat must be sorted from the chaff."

"First Lord!" A man's cry from behind them was nearly lost among the sounds of battle, lost within the vast loneliness of the decimated hall. Ean turned

*to see a man running towards them, sword in hand. He knew his name...
Cristien...but he didn't know how he knew it.*

*"First Lord," Cristien staggered to a halt. Blood caked one side of his head;
his neck and shoulder were soaked in it. "We've found them."*

*Björn turned a heated look to Ean. "Treachery lies upon the path of the
indolent and cowardly." Condemnation rode the crest of Björn's fury. He
squeezed Ean's shoulder. "The brave must ever face the darkest road. I would this
bloody job didn't fall to you, my brother."*

*"As would I, my lord," he answered tightly, holding his gaze, for he knew
with grim resolve—with everything in his soul—that the coming battle would
be his end.*

*Their locking of eyes spoke volumes when no words of farewell would suffice.
Björn seemed to search Ean's gaze with his own, and then he grabbed him into a
fierce hug. The embrace was unexpected, and rough, and it brought a clenching
sense of grief, but Ean clutched his lord in return, for what else could he do?*

*Releasing him, Björn took hold of both shoulders. Ean saw the anguish in
his gaze, and it only served to disturb him more, but they were both resolved to
this path. They had been upon it too long to change course now.*

Björn said, "May we meet in the Returning, Ar—"

Ean jerked awake and sucked in his breath with a throaty gasp. He was alone
in bed. For the briefest, heartbreaking instant he thought *he'd* somehow
survived the battle while Isabel had not.

Lucidity returned as Ean looked around the dim room, recognizing
his bedchamber in T'khendar, remembering himself as he was now...
whereupon he realized it had only been a dream.

But was it? He let out a nervous laugh, hearing the unease in his own
tone.

Shade and darkness—I can't even convince myself!

Ean pressed palms to eyes. This dream, like so many others, had held
the visceral quality of truth. He could still see the anguish on Björn's face,
feel the emotions of that night, agonized and cutting...

When he lowered his hands from his eyes, a Shade was standing at the
foot of his bed.

Ean started and then, settling, exhaled in aggravation.

"The general will meet you today in the Hall of Heroes," the Shade informed him tonelessly. He faded before Ean could complain about the invasion of his private chambers.

Unnerved more by the dream than the ephemeral creature—though Raine's truth, it was certainly unsettling to wake and find one of them standing between himself and the sun—the prince ran both hands through his hair. Where was Isabel?

He felt for the bond and sensed her, distant but hale. He wished she'd been beside him still, wanting the feel of her satin skin as well as the reassurance of her presence. The haunting dream lingered in his thoughts like a miasma clinging to the morning to cast a pall upon the day. He feared, as with his earlier dreams, that this one also heralded a flood of new memories, and he instinctually feared them greatly.

Moreover, he was certain that he had *reason* to fear them.

Still, the last thing Ean wanted was to keep Markal waiting. Idle moments only stirred the wielder's active mind towards perilous mischief—at least as far as Ean's training was concerned—so the prince hastened to dress. When he opened the door to his chambers, he found another Shade waiting for him in the hallway.

Ean drew up short with a grimace.

The Shade steepled fingertips, pressed them to his lips and bowed. "The general thought you might need assistance finding your way to the Hall of Heroes."

Ean couldn't shake the underlying sense of unease that had a grip on him that morning. If only Isabel might've been the one to wake him instead. He gave the Shade an uncertain smile. "The general would be correct in that assessment."

"If you will permit, my lord, I shall escort you there."

"I gratefully accept your offer."

Thus tasked, the Shade led away down the passage. All the while Ean followed him through the maze of palace corridors, the creature kept his silence, leaving the prince at the mercy of turbulent thoughts. He couldn't push the ominous dream from his mind. The images nagged him relentlessly until he couldn't help but wonder where the battle had taken place. Who were the thousands of men who'd lost their lives beneath that shattered dome?

He was so consumed with these questions that he hardly noticed they'd arrived until they'd been standing still for some few moments, whereupon the Shade at last murmured, "The Hall of Heroes. I leave you now, my lord," and faded.

The prince stood for a heartbeat longer, staring at a pair of tall mahogany doors. They were carved with a great battle scene of men waging war upon one another. He found the melee faintly unsettling, and the feeling puzzled him until he realized that he might've actually *been* at the very battle that the doors were depicting.

After this, he somewhat lost his appreciation for art, such admiration being replaced by a heavy and inexplicable feeling of guilt. He opened the doors into the Hall of Heroes with his shoulders hunched against the weight of his past.

Three rows of soaring columns ran the length of the long hall, which was sheathed entirely in white marble. Along the right-hand wall, tall, vaulted windows let in the eastern light. The long rays of morning fell short of the westerly wall to his left, which was adorned with every weapon conceivable by man. Wall sconces and chandeliers lit the hall with a cold, pale light, which Ean instantly recognized as the fifth strand at work.

Seeing no one, Ean walked along the wall, marveling at the collection of weaponry. Swords of every manner and make hung among mace, flail, spear, halberd, staff, or dagger. He saw wood and metal rods linked with chain; iron shuriken; crossbows, longbows and wickedly barbed arrows and bolts…a dizzying display.

Halfway down the wall, he reached a grouping of Merdanti weapons. The night-black daggers and swords seemed to anchor the entire collection, which spread to left and right, as if forming the coal-dark body of a great winged moth. There must have been fifty Merdanti weapons arranged in an irregular pentagon. Ean finally recognized the shape, with a gulp of unease, as the exact outline of the stars that formed Cephrael's Hand. He didn't think it was a coincidence.

As he studied the collection of onyx-black blades, one particular sword caught his eye as truly as if his soul had been bound within its forging. Suddenly riveted to the blade, Ean waked to the wall and reached up to grasp the hilt. It hung just low enough that he could reach it if he stood on tiptoes. He strained for a moment to grasp the pommel, fingers just brushing the cool stone hilt, and then with a bound, he had the weapon in hand, and—

It fell with a thunderous clang onto the marble stones, all but yanking his arm from its socket as it ripped from his hold.

Shade and darkness! The damnable thing is heavier than an anvil!

With the embarrassing echo of the sword's crash still resounding through the hall, Ean bent and tried to pry up the hilt from the floor, but it was a strain to lift enough of it to get even a finger underneath.

"It takes a flow of *elae* into the blade of a sentient weapon to waken its song," an unexpected voice explained. Ean slowly straightened to find the *drachwyr Ramuhárihkamáth* approaching—*not the g*eneral Ean thought he was meeting.

Tall and sleek, dressed in his usual charcoal vest and black tunic and pants, and with his dragon-hilted greatsword extending above one shoulder, Ramu struck an imposing figure.

Ean nodded a silent hello. He was both embarrassed and infuriated by his inability to recall even the most basic knowledge of *elae*.

Instead I'm bombarded by the emotions of a man who's been dead for three hundred years!

"I should've known that," Ean admitted as the *drachwyr* came to a halt before him. Looking back to the weapon lying like a long blemish upon the pristine marble floor, Ean added uneasily, "Especially since I'm…fairly sure that sword belonged to me."

Ramu eyed the blade circumspectly. "I believe, in fact, that it did." He bent and retrieved the weapon. Straightening, he flipped the sword into the air, caught the blade in one gloved hand, and extended the hilt towards Ean. His dark eyes were compassionate. "A flow of *elae*. You'll remember, I think, once your hand finds its place."

Ean wasn't so certain, but he was grateful for Ramu's kindness—such a far leap from Markal's churlish instruction. With the *drachwyr* still holding the blade, Ean wrapped his hand around the hilt, feeling the cold stone—so impossibly hard and unyielding. It immediately began leeching the warmth from his fingers.

He experienced no flash of memory upon taking firm hold of the hilt—the room did not suddenly drip with blood, nor did the sounds of remembered violence accost his consciousness—but something *did* happen when he felt the sword once again in his hand. A sort of…recognition, as if the weapon remembered him, even as he'd remembered it.

Before he knew what he was doing, Ean had wrapped his mind around the blade. There was no other way to describe the embracive feeling than to say that the sword hovered within his awareness more like a third appendage than a foreign substance forged of mineral and magic.

He hardly realized he'd drawn it from Ramu's grasp before he was slowly slicing the air, testing its weight, and listening intently as the weapon hummed within his consciousness, the Merdanti 'song' Ramu had mentioned.

When Ean finally roused from this reunion, he lowered the weapon to his side. The blade felt light in his hand, no heavier to wield than his own arm. The prince lifted wondrous eyes back to Ramu.

"Is it always like this?" he asked, somewhat startled by the unexpected exhilaration he was experiencing just holding the weapon in his hand. His gaze strayed to Ramu's blade, which hovered behind the drachwyr's shoulder.

"When one wields a sentient sword, he touches the elemental power of the very realm. So yes," Ramu answered with a shadowy smile, "it usually is."

The tall *drachwyr* moved closer to the wall and looked it over with hands clasped behind his back. "These are the weapons of heroes, those who fell." He gazed upon the multitude of arms as if remembering each and every man whose life they represented in trade. "We hold them here in trust, to be reclaimed in the Returning."

Ean looked to him sharply. "How many have been reclaimed?"

Ramu turned a grave look over his shoulder, yet an undeniable insouciance hinted within the depths of his gaze as well. His eyes flicked to Ean's blade and back again. "One…so far."

Ean gave him a pained look in reply, to which Ramu chuckled good-naturedly.

He moved to clap Ean on the shoulder. "You have not changed, my friend. That is good to see."

"Is it?" Ean held his gaze. "Markal wouldn't have me think so."

"Markal sees only the pupil—"

"Who failed him," Ean supplied tightly.

But Ramu shook his head. "I fear you have the wrong of it, Ean. Markal feels he failed you."

Ean stared in astonished silence.

Ramu looked him over with his dark eyes. They were like depthless pools out of which the sentient realm observed the inept fumblings of men. "You two are more alike than you know," he remarked with a smile hinting in his unfathomable gaze. "I've told Markal this many times—though he ever argues the point with me—but both of you, in your peculiar egocentricity—and I intend no slight by so saying, Ean—are all too willing to assume responsibility for the evils of the world. Markal believes any pupil's failure is his failure as an instructor. And you, my friend," and here he gazed quietly but forcefully upon Ean, "you have ever believed that any failure in the First Lord's game is your failure alone."

Ean stared at the *drachwyr* in silence. It was a difficult truth to realize that Ramu—whom he'd met only once—knew him better than he knew himself.

"But come, Ean. Markal asked me to work with you today as we restore the *cortata* to you."

Ean tried to shake off the anxious feeling that always accompanied references to the man he used to be. "The *cortata*," he murmured, frowning. "What is it?"

"You might think of it as an Adept's version of the Dance of Swords. It is an age-old training routine taken from the *Sobra I'ternin*. I'm told you saw part of it being practiced in the courtyard on the same day we met."

Ean remembered watching Isabel leading a class through a series of complicated, interconnected steps and motions that had indeed reminded him of the Dance of Swords. "The *cortata*," he repeated.

Ramu walked to the center of the vast hall and turned to face Ean. "The *cortata* is itself a pattern, but it must only be wielded with a talisman."

Ean followed him with his gaze. "Why?"

Ramu considered him quietly. "What do you remember about the use of talismans?"

Ean grimaced. "Markal and I have been working with them as regards the Seventeenth Law: *The use of talismans must focus force without limiting scope.* Whatever that means," he added under his breath, shooting the *drachwyr* a disgruntled look. The Seventeenth Law had already proven far more complicated and aggravating than it seemed upon first inspection.

He was relatively certain now that he had only ever maintained an adversarial and combative relationship with the Laws of Patterning.

"Talismans, of themselves, may have little or no power," Ramu echoed Markal's words as he reached across his shoulder and drew his sword with a quick circling of his arm. He aligned the blade towards Ean and sighted down it. "By the Seventeenth Law, talismans become a focal point for channeling the force of a working."

He lowered the weapon and swept it to the side. "The moment you summon *elae*, you gather a grave quantity of potential force within your own sphere. The use of a talisman gives you a means of channeling this potential force to more effectively guide it along the framework of your intention." Ramu spun his sword around in his hand and caught his blade up casually beneath his arm. "Think of it as channeling a river through a canyon as opposed to allowing it to flow across a wide delta."

Ean had heard this explanation before from Markal, and he followed with the same question, "Why couldn't *I* just be the talisman?"

Ramu nodded, granting credence to the legitimacy of his reasoning. "Yes, it would seem the obvious answer. Yet if you became the talisman, the collected force of your working must channel through your body. With the workings you've done so far, that might not seem problematic, but by the end of today, I think you will have a better understanding of the inherent flaws of such a course."

He gestured to the weapon in Ean's hand. "Since you've chosen your talisman for today, we can begin the *cortata*." He turned his back on Ean and looked at him over his shoulder. "Follow and mimic my motion as exactly as you can."

Thus did Ramu begin.

Ean's eyes were glued to the tall *drachwyr* as he began the Adept Dance of Swords. The sequence seemed very different when performed while holding a weapon than it had while watching the Adepts in the court with Isabel. Ean had barely begun following along with Ramu before he began to sense the power inherent in the *cortata*. He realized he was forging the pattern with each sweep of his hands, with every twist and turn. He wasn't consciously drawing upon *elae*, yet it began collecting around him.

"The *cortata* can be summoned through any strand of *elae*," Ramu advised as he lifted his sword overhead with two hands and then slowly sliced down through the air. He stepped to his right and turned slightly in the same direction, and one hand swept the blade in an arc while the other lifted outwards and upwards. He made every motion slow and deliberate that Ean might mimic it exactly. "But it is at its most powerful if wielded through the fifth. Much like the Merdanti weapon in your hands, the *cortata*—itself a weapon in pattern form—draws upon the power of the realm."

Ramu brought both hands to the hilt of his greatsword and lifted the blade above his head and over behind him. He ducked low and slowly turned a circle.

Ean followed, laboring to keep his balance in the awkward position.

"The fifth being the most powerful of the strands of *elae*," Ramu continued as he rose again and circled his sword around in a deadly sideways slash, "the *cortata* is at its most potent when wielded with the fifth. Its power diminishes as you move up the strands from five through two, until it becomes completely powerless in the first."

"Why?" Ean followed Ramu in bringing his sword up above his head again. He stepped backwards as he mimicked the *drachwyr's* motions, and turned another slow circle.

"Because the *cortata* is a destructive pattern," Ramu answered while sweeping his weapon in a diagonal arc, "the antithesis of the first strand."

They retreated to silence after this, for the *cortata* became more complicated, and Ean had to focus carefully on following Ramu's motions. Eventually the practice became meditative, and soon Ean knew only the motion, the ever-present hum of his sword deep within his consciousness, and the feeling of *elae* surrounding and infusing him.

It took the better part of an hour to move through the motions with the deliberateness of the pouring of thick honey. Finally Ramu extended his sword in front of him and took hold of the hilt with both hands again. He raised the flat of the blade before his eyes, pressed the cross guard to forehead and then lips, and bowed.

Ean mimicked these motions. As he straightened, he sensed power draining away. It was a strange feeling that fell upon him then: a sense of accomplishment in having completed the entire pattern, and an unexpected sense of loss for the same reason.

Ramu smiled. "You sensed, perhaps, the meditative state that accompanies the *cortata*?"

Ean lowered his blade beside him. He felt unaccountably drained. "Very much so."

"No doubt, also, you felt *elae* accumulating."

"Absolutely."

"Very good. Now we do it again, but with our intent as a channel for the power the *cortata* summons. In other words, we must now *intend* for the *cortata* to assist us in accomplishing a specific end."

Ean frowned. "How do we do that?"

Ramu settled him a regretful look. "I must apologize to you now for what I am required to do."

Then he attacked.

In retrospect, Ean decided no experience in the world brought one so close to the dark grace of death as watching the Sundragon Ramuhárihkamáth rushing towards you with his liquid black eyes pinning your soul and his deadly blade raised for the claiming.

But in that moment, all Ean had time to do was bring up his sword to deflect the *drachwyr's* downward stroke.

Their blades clashed with a resounding clang. The hum of the Merdanti stone rippled the air, and Ean felt the force of Ramu's strike reverberating down through his bones into the stone beneath his feet. The blow sent him staggering backwards. The *drachwyr* pressed Ean with focused intent, and he struggled to deflect each powerful stroke. Ramu advanced like an avalanche, and the prince tumbled at its stormy edge. Every blow of the *drachwyr's* blade slammed and battered Ean with thunderous force. Even calling upon *elae* to give him strength, he couldn't match the man.

Still, the prince was sure they were merely sparring, despite the force of Ramu's advance—that is, until he faltered. He expected Ramu to compensate accordingly, but the Sundragon took advantage instead and marked a gash in the meat of Ean's shoulder that would've been worse but for Ean barely jerking away.

The prince staggered, both from the blow and with the dawning realization that the man might actually kill him. He lost a precious moments trying to find some equilibrium in the realization.

Ramu almost caught him again, and as Ean leapt back, the *drachwyr's* blade sliced Ean's thigh, marking his flesh in a thin stripe of blood.

Ean knew on some level that this was no different than what Isabel had done—requiring dire necessity to rouse the instincts and long years of training yet buried beneath the veil of death—but the knowledge served only to rouse an underlying sense of desperation, for he was dreadfully overmatched in facing this ancient, elemental creature.

Ramu pressed him back through the hall with a sequence of strong over-handed blows that shuddered through Ean's arms and shoulders. He felt like he was trying to stop an oncoming galleon ship with his arms, such was the unyielding force of Ramu's attack.

Slam! Slam! Slam! Slam!

Each blow clanged violently in Ean's skull, while the Merdanti hum had started reminding him now of the Whisper Lord's virulent screech. He soon labored to draw breath in his lungs, his arms ached deep in the bone, and blood soaked his shirt and side—and still Ramu pressed him relentlessly. Ean had no time to form his own advance, no time to think, only to react, for the *drachwyr's* pace in battle was so furious as to truly lead the charging avalanche down the mountainside.

A powerful blow suddenly made Ean stumble. His ankle turned, his hold upon his weapon slipped, and Ramu's blade took him. Fire erupted across his chest, and Ean cried out, diving and rolling desperately away before the next round of that circling blade claimed more than a bit of flesh.

It was then, as he stumbled back to his feet looking for his sword, that he knew that Ramu *would* kill him; that whatever the general's intentions for this battle, they led unequivocally to this truth.

Seeing Ean's defenses waning, the *drachwyr* lunged, his blade a bolt aimed for the prince at its bull's-eye. Time seemed to slow in that moment. Ean saw the blade coming for him. He knew the heat of its kiss, and feeling only the dread of encroaching disaster, he thought of Isabel. It was naught but a split-second flash, but it held all of the guilt and anguish of having failed her already too many times. Just as the blade met with the cloth of his shirt, just as he knew this would be his end and he would fail her again, Ean finally pierced the veil.

Multiple patterns flooded into his mind, and with them *elae*. Instantly he remembered how to wield *elae* in battle, how to channel it into the force of a violent intent, how to mold the formless power to his will while battling multiple enemies.

Diving into an *elae*-fueled roll that would've been impossible to manage only seconds before, Ean swept up his sword and narrowly deflected Ramu's weapon. The *drachwyr's* Merdanti blade still ripped into his tunic and his flesh besides, but its touch might've been far more deadly.

Elae channeled into Ean like the returning tide…

He launched into the *cortata*, sensing already which part of the pattern they were upon—for he saw now that this entire time Ramu had been performing the *cortata* sequence, yet only in that moment could Ean finally recognize it. He met Ramu's blade with his own, and they fell into the dance.

Now Ean knew the motions exactly. Now he knew before Ramu's blade came towards him where he must go to meet it—or avoid it altogether. Now he understood the intricate footing, the slight shifts of balance, the twisting spins that took one beneath the guard of his opponent or out of harm's way. Now he felt the pattern working, channeling into him, through his weapon, its power directed into the force waged in each blow of his sword; and he remembered how to wield the *cortata* in pieces, even non-sequentially, without losing the power gained through working the entire pattern.

As fast as they moved now in the sequence, Ean did not tire. He was merely a conduit. The lifeforce passed through him and into his blade, and the weapon became the channel along which he directed the force of the inexhaustible power that was *elae*. Ean lost all track of time—indeed, there was no time, there was only the *cortata*.

Suddenly, unexpectedly, they came to the pattern's end.

Ramu stepped out of Ean's reach, swept up his blade before him in an elegant gesture, and bowed.

Gravely, Ean returned his regard, feeling odd and out of sync with time, with the world around him…and yet wholly more *himself*.

Elements of the man he'd once been had found a new place. More pieces had been restored to the King's board of his life, even ones he hadn't known were lost.

Ean stood holding the dark-eyed gaze of the Lord of the Heavens. He understood now that the *cortata* had been his to command once—indeed, he'd known its dance for decades—and having it restored to him was deeply meaningful. His wounds were afire, his tunic was shredded and soaked in blood, but Ean knew only gratitude.

Staring at the *drachwyr* at a loss as to how to communicate such thoughts, he managed, "Thank you."

Ramu nodded in reply. He swept his sword before him, focusing upon the blade, and Ean heard a hiss and saw smoke release from it as Ramu sheathed it in the scabbard on his back, cleansed now of blood. Whereupon, the *drachwyr* offered, "Shall we break our fast together? I believe there is one who would tend to your wounds," and he nodded towards the far end of the room.

Ean turned a look over his shoulder, his heart suddenly quickening in anticipation, yet it was not Isabel who waited at a round table set with a meal, but another. His eyes widened.

"*Ma dieul*," Ramu called pleasantly to Björn. He motioned Ean onwards, and the prince limped to join the First Lord at a table draped in white linen.

Ean wondered where the table had come from. He was certain it hadn't been there when he'd first entered the hall. Of course there had been plenty of time while he battled the Sundragon to cart in a table and set it with a meal, but that he'd noticed nothing of this happening was a little disturbing.

Björn looked Ean over as the prince hobbled near, and his raven brows lifted. "You went easy on him, Ramu."

"I dared not incur the Prophetess's wrath, my lord." Ramu flashed a twitch of a smile.

Ean looked to the *drachwyr* feeling unnerved. That had been going *easy* on him?

"Ean, come," Björn beckoned him over. "I would that you not remain so wounded—unless it pleases you to do so?"

"No…thank you," he answered while still looking uneasily at Ramu, "I gladly accept your Healing."

Björn placed his hands to either side of Ean's head, and the prince closed his eyes. The shared pose seemed suddenly familiar, and Ean realized he'd assumed it many times before. He soon felt warmth suffusing him. Moments later his wounds started tingling.

This Healing felt very different from Alyneri's ministrations. Her touch was the kiss of moonlight, while Björn's in comparison felt like the scalding desert sun. It was more unsettling than unpleasant, for Ean realized that what he was truly sensing was the difference in the amount of power Alyneri might draw at her most desperate, compared to what the First Lord held readily available.

When Björn withdrew moments later, he nodded Ean towards a marble urn and washbasin. While Ean cleaned away the results of the morning's sparring, Björn held up a tunic of heavy grey silk worked all over in thread-of-silver. "I thought you might have need of this."

Ean gratefully accepted it, surprised and touched by the First Lord's consideration.

Then did they break their fast together.

Dining with the First Lord always made for a pleasant experience, for the man was interested in everything under the sun and harbored a vast knowledge of the world. He and Ramu spoke idly but at length about the long-dead kingdom of Gahanda, which had been absorbed by the Empire of Agasan in a vicious and bloody war while Björn still held the Alorin Seat. Ean found it both wonderful and strange to listen to events that had occurred upwards of five centuries ago being spoken of through personal experience.

To know these men had lived for so many lifetimes…being himself a moon short of ten and nine, Ean couldn't even imagine it.

It wasn't until the meal was finished and he was following Ramu back towards the center of the hall to continue training that he began to wonder why the First Lord had come to eat with them. He'd mentioned nothing of dire importance to their training…

That's when Ean realized the truth, and it brought him to a standstill: the only logical reason for Björn van Gelderan to have attended him that morning was to be on hand, in case Ramu had injured him so grievously that Björn's skills alone might be needed to restore Ean to life.

The enormity of this realization—that these men would do *anything* to restore to him whatever power and skill he once possessed…Ean could barely process it. He hardly noticed that he'd stopped walking. He pushed a hand through his hair and kept it hovering there. This conflict might've been spoken of in the guise of a game, but clearly its players were not cavalier about their roles.

In the First Lord's game, people truly played to the death.

Ean might've reached this conclusion already, having himself passed that line of demarcation three times—but those had been *other* men's lives, no matter that he'd been wearing their identity at the time. He still had difficulty time connecting past with present in any way that seemed real; and he certainly couldn't easily embrace the same gritty reality as was maintained by those who'd been playing the game unendingly for eons. Ean had rather glibly accepted the concept of being eternally bound to a single quest until it slapped him painfully in the face—which it seemed to be doing repeatedly since arriving in T'khendar.

Rousing from these thoughts, Ean saw that Ramu had already reached the center of the hall, so he jogged to catch up with him.

The *drachwyr* said as Ean neared, "You noticed, no doubt, how the use of a talisman in the *cortata* was of benefit."

Ean nodded as he came to a halt before Ramu.

"Now we'll explore the use of the *cortata* and our talismans in a practice that is much closer to the requirements of actual battle."

Ean welcomed the challenge. Anything he could learn from Ramu would be of value, and the practice would be a worthy distraction from the underlying and inexplicable sense of guilt that had been relentlessly hounding him since waking that morning. He didn't seem able to retrieve any part of the man he'd once been without also compounding that feeling of guilt.

Ramu drew his weapon with a fluid sweep of his arm and leveled it before Ean. "In battle with other Adepts, one is most likely required to wield numerous patterns at once. Now we will perform the *cortata* while also working the fifth. You must apply the Laws as required to counter my working. Begin."

Ramu launched into the *cortata* with no less ferocity than he had exhibited earlier. Ean found the *cortata*, and they flowed into the Adept Dance of Swords as *elae* began pooling around them. This time it Ean easily fell into the focused and meditative state of the *cortata* even while fending off Ramu's earth-trembling blows. While working the *cortata*, his energy, like *elae*, seemed boundless.

And then it began to rain.

At first, Ean just admired Ramu's ingenuity and skill. It was hard not to stand in awe of the Lord of the Heavens.

Without missing a step in the *cortata*, Ean began considering how to counter the *drachwyr's* working. In a moment when their eyes met over clashing blades, Ean formed his first pattern and molded it around his intention. Then he cast it forth. A heavy wind came screaming through the hall, but all this accomplished was to send stinging rain into his face. He let the wind blow itself out while he decided upon another tactic.

Ramu's rain soon had him drenched, and the stone hilt of his blade slick became in his hands. It finally occurred to him to shift the structure of the air to protect himself from it. Ean held this shield happily, relieved to be free of the constant barrage of water against his head, but as they completed one section of the *cortata* and launched into the next, Ean realized this was not the type of response Ramu was seeking from him.

He released his protective pattern and suffered the rain again while he searched for another means of countering Ramu's working.

The meditative state of the *cortata* allowed for thought much clearer and deeper than any form of mortal combat training, for working the pattern through its accompanying motions now came as second nature, leaving Ean's attention free for patterning of a different sort. Still, he had difficulty envisioning a way to balance Ramu's rain while maintaining such a furious pace through the battling sequence.

Ean's next attempt to balance Ramu's working turned the moisture in the air to fog but was ineffective in stopping the rain. Frustrated, he let his mind empty to focus on the prime balance of the *cortata* itself.

"You violate the Ninth Law," Ramu advised during a moment when their blades met and their faces came close enough to feel the *drachwyr's* breath tingle upon his skin.

They separated again, following the sequence, and Ean realized he was right. That pesky Ninth Law.

Do not counter force with force; channel it.

Almost at once he had an idea. As an Adept of the fifth strand, Ean instinctively thought with the necessary patterns to change water to any other form. All he required was a clear concept of the effect he wanted to create—application of the First Law—to change Ramu's rain to ice and then, with careful consideration—the slightest shifting of his conceptual imagery—to snow.

He formed his intent and cast it upon the world. He kept this up long enough for the snow to build into drifts at their feet, forming a sort of pattern in itself upon the marble tiles as they continued their exact dance through the *cortata*, but the effort of constantly keeping this working in play soon started draining his energy.

That's when he realized that he could do more than simply channel Ramu's force into a new form. Ramu was already changing the structure of the air in the room with his working. Ean had merely to augment the *drachwyr's* alteration with his own new layer—one pattern of intent imposed upon another, but using the same energy already summoned by the first.

Almost as soon as he began the working, the air grew colder. Soon the snow ceased altogether, but still the chill grew, becoming so intense that it even disrupted Ean's mental calm.

He began to feel *elae* pulsing through him in time with his heart, and still he drew upon the lifeforce, channeling it through the blade in his hand, through the *cortata* sequence. The sun continued its slow motion through the sky, long rays shifting in the tall windows as the orb made its way across the heavens, but within the Hall of Heroes, the passing of the day was measured only in the number of times Ean completed the *cortata*.

The snow had long stopped, replaced by ice that blossomed before Ramu's rain could form. Ean's breath came as frost and his body felt as lead, but he ignored the freezing temperatures as much as the pounding in his skull and pushed through the sequence again…and again…discounting utterly the growing unease that tugged at his consciousness, until—

Ramu twisted away suddenly in a motion that Ean recognized afterwards as a means of safely discontinuing the sequence without completing the pattern. The prince lowered his sword to look inquiringly upon the *drachwyr*—and staggered.

Ramu moved to catch him before he fell. He lowered Ean in his arms and helped him sit on a floor that seemed a solid lake of ice. Ean's head was suddenly swimming, an abominable ringing had started in his ears, and he felt both burningly hot and frighteningly cold at the same time.

"A fine application of the Ninth Law," Ramu murmured over the chattering of Ean's teeth. The prince hugged his elbows and willed the room to stop spinning around him. "It was not, however," Ramu added with a quirk of a smile, "the best example of the Fifth Esoteric."

Ean pushed his head between his knees and focused on not throwing up. "What's the Fifth Esoteric?" he managed while watching his breath frost in the air.

"To understand the Fifth Esoteric, we must begin with the Second, which introduces us to the concept of Absolute Being. This idea encompasses all that you are and more, for it includes the concept of the space which a wielder might control by expanding his zone of influence."

"Is this supposed to make sense to me?" Ean knew his head was going to explode any minute, and he wasn't sure he wanted his last moments alive to be spent trying to figure out impossibly cryptic rules.

Ramu chuckled. He looked to the table where they'd broken their fast and called forth an empty goblet from its quiet respite. A loud crack echoed through the hall as the goblet ripped free of the icebound table and flew towards them. Ramu caught it out of the air, shattering the nimbus of ice that had encased it. A moment's concentration upon the cup soon resulted in swirling dark liquid that filled to the brim. "Here, Ean." He extended the wine to him.

Ean managed to take the chilled goblet and drink, grateful just for the show of compassion. Though the strong wine warmed his stomach but little, yet he soon felt slightly less askew. He looked around the hall and—

The scene was astonishing... terrifying.

At first Ean didn't know what to make of what he saw. He stared uncomprehendingly at the milky white ceiling, the slick and shimmering columns, and the myriad crystalline designs crackling the high windows.

The entire vast hall had become encased in ice.

Turning the other way, he saw icicles hanging from the weapons on the wall and even larger ones from the ceiling. The floor was a solid sheet of bluish ice from door to door. Looking back to Ramu feeling immensely discomfited now, Ean asked, "*I* did this?"

"Perhaps not exactly the effect you had envisioned?"

Unsettled, Ean drank more wine. "I..." he tried pushing a hand through hair but instead found frozen locks bound in a thin sheath of ice. He looked at the particles of ice on his hand and shuddered. "No," he whispered then. "I meant merely to rechannel the force of your working. I thought of the super-chilled winters in Edenmar when the air was often too cold even for snow to fall."

"*The wielding of patterns is governed by the boundaries of Absolute Being*," Ramu said. "This is the Second Esoteric. It means, in simple terms, that we as wielders are limited by the amount of force we can control. The Fifth Esoteric further refines this concept by stating that '*Absolute Being must equal the scope of a wielder's concept of effect.*'"

Ean grimaced. "Should I pretend to understand what you're talking about, or...?"

Ramu gave him an amused look. "All of this means that if you intend to encase an entire hall in ice, Ean, you must first expand your *self-being*—a term used to express the amount of space a wielder might occupy with his mind—to incorporate the entire hall. Otherwise, *you* fall prey to your own intended effect, for you have set your working *outside* the limits of yourself."

Ean downed the last of his wine and lowered a shaking hand. His head had finally stopped spinning, but he had to clench his teeth to keep them from chattering, and his body kept trembling in violent spurts. "I think...I understand."

Ramu sheathed his sword and helped Ean to stand. He carried the prince's Merdanti weapon on his behalf and began walking them slowly towards the doors.

"Think of it like this, Ean: if you bake a cake using a bowl too small for the batter, it will spill out over your hands and onto the table. You become the effect of the thing you created. If you try to herd a flock of sheep that is larger than you can easily control without the help of a sheepdog, the sheep readily slip away and you must spend hours chasing them down—again, you have become the effect of the original thing you set out to control.

"The same is true with *elae*. You can draw it endlessly to you, especially while wielding the *cortata*, but if you draw more than you can easily control, then it slips out of your grasp. Moreover, drawing that much of the lifeforce without controlling the implementation of its force—without sending it through an exact channel—is exhausting and the surest way to meet a quick end. The Esoterics explain that a wielder need not be limited *if* he is capable of expanding the force of his own being. It is really quite simple."

Ean felt it was anything but, though he nodded politely to Ramu anyway.

Now that *elae* had all but abandoned him, Ean was feeling the effects of his causation all right. Every muscle in his body ached. His arms twitched at inappropriate times, and he felt like his bones were frozen solid. Yet, he needed to understand what had happened so he would never made the same mistake again.

"How would…" he began haltingly, stammering through chattering teeth, "how do you o-occupy space with the f-force of your b-being?"

Ramu glanced to him with his dark eyes hinting of mirth but revealing only patience. "You might begin by expanding your awareness to fill the room. It is an activity you would find merit in practicing," and compassion or no, he couldn't help adding with the quirk of a smile, "…that is, after you warm up a bit."

"I feel like my blood is f-frozen."

"The aftereffects of drawing more *elae* than one can direct," Ramu noted. "Unfocused power rages through like a swollen river, stripping away one's own supply of the lifeforce, leaving you as you feel now. A mild case, considering."

"Mild?" Ean croaked in protest.

Ramu gave him a telling look.

As they neared the doors, which glistened beneath their layer of ice, the Lord of the Heavens sent the fifth to open them. They broke apart with a shattering icefall and opened to reveal a Shade just then congealing on the other side.

"General Ramuhárikhamáth," he bowed to Ramu in the usual fashion. Then he looked to Ean. "I have been sent to escort you back to your apartments, my lord, if you would like my assistance."

Ean didn't have the energy to answer, so he just let his head hang slightly by way of acceptance.

Ramu chucked beside him. "A good day's work." He lifted Ean's Merdanti blade and spun it to extend the hilt to him. "Your sword, Ean?"

Ean couldn't conceive of calling even the small amount of *elae* it would take to hold the weapon, and he despaired of carrying it. Ramu must've read this from the terrified look on his face, for he swirled it around again and caught the blade beneath his arm like a riding crop. "I'll place it back on the wall. You will know where to find it if you desire."

"Thank you," the prince whispered. Then he lifted his head to meet the *drachwyr's* gaze and said again, more exactingly, "*Thank you.*"

Ramu nodded. His ageless gaze seemed to understand that Ean might never find words of gratitude enough to encompass all they had accomplished that day. Smiling, Ramu bowed a farewell, and then Ean was following the Shade down the long alabaster passage, just focusing on putting one numb, frozen foot before the other.

FORTY-EIGHT

"A man's intelligence may be measured by his ability to deceive."
— Shailabhanáchtran, Maker of Storms

RIVAS'RHAKÁRAKEK, THE SHADOW of the Light, flew high above the Kutsamak. In the harsh light of the desert afternoon, his shadow floated across mottled ridges and dove into deep, shaded canyons. It slid down the sides of sheer cliffs and glided up vertical rock faces, and everything it fell upon—whether tree or stream, dumb beast or dumber man—was known by Rhakar.

As he flew, the strong desert sun glinted off Rhakar's coppery scales, making his hide sparkle blindingly. From the ground, he often seemed a soaring comet perusing the daylight skies of man, burning so vividly as to challenge the sun in brilliance. There were many who claimed his sparkling hide was the reason the Sundragons were so named. Rhakar knew better.

He didn't often fly this quadrant of the Kutsamak, for it was far from the lines of war—farther still from Raku—and no armies marched among its dry wastes. But that day he didn't search for archers in hidden lairs or soldiers concealed in ambush. That day, he sought villains of a different mold, and he wouldn't cease his search until he found them.

Rhakar was good at finding things. The meaning of his name hinted at this truth, for while light could illuminate dark corners, so also could too much brilliance sometimes conceal, being so bright as to chase all the shadows from the world, obscuring the secret things they sheltered. Rhakar could see into the shadows with or without the light to guide his search. He suspected it would be in shadows where he'd find his quarry.

It went without saying that he *would* find them. Had he not already once discovered Trell of the Tides in such a place of shadows, where none other might've thought to look? Indeed, he'd found him before and would do so again, though it chafed at him that he must twice look to save the life of the same inconsequential man.

Men. They were fragile creatures, really. Would that the First Lord was less enamored of them. His brothers, too, seemed woefully taken by some apparent charm that the races of man seemed to exude. Especially Náiir.

Rhakar was not so duped. He saw humankind for the fleshly creatures they were—frail and mortal, they withered in a week without water and were capable of enduring but the slightest variation in climate or temperature without expiring from one end of the spectrum or the other. He didn't see their appeal, particularly.

Oh…Ramu lectured tediously on the importance of humans as one of the Maker's child-races, prattling on about how humankind was blessed with a simplicity that was inherently divine; and his sister Jaya disserted on the subject with inexhaustible patience, trying to help him see the value in their fragility.

While Rhakar begrudgingly recognized some shadow of their Maker in the races of man, their 'inherent divinity' was so fleeting and long-derived— so distant in relationship—that he felt little compunction over harming the pitiful things when situation or Balance called for it. Mostly he enjoyed the diversion.

This dark delight was another aspect of his name. The Shadow of the Light. Or so Jaya sermonized. She felt that their unique and true purpose for existence was to understand the deeper meanings of their names via exhaustive questioning and introspection—for each of them had been named specifically by their Maker.

Jaya believed that in understanding their names, they might better understand the Maker's will for their existence. She'd made a religion out of this idea and had spent centuries refining and codifying it into tomes of complex syllogism and symbolism.

Rhakar could not have been less interested in her philosophy. He had his own philosophy: Find his quarry. Question it. Kill it.

Simple.

Look for Saldarians, Náiir had told him in their unique way of communicating across distance and even time, should the need arise. *Find Trell.*

While he flew, Rhakar kept a tendril of the first strand burning in his awareness, both to lead him to things living and to alert him to Trell's presence among them. Having found the man before, he would easily recognize his unique life pattern again. But Rhakar sensed it nowhere within the boundaries of his awareness—not even a trace upon the currents.

Still, a strong emanation pulled him northward, what could only be a host of men and beasts. It seemed unlikely there would be one among them with the ability to hide Trell's presence on the currents, but Rhakar would leave no trace uninspected, no clue uninvestigated, nothing to chance.

He came upon the party from the south, so he hid from them in the face of the sun, being careful to ensure his telltale shadow was likewise cast far from where they rode. He saw a score of men, all ahorse; four were bound, and one was unwell. Rhakar could smell the blood soaking the latter's bandages while still miles away.

The rider in the lead appeared as any other, yet upon closer inspection, Rhakar sensed something of the second strand in him—a Nodefinder, like as not.

But the man dressed all in black who was riding just behind him was so bound with *elae* that the lifeforce clung to him. Indeed, the currents glommed in great sheets about his presence, clutching and binding, only to be ripped from his person and carried forward again on their usual rushing path. The man was a boulder in the raging Cry, catching the flotsam of the river in constant storm.

Rhakar was at first intrigued, and he sought more of the man's mind so as to learn what patterns might engender such a reaction in the currents. However, the briefest inspection of the patterns layered upon the man so disgusted him that he quickly abandoned all interest. The man was lost, not long for this world.

Among the others—Saldarians all, in Rhakar's experienced estimation—Trell clearly was not.

Which begged the question: where was he? Perhaps one of these Saldarians could tell him—with the proper motivation.

Rhakar inwardly smiled. The day was turning out to be interesting after all.

He spent an idle while choosing the direction from which to best surprise them and then dove low, spearing down with lightning speed to level out just a handspan above a mountain ridge, close enough that his furnace breath stirred billowing dust. Yet this upsurge was but a tuft compared to the swirling storm of sand and dirt raised in his wake.

He came at them from the west then, where the sun's falling rays as yet speared pain into fragile eyes, encouraging men to turn their gazes elsewhere; and he came at them fast, rising suddenly above the ridge to blanket them with his shadow and the radiant heat of his sun-scorched form.

The men scattered in a panic, shouting and cursing, their horses rearing with screams of protest, a mad flutter of chaos. Trained soldiers tended to stand their ground—futilely perhaps, impotently to be sure, but with honor intact—but Saldarians routinely fled like cockroaches exposed to the daylight.

As he rounded the ridge, Rhakar selected one of them: a squat rider ripe for the plucking. He twisted and dove with faultless aim, and his taloned feet snared the man, who screamed like a speared pig.

Rhakar clutched the man's mortal body close to his belly, and then his powerful wings were pounding the air, climbing out of the ravine, rousing whipping torrents of dirt to obscure the eyes of any who might dare some meager, if ultimately inconsequential, response.

Thus he was startled when he felt a sudden shock of the fourth hit him from below. It was a powerful stroke—if harmless to him and strangely aimed—yet it drew his fiery gaze below as he flew away, interested to know its source. The man in black stared up at him through the swirling sand, unruffled, hands at his sides, and Rhakar named him now for what he was.

A wielder, if one of a strange and unnatural makeup.

Curious. The briefest inspection of the pattern the wielder had worked showed Rhakar that the attack had not been aimed at him at all but at the man he'd stolen away. This earned the wielder some small shadow of respect, for it demonstrated intelligence and a cool head. It was a strong leader who, in the thick of attack, would think to prevent the enemy from learning their secrets by killing his own man—never mind that the attempt had failed.

Still, the wielder clearly could not work the fifth, else he would've done so already. Rhakar gave him no more thought.

He banked in the rising east wind and flew towards the southern cliffs, looking for one that offered a spot for landing. And interrogation. The man in his claws was whimpering, and Rhakar loosened his grip slightly. This seemed not to help much, for now the man screamed instead.

As he soared over a crumbling ridge, Rhakar spied an outcropping of rock that offered ideal conditions for what he required. Ignoring the shrieking man in his grasp, he shifted his wings and headed for it.

Sharpe swam in a world of pain.

Pinned within the massive dragon's talons, speared and bleeding, he whimpered in the rushing air, which beat across his skull with driving force, the wind coming so fast and hard he couldn't even open his eyes. It seemed an interminable flight, with every moment spent in agony, every breath a struggle through a chest and lung pierced by the dragon's claw. Another impaled his stomach, and a third passed through his thigh.

Worse was the burning. This was the pain that kept him screaming. He wasn't sure how it had happened—some fiery, vengeful force had blasted into him as the dragon was dragging him upwards through the skies—and now he felt nothing but searing pain and emptiness where his feet should've been.

When the creature finally set him down on the rough rock and withdrew his claws, Sharpe screamed anew, for he felt every inch of each talon as it slid languidly from his flesh.

Lying on a slender ledge just inches from the cliff edge, Sharpe waited for death. The dragon hulked over him; it was so massive that he couldn't discern its shape, though he knew its barbed tail hovered near. Its wings caught the wind as the beast settled, the sound a whirring rasp of a thousand snakes rushing through the dry grass. Sick with vertigo, Sharpe looked up to find the beast staring down at him, golden eyes large in a body scaled in flames.

Terror choked Sharpe's every breath.

WHAT IS IT YOU DO IN THESE FORBIDDEN LANDS? The voice boomed through his mind, and intrusion that felt as an anvil upon his brain, crushing in its power.

Sharpe had no option but to answer, for his mind was immediately dominated by the dragon's will, as impotent as a fly pinned beneath a man's finger.

"*Captives...*" he gasped through lungs that refused to fill, through the fire that still seemed trapped in his shins, "*...bait.*"

The dragon stared compellingly at him, and Sharpe closed his eyes rather than endure its fiery observation. A fit of bloody coughing choked him, and he prayed in each moment that it would be his last.

Even knowing he was doomed...the experience of looking up into the dragon's golden eyes, knowing the creature was clawing into his mind with some terrible magic—this was more frightening than any torment death could claim.

WHERE IS THE ONE THEY CALL TRELL? I DID NOT SEE HIM AMONG THIS PARTY.

The thought pounded into Sharpe's skull, and pain radiated through him like a jagged dagger dragging along his bones.

It was at least a minute before Sharpe realized the pathetic scream echoing hollowly in his broken ears was his own, and a minute more before he managed to stop. He had no idea how long it took before he fashioned his answer. Every moment was a terrorized agony.

"*M'Nador...*" Sharpe finally gasped, a bare whisper. He realized in a sickly moment of clarity that what he'd thought was the red haze of sunset flaming the sky was actually his eyes hemorrhaging. Likewise, the echoic kettledrum sound of the wind was due to his ears filling with blood.

The world spun wildly as he stared up at the dragon. Its fiery eyes began to swim and multiply before his vision. And still the creature demanded further answer to its question—Sharpe felt the rest being drawn out of him as if hooked by lure and line. Drawing in a shuddering breath, he croaked in the last, "*To Radov.*"

It may have been hours that he lay in broken agony praying for death, or mere seconds before the dragon granted his unspoken wish. But the beast at last opened its mouth upon him, and Sharpe cringed, expecting some flaming eruption that never came.

What he did see there was far more terrifying.

A sun burned within the dark, cavernous opening that was the dragon's maw. *That's why they call them Sundragons!*

Sharpe had time to look with scalded eyes upon the sun boiling in the dragon's mouth, time to feel his flesh begin to sear, crisp, and flake from the bone, and then his skull exploded.

Leaving the charred husk that had once been a man upon the lonesome cliff, Rhakar drove his wings through the rising heat of late afternoon to regain the high skies where the air grew thin.

He misliked what the man Sharpe had told him.

Mithaiya... Rhakar reached out across the aether to find his sister's life pattern upon the wavering strands of time, which bound all existence.

Silence lengthened while the wind thundered through his wings. Then came her reply—distant, faint.

Rhakar...

He told her his news, knowing she would reach Ramu and he in turn the First Lord. Then he contacted his brother Náiir with the same report.

He might've returned to his patrol then, but something gnawed at him. He didn't have the prescience of the First Lord's zanthyr, but Rhakar knew well when instinct spoke. He'd lived too many long centuries and endured too much to question that voice.

So he tilted his wings and rode the turbulent desert currents back towards the valley and the unusual wielder who still snared his attention.

Işak'getirmek shielded his blue-grey eyes with one hand and watched uneasily as the Sundragon disappeared over the ridge with a mindlessly screaming Sharpe in tow. Perhaps more troubling than the dragon's inexplicable attack was the feeling that suffused him upon watching Sharpe agonizing in its grasp as the dragon was flying away.

Vindication...

Whyever did he feel *vindicated* in knowing that Sharpe was meeting his due? It related somehow to the fact that Sharpe had put three darts into Fynnlar val Lorian. It was all backwards and wrong, yet he couldn't deny the feeling.

As the heavy thumping of the dragon's wings faded into the distance, the Saldarians emerged from their places of hiding, albeit tentatively, suspiciously. Of the twenty in their company, only Işak had held his ground.

His prisoners had used the moment to attempt an escape, which he'd quickly thwarted with a net of compulsion cast wide. They writhed in the dirt now, enduring his displeasure. Their untimely break had caused him to muddle his aim of the fourth-strand working he'd intended for Sharpe. Işak was fairly sure the bolt of concentrated energy had missed most of him, which meant…

He wasn't sure what it meant.

The entire encounter baffled him.

Joss finally managed to wriggle out from beneath the low ledge he'd hidden under and made his way through the chaos of scattered Saldarians to rejoin Işak. "Bloody ill-luck for Sharpe." He cast a heated gaze in the direction the Sundragon had gone. "We're naught but a sprint away from that node."

Işak slowly turned his gaze from the distant sky to look at Joss. He wore a layer of dirt that might've been from the dragon's generated windstorm, or perhaps from having plastered himself beneath the sliver of a ledge. "Round up the men and horses," he said tightly, still on edge.

Işak's own mount had reared on him the moment the dragon erupted over the mountainside, and due to his bad leg, Işak had been forced to abandon the steed. He hadn't dared attempt to control a frightened horse amid twenty terrorized men while subduing four prisoners with compulsion *and* fighting a Sundragon. Işak knew his limitations.

He cast Joss a sideways glance and added darkly, "And hurry up about it."

"Some of the men are hurt," Joss grumbled, looking sullen. "Huric might've broken his leg. It should be set."

Işak speared him with a dangerous look. "Get him on his horse."

"Why?" Joss threw a hand to the sky. "The damnable beast is gone! It's no doubt making a fine snack of Sharpe as we speak! What's so bloody pressing?"

Işak drew in a deep breath and exhaled slowly. What could he tell Joss? That Dore's paranoia over anyone remotely related to the Fifth Vestal had engendered a need to teach Işak all possible spells to escape the Vestal or any of his liegemen? And that whoever else they may be sworn to, the Sundragons were sworn first to Björn van Gelderan?

How could a man like Joss possibly understand the transference of knowledge that came with being bound to Dore Madden, how his insanities and understandings both had filtered across the bond?

Işak knew, because Dore knew, that a Sundragon would never stop until he had achieved his goal—and especially Şrivas'rhakárakek, which this undoubtedly had been. Dore said Rhakar was always sent to do Björn's dirtiest work, though why the Fifth Vestal would've involved himself in Işak's business was anyone's guess.

"Get the men ready," Işak repeated, suddenly fearing that they'd already lingered too long. His gaze and tone simultaneously invited challenge and warned against such an ill-advised response.

Joss gave him a look of sour accusation but turned to do as tasked.

Işak looked back to the sky. He didn't understand why the dragon had come. It hadn't been to rescue the prisoners—the creature had patently disregarded them—and it hadn't had anything to do with him personally, for the dragon had all but ignored him. And despite all tales and Joss's assumption to the contrary, Işak well knew that Sundragons would never feast upon the flesh of men.

Thus he could only conclude that the dragon had come in search of Trell val Lorian.

Trell...

Işak marveled at the mysteries that encircled the prince's life. He wondered, too, if he would rue the day Trell crossed his path. But one thing was certain: the prince had the favor of a god—Raine's truth, a god had already rescued the prince from sure death in the Fire Sea. What lengths then would this god take to track Trell down again? Might he send a Sundragon in search?

Unsettled by the possibility, Işak called a first-strand pattern and cast it upon the currents. It occurred to him, as he began getting tentative readings back from the pattern's ever-expanding reach, that this was very likely the same pattern the Sundragon had used to find them.

Oh, he knew more than any mortal should about Sundragons. Dore had lectured tirelessly and with dreadful insistence about their talents and their weaknesses... especially their weaknesses, which were few enough in Dore's estimation to count on one hand. But one thing Dore had stressed time and again was that Sundragons could not travel the nodes. If the dragon returned—and Işak's gut told him it would—he had to buy them time to escape.

Joss was just approaching with Işak's mount in tow when Işak felt a mental tug, his first-strand pattern resonating strongly. He'd been right to fear. The dragon was returning.

"Get Waryn to prepare the node for travel," he hissed in a low voice as he took his reins from Joss. "And tell him he'd better be bloody quick about it!"

Joss looked alarmed. "What's wrong?"

Işak gave him a black look. "The dragon returns."

"*Shade and darkness*, what do we do?"

"*You* get the men across the node." Işak looked back to the sky and added grimly, "…I will deal with the dragon."

"What do you mean, you'll 'deal' with it?" Joss grabbed Işak's arm. "Don't be a fool! No man can fight a Sundragon!"

"I can fight him." Işak held his gaze evenly.

Joss frowned and released his arm—he was never comfortable touching Işak anyway. "As you will then," but he sounded dubious, his frustration evident in tone and manner. "Then what—?"

"*Just get the men out of here, Joss!*"

Perhaps it was the desperation in Işak's tone that finally got through, but Joss's face went slack, and he rushed off, shouting orders at high pitch.

Işak looked back to the west. He had a vast repertoire of patterns that Dore had made him learn through threat and torture and pain. Sometimes the patterns themselves had been as painful to learn or work as the punishment being held over him. But outside of the fifth, which Işak could not work, only one pattern was truly effective against a Sundragon—according to Dore—and even then it was only effective once, for afterwards the creature would be alert to it.

Işak made ready with this pattern while his men regained their horses and lined up to cross the node. They moved single-file and vanished with a step.

Işak brought up the rear of the line, backing towards the node, acutely aware of the risk he was taking. And yet, if he failed and the dragon claimed him as he'd surely claimed Sharpe, who could say if such a death might not be preferable to an eternity bound to Dore Madden? Işak pondered this in ill humor while the line of escape seemed to shrink at an alarmingly slow rate.

Only half the men had crossed when the resonance of Işak's first-strand pattern grew so painful that he had to release it, knowing the dragon came too near. He kept his eyes pinned on the western hills, sparing only an occasional glance for the agonizingly long line still between him and the node.

Then he saw him.

A man approached from out of the shadows.

Tall and powerfully built, he wore a greatsword behind one shoulder, its black stone hilt carved in the likeness of a winged dragon. His long raven hair was pulled back from a wide widow's peak, and his gaze was just as fiery in human form as it had been whilst flying the skies.

Here then was the fearsome Şrivas'rhakárakek *in the flesh!* Dore would've pissed himself.

Heart racing, Işak released his pattern.

Rhakar saw the Saldarians and their prisoners vanishing one by one, obviously crossing a node. But he let them go, for the man he wanted followed at the end.

This one Rhakar would not harm—unless he must—for now that he'd fixed his attention newly and firmly upon the young wielder, Rhakar saw that he was surely a Player.

*Oh…*men rarely knew they played in the First Lord's game, but Rhakar could always tell. An aura surrounded such men or women. They had an almost indefinable quality to their life patterns that made each one ring with a certain faint chime, a harmonic of the greater chord resonated by the vast pattern that was the First Lord's game itself.

It changed a man, being part of the First Lord's game. Whether *he* knew it or not, his pattern was inalterably transformed.

Rhakar fixed his gaze upon the wielder and strode towards him purposefully. He knew the man held *elae*, but clearly he could not work the fifth, so Rhakar spared no inspection for the fourth-strand pattern the man was holding in his mind.

When the wielder released it, Rhakar easily batted it away with a mental sweep, and yet—

Impossible!

A mental cage sizzled into being. Powerful bindings spider-webbed in lightning streaks to ensnare his thoughts.

Rhakar staggered beneath the onslaught and fell to one knee, shaking his head as his vision clouded with spiraling pathways. He knew this pattern. It was old…he'd not seen it used in centuries.

The pattern was a trap, of course, a maze that could only be escaped by mentally tracing its endless curves and alleys. Yet to do so itself was deadly, for the more mental energy one put into the maze, the stronger the maze became. The maze likewise required increasing attention—greedily, thirstily, it was an insatiable beast that demanded a man pour in ever more of himself until his mind was entirely devoured within it.

Rhakar regarded the wielder, who was growing blurred beyond his vision now, with a new appreciation. How ingenious he'd been! Beneath the puny pattern he'd thrown at Rhakar had lurked one with real bite. A wielder without the fifth might not harm a creature of Rhakar's ilk—*no*—but he could occupy the dragon's mind with fourth-strand trickery that was just as incapacitating. Which is exactly what this wielder had done.

Rhakar pitched forward yet again and pushed a hand to the earth to steady himself. The labyrinth was urging his attention, and it was a hellish battle to deny its will. He looked up and forced himself to focus on the wielder standing ten paces away from him.

The man was staring back.

Rhakar wondered how such a youngling as this had found the pattern of the Labyrinth. To his knowledge, there were few living wielders who recalled it. The man's hand had been well played though; Rhakar never would've imagined him harboring knowledge of so vicious a pattern.

"I'm…sorry." The wielder's low voice sounded strangely tormented.

Rhakar wondered how gruesome his own expression must've been to have elicited such an apology. He knew the man meant it, though, even as he could tell the wielder was himself surprised that he'd offered it.

Then the Labyrinth had him. Rhakar collapsed onto his side, unable to respond lest he lose what tentative hold he had left on his own mind. He watched through a blurred haze as the wielder turned and crossed the node, leaving him alone in the darkening valley.

Twilight had just fallen when Rhakar escaped the Labyrinth, at last breaking the pattern into shards. *Elae* bled out of them and they dissolved, their meaning and power lost.

It was never a question that Rhakar would escape the maze. He'd many times fought the Labyrinth—as youths, he and his sister Mithaiya had used it relentlessly on each other—but the stronger one's mind became, the more compelling the maze. Rhakar was pleased that he'd broken it as quickly as he had.

Never mind that Balaji would've claimed he should've done it in half that time and Ramu would've arched a brow and asked why he'd allowed the maze to capture him in the first place. Rhakar thought his two oldest brothers were often impossible in their imperiousness, but he vowed neither of them were as insufferable as the First Lord's zanthyr.

Shaking off the last vestiges of the pattern, Rhakar sprang to his feet. He walked to where the young wielder had last stood and stared down at the stark line where myriad boot prints ended abruptly in the night-pale earth.

There had been a popular rumor passed among the wielders of the Fourth Age, those who'd last walked in the Citadel halls and tested for their rings before the Hundred Mages...the last generation known to have worked the Labyrinth. As he gazed upon the trampled earth, Rhakar wondered if the young wielder had been instructed by such a one.

There *were* survivors from the Citadel living outside of T'khendar, and his young wielder had worn scars that hinted at a mentor from the Fourth Age.

If the young man *had* mentored with such filth as Viernan hal'Jaitar or Dore Madden, however, he was sure to have been taught the same falsehoods.

Rhakar smiled.

Then he summoned the second strand and crossed the node.

FORTY-NINE

*"Therein lies the challenge of the game—that men are free to
choose, that you cannot always predict what a man will do."*
— Dhábu'balaji'ṣridanaí,
He Who Walks The Edge of The World

KJIERAN LAY IN the surf of dawn's high tide letting powerful
waves thunder down across his naked body. While he lay in this
tumultuous churning of sea and sand, the sky had brightened to
powder blue and the clouds had lost their gilded luster.

The flesh of his hands was pruned now, while his shoulder-length dark
hair had become a ragged, tangled mess of weeds and sand; but the crashing
waves had scoured the necrotic flesh from his legs and hips, and now his
lower body shone blackly each time the waves dissipated.

Kjieran gazed down at his legs in morbid fascination. Without the
obscuring tissue, the ropy muscles of his thighs bulged grotesquely. What
was he made of now that this stony flesh, dark as onyx, flexed and extended
though no life ran through his veins? Had such monsters as he was becoming
ever existed in legend, perhaps in the Age of Fable, when Warlocks from the
Shadow Realms were rumored to have coupled with the sorceresses of Vest?

Looking at his legs and hips, now completely transformed, Kjieran
imagined himself a fortnight hence, once the rest of his body had succumbed
to Dore's Pattern of Changing. The vision made him shudder.

Kjieran stood and dove into the surf. He swam out past the rocks to
let the deep water cleanse the sand from his hair and ears and cleanse his

spirit of the gruesome foreboding that so often held him in thrall these days. His legs were heavy in the water, and he couldn't float as once he'd done. But he didn't tire of swimming, no matter how strong the current, and the enveloping water was a comfort to his battered soul.

Kjieran thought often of the Prophet now. The more his body succumbed to Dore's pattern, the stronger he felt Bethamin's bond clutching him. A perpetual awareness of the Prophet was growing within him, and though the man had so far honored his promise not to invade Kjieran's thoughts, still Kjieran remained constantly aware of him in subtle ways. Every day Kjieran grew to better understand the Prophet's mind—*how* he thought, if not why—and every day Kjieran became more certain that there could be no escape from him.

As he swam in the cold sea, Kjieran marveled that he clung yet to life at all. If the Prophet's theories were true, he should long ago have embraced death. Yet something within him drove him to survive, some strength of will that demanded he endure.

Purpose held him—the driving need to solve the mystery of Sebastian's death and Trell's disappearance, the resolute conviction that he must save his king. This purpose, this promise...these ideas chained Kjieran to life more surely than the Prophet's binding ever could.

Finding himself far from shore, Kjieran dove beneath the waves and turned onto his back, letting his raven hair float freely around his face as he sank ever deeper. Looking up at the sparkling surface, he felt himself drifting slowly downwards until his feet struck the sandy bottom and the sun shone as a diffuse flame wavering far above. It felt strange to anchor in the sea floor and need no breath, hear no heartbeat, feel no painful burning in his chest or pressure in his ears. He might've stayed there forever with naught but the sound of the whispering sands for company, letting the tiny sea creatures make their homes in his hair, crustaceans attaching to his stone body—or at least until the Prophet claimed his will and drew him forth... until there was no other end but the death of his soul amidst Bethamin's devouring lust.

Yet he couldn't bring himself to give in yet to death.

Always within him sparked the tiniest fear of leaving this life—even the horrific life left to him. Certainly the ability to embrace death would've come as a relief, and yet the contemplation of death was in itself more terrifying than any pain he had yet endured.

One would think this proved that a man strove for survival, not death, as his ultimate end. Yet Kjieran knew, because he *knew* him now, that the Prophet would never see it that way.

The sun was high by the time he walked out of the sea.

Looking down at his Merdanti legs, Kjieran felt half sea-creature himself, a Wildling spawned in the darkling deep. His tunic and pants lay where he'd left them, warming on a rock. He'd taken to wearing the Nadori *shalwar-kameez* for their ease of movement as much as for the way the loose silk hid what he was becoming.

He faced a long walk back to the palace from his secluded beach. Time enough to decide upon his next course of action.

Since his foray into the Assassin's Guild, Kjieran had barely dared venture into the palace. He'd stayed far from the Court of Fifty-Two Arches—which was being watched day and night by hal'Jaitar's spies— and had spent much time in his rooms scratching and twitching and being generally miserable, worrying over Trell's state and what would become of the prince once he fell into hal'Jaitar's hands.

Kjieran's inability to reach his king with any sort of warning greatly distressed him, while his visits to the Prophet's mind were growing ever more unbearable. He'd received no notice from hal'Jaitar detailing when or where he was expected to perform the assassination of his king. He wondered if he ever would get such a missive. More likely the man was preparing his forces to descend upon Kjieran at the first sign of aggression.

It bothered him most that he'd heard nothing from hal'Jaitar in any capacity—especially after the scene in the Guild Hall. The wielder remained suspiciously silent, and his usual spies had been recalled from watching Kjieran.

There was a chance, of course, that hal'Jaitar was still occupied with searching for the man who'd infiltrated his sacred sanctum, that he didn't know it had been Kjieran and had his forces deployed to this end. But somehow Kjieran didn't think so. He feared that hal'Jaitar suspected him and was only lying in wait, the viper coiled for a retaliatory strike.

Kjieran's hands twitched as he walked.

It was a stony path he followed along the arid cliffs north of the palace, and all the while he traveled, his right hand clutched his amulet, safe beneath his tunic. It was his only comfort, his last tie to a humanity that had abandoned him. He hardly noticed he was holding onto it until once he saw his shadow. After that, he forced his hands to his sides and kept them there, lest he draw undue attention to the talisman.

He saw the Ascendant while still high on the road that led down to the palace's north gate. Kjieran couldn't be sure if he could see so clearly due to a new sharpness of sight or merely because the man was standing in the sun, with the strong daylight glaring off his torc and wrist cuffs as brightly as across his shaved pate.

By the time Kjieran could make out the spiraling tattoo on the Ascendant's forehead, the man had risen from his perch on a limestone statue of a lion and was standing squarely in the middle of the road, forcing all others entering or exiting to veer around him and earning black looks from the palace guards.

Guessing that the Ascendant had been waiting for him but not the reason why, Kjieran took the man by the arm and drew him from the road. The maneuver narrowly prevented an imminent collision with a wagon laden with carpets, upon which sat four black-eyed Nadoriin in crimson-chequered *keffiyehs*. None of the men had seemed the least bit squeamish about running them down.

The Ascendant glared at Kjieran as if affronted by this attempt to save him from injury. "I've been standing here for hours on the lookout for you!"

He was hairy as a bear and slightly paunched, with a fold of tanned fat hanging over the heavy gold chain that secured his *shendyt*, that tri-folded kilt of linen that all Ascendants wore. His forehead shone with the spiraling tattoo of the *aggreitha*, marking him as one of the researchers and scholars who acted as the Prophet's scribes.

"How did you know I would be coming this way, Ascendant?" Kjieran clasped his twitching hands behind his back.

"I didn't. The Brother Noll's been watching for you at the South Gate, too. At least he's standing in the shade." Settling Kjieran a suspicious glare, he demanded then, "What business for the Prophet possibly drew you north, Envoy? There's nothing but rock and sea for miles."

"When last I checked, my business was not also yours, Ascendant. What is it you want?"

The man glared daggers at him. Ascendants were not accustomed to being challenged—the best of them were naught but low-breed peasants whose innate hatred of authority led to its inexcusable abuse as soon as they were given any. Ascendants were men who had *chosen* to embrace Bethamin's doctrine, and Kjieran had yet to meet a one with some redeeming quality.

"Marquiin Yveric sent us in search of you," the Ascendant groused by way of particular complaint. "That was ere dawn, and it's been hours since. I expect he may be dead by now—*Lo but the Prophet sayeth it so!*"

Kjieran's hands twitched behind his back, this time with a violent desire to choke the insolent man, but he replied only, "Take me to him."

The Ascendant settled him a baleful glare. "Tis a fool to order twice what a man's already been sent to do." He turned and stalked back through the palace gates.

Kjieran followed, feeling turbulent and fractious. Yveric's possible deterioration concerned him as much as his constant fear of hal'Jaitar's spies. But even with so many swirling concerns clamoring for attention, Kjieran's concentration was repeatedly interrupted by the brand on the Ascendant's back.

Kjieran had seen its like many times, for all of Bethamin's Ascendants had been marked with such tattoos. The mark was a twisting, thorny pattern, as like unto darkness as billowing curls of smoke or the plunge of Black Krinling oil into clear water; a malevolent yet meaningless pattern—at least in its inability to harness *elae*.

Yet looking at the pattern now through eyes seasoned by a bond to the pattern's maker, Kjieran saw something new in its construction. Far from meaningless, the pattern encapsulated the Prophet's entire doctrine. Within its swirls lay tomes of knowledge; yet the truth it concealed—or rather *revealed* to those who understood its language—was so antipathetic to *elae* that Kjieran's Adept mind had been incapable of recognizing even a shadow of its existence without Bethamin's understanding to give it context.

Suddenly the darkness of the pattern chilled him, and he forced his eyes to look away and not return to it.

Agitation was thrumming through Kjieran by the time he reached

Yveric's room. He come to feel an unexpected kinship with the Marquiin, and he didn't want him to pass into the beyond without saying goodbye.

It was to his great relief when he knocked and heard Yveric call for entrance. Kjieran opened the door to find Yveric lying on the floor before the open screens, his body covered in blankets and his back to Kjieran. The sun had not yet fully reached his room, but Yveric clearly lay in wait for it.

"Soon, truthreader," the Marquiin whispered hoarsely. "Soon I am gone."

Kjieran came slowly inside and closed the door. "Is there anything I can do for you?"

Yveric laughed wetly, a whetstone grinding against itself. "What could you do?"

As Kjieran neared, he saw the man's lips and teeth were stained with blood. Sitting down in view of Yveric's gaze, Kjieran leaned against the wall and hugged knees to his chest. His legs were stone beneath the silk of his pants, like the Prophet's marble flesh. Inside, he felt barren and cold.

"I don't know what you believe, Yveric," Kjieran observed tonelessly, disheartened by the man's condition. "Would you be offended if I prayed that we should meet again in the Returning?"

Yveric coughed violently, a spasm that lasted many minutes and brought a surge of blood into the cloth he held to his mouth. When he had recovered but shallow breath, the Marquiin pinned his unsettling ebon eyes on Kjieran. They were alert and lucid and immensely disturbing. "You don't see it, even still?"

Kjieran shook his head. "See what?"

"Once our master's Fire cuts us off from *elae,* the line is severed forever. There *is* no Returning. There is no new life as an Adept."

Kjieran gaped at him. Never had he imagined such an incomprehensibly vicious end. Always in the back of his mind he'd believed there would be some future life for him...for whatever part of him moved on. But Yveric's words resonated with too much truth to doubt.

Kjieran closed his eyes and laid his head back against the wall, feeling ill. Would he have chosen this path if he'd known it would mean the ultimate sacrifice? If he'd understood then that there would be no Returning, that he would fade into the aether, his spirit unmade?

"Thought you knew," Yveric gasped.

Kjieran opened his eyes to find the man still watching him.

"Thought you knew the lady," he whispered, "that day you came... thought she'd sent you."

Kjieran shook his head, uncomprehending. "No one sent me, I told you that."

"She said you'd be coming, see." Yveric barely found room for breath around the fluid in his lungs. "Said you'd say...what you said. I didn't believe...until you came."

Kjieran began to feel very unsettled by this talk. "Who is the lady, Yveric?"

"Has a message for you, too." The Marquiin closed his eyes. "Said neither she nor the goddess can reach your dreams...said for you to take off...amulet."

Kjieran stared at the man, suddenly dismayed. He spun a fast look around, certain suddenly that this was some devilish trap, a ploy by hal'Jaitar to blackmail or otherwise manipulate him. He resisted the urge to grab the amulet.

The Marquiin had opened his eyes and was looking at him again. "Whatever it is...you wear, they can't reach your dreams because of it."

Neither, apparently, could the Prophet. But how could Yveric know about his amulet?

Growing agitated, Kjieran took hold of the Marquiin's shoulder. "Who is this lady?"

Yveric smiled a bitter, loathsome grimace full of bloody bone. "A figment...a delusion...a dream."

"A dream." Kjieran relaxed and released Yveric's shoulder, but he felt unnerved. He was certain he'd never drawn attention to his amulet while in the Marquiin's company, and to be sure he'd never told a soul of its existence.

"*Kjieran van Stone,*" Yveric abruptly spoke his name like a grave calling, his tone suddenly hale and powerful and so unexpected from this shell of a man.

Kjieran's eyes flew to his, startled and shocked.

The sun had finally reached the room, and long rays fell now upon the Marquiin's blighted face. "She says..." he spoke through lungs drowned in blood, forming the words with a desperate force of will, "...there may be a way."

Something in the man's voice, in the flotsam of his tortured thoughts…
there was some whisper among the madness that spoke of truth.

"A way to what?" Kjieran grabbed the Marquiin's arm again.

"I'm cold, truthreader," Yveric whispered.

Then he died.

Kjieran took his time getting back to his rooms. He was disheartened over
Yveric's death and seething at the callousness of the Ascendants, who had
refused to do more than cart the man's body out to be dumped at sea.
Kjieran had said the Rites for the Departed over Yveric before he'd called the
Ascendants to attend to him, but it brought little consolation.

Kjieran feared meeting Yveric's same end on many levels. A part of him
wished another might be there to likewise witness his own death…to walk
with him to the Extian Doors. But if what the man said was correct—and
Kjieran had to believe it was, for *elae* had resonated with its truth—then
Yveric was gone for eternity. There would be no Returning for him, no new
life. He'd been forever severed from *elae*.

This truth was so disturbing that for the first time Kjieran honestly
desired death. Were he to somehow find his way across that threshold now—
before Dore's pattern finished its work, before the Prophet's bond became a
granite sarcophagus for his soul—if he might perish precipitously, he retained
a chance of rebirth. The very idea seemed so hopeless…

It was in that moment that he saw his king.

Kjieran had just entered the arcade bordering the pink marble Court of
Penitence and its jade Pillars of Jai'Gar. There, before the Pool of Purification,
surrounded by a score of knights, stood Gydryn val Lorian. The Dannish
contingent shared the poolside with a host of others—for despite its off-
putting name, the Court of Penitence was a popular locale for pretentiously
pious ladies, as well as the dark-eyed courtiers who preyed upon them.

The king had stopped to view the pillars—Kjieran glimpsed him standing
among his red-coated personal guard—and he remained a striking presence.
Gydryn soon set off again, seeming the dark-coated eye in a hurricane of red,
so close and yet completely unreachable.

The moment was heartbreaking.

However am I going to manage this?

Kjieran could no more bring himself to raise his hand against Gydryn val Lorian than he could against himself; yet if he didn't do *something* soon, he feared the Prophet would compel him into the act, and all would be lost.

As Kjieran stood immobilized, struggling with these uncertainties, he saw a shadowed form move away from a column across the way. Kjieran caught just a sliver of the man's thoughts, but that sliver was mirror clear.

Trell val Lorian.

Kjieran called upon his pattern of shadows, draped it about himself like a cloak, and followed.

It wasn't easy to hold the pattern that day. *Elae* felt like sand between his fingers, and he kept breathing deeply of it that he might maintain a reservoir to fuel the working. Kjieran knew that Dore's pattern was slowly overtaking *elae*, each foothold claimed upon his person becoming stronger than the last.

He faced this truth with grim resignation; it was an eventuality as inevitable as nightfall, as the inexorable motion of the tides.

There may be a way...

The Marquiin's admonition haunted him. Who was this lady that came to madmen in their dreams, prophesying salvation? Or if the dream was but a dream, how had Yveric known of the amulet? Their final conversation still had Kjieran disturbed, for Yveric had been lucid, and his words rang with truth.

Yet Kjieran dared not chance removing his amulet; it was his last lifeline to *elae*.

The man Kjieran followed was singularly focused, and Kjieran followed him deep into the bowels of the palace, down and through narrow, stone-lined corridors where servants scurried and Saldarian sell-swords drank and pissed and gambled. Past storerooms and cellars into a twisting service tunnel that eventually emptied into the lower city.

When Kjieran realized they were no longer in the palace, he began to wonder just what business the man was upon that it took him so far from hal'Jaitar's domain. Wondered, that is, until he saw a great building rearing at the end of a narrow street and realized with a sinking unease that *all* of Tal'Shira was hal'Jaitar's domain.

Kjieran slowed as he faced the building he'd come staggering out of several nights past; beneath it, in a secret subterranean cavern, lurked the halls of the Assassin's Guild.

The street led to an ironbound door, which Kjieran's spy quickly opened with a trace-seal to slip within. All around Kjieran, high stone walls blocked the daylight, with no retreat but the windowless corridor down which he'd just come. A high balcony of wrought iron stood three floors above him, but it was out of reach with no trailing ladder.

Kjieran looked around anxiously. His senses were not so acute as once they'd been, but he knew something was amiss.

Once, he might've crafted a pattern to reveal the currents and show him what else was being worked in his presence. Once, he might've worked many patterns at once. Now he could barely manage his single pattern of protective shadows.

Still, he was a truthreader, and all such Adepts had instilled within them a keen sense of the *truth* of things. Kjieran perceived a falsehood in that narrow street. He saw only one way to find out what it was.

He released his pattern of shadows.

As soon as the darkened veil slipped off his vision, a host of additional shapes materialized—six big men, with a seventh garbed in wielder's black. Now Kjieran saw that the wielder had been hiding the brutes with a similar illusion— hiding their thoughts as well as their forms—that Kjieran might sense nothing of them.

"Recognize this place, *truthreader*?" The wielder wore a black *keffiyeh* banded with a gold *agal*, and his rounded nose and slightly upturned eyes marked him as Bemothi, in keeping with his accent. "Seen it recently, perhaps?"

There was no point in dissembling. They had lured him there with thoughts of Trell. They knew what purpose he was about.

Kjieran looked around but didn't see hal'Jaitar. "I would speak to your master." In the same breath he loathed his own foolishness and wondered how he could possibly avoid this disaster.

"Oh, but my master takes ill interest in northern spies. Unless…he might hear a confession."

Kjieran looked around at the six men looming near. They were all heavily armed, and any one of them seemed capable of breaking his neck like a twig. "A confession? To what end?"

"Perhaps to learn why you've really come to M'Nador, Kjieran van Stone. Who do you work for? Why do you seek news of Trell val Lorian?"

"I serve the Prophet," Kjieran said numbly.

The wielder laughed. "Yes, and who else?" His eyes flashed with this question, no doubt one hal'Jaitar shared. "How many masters have their hooks in your tongue?" When Kjieran gave no answer, the wielder smiled. "So there *is* another. My master thought as much."

He moved away from his men while eying Kjieran speculatively with his slanted almond eyes. He appeared to be in his third decade, but Kjieran suspected he was far older, for a glance at his hand had revealed four Sormitáge rings. No man became a wielder who did not work the Pattern of Life, for mastery of the craft was more than one lifetime in the gaining.

Even if he'd possessed full use of *elae* and had all of his faculties about him, Kjieran would've been outmatched in facing this wielder.

"My master perceives all manner of patterns upon you, truthreader." The other Adept walked a slow circle around Kjieran with his hands clasped behind his ebon robes. "He would know how you defeated his poison and what power you worked in the Hall. Confess these things...confess what mischief you're truly about, and he might be convinced to spare your life."

Kjieran broke into a humorless smile. "If I thought your master capable of that, I might even be tempted."

The wielder settled him a grim smile. "It seems then that we've come to the end of our meeting, Kjieran van Stone."

He nodded to his men, who descended upon Kjieran. Strong fists pummeled him, as did knees and elbows, feet and bludgeons. Kjieran wallowed in the dirt helplessly, and still they kicked and beat him. Even with half of him already changed, the pain was excruciating.

He made no attempt to defend himself.

In some small way, pain's fiery warmth was a welcome relief from the frozen void that was the Prophet's bond. Kjieran knew he might at any time seek the Prophet through this link, might know—as he had known in the Hall—how to wield his grave power and escape this punishment. But he didn't reach for Bethamin.

In fact, he tried with everything he was to keep the Prophet from sensing what was being done to destroy him.

A great part of Kjieran desperately craved the idea that this could be his end. All thoughts of his king, of his mission—anything and everything he cared for vanished in light of his suddenly overwhelming yearning for death. He sought it so completely that even his own honor fled from the ferocious face of this desire. So he let them do their worst and prayed all the while that they would be successful.

Eventually the pummeling ceased and two of them yanked him up to hang limply. The world swam; pain consumed every part of his being, while his legs felt numb and cold and rock-heavy. He hung his head, seeking oblivion.

"Do it," growled the wielder.

Something cold and sharp speared inside him. He felt the blade slicing through the flesh of his abdomen, as yet unchanged by Dore's violent working; felt his insides opened to the alley's foul air. He heard a horrific scream escape his throat.

They dropped him in the dirt. Kjieran lay there staring dully at the dry earth.

The wielder came to stand over him. "My master sends his regards, *truthreader*."

Two fast but heavy clicks accompanied these words. Kjieran's body twitched violently as two crossbow bolts found their way into his heart.

Someone reached down and grabbed his head, twisting it roughly that his eyes might stare upwards, that he might focus upon the black-robed figure standing on the high balcony. *Hal'Jaitar*.

Then they left him.

Kjieran laid for a long time in silent despair, so consumed with pain yet numb with hopelessness that he couldn't find the will to form a thought. As the hours passed with the failing day, his mind drifted and awareness slipped towards unconsciousness—yet even a blessed oblivion was denied him. Pain and exhaustion mingled, leaving him disoriented and confused.

He felt inconsolably alone.

Kjieran never knew why he called for the Prophet then. Perhaps in his agonized condition, in the confusion of waiting for a death that had disavowed him, he sought companionship during the hours that should've been his last...so he sought the only living soul his agonized mind could reach.

My lord...

In moments, the Prophet's awareness opened to him.

Kjieran...Kjieran! What has happened?

Kjieran recalled the brutal memory for the Prophet's inspection.

Immediately Bethamin drew him within his own consciousness. The world took a different shape, and suddenly the Prophet was kneeling at his side. His hands—strangely warm—lifted Kjieran's shoulders, and he cradled Kjieran's head in his lap.

"I don't understand." Bethamin's dark eyes were uncommonly vivid, his tone sharp. "What happened?"

Kjieran tried to focus, but it was so hard when confusion clung to every thought. A jumble of images bounced across the bond. He saw the Prophet react, saw his gaze tighten, his dark eyes burn with cold fury. "*WHO DARES HARM YOU?*" The thunder of Bethamin's anger shook marble dust from between the massive stones of the chamber.

"Hal'Jaitar," Kjieran whispered.

He had no reason to feel weak, for they communed now out of time and wholly in the Prophet's mind, but some residual awareness of his body made it hard for Kjieran to find strength or mental clarity.

The Prophet smoothed a strand of raven hair from Kjieran's forehead. "Why did you not call upon me for aid?" His tone was dangerous and dark, full of injury and accusation. Oddly, Kjieran thought he sensed real concern in the man's manner, in the reverberation of his thoughts. Could it be that the Prophet actually *cared* about him?

He held the Prophet's gaze, feeling wretched and distraught. He hadn't the energy to craft a lie. "To my great shame, my lord, I sought to know what would happen…to know if my body could still be injured or if I would pass on. I regret that my human soul is so frail, my will so weak…I regret that I sought to know such things."

The Prophet trailed his fingers down Kjieran's face, pressed his thumb hard upon his chin to part his lips. Anger was rolling off him in waves, the storm of his thoughts amassing chill clouds of power.

"This Viernan hal'Jaitar, Radov's wielder," he said in a low voice, his dark eyes like imploding stars, "I will make him suffer for this."

Kjieran closed his eyes and let the Prophet's anger wash over him. It felt…cleansing. The part of him that was still himself shuddered in this knowledge, for he saw that he was changing, *becoming*…but in that moment of heartbroken misery, he couldn't prevent it—he didn't even want to. In that moment, Bethamin owned him wholly.

He opened his eyes to find the Prophet's lips close, his mass of braids a curtain enclosing them both, his large eyes desiring.

Abandoning the whispered warnings of his shattered soul, Kjieran reached for him.

He regained consciousness with a gasp.

Sunset flamed the sky above him. The bloody clouds felt an unwanted reminder of the copulation he'd just so willingly embraced.

I made love with a monster.

The knowledge sickened him.

As he regained awareness of where he was, of what had been done in that abandoned alley…Kjieran clutched at his chest, suddenly desperate.

But the tiny medallion was still there, safe around his neck. It seemed the brutes had merely meant to punish and kill him, not to rob him of what little he possessed.

I shall remember this one grace when I exact the Prophet's vengeance upon you, Kjieran thought.

Hearing the thought, Kjieran shuddered, for he saw that this had not been his thought at all, but the expression of some…*other*. The *other* that he was becoming.

A sudden awareness work within him—the terrible knowledge of what had been taken from him, the horrors that had already been exacted against him…and what was yet to be.

He'd sought the Prophet in his last moments and consummated their bond!

Though it was only in thought and not in physical deed, yet it seemed no less real for lack of the Prophet's seed or their mark upon the tides of *elae*.

He'd sought comfort in the Prophet's arms, had accepted his love, and had returned to life less human because of it. Something *else* had come back with him.

Kjieran loathed the thing he was becoming, loathed that he'd been so weak as to seek solace in the arms of the Prophet Bethamin. Kjieran lay consumed by grief while the world spun crazily, and then his shoulders began to shake with his sobs.

He wept there in the alley for all he had lost.

Eventually his tearless gasps abated. Eventually he realized he had to get up and continue on, for even the grace of death had turned its back on him.

Desolate, Kjieran rolled onto his back and stared at the fletching on the bolts still protruding from his chest. It seemed another man's hand that reached up, and with a strong tug, ripped them free. He sent the shafts clattering into the wall.

Pressing both hands to support his ruptured abdomen, Kjieran sat up and assessed the damage. His gut was a shambles, ripped from hip to hip. More horrifying still was that it seemed the wound of a rotten fish, bloodless, with all of his vital organs hanging dark and unhealthy within the cavity, long dead. His body had become as inanimate clay just waiting to be molded, waiting for the fell magic to spread into its dull substance, to fashion it into Dore's Merdanti blade.

Pushing one arm across his ravaged belly, Kjieran struggled to his feet. Night had fallen, and the streets were dark. Seeming a beggar in ripped and soiled clothes, he made his slow way back to the palace.

It took a great effort to hold *elae* and drape himself in shadows. The lifeforce kept slipping out of his grasp, seeping out of the holes in his body. No longer a vessel for *elae*, his body was a sieve. He took some comfort that he could call the lifeforce at all, and strangely did not despair in how little of it he could control.

Still, it was slow going. He dared not let a soul see him return—never mind the questions he would get from the guards, he couldn't afford to alert hal'Jaitar that he lived—but he also couldn't keep up the obscuring pattern for long. Accordingly, he moved in spurts, one street, alley and tunnel at a time.

When he finally reached his rooms, they'd been ransacked. He locked the door nonetheless, and after some searching, uncovered his little box of needle and thread from a pile of clothing dumped beside his chest of drawers. He ripped off his tunic and let his britches fall around his feet. Taking the black thread in hand, Kjieran began stitching himself back together.

While upon this task, he made some decisions.

Some *thing* had come back with him from that foray into the Prophet's mind, a new awareness birthed in their sex. It was a cold and heartless entity, and the innocent truthreader in Kjieran had shied from it at first. But as he slowly pierced his dead flesh and tied off each knot, pierced and tied with painstaking care, he couldn't keep from glancing every so often to where the thing crouched in the corner of his mind.

A wild and volatile thing, yes, but one that might be at his command, if he was brave enough to compel it.

Oh, he knew it would attempt to control him equally, that they might wrestle over every choice and action, but he also somehow knew that so long as *elae* was with him, he would be the victor.

The Prophet had consumed the last of his innocence. He would make that sacrifice worth something.

So while Kjieran sewed his flesh back together, he talked to this new entity that lurked in his mind, timidly at first, but then with growing surety. When at last he tied off the final knot of his sutures and snapped the hanging thread, he had formed something of a plan. It was dangerous. He never would've attempted it before coupling with the Prophet, but he saw now how little he had left to lose.

He would only be worthy of himself if he succeeded in saving his king.

Standing then, straightening with his resolve, Kjieran walked to the carved wooden screens that acted as doors between his room and the night. He hadn't realized until that moment that he'd been operating in darkness, but the moon was high and cast a glimmering reflection on the wavering sea.

Thinking upon his recent intimacy with the Prophet, Kjieran wondered if there was such a place as the furthest level of Hell, or if in truth, Hell had no end. Every time it seemed he could cast his nets no lower, still they snared some new atrocity to subjugate and torment him. Hours ago he'd been ready for death, sure he would at any moment stare upon its misshapen face. Now death seemed impossibly out of reach, an impotent phantom with naught but moonlight for substance.

All the better, for he had things to do.

Hours passed before he found his bed that night, but finally he had only one thing left to do before lying down to sleep.

Kjieran took off his amulet.

FIFTY

*"Partaking of Alorin's tender flesh has roused in them an
insatiable hunger for worlds they were never meant to know."*
– Jayachándranáptra, Rival of the Sun,
on the Malorin'athgul

TRELL PITCHED TO his knees on the marble floor. Someone
ripped the hood from his head, and he inhaled free air for the first
time since departing camp in the Kutsamak.

As his eyes adjusted to the light, Trell blinked and looked around the
long, rectangular room, whose walls were decorated in elaborately carved
soapstone panels. High windows admitted long shafts of afternoon light,
which illuminated the four marble lions that demarked the corners of a
sunken floor. Each massive animal held a paw upraised, jaws forever open in
soundless roars.

"Unshackle him."

Trell looked over his shoulder to see a man standing just inside the doors
at the near end of the room. He wore robes of ebon silk and a matching
keffiyeh and black-corded *agal*. As the man approached, Trell noted eight
Sormitáge rings gracing his long fingers. They announced his identity better
than any introduction.

Muttering something unintelligible, the Saldarian guard released the
iron cuffs binding Trell's hands.

He gingerly massaged his wrists and got to his feet.

"Leave us," commanded the wielder.

"But my lord—"

"I said *leave us!*"

The Saldarian ducked his head and skulked away. Trell watched him go with the shadow of a smile hinting on his lips. How fearful did these Saldarians think him if they imagined he'd take on Viernan hal'Jaitar with naught but his bare hands?

Hal'Jaitar must've reached the same conclusion, for he looked to Trell with one ashen eyebrow raised. "It seems you made quite the impression, Prince of Dannym."

The wielder stopped beside one of two sofas, velvet-covered and low-backed. A table sat in between. Four glasses and a silver teapot were resting on the table. The pot's curving spout was emitting a faint tendril of steam. Hal'Jaitar indicated the sofa across from him with an open hand. "Won't you join me?"

Still rubbing his wrists, Trell walked slowly to the sofa. His entire body ached from bruises old and new. The trip east had been rough, the Saldarians' treatment of him just shy of brutal. He was fairly sure one of his ribs had been fractured.

Every breath exacted pain in the claiming, every motion required an effort of will, but he'd be damned if he'd let Viernan hal'Jaitar see him hurting.

As Trell was slowly lowering his body onto the cushion, the wielder leaned back in his seat and crossed his knees, clasping fingers in his lap. "Let us assume we know each other," he said with his piercing dark eyes pinned on Trell. There was naught of amity in his gaze, belying his mild tone. "Imagine we have met again after many years abroad. What then might you tell me of your travels?"

"You mean, since you sent men to assassinate me and set fire to my ship?"

Viernan's expression darkened. "So you do remember. They told me you claimed no knowledge of your past."

"I know only what the wielder Işak intimated." Trell gave hal'Jaitar a smile full of promised retribution. "But now you've confirmed it. Thank you."

In the angry silence that followed, Viernan returned the twitch of a smile. "Well played, Prince of Dannym. You take the point."

He stared at Trell coldly then, holding the prince's gaze, two players regarding each other across the King's board. Eventually Viernan's smile returned, wider this time, revealing long teeth yellowed with age. He indicated the tea service on the table between them. "Let us take tea together as allies are wont to do."

"Allies who try to kill each other." Trell eyed the tea skeptically. "I think I'll pass."

Viernan speared him with a narrow look full of venom. "You are too like your older brother. He, too, was insolent. He, too, thought himself beyond my reach."

Trell stared back at him working the muscles of his jaw. He knew Viernan hal'Jaitar's reputation—the Emir's forces had been battling Viernan's wielders for months. But in that moment, Trell didn't care that the man was insanely dangerous, or that his gold rings bespoke of untold abilities. All he knew was that this man had stolen years of his life *and* apparently was claiming to have played a role in his brother Sebastian's death.

Trell bent to rest elbows on his knees, the better to meet Viernan's glare. His calm demeanor belied the shock he felt. "To think," he remarked in a low voice, wolf-grey eyes pinned unerringly upon the wielder, "...all this time, everyone suspected the Khurds were to blame for our deaths, when it was you." He shook his head as if with admiration, but he was dangerously angry. "Score a point for Viernan hal'Jaitar."

The wielder said nothing, but he didn't need to, for as Trell considered the matter, more pieces clicked into place.

"Of course. Now I see." He sat back slowly in his seat. "Let us return eight years into our mutual past. M'Nador's lingering war with the Akkad has interrupted Radov's mining operations in the Kutsamak, and the royal coffers are growing sparse. The Congress of Princes is fractious and ever with an eye towards overthrow—Radov wouldn't dare go to them for aid. He knows he can't rouse a mercenary force large enough to defeat the Akkad, so he must call upon the Triad pact."

Trell pressed a finger thoughtfully to his lips. "But how to convince his neighborly monarchs to help? Radov needs more than a token force to defeat the Seventeen Tribes. He needs the bulk of Dannym's army." He raised his finger as if with sudden inspiration. "Of course! What better way to secure his allies' support than by assassinating their children and blaming his enemy?" He cast Viernan a look of merciless accusation. "The essence of war is deception, eh, Consul?"

The wielder's gaze in reply to this speech was chilling, but he clearly would not be baited into another confession.

Abruptly Viernan stood and began walking the circumference of the sunken floor with his hands locked behind his back. "Let's speak of Işak'getirmek." He speared a look towards Trell. "What happened between the two of you? He defeats you in battle and suddenly you're compatriots, sharing secrets in the dark?"

"Işak?" Trell wore a baffled frown as his eyes followed Viernan around the room. "What do you care about him?"

Viernan spun with a sharp glare. "You will answer my questions, Trell val Lorian, or be asked them again by His Highness's Questioner, who is not so patient!"

Trell shrugged. "We barely spoke at all."

"Yet in this bare exchange you managed to uncover truths we've effectively hidden for half a decade!" Viernan swung heatedly to face him. "You will tell me *now*." He pointed a finger and stalked towards him. "Where have you been these past years? How did you survive?"

Trell felt the compulsion impinge upon his mind, a fiery poker to his thoughts. It assaulted his stomach with a sickly heat, but as he'd been fed little for days, there was nothing to react to it. And he'd fought worse in Işak's patterns. Much worse.

"As I told your men," he hissed, reflexively hunching his shoulders against the mental attack, "I remember nothing of my past."

"*Lies!*" Viernan waved an airy hand, but his compulsion became a fiery iron fist in Trell's intestines and a forge consuming his brain. "*You* would have me believe you just appeared with the black-sheep cousin with no memory of your life? Why not claim you were in T'khendar and flew back here in the arms of a Shade!"

Trell sucked in a shuddering breath and fell sideways on the couch, bent nearly double from the force of Viernan's compulsion. He lifted his gaze to the wielder and cast him a sharp smile through gritted teeth. "Can they do that?"

Viernan gazed broodingly at him. Abruptly the compulsion ceased, and the pain vanished as instantly as it had come. "So you will not easily divulge the truth." He started pacing again. "Therefore you must be protecting someone. But is it yourself...or another?"

Trell pushed himself back into a sitting position with slow care. He fixed his gaze on Viernan and reflected on the irony of his situation.

Had he been defeated on the lines, abducted in battle, this confrontation would've had its place...but he wasn't there as a leader of the Converted, hostage of war—they knew nothing of that. He was there but for the happenstance of a royal birth.

Yet Trell recognized that Viernan hal'Jaitar *was* his enemy in every way—it wasn't the Nadoriin at large, or the Saldarians...perhaps not even Radov. *Viernan* stood behind this conflict.

Trell shook his head, amazed at the winding path of Fate. All of his years...years of amnesia, years of battle, his recent quest...everything that had come before—all of his conflicts and choices—they had still brought him to this seemingly inevitable confrontation.

What really twisted incredulity was that the Mage had foreseen it—of this, Trell was certain. He'd glimpsed but a shadow of the Mage's plan in the moment of parting with Alyneri, but the section of the pattern he had seen...

"The truth is coming, Viernan," Trell said quietly. Somehow he knew that events continued to unfold in the world around him, the Mage's leviathan plan moving inexorably forward.

He lifted his gaze to meet the wielder's vehement stare. "How long do you think you can keep up this charade? My father must be in Tal'Shira by now. Care to wager on whether he'll keep his army in Taj al'Jahanna once he learns of your betrayal?"

The wielder arched a brow. "What makes you think he will?"

Trell barked a laugh. "How can you imagine he won't?" He leaned back slowly on the couch, the better to support his aching side. "That will be a problem, won't it?" He pressed a thoughtful finger to his lips. "How will you ever retake Raku without the Dannish army? Radov's forces are spread too thin. The Emir has too many, and his Converted fight like banshees— unlike those Saldarians." He clicked his tongue in mock sympathy. "Not turning out so well is it, that pact with the Prophet? Maniacs *can* be unpredictable—"

"As amusing as this conversation is, Prince of Dannym," the wielder interrupted with a withering smile, "we grow short on time."

"Yes, I suppose *you* do," Trell agreed, and all pretence vanished from his manner, revealing only the solid core of determination beneath.

Viernan's dark eyes were coldly calculating. "You are too intelligent for your own good, Trell val Lorian."

"So it would seem," Trell agreed soberly. For all his cavalier demeanor, he knew what would be awaiting him in the shadowed, soundproof cells of Radov's dungeon.

Viernan clapped his hands, and the doors at the back of the room opened. Trell guessed their meeting was over. As the Saldarian approached with clinking irons in hand, Viernan cast Trell one final look of searing curiosity. "How *did* you survive?"

The Saldarian grabbed Trell up off the couch and wrenched his arms behind his back.

The prince looked up at Viernan under his brows. "Fate chose a different role for me, Consul."

"Strange," the wielder remarked with eyes like black orbs gleaming with cold malice. "For a favored child of Fate, Cephrael's hand seems to have dropped you right back where you started."

The Saldarian jerked Trell upright. He tossed his dark hair from his eyes and replied with a wry smile, "If it was Cephrael returned me to your doorstep, Viernan, you can be certain He had his reasons."

Then the Saldarian was shoving the hood over Trell's head and dragging him away, but not before he noted with deep satisfaction the shocked expression on Viernan's face.

FIFTY-ONE

"If you want a pattern to be eternal, unbreakable, irreversible,
you bind it with the fifth. Love often feels the same."
— The First Vestal Alshiba Torinin

H IS MAJESTY GYDRYN val Lorian paced at one end of the hall
with hands clasped behind his back. Six of the king's remaining
knights—those who hadn't gone with Duke val Whitney—stood
near the wall with gauntleted hands resting on the hilts of their swords. They
had all been waiting for far too long, which helped the king to summon real
heat when at last Viernan hal'Jaitar walked through the doors.

"I will stand for no more of this, hal'Jaitar." Gydryn turned to face the
wielder as the latter strode sinuously across the hall, each step stirring the
voluminous silk of his ebon robes.

"Pray tell, no more of what, Majesty?" Viernan asked, smiling benignly.

"Of Radov's stalling." The king made sure the disapproval was evident
in his tone. "And where *is* your prince? He is conspicuously absent at a
meeting called by him directly."

"A touch of fever, Majesty. He sends his gravest regards…and me…to
attend your needs."

"My *needs?* I've been here for a score of days and still there's no word
from your prince on when this parley shall commence. My kingdom suffers
constant threat of danger, Viernan. I came at Radov's urgent request, only
to sit and await his pleasure. My men endure this stifling heat and the
ever-corrosive effects of boredom while you and your prince deliberate?"

Gydryn brandished his hand with outright fury. "I will not abide it, Viernan hal'Jaitar!"

"Your Majesty, I confess His Highness is most aggrieved by the delay," Viernan returned, though his dark eyes were all too reminiscent of a predator's watchful gaze. He motioned to a low table surrounded by four low-backed chairs, where a tea service had been set. "Won't you take tea while I explain what little I know?"

The King eyed him disagreeably. "Very well." He walked to join the wielder and took a seat across from him. Viernan poured tea into two glass cups rimmed in gold, and raised his to the king. "May this war find a swift and sure end upon the blade of our alliance."

Gydryn took up his cup to make the toast, but he lowered it again as Viernan drank. "Speak then," rumbled the king. "I would know what keeps us from pursuing the purpose of my journey."

If Viernan noticed the king's untouched tea, he did not remark upon it. "Whispers, your Majesty," he advised warily instead. He set down his glass and sat back in his seat, crossing one knee and clasping hands around its bony protrusion. "Whispers of plots and intrigues, of assassination."

Gydryn frowned. "Threats against your prince?"

"We are unsure as yet of the target," Viernan murmured, "but it forestalls progress while we investigate. However, preparations for the parley continue. I myself was not too long ago upon the site inspecting the progress. Tents have been erected, supplies loaded in…all stands ready but for any and all possible steps to ensure the safety of the parley's members."

Though he smiled at this utterance, Gydryn knew better. There was ne'er a shadow of amiable intent in Viernan hal'Jaitar. His repertoire of smiles was but a cache of deadly needles, each focused to draw the blood of a different emotion through the veins of conversation.

"Too well does my prince remember how ill-prepared we were when last we attempted to reason with Abdul-Basir," Viernan noted then, his smile sharp and cutting, "…and how much was lost as a result."

Gydryn's expression darkened at the reference to his first-born son, Sebastian, whose life had been claimed by Basi assassins in the aforementioned meeting—or so hal'Jaitar certainly expected him to believe.

Rather than rising to this taunt—for it was surely an attempt to rouse his ire, that hal'Jaitar might learn something of the king—Gydryn stared fixedly at the wielder. "I mislike the ills I find in your prince's domain." His gaze and tone were fierce in accusation. "Saldarians running rampant, Ascendants spreading Bethamin's doctrine of filth uncensored and unchecked." He leaned towards hal'Jaitar and set his untouched tea upon the table. "If I didn't know better, Viernan, I might be inclined to imagine your prince has formed a pact with the Prophet Bethamin."

Viernan gazed at him quietly. When he spoke again, his smile was wan and his eyes unkind. "How foolish you must think us, dull-witted heathens lacking in couth and culture."

Gydryn stood and looked down at the man. The lie came easily to his lips. "General Loran val Whitney is on his way to Taj al'Jahanna to ready my troops for departure. He awaits but word from me to evacuate."

Viernan's smile withered, replaced by cold anger. "I hope you have given no such word, Majesty."

"Three days," Gydryn turned and strode for the door. "Radov has three days to secure the parley, or my army and I are leaving." His knights marched forth to surround their king, and all departed.

Radov abin Hadorin, Ruling Prince of M'Nador, paced restlessly behind the carved soapstone screens that secretly opened upon the Hall of Seas, where his Consul, Viernan hal'Jaitar, was meeting with the King of Dannym.

Belloth take those damnable val Lorians!

He really should've had both of the older boys beheaded when he'd had the chance, as Viernan had pushed him so vehemently to do. He could've dumped their heads in Duan'Bai and blamed the deaths unquestionably on Abdul-Basir. But then...well, he'd tried having the middle prince killed and that didn't seem to have worked out well for anyone. Viernan didn't know everything.

Radov spun on his heel and stalked back in the opposite direction with hands clasped behind his back, his footfalls muffled by thick Veneisean carpets. Those Veneiseans knew how to weave a good carpet even if their military was as worthless as a camp whore with the pox.

Even when he was in a mild humor, which was a rarity of late, Prince Radov was a fierce-looking man. His aquiline nose extended from a heavy brow that shadowed deep-set eyes, and he wore a goatee that left his face clean to better view the intricate tattoos adorning his lower jaw. The tattoos extended down his neck and met in a jagged-edged design, glimpsed that day between the open folds of a *kameez* of crimson silk worked all over with jet beads. He wore a large ruby in each pierced lobe, and a gold band at the top of each ear, and to court he wore a royal *keffiyeh*, but today had chosen a simple black one striped with gold.

Radov rubbed his brow. The king in the other room was already giving him a headache. Jai'Gar be praised that Viernan had the foresight to encourage Radov to feign illness rather than deal with these sniveling Northmen. All any of them ever did was complain about the heat. He would've sent them all back to the wilderness they called home long ago, except a solid few knew where best to stick their steel to kill a Khurd and had passing good aim with a crossbow.

Still, his head *was* pounding.

Radov spun a desiring look towards the crystal bottle that rested upon a near table, its liquid contents clear and bright. He licked his lips. His hooded eyes examined the bottle as if it was a virgin disrobing before him, and his tongue flickered at the edge of his teeth as he considered the liquid's fiery touch.

By Jai'Gar, but the bottle called out its own name, the wanton cry of a prurient nymph: *Absinthe…absinthe…*

The powerful distilled spirit was useful for cleaning resin off an axe and starting fires. Viernan claimed it wasn't fit for human consumption, though the Veneiseans drank it by the barrel. Merely a spoon of it in a glass of water brought a lightening to the head—and this was how the Veneiseans took it, watered down or mixed—yet Radov poured himself a glass and sipped it straight.

Viernan would be furious with him. The man was outspoken about the evils of the *'vile drink.'* But he didn't answer to Viernan hal'Jaitar. *Radov* was the Ruling Prince of M'Nador! What Viernan didn't understand—what Radov couldn't tell him—was that the Veneisean spirit was the only thing that quieted the abrasive voices in his head.

Radov cast a sooty glare past the concealing screen to where Viernan was now talking with one of his spies. Viernan and his damned intrigues. Radov couldn't spit in his own palace without hitting a spy.

Hal'Jaitar was just then saying, "…find val Whitney and the Dannish knights. I would know if they've departed as the king claimed…"

Radov frowned. When had the king departed? He realized he couldn't remember Gydryn and his knights leaving the room.

He looked at his glass and found it startlingly empty. He set it down on a table with sudden revulsion. Viernan was right—the stuff was the drink of the damned...no doubt a trick of Indora's spies. Hadn't the absinthe first come to him as gift from Veneisea's decadent queen?

No! *No*...he refused to believe his memory troubles stemmed from the absinthe. It was that Bethamin's fault!

Yes, Bethamin was definitely to blame.

No matter what complaint Radov conceived—the lingering war, his financial problems, the lesser princes and their petty politics—and a bunch of whining, nagging bitches *they* were—whatever the issue, Radov blamed it unerringly on Bethamin. The man had...*done* something to him.

Ever since that Prophet's grey hound dared put his leprous hands on Radov's royal person...every night since, his dreams had been haunted. After so many sleepless nights, it was getting so he couldn't think straight— never mind how his appetite had abandoned him. Everything he ate tasted of ash and cyanide. He was losing weight.

His once-favorite daughter—*the ungrateful whore!*—had run away, and this after he'd spared her life. Granted her mercy! But mercy only gained one a knife in the back. Viernan was always saying that.

Viernan...he was ever a bad taste in Radov's mouth. Fennel...like fennel. *No, not fennel.* Wormwood, maybe. In any event, Viernan couldn't be trusted. Radov knew that Viernan would betray him, but not yet...not yet. He had an agenda, Viernan did. The man was nothing if not conniving. Radov made him legitimate. Viernan could do anything in the prince's name. And where would he be without Radov? Just one more relic from a bygone era—*one of the Fifty Companions*...

Radov snorted at the moniker. Whatever had any of them done except manage not to die? Like those damned Sundragons. They just wouldn't die, no matter what you did to them. Viernan was always promising to do something about the Belloth-spawned dragons. Radov knew he would've won the war by now if not for those hell-forsaken beasts...*and the Mage.* The Emir's Mage.

But the Mage...Radov didn't understand his magic. Viernan didn't even understand his magic—at least he pretended not to. In any event, Radov preferred not to think about the Mage.

That's why he needed Dannym's army. He needed well-trained men—and lots of them!—to retake Raku. The Prophet had given him big promises of weapons and men. Then he sent Saldarians. *Saldarians!*

A pox on the lot of them. They were useless in battle. Undisciplined. Erratic. Except for terrorizing the countryside—this they did well, so he let them do that. What if they ravaged villages on the wrong side of the lines here and there? Radov was the first to admit it was hard to tell the bloody peasants apart—Basi, Khurd, Telnadi, Nadori…they were all inbred rabble. Radov couldn't be bothered with reining in the Saldarians.

No, the problem with the Dannish army was the Dannish general. Yes, the problem was leadership. The Northmen were too bloody stubborn. A press! That's what he needed! An *all-out press* for Raku. An over-the-ramparts unyielding assault—wave upon wave, until that damnable Basi and his upstart Converted had become pulp beneath their boots. A press would regain the oasis. The Khurds wouldn't know what hit them.

Only…that craven Loran val Whitney refused to do it! Complaining instead about the potential death toll. It was infuriating. This was war! The men were soldiers! They were *supposed* to die.

Yes, the problem was definitely one of leadership. The leadership had to go.

Abruptly a soapstone screen between Radov and the Hall of Seas swung inward on well-oiled hinges. Radov spun to find Viernan standing in the portal. The wielder's dark eyes immediately narrowed with black disapproval.

Radov followed the wielder's gaze downwards to the half-empty glass in his hand. When had he poured another? By Sherq's ill wind, the absinthe was the least of his problems.

"Gydryn is suspicious." Radov took another sip of absinthe in the face of Viernan's displeasure. What did he care what the man thought? *He* ruled in his own kingdom, not Viernan hal'Jaitar.

"That is doubtful." Viernan let the concealing screen close behind him and moved on into the room.

"Are you certain he suspects nothing? He sounded suspicious to me."

"Even should he suspect something, my prince, what can he know? The king merely bristles at being kept waiting, and at finding Bethamin's dogs milling about. But he can have no proof of your alliance with the Prophet, nor with Morwyk."

"Morwyk…" Radov hissed into his drink. "I know he means to betray me." He shot Viernan a dark glare, daring him to argue. "*I* act upon the deeds Morwyk is too cowardly to own, make it simple for him to claim all he covets…" The prince shook his head and snapped vituperatively, "He will raise arms against us, Viernan! Mark my words!"

"Let Morwyk have his fantasies," the wielder murmured, still eyeing the absinthe in Radov's hand like a jealous mistress. He walked to an armchair and settled in, crossing a knee as he rested hands on either chair arm. "Dannym only thrives because the val Lorian line keeps it strong. Even that lunatic Bethamin sees this truth. The bloodline is old—as old as your roots, my lord—dating back to ancient times, to Agasan and the first families. It is the strength of Gydryn's blood that keeps his kingdom hale. When the val Lorian line is broken, the kingdom will wither. Morwyk inherits a dying reign."

Radov was somewhat mollified by this thought. He would like to see Morwyk thwarted. The man was above himself and far too chummy with Bethamin.

Seeing he had the prince's attention, Viernan dropped his voice low, his words as the whispering of prophecy as he continued, "And when Morwyk finds his new kingdom disintegrating, his armies in revolt, duchies splintering away…then, my lord, *then* will Morwyk come crawling back to you…destitute, desperate, ready to shed his blood for you. Then, my lord, shall you own him wholly."

"Yes," Radov whispered into the glass held close to his lips, and the nymph whispered back, *yes…absinthe…*

Radov enjoyed thoughts of the high and mighty Stefan val Tryst groveling at his feet, abasing himself before the entire Congress of Princes… *receiving Bethamin's Fire…*

The Prince's dark eyes gleamed at this thought—for truly, only the latter would be a severe enough punishment for all the trouble Morwyk had caused him.

How *dare* Morwyk think of betraying him after all Radov had done to aid his aims! He would *crush* the man! Crush him with his armies! His massive armies! For a moment, Radov saw himself riding at the head of a force like none had seen outside of Agasan.

Yes!...absinthe...

But no. *Wait.* Radov vaguely remembered hearing Gydryn say something about leaving with his army.

He spun to Viernan. "Gydryn threatened to leave! The king must know of his son!"

Viernan was sitting in the armchair resting his chin on one hand. Radov got the distinct impression that the wielder had been listening to his thoughts.

"Impossible," hal'Jaitar returned. "If he knew we had Trell in custody he would've been in here with all fifty of his knights brandishing weapons, not merely making threats."

Radov didn't like the way Viernan was looking at him, all smug and condescending. Viernan was going to turn on him, sure as silver. But not yet. Not yet. They could still use each other.

But the man had to stay out of his head. It wasn't right, poking around in other men's minds. That's why he wouldn't abide truthreaders in his presence. Dung beetles, the lot of them! Sneaking through the shadowed crevices and corners of people's skulls. It wasn't natural! Bethamin had the right of that.

Yes...absinthe...

A knock came upon the door, oddly repetitive, and Viernan called for entrance. It was his spy come back to make his report.

Radov didn't like spies. They were just as bad as truthreaders...hiding in the shadows, stealing secrets. Like rats. Yes, rats. It wasn't natural for men to be as rats. Spies were unnatural. Just like truthreaders. Would that Bethamin had worked his foul trick on all the spies too.

"It is so," the spy meanwhile told Viernan. He'd barely acknowledged Radov, which made the Prince bristle until he remembered that actually the man had bowed respectfully low. "Forty knights left during the night."

"*Why was I not informed of forty men and horse departing the gates?*" Viernan's gaze was as viperous as his tone.

Radov reflected that if Viernan's eyes were daggers, he'd have just speared the spy to the wall. The latter looked unruffled though. He was a cool character, that one. Probably an assassin. They were a cold-eyed, cold-blooded crowd, the lot of them.

"The knights left in small groups, my lord," the spy meanwhile replied, "two and three at a time. Some volunteered to go along with the patrols, pleading boredom. Later they broke away." He made a face and offered, "You want us to track them all down?"

"No." Hal'Jaitar irritably waved the man off. "I know where they've gone. The king has told us his intentions." He strummed his long fingers under his chin while he contemplated. After a moment of silent stroking, Viernan focused his gaze on the spy again. "Get a force to Taj al'Jahanna. I want Loran val Whitney and all of his knights under constant surveillance. None of them are to move without my approval."

The spy grimaced. "How are we supposed to accomplish that?"

Viernan leaned towards the man and pinned him with a murderous gaze. "Get them all drunk on wine and women. Give them a case of dysentery. I don't *care* how you do it, but ensure that Loran val Whitney and his knights *remain* in Taj al'Jahanna!"

The man ducked a bow to his master and then another to Radov, who waved him brusquely out of the room. When he turned back, Radov noted that Viernan had that look again. Like *he* was in charge.

Radov wasn't sure how to deal with Viernan. One didn't merely *deal* with wielders. You couldn't easily plot the demise of a man who could read your mind—at least, Radov suspected Viernan could. The man had *eight* Sormitáge rings. He wasn't sure what Viernan could do. Wielders couldn't be trusted any more than truthreaders or spies. They were all of them rats. Would that he could poison the lot of them *en masse*. And all the val Lorians with them!

Speaking of val Lorians.

"What of the prince?" Radov demanded of Viernan without looking at him. Let the man know his displeasure. "I would see that Raliax fellow tortured and beheaded for this. Perhaps stoned." Radov's eyes searched the room, envisioning the man's demise. "Whipped and *then* stoned…"

"Raliax failed you," Viernan agreed, "but perhaps we can turn Trell val Lorian's survival to our advantage."

Forgetting he'd vowed not to look at Viernan, Radov spun him a fast glare. "How?"

"We need the Dannish forces to end this war with Abdul-Basir. The Veneisean armies, too long stalled at the Cry, have begun a retreat back to their bitch mother to nurse their wounds. *Useless!*" Viernan made this last a drawn out hiss through his yellowed teeth. "But with Dannym's forces at our command, my prince, we shall regain Raku."

"Not with those bloody dragons," Radov grumbled.

"Leave the dragons to me."

Radov arched a brow at Viernan. He really was getting above himself if he thought he could fight a Sundragon. Radov wondered if Viernan was still fit to perform his duties. Surely any man with an ego so inflated was naught but a liability. Maybe he should release him now...it might be safer...*but no*. He needed Viernan. Viernan... *handled* things. Like that bloody parley. What a farce that was!

"Gydryn was complaining about the parley," he murmured to his absinthe, held close to his lips. "He wants us to go through with it."

"The parley is a trap for you, my lord," Viernan assured him. "Though supposedly on neutral ground, my people tell me the valley is watched around the clock by the Emir's scouts. Tis a ruse to lure *you* into the open, so the Basi might dispose of their most dangerous enemy."

Radov cast him a bland eye. "Tell me something I don't know, Viernan. Isn't that what I pay you for?"

"Ah, yes I see your point, Highness." Viernan gave him a sly smile. "What has worked once will work again. Your wisdom always impresses me, my prince. We will use the parley as we have in the past—stage an assassination and blame it on the Basi."

Radov frowned. "Whose assassination?" He didn't see how killing Trell val Lorian at the parley would get them anywhere. Too many questions. Where had the boy been all this time, anyway?

"The val Lorian prince has proven resilient to my questioning about his past," Viernan muttered as if in answer to this question.

Radov wanted him out of his head! "Assign him to Taliah," he muttered, casting the man a glare of accusation.

"Yes, of course. Taliah could gain us the information we need." Viernan pressed forefinger to temple and rested his chin on the others. "She is quite efficient in her Questioner's duties. But there is so little vengeful satisfaction in her work. Who delights in plucking the low-hanging fruit? No, my lord, Taliah's work is effective, but...I think I have a better way to gain the answers we seek. Yes..." and his gaze became suddenly bright, his smile adder-sharp. Radov knew that look. It was the one Viernan got when he was planning something nefarious.

"And then my lord," the wielder continued, lifting those dangerous black eyes to meet Radov's suspicious gaze, "then we shall set into motion your brilliant plan. When all is done, Loran val Whitney will be begging us to lead the Dannish forces into a press on Raku."

"And if he doesn't?"

Viernan smiled humorlessly. "Have you not said the trouble with the Dannish army is the Dannish leadership?"

Radov suspected he'd *thought* it more than spoken it, but he really couldn't remember. Since that Belloth-spawned Marquiin had dared touch him, his mind had become a storm of fearful, confusing images and violent thoughts, clashing and gnashing and tearing each other to bits. None of the vying factions that occupied his mind had the least sense that he was in charge. He tried to stay out of his head as much as possible.

Radov stared into his empty glass. The absinthe was quiet now. He felt a little unsteady on his feet and decided a nap was in order. Dropping the glass upon the carpet from fingers suddenly gone numb, Radov staggered across the room. When he reached the door, he pressed one hand to the frame to still the floor beneath him and turned Viernan a glazed look over his shoulder. He wasn't sure anymore what he was agreeing to, only that if Viernan had planned it, he'd better go along. Wasn't that what he paid the man for?

"Let it...be so," Radov mumbled. Then he staggered through the door and collapsed into the arms of his guards.

FIFTY-TWO

"There is something dead inside him—and it lingers there, watching."
— The Nodefinder Devangshu Vita,
on Dore Madden

İŞAK'GETIRMEK STOOD AT a tower window staring out into the night while his left hand worked a length of string into elaborate knots. This habit was one of the few pieces of himself he'd retained from before N'ghorra. Usually it calmed him, allowed him to focus his thoughts while working out the nervous energy that came in consort with a mind hostilely occupied by another man's will. But on that night, it seemed every knot represented another mystery…another lie.

Işak and the Saldarians sheltered in the keep of Count Basil of Doane, one of the Karakurt's wealthy patrons. They'd meant to stay the night and move on, but Işak needed time to question his prisoners and collect his thoughts…time to understand what was happening to him. And to decide what to do about that damnable Sundragon.

Beyond the shadow of the high tower keep, a full moon shone upon a dark mountain lake whose waters seemed formed of captured night. Jutting mountains surrounded the valley where they sheltered, the slopes of which were furred with hemlock and pine, aspen and fir.

Işak had been standing at the window for hours. He liked to tell himself it was to facilitate the first-strand pattern he was working in search of the Sundragon, but the larger part of him confessed to a different truth.

He couldn't take his mind off of Trell val Lorian, despite the fact that every time he thought about their meeting, his head exploded with pain.

Submitting to the throbbing for a moment, Işak pushed an elbow against the edge of the window alcove and rested his head on his forearm. He willed the agonizing ache to stop but knew it would remain, even as the images now lodged within his consciousness remained, memories and pain inexorably mingled.

Increasingly, Işak cursed Dore Madden and Trell val Lorian both, for each man represented an opposite end of the malicious path that had him pinned.

Just like that bloody Sundragon.

Işak couldn't see Şrivas'rhakárakek in the darkness, but he knew he was there somewhere, for the first-strand pattern he worked still resonated with the dragon's powerful presence. Işak wasn't sure how Rhakar kept following them—he'd spent many an hour during their journey from the Kutsamak to Doane imagining how he would break the news to Dore that Sundragons *could* in fact travel the nodes—but he suspected the Sundragon's steady tracking had something to do with him, that the creature was able to find him specifically on the currents.

Why was the dragon following them?

This question tormented him endlessly. Rhakar seemed not to care about Işak's prisoners—certainly not enough to free them. What then did he want? For that matter, why had he attacked Sharpe in the first place?

Işak had been certain the creature had first come in search of Trell val Lorian; yet clearly Işak didn't have the prince in his possession now, so why was Rhakar still following him?

He heard Joss's heavy boot steps coming up the stairs outside his tower room, and he straightened just moments before the man arrived.

Joss planted his body close to Işak and tried to see over Işak's shoulder through the window. "Is he out there?" Joss growled low into Işak's ear, his breath coming sour from a mouth too near.

Işak leveled an irritable stare over his shoulder. "Do you want to work the pattern or should I?"

Joss looked him up and down disagreeably, but he backed off. "What does he want? Why doesn't he just come for us?"

Işak shook his head and turned back to the night. No matter how many times he asked himself the same questions, he found no answers.

"Could've been in Tambarré by now," Joss muttered.

"And how do you think the Prophet would feel about finding a Sundragon in his city, Joss?" Işak's temper was riding a fine edge.

"But that's the whole point! Let the Prophet take care of the Belloth-spawned dragon. He's not our problem."

"Not our problem." Işak shook his head and looked coldly upon the man. He thought of trying to explain to Joss how returning to Tambarré with a Sundragon in tow would be as grievous a mistake as bringing the Emir's entire army to the Prophet's doorstep and handing them the temple keys. He thought of asking Joss to speculate on their chances of survival when Bethamin learned of such treason, and perhaps elaborating for the man on the Prophet's unique interpretation of forgiveness.

But he quickly realized how futile such a discussion would prove. Joss and his crew were base ruffians, there for the spoils and the coin and an occasional chance to spill their seed in a woman unlucky enough to get caught in the crossfire. They had no idea what the Prophet could do to a man. They knew almost nothing of Dore Madden.

"We can't return to Tambarré without Ean val Lorian." Işak reined in his temper; it would only be wasted on a man like Joss. "We keep to the plan as originally devised." *Traps within traps…*

"The plan was to keep moving," Joss grumbled. "We've been here for—"

"We'll move on when I determine it's safe to do so!" Işak snapped, bristling at the man's insubordination.

Privately, he admitted that doing anything was likely better than sitting and waiting—especially for men like Joss, and especially when the waiting involved contemplation of a dragon eating you as it had eaten your friend such a short while ago that his body might still be digesting in its gut when you joined him there. He envied Joss such simple fears.

Işak turned back to the silvering lake and the night. "You're wasting my time. Why have you come to me?"

"There's a crafter here says he has the commission you requested," Joss answered resentfully.

At last! "See that he's paid for his efforts and have the package brought to my chambers." When Joss just stood there, Işak turned him a strange look. "Something else on your mind?"

Joss looked down at his boots and shuffled his feet. "Count Basil has a large shipment departing in the morning for Kandori," he said to the floor. "He wants to make sure you think it's safe to...you know, move it...with the dragon and all."

"I doubt a Sundragon cares overmuch about the business of an obscure count. What's in the shipment?"

"How am I supposed to know?"

Noting the sudden shift in Joss's tone, which had become instantly defensive, Işak arched a raven brow.

Joss withered beneath his stare—he'd watched Raliax writhing in the dirt beneath Işak's compulsion, and he was smarter than his predecessor, or at least less consumed by ego. "Oh, all right..." Joss glared at him. "The count says cider," and he added sharply under his breath, "but I ain't never seen a barrel of cider so heavy it takes six men to lift it onto a wagon—"

Işak sighed. "Get to the point if you can find it."

Snapping shut his mouth, Joss glowered belligerently at him. "The way I make it, title or not, nobody lives like this from sellin' cider. There's supposed to be gold in this part of the Assifiyahs—"

Işak gave him a cutting look of warning. "If you steal from Count Basil of Doane, you pilfer the Karakurt's own coffer. Attempt such at your own peril."

Joss threw up his hands. "I'm only *saying*—"

"How large is the shipment?"

Joss exhaled in frustration. "*Four* wagons." He gave Işak a flat stare that made clear his desire for alternative leadership.

"Tell the Count it's safe for his shipment to depart in the morning, and that we'll be leaving with it. We make for the Castle of Tyr'kharta. Ensure the Nodefinder and your men are ready."

Joss glared bitterly at him and stalked out.

As the man's footsteps were fading down the stairs, Işak attempted to work his first-strand pattern again. But it was no use. The concept wouldn't form, and now the package the crafter had delivered was consuming his thoughts.

Making his way to his chambers, Işak found the item he'd commissioned lying on a table. He unwrapped it with growing trepidation. Then he stared down at the molded velvet mask lying in a bed of silk while Dore's worms twisted in his mind and apprehension clenched in his stomach.

He didn't entirely understand the motivation that had driven him to commission the mask two days prior.

Işak had never worn his scar with shame, yet ever since facing Trell val Lorian, his disfigurement had felt a brand of degradation. It was more agonizing now than ever before—in N'ghorra, such marks had been badges of pride.

But now...

Taking up the molded velvet mask with rueful misgiving, Işak moved to a standing mirror and held it against his face. It fit well. Too well—though that had been the point of letting the crafter make a plaster cast of his face, to be certain of its form.

Işak had paid handsomely to have the mask made and delivered so quickly, using the cover of the Sundragon's presence to delay their departure. The mask covered the top half of his face. It looked like him, and yet...not. It was perfect.

Işak hated it.

More and more, Işak looked upon the day he'd encountered Trell val Lorian as a pernicious stroke of Fate. The intricate latticework supporting the illusion of his past had been fractured during that meeting. Somehow a boiling geyser had been uncapped, and now it spewed a striated mud of warped memories. Işak's mind felt like formless clay too saturated with confusions to hold any shape. The new uncertainty of his past tormented him endlessly now. He'd never thought to question it until Trell had appeared and shattered everything he knew...or thought he knew.

New ideas—*frightening* ideas—had sprouted from the sluggish memories that now oozed forth. Işak couldn't dig the ideas out, no matter how he tried, so they thrived in the broken vessel of his recollection... possibilities that grew ever more likely the longer they remained, the more he had time to reflect upon them and despair.

The truth most damaging to his psyche was in knowing that he *should have* wondered, *should have* questioned long before now, and it sickened him that he'd never thought to do so.

But why would I, when my memories seemed so real? He'd asked himself this question over and again as he lay in tormented sleeplessness, his head a blazing fury.

Only because you're Dore Madden's favorite toy.

But now…now he had the mask and could question his prisoners. Now he would know whether his awful suspicions were correct.

Knowing the truth would change nothing, of course. Even were the facts as he suspected, he was bound to Dore until the end of his days.

This was the cruelest truth of all.

Işak secured the silk ties of his mask and drew up his hood as he headed out. He'd been wanting to question the Lord Captain Rhys val Kincaide. Just yesterday he'd stood for more than an hour outside the door to the cellars where the prisoners were being held, willing himself to go through. But in the end, he hadn't been able to do it.

Every time he thought of asking the questions that haunted him, his head exploded with pain and his stomach turned so sickly he feared unconsciousness. The headaches he could bear; the looks he garnered in such moments were the infuriating part.

Işak told himself the mask was meant to hide his expression, that the captain might not see him in a moment of weakness and read into his thoughts; but a deeper part of Işak understood that this was not the reason he'd commissioned the mask.

Whatever the mask's true purpose, Işak was safely bound to anonymity as he swept down from the keep tower and through the castle halls, a hooded specter. The Count's people already gave him a wide berth, with servants backing to the walls to let him pass, but now they watched him go by with dreadful unease, their gazes betraying both fear and accusation.

Oh, they knew him as a wielder, as the leader of the Saldarians, and they whispered of his magical battle with Rhakar—the tale having spread rapidly from the mouths of his men. The privileged within the count's inner circle even knew him as a favored minion of the Karakurt. But none of them understood the mask.

Işak gave no heed to their speculations—what did he care what they thought of him? It was his own conscience whose speculation he couldn't bear.

The prisoners were being held in separate rooms in the count's 'dungeon'—little more than a row of windowless storerooms repurposed for incarceration. But the doors were thick, and the chains—recently installed to secure each man to the walls—were strong.

The two Saldarians who'd drawn the night shift were dicing as Işak started down the long flight of stairs. When they saw him, they exchanged a look and rose from their game.

"They been quiet," the first man told Işak. He had a knife scar making a jagged white part unevenly through his reddish hair. He frowned at Işak's mask, the sort of blankly uncomprehending look assumed by the not-so-bright when they're trying to access the part of their brain normally used for thinking.

The other Saldarian, a giant cornstalk of a man named Vincent, clicked the dice in his hand and watched Işak with blatant mistrust.

"Which cell is the Lord Captain's?" Işak asked him.

Vincent thumbed over his shoulder. "Fourth one down."

"Open it."

The Saldarian plucked a ring of keys from a hook on the wall and ambled down the barrel-vaulted hallway, ducking to the side each time he passed a hanging lamp, lest the iron bang against his head. Stopping before the fourth rounded door, he unlocked and then hauled it open with a squawking protest of hinges.

"Leave us." Işak moved inside.

The man shrugged and left.

Işak pulled the door closed behind him and then waited with his ear to the wood—as well as a flow of the first strand—listening carefully until he was certain Vincent had retreated.

Then he turned to face the captain.

Rhys val Kinkaide sat in the corner with one bandaged leg extended, the other knee bent, and an arm draped over the latter. His wrists and ankles were shackled, and heavy links trailed back to the wall. The beatings he'd endured had not exactly softened his demeanor; if anything, he looked more dangerous in the chains of captivity than he had when bound in rope alone.

"Lord Captain Rhys val Kincaide." Işak moved further into the dim room, which held the musty odor of potatoes in its earthen walls. One hand worked his ever-present string into elaborate knots, a chain of lost memories. "I have questions for you."

When the captain said nothing, Işak posed, "Your Prince Ean...what kind of man is he?"

The captain watched him in silence.

Exhaling a sigh, Işak leaned one shoulder against the wall. "Captain, you know I can compel any knowledge I require out of you, and might I remind you, my patterns are not nearly as pleasant as those of a truthreader."

Rhys looked belligerent, but after a moment he answered, "He is a better man than you have hope of ever becoming."

"Indeed, that is undoubtedly true, for I claim no such lofty aspirations." Işak pushed off the wall and began to pace the short length of the cell with knotted string clasped behind him. "Will he come for you? I think that is the answer I'm most interested in having." He turned his gaze on the captain, feeling uncommonly secure behind his new mask. Odd that velvet cloth could prove more sturdy protection than shield or buckler or mail, yet what Işak hoped to safeguard was nothing that metal might defend.

Rhys watched him in his solitary pacing. "He will come," but there was warning in his tone, and anger aplenty in his gaze.

"And what do you know of his talent with the art?"

"Nothing I understand."

Işak gave him a curious look. "Who trained him as a wielder?"

Rhys shrugged. "The zanthyr a bit. But that was after His Highness did... whatever he did to that Marquiin."

"Ah yes, the fateful deed." Işak looked him over. "What can you tell me of it?"

"I've just told you all I know."

Oddly enough, Işak believed him. Rhys val Kincaide struck him as a simple soldier, steady and forthright in his loyalties. Not one to attempt to deceive—though he'd no doubt the man would happily wring his neck if given the opportunity.

"What's with the mask?" Rhys' bearded upper lip lifted in a sneer. "Afraid to let the light find your face for what it might reveal?"

Işak cast him a bland eye. "How little you know of me, Captain."

"I know a man who's hiding when I see one." He shifted in his corner and winced as he adjusted his injured leg. "I hear that dragon's still out there. He must've liked the taste of that Sharpe fellow. I vow the more deserving of death, the tastier they are. No doubt he's salivating over *you* something fierce."

"But we're speaking of Ean today, Captain," Işak reminded him with a humorless smile. His temper was oddly rising beneath the man's taunts. Something in the captain ground against his deepest aggressions, as like towards an overbearing father too quick to punish and oft unjustified. "How fares your youngest prince with a blade?"

The captain barked a laugh. "As if you'll meet him fairly in battle." He spat at Işak's feet. "He'll take you left-handed."

"I welcome the challenge," Işak replied, his gaze growing colder still.

Rhys laughed loudly that time. "Aye, so will he. In that you're well paired."

Işak was fast wearying of the haughty captain, though it bothered him doubly that the man could so easily fray his temper. Worse, he suspected that the captain knew his questions about Ean were but a pretense.

Indeed, the purpose for which he'd sought out Rhys was intimately connected to the reason he wore the mask to do it. Işak's head was already pounding in anticipation of this discourse, making conversation increasingly difficult.

Recognizing his growing liability, Işak pushed on. "How long have you served Gydryn val Lorian?"

"All my life." Rhys gave him a look of proud defiance.

Işak affected his most benign tone. "I'm interested in the story of your Prince Sebastian." He turned to pace in the other direction, hands clasped behind him, his left hand unweaving the knots that now entirely bound the string. "What really happened to your king's firstborn son?"

Rhys gave him a long look. "Prince Sebastian was murdered. It's no secret."

"The whole story, Captain, if you please."

Rhys frowned. His gaze took in Işak's string and its knots and narrowed. "It was eight—maybe nine years ago now," he answered while his pale blue eyes followed Işak in his pacing. "His Highness went as his father's emissary to a parley in M'Nador, supposedly called by the Akkadian Emir—"

Işak's head exploded upon this statement, bringing new levels of torment. He pushed a hand to the wall and barely gasped out, "Yes—yes, *and...?*"

The captain's brow furrowed as he watched him. "No one knows for certain. Purportedly Basi assassins murdered our prince. Radov claimed to have caught and disemboweled the bastards, but there was no hearing held before a truthreader to confirm their guilt, and the body was never found."

Brain rupturing, Işak tried desperately to focus. "*Whose* body, Captain? Please be clear."

"Why, the prince's body, of course. The whole bloody affair supposedly took place in the midst of a sandstorm—the Nadori claimed it was how the bastards snuck up on their camp." Rhys shook his head and growled, "It was treachery no matter how you cut it."

...the prince's body...

These words stabbed as knives into Işak's gut, making him *very* ill. "And...who was blamed for this treachery, Captain?" He felt weak with dread.

"Who was blamed?" Rhys sounded aghast. "The damned Basi were blamed!"

Işak saw spots before his vision, his head now a blinding agony. "No one else?" he managed a threadbare voice. "No one...of the kingdom?"

"Who was there to blame?" the captain balked. "All of the men who went with our prince were killed. His Majesty has ever blamed himself."

Işak sank against the wall, his breath coming raggedly, pain wreaking his consciousness. Whatever patterns yet clung in concealment of his memory, they bit with a vengeance to prevent his continuing down this path of inquiry.

It was with the greatest force of will that Işak pushed back his hood and used the same shaking hand to untie the ribbons of his mask. He held the molded velvet in place while the captain watched him with suspicion deepening the severe angles of his face.

Finally, battling a loathsome sense of dread, Işak stepped forward into the dim light. "Tell me, captain," and he lowered the mask with a shaking hand, "do you know this face?"

Rhys recoiled.

Işak stared at the captain in return. Rhys' his horrified expression was answer enough.

"What is it you work here...some foul trick?" the captain found anger where compassion would've suited better. "You think to fool Prince Ean with a string of knots and an ill-conceived illusion? He will know his own—"

"Captain, *do you know this face?*" Işak's demand rumbled through the cell, borne on currents of the fourth. The air crackled, and dust fell from the mortar between the stones.

The working compressed the captain's body into the corner, and he gritted his teeth against it. "*Yes,*" he snarled, glaring now with undisguised hatred, "but *you've* no right to wear it. It belongs to a dead man."

Indeed it did.

Işak fled from the cell, staggering into the walls in his haste to be away, to leave behind him that horrible truth and all it implied, a single thought pummeling him as he made a punishing retreat to his chambers.

Oh, Captain, Captain…if only you knew!

FIFTY-THREE

"A man knows nothing of courage until he's killed in another's name."
— The Adept wielder Viernan hal'Jaitar

KJIERAN VAN STONE slipped from the shadows to follow the man in the black-chequered *keffiyeh* as he headed away from the Court of Fifty-Two Arches.

The day knew a stifling humidity, the leading edge of a storm that darkened the eastern horizon. Sherq, god of the east wind, only ever brought ill weather to Tal'Shira. The brine-laden air crackled with static, and Kjieran was on a countdown.

The hourglass sands of his life were pouring swiftly through the narrows of opportunity. He had but few precious grains of time in which to act. A day, perhaps two.

The Pattern of Changing had now claimed his torso up to his chest, and both of his arms and his shoulders. Its darkness was spreading across his back now. An hour in the sea had scoured away the necrotic tissue that had once been his skin. He could count the remaining flesh in inches.

No longer did he fear his presence upon the currents or what they might reveal of his activities. By the time anyone read them, it would all be over.

Kjieran closed the distance between himself and his quarry. As the man passed a narrow alley, Kjieran took three leaping steps, grabbed him around the neck, and spun them both into the shadows.

He'd caught the spy off-guard, but the trained man reacted quickly. He slipped from Kjieran's grasp and attacked in return, brandishing a knife from somewhere in his robes. Kjieran used his arms as a shield from the spy's onslaught of steel, but the *other* in him…

It knew better how to fight.

His own hands became his swords, his feet as powerful as crossbow bolts, and his forearms and elbows as bludgeons that bashed and crushed. In seconds, he sent the spy spinning into a wall. The strength in his new limbs was astonishing…and terrifying. A breath of wind later, he'd pinned the man to the ground beneath him.

Kjieran pushed his fingers into the truthreader's hold and summoned *elae*. The lifeforce remained barely within his reach—he was only able to control it by drawing in huge gulps. He therefore used a bucketful when a teaspoon might've sufficed and ripped the knowledge he desired out of the man's mind. The fine mental tooling that was a truthreader's finesse was quite impossible for him now.

He didn't mean to kill the Nadoriin—it came as a shock when he removed his hand and found dead eyes staring back—nor did he mourn him. This man had served hal'Jaitar, and for that he deserved his end.

Kjieran hauled up the spy and slung his body across his shoulders. Straightening beneath the man's not inconsiderable weight, he carried the corpse through the winding alleys until he found one that opened upon a drainage ditch. He stripped the man of his fine robes then, of his *keffiyeh* and *agal*, and pitched his naked form into the stinking darkness of the sewers. Kjieran's own garments followed into the sluice. When he emerged from the alley, he was wearing a dead man's identity.

But this hardly differed from any other day.

Kjieran pulled the long fold of the spy's chequered *keffiyeh* across his nose and mouth and headed off. The linen smelled of the man's fetid breath, of the curried lamb he'd eaten for lunch and of the particular scent of sand that permeated everything in the desert; but the cloth protected his identity from inquiring eyes.

From the spy's thoughts, Kjieran had learned that the secret offices of hal'Jaitar's clandestine operatives were reached through an alcove off one of the busiest passages in the palace. He made his way along the crowded strip and then slipped between two virginal statues, which demarked the alcove.

Finding that he was well concealed from the flow of bodies, he pulled the stinking *keffiyeh* off of his head and faced the bare wall. It took more than a dozen attempts to craft the trace-seal he'd stolen from the spy's mind, but he finally heard a click, and the stone wall slid ajar. He slipped silently through the parting and emerged onto the highest landing of a vast atrium. Five floors fanned out beneath him. Kjieran had no idea where to find the stairs leading down to the next level. Even a few days ago, this might've seemed an insurmountable barrier, but now…

He waited until all of the lower balconies were empty of eyes. Then he swung himself over the railing.

The downward plunge came faster than he'd anticipated. His robes whipped up around his head, and he landed blind with a resounding clap of stone against stone, which surely the entire building must've heard. He scrambled to untangle himself from his robes and sought the shadows.

When he saw two armed guards approaching, Kjieran concealed himself until they'd walked passed. Then he grabbed both by the back of their necks and slammed their heads together. They slumped in his arms.

Kjieran dragged them into the shadows and ruthlessly dredged their unprotected minds for the knowledge he sought. From one he gained an understanding of the labyrinthine passageways of the Shamshir'im's headquarters. From the other.

Trell!

Kjieran straightened and looked around to get his bearings. He knew that his working had left the guards' brains as slush. The truthreader in him recoiled at this understanding, but Kjieran had buried any thought of mercy in a far and fallow field. He left the men where they lay and moved on.

He made his way deep among the twisting passages, avoiding others when he could, allowing the *other* in him to kill when facing no other choice. He finally gained the narrow spiral of stone steps he'd been searching for. They ended before a single iron door. Four kicks later, the door slammed against the wall amid a scream of metal hinges.

Kjieran stepped into Trell's cell.

He'd endured so much to reach that moment—Dore's working, the Prophet's raping of his consciousness, the slow devouring of his ravaged body, the corruption of his spirit—yet none of it had prepared him for this first sight of Trell.

A sickly pit opened in Kjieran's stomach. He rushed across the room to where his prince hung, nailed to the wall. He took Trell's head in his stone fingers—*oh so carefully!* as if handling a delicate butterfly—and found that he lived.

With vengeance blackening his gaze, Kjieran seized the six-inch spike that impaled Trell's right hand and yanked it out of the stone. He flung it so violently across the room that it chipped the rock on the other side of the cell. Five other spikes followed in its blistering wake, and the prince collapsed into his arms.

Kjieran lowered Trell's unconscious form to the floor and looked his prince over. The villains had clearly taken great care to ensure the gravest punishment with the least risk of life. The spikes had been placed so they'd severed no vital arteries, and someone had healed the worst of the wounds around the spikes, that they might bring enduring pain.

Now he'd reopened those wounds. Blood seeped from Trell's arms to mingle with Kjieran's tears. Angry bruising on Trell's bare chest showed that someone had healed other wounds as well, though surely with no kind intent.

The prince stirred, and his eyes fluttered open. They were bloodshot and bespoke of unreasoning pain.

"Your Highness," Kjieran murmured wretchedly.

It took a moment, but then Trell seemed to focus his gaze on Kjieran. "I know your face..." his voice came as a rough whisper, "but I don't...know you."

"I'm Kjieran van Stone, Your Highness." Grief and guilt mingled thickly in his throat. "I'm sworn in your father's service. I was there when Raine D'Lacourte truth-bound you—would that Cephrael had closed his eye that abject night! We have none of us forgiven ourselves for what became of you."

Trell closed his eyes and managed the barest shake of his head. "I was upon my path. No one could have prevented it."

Kjieran gazed at him, feeling buffeted by the conflicting winds of misery and wonder. "Five years—*five years* we thought you dead! My prince...where have you been?"

A wave of pain shuddered through Trell, and he shut his eyes again. "The Akkad—"

"How *touching*," came a sudden voice from the doorway.

Kjieran spun his head to see hal'Jaitar standing in the threshold. The *other* within him reared to fight—

And Trell screamed. His body went rigid in Kjieran's arms, and he began to shake.

"Tread carefully, Kjieran van Stone," hal'Jaitar warned, even as four others entered behind him: the wielder from the alley, two of the thugs who'd gutted Kjieran, and a crimson-gowned woman with long, raven hair.

"Taliah has the prince's pattern." Hal'Jaitar's gaze shifted from where Trell writhed in breathless agony to the woman in crimson silk, who was standing with her dark gaze fixed on Trell. "She can kill him with a thought."

Agonized, Kjieran quelled the rearing *other*. He wouldn't risk the prince's life, and now that he knew the woman's identity, he knew also that hal'Jaitar's claim was no bluff.

Here then stood the Adept who had overseen Trell's torture and his subsequent healing, for Viernan's daughter, Taliah hal'Jaitar, was a Healer by birth. Her abusive use of her talent, however, was as loathsome and unforgivable as Bethamin's scourge upon *elae's* fourth-strand children.

"Quite the conundrum, isn't it?" Hal'Jaitar watched Kjieran as a viper might regard a threatening hawk. "Call forth your master's power, and you *may* destroy us with it...but is your strike faster than mine? Faster than Kedar's?" and here his dark eyes indicated the wielder Kjieran had last seen in the alley. "Faster than Taliah's when she already holds the prince's life-pattern in her thoughts? Care to wager on it, *truthreader?*" The contempt in his tone was thick.

Kjieran lowered Trell's body to the floor and stood up cautiously. He felt as if he balanced on a tiny skiff being swamped by a hurricane sea. Everything was going incalculably, inconceivably *wrong*.

Viernan moved further into the cell wearing an expression of triumphant condescension. "Did you really think you'd fooled us?" His dark eyes speared Kjieran with contempt. "Kedar's men gutted you like a pig, but you bled not a single drop. And in the Guild Hall...did you imagine *I* would not recognize *deyjiin? I* who lived through the Adept Wars, who witnessed with mine own eyes the foul power birthed in the hands of Malachai's Shades?"

He settled Kjieran a derisive sneer. "*I* have known your every move since Dore Madden brought you forth from Tambarré. Your little interlude with that wretched Marquiin, the lengthy sea excursions to scour the flesh from your bones—there is *nothing* I don't know of your activities, Kjieran van Stone!"

Trell moaned beside Kjieran, who in turn felt his entire world slipping away—the seas were deepening fast above his head now, the light of hope growing ever more distant.

"What I don't yet understand is *how*." The Consul cast a slicing look up and down Kjieran's form. "You haven't appeared on the currents since you arrived. How then are you striding Tal'Shira's halls, when as far as *elae* is concerned, you *don't exist*?"

Kjieran gazed brokenly at him. He was desperate to help his prince, hal'Jaitar had him caught between his pincers with his scorpion tail poised to strike. Kjieran dropped his gaze. "What do you want from me, Consul?"

"I want *answers!*"

Kjieran turned an agonized look at Trell. "Then make her release him—*heal* him."

"You will tell me what I want to know," hal'Jaitar returned, "or Taliah will boil the prince's blood in his veins. Have you ever seen a man when he's been boiled, Kjieran van Stone?"

Trell screamed again, and his body went rigid.

"*STOP!*" With Kjieran's sudden desperate fury, the vicious *other* launched out of his control. Cold power erupted out of him.

Hal'Jaitar threw up his hands and cast a shield of protection over himself and the others as *deyjiin* ripped through the room, thunder without sound.

Trell screamed even more terribly than before, while the *other* launched Kjieran's body towards hal'Jaitar with hands as claws—

A sword caught Kjieran across the side of the head, dropping him hard to the stones. The room shuddered, and stone dust showered down.

Shocked silence descended with the dust, and Kjieran pushed up to elbows to find the black-robed Kedar holding a Merdanti blade over him.

Hal'Jaitar wore an expression of black excoriation. "Fight us now and everyone dies," he growled, chest heaving.

Kjieran slowly got back to his feet. The blade had only stunned him, but Trell still writhed on the earthen floor, and he couldn't bear it. He looked to the Consul; his desolate gaze bespoke his willingness to destroy all of them to save Trell more suffering. "Make her stop."

Hal'Jaitar considered him with a frown and then a glare. "Taliah," he said in a voice like grinding gravel.

Taliah shifted her eyes to him in agitation. A moment later Trell stilled and exhaled a shuddering breath.

"*Heal* him." He held hal'Jaitar's venomous gaze, but he saw in the exchange that the wielder understood: Kjieran had become the wild, cornered wolf; he would chew off his own paw to see his will done.

"Healing takes time," hal'Jaitar hissed, but he flashed a brusque look at Taliah to see it done. Then he settled Kjieran a piercing glare. "Now... explain."

In that moment, Kjieran committed himself to salvaging *something* of his king and his prince...something of himself.

So he forced back the fear and the *other*, which were both fighting for his attention, and confessed, "Dore Madden has long sought the pattern Björn van Gelderan used to create his Shades. He designed a Pattern of Changing, merging the fifth and the first to create..." and here he paused, swallowed sickly, "...what I am becoming."

Hal'Jaitar eyed him narrowly. "Which is?"

Kjieran lifted colorless eyes to meet his gaze, feeling naught but empty desolation where his soul had once resonated. "A weapon."

Hal'Jaitar broke into a low chuckle, one that grew in volume and spirit until his cold laughter resounded in the stone chamber. "*Dore Madden!*" He flung out one arm. "Your insanities have borne incredible fruit!"

Abruptly he swung away, eying a grieving Kjieran over his shoulder as he paced with hands behind his back. "There were rumors, of course. Whispers of how that lunatic, Madden, was creating some sort of weapon for the Prophet. We never imagined the weapon would be alive." He looked Kjieran up and down with his black eyes. "Then again, one must use the term loosely."

Kjieran bowed his head, gritted his teeth and tried desperately to hold back a crushing wave of despair. Viernan hal'Jaitar had outwitted him at every turn. Had he *ever* stood a chance?

"But this does not explain *you*, Kjieran van Stone," the wielder meanwhile remarked. "How is it you live and walk and breathe?"

"T'were better you asked Dore Madden to confess such sins, for I understand them but little. I know only that...only that..." *Dear Epiphany*, it was so hard to say, "...that my spirit is somehow now...bound...to the Prophet."

"Miraculous." Hal'Jaitar exchanged a telling look with his wielder, Kedar.

Trell groaned, then stirred, and Kjieran turned to see the prince pushing up on one elbow. The gruesome and bloody holes in his arms were now covered by regrown flesh. Taliah was powerfully skilled indeed to heal him without touch.

Hal'Jaitar pinned his gaze on the prince, who returned his stare in kind. "I'm still waiting for Fate to come and rescue you, prince of Dannym."

"That's...odd." Trell rolled onto his back, his voice betraying his exhaustion. "I'm not."

Hal'Jaitar gave him a surprised look. "No?"

Trell pinned the wielder with a look that spoke volumes. Kjieran thought he might've even seen a shadow of humor in his gaze. "It's not me He's coming to claim, Consul."

Hal'Jaitar's expression darkened. Kjieran saw the malice in his eyes deepen and take root in punishments as yet unimagined. He feared for his prince, and he railed against his own unforgivable failures. All the world seemed to teeter at the edge of a sliding cliff.

"Kjieran van Stone," hal'Jaitar remarked, and Kjieran turned back to him. "Your time has come."

Kjieran wanted desperately to unleash the *other's* wrath, but he dared not do so again—not with Taliah so close and Trell in harm's way. Not with hal'Jaitar and Kedar still holding *elae*. "Release the prince," he said. "Then I will do what you ask."

Hal'Jaitar laughed at him. "I will do what I will with my own prisoner, Kjieran van Stone," he declared with a piercing glare, "and you will comply with my desires without question or defiance, or *this* prisoner of mine, with whom you so tragically and impotently concern yourself, will meet his end via the most gruesome and ignoble means imaginable."

Kjieran gritted his teeth. "And what is your will, Consul?"

"Ah, but you know that already. The time has come to carry out your master's order and eliminate Dannym's king. Oh, yes," hal'Jaitar returned Trell's burning gaze with a supremely triumphant look, "your dear father has become a stump in the marching path of progress, my prince. But don't dwell too long upon his fate, for you'll need all of your attention just to stay alive."

A brusque wave from hal'Jaitar, and Kedar's two thugs moved to take

Trell in hand. Hal'Jaitar turned back to Kjieran as they were grabbing the prince up.

"Kedar waits to escort you, Kjieran van Stone." He motioned to his wielder. "You will be told what to do when the moment is nigh. You *will* do this, Kjieran," he emphasized then, holding him in the thrall of his terrible gaze, holding him by the threat in his tone and the fourth wielded in binding, "or I give you my solemn oath that your dear Trell val Lorian will live a *very* long life in my daughter's care and suffer grievously during every moment of it."

In that moment, Kjieran understood that he would have to choose. He could not save both his prince and his king—Raine's truth, he might not be able to save either of them.

He turned a stricken look to Trell, whom hal'Jaitar's thugs now had in hand. Though Kjieran's talent had nearly abandoned him, still he heard Trell's powerful thought as their gazes locked, the sentiment offered this time in consolation: *I am upon my path, Kjieran...*

For a desperate moment as Kjieran held his prince's gaze, understanding passed as wine between them.

Share with me this drink to fate, Trell's grey eyes seemed to say while the men roughly bound his hands behind him, *that we might face it bravely and with honor, and never fear our road.*

Grief settled as a heavy stone deep in Kjieran's heart. He knew he would never see his prince again.

Then they were carting Trell away, with Taliah in the lead.

Kjieran looked back to hal'Jaitar. "And once I've done as you ask?"

The wielder's lip curled in a sneer. "You think to bargain again?"

"No, Consul. Only to caution you."

"And what would be this warning, truthreader? Another dire prophecy like the ones your prince so glibly spouts?"

Kjieran glanced to the broken doorway, where the wielder Kedar was awaiting him. "No," he bowed his head, "only...lest we forget, Consul," and here he lifted hal'Jaitar a look of dreadful sincerity, "there is Balance in all things."

FIFTY-FOUR

"He is neither the captain nor the helmsman who
steers our ship. He is the compass."

– The Second Vestal Dagmar Ranneskjöld,
on Björn van Gelderan

GYDRYN VAL LORIAN pressed fists to the marble desk in his chambers and stared down at the pale stone. In his mind, the conversation he'd just had with Viernan hal'Jaitar replayed endlessly, while in his heart, grief and hope warred for purchase...

"Your Majesty, we have news of your son."

Gydryn had barely entered the salon of Viernan hal'Jaitar before the consul was coming towards him with this declaration.

The king frowned. "News of Ean?"

"Of Trell."

Gydryn blinked. "I beg your pardon?"

"Your Majesty...he lives."

The king's expression had darkened. "First these claims of Radov's ill health, and now you insult me by naming my dead child? Each of your lies is less plausible than the last, Consul."

"I assure you, it is true, Your Majesty." Viernan's expression affected a level of compassion which Gydryn suspected he was quite incapable of actually feeling.

Hal'Jaitar motioned the king towards a grouping of low-backed chairs as he explained, "We have long followed whispers that your son lived as a hostage in Duan'Bai. *How*, we yet wondered. If he survived the shipwreck, why have we seen naught of him?" Viernan took a seat across from the still standing king. "And then the Emir's Mage made his presence known, and the stormy skies of mystery cleared. Powerful and cunning, the Emir's Mage has only recently revealed himself, but we suspect he's been advising the Emir for many years."

Gydryn felt a chord of tension stringing through him, anchoring him in place. "What does this have to do with my son, Viernan hal'Jaitar? My patience grows thin."

"The Emir's Mage is the reason your son remains lost to you, Majesty." Viernan sat back and eyed the king sagaciously. "He worked a terrible pattern upon your son to make him forget his identity. Majesty…Trell remembers nothing of his life before the shipwreck. He's been hiding in plain view these many years our enemy's ranks. Only recently was he positively identified, a simple soldier."

Gydryn stared at the man, searching for words that wouldn't come. If even a fraction of it were true…

"I dared not speak of this before." The Consul's dark eyes regarded Gydryn with well-crafted concern. "Not before confirming the reports, but at last we have eye-witnesses who have identified your son—witnesses who will hold up even to a truthreader's incontrovertible inspection."

Gydryn stood speechless.

"Your Majesty, this is the reason we've been holding off on the parley. Now, having confirmed the reports, His Grace hopes to use the parley as a means of demanding your son's return to you. Abdul-Basir requested this truce, never anticipating we knew of his treason. While Prince Radov would hear his terms, yet we will grant the Emir nothing unless it includes your son's immediate return…"

That had been less than an hour ago. Now Gydryn found himself much at odds.

Was it possible?

With a heavy heart, the king walked out onto his balcony. His knights kept a vigilant watch there, as well as in the hall—in the palace of a foreign prince, anyone could be a spy. Nodding a greeting to his loyal men, the king leaned elbows on the balustrade and gazed out over the azure bay.

Could it be true? Could Trell be alive?

For all Viernan hal'Jaitar could be trusted as much as a viper in a rabbit warren, he was far too savvy to make such a claim without a truth to support it. How much truth was the question Gydryn now battled with, and whether it was enough to warrant delving deep into the well of his sorrow and attempting to salvage something of hope from those depths.

His heart wanted desperately to investigate Viernan's claim, but this would cause further delay and introduce potential new complications. It would give Viernan hal'Jaitar time to gather intelligence and learn of Gydryn's true activities.

They faced off across a King's board, he and hal'Jaitar, and while their strategies varied, the end they sought was the same: survival for their respective kingdoms and their way of life.

The king had made his initial feint in approaching hal'Jaitar with threats of evacuation. Hal'Jaitar had taken the bait. Now, whether true or not, this news of Trell was merely the wielder's next play.

So while his heart bled at the possibility, his head knew that a game of Kings was never won by merely reacting to an opponent's single move. No, any strategy of Kings must encompass the entire game and take into account a multitude of moves and counter-strokes. And once set into motion, it must be played out to its end.

The king exhaled a sigh as he stared at the shimmering waters. He wondered if there truly was some divine plan that justified so many sacrifices. Errodan had read lengthily of the writings of Epiphany's Prophet, and she believed strongly in the idea that a greater purpose was guiding the tragedies of their lives, that each chain of cause and consequence was somehow woven into the fabric of a larger pattern. She believed an individual was beholden to discover his purpose, his part to play in the great pattern, and to have faith until such time as this purpose became clear.

Gydryn saw the value in this ideal…how it could give a man hope when all the world seemed winter-bleak and the future held naught but empty despair—but he couldn't live that way.

So long as men were free to do ill or good to their peril or success, terrible things would happen in the world. There was no larger pattern in Gydryn's view—no Maker sat in the clouds playing with their lives as if upon a King's board, all of the trials and betrayals somehow part of his master strategy. No, if there was a purpose to be found amid the grave consequences of life, it was only what purpose a man made for himself.

Gydryn bowed his head and closed his eyes for a grieving moment. He knew what he had to do.

Whether or not his son lived, whether Trell knew anything of his past or had walked away from it knowingly—whatever had happened in the intervening years—he would be a man now. He would've made his own choices to live by or regret. He walked his own road. Gydryn couldn't allow the possibility of Trell's survival to alter the course already set.

If his son lived, he was on his own.

The king straightened and turned to his knights. "Prepare for departure to the parley. We leave with Radov at dusk."

The royal party gathered inside the palace's parade yard, where the ruling prince made a riotous ceremony of their departure. Fire-juggling acrobats, dancing girls, and sword-swallowing performers entertained the troops while Gydryn was forced to take ceremonial tea with the prince beneath the blowing tassels of a colorful domed tent.

Then came numerous speeches from Radov's puppet council, each alternately praising his leadership through the trials of a long and difficult war and toasting the end of the hostilities by means of a diplomatic solution, which would ostensibly be gained through Radov's skilled political maneuvering.

The ceremony concluded with a tedious prayer led in sections by the priests of five fractious sects. All of them looked resentful at having to either precede or follow their brethren, and each attempted to surpass the one before with litanies of pious quotations and lengthy prayers.

Finally, it was somehow determined that Jai'Gar had given his blessing and all were allowed to leave.

As the king emerged from the tent to return to his men, hal'Jaitar approached through the mass of councilmen and courtiers, nobles and aides. Falling into step beside the king, he clasped his gold-ringed fingers before him and murmured, "Prince Radov and his knights will leave ahead to secure the way, Your Majesty."

Gydryn spared him a sidelong glance. "I understood we would all be traveling together."

"My prince is concerned for Your Majesty's safety, especially with so few knights remaining at your side."

Gydryn turned him a look, for he'd noted the disharmonic strains underlying hal'Jaitar's tone. He replied in kind, "I appreciate his thoughtful regard."

Hal'Jaitar nodded in acknowledgement of the prince's greatness. "We are sending men along to augment your remaining guard. It can be a dangerous journey. The treacherous Basi ever seek an opening to attack." As they were passing Radov's assembled council, hal'Jaitar he added significantly, that the Council might later bear witness, "Whatever happens, Your Majesty, do not leave the road."

Then they'd departed.

As he and his knights assumed their assigned place in the column, Gydryn could barely see the Ruling Prince of M'Nador at its head, nearly a mile distant.

They would be traveling during the night hours, for the scalding desert sun struck an armored soldier as deadly as any archer's arrow. Soon the sun had fallen behind the Kutsamak, giving the air a golden sheen. The cloudless sky flamed red, and then night's shadows crept forth, freed from their places of hiding.

If Gydryn squinted, he could just make out Radov's colorful, multi-tasseled *keffiyeh* heading the column as the latter snaked westward through the twilit hills. Torches carried along the column bobbed and shimmered, leaving trails of their own wavering heat to challenge that of the dying day, while the cavalrymen riding behind the king wore black upon black and seemed already to be draped in the curtain of darkness that rapidly chased from the east.

Gydryn gazed towards the sunset with the unwelcome suspicion that hal'Jaitar intended for this nightfall to become his last. *Oh,* he trusted his men beyond question and he knew their skills, but he also knew hal'Jaitar— and Raine's truth, he'd made it easy for the wielder to act against him, hadn't he? Practically serving himself up for the feast as a regretful, if necessary, diversion.

Yet if his life was forfeit in the salvage of his kingdom, so be it. No one man stood greater than the people he led; his life was no less important than those already sacrificed.

"Daniel," the king murmured to the knight riding closest beside him.

He turned his helmeted head at once. "Sire?"

Gydryn cast him a sidelong look. "If something should happen here tonight, if we should become separated, you must rally the men and make north in all haste for the Pass of Ryohim. Beyond it, turn west and find the fortress of Nahavand."

Daniel looked understandably troubled by this order. "Sire...surely you don't expect—"

"What I expect is for you to follow my instructions," the king growled.

Daniel gazed upon him with a frown of trepidation. Then he dropped his gaze. "Your will be done, Majesty."

The king looked back to the road with only the muscles of his jaw breaking the stillness of his form...clenching and unclenching.

Swathed in the black robes and *keffiyeh* of the Nadori cavalry, Kjieran van Stone sat on his horse in the sweltering late afternoon sun, head bowed, while Radov and hal'Jaitar played at being allies with his king.

He felt...numb. Betrayed. As if all the promises ever made to him had been lies, his entire lifetime a foul trick.

The Prophet's doctrines now seemed frighteningly true. What hope was there in this life? One merely walked a rigid path towards death, and all the joy to be found upon it was illusion.

Hal'Jaitar held all the cards in their game of Trumps, fully embodying the role of the hated sorcerer, and Kjieran's hand was reduced to a single knight. Only Raine's amulet and Kjieran's battered will stood between them now, and he feared the latter would soon be claimed by the Prophet.

Kjieran shook his head bitterly and clenched his teeth. His hands were steady where they clutched his reins.

He felt Bethamin's bond at all times now, even when he knew the man wasn't looking in on his thoughts. Beneath his robes, his flesh was nearly consumed. The explosion of *deyjiin* back in Trell's cell had somehow catalyzed the process of changing, and now Kjieran's face and a pale circle on his chest—where Raine's amulet lay—stood as the last bastion against Dore's pestilential pattern.

Kjieran knew the denouement of his entire path—his life's greatest effort—was nigh.

He stared at the pommel of his saddle, thinking of his last conversation with the wielder, Kedar. The Bemothi had detailed hal'Jaitar's demands as he'd watched Kjieran dressing in the robes worn by a hundred other men.

"We've set a little surprise for your precious king," the Bemothi had claimed, his dark eyes sharp upon Kjieran's strange and unsettling new form. "When the attack begins, you're to find him and make sure he doesn't live to see the dawn."

Because Kjieran had given him a traitorous glare, Kedar added, "My master has assured me that your king will die either way, *truthreader*, but if you're not seen to be the one taking the king's life, my master will make your prince pay dearly."

Kjieran had no doubt Trell would be paying dearly, no matter what actions he personally took, but he dared not rouse Kedar's suspicions by further defiance. So he'd merely nodded and done as Kedar ordered him.

They'd set off as the sun was sinking below the rim of the world. Kjieran rode among the tallest of Radov's Nadoriin. These base men laughed and joked in the desert tongue, sharing lewd commentary of shocking acts that were abrasive to Kjieran's ears. He'd never before been grateful for *elae's* increasingly distant whisper, but it was an admitted relief not to have to listen to their thoughts as well as their crude words.

The desert heat faded with the dying light, and night swept in upon the tide of a rising wind. It whispered and danced among the long procession that snaked through the dunes. And somewhere between Tal'Shira and midnight, Kjieran hardened his resolve.

This would be his last effort to save his king, his final act towards salvation. Honor rooted him to this purpose. Will kept him upon its path. Faith drove him forward and made him never think of turning back.

But of hope…he had none.

A moon just shy of full shone down upon the Nadori desert as Gydryn val Lorian and his knights made their way deeper into the Sand Sea. They followed an ancient road that was waging a vigilant war against the ever-shifting dunes, each fighting to claim the space of the other. The steady plodding of horses, the jangling of harnesses, the occasional squeak of leather or the chink of mail—these were the only sounds as the men passed quietly through the desert night.

Above, the sky was a dizzying kaleidoscope of stars. The luminous moon cast enough silvery light to illumine the hills and shadow the valleys, making a monochrome patchwork of the broad expanse of dunes. The repetitive percussion of the moving column, the torches' wavering flames, and the ever-lengthening night lulled the men into a trance-like daze, neither asleep nor fully awake. Only the scouts remained wakeful as they ranged far afield of the main column.

Thus they were the first to die.

So the attack came without warning. One moment the blanket of night lay in quiet slumber, the next it was awash with assassins hollering a startling tongue-trill from atop horses that came careening down the dunes.

They descended on the column from all sides and scattered the troops amid blood and steel, immediately cutting off Gydryn's section from Radov's. The Dannish knights surrounded their king, while the cavalry fanned out to meet the marauders with flashing scimitars and angry shouts. Yet as the lines were broken and men became scattered and their torches extinguished in the sand, Gydryn found it increasingly difficult to tell Nadoriin from marauder.

Gydryn spared a glance towards the front of the column to see how Radov fared and—

Gone!

The king stood in his stirrups to get a clearer view, but his eyes didn't lie. The dead lay as dark petals among the fallen torches, but the ruling prince and his men had vanished.

Suddenly the marauders broke the line of Gydryn's knights, and the king could spare no more thought for Radov. He drew his sword and took the first man who came at him through the heart. The man tumbled from his mount, joining the morass of dying men already staining the sand.

Another marauder broke through, and Gydryn fought him off with three powerful strokes. His knights managed to close the breech then, and in the momentary respite, the king spared another glance westward, seeking Radov and his missing Nadoriin. Had they been chased off, scattered, *captured*? What had become of them?

"Sire!"

The King swung around as a second wave of assassins stormed over the dunes with tongues trilling in that ear-piercing call. The sight brought a sinking feeling, a flash of debilitating dread, but then Gydryn hardened his resolve.

"Fan out!" he shouted. His knights could ill afford to become trapped and surrounded, for there would be no quarter to be found among these marauders.

His dutiful knights complied, though he felt their reluctance radiating, as if their armor was a resounding gong for their discord. But soon Gydryn was raising his blade to fend off an approaching attacker, and thereafter he knew only the ringing of steel.

Another marauder's horse careened close to the king, near enough to smell the beast on the wind of its passing. Gydryn swung his blade and tool the would-be assassin across the chest. He cried out and toppled from his mount, which in turn spun away to ram into another rider, knocking him from the saddle. He shouted in anger as he fell. Gydryn heeled his horse over and speared the man through before he'd regained his feet.

Thus did the battle proceed.

The king lost sight of his knights, lost count of the marauders he met and battled and dispatched as the melee ranged far afield of the road. His hands and vambraces were soon blood-drenched, his sword slick with it. The acrid tang of the humour filled his nostrils, mingling with the baser odors of death, of excrement and the sweat of men and horse. In the moonlight, the fighting men seemed a choppy sea, mercuric blades flashing as waves, and with no relief in sight.

The king treated each marauder he met as thought theirs was the whole conflict—in that moment, he knew only the one man and their fierce contest. When the man fell, violently or unremarkably, sometimes clutching upon the king as he sank into death, often staggering away to find his solitary end, Gydryn thought of him as one more dark stone in the battle jar. A vessel that was barely a quarter full.

He'd just claimed another assassin's life and stood awash in the unwelcome warmth of the man's blood when the barbarian stormed him.

Kjieran was riding far in the rear of the slow-moving column when the attack began. He heard them first, those trilling tongues in a high-pitched death cry, and then they came pouring over the distant dunes as ants descending upon a feast. Kjieran spotted his king, safe within the circle of his knights, and was taking up his reins to rush to his side when two blades descended across his gaze.

"We got orders to see you make no mischief," said the giant who was riding on Kjieran's left.

Kjieran turned him a cold glare. "And I have orders as well."

"Kedar said you'd say that," the other giant remarked. "He said we weren't to let you free, no matter what you claimed. He said he'd be watching."

Kjieran had the urge to spin around to see if indeed the wielder was observing them, but even had he done so, the night easily protected those who sought anonymity.

Far in front of him, the king's men were holding off the marauders with the help of Radov's Nadoriin, but for how long?

Kjieran ground his teeth at hal'Jaitar's artfulness, deft and cunning. Had he *ever* intended for Kjieran to harm the king? Or had hal'Jaitar meant only ever to distract him, to keep him occupied and out of his way—*so that his own men disguised as marauders could do the deed instead.*

Kjieran cursed himself for not suspecting this truth sooner. A man like hal'Jaitar would never trust someone outside his circle with such an important act as treason.

Kjieran watched the wielder's elaborate deception playing out with his jaw clenched. After a battle such as this, with few witnesses to speak against him, hal'Jaitar might assign blame for King Gydryn's death to whomever he chose.

In that moment, Kjieran remembered his dream.

He'd been afraid when he took off his amulet to sleep, afraid that he would wake wholly the Prophet's creature, but *she* had found him instead.

"This is your path, Kjieran," she'd told him as he gazed in dreamscape upon the goddess's ethereal, ever-shifting form, observing a dazzling metamorphosis occurring before his eyes. *"It was always meant to be you who walked it. If you cannot find the will to see it to its end, to where it merges with the greater pattern, then all of the branches that would've grown from that joining will never be."*

In that moment, as Kjieran recalled Epiphany's admonishment, assigned equally as warning and duty, a renewed purpose surged to life within him.

And the *other* reared to fight on its behalf.

Kjieran's hands flashed. He grabbed the offending swords by their blades and wrenched them free of their owners hands. Then he flipped the weapons in the air, caught the hilts and drove the blades in dual killing blows, taking one soldier through the heart and another through the neck. They toppled.

Kjieran spurred his horse through the opening their deaths provided.

Another wave of marauders came pouring shrilly over the far hills as Kjieran spurred his horse towards his king in a blaze of sand. Kjieran sought to keep his king in sight as his mount dodged and slid around fighting pairs, but swords and soldiers kept intruding across his line of vision.

And then the sand exploded in front of him, and a figure appeared.

Kjieran's horse reared with a whinny of protest, and he tumbled from his saddle. Landing on his neck and shoulders, he flipped over backwards and onto his stomach, momentarily dazed. A hand grabbed him by the collar of his robes and yanked him up, and Kjieran focused on Kedar's black gaze.

"*Foolish*," the latter snarled.

Kjieran felt *elae* pouring into him and both wondered and despaired that it had no effect. He watched disconnectedly as his own ebon hand reached out and grabbed Kedar's neck, watched as his stone-hard fingers closed around living flesh. Kedar retaliated with a blast of raw energy that sent nearby men tumbling like leaves and forced Kjieran back. The *other* drew deeply upon the Prophet's dark power, and Kjieran raised his hand to wield it—

The Prophet's violent presence flooded into Kjieran's mind. He sucked in a painful breath and fell to his knees, pushing hands to his suddenly exploding head. A breath later, he found himself lying prostrate before his master, once again in the antechamber of Bethamin's mind.

"YOU BETRAY ME, KJIERAN!" A tidal wave of fury pounded Kjieran's consciousness.

He shuddered beneath the force. "No, my lord!"

"WHAT THEN IS THIS YOU DO?" A terrible weight descended,

constricting Kjieran's chest, sending shards of pain coursing through his body.

"I would have vengeance in his death!" Kjieran gasped, despairing that the lie came so easily to him.

Anger rolled off of the Prophet in waves, and Kjieran let out another anguished cry as a force pressed him down, down…flat against the stones. He feared his ribs would shatter, and he knew that back in life, his real body was being similarly crushed. Even Dore's pattern offered flimsy protection against the Prophet's displeasure. Kjieran whimpered in agonized entreaty, "My lord—I would have him…*suffer*…"

The vigor of Bethamin's disapproval abated slightly, and the Prophet's voice floated to him across space and time, distant and yet too near as their minds melded within the pattern of binding. "I must be able to trust you, Kjieran."

Then you should not have destroyed and corrupted me with your touch!

"My lord…" Kjieran drew in a great shuddering breath. The delicate bones of his cheek were still forced painfully against the cold stones of Bethamin's mental chamber. "You granted me the freedom to carry out your will. Do you deny it to me now?"

"This is what you claim to have been doing?" The Prophet sounded dubious, his favor relentlessly withdrawn. "I know your mind, Kjieran—your thoughts crossed freely to me upon the bond. You meant to save this king from a certain end."

"Yes, my lord." Kjieran confessed brokenly. A part of him was genuinely contrite—that portion of his soul which felt Bethamin's wrath as a shattering loss and wanted only to please him, to regain his favor. A much smaller yet still determined part, however, railed against this subjugation, knowing it meant eternal bondage.

It was from this place that he found the courage to reply. "I crafted a dramatic deception…the better to draw out the king's pain."

"I did not think such vengeance within your ken, Kjieran."

"I admit that I've changed in becoming your weapon, my lord." Kjieran added in a threadbare voice, "How could I not?" There was no need to point out that if the Prophet had wanted to keep him pure, he shouldn't have let Dore Madden at him, for this was evident, and Bethamin was no fool.

Kjieran drew in courage with his breath and whispered, "What you saw, my lord, was me claiming my right to take my king's life while defying the right of any other to do so. Gydryn val Lorian must be—" Kjieran stumbled over the words, lest his true intentions come through too desperately, "burned, my lord. He must be *punished*."

The crushing weight of Bethamin's anger at last withdrew. Trembling, Kjieran pushed unsteadily to hands and knees.

"Look at me, Kjieran."

He sat back on his heels and lifted his colorless eyes to meet the Prophet's scalding gaze, which licked over him like flames, leaving traces of heat everywhere it touched. The fury was absent from Bethamin's dark eyes now, but other terrible emotions took its place, and Kjieran trembled to imagine the thoughts that had birthed them.

The Prophet cupped his chin and lifted him to his feet. "You gave yourself to me freely," he murmured, his dark eyes hot upon Kjieran, a flood of confusing emotions crossing the bond to accost him with their sharp hunger, "so I give you this in return."

And he fastened a kiss upon Kjieran's mouth.

In the waking world, Kjieran's eyes flew open. He emitted a silent scream as Bethamin's power flooded into him, filled him, spilled out of him, his master's corruptive seed overflowing into the fragile, virgin world.

When blackness cleared from his vision, Kjieran found himself on hands and knees. A host of armed men were surrounding him, with Kedar centermost among them. They were all watching him uneasily, swords leveled, their stance showing a readiness to act at the least provocation.

In a single motion, Kjieran rose. The men all took reflexive steps backwards in a sudden jangle of shifting mail.

Kjieran settled his colorless eyes on Kedar. He suspected from the man's infuriated glare that the wielder was working some kind of pattern meant to contain him.

No one could contain him.

Kjieran felt swollen with Bethamin's power. He'd never before been entrusted with its discretionary use, but now he inherently understood how to wield it.

Somewhere beyond these men, Kjieran's king was fighting, possibly dying. Kjieran reached out and found his king's precious life pattern and isolated it in his mind to protect Gydryn. Then he fastened a merciless gaze on Kedar.

His colorless eyes blackened at the edges with the violet-dark sparkle of *deyjiin*. Then he opened his mouth and released the flood of Bethamin's wrath upon the world.

The marauder who came towards Gydryn was a beast of a man. Standing a full head taller than the king, he wielded his scimitar as a barbarian wields a club, beating and bashing with ferocity at anyone in his path.

He reached the king and drove him back with a barrage of over-handed blows, casting Gydryn forth as leaves before the storm. And all the while, more marauders poured down the dunes singing their sharp trill, until the night became saturated with the sound. Horses flew wildly past carrying flailing riders; scimitars flashed in the night; men screamed and blood-mist stained the air. It was chaos.

Just when Gydryn thought he might be gaining the upper hand on the giant, a rider flew behind him with a shrieking trill, and his razor-edged blade pierced the king's hauberk. Gydryn staggered and gasped as fire traced a line across his back, and the giant's blade took him through his left side. Before he could turn to defend himself, the giant stabbed him again in his right shoulder.

Gydryn fell to his knees. The shock of three grievous wounds rapidly overtook his senses. Emotions surged through him confusingly, thoughts that couldn't fully form amid a fog of pain. Some part of him recognized the danger in this disconnectedness, but he could do nothing to change it.

Gydryn blinked, watching as the giant came and towered over him, his hulking features grey in the pitiless moonlight. He lifted his blade and—

Light flared, searing the king's eyes and leaving violet spots before his eyes. He almost didn't believe them when the giant standing over him dissolved into ash.

Gydryn shoved an arm across his face and spun away. Ash choked him, bitter and stinging. As he blinked the blackened remains of flesh and bone from his burning eyes, he beheld a gruesome scene.

In every direction, men were...*evaporating*.

Coughing a bloody froth that tasted of acid and char, the king collapsed onto his side, staring but not understanding as the battling men became strangely shadowed and then dissolved in tumbles of billowing ash, their desiccated forms simply unable to hold shape any longer. Weapons fell soundlessly to the sand. What horses had not been claimed fled the scene with equine screams, sensitive to whatever evil power was at work.

Gydryn inhaled a painful breath and pushed up on one elbow to gain vision of the larger field. He searched for anything that would explain what he'd just witnessed, sought any signs of life, but even the bodies of the already dead had been disintegrated. No evidence of the battle remained, save a field littered with swords.

Until—he saw him then. A dark figure rounded a distant dune, his cloak floating on the wind. Gydryn watched the figure slowly closing the distance between them, a long walk across sands blackened with the slag of hundreds of men and horse.

The figure reached him and in one motion bent and scooped up his weakened form into arms as unyielding as stone. "My king," he pronounced wretchedly. His voice was the whisper of wind beneath the dark strands of his blowing hair.

Gydryn could barely draw breath for the pain that consumed him; certainly not enough breath to form a reply. He sagged in the man's arms, shocked and confused. When the stranger began to run, the torture proved too great for Gydryn, and he embraced unconsciousness.

When the king roused again, he found himself sitting upon a cantering horse, with the man's ebon-black arm wrapped solidly about his chest, strong as any band of iron. And dawn was upon them.

The king sought words, sought coherent thought to form into such, but the shapes wouldn't come to his tongue. He felt a choking weight in a mouth too dry with the dust of the dead. Gydryn's gaze dimmed again, and he tumbled once more into darkness.

He finally regained consciousness in the heat of the deep afternoon as the cloaked stranger was half-carrying, half-dragging him up a steep dune. The scalding sun blinded him, and the burning sand scoured his wounds, eliciting a moan that hardly sounded his own. At last the stranger slung him down on the side of the dune and stalked away.

Gydryn would've bartered his soul for even a trickle of water. Pain seemed to come from everywhere at once, seeping out of his very pores to taint his breath.

He followed the stranger with his gaze as the man descended into the bosom of the dunes, towards a vast collection of striped tents, and one by one began ripping them down.

Kjieran dropped the king on the side of the dune and set off towards the host of tents that had been erected for the parley. With every step, he sunk to his knees in the sand.

The sun was a blistering inferno above him. It drew forth heat from the scalding sand, baked the air, and roused a furnace wind. Yet Kjieran's struggle with the elements could not compare to the ravaging fury berating his consciousness.

The Prophet knew. And no dissembling would assuage his fury.

Kjieran didn't know how much Bethamin had gleaned of his true intentions, but he knew Kjieran had deceived him. Now the man fought to gain control over Kjieran's body and mind.

Kjieran fought back with everything that he was.

The Prophet repeatedly threw bands of compulsion across the bond, but thanks to Raine's amulet and Kjieran's vigilance upon his thoughts, Bethamin's compulsion fell short in the waters of Kjieran's consciousness; yet each attempt struck those waters with hurricane force, the power of his fury as sleet sheeting across the sea. It numbed thought and turned every action into a sluggish battle for control.

Kjieran clenched his jaw and pressed ever onward. Every thought—every ounce of will he could muster—he focused upon completing one action at a time. He managed each with a snarl of defiance broken by gruesome cries of pain, for his mind was being repeatedly fractured by patterns that sought to bind him, by the throbbing rage of the man who sought to own him, and by his own conflicted emotions—loyalties and betrayals as a bewildering jumble of purposes whose aims were rapidly losing shape.

Kjieran's head felt an exploding sun. He just focused on putting one blackened foot before the other. One hand and then the next grasped the striped cloth canvas and tore the tents down, one by one, until he'd gathered the entire structure into a massive tower of wood and striped canvas, snapping in the furnace wind.

YOU WILL STOP THIS, KJIERAN!

Bethamin's will impaled Kjieran's mind in a violent rape of his determinism. He staggered and fell to his hands and knees and screamed.

Compulsion drew forth unwilling emotions as a needle drew blood, and Kjieran writhed in the sand, his body shaking and twitching. He could do naught in that moment but gaze upwards at the blinding sun, knowing only the piercing agony of Bethamin's disfavor and the intensity of his unrelenting determination to own him.

But as before, the Prophet's attempt to claim him failed. As the force of his last working faded, Kjieran regained himself. Trembling, he attempted to push to hands and knees but collapsed again with a sharp gasp.

All of his ribs had broken.

Several minutes passed before he found the will to move. When he did, pain blazed violently, but he welcomed it that time. Its heat was a cruel, if potent, reminder that part of him could still be harmed, that some portion of him yet walked *elae's* path.

Kjieran lifted his gaze across the clearing and focused on the supply tent. Grunting with effort, he lifted his body from the sand and staggered towards the tent with determination as his only fuel.

The Prophet snarled damnations at him from the other end of their hateful bond, but the only thing Kjieran feared was failing in this, his final task. He dragged a single barrel from the supply tent towards the mound of canvas and wood, and then, gritting his teeth, he heaved the cask atop the towering pile. The barrel split upon landing, and a clear liquid spewed forth to quickly soak into the striped cloth.

Absinthe. Drunk in quantity by Radov's troops, it had been stocked for the parley's concluding feast. Kjieran would put the volatile spirit to better use.

KJIERAN I DEMAND YOU CEASE UPON THIS COURSE!

Bethamin sought to drag him into his own mind once more, but Kjieran resisted fiercely. Should he fall beneath the Prophet's will this time, he suspected there would be no return to consciousness.

Bethamin's battering will lashed him repeatedly, as if to expurgate his defiance. Kjieran gripped his medallion and clenched his teeth and stumbled back in a faltering, drunkard's slog to assess the pyre.

Holding onto himself with a will he'd never imagined possible, he pointed his fingers towards the barrel and reached for *elae*.

It was as painful as trying to draw breath under water. All the while, the Prophet's whip cracked against Kjieran's consciousness, bringing stinging tears of pain and betrayal, commanding contrition—all of these intermingled with Bethamin's immeasurable fury.

Kjieran desperately sought *elae* though this onslaught like a drowning man swimming for the surface. And then, with a surge of elation, he felt the lifeforce finally in his grasp. It was just the tiniest tendril, but it would be enough.

He cast a spark of the fourth strand towards the absinthe-soaked canvas and collapsed to his knees as it arced through the air and trailed downwards...

Searing heat buffeted him.

The wind of the explosion sent sand scouring across Kjieran's form while the its fury echoed against the surrounding cliffs. Kjieran dragged himself to his feet and stumbled across the clearing towards Gydryn's inert body. He dropped to his knees at his king's side.

"Sire," Kjieran gasped. Bethamin's infuriated will was repeatedly bombarding him. He knew he had but minutes left, may Epiphany not desert him just yet.

The king blinked open bloodshot eyes. His life, too, lay in Epiphany's hands.

As Kjieran gazed at his king Gydryn seemed to finally recognize him. His eyes widened and his lips formed a dry whisper too faint to be heard above the roaring pyre, whose heat was now more intense than the scalding sun's.

Kjieran took a water flask from his belt and held it to the king's cracked lips, letting a trickle of liquid moisten them. The king drank what he offered, but his eyes never left Kjieran's.

Bethamin's presence filled Kjieran's mind; the Prophet would have him any second. Already each moment seemed twice as removed from the end of his path as the one that had come before, as if the Prophet was hauling him backwards, away from the death he so desperately sought. Time grew frighteningly short.

Holding the king's astonished gaze, Kjieran looked down at the bulging muscles of his blackened chest. Just a circle of pale flesh remained where Raine's amulet lay. Tears streamed down Kjieran's face as he pushed fingers into the king's shoulder, eliciting a gasp of pain from him.

He stared hard into Gydryn's eyes, willing him to understand, not daring to speak—barely daring even to think—and scrawled across his own ravaged chest:

he sees what I see

The king's eyes widened.

"Sire." Kjieran managed a raw rasp, barely able to summon the will to form the words. "Trell lives. The acts against your sons...it was *Radov*—"

Abruptly the fury and violence of the Prophet's contention pierced Kjieran's mind, and he screamed a raw and despairing cry. He yanked Raine's amulet free of his neck and shoved it into Gydryn's bloody hand.

Then he tore himself away.

Bethamin filled him as he fled in a staggering gait, nearly blind, his mind only moments from domination. As he neared the burning pyre, Kjieran took a running leap and flung his body high upon the flames.

The Prophet thundered in outrage. Kjieran voiced his fury, howling as he sank into the pyre amid an eruption of fire and smoke. His dark hair exploded in flames. The flesh of his face charred and blackened and peeled away, revealing the ebon skull beneath. Only then did Kjieran succumb to the flames, to the guilt and grief and fear. Only then did the Prophet abandon his impotent fury and grow silent...still.

Time seemed to ebb and wane. What few remaining living parts Kjieran possessed soon boiled away, leaving him in silent agony, unable even to cry out, pinned to that petrified flesh in darkness. He couldn't know if it would work, this plan. He lay in blind agony with every moment bringing a new level of terror.

For this was his last hope. If his plan failed, his blackened body would emerge from the charred pyre of dying flames seemingly unscathed but for the utter corruption of his soul.

Kjieran desperately wished that Bethamin would leave him to his despair and his grief, that he might meet his end in peace and be spared finally from the Prophet's lustful desires. But the man's presence remained, hovering within his consciousness, drinking in his desolate thoughts.

At last the pyre shuddered beneath Kjieran, and his ravaged body tumbled into the deep well of coals. A geyser of fiery cinders and smoke erupted to join the billowing clouds already darkening the sky, and new flames sprouted where others had ebbed. As the heat of the fire's core latched onto Kjieran's mutated flesh, its hunger at last proved superior to Dore's patterns.

Kjieran thought he'd traveled the gamut of pain's many forms, yet he realized in that moment that he'd barely begun to explore them. As he opened his mouth in a soundless scream, his jaw dissolved to cinders. He tried to flail his arms, but his stone hands melted. Only then, as Dore's very pattern caught the flame, did Kjieran finally fade from consciousness.

His spirit withdrew from the world of men. Kjieran stared into the dark void of unmaking, desperate for the oblivion death offered. And then…

A flicker in the darkness.

Into the void, a spark erupted. A too-brilliant form with wings of shimmering light blossomed before Kjieran's gaze. He shied away from it, fleeing it and the void of unmaking.

And he heard her voice. It was the music light itself might make if it could manifest in sound.

Kjieran van Stone.

Kjieran wept at her divine summoning. He knew he hovered close to the shadows—so close that their kiss was a chilling caress, the promise of unmaking a dreadful temptation. The line he tread between *elae* and *deyjiin* grew ever thinner; the thread binding him to the Returning all but non-existent. He would rather become unmade than spend his eternity bound to the Prophet Bethamin.

But the goddess flamed before him, and her light drew his spirit back from oblivion—likewise her searing demand:

Kjieran van Stone, would you bind yourself to me and know rebirth?

Kjieran despaired. *I am bound to another already, my lady.*

But this binding was done against your will, she told him in the way of spirits, her shimmering form shifting so rapidly that Kjieran saw multiple shapes coalesce and dissolve again. *It cannot last.*

Kjieran's soul trembled as he confessed his deepest fear, *But the working was bound with the fifth.*

The goddess shimmered and blazed. *The fifth cannot bind the soul once the shell is gone.* She glowed so brightly that he could barely look upon her. *But I can...should you wish it.*

The barest hope sparked within Kjieran. He knew that she had spoken truly, for she was the lifeforce of thought and of creation, the kinetic energy of the second strand and even the wildly variant aspects of the third—she was every strand but the elemental fifth. She was Life.

She was *elae.*

My lady, Kjieran gasped into the void, which had become saturated now with light, *I would bind myself to you a thousand times and again.*

Her shimmering wings enfolded his battered spirit, and Kjieran became blinded by brilliance, by a flooding warmth, by the sudden acute awareness of the millions of souls who had bound themselves to her and been reborn.

Finally then did he feel the bond with Bethamin dissolving as Dore's fifth-strand pattern at last seared away. The Prophet's anguished wail faded to a whisper and was gone.

The last thing Kjieran knew was the bliss of Epiphany's final blessing.

Then let it be so, Kjieran van Stone.

Gydryn val Lorian lay dying.

As he labored over each indrawn breath, he clutched the amulet Kjieran had given him and marveled at the mighty forces of fate that had brought them together for their mutual ends. He'd watched Kjieran's black-robed figure fling itself onto the flaming pyre, watched as his shredded garments were consumed in smoke and flame. He'd prayed for him, whispering the Rite for the Departed as the sun slanted towards the surrounding ridge and smoke billowed upwards to pollute the sky.

Gydryn expected his end approached as well. As the day lengthened and waned, he faded in and out of consciousness. Sometimes he dreamed. At one point, he thought he saw dark riders atop the far ridge, their silk garments swirling and snapping upon the winds. He'd felt a glimmer of hope stir in his exhausted soul, but then he'd looked a second time and realized the forms were only shadows cast by the falling sun.

With dulled senses, he spent some time pondering the mystery of the words Kjieran had scrawled upon his chest and wondered at the news the once-truthreader had delivered of his sons; but in the end, thought itself became too difficult. Gydryn abandoned it and let his attention wander as his life waned.

He must've drifted off, for when he opened his eyes again, a shadow lay upon him.

The shadow of a man.

Gydryn blinked abrasive sand from tearing eyes and lifted his gaze towards the silhouette standing between him and the sun. Piercing brown eyes stared down at him beneath a black and silver turban. The Khurd pulled his scarf free to reveal the angular features of a man in his prime, with a strong jaw shadowed by a close-cut beard.

"Prince Farid!" Another dark-eyed Khurd came running, but he drew up short as his gaze befell Gydryn. "Is *that*—?" The man cut off his own question, his heavy black brows furrowed in surprise.

Prince Farid's eyes never wavered from the king's. There was little of amity in his inscrutable gaze. He spun in a swirl of silk. "Take him."

Hands reached for Gydryn, the world spun crazily, and the dying king fled into the darkness of oblivion.

FIFTY-FIVE

"Everything was going as planned until they showed up."
– The Adept truthreader Cristien Tagliaferro on the Paladin Knights'
invasion of the Citadel of Tiern'aval

"ENOUGH." EAN DOUBLED over. He rested hands on his knees and looked up under his brows at Markal, who was standing across the field.

They worked that day in a high meadow overlooking Niyadbakir and its majestic mountains. A storm was rising in the south; charcoal clouds had amassed against the mountains' jagged emerald reaches, and the mottled sky between was becoming a battleground; the storm clouds were advancing into the sun's dominion, only to be broken apart by powerful shafts of arrow-light piercing down to the valley.

And Ean was tired.

Tired of this training, tired of Markal's unrelenting condescension and their inevitably contentious relationship...tired of trying to remember the life and education of a name he hadn't claimed for centuries.

"I don't see why we keep having to do this," the prince complained. The statement encapsulated his entire outlook at the moment.

Markal settled his staff between his feet. "That has ever been your problem."

Ean gave a frustrated sigh. "We've been at this since dawn. I've made you do a hundred different things. Surely I've proven I can work compulsion patterns."

Markal rested both hands on his staff and gave Ean a nightmare of a frown. "As usual, you fail to grasp the point of the lesson, Ean val Lorian. *Patterning is most effective at the level of thought,*" he quoted the Sixth Law of Patterning. "But we are not merely working with the Sixth Law. We are also working with the Ninth Esoteric."

"Which is about as comprehensible as Cyrenaic hieroglyphs!" Ean threw up his hands and walked a frustrated circle.

"*Pure concept always overwhelms linear translation,*" Markal stated, as if the Ninth Esoteric would somehow become clarified in repeating it for the tenth time. Then he added critically, "If the Esoterics were so simplistic a child could understand them, they would not be named the Esoterics."

"And the mouse said to the tiger, come hither and I shall tickle your ear," Ean muttered, which statement he felt was just as helpful.

Markal arched a mordant black brow. "If you are so obtuse as to only comprehend *simple* concepts, Ean val Lorian, go back to your arithmetic and the abacus and leave Patterning to those with the wits to apply its laws properly."

Ean glared sootily at him. There was really nothing he could say to that.

After a moment of staring fractiously at each other, the prince grumbled, "Did we *ever* get along?"

Markal arched brows and turned his back on him. "Have you ever done as you were instructed?"

"Possibly!" Ean called after him, though he privately doubted it.

Markal retook his position ten paces away. "So, since you're so certain of your understanding of the interrelationship between the Sixth Law and the Ninth Esoteric, let us proceed."

"Actually, I believe I said exactly the opposite."

Markal extended his staff like a sword before him. "I will now work the compulsion, and you will counter it by applying these laws."

"How am I supposed to apply—"

A sudden force bombarded him so powerfully that he dropped to his knees and doubled over, and still the pressure forced him down…down… until his body was flat and his check was pressed firmly into the grass.

Eventually Markal came and stood over him—long after Ean's jaw had started aching, long after he thought his bones would shatter from the invisible monster squatting on his spine.

"*This* is compulsion," the wielder informed him critically. "This is but a fraction of what they will throw at you. *They* will include thought layered with Form. *They* will have you thinking you are dead already—or worse."

Markal released the pattern, and Ean sucked in a shuddering breath and rolled onto his back.

Markal watched him gravely. "You must be ready and alert for compulsion, Ean. *Ever* alert. It is a wielder's prime weapon, for a *man's* greatest weapon is his mind. Attack that, subdue *that,* and he becomes as putty to your will—far more useful than a sword when wielded with finesse and intelligence."

Markal retreated across the meadow. Ean lay staring at the charcoal clouds trying to rein in his instinct to snuff out the man like a flame between his fingers. He *could* do it—he had the ability, he had the *knowledge*…or mostly he did.

Ean was growing increasingly frustrated by his inability to immediately access what was supposed to be second nature to him, while growing decreasingly willing to endure Markal Morrelaine's instruction with the objective of reclaiming it.

Eventually the prince rolled back to his feet. He leveled Markal a smoldering look that mostly conveyed his desire for retribution.

Markal arched a brow. "Again."

That time Ean readied himself. He embraced *elae* and crafted a mental shield to protect his mind from patterns of the fourth. When he sensed Markal wielding a fourth-strand pattern within the amassing tides of *elae*, Ean snared the pattern and pulled it apart like a violently unwinding a spool of thread.

"No, no, *no!*" Markal slammed his staff into the earth to emphasize each exclamation.

"Why no?" The rebuke honestly startled Ean. "It worked, didn't it?"

Markal cast him a look of supreme disapproval. "We are here for you to apply the Ninth Esoteric, Ean val Lorian, not to play at cat's Cradle. '*Pure concept always overwhelms linear translation.*' Again."

"You know, if you'd ever bother to explain *anything*—"

And a second later Markal had him on the ground, that time drooling into the grass.

When the wielder once again released Ean from his compulsion, the prince gathered enough self-respect to spit the grass from his mouth and cast Markal a baleful look as he got back to his feet.

"*Patterning is most effective at the level of thought,*" the wielder reminded him imperiously.

Ean resumed his place, feeling ill-used and mistreated and generally sullen. He couldn't quite hold back the accusation that escaped him as their gazes locked. "You take perverse pleasure in tormenting me, don't you?"

Markal stiffened. "Pleasure?" His expression darkened. "You think I *relish* watching the most gifted student I ever had the honor of instructing floundering like a mindless carp on dry land?" Abruptly he stalked towards Ean looking as dangerous as the thunderheads looming above. "You think I do this out of *choice*? That *this* is how I desire to interact with you? Saying little, *teaching* less, with my hands bound behind my back and the irons of Balance *chained around my balls?*" This last came out in a veritable roar.

Ean stood stunned.

Markal stopped nose to nose with the prince with the fifth singeing and snapping as it rolled off his thoughts. "And *you,*" he shook his staff at Ean's head, "with your incessant whining and complaining, like a petulant child set begrudgingly to task. What is it you think we *do* here?"

Ean felt scoured. The wielder's words had stripped him of his anger, of his vengeful desires—of all the petty emotions the man had rightfully accused him of. He knew only the shame of ignorance and the galling embarrassment of his own immaturity thrown into stark illumination.

"I...wronged you," Ean confessed after a moment of contrite silence. He felt ashamed at his actions and even more so by the bitter enmity he'd so unjustly harbored against Markal. "I thought—oh, it doesn't matter what I thought."

Markal regarded him with grave solemnity. "We all have our roles, Ean val Lorian. Like them...or despise them," and his scowl, which only deepened the shadows of his brown eyes, clearly conveyed the opinion he held about his own particular role. "Destiny governs us all, prince of Dannym. Some of us are destined to live long lives of toil and tribulation; others live but for a single purpose and die by its end." Markal turned on his heel and walked back to his place.

Ean watched him crossing the meadow, feeling a different sort of shadow upon his soul. "Who decides our destiny?"

Markal reached his mark and turned to face the prince. "That depends on whose game you're playing." He fixed Ean with his gaze and returned them to their lesson. "*Patterning is most effective at the level of thought*—this is the law we seek to apply. Since this morning's instruction has so far been unfruitful, let us pretend you are…well, *you*, and I shall for the moment be your enemy as he may more truly appear."

For the moment? Ean caught himself at the thought and quickly quelled it, for he realized now that Markal was suffering just as grievously beneath the yoke of Balance.

Then he had no more time to ponder such things, for Markal threw a compulsion pattern at him. Ean snared it and unworked it, despite knowing the man would be wroth with him for choosing that line of defense.

Rather than stop to scold him, however, Markal immediately threw another pattern. Again Ean unworked it. But before he had it fully undone, Markal had thrown another, and very soon another…and *another*. Ean had his own mind shielded from the fourth strand as he worked to mentally dodge and catch each pattern, starting it unraveling before catching the next. But Markal's patterns were soon coming too quickly, and Ean strained to keep his own mind shielded while unworking so many patterns at once.

The patterns kept coming.

Ean had to draw more and more *elae* to defend, protect and unravel—until there were too many patterns coming at him, too many still only half undone. Too much force. Too much random motion swirling within his consciousness.

His head started pounding with the strain. He tried to expand his sense of self, as Ramu had advised him, yet this only resulted in his feeling stretched too thin. In the effort to expand and contain simultaneously, his hold on the pattern that protected his mind slipped—

Markal's patterns bit with a vengeance.

The malevolent pattern immediately feasted on Ean's thoughts and disgorged painful commands that forced the prince's body to the earth.

Ean gasped and dropped to his knees. Everything fell apart—his shield dissolved utterly, whereupon the remaining vestiges of Markal's half-worked patterns also descended on him.

Ean floundered helplessly within this barrage of torments, unable even to *find* the lifeforce—unable even to *think* of it—and utterly incapable of seeing beyond the horrific images being shoved mercilessly into his consciousness. More painful than the images, however, were the commands the compulsion patterns made him believe, for they preyed and expanded on his own deepest fears:

Your flesh is burning. Your bones are shattered.

Isabel is dead...

No hope, said the patterns; and weeping, Ean knew there was none.

You are ruined, said the patterns, and Ean knew it was so.

And then...something...*shifted.*

The breath of a breeze stirred the curtain of memory, and Ean glimpsed beyond the veil. In that moment, he knew that he'd experienced this before, this *decaying* of his will. Moreover, he realized that he could throw it off—in fact, that he *must* do so at all costs. Desperation—*necessity*—seized him—

The veil parted.

Knowledge flooded into Ean's mind as if a dam bursting wide. Brilliant, abounding knowledge came on in voluminous waves. Suddenly Ean could see in stark illumination the patterns Markal was wielding against him. He could see their intertwined layers of form—the connective tissue of *elae*—holding the compulsion in place.

He remembered that such tissue could be severed, and how to make it so.

Do not counter force with force, channel it.

Ean heard the echo of the Ninth Law as spoken by a different Markal, in a different era, when the wielder had been his mentor and friend, when Ean had led another man's life.

But he knew how to escape now—knew far more than he wanted to, suddenly, about compulsion and its many forms. That door had been reopened.

Nay, it had been *obliterated.*

With precise certainty, Ean grabbed hold of the nets of compulsion—*took hold of the patterns themselves*—and used their own power to set them spinning. A mental knife comprised of the fifth severed them in a splay of brilliant energy.

The patterns shredded, and Ean was free.

He pushed to his elbows and then, somewhat unsteadily, to his feet.

A part of him felt as if inebriated, still reeling from the vast cacophony of malignant thoughts that had held him in thrall only seconds before.

With his newly restored knowledge had come the understanding that the patterns Markal was using him were some of the most vicious ever devised, but this was not what had him so shaken.

No…it was a realization that came with his newly restored understanding: his true gift was not in *unworking* patterns. It was in his ability to *see* them.

Some few wielders in history had been born with the unusual ability to unwork patterns, but being able to *see* a pattern *while it was being worked by another wielder*—this talent made him utterly unique.

Ean understood now that this gift had also forever been his liability, for it produced a tendency to think in 'linear translations' rather than in 'pure concepts'—Markal's very point from their lesson that day.

But it stood also as a great boon, because in seeing the patterns, Ean knew instantly how to unwork them.

Indeed, he had but to view a pattern to know its entire concept— including what strands it was comprised of. He could see how to pick any pattern apart, how to find the tiniest frayed end within it and unravel it all.

This then formed the crux of his talent, what made him unique among wielders, and undoubtedly why Björn needed his particular participation in his game.

"I perceive that a light has suddenly been lit in the vast cavern of your obstinacy," Markal observed.

Ean cast him a long look. He reminded himself that Markal was trying as hard to help him as he in turn was trying to pierce the veil—and that indeed, they had succeeded just then in regaining a crucial part of what Ean had lost. Yet with this knowledge regained, so also had an old sense of dignity been restored, and Ean would not suffer its diminishment again.

"You're right." The prince met Markal's gaze and brushed grass from his hands. "Just now, much returned to me." He cast the wielder a conflicted look. "I understand that this…process of ours may be the fastest way to restore my knowledge, so I'll forgive the working you just forced on me. But I can't endure this any more, Markal."

Markal arched a black brow. "Think you're ready to face the Malorin'athgul, do you?"

Ean held his gaze. He thought about that moment when Markal had so brutally subverted and used his own mind against him. In that dreadful instant, Ean had remembered being another man, living another life, and he'd recalled a vow Arion had made in blood to never allow his will—or his power—to be usurped by another.

"I don't know." Ean dropped his gaze, all too aware of the mental casks that were still breaking open, knowledge spewing as wine from barrels burst. "But I know there's nothing more you can teach me that will help, if and when I do."

Markal leaned on his staff and regarded Ean with deep concern in his dark eyes. "Then you are perhaps at last upon the path."

The prince felt inundated now by the ever-growing deluge of Arion's memories, which continued their flood of restoration. But one overarching desire accompanied them all: a need to pronounce a vow which Ean realized had been lacking for a painfully long time.

He crossed the distance to where Markal stood leaning on his staff. Planting his feet before his teacher of ages old and new, he extended his hand. "Thank you."

Markal clasped wrists with him, but only his troubled gaze spoke in reply.

Björn van Gelderan, Fifth Vestal of Alorin, stood before the tall windows of his study with his hands clasped behind his back, gazing out at the advancing front of a thunderstorm.

Raine D'Lacourte, Fourth Vestal of Alorin, sat in an armchair in the corner observing his oath-brother, while Dämen, Lord of Shades, gave his report. Raine was a guest at this briefing—indeed, he was welcomed everywhere now, invited to act as Björn's constant shadow. It was surreal.

So many centuries had passed, yet Raine found his oath-brother to be essentially the same, as if the intervening years had been but a blink of the eye. It appeared to Raine that the usual deleterious effects of centuries of life and loss merely hit Björn and bounced away, as light reflecting from a mirror, leaving no trace.

In fact, this scene was so like countless others he'd witnessed centuries ago in Illume Belliel that Raine could simply close his eyes and see the same images played out upon a different background. In the cityworld, Dämen would've been but one of hundreds in Björn's service come to give news of their activities, intrigues, successes. Raine recalled many an afternoon spent in Björn's chambers being privy to such conferences. Björn *had* trusted him, and yet…to think of the intrigues Björn let Raine sit in council upon—*the rise or fall of entire kingdoms, empires even!*—yet knowing he had not trusted him with the truth of T'khendar…it gave a new depth to the enormity of his oath-brother's game.

In Illume Belliel, Raine had followed the conversations he'd been overhearing, but there in T'khendar it was all shades of incomprehensible. It wasn't just the often disjointed communication between Björn and Dämen, statements formed of incomplete sentences, as if they were finishing the rest in their heads.

No, it was more that Raine knew he was still missing an underlying grasp of the foundation of the game overall—the objectives, as it were—and without those, every move just baffled him.

"What of the Sylus node?" Björn cast Dämen a look over his shoulder. He wore a heavy silk tunic in dove-grey, belted over slim black pants. The light in the room was growing ever dimmer from the storm rolling in, but still Björn's oathring sparkled as if held to the sun.

"Franco Rohre has been given the task, as you required, *ma dieul*," the Shade replied.

Björn arched a brow over the shadow of a smile. "Then he accepted the assignment?"

"Not without expressing his immense trepidation and disagreement."

Björn's smile deepened. "I wonder if even this will prove a challenge for Franco? Doubtless, he'll one day be grateful to have gained the skill."

Though Dämen's sculpted silver features remained impassive, Raine sensed an underlying unease in the Shade regarding the topic of the Sylus node—wherever *it* was. This gleaned perception was the best Raine could accomplish, for it was impossible to read the mind of such creatures. From a truthreader's perspective, their minds simply didn't exist. The man was standing there having a conversation, but his thoughts originated… elsewhere.

Dämen *looked* uncomfortable, however—twitchy, his attention dispersed—which manner gave Raine some insight into his state of mind.

"*Ma dieul*," the Shade said after a long, discontented silence, "will you truly let them take you? After all that has happened?"

Björn considered the question with the slightest of furrows between ebony brows. Then he turned from the windows, walked across the room and slung himself into a violet-hued armchair, settling his chin in hand. "If my path leads there, Dämen, then I will follow it, as ever I have."

The Shade looked highly dissatisfied with this answer.

Raine understood little of this interchange. He'd been invited there not to understand the inner workings of Björn's activities so much as to realize what he already knew: that Björn was still Björn, untainted by time or the elements or *deyjiin*...or even by Raine's own betrayal—much to the truthreader's lingering chagrin. His oath-brother remained as constant as the slow turning of the cosmos itself, and Raine was now ideally poised to endure the everlasting guilt of his forgiveness.

Dämen was just opening his mouth, perhaps to make some further protest, when his attention caught across the room.

Raine turned to follow his gaze and found Isabel standing in the threshold. She wore a high-collared gown of forest green with a darker cloak folded across her arm. As always, a raven-dark blindfold bound her eyes. Still, she looked as radiant as the sun. Her presence suffused the room with a certain serenity that Raine associated with Isabel alone.

Raine stood from his chair at the same time that Björn did. "Isabel," the latter smiled and opened his arms to receive her, "you bless us with your presence."

Smiling beneath her blindfold, Isabel crossed the room and planted a chaste kiss upon her brother's cheek. "And you are ever a boon for my self-esteem," she murmured sweetly.

Björn gave her attire a sweeping look and asked with arched brow, "Going somewhere?" Raine saw something in Björn's gaze that he couldn't quite decipher, but Isabel seemed to know it, for she took her brother's hand as a sort of answer and turned silently to the doorway—just as Ramuhárikhamáth, Lord of the Heavens, crossed the threshold.

"*Ah...*" Björn murmured. He slowly retook his chair, and Isabel moved closer to his side, still holding his hand. "Ramu, what have you?" the First Lord asked then, his expression unreadable.

"Ill news of Trell val Lorian, *ma dieul*." Ramu explained then how Balaji had contacted him with news of Trell's capture as learned from the Healer Alyneri d'Giverny.

"Rhakar says Trell has been taken to M'Nador—to Radov," Ramu concluded with a frown, "which we all know means Viernan hal'Jaitar. The Saldarian crew who captured Trell took the rest of the prince's party hostage—to what end, we yet don't know. Rhakar followed them to observe and report."

"I believe I might shed some unfortunate light upon the mystery," offered an entering Dagmar. He held up a folded letter. "This just arrived from your contact in the Cairs, First Lord. It says four of Ean val Lorian's companions are being held hostage in demand for his surrender at the Castle of Tyr'kharta, on the Kandori-Saldarian border."

"*Taken?*" growled yet another voice. Raine looked back to the doorway to find Ean standing there—truly, was the entirety of Björn's counsel to converge upon his study in the same moment?

Yet…something had changed in the young prince. Anger was radiating out of him, its force doubled for being carried also on the tides of *elae,* but this wasn't what struck Raine. For the first time, he recognized something of Arion Tavestra in the prince's presence. It was not exactly a comforting observation.

"'Tis well you're here to receive this news, Ean," the First Lord meanwhile remarked, "ill though it appears to be."

"Indeed," Dagmar eyed the prince as the latter moved into the room, "for there's more." He handed the letter to Björn and gave the rest of them a significant look. "The felons have demanded that Ean should arrive alone upon the hour given, or they'll take the lives of his companions, starting with the Lord Captain Rhys val Kinkaide. They warned that they'll know if Ean should bring others with him or otherwise attempt to deceive them."

While everyone was absorbing this news, Ramu observed dolefully, "First Lord, Rhakar says the wielder who leads this Saldarian crew is skilled and not to be discounted. While Rhakar couldn't be certain who the man serves, he believes he may have been trained by one from the Fourth Age."

"Yes," Björn murmured, looking regretful. "Undoubtedly."

Raine wondered if Ean would ever be free of the plague of factions warring for the chance to kill him. Which reminded him… "The Karakurt's operatives have long sought Ean," he said, turning a regretful gaze to the prince. "This treachery has the stain of her hand upon it."

"It would be ill-advised for you to attempt to free your friends from such an obvious trap," Ramu cautioned.

The room fell silent as everyone considered this truth, while beyond the windows, thunder sounded close and near, and the storm broke upon the world. A sudden torrent of rain pelted the glass doors and ran in rivulets to pool on the balcony tiles. Björn sent the fifth into the lamps, which swelled into a soft glow.

"Is there any remark as to why this interest in Ean?" Isabel finally inquired of Ramu and Dagmar both. "What crime do they place upon his shoulders?"

"It states the Prophet holds a claim upon him," Dagmar answered.

"The Prophet?" Raine turned Ean a swift look of inquiry.

The prince grimaced, and his gaze darkened with obvious chagrin. "It happened in Acacia." He dropped his chin to his chest, his features tense, hands clutched at his sides. "I unworked the pattern that bound Bethamin's Marquiin to him—I hardly realized what I was doing," he added hastily, and he turned an apologetic look to the First Lord, as if beholden to him for some misuse. "I was new to my returning talent and became lost in the moment. The Adept died, and the Ascendant working with him escaped into the river." He exhaled heavily. "I had thought—hoped—him dead as well."

Isabel shook her head. "If you freed a truthreader from Bethamin's blight, Ean, then you saved his soul from oblivion. Harbor no regret over the act."

The prince lifted his gaze to her. "I regret only that it's now brought my friends to harm," he replied tightly.

The room fell silent again, whilst the storm seemed to grow disproportionately louder, its temperament worsening as their outlook diminished. Into this silence, Björn said, "You must decide what you will do, Ean."

Ramu's expression became troubled, and when the Lord of the Heavens frowned, the whole world fell beneath a shadow. "The Prophet Bethamin..." he turned his gaze upon the prince. "He is not a man to engage with lightly,

Ean. Should you fail in the task of saving your friends, it is into his hands you would be delivered. Are you ready to do battle with such a one?"

The potentiality of this consequence also greatly disturbed Raine. "I beg you think carefully upon this, Ean," he urged. "You know what we suspect of the Prophet and his interference with your family's rule. Having encountered his Marquiin, you must know also the grave effects of Bethamin's power. This trap is obvious, and your success is by no means assured."

"I agree." Dagmar frowned as he regarded the prince. "You must consider the enemies you would face."

Raine added, "The Prophet is cunning and deceitful and works wholly toward his own ends. Such men have no honor. Your friends may already be dead."

Ean shifted his gaze to meet Raine's, whereupon he saw that the prince was deeply affected by the choice lying before him. Yet Raine could read nothing of Ean's thoughts—this, too, was telling of the change the prince had undergone.

"You would have me abandon them," Ean said, flicking a concerned glance from Raine to Ramu.

"We have all sacrificed beyond measure in this endeavor," the Lord of the Heavens remarked candidly, his tone reflective of the steadfast conviction that ever guided him. "You should understand this better than most, Ean."

"And would I sacrifice my friends," Ean argued, growing agitated, "you would have me forsake my honor as well!"

"We would have you make an informed choice, Ean," the First Lord soothed. "That is all."

Ean turned him a desperate look. "But *I* can't see the path ahead! I don't know how this choice wil affect the game. You choose for me."

"It is not our choice to make, Ean," Isabel advised. Her presence ever felt a light within the darkness, the flickering flame guiding the way into the bleak beyond. "This decision lies upon your path, love of my heart. Not ours."

Ean turned a tormented look from Isabel to Björn, with reticence and urgency both commingling upon his features. Yet strangely, Raine got the distinct impression that choosing to save his friends wasn't the decision Ean was wrestling with.

"First Lord…" the prince's voice sounded choked, "may I have a word alone?"

"Of course." Björn stood and motioned Ean towards the balcony, whereupon the raging storm suddenly waned. The rain faded from a downpour to a faint pattering, and by the time Björn was escorting Ean out of doors, only a humid wind remained.

Ean followed Björn outside into the nascent calm, while within a different storm raged. Some might've observed that the world seemed cleansed, but the low, tumbling clouds felt like a tomb to Ean.

'Players make their moves at will, reassured only by their own resolve, facing dire consequences, protected by no one, and shielded by nothing but the force of their conviction.'

The zanthyr's indelible words from so long ago kept running through Ean's mind, for there he stood facing yet another choice that could easily result in the death of someone dear to him. He reflected that he really despised the zanthyr for always being so right.

Björn glanced to him, seeming keen to his state of mind. "There are countless choices that will be made in the coming days, Ean." He clasped hands behind his back as they walked side by side. "With each new choice, the balance of the game could shift, but therein lies the challenge of the game." His very blue eyes searched Ean's for understanding. "Your choices are but drops within the sea, your role one among many, my friend. These paths are ever changing, ever fluctuating. The future is always in motion."

Ean exhaled a troubled breath and looked up at the smothering clouds. He felt somehow connected to the slumbering storm, as though the First Lord's presence becalmed him but momentarily as well, for a part of him was still battling the three-headed demon of guilt.

He stopped walking and turned to Björn. "I want to give you my oath."

Björn stopped and looked at Ean in puzzled silence. "Thank you, Ean," he said after what felt an interminable assessment. "But I do not doubt your fidelity."

"Then…you will accept my oath?"

Björn shook his head and his gaze tightened slightly. "No."

It was denied in the kindest imaginable tone, but still Ean felt shattered by his refusal. "But…why?"

Björn looked deeply into his eyes. "Because I sense you are as yet uncertain what this oath entails."

"It doesn't matter what it entails." Ean felt a sudden desperation to convince him to accept his oath that he might divest himself of the ever-growing chasm of its absence. "Whatever you require, I will give it."

Björn drew in a deep breath and let it out again evenly as he considered Ean. After an uncomfortable moment of this, he asked, "What is an oath?"

"A promise," the prince returned tightly. "A binding promise."

"But what binds it?"

Ean clenched his jaw. He saw where the First Lord was going with this now, and he didn't like it. "Honor, my lord."

"Honor," Björn repeated with a solemn nod. "When all the trappings are stripped away, an oath is bound first and foremost with honor."

"But is it not honorable to give one's oath?" Ean still wished he might persuade Björn to accept his. Whatever part of him had known the bond of this oath before now missed it painfully. He felt as if he stood upon a barren landscape scoured raw by the winds of their forgotten friendship.

"If an oath isn't given to someone else does that make it any less of an oath?" Björn posed in return. "Why must something be said to another before it becomes binding? Should not the force of our own conscience dictate our purpose and be damned if it should matter whether or not another has heard it?"

Ean turned his gaze away in begrudging admission, for there was no disputing this truth.

The First Lord took him by the shoulders. "You have never needed another's approval to act as your conscience dictates, my old friend." He gave Ean a look of soft amusement. "I dare say you needn't start now."

Ean clenched his jaw and nodded tightly.

Björn gave him a look of encouragement. "I will see you again, Ean," he said with a squeeze of the prince's shoulders, "whatever your choice."

"*Rad nath*, First Lord." It was an unexpected response—the phrase had just come to him.

But Björn seemed pleased by the expression. He nodded farewell, and a moment later, Ean found himself standing alone.

The moment reminded him unhappily of a similar parting, the one in his dream, where a battle had raged and good men had died, where he'd carried a blood-drenched Merdanti sword and said goodbye to the First Lord on the broken stones of a shattered dome. He knew that battle had taken place in the Citadel on Tiern'aval, where Arion was thought to have died.

Then, as now, Ean-Arion had been surrounded by friends who would've given their lives for him; but then, as potentially now, it was Ean's life that was forfeit to Fate's whim.

Death's path might be walked by all men, but never more than one man at a time.

Ean felt a strange duality in this recognition, a renewed connection to the person he'd once been. Ever had he walked with an army of the truest friends at his back, and ever had he walked alone.

Björn returned to the room in silence, his expression unreadable, and a few minutes later, Ean arrived. Raine saw sadness and determination both reflected in the prince's gaze.

"I will go after them," Ean announced to the room at large.

"Then you'd best go at once," Ramu advised, "for surprise will be in your favor."

Dagmar agreed. "They won't be anticipating you for another many days—no doubt they expected it would take that long for their ill-begotten missive to find its way to you."

Isabel went over to Ean and kissed his cheek. She murmured something in his ear, and he nodded, but his expression grew even more tormented than before. "Go and prepare," she said quietly. "I will join you soon."

Looking gravely conflicted, Ean glanced to the others by way of farewell and then departed.

When the prince was gone, Raine murmured through a frown, "I should go with him."

Isabel turned him a grateful smile. "And you would serve my true love well," she replied, "but my brother needs you here, Raine."

Your talents will be needed elsewhere, friend of my heart…

Raine couldn't tell if she'd given him the thought or if he'd plucked it from her consciousness—in either case, she'd obviously wanted him to hear it.

"I gather you intend to follow Ean into the fray, dear sister," Björn said drily, but concern clouded his gaze.

She looked back to him. "Unless you have someone more qualified in mind," and she arched one delicate eyebrow in inquiry.

Björn stood and took her by the shoulders. "None," he whispered and kissed her upon the forehead. Then he looked into her blindfolded eyes with a slight furrow between his brows. "So long as you are clear where the line between Isabel and Epiphany's Prophet is drawn, sister of my heart."

"As certain as you are on the boundaries of Balance, dear brother," she returned with a tart little smile.

Björn gave her another kiss and released her.

"Isabel, I confess I'm troubled by what else to divulge to Ean," Ramu admitted as Björn was retaking his chair. "He missed hearing my earlier report of Trell, but I vow he will not well receive the news that his brother and companions both are in dire peril."

"You mean you think he'll try to save them all," Raine amended.

Ramu turned him a telling look that confirmed this had been his thought exactly.

"Trell walks upon his path," Isabel answered Ramu. "It is too soon for his to cross Ean's."

Ramu nodded at this.

"I will go now to help him prepare," Isabel announced. "Might you join us in our departure, Ramu? There is much of your knowledge Ean would benefit from."

The Lord of the Heavens bowed graciously. "I would desire nothing else, my lady."

She nodded gratefully and took her leave.

When Isabel was gone, and all in the room seemed diminished for want of her, the rain started again, rubbing salt in the wound of her departure.

Dämen observed then, "First Lord…I mislike this course of action."

"And I as well, Dämen," the First Lord agreed. He sat slouched in his chair with his chin resting on one hand. "But you must argue with my sister upon the matter. It was clear from the moment of her arrival tonight that their departure was imminent."

The Shade seemed not to take his point, or else to ignore it. "Ean has just been returned to you, *ma dieul*, and yet he now heads into an obvious trap engineered by a wielder in the service of the Prophet Bethamin. What reassurance have we that 'tis not your enemies behind this venture, who even now plot his end?"

"If that is his path, Dämen, he must walk it," Ramu returned bluntly.

"It is his choice to go, Dämen," Björn pointed out more gently. "We are neither his masters nor his jailers—I would that you keep this in mind."

"But a mere word from you would change his mind, *ma dieul*," the Shade urged.

Thunder sounded close, rattling the windowpanes. Raine thought it a fitting accompaniment to the general mood in the room.

Björn shifted in his chair and frowned at his Lord of Shades. "We presented Ean's path to him twice before, Dämen, and you saw where that got us. The more we tried to influence him, the deeper he sank into the rut of past mistakes. Should we allow Ean to forge his own path this time, perhaps he won't be bound by the same pattern of error."

"It is a grave risk you take, First Lord," Dämen grumbled.

"Is it?" Björn glanced to Raine before settling his gaze back upon his Lord of Shades. "Or is it application of the Fifth Law? *A wielder is limited by what he can envision.* If the path is dictated to Ean by another, then he's restricted by their knowledge, foreknowledge, or lack thereof. Yet if we leave the path open before him—not showing him the way, merely giving him a light by which to see," and here Björn's gaze grew bright with possibility, "*then,* left entirely to his own devices, protected by no one, bound to nothing but his conviction...*then,* Dämen, when necessity calls, might Ean make a different choice which would otherwise be against his nature? A *new* choice. One *they* do not expect? Balance, Dämen," Björn concluded with a nod. "It is ever our guide."

He rose and walked to the doors then, and his gaze drew their collective attention to the storm, which raged once more as if it had never broken. "Of all the paths that spread before us," the First Lord observed, clasping hands behind his back, "Ean's pulls him inexorably forth. He is as bound to it as he is to my sister, and she to him." Glancing over his shoulder at the rest of them, Björn admitted, "I have often wondered if theirs was not somehow the same path."

"I have wondered that as well, First Lord," Ramu confessed. He bowed then, and his gaze gave farewell to all as he murmured, "If you will permit me, I shall join them as they depart."

Björn nodded quietly, and the *drachwyr* left them.

"And I must prepare the node," Dagmar observed, adding with a nod of farewell, "Brothers."

As Dagmar was leaving, the Shade bowed deeply, as if burdened by the weight of his contrition. "Your pardon, First Lord, I will depart to my tasks."

Raine wasn't sure exactly what the creature was apologizing for, but Björn seemed to understand. "Influence, not interference, my friend. It is the most we can do."

"*Rad nath, ma dieul,*" intoned the Shade. His form faded until only the memory of it remained.

"And what of your thoughts, brother?" Björn inquired then, turning to Raine.

The Fourth Vestal looked to where his oath-brother stood before the tall windows, framed by the storm raging in the world he made. There was a grave beauty to Björn van Gelderan in any temperament, but especially when he smiled, as he was doing just then.

Still marveling on the unreality of his current existence, Raine shrugged. "Isabel has chosen to go with Ean. Whatever the reasons behind her choice, I trust her decisions." Then he added with a wry smile, "Truly, I think I would rather face down the Malorin'athgul than cross your sister once she's made up her mind about the path she intends to follow."

"Wise, Raine," Björn murmured. He turned to look back out at the storm, still smiling. "Very wise indeed."

FIFTY-SIX

"To him who is determined, it remains only to act."
— Ramuhárikhamáth, Lord of the Heavens

EAN FROWNED INTO the rain. The storm seemed a mirror of his mood, of his very temperament: turbulent and brooding, violent, reckless, haphazardly attacking the world; making up for what it lacked in strategy by the force of its determined effort.

"Come, Ean." Isabel called him away from the window and held up the last of his garments to be donned ere their departure.

He joined her in front of a standing mirror, whereupon she helped him into a heavy suede vest lined in fleece and then fastened on his baldric and belt. Ean realized just how long it had been since he felt the familiar weight of his sword at his hip. He hadn't exactly missed it—he certainly hadn't needed it in T'khendar, only wishing he'd had it a time or two that he might've possibly used it against Markal.

Yet seeing the sword at his side again brought thoughts of the zanthyr, and the recognition that, like Isabel's staff, Phaedor had constructed this sword especially for him.

Looking at the baldric in the mirror, at his father's sigil so vividly embossed in the leather, Ean felt a pang of regret. It seemed a different man's accoutrement suddenly...another man's life.

Isabel settled his navy cloak upon his shoulders and fastened the braided clasp. "There." She smiled up at him. "You look yourself again."

Ean gazed past her to take in his reflection. Cinnamon hair fell across grey eyes, and longer strands framed a lean jaw shaded with scruff. The charcoal clothes he wore were not the garments of a prince, but the blade he carried was. "Do I?" he asked as he stared into his own eyes. "I'm not sure I even know what that means."

"Simple words," she replied with a knowing smile. "You make them too complex."

Ean shook his head. He'd thought that piercing the veil and regaining Arion's memories—even partially—would've restored some sense of self, that he would now become this other person who was bold and defiant and calmly confident of his power. Instead, he felt just as confused as ever about who he really was and what he should do. The only thing that seemed to have grown more certain was his potential to harm those he loved.

"Isabel," he murmured miserably, staring at their combined reflection, which seemed suddenly the only thing that wasn't spinning in a whirlwind of guilt, "how can you know me so completely when I barely know myself?"

"I have the benefit of never having lost my memory, my lord."

He turned to her and took her hand. "You torment me." He closed his eyes and pressed lips to her captured palm. "Today of all days, I cannot bear it."

She let him have her hand. "But do you not know me equally, my lord?" she posed in reply, teasing his tormented gaze with a smile suggestive of all they'd shared. "Did not your soul know mine in the first moment of reunion?"

"Yes," he admitted, because it was true.

"Would you deny our history, the recognition that we feel in each other?"

"No. Never."

She slipped her hand free of his and placed it upon his cheek instead. "You put too much importance on the man that you once were and not enough on the one you are becoming." She gave him a kiss then and slid her fingers beneath his chin as she turned away, inviting him to follow her out of their apartments.

Their things had already been taken in preparation for departure, and now Isabel led Ean to the Nodes. That she accompanied him both comforted and disturbed him, for while he couldn't conceive of walking his path without her, still, he knew he'd be constantly concerned for her safety.

Down the endless hallway, they slipped through a door that looked like all the others and emerged into an open meadow. Judging from the long grass damp with rain, Ean assumed the storm had already passed through this part of the world. Now a moon just shy of full bathed them in alternating shadow, shining intermittently through a clearing sky to illuminate a wide meadow.

Where the Lord of the Heavens awaited.

"Ean," Ramu bowed slightly as they approached, "knowing how you struggle with memory, I would share with you some of my experience in battling wielders of the Fourth Age. If you would hear it."

"I welcome your advice," Ean returned. While he'd regained much with Markal that afternoon, still he knew he had literal ages yet to reclaim of Arion Tavestra's knowledge, and anticipating the conflict to come was making him tense and edgy. He took Isabel's hand in his as the three of them walked through the meadow.

Ramu began, "Always search the currents for patterns before advancing…" and thereafter embarked upon what became a litany of vital cautions. "Keep your thoughts warded at all times. Do not use *elae* when the strength of men will suffice. Never let yourself fall beneath a compulsion pattern. Always keep the lifeforce within your grasp. Stay guarded against the Labyrinth…"

As Ramu rattled off the ever-lengthening list, Ean felt each as a painful echo of his past mistakes.

"I need likely not remind you to never use the fifth when the fourth will suffice," Ramu said as they neared the crest of the hill they'd been climbing, "for when you wage the fifth in combat, you walk the knife-edge of Balance over an abyss from which there is no return." His dark eyes were compelling as he held Ean's gaze. "Make no mistake, Ean—no manner of craft will save you from this abyss, should you falter."

Ean felt this truth too nearly. Instinct said he'd violated it more than once to grave and wretched consequence.

"If you do intend to work the fifth," Isabel noted from Ean's other side, "you must be alert to patterns within patterns, for wielders who cannot work the fifth are ever wary of those who can."

"Just so," Ramu agreed. "Fourth Age wielders especially developed all manner of traps to ensnare a fifth-strand Adept or any wielder who dared attempt to use the fifth in combat."

Ean turned him a puzzled look. "Do we know the wielder who has my men cannot use the fifth?"

"If he could, he no doubt would've used it against Rhakar," Ramu replied, "and their reasonably amicable encounter would've ended differently."

Ean frowned at him. "But if Rhakar already engaged with him, why didn't…" The question hung unspoken, for he realized even in the asking that it would go unanswered. Whatever role the *drachwyr* played in the First Lord's game, it didn't involve saving Ean's friends.

The whole situation reeked of wrongness.

Why were they letting him walk off into an obvious trap? How did they expect him to succeed all by himself? Too well he remembered his promise to hunt down the Shade who he believed had slain Creighton…how he'd threatened to take on the Fifth Vestal all on his own! It was testimony to Raine's forbearance that he hadn't laughed that brash young prince from the room. Yet here now Björn was sending him off to pursue an equally outlandish and uncertain course.

They rounded the hilltop and came in view of two men standing beside a pair of horses, one dark, the other silver-pale in the moonlight. Ean's heart did a little jump upon recognizing the horse's silhouette.

"Caldar?" He released Isabel's hand and jogged across the meadow to greet his proud stallion, who neighed and tossed his head as Ean neared. The prince slipped an arm around the stallion's neck and stroked his nose, murmuring astonished hellos, so overwhelmed to see his treasured horse in such an unlikely place.

Eventually he recalled himself and turned to the two men who were waiting with the horses—Dagmar and Franco Rohre.

"Ean," the Second Vestal said warmly then, "I see you found an old friend."

Ean looked at him in open wonder while he rubbed the stallion's nose. "Is this your work, my lord?" He spared a glance for Isabel, who was coming up beside him, and reached for her hand.

"Sadly, I had little part in this happy reunion—only to bring your mounts from the stables."

Isabel placed her hand on Caldar's nose in silent greeting and observed quietly as she did, "You will surely know the source of Caldar's presence here if you but think upon it, Ean."

Indeed, it was the work of a bare moment to conclude the only possible *who*, though it brought no understanding of *how*. Exhaling a perplexed sigh, Ean shook his head. "He never ceases to bewilder, does he?" He didn't think he would ever understand the depths of Phaedor's foresight.

Isabel blessed him with a smile by way of understanding. Then she gave her attention to Dagmar. "We're ready."

"As are we, my lady. Franco has completed the work. It was good practice before tackling the Sylus node, I dare say, and well done."

Franco grimaced, but he managed a muttered, "Thank you, my lord."

"What work is this?" Ean asked.

"Rerouting a node between the realms," Dagmar said with a broad smile of approval.

Ean arched brows at Franco. "You can do such a thing?"

When Franco merely grimaced again in answer, Dagmar chuckled and clapped the espial on his back, offering on his behalf, "Tis not a task to be undertaken lightly nor by the faint of heart."

"Would that mine had been less stalwart," Franco grumbled. "I might've avoided the assignment altogether."

Isabel turned her blindfolded gaze to the espial. "None have proven more capable or faithful, Franco. Do not doubt yourself so."

"I fear the virus has reached the marrow, my lady," Franco returned grimly. "It's too deep to be killed off now."

She reached a hand to cup his cheek. "There is more than one way to cleanse a man of his malaise," and her enigmatic smile seemed portent and absolution both.

Unsurprisingly, this sentiment did not seem to cheer Franco in the least.

"Well then," said Dagmar with his usual robust humor, "let us proceed."

Saying farewell to Franco and Ramu, Ean and Isabel took their reins in hand, and then Dagmar was ushering them across the node.

They emerged beneath moonlit darkness into a snowbound wilderness of luminous ice. A bracing wind swarmed around them, whereupon Ean became instantly grateful that Isabel had made him bring his heavy cloak and fur-lined gloves. Blinking into the stinging wind, Ean saw a man approaching out of the snow-filled darkness.

Tall and broad of shoulder, his silhouette struck so similar a form to Rinokh's that Ean was at once transported to the fateful night that the Malorin'athgul had invaded their camp. The prince stiffened, but Isabel placed a hand upon his arm, and he realized that of course this could not be Rinokh. Still, the unsettling vision and the painful memories it had evoked did not immediately depart.

"I entrust you to capable hands, my lady." Dagmar nodded towards the approaching man.

Isabel kissed Dagmar's cheek to show her gratitude.

Dagmar smiled at both of them by way of farewell and vanished with a backwards step.

"My lady," came a deep voice, and Ean turned back to find a Sundragon closing in on them.

Up close, with his jet-black hair and slightly rounded nose, he resembled Ramu more than Rinokh, but his features were fiercer than Ramu's, with a heavy brow hooding penetrating yellow eyes. He had the sort of build that lent itself to power over grace, yet he moved as agilely as the zanthyr.

Isabel squeezed Ean's hand. "Ean, may I present Şrivas'rhakárakek, Shadow of the Light."

"My lord," Ean greeted with a slight bow.

Rhakar looked him over with one sweep of his fiery eyes. "You are like your brother," he remarked in a deep voice somehow reminiscent of a waterfall's elemental thunder, "the one I found in the well. The First Lord thinks very highly of that one to have sent us in search."

Ean blinked at him, unsure how to respond to such a greeting.

Isabel squeezed Ean's hand encouragingly. "Rhakar, might you illuminate us with what you've learned in your observations of this mercenary troop?"

"As you wish."

The *drachwyr* motioned them to follow and turned to lead away into the night, back in the direction from which he'd come. "I've been concealing my presence on the currents since following them here," Rhakar advised in his deep rumble. "The better to observe them unnoticed. The Castle of Tyr'kharta is sorely lacking for men considering who they're baiting to their trap—no doubt this young wielder intends a proper army to arrive before week's end."

"*Army?*" the prince croaked.

Rhakar settled him a level look. "I sense dismay in you, Ean val Lorian, but it should be a small task for a ringed wielder to take on a few hundred men."

While Ean was digesting this staggering idea, Isabel noted, "He is a lad, the wielder you followed?"

"By my estimation, not more than twenty and eight."

Ean thought such an age warranted a different appellation than 'lad,' but he conceded when you were thousands of years old, twenty and eight probably seemed a raindrop in the well of time.

"Tyr'kharta is a busy place under the cover of darkness," Rhakar continued. "Whatever it is they are about, they dare it not when common eyes might easily see. I don't think your young wielder is involved in the greater dealings of this place. There have been…altercations, and the second strand currents are awash with activity."

Ean frowned. "You mean—"

"The nodes into the castle are in heavy use," Isabel explained. Then, to Rhakar, she asked, "Have you any other ken of this wielder Ean must face?"

Rhakar turned her a telling look, his yellow eyes fierce. "I have never seen a man so wound through with compulsion, as like a mutineer bechained and cast into Tethys' depths." He shifted his yellow-eyed gaze to Ean. "You will see what I mean when you face him."

"But he cannot work the fifth?" Ean asked.

"Not that he revealed to me—and he's been busy seeing that you won't either. I've not witnessed so many patterns used in warding since before Tiern'aval fell. You're lucky the lady needs no protection and conceals herself well upon the currents, for such patterns as this wielder has conceived would occupy even the mightiest of us. Here now."

They emerged from the forest onto a jutting precipice, where the trees thinned. The wind howled along the cliff, tearing at hair and cloaks and stealing their breath with its bracing chill.

Far aloft in the distant sky, a waxing moon shone down through the crystalline night, illuminating a forested valley blanketed in snow. Low upon the far mountainside, the lights of a sizeable castle glowed, multiple windows winking golden or pale-white behind glass half-frosted over. Along the exterior wall of what was presumably a great hall, arched, stained-glass windows hailed as brilliant gems. They cast colorful shadows onto the wavering black waters of a wide river that hugged the castle's base.

"Tyr'kharta," Rhakar rumbled. "It is garrisoned with Saldarians. Expect some resistance."

Ean thought this a sizeable understatement. Even now he could see dark shapes moving among the castle parapets and other shadows passing beneath the colorful lights bordering the river—guards on regular patrol.

"Do we have any idea where my men are being held?" Ean asked. Then he added heatedly, "Shade and darkness, do we even know if they're *in* there?"

Rhakar observed him steadily, and Ean did not like his intimation as he answered, "You will uncover these truths when you enter, Ean val Lorian."

"Thank you, Rhakar," Isabel said. "You have helped us greatly."

Rhakar nodded as if this was abundantly clear. "Take care with the outermost ward," he remarked. "It lies this side of the river."

"Yes, I see the pattern," Ean murmured. He was in fact already unworking it—it settled his mind to have something to do. "I have it nearly undone…"

His comment drew Rhakar's eye. "Then you have regained Arion's talents," he observed with a measure of new appreciation in his tone. "My brother Náiir and I had wagered upon the matter. I fear Náiir has won the bet."

Ean blinked at him. Could the man really be so callous as to have gambled against the likelihood of his Awakening?

"Delicacy is not one of Rhakar's strong-suits." Isabel laid a gloved hand on Ean's arm. "He meant no insult."

To which the Sundragon looked at Ean as if wondering how anyone could be offended by aught he'd said.

Ean gathered himself and shook his head. "No," he replied, feeling slightly unbalanced in Rhakar's company. "No offense taken."

Rhakar seemed not to care one way or another. "Ramu tells me you must enter alone. Therefore, I bid you fair hunting. Farewell, Lady of the Light, and your shepherd too."

With that, he turned and retreated into the darkness.

"What did he mean by that?" Ean gazed after him with a frown. On the one hand, he was slightly relieved that Rhakar had gone, for the man unsettled him, and yet…he would've liked to have had his aid.

"It is an old name of mine," Isabel meanwhile answered. "The *drachwyr* remain fond of it."

She moved nearer to him then, and Ean drew her close and enfolded her within his cloak. Resting his chin upon her head, he let his gaze drift back to the castle and wondered not for the first time what in Tiern'aval he was doing attacking a fortified stronghold with naught but an intermittent memory as ammunition. Yet Ramu and Rhakar both believed such an endeavor to be a minor task for a trained wielder.

Ean consoled himself that surely Björn must believe this too, else he wouldn't have let him leave, but he couldn't bring himself to trust wholly to such a truth. He knew the Vestal's ideas of Balance too well for the illusion to be entirely convincing.

Before he'd faced Rinokh, Ean had been certain of his own infallibility. Now he feared any mistake would be his last.

"Are you ready for this, Ean?"

"I have to be, don't I?" He was desperately aware of Isabel's closeness, of the lifetimes he'd failed and lost her. He stared at the distant castle, coldly luminous and laden with deadly patterns, and dreaded going there. The whole enterprise felt entirely *wrong*. "It seems my path has ever led into ruin," he murmured.

"It is not the path that destroys you but the choices you make upon it."

Ean exhaled a heavy sigh. "Then let me make no choice that keeps me from your side."

"Epiphany willing, it will be so," Isabel agreed, and she lifted her head and kissed him to seal the prayer.

Thus did they head into battle.

Işak'getirmek paced the length of Tyr'kharta's great hall with shoulders hunched, hands clasped behind his back, and cursing Dore Madden with every breath.

He waited in a state of agitated malcontent, his limbs twitching beneath the compulsion to confront the stranger who was approaching. Işak's first strand pattern had confirmed that a single presence was moving through the night—untimely though his arrival was—and he dreaded that the intruder might actually be Ean val Lorian.

Oh, the irony! Işak understood better now of Dore's corrupt and malicious sense of humor. He'd never quite grasped the undertone of delight Dore had exhibited in setting him to the task of apprehending Dannym's prince, but now that the Lord Captain had confirmed his suspicions, Işak held a grim new understanding of the depths of Dore's depravity.

Along the length of the hall, tall candles burned in iron chandeliers. Their light cast colors through the vaulted stained-glass windows out into the night, but within the vast hall, deep troughs of lingering darkness remained. Işak paced within one such tunnel of shadows.

He'd experienced a momentary lightening in the emptiness of his soul when they'd come to Tyr'kharta and he no longer sensed the Sundragon in pursuit, but the relief was a transient flash, the spark of a dying star as it fell across the sky.

Nothing could truly alleviate the churning devastation that ravaged him. His velvet mask concealed the horror that his features could no longer hide, but his grieving soul bore no such shield. Its gossamer flesh had been laid bare to the sun of searing truth, and the blistered remains bled endlessly.

Işak had learned from Dore that memories could be occluded, buried, hidden beneath veils of the fourth as dense as a vat of pitch. It was a terrible thing to do to a man. Far more brutal, however, was giving him *new* memories to supplant the old, for the two would ever be at war, the man himself split, fractured, ever denying pieces of himself. Even as Işak was now.

He'd thought himself beyond the capacity for tears...that the horrors of N'ghorra, compounded tenfold by Dore's vicious indoctrinations, had bled him dry of grief, but understanding now the enormity of what had been done to him, Işak found that tears

could still come.

The mask hid them the same way it hid his shame, even as it hid a visage he could never again claim with its proper name. Dore had taken everything from him save the will to see the man himself lying in pieces at Işak's feet. He vowed to his charred and bleeding soul that somehow...some way...he would free the world from the scourge that was Dore Madden, even if it meant his own end—praying, in truth, that this is exactly what it would mean.

The first-strand pattern Işak was working resonated again. His quarry neared.

His hands twitched at his sides, guided now by Dore's implanted will, by the patterns that were claiming Işak's body without his consent. The moment was nigh, Dore's clock of compulsion winding down to the fateful hour of reckoning. Işak wondered if he would still be sane when all had been said and done…if indeed he dared profess to sanity even now.

The first-strand pattern vibrated more strongly in his skull. Işak marveled that the man had not yet crossed one of his wards—how could he be so close without hitting them?

Had any of them been tripped or even attacked with *elae*, Işak would've known. He'd spent countless hours meticulously connecting his wards into a vast web, as Dore had taught him to do, so that any attempt to break or alter one ward would set the whole web buzzing. Moreover, to conceal his own activities, Dore had long before cast his own nets about this castle to snare unwanted eyes and turn away their interest. Yes, Dore Madden was hiding much beneath Tyr'kharta's icebound halls, which made it the perfect place to lay a trap for a prince.

Yet it seemed the man came on without disturbing a single ward.

A distant horn sounded—the Saldarians' alarm—which meant the stranger had reached the castle and now battled his way towards Işak.

He cursed heatedly. How could the man have evaded his wards? Had he some skill unknown even to Dore Madden?

Işak had no way of learning what was happening beyond the hall without revealing himself and disrupting his own traps. He growled in fury to be so captive to his own devices.

At least he'd prepared for this contingency. Işak took some consolation in this. The moment the alarm sounded, the Nodefinder Waryn would act—no doubt he'd already done his duty and was now half a world away with Işak's prisoners in tow. If it was Ean val Lorian who approached, he wouldn't find his men waiting for him.

Only Işak.

He spun and stalked back towards the far end of the hall, thinking again through the intricate trap he'd constructed for Ean val Lorian.

When he and the Karakurt had first devised their plan, she'd told him not to underestimate the prince, that whatever else he might be—burgeoning wielder or aught unknown—Ean was either very skilled or uncommonly lucky. The prince had several times eluded or escaped her own assassins, when by all rights he should've died.

They had therefore taken due precaution, layering plans within plans to ensure that whether Ean came wielding great power or extraordinary luck, their leverage would not be lost.

However, Işak had taken steps beyond even this level of planning—for whatever else Dore had done to him, he'd trained Işak to be paranoid, to consider otherwise unforeseen occurrences, the perils of misjudgment, and a wielder's inevitable trickery. So while he fumed at his sudden powerlessness, he yet knew that in the final confrontation, he would prevail. Much to his soul's utter ruin.

Ean stole down the dim stone passageway beneath the Castle of Tyr'kharta, sword in hand. His *elae*-enhanced awareness was moving far in advance of his person, so that he'd already unworked each ward long before he and Isabel reached it.

She walked confidently in his shadow, carrying her Merdanti staff. In her blindfolded state, she saw better in the darkness than he could with naked eyes, and she often warned Ean of approaching guards in time for him to fell or silence them without raising an alarm. Thus did they progress from the moonlit night into a different darkness among twisting passages and cold, dim tunnels.

"Two guards, right passage," Isabel murmured, a bare whisper, and Ean drew up short and pressed back against the cold stones just shy of the intersecting hallway.

The guards' boots fell softly, but Ean was also keen to them in subtle ways, his perception sharpened to a fine point with *elae* infusing his senses. The guards stepped past the prince and noticed his presence too late. He had them just as they began to turn. The first fell without ever drawing his sword, the second but a heartbeat later.

Isabel knelt and placed a hand on the first one's face, finding the truthreader's hold. Three breaths, and she moved to the second man. Frowning then, she sat back on her heels. "A foul craft pervades this place,

Ean. These men know nothing about your friends and too much about a host of tortured others."

Ean felt a controlled fury filtering from Isabel across the bond. He had never seen her display aught but compassion, and the power roused in the wake of her anger startled him.

"The patterns of warding are inconsistent," he said by way of mutual discord. His own unease over the entire endeavor grew ever more potent. "Layered…as if worked at different times by different men."

Isabel rose. "Lead us on, my lord," she said, but her tone had become as steel.

They moved off down the passage again, but Ean couldn't regain his focus. Instinct told him something was very wrong. He gazed into a corridor of shadows trying to discern one from the next.

"Ean," Isabel warned in a low voice. Then: "*Ean!*"

Too late he heard her. He stepped into a pinwheel chamber of intersecting hallways, and Saldarians flooded in.

Ean swung his sword to block the advance of a giant cornstalk of a man. Their blades met and scraped, but Ean dodged and spun, and the man fell back in blood. Two others came on to take his place, and more men were arriving still. Ean was too conscious of Isabel in harm's way, and as a third troop came in from the left and Ean swung furiously to deflect a host of blades, he cursed his single moment of unawareness. He was so immediately outnumbered that he reached in desperation for the fifth—

Then Isabel was at his side, spinning her Merdanti staff. Two men fell to left and right while Ean fended off the blades of three others. A fourth cried out from behind him as Isabel sent him flying into a wall, where he collapsed. Two others immediately joined him in motionless silence.

Ean spared a startled glance for her, narrowly dodging a blade in the doing. In that moment, he saw her send a man spinning with one end of her staff and then strike another across the back. Ean recognized the *cortata* in her movements and cursed himself for not calling upon it sooner.

He amended this error at once.

The *cortata* brought clarity and a renewed and revitalized awareness. He worked meticulously through the mass of Saldarians then. When at last Ean lowered his dripping blade, two-dozen men lay at his feet. Some sprawled unconscious, many labored with their final breaths. But there had been others who'd gotten away.

Breathing hard, Ean looked to Isabel. She was kneeling beside one of the fallen with her hand across his face, reading him before he passed. Ean couldn't recall if he'd known that she could work the fourth strand as easily as she worked the first and second. No wonder Rhakar and Ramu hadn't feared for them in this action. It wasn't one wielder storming the castle. It was two.

Isabel's lips pursed in a thin line. She rose and settled her staff two-handed before her toes.

Ean frowned at her stance. "What is it?"

Just then a distant horn sounded.

Isabel turned her blindfolded gaze to Ean. "Go. Find him."

Ean felt an immediate and extreme protest at the idea of leaving her side.

"We cannot do what must be done here if we stay together," she reasoned, knowing too well his mind. "You feel it too, Ean—the pervasive sense of wrongness in this place. It is the call of Balance seeking to be righted."

Ean made to protest, but she pushed three fingers across his lips. "Cephrael calls you to arms, my love. Can you not hear his war cry?"

As much as he wanted to argue with her, he knew she guided him true. That throbbing *wrongness* had been accosting him ever since he set foot upon this path. But if he failed in whatever was to come... Conflict raged across his features.

"Love of my heart," Isabel murmured, just as the horn of alarm blew again, "you know the way." She took up her staff and spun it before her as if readying to strike *him* if he did not leave at once.

Ean rather imagined she would do it, too. He gave her one last look and ran.

As Ean's running steps faded, Isabel walked among the bodies at her feet. The long hem of her dress brushed the limbs of the dead as if paying final respects, the echo of a sweeping evergreen bough as conducted in the ancient and sacred Rite for the Departed.

Elae fueled Isabel's vision, revealing a shimmering world of iridescence.

She saw men illuminated not by light but by the varied, pastel-hued strands of the first strand. The otherwise dim hallways appeared to her in a golden sheen, the sputtering lamps glowing luminous as the moon. Only the men at her feet were diminished, some by the blackness of their souls, others by death's encroaching shadow.

Stepping carefully among the fallen, Isabel came upon one whose life-pattern still shone brightly. Here was a man who could be saved—the threads of his life rewoven to serve a higher purpose.

Kneeling at his side, Isabel placed her palm to his chest in the Healer's way. *Elae* surged through her and into him, channeling along his life-pattern in obeisance of her will.

A moment later, his eyes flew open and he gasped, "My lady!"

"Dorn," Isabel murmured. "We have work to do." She extended her hand to help him to his feet, and they set off together.

The prince rushed through Tyr'kharta's upper levels towards the wielder he sensed waiting. He had the man in his sights now, even as he suspected the other likely had him. The man's life signature appeared as a strangely wavering image among the first-strand pattern Ean was working, a ghostly apparition barely glimpsed, a seeming mirage.

Ean understood now what Rhakar had meant when he'd first spoken of the wielder; for the fourth strand of *elae* bound the man so completely that Ean could barely see *him* at all. Yet there was no missing his presence on the currents—*elae* snarled and eddied around him so that he stood out like a beacon.

The prince kept the *cortata* close now. He spun into and out of its pattern each time he met, clashed with and ultimately dispatched those unfortunate enough to cross his path. He cast his awareness ahead and around him, and set patterns to unraveling far in advance of his coming, so that they were falling apart as cobwebs as he passed.

And he realized that he'd done this before—that he'd many times progressed through an enemy's stronghold in just this manner. The more he allowed Arion's knowledge to emerge, the wider the trench of its path to restoration, the faster the flow of memory. It was *doing* that restored his knowledge, *need* that brought it forth, and working the patterns themselves that gave Ean certainty.

By the time he reached the tall double doors leading into Tyr'kharta's grand hall, Ean no longer had to think about what he was doing. He had regained his wielder's instincts.

The prince slowed before the vaulted doors and scanned for patterns, his senses on full alert. This was where his talent boosted him far beyond the skill of other wielders, for while they had to rely on the currents to hint at what lay in wait, Ean could see the patterns hovering in the aether as clearly as a Nodefinder would gaze upon the nodes.

Ean unworked the three wards he found upon the doors, and while these were dispersing, he cast his awareness beyond them, into the hall. Patterns layered throughout it, lying thick as cobwebs in a cave. This much he could tell.

As he stood facing the tall doors, with the still-unraveling patterns swirling around him, the prince suddenly felt himself transported to a different hall where fires raged, where the First Lord went to confront a band of deserters and Ean/Arion stood to battle a traitor of a different color, and—

Ean realized that he'd done *this* before, too...this study of his enemy from beyond closed doors, studying his pattern to better know his opponent. He recalled something else as well:

Arion Tavestra did not die on Tiern'aval.

Stunned to know it, yet *knowing* it completely, Ean felt his mouth go dry.

Yet if I didn't die on Tiern'aval, then where?

Before he could spend any more time pondering the mystery, the last of the wards on the doors dissolved, and necessity forced Ean to concentrate on the moment.

He pushed through the doors and entered a vast vaulted hall, dimly lit by high chandeliers. Now he could see the patterns spider-webbing the chamber, heavy iron traps for the wolf who walked the powerful strands of the fourth and fifth. There were smaller snares for rabbits of the first and foxes of the second. Even patterns of the third strand would be caught by a broad net set to plunge down upon any wielder who dared cause the slightest tremble in the net's gossamer strands. As Rhakar had warned, Tyr'kharta's wielder had been busy.

Ean wondered if the man had somehow protected himself from these many snares, or if he truly intended to meet only in hand to hand combat—for Raine's truth, neither of them could wield the lifeforce with so many patterns in place.

In either event, the prince knew the man would be unprepared for him. Walking further within, he plucked at the closest isolated pattern as if at a harp string and started it unraveling.

"Ean val Lorian…" the voice floated to him from out of a void of darkness, from the deep shadows that collected in pools down the length of the chamber and beneath the wall of high, stained-glass windows. "The Lord Captain assured me you would come. I must admit some disappointment to find you possessed of such foolish notions of nobility."

That voice!

It had to be illusion. Ean moved into the chamber, remaining deeply sensitive to the patterns fluttering in his wake. He treated them as fragile moths and was careful not to disturb their integrity by working *elae*, for though beautiful in their intricate construction, each was poison to the touch.

"Who are you?" Ean kept the *cortata* hovering close within his consciousness. "Show yourself."

The man moved from the shadows into a circle of light. Tall and broad of shoulder and with dark hair, he stood similar to Ean in height and build; but unlike the prince, he moved with a slight limp, and a velvet mask concealed his face.

Something in the man's motions unnerved Ean. He lifted his blade and held it warily. "Who are you? Do I know you?"

"Call me Işak." He moved further into the light. "You're very like your brother with these grand notions of honor. I recently encountered the illustrious Trell val Lorian, back from the dead, as it were. That is, before he was taken to M'Nador to face Radov's wrath for not having the decency to die the first time—*Oh*…you didn't know." Işak smiled at the look of shock on Ean's face. "Yes, your dear brother was first among the men I captured."

For all the shock of this pronouncement, Ean barely registered what the man was saying, for his *voice*… He knew it must be some kind of illusion, yet if so, it had been extraordinarily well crafted.

He cast his awareness towards the patterns floating around the room, searching for any that would hold such a deceptive illusion in place, but found none.

Returning his attention to the wielder's life-pattern then—barely discernable beneath a mass of corrupted, intertwining patterns of the fourth—Ean perceived something of the man himself that awakened strange feelings.

What's happening here?

Forced himself to focus, the prince chose an isolated fourth-strand ward and started it unraveling. It would give his mind something to do beyond worrying over perceptions that made no sense.

Işak meanwhile stopped in the center of the circle of light and drew forth a black-bladed weapon. "Merdanti...yes," he observed, noting the prince's gaze on the blade. "It appears that yours is not. Pity." He toyed with his sword in a display of skill. "I had hoped for a fair battle. The captain said you could hold your own with a blade."

Ean stared at him oddly, at the practiced pattern of loops and spins he was making with his weapon. It, too, was familiar to him. He tried to shake the feeling of kismet that held him inexplicably in thrall, but he felt as if he stood suddenly on a threshold...*nay*, on a precipice, from which myriad branching paths extended. Ean desperately wished he could understand how the man was working these illusions, and why he felt such odd feelings of fate and connection to him.

Focus, damn you!

Ean pointed his blade at Işak. "There can be no fair match between us."

Işak stilled his sword at this reply. "That's true." His tone revealed a well of bitter torment. "For how can anything be fair when all have named you and forgotten?"

Chills striped Ean. Such words...in *that* voice...

But...can it be possible?

Abruptly Ean started forward, intent now upon reaching the man, upon seeing his unmasked face and looking into his eyes. Now he cared not if he disturbed Işak's patterns. Rather he mentally leapt for all he could reach and started them rapidly unraveling, an outlet for the riotous energy that was suddenly thrumming through him.

Işak grew agitated. "Stay back!" He threatened Ean with his blade extended. "Stop or *face your death, Ean!*"

Such fervent desperation filled this last exclamation that Ean came to a standstill.

He'd halted just beyond the circle of light, while the dissolving energy of countless patterns showered down over him. Wondering what in thirteen hells was happening to him, Ean exhaled and murmured, "If that is so, then let us face death together."

He rushed into the light.

Işak uttered a growl of reproach and sprang to meet him. Their blades clashed, sparked and then separated roughly as each man pushed off the other. Ean's blade sang as true as any black-bladed Merdanti weapon, and with his mind wrapped around it, he knew the thrill of rapport with a sentient blade. He spared a second to marvel that even a world away, Phaedor was still protecting him.

Işak came at Ean again with his sword sweeping up from the left. Ean parried with a downward blow, and the subsequent clanging and scraping of their blades formed a rapid percussion. Ean drew upon the *cortata*; yet he recognized at once that Işak also followed its dance, and as their fierce interplay continued, Ean noted that they were well matched.

What Işak's limp lost him in coordination, he made up for in sheer strength, while Ean's agility and alacrity with the lifeforce kept him apace. But most surprising was that their fighting styles were nearly identical— almost as if they'd shared the same swordmaster—and it was nigh impossible for one to get the upper hand over the other.

The fight might've continued for hours, with both of them using *elae* to fuel their blades, but Ean grew ever more disturbed. His instincts veritably shouted the wrongness of this course.

Finally, he spun out of the *cortata*, out and away from Işak, trying desperately to make sense of what he was experiencing. They stalked one another then with chests heaving, their steps tracing the outer circle of light.

To buy himself time to interpret the perceptions bombarding him, Ean posed, "My men. Release them, and I will spare your life."

Işak laughed, but there was only despair in it. "By now your men are kingdoms away—did you think us so foolish as to keep them here?"

Again the voice—it tormented him so! Ean tried to clear his mind of the man's impossible voice, which was proving every bit as effective at incapacitating him as any pattern of the fourth. Worse was the feeling of misdoing that bit and clung like a viper's fangs, staying his hand when he should've been free to slay, to wreak vengeance.

Instead, he found himself divided between his duty to his loyal soldiers and a desperate need to confirm his suspicions of the identity of the man standing before him.

Suddenly Işak hissed a foul curse. His gaze darted around the hall, and Ean watched him grow more agitated still, the muscles in his arms and neck twitching.

"*Ah Cephrael, no!*" Işak had finally realized that his patterns were disappearing. He pinned the prince with a frantic look, eyes wild behind his mask. "*Shade and darkness,* don't you see what you've *done?*"

His words and tone perplexed Ean. The man sounded horrified where anger should've ruled. Yet he'd been right in noting that the only patterns that remained in the room were those seeking use of the fifth. Ean knew better than to risk touching them even in unworking—for he was an Adept of that elusive strand, and it was too likely that they would trigger at the merest whisper of his mental touch.

"You damn fool—*fool man!*" Işak turned frantically around as Ean watched the last of the other wielder's patterns dissolving away. "Those traps were all that protected you from me—"

Suddenly Işak staggered, as if beneath a powerful force. He seemed to haltingly recover, shook his head from side to side, and then—

Compulsion pounced upon Ean.

He'd fallen to one knee before he even realized that the pattern had hold of his mind, and it was a harrowing length more before he concluded that his body was not actually on fire.

Never was he so grateful for Markal's brutal training than in that moment, as he watched the masked wielder coming ominously towards him across the circle of light. Still, ripping the pattern off of his mind felt like he was ripping out his own heart. Ean stared into the blazing inferno that was the compulsion pattern, risking its searing heat and blinding light both, and though the pattern told him he was already burning, already dying, still he wrapped a mental hand around it. Pain flared through his entire body as the pattern surged to engulf his mind, and Ean cried out.

Then he squeezed. Squeezed until the pattern bled *elae* through his mental fingers, until the flames dimmed…and were extinguished.

Just as Işak reached him with his sword raised for a killing blow.

Ean launched up under Işak's guard and grabbed his descending wrist with one hand. With the other, he ripped off Işak's mask.

The face that stared at him could not have been more horror-stricken than Ean's own.

The prince fell back, staggered by the sight.

Işak roared in outrage. He swung his Merdanti blade, aiming for Ean's neck. The prince dove, rolled, scrambled for his sword—and simultaneously called the fourth to form a wall between them.

A band of energy rocketed upwards and blasted Işak backwards through the air. He landed in a skid, and his sword clattered away into the shadows.

Shaken by the encounter, Ean pushed slowly to his feet. It wasn't for his own safety that he'd raised the shield. There was a terrible truth lurking in that room, and he would brook its concealment no longer.

Holding his blade low, Ean approached the shimmering barrier. His eyes were glued to the man lying just beyond it—how could they not be?

"It *is* you, isn't it?" Looking upon Işak's face felt impossibly painful.

Işak pushed to his hands and knees, looking dazed.

Ean made the shield move before him and advanced towards Işak. His entire focus had shifted. He was no longer there to seek vengeance upon a kidnapper; he wondered now if he ever truly had been.

"*Dear Epiphany.*" Ean pinned Işak with his gaze. "*Sebastian?* Where have you been all this time?"

Işak choked back a despairing cry. He hung his head, and his voice was hoarse with grief as he answered, "N'ghorra."

But he gave Ean no time to compute this dreadful truth, for in the same moment he launched to his feet and flung a pattern of the fourth towards Ean's barrier. The blast exploded in a blaze of sizzling light.

Ean struggled to keep his shield in place. "*N'ghorra,*" he nearly choked over the horrific word. "They did *this* to you there?"

Işak lifted his gaze to meet Ean's and the prince saw both fury and desolation there. Then Işak threw a barrage of raw power towards Ean, the harvested energy of the fourth.

The prince altered his pattern to absorb it. The forceful reverberation of his own working cast Işak stumbling, and Ean watched him trip over his debilitated leg and fall.

"*Sebastian...*" Ean pressed forward with pity and fury both infusing his tone. "*Who* did this to you?"

"Stop calling me that!" Işak snarled. He fled into the shadows, dragging his bad leg.

Ean rushed after him. "Let me *help* you!"

He chased Işak down a wedge of darkness between a row of columns and the tall, stained-glass windows. He could hear the man moving ahead of him, possibly heading for the doors. Only then did Ean notice the shouting of men from elsewhere in the castle.

Instinctively, he cast an illusion before the doors, so that any who approached might believe them locked. Finishing this, he scanned the darkness for Işak and—

The man crashed into him from behind, taking him down with a painful crushing of shoulder and hip again immutable stone.

They struggled, with Sebastian grappling for Ean's sword and he in turn trying not to injure the other man—for Raine's truth, he'd clearly been harmed enough already. But their tactile contact gave Ean what he'd been wanting all along—a clear view of Sebastian's life pattern.

Ean dove deeply into Sebastian's mind and saw the hundreds of spiny tendrils sunken into his mental flesh, saw how they speared and stabbed and bled him mercilessly; how they held him captive to another's will. He saw, too, that many of these patterns were bound with the fifth, which brought a devastating understanding.

But those patterns that weren't so bound... Ean didn't bother trying to discern what they were doing—it was enough to know they were malicious and parasitic and Sebastian was their innocent host. It was like digging for the man in a pit of quicksand, where the vile stuff was already far above his head, but Ean grabbed a mental handful of patterns and ripped them out like weeds, casting them forth into unraveling.

Işak cried out and rolled off of Ean. He snatched up his dropped sword as he staggered to his feet and backed away, blade extended in a shaking hand. His eyes were wild, and his head jerked sporadically, alarmingly, not unlike a maddened animal.

Overcome by the terrible understanding he now held, Ean also got to his feet. He held his blade at his side and looked Sebastian in the eye. "I will not fight you."

"Then you are a fool." Sebastian's eyes bore into Ean's while the ropy muscles of his neck twitched and jerked. "I am bound to my course. You cannot stop it."

"We don't know that." Surely there was providence in his coming here, in this meeting. It couldn't be by chance. "Even now you *must* sense something of what I've just done to help you." Ean tried not to despair at having been able to do so little. "Do you remember nothing of me? *By Cephrael's Great Book*, Sebastian—"

"Don't you see it doesn't matter, Ean?" Sebastian very nearly wept. "I am *bound* to him with the *fifth*!"

"But I can *help* you—"

"THERE IS NO HELP FOR ME!" Sebastian launched at Ean with his sword held high.

The prince met him blade to blade, and the match again drew out the best in both of them—but Ean wouldn't risk harming Sebastian. He called up another pattern of the fourth, this time layered with Form—a difficult and artful working to accomplish with the vast, formless energy of that strand while also engaged in battle.

When he had it ready, Ean threw himself roughly back, and a shimmering veil speared up to enclose Sebastian in a ring of power.

The wielder spun furiously around, trapped by the crackling energy. He tried a desperate counterattack, but Ean saw the pattern in his mind before he even had it fully formed, and he ripped it out of his consciousness.

Sebastian shouted a slew of curses then, vituperative and fierce.

Ean approached the barrier. He lifted one hand in entreaty, his gaze pleading. He had to make Sebastian somehow see what he knew already to be true—that theirs was not a chance encounter, that this reunion must serve some purpose, even should that purpose be the undoing of too many years of violent injustice.

"Can we not talk?"

Sebastian hung his head, but his shoulders and arms still twitched as violently as if lightning was trapped within his flesh. "If I cannot compel you," he ground out through gritted teeth, "I *must* kill you." He raised his gaze to meet Ean's, and his eyes were vivid with pain. "This too is bound with the fifth."

Then he released his pattern.

He'd hidden it well that time—Ean hadn't sensed him forming it at all. A volcanic force seared through Ean's shield and thrust him staggering backwards.

The prince threw up a desperate pattern to protect himself as the working roared like a hurricane through the great hall. The massive doors burst in a splintering staccato, the chandeliers ripped from the ceiling, and the hall went dark just before the iron rings crashed resoundingly on the floor.

And still the eruption raged.

The roof strained and whined. Then, with a groan of protesting metal, the stained-glass windows shattered. Ean made his shield more solid and threw himself behind a column just before razor shards of glass exploded in every direction.

As the deadly shower quieted, the prince cast his awareness desperately forth, but save for the patterns that yet hung in place seeking whispers of the fifth, the room stood empty.

Ean got to his feet and looked grimly around, his lips set in a thin line. For all the devastation around him, he knew that the ferocity of that *elae*-storm had been but a whisper of wind compared to the patterns that held Sebastian's mind in thrall.

Ean walked to the twisted frame of one of the shattered windows and stared out. Beyond, lay the luminous night and the river, its dark waters lurking twenty feet below.

A commotion from the near passage drew Ean's sudden gaze, and he turned to see four men rushing through the splintered doors. They each held a torch in one hand and a sword in the other, and Isabel walked between them. "Stay here and guard us," she told them. The men promptly turned shoulder to shoulder before the doors.

Isabel's Merdanti staff tapped a quiet cadence to her steps as she approached. "Your men are gone, Ean. It appears that a Nodefinder took them away when first the horns blew in warning." She halted at his side and seemed to consider him, whereupon the slightest furrow creased her fair brow. "But this, I do not think, is what troubles you."

Ean turned and pinned a tormented gaze back upon the shadow he'd been watching cross the river. He could just make out the shining end of an oar as it lifted and dove into the mercuric waters.

"I have to go after him, Isabel." Ean swallowed back powerful emotions and turned her an agonized look. "I won't let him suffer like this—I won't see such unforgivable use of *elae*!" He shook his head in desperate fury, his gaze haunted by what he'd witnessed, what he now knew. "Whoever I once was, this is the man I am now."

She placed a consoling hand upon his arm, and he covered it roughly with his own, gripping her fingers even as grief gripped his soul.

"I have to go after him, Isabel," Ean said again, looking back to where the shadowed form now climbed the far riverbank. "He's my brother."

EPILOGUE

WHEN HE LATER looked back upon them, Tanis found his early days of travel with the zanthyr to be something of a blur. Phaedor was taking them deep into a high mountain range that Tanis didn't recognize, and the zanthyr spoke neither about their whereabouts nor their ultimate destination.

Still, Tanis had never felt such happiness as he felt traveling in Phaedor's company. Within his protective shadow, the lad knew sure safety. It didn't matter where they were going, for Tanis would follow the zanthyr anywhere. Only his curiosity suffered.

As they traveled, the zanthyr told him somewhat of their companions—of Prince Ean's waking and the battle at the Temple of the Vestals, and of Her Grace returning from a near fatal kidnapping with the seemingly resurrected Prince Trell in tow—which incredible fortune Tanis would have disputed outright if it had been anyone other than Phaedor telling him.

But beyond speaking of these things that had come to pass while Tanis traveled with Pelas, the zanthyr kept silent. Tanis's days with Pelas had been full of discussion. Now he had long hours amid vast snowy reaches to dwell within his own thoughts.

In these times of lengthening silence, where the patient trod of their horses' hooves marked the ticking of the minutes and hours, Tanis couldn't stop thinking about Pelas...except when he couldn't help wondering about his mother. Thoughts of Pelas came with feelings of regret and loss and an immense worry over whether he'd done the right thing in leaving him. Never mind that Pelas was an eternal creature thousands of years old and surely could make it through life on his own. The lad knew Pelas yet needed him, and it pained him that he'd abandoned him so.

On a brighter side, when he wasn't fretting over Pelas, Tanis pondered the mystery of his mother with fascination. He spent many hours huddled in his fur-lined cloak—a gift from the zanthyr—wondering who she was, *where* she was, if she lived, and whether they would ever meet again. Then there were the questions of why she'd sent him away, whether he was really Agasi by birth, and why he'd been taken to the Lady Melisande to raise. So many, many questions. So many possibilities.

Until Phaedor had told him of the promise he'd made to his mother to protect him, Tanis had barely conceived of her as real. The only bit of memory he had of her was the vision Alain had helped him find so long ago in Chalons-en-Les Trois. Accordingly, she'd felt more dream than substance to the lad. But suddenly now his mother was a woman to whom the zanthyr had sworn a sacred oath—suddenly his mother was flesh and blood, and fifteen years worth of questions Tanis never knew he'd held had simply appeared, demanding explanation.

The lad knew the zanthyr well enough to understand that getting answers out of him was a game of chance. If the dice rolled in his favor—that is, if the stars were somehow correctly aligned and Fortune turned a favorable eye and the wind had the right flavor or something equally indefinable and ridiculous—then Phaedor might deign to answer a question more serious than what they'd be eating for dinner. But the likelihood of all of these unknown mystical factors somehow occurring in the exact moment that Tanis decided to ask a question was like expecting the sun to set amid the same striated curtain of clouds each night.

Still, he was too young and optimistic not to try.

The sun had barely risen on their second day together when Tanis broached the subject. "My lord," he said as they rode along a frostbitten path through stony foothills coated in rime and with the snowy peaks of the great mountain chain looming ahead of them, "will you tell me of my mother?"

The wind lifted and tossed Phaedor's raven curls as he sat upon his black stallion, spinning them into wild designs. He glanced over at Tanis wearing an endlessly unreadable expression—and to the lad in that moment, all the world seemed to turn around the zanthyr. Tanis remained ever in awe of this utterly mysterious and magical creature; no one made so indelible an impression or was so seemingly immutable as Phaedor.

Just when Tanis thought his question would fall into the zanthyr's Cavern of the Eternally Unanswered, Phaedor inquired in his deep purr-growl, "What would you know of her, lad?" His voice rumbled into the frigid morning like the resonant baritone of a mountain cave greeting the frost-bound meadow.

Tanis brightened with sudden excitement. "Well...everything!"

Phaedor grunted and turned back to face the path ahead. "Such would take a lifetime," his breath clouded in the frosty air, "and still I couldn't do her justice in the telling."

Tanis worked hard to quell his eagerness, or at least to knead it into something slightly less uncontainable that he might pose an intelligent question before the zanthyr lost interest or otherwise peremptorily ended the discussion. "Is she...I mean is she..." He wetted his lips and tried again. "What I meant to ask is..." The question lay right there, yet the lad found to his dismay that he couldn't utter the words.

Phaedor turned him a look of understanding, though regret also threaded within it. "She lives, lad."

Tanis exhaled a great explosion of relief—only realizing in that moment that he'd been holding his breath. He gave the zanthyr a painfully naked look of hope. "And my..." He had to clear a sudden frog in his throat. "My, um...father?"

The faintest hint of a shadow crossed the zanthyr's face. "Your father is...not as you remember him."

"I don't remember him at all." Only Tanis's mother stood out clearly in his mind—her large, colorless eyes, so like his own; her beautiful smile and voice so full of love for him.

Phaedor grunted and looked back to the trail. "That is well, then."

Tanis gave him a long look, wondering at the duality of meaning within his words. Never a moment passed when Phaedor said something that didn't also mean something else entirely—he spoke almost exclusively in ambiguities that held multiple meanings. "Do we go to see them now, my lord?" Tanis couldn't quite conceal the hope in his tone.

"We walk upon your path, lad," the zanthyr replied, which didn't seem an answer at all—at least not to the question Tanis had been asking.

The lad shifted his gaze to the jagged mountains rearing before them and thought his path was leading to places indecently cold. "Do you know when I will see my parents again, my lord?" he asked as he stared uncertainly at the razor-sharp peaks.

"You speak as if I see the future, truthreader."

"Only one part of it."

The zanthyr arched a raven brow. "And you imagine somehow that I do?"

"I know that you do," Tanis returned, giving the zanthyr a hard look. "I just don't know how much of it you see."

The zanthyr turned forward again, but the shadow of a smile hinted upon his lips. "So it seems I'm a Seer now, too," he observed in veiled amusement. "Fascinating, the number of human attributes you ascribe to me."

"More like preternatural," Tanis muttered, to which the zanthyr really grinned.

It was evident Phaedor wasn't going to expound on this topic, however, so Tanis posed a different question—it wasn't as if he didn't have a hundred of them already lined up. "Why did you bind yourself to me, my lord?"

It was such an astonishing truth the zanthyr had spouted off so nonchalantly to Pelas—he might've been merely commenting on his appetite or the length of his hair.

"The answer should be obvious to anyone with the least knowledge of binding."

"Apparently I've less than the least knowledge of it," Tanis returned with a shrug. He gave the zanthyr a tart grin.

Phaedor pinned him with a dark eye, beneath which Tanis felt his bravado measurably withering. After a long, uncomfortable moment of this inspection, wherein all semblance of Tanis's impudence scurried for cover, the zanthyr finally replied gravely, "For your protection, lad."

Each word landed heavily upon the boy, such that their significance claimed a stronghold within his thoughts. But four words, yet Tanis felt battered by the enormity of their meaning.

He thought of his immunity to both Bethamin's Fire and Pelas's dark power and gulped a swallow. Could Phaedor's binding be the source of this immunity? He knew nothing of the theory of bindings, but he'd heard enough stories of them to know that such feats were possible.

He'd gained the truth, yet not without cost. The zanthyr misliked answering questions, and he had a knack for making Tanis feel horribly unworthy whenever the lad managed to force an answer out of him. Exactly as had happened just then. Tanis dropped his gaze and stared at his reins. "I'm sorry."

Phaedor gave him a tolerant look by way of absolution.

"But you would have me making assumptions!" Tanis blurted as an afterthought. It was a feeble attempt to justify his requiring a truth from Phaedor that, in retrospect, he might not have been ready to know. It didn't help him feel any better about having done it, but now the zanthyr was expecting him to make a point, so he looked back to him and muttered, "Assuming things isn't such a good habit, you know. Assumptions are rarely accurate."

"Instincts, however, often are."

Tanis thought of all the strange choices he'd made lately and wasn't so sure his instincts had been at all trustworthy. He asked, perhaps a bit more belligerently than he intended, "Why can't you tell me more of my parents?"

"All knowledge must be gained in its proper time and place, lad." Phaedor gave him a tolerant look. "Balance often hinges on a natural progression of events, on knowledge gained in its proper order and circumstance." Tanis must've looked immensely dissatisfied with this answer, for the zanthyr chuckled. "Your questions are not unanticipated, Tanis. I would answer more of them if I dared."

"Would you?" the boy challenged. He'd heard the underlying truth of that statement, and it didn't exactly match what the zanthyr had said. Not that what he'd said was untrue. This was the problem with asking questions of the zanthyr.

In answer to the lad's challenge, Phaedor flashed a wide grin, exposing the tiny fang teeth in the corners of his mouth. The sharp smile was a reminder to Tanis that for all his seeming omnipotence, for all his apparent adherence to the laws of Balance, the zanthyr was still a feral creature— fierce, and wildly unpredictable.

"That's what I thought," Tanis grumbled.

The zanthyr shrugged unapologetically. "To live within the swirling mists of mystery is ingrained in my kind, Tanis. We cannot but follow our nature."

"Maybe," the boy answered, casting him a dubious look, "but that doesn't mean you don't enjoy tormenting the rest of us with one of your more insufferable attributes."

The zanthyr flipped his raven hair from his eyes and cast the boy a sidelong glance, his sparkling emerald gaze full of amusement but also infused with endless wisdom. He ended that day's discussion with the admonition, "There are few mysteries left to the ancient races, Tanis. Would that humanity better understood their value."

Over the next few days, the zanthyr led Tanis deep into the mountains. They rode hard during the daylight hours and slept harder each frosty night, warm within the violet folds of a small but richly constructed tent that the zanthyr would set up just before sundown. They spared little time for talk during those days, for they traveled upon perilously thin trails whose crumbling edges showered pebbles into vast canyons of cloud-mist, their walls hugged tightly by firs permanently bound in ice. Too, the zanthyr never was much for idle conversation, even had they not been covering such treacherous terrain.

But despite his yearning for answers, Tanis was heartened, for the knowledge that his parents lived now blazed within his heart. It warmed him as much as the fur-lined cloak the zanthyr had given him.

The lad thought long on the things Phaedor had told him, and especially on the zanthyr's comment on the value of mystery, but Tanis couldn't quite find it in himself to appreciate the concept as Phaedor did. He had too many burning questions that seemed to fair singe him from the inside out. Thus, Tanis persisted in his questions at every opportunity, for not asking them at all felt worse than being told nothing in reply.

So it was that they were camped one frosty evening on the edge of a swift-rushing stream banked in snow, eating a dinner of fresh-speared trout fried to a crisp, when Tanis asked the zanthyr, "My lord?"

Phaedor looked up beneath the spill of his raven hair to spy Tanis juggling a piping hot piece of fish between two hands and blowing gingerly on his fingers in between. He stifled a smile. "Yes, Tanis?"

The lad popped the fish into his mouth, sucked in a cooling breath around the steaming flesh, and finally mumbled while chewing, "My lord, why did you enchant the dagger you gave me? And don't say it's an obvious question," he hastened to add, angling a look at the zanthyr with his bright, colorless eyes, "because I don't expect an obvious answer, so therefore it can't be an obvious question."

The zanthyr gave him a skeptical look. The near firelight played across his statuesque features and heightened the mysterious quality of his emerald gaze.

"It's just..." Tanis screwed up his face as he tried to think of how to better phrase his question. He settled both elbows on his knees. "What I mean is, did you give me the dagger because you knew I would be needing a dagger that would keep returning to me? But no," he answered for himself, frowning at the flames, "you'd have needed to know ahead of time that I would get into trouble, unless—oh, wait...did you maybe enchant it somehow after the fact, after you knew I was with Pelas? Actually—wait... *did* you know I was with Pelas?"

"Are we still talking about the dagger?"

Tanis gave him a flinty look. "How much *did* you know beforehand, my lord?"

Phaedor leaned on one elbow and extended long legs to the flames. "I knew that boys are wont to lose things." He balanced the razor-sharp point of another of his daggers on the end of his fingertip and glanced at Tanis over the hilt. "And a dagger that returns despite a lad's best efforts to misplace it is something any earnest boy of good intent should have."

Tanis was unsurprisingly dissatisfied with this reply. He'd long noticed that the zanthyr was very good at making you think he'd answered your question when he really hadn't answered it at all.

"Are you upset that I gave the dagger to Pelas, my lord?"

"It was yours to do with as you would, Tanis."

"Except lose, apparently," the boy pointed out, frowning at him.

Phaedor gave him a shadowy grin. He sent his own dagger flipping three times before catching the point on his fingertip again.

There was something about his nonchalance that suddenly made Tanis *really* want to know the truth.

Tanis had tried truthreading the zanthyr before to no avail, though he could sometimes tell when Phaedor was telling the whole truth and when his words merely masked a deeper truth running beneath them. But Tanis had recently had luck working his talent with Pelas, and this emboldened him to the possibility of success of the same kind with the zanthyr. So he focused all of his will and asked again, working his most powerful Telling, "*Did* you know I would meet Pelas, my lord?"

It should have produced an answer from even the most rigid of opponents, but Phaedor merely chuckled, long and deep, a sort of dangerous purr-growl that could make your hair stand on end. He peered at the lad from beneath his raven curls and murmured in a decidedly ominous tone, "Trying your Adept skills upon me, are you, truthreader?"

Tanis gazed unhappily at him. "It worked on Pelas."

Phaedor made his dagger vanish with a flick of his wrist and tilted his head to regard the lad curiously. "Why should you need reassurance, Tanis? It was your choice to give Pelasommáyurek your dagger, just as it was your choice to follow him in the first place, as it was to leave him when the time came."

Tanis eyed him askance. "You're implying that all of these decisions were of the same quality or nature, but—"

Yet even as he thought to deny it, he realized that it was actually true. Phaedor had already told him that instincts often led one to the right choice. Tanis had dismissed the notion at first, but now that he'd had some days to ponder it, he was more willing to admit that *some* instinct—for good or ill—had guided him from the moment he'd laid eyes on Pelas.

Then another thought struck him, and he gave the zanthyr a sooty look. "Is this what you were referring to when you said instincts were rarely wrong?"

Phaedor's emerald gaze glittered, which was an answer in itself.

Tanis frowned down at the half-eaten fish lying on a fir branch across his lap. Phaedor often spoke in mysteries, but sometimes the lad understood the truth running beneath his words, even if the words themselves made no sense. Perhaps it was an aspect of the magic that bound them together, or perhaps the zanthyr was merely pushing the truth across to him purposefully, mind to mind, allowing him to see it. Whatever the cause, Tanis was suddenly certain of one fact: he *was* being guided.

Moreover, the more he accepted this truth, the louder his instincts seemed to say that a higher purpose was influencing the strange events of his life, or at least…he wasn't sure, but he got the sense that there were things he was meant to do.

Maybe that's what the zanthyr meant when he said we're following my path.

The idea gave him sudden chills, though the fire felt warm on his face. "I just have to trust, don't I?" he asked softly into the darkness.

"We all do, lad," came the zanthyr's deep reply.

For every mystery that the zanthyr saw fit to comment upon, many more never came so close to resolution. Some, Tanis didn't even bother asking, such as why they were traveling by horse through icy, mountainous terrain as labyrinthine as a mirror maze when the zanthyr might've just called a portal and used the dimension of Shadow to transport them to their ultimate destination. Tanis was bright enough to know that if such could've been done, the zanthyr probably would've done it, so he rightly assumed that wherever they were headed, this was the way to get there.

Other questions—like the nature of Phaedor's relationship with Tanis's mother or what lay in store for them upon arrival at their destination— continued to go unanswered despite the lad's best attempts to draw those answers forth. This was due to those answers being categorized within the infuriating classification of "maintaining Balance."

Tanis thought Balance was entirely too convenient an excuse for not having to answer any questions. Knowing the zanthyr's disposition towards questions in general, which was not far afield of Rhys' disproportionate loathing, he found the explanation highly suspect.

He had been brooding disagreeably over the concept of Balance for more than a few days of travel when they finally emerged from the maze of mountain passes onto a ridge that opened upon a panoramic view.

Beyond and beneath their high vantage spread a lush, forested valley. It formed an emerald blanket that jutted up against a dark blue sea. Spanning many miles between snow-capped ridges and ocean, the canopy of trees was interspersed with rolling green hills and meadows dotted here and there with what Tanis at first assumed were sheep but which he later realized were horses.

The zanthyr halted their mounts at the edge of the cliff and gazed silently across the pristine valley, his emerald eyes greener even than the trees beneath them, his thoughts more distant than the cloud-rending peaks at their backs. The zanthyr always maintained an effortless remoteness, even when he was being kind—which he always was to Tanis.

The lad drew rein beside Phaedor's black destrier and gazed appreciatively out over the vista. His thoughts and musings of malcontent were momentarily forgotten in light of the incredible view.

"Where are we?" Tanis asked, smiling with wonder, for the valley and its distant sea were lovely in so many ways.

"Home," the zanthyr murmured. He gave the boy a sidelong glance full of meaning and led away down the trail.

Loran val Whitney, Duke of Marion and Dannym's General of the East, sat his warhorse at the top of a rise, frowning down at the fortress of Nahavand. With the sun slanting low in the west and casting its powerful rays directly on the fortress walls, Nahavand seemed a near mirage—yet still a sight to behold.

The high, crenellated wall both emerged from and ended in the mountainside, and the fortress's great towers were carved from the unforgiving stone. The detail of their construction, the ornate figures depicted among the richly carved walls—this was the work of master craftsmen, reminiscent of an age when kings didn't just stack stones atop each other with a bit of wet sand and call it a castle.

Loran suspected that Nahavand had seen eons come and go—certainly it had been standing longer than Radov abin Hadorin's reign. Nahavand's ancient engineers had taken care with its placement and design, utilizing the natural landscape to provide both protection and advantage. A trained eye easily saw how a small force could hold such a fortress indefinitely against a much larger host.

Nahavand was a treasure, yet the Nadoriin had apparently abandoned it without a backwards glance.

Loran's knights were investigating the fortress. Some ranged north and south on horseback along the perimeter defense, while others had lit torches and ventured through the open portcullis and into the keep.

Loran scratched his dark-haired head.

"I need you to go to Nahavand personally, take command of the forces there and fortify the outpost... You must make it defensible, Loran, and fortify it well."

His king's order—baffling words when faced with the truth. Nahavand boasted no force in need of Loran's leadership. All signs indicated the fortress had been deserted for many moons.

Knowing Gydryn val Lorian well, Loran understood what his king wanted him to do at Nahavand, though he didn't understand why he'd been given the task under such subterfuge and misdirection.

Loran's discerning gaze noted places in Nahavand's wall which required repair. Some of the crenels were crumbling, and one of the portcullises was stuck halfway up. Then there were supplies to consider, quarter to be found for the men and horses, fresh water and weapons…

Nahavand's foundation was solid, but much work would be needed to fortify it well. Still, from the looks of it, the fortress could easily protect a few thousand men.

"…it will play a vital role in the coming conflict…"

Loran exhaled a measured breath. *Gydryn…*he thought grimly, jaw clenched with misgiving, *I pray you know what you're doing.*

Then he set heels to his mount and embarked upon the monumental task that his king had assigned him.

END OF BOOK TWO

A Pattern of Shadow & Light continues with Book 3, *Paths of Alir.* Look for it in bookstores, available now.

KEEP IN TOUCH

If you enjoyed *The Dagger of Adendigaeth* and would like to support the author, please consider leaving a review on Amazon.com, Barnes & Noble, Goodreads, the iBookstore, or wherever you purchased the novel.

Stay in touch with Melissa via these social sites, and make sure to sign up for her newsletter for updates on the release of future books in *A Pattern of Shadow & Light*.

http://melissamcphail.com

http://Facebook.com/cephraelshand

http://twitter.com/melissagmcphail

http://pinterest.com/melissagmcphail

http://www.goodreads.com/melissagmcphail

GLOSSARY OF TERMS

UNDERLINING WITHIN DEFINITIONS denotes words that may be found in this glossary.

Adendigaeth (aden'– di gay'uth) [Old Alæic] 1 Rebirth, regeneration 2 A festival in celebration of the Winter Solstice lasting varying lengths but traditionally ending on the Longest Night.

Adept (a'-dept) n. [Old Alæic] 1 One born with the instinctive ability to sense and compel one of the five strands of *elae* 2 A race of such persons, each with attributes intrinsic to the strand of *elae* that modified them *[an adept of the third strand]* 3 A Healer, Nodefinder, Truthreader, or Wildling.

Angiel (ahn gēl') n. [Old Alæic] The Maker's two blessed children, Cephrael and Epiphany, who were made in the Genesis to watch over His worlds.

Ascendant (ah send'ent) [Cyrenaic *ascendere,* to climb] A priest or cleric serving the Prophet Bethamin. Ascedants are marked by tatooes denoting their rank and function.

Avieth (ay' vee uth) [Old Alæic, bird] n. A third-strand Wildling race of shapeshifters with the ability to asssume two distinctly separate forms: human and hawk.

Awaken (ah wā' ken) v. [Old Alæic] Adepts who have Returned awaken to their inherent abilities usually during the transition of puberty but sometimes as early as two years of age.

Balance (bal'ans) n. [<Veneisean <Cyrenaic, *bilanx* two+scale] The term used to describe the highest force of cause and effect in the realm of Alorin; the natural laws of the realm which define how far the currents may be twisted out of their natural paths by wielders of *elae* before manifest retribution is incurred by the wielder. These laws are of much consideration among the various Adept Guilds and a topic of intense speculation and theorization.

Cephrael (sef'ray-el) n. [Sobra I'ternin] The Maker's blessed son. Ascribed as the Hand of Fate, Cephrael is responsible for administering the Maker's ultimate justice. See also Angiel.

Drachwyr (drak´wēr) n. [Old Alæic] An Adept of the fifth strand of *elae*: the drachwyr were banished to the icy edges of the realm in the year 597aV. Also called a Sundragon.

Elae (e-lā´) n. [Old Alæic, *elanion,* life, force; the power of life] 1 The itinerant (roaming) energy that, in its accumulation and formation, creates the pattern that becomes the foundation of a world 2 Pertaining to any of the five codified strands of this energy, each with distinctly separate attributes.

Epiphany (ē pif´fany) n. [Sobra I'ternin] The Maker's blessed daughter. Epiphany is the speaker of the Maker's will and is often turned to in prayer by those seeking divine blessing. See also *Angiel*.

Espial (espy´-al) n. [Cyrenaic *espyen* <es − + *spähen,* to spy] See also Nodefinder. The term used to describe a Nodefinder of the highest degree who has gained license from the Espial's Guild to travel between the realms.

Fhorg (forg) n. [origin unknown] One of the Wildling races most notably known for their use of blood magic.

Healer (hēl´er) n. [Old Alæic *haelan* > *hal* whole] An Adept of the first strand of *elae* who has the ability to see the life patterns of living things and compel the creative forces of the first strand to alter them.

Leis (lay) n. [Old Alæic *leis*] The shortest pathway available to a Nodefinder when using the pattern of the world to travel, often connecting spaces within a small geographic area.

Marquiin (mar kwen´) n. [Myacenic, chosen] A truthreader who has been chosen by the Prophet Bethamin to be cleansed in a "purifying" ritual involving, in part, the insertion of Bethamin's Fire into the Adept's mind.

Merdanti (mer dan´tē) n. [Agasi] 1 An impossibly hard black stone named for the region of Agasan in which it is found 2 A weapon forged using the fifth strand of *elae* and made from this stone.

Malorin'athgul (muh lor´en − ath´gool) n. [Old Alæic, they who make the darkness] A race of beings from beyond the known realms of Light who were birthed by the Maker to balance Creation by unmaking the universe at its far unraveling fringes while it is constantly expanding at its core.

Na'turna (nah toor'nah) n. [Old Alæic < *nare turre*, of the earth] A non-Adept; mortal.

Node (nod) n. [Old Alæic *nodus*, knot] The points where the pattern of the world conjoins. Nodes connect places in vastly different geographic regions and allow a Nodefinder to travel great distances within a few steps. In the realm of Alorin, nodes also connect to the neighboring realm of T'khendar due to the nature of the latter's formation.

Nodefinder (nod-fin'der) n. [Old Alæic *nodus*, knot + *findan*, find] Adept of the second strand of *elae* who sees the points where the pattern of the world conjoins (called nodes) and can use these points to travel vast distances; see also *Espial*.

Patterning (pat'ərn·ŋ) v. [Veneisean *patrun*, patron, hence something to be imitated, pattern] The codified methodology encompassing the use of patterns to compel the strands of *elae* to move against their natural course, an action (also called *wielding*) which is often erroneously referred to as magic.

Raedan (ray' dan]) n. [Old Alæic *raedan*, to guess, read, counsel] 1 One trained to read the currents of *elae* and thereby able to discern the workings of patterns and their effects throughout the realm.

Realm (relm') n. [Veneisean, *realme* (altered by assoc. with *reiel*, royal) < Cyrenaic, *regere*, to rule] 1 A kingdom 2 One of the thousand linked worlds, each represented by an elected Seat and four Vestals in the governing cityworld of Illume Belliel 3 The realm of Alorin.

Return (Returned, Returning) (rē turn') n. [Agasi, *strônd*] An Adept who has died and been reborn. See also Awakening.

Sobra I'ternin (so' brah – e turn'en) n. [origin unknown] The ancient text, most often attributed to the *angiel* Cephrael, which details the natural laws of patterns in thaumaturgic application. The book is itself written in patterns and has yet to be fully translated. Many Orders are dedicated to its study, translation and adaptation for use in the Adept Arts.

Strand (strand´) n. [Agasi, *strônd*] 1 Any of the parts that are bound together to form a whole *[the strands of one's life]* 2 Referring to any of the five composite aspects of *elae* and its five attributive fields of energy (respectively: strand 1:creative energy, 2:kinetic energy, 3:variant energy, 4:energy of thought, 5:elemental energy).

Thread (thred) n. [Old Alæic *thræd*, to bind] A colloquial term used when speaking of a group of four men of a specific race, as opposed to a String, which is a grouping of six.

Tiern'aval (teer´ – navol´) n. [origin unknown] An island city, one of the Free Cities of Xanthe, which vanished at the end of the Adept wars circa 597aV. The city's fate remains a mystery.

T'khendar (tuh – ken´dar) n. [origin unknown] The realm created by the Adept wielder Malachi ap'Kalien out of Alorin's own aether, which sacrilegious act resulted in fierce denouncement from the Council of Realms and indirectly, his later madness.

Truthreader (trooth´ rēd er) n. [Old Alæic *treowe*, true + *raedan*] An Adept of the fourth strand of *elae* who is able to hear (and sometimes see) the thoughts of others and is thereby able to discern the time, place and form of any occurrence in their memory, i.e. its truth.

Tyriolicci (teer´e-oh – lee´chee) One of the Wildling Races of the Forgotten Lands. See Whisper Lord.

Vestal (vest´-al) n. [Cyrenaic, *vestir*, to endow] 1 An Adept elevated and empowered with the responsibility of enforcing the laws, regulations, activities and codes of his respective strand of *elae,* and of overseeing all Adepts subject to it 2 one of five highly-trained and advanced Adepts elected as voting members of the Council of Realms, ranking just below the Seat of the realm in authority.

Weld (weld) n. [Cyrenaic, *welden,* to be strong] The most major joints in the pattern of the world. All leis and nodes connect through a weld, thus a weld allows travel to any location. Welds also form the joints between the realms and thus allow travel from realm to realm.

Whisper Lord n. [Collq.] One of the Wildling races (also called Tyriolicci) known for their frenzied fighting style and ability to make small skips through time.

Wielder (wēld´ər) n. [Cyrenaic, *welden,* to be strong < Old Alæic, *valere,* a show of strength] A person of any race who uses patterns to compel one or more strands of *elae,* thereby influencing the strand's properties to create the effect he has postulated; a sorcerer in the realm of Alorin. Adepts and men alike become wielders through intensive training and study.

Wildling (wahyld´-ling]) n. [Old Alæic *wilde*] 1 (Collq) An Adept of the third strand of *elae* 2 Any of the twenty-seven non-human races whose native abilities are attributed to the third strand of *elae* but who may or may not be possessed of paranormal abilities.

Zanthyr (zan´thur) n. [Old Alæic] An elusive Adept of the fifth strand of *elae*; zanthyrs can shapeshift between two forms: one human, one animal. Some have been known to work *elae* as wielders, but the extent of their abilities is unknown.

DRAMATIS PERSONAE

THE FIVE VESTALS:

Alshiba Torinin—the First Vestal, an Adept Healer and the Alorin Seat

Dagmar Ranneskjöld—the Second Vestal, an Espial

Seth nach Davvies—the Third Vestal, an avieth of the Wildling races

Raine D'Lacourte—the Fourth Vestal, a truthreader and *raedan*

Björn van Gelderan—the Fifth Vestal, branded a traitor

MEMBERS OF THE ROYAL FAMILY OF DANNYM

Gydryn val Lorian—King of Dannym

Errodan Renwyr n'Owain val Lorian—Queen of Dannym

Ysolde Remalkhen—the Queen's Companion; a Fire Princess from Avatar

Ean val Lorian—Prince of Dannym, the youngest son

Trell val Lorian—Prince of Dannym, the Queen's treasured middle son

Sebastian val Lorian—oldest son (a victim of assassination)

Creighton Khelspath—ward of Gydryn, blood-brother to Ean (now a Shade)

Ryan val Lorian—brother to Gydryn, posted as Dannym's Ambassador to Agasan

Fynnlar val Lorian—son of Ryan, a prince of Dannym

Brody the Bull—Fynnlar's bodyguard

IN THE KING'S CABINET & GUARD

Morin d'Hain—Spymaster

Donnal val Amrein—Minister of the Interior

Mandor val Kess—Minister of Culture

Vitriam O'reith—truthreader to the King

Kjieran van Stone—truthreader to the King (assigned as a spy to Bethamin's Temple)

Rhys val Kincaide—Lord Captain of the King's Own Guard

Bastian val Renly—a lieutenant of the King's Own Guard

Cayal—a soldier of the King's Own Guard

Dorin—a soldier of the King's Own Guard

OF THE PEERAGE & THEIR HOUSEHOLDS

Gareth val Mallonwey—Duke of Towermount and General of the West

Tad val Mallonwey—Heir to Towermount

Katerine val Mallonwey—daughter of Gareth, engaged to Creighton Khelspath

Lisandre val Mallonwey—daughter of Gareth

Loran val Whitney—Duke of Marion and General of the East

Killian val Whitney—Heir to Marion

Melisande d'Giverny—mother to Alyneri (*deceased*)

Prince Jair—Prince of Kandori, father of Alyneri (*deceased*)

Alyneri d'Giverny—Duchess of Aracine, an Adept Healer

Tanis—an Adept truthreader, Melisande's ward

Farshideh—a Nadori midwife, Seneschal of Fersthaven (*deceased*)

Stefan val Tryst—Duke of Morwyk

Wilamina—Dowager Countess of Astor

Ianthe d'Jesune val Rothschen—Marchioness of Wynne

Wilem val Rothschen—Marquess of Wynne

The Contessa di Remy—wife of the Agasi Ambassador's Aide

On Trell's & Alyneri's Travels

Yara—an old Kandori woman

Lord Brantley—Earl of Pent, liegeman to the Duke of Morwyk

Ghislain

Haddrick—an Adept truthreader and pirate of Jamaii, cousin to Carian vran Lea

D'Varre—Guildmaster of the Nodefinder's Guild of Rethynnea

Gerard—an Espial

In T'khendar

Balaeric de Parma—a pirate from Alorin, now a gypsy Iluminari

Carian vran Lea—a pirate of Jamaii, an Adept Nodefinder

Gwynnleth—an avieth from Elvior

Isabel van Gelderan—Epiphany's Prophet, sister to Björn van Gelderan

Julian d'Artenis—a fifth-strand Adept from Jeune, Veneisea

Markal Morrelaine—a wielder, one of the First Lord's three generals

The Council of Nine

Björn van Gelderan—the First Lord and Alorin's Fifth Vestal

Cristien Tagliaferro—an Adept truthreader

Anglar Tempest (*deceased*, revived as a Shade)

Dunglei ap'Turic (*deceased*)

Parsifal D'Marre (*deceased*)

Arion Tavestra (*deceased*)

Markal Morrelaine—a wielder, one of Björn's three Generals

Ramuhárikhamáth—a *drachwyr*, one of Björn's three Generals

Malachai ap'Kalien (*deceased*)

THE WARRING PRINCES & THEIR ALLIES

Emir Zafir bin Safwan al Abdul-Basir—Akkadian Emir, Unifier of the Seventeen Tribes

Rajiid bin Yemen al Basreh—Prime Minister of the Akkad

Radov abin Hadorin—Ruling Prince of M'Nador

Viernan hal'Jaitar—Radov's wielder (see The Fifty Companions)

Raliax—a Saldarian mercenary

The Prophet Bethamin (also known as Darshan)

Dore Madden—an Adept wielder serving the Prophet (see The Fifty Companions)

Işak'getirmek—a wielder bound to Dore Madden

The Karakurt—a female truthreader, leader of an infamous ring of assassins

AT THE FIRST LORD'S SA'REYTH

Vaile—a zanthyr

Leyd—a zanthyr

Loghain—a Tyriolicci (of the Wildling races, called Whisper Lord by the races of men)

THE FIFTY COMPANIONS (THOSE KNOWN TO BE LIVING)

Pavran Ahlamby—a truthreader

Usil al'Haba—a Nodefinder

Elien ap'Gentrys—an Adept wielder

Gannon Bair—a truthreader

Karienna D'Artenis—an Adept Healer

Laira di Giancora—an Adept Healer

Mian Gartelt—an Adept Healer

Viernan hal'Jaitar—an Adept wielder

Socotra Isio—a Nodefinder

Ledio Jerouen—an Adept Wildling

Dore Madden—an Adept wielder

Mazur of Elvior—an Avieth of Elvior

Franco Rohre—a Nodefinder

Delanthine Tanner—an Adept wielder

Thessaly Vahn—An Adept Healer

Devangshu Vita—a Nodefinder

Niko van Amstel—a Nodefinder

THE MALORIN'ATHGUL

Darshanvenkhátraman (Dar´shan – vin ka´tra mahn) called Darshan
whose name means Destroyer of Hope

Pelasommáyurek (Pe´las – oh my´yur eck) called Pelas
whose name means Ender of Paths

Rinokhálpeşumar (Rin´och – cal pesh´oo mar) called Rinokh
whose name means The Mountain That Flames

Shailabhanáchtran (Shale´ – ah bah nock´trun) called Shail
whose name means Maker of Storms

THE SIX SUNDRAGONS (DRACHWYR)

Dhábu'balaji'şridanaí(Da´boo – ba lah´gee – shree´da nye) called
Balaji
whose name means He Who Walks The Edge Of The World

Şrivas'rhakárakek (Shree´vas – rah kar´akeck) called Rhakar
whose name means The Shadow Of The Light

Jayachándranáptra (Jai´ah – shan´dra – nap´tra) called Jaya
whose name means Rival Of The Sun

Ramuhárikhamáth (Rah´moo – hareek´amath) called Ramu

whose name means Lord of the Heavens

Amithaiya'geshwen (Ami-thi'ya – gesh'win) called Mithaiya

whose name means The Bosom of God's Nectar

Náeb'nabdurin'náiir (Ni eb'– nab dur'en – ny'ear) called Náiir

whose name means Chaser Of The Dawn

THE SEVENTEEN GODS OF THE AKKAD

Jai'Gar—the Prime God

Azerjaiman—the Wind God

Sons of the wind god—North son, Shamal; South son, Asfal; East son, Sherq

Daughter of the wind god—West daughter, Qharp

Shamash—God of Travelers and the Poor

Inanna—Goddess of War

Naiadithine—Goddess of Water

Enlil—God of Earth and Agriculture

Inithiya—Goddess of Restoration (Spirit)

Angharad—Goddess of Fortune (Fate)

Thalma—Goddess of Luck (Virtue)

Huhktu—God of Bones

Baharan/Baharani—The two-headed God of Blood/Goddess of Birth

Ha'viv—the Trickster God, patron of thieves

CPSIA information can be obtained
at www.ICGtesting.com
Printed in the USA
LVOW13s1752280318
571473LV00009B/329/P